CARTER

'Wholly original ... Gold's [...] of the great illusionists and escapologists ... and his plot garish, crude, infernally clever – is precisely honed to the task: it is a triumph of misdirection, a nest of boxes constantly springing fresh surprises. Stage illusions were a popular art; they worked at pace, with drive and rolling drums. Gold's prose has precisely that energy. He creates his own rich, strange world where anything is possible, where characters from fact and fiction mingle ... he leaves himself with only one resounding problem at the close. After such a debut novel, what does he do for his next trick?' Peter Preston, *Guardian*

'It's a long book, but reads like a novella, such is the pace and action Gold manages to pack into it ... His role is as much grand illusionist as author, and as he misdirects, misinforms and ultimately reveals his truths, the reader can only applaud. This is a terrific novel of the Jazz Age that entertains, informs and moves. Gold has tackled a difficult subject for his debut and succeeded brilliantly.' Jim Driver, *Time Out*

'I've had the most fun this year with *Carter Beats the Devil* – a first novel full of romance and adventure, with a fantastic smoke-and-mirrors plot. I recommend it to anyone who wants to brighten a murky winter.' Helen Brown, *Daily Telegraph* Books of the Year

'What really sparkles is Carter's introduction to the world of theatrical magic. Live entertainment is now so frequently gazumped by its widescreen, digitally enhanced competition that a depiction of the golden age of variety performance could have appeared twee. Gold avoids this, showing a nation hungry for simple escapism from the restrictions of prohibition and that awful vanishing act where a generation of young men disappeared in the battlefields of France' Christian House, *Independent on Sunday*

'I found myself unable to stop reading. It is a magnificent achievement. The plot is endlessly inventive and surprising and pulls the reader through some very complicated events in the most compelling way.' Charles Palliser

'Glen David Gold's *Carter Beats the Devil* is a big, mischievous, intelligent read – nice to see a bit of magic in fiction again' A.L. Kennedy, *Observer* Books of the Year

'A mischievous, magical debut' Hepzibah Anderson, *Daily Mail* Books of the Year

'The prose breathes the very air of the burlesque house – the mixture of cheap glamour, false bonhomie and the faint hum of sexual tension ... Gold excels at the psychology of working the crowd, and the collective comforts of deceit ... The novel weaves biography and fiction with a seamless ease, history making various cameos and then being made to vanish like a dove into a handkerchief. Writing is thus the ultimate trompe-l'oeil: pick up a word, any word, and Gold will tell you what it is ... To make the performance even more mesmerising, the book is also partly a thriller.' Graham Caveney, *Independent*

'[A] remarkable novel, a combination of paranoid conspiracy thriller, period romance and meditation on the nature of art ... Gold is an inventive plotter who does not push the parallels between conjuring and fiction, but clearly loves the thrilling game of sudden revelation common to both ... Part of the art of illusion is misdirection, putting things in plain view, and ensuring that people will not notice them until the right moment. Gold uses this technique with great skill – the triumphs and disasters of his hero come from nowhere only if one has been lulled into failing to pay attention to details' Roz Kaveney, *Times Literary Supplement*

'This is a novel that rescues the ephemera of history, puts them centre stage and shines a bright light on them. It is this spectacular recreation of a lost world that stays in the mind long after the last page is turned and the curtain comes down.' Adam Lively, *Sunday Times*

'History coloured by a wonderfully fertile imagination, it is a wry-humoured whodunit with a dazzling sense of suspense, it is a romantic tribute to a different age and, at its heart, it is a moving testament to the power of love over loneliness ... Awesome ... his timing and touch are immaculate as he creates one of the most diverting reads of the year ... Simply brilliant ... By turns fearful, intriguing, emotional and confounding, but whatever it is, *Carter Beats the Devil* is never less than wonderfully entertaining.' *Irish Times*

'As a portrait of the Golden Age of Magic, it works brilliantly ... Equally good, in a very different vein, are the accounts of Carter's love life ... Gold has captured the high-wire excitement of the age' Julia Flynn, *Sunday Telegraph*

CARTER
BEATS *the* DEVIL

A NOVEL

GLEN DAVID GOLD

SCEPTRE

First published in Great Britain in 2001 by Hodder and Stoughton
First published in paperback in Great Britain in 2002
by Hodder and Stoughton
A division of Hodder Headline

A Sceptre Book

A CIP catalogue record for this title is
available from the British Library.

ISBN 978-0-340-79499-9

Typeset in Monotype Sabon by
Palimpsest Book Production Limited,
Polmont, Stirlingshire
Printed and bound in Great Britain by
Clays Ltd, St Ives plc

Hodder and Stoughton
A division of Hodder Headline
338 Euston Road
London NW1 3BH

CARTER
BEATS *the* DEVIL

A NOVEL

GLEN DAVID GOLD

SCEPTRE

Typeset in Monotype Sabon by
Palimpsest Book Production Limited,
Polmont, Stirlingshire
Printed and bound in Great Britain by
Clays Ltd, St Ives plc

Hodder and Stoughton
A division of Hodder Headline
338 Euston Road
London NW1 3BH

For my assistant,
the mysterious Miss Alice

Thursday, August 2nd, 1923, at 8 o'clock p.m.

MUST END TONIGHT COME SEE TONIGHT WILL END TONIGHT

CARTER
THE GREAT

— AND HIS FULL COMPANY —

*returning from a triumphant tour
to the far reaches of the globe*

*in three acts of mayhem,
magic & mystery*

TO-NIGHT'S PROGRAMME

OVERTURE

ACT I:
METAMORPHOSIS

A cascade of thrilling illusions:
Metempsychosis, Fly-to, Gone!, the
Enchanted Cottage, a Night in Old
China, and the Ducted Mystery of
the Elephant.

~interval~

ACT II:
AN INQUIRY INTO THE
SPIRIT WORLD

A baffling séance in which MADAME
ZORAH KNOWS ALL, SEES ALL, TELLS
ALL. Telepathy, clairvoyance, spirit
manifestations, thought transference.
Before the curtain rises, please submit
your questions to Madame Zorah in
writing, including your full name so
that she may better bring to bear the
force of her psychic powers.

~interval~

ACT III:
CARTER BEATS THE DEVIL

The management requests that,
due to the intensified nature of the
performance, no patron reveal details
of Act III, "Carter Beats the Devil".

~curtain~

ORCHESTRA $8.00 / CIRCLE $6.00 / PIT $5.00 / 1ST GALLERY $3.50 / 2ND GALLERY $2.50.
NO STANDING ROOM TICKETS. NO REFUNDS. NO SEATING OF LATE ARRIVALS.

*"Puisque toutes les créatures sont au
font des frères, il faut traiter vos bêtes
comme vous traitez vos amis."*

Charles Carter, S.A.M. #532,
is represented by Carter and Company,
San Francisco.

Carter Beats the Devil

OVERTURE

The most beautiful experience we can have is the mysterious. It is the fundamental emotion which stands at the cradle of true art and true science. Whoever does not know it and can no longer wonder, no longer marvel, is as good as dead, and his eyes are dimmed.

— ALBERT EINSTEIN

On Friday, August third, 1923, the morning after President Harding's death, reporters followed the widow, the Vice President, and Charles Carter, the magician. At first, Carter made the pronouncements he thought necessary: 'A fine man, to be sorely missed,' and 'it throws the country into a great crisis from which we shall all pull through together, showing the strong stuff of which we Americans are made.' When pressed, he confirmed some details of his performance the night before, which had been the President's last public appearance, but as per his proviso that details of his third act never be revealed, he made no comment on the show's bizarre finale.

Because the coroner's office could not explain exactly how the President had died, and rumors were already starting, the men from Hearst wanted quite desperately to confirm what happened in the finale, when Carter beat the Devil.

That afternoon, a reporter disguised himself as a delivery man and interrupted Carter's close-up practice; the magician's more sardonic tendencies, unfortunately, came out. 'At the time the President met his maker, I was in a straitjacket, upside-down over a steaming pit of carbolic acid. In response to your as-yet-unasked query, yes, I do have an alibi.'

He was almost immediately to regret his impatience. The next day over breakfast he saw the headline in the *Examiner*: 'Carter the Great Denies Role in Harding Death.' Below was an article including, for the first time, an eyewitness first-person narrative from an anonymous audience member who all too helpfully described the entire show, *including* the third act. He could not confirm whether, in fact, President Harding had survived until the final curtain. After a breathless account of what Carter had done to the President, the editors reflected on Lincoln's assassination at Ford's Theater fifty-eight years beforehand, then made a pallid call for restraint, for letting the wheels of justice prevail.

Carter, a sober man, knew he might be lynched. At once, he ordered his servants to pack his steamer trunks for a six months' voyage. He booked a train from San Francisco to Los Angeles, then transit on the *Hercules*, an ocean liner bound from Los Angeles to Athens. He instructed his press agent to tell all callers that he was seeking inspiration from the priestess at Delphi, and would return at Christmastime.

Carter was chauffeured from his Pacific Heights mansion to the train station downtown, where a crowd of photographers jostled each other to shoot pictures of him. As he boarded the Los Angeles-bound train, he made no comment other than to turn up the collar of his fur-lined coat, which he hardly needed in the August heat.

By the time the train arrived in Los Angeles, Secret Service agents were posted at all exits. They had just received authorization to detain Mr Charles Carter. But this posed an unexpected challenge. Though they saw several pieces of Carter's luggage leaving the train, Carter himself was nowhere to be found. His servants were halted, and his bags opened and searched right on the platform, but law enforcement concluded that Carter had slipped away.

Passengers boarding the *Hercules* were given the professional bug-eye by agents who'd received copies, by teletype transmission, of Carter's publicity photograph. Since these images featured him in a silk floral turban, with devils drawn onto his shoulders, and his face thrown into moodily orchestrated shadows, they also received careful descriptions of what Charles Carter actually looked like: thirty-five years old, black hair, blue eyes, Roman nose, pale, almost delicate skin, and a slender build that allowed, it was said, exceptionally agile movement. Informants could not say for certain whether Carter was the type of magician who was a master of disguise; San Francisco's law enforcement was of the opinion that he was not. He was, they thought, the type who specialized in dematerialization. This did not set the agents' minds at ease, and when every passenger had been examined, they were no closer to catching their man than they had been on the train. He had not stowed away with the crew, nor with the luggage – both had been examined minutely.

Finally, the agents concluded he had been scared off by the attention. The *Hercules* was allowed to sail, and as soon as it cleared the breakwater, the harbormaster saw through his binoculars the unmistakable form of Charles Carter, in bowler hat and chinchilla coat, sipping champagne and waving adieu from the aft deck.

Authorities on board and at every port along the way were alerted to Carter's presence, but even the most optimistic federal agent suspected the magician would never be found.

This was hardly the Secret Service's first disaster, only the most recent. Morale among all government bodies had plummeted during the twenty-nine months of the Harding administration. As one scandal followed another, it became apparent that in stark contrast to President Wilson, Harding tolerated corruption. In short, the whole government to a man realized that only bastards got ahead.

For Agent Jack Griffin, this philosophy was no adjustment whatsoever.

On the evening of Carter's performance for President Harding, Griffin had been told to report to the Curran Theatre. Though his duties – 'analyze local grounds for all malicious forces' – sounded important, he knew he was superfluous. The Curran was undoubtedly secure: magicians took extraordinary precautions against competitors' stealing their secrets. Furthermore, a follow-up detail would double-check the entrances, exits, and the President's seats. Nonetheless, Griffin would make a thorough report; after a twenty-year cycle of probations and remedial duties, he remained determined to show he couldn't be broken by lame assignments.

The Curran, a monstrous and drafty theatre, had just been

refurbished to accommodate pageants, top-flight entertainments, and prestigious motion pictures. The orchestra pit had been expanded to seat one hundred musicians and a projection room had been added in the back balcony. The old Victorian motifs – a ceiling mural of pre-Raphaelite seraphim, for instance – had been co-joined with Egyptian themes. The walls now rippled with hieroglyphs and the apron of the stage was flanked by huge plaster sphinxes whose eyes glowed in the dark.

Since Harding was coming to San Francisco as a stop on his Voyage of Understanding, an effort to refocus his tired administration, he would likely come onstage during the evening, perhaps even volunteer in one of Carter's illusions. Thus Griffin was to determine which act might be most dignified for the President.

He came to the Curran in the late afternoon, while workmen were testing filaments and maneuvering black draperies into their places. He interviewed Carter's chief effects builder, a stooped old man named Ledocq, a Belgian who wore both a belt and suspenders, and who frequently scratched just above his ear, threatening to dislodge his yarmulke. Griffin wrote in his notes 'Jew.'

Ledocq wouldn't let Griffin examine any of the illusions onstage, but he described the effects in detail: the show opened with 'Metempsychosis,' in which a suit of armor came to life and chased one of Carter's hapless assistants around the stage. (As this seemed like tomfoolery to him, Griffin noted that Harding should probably not participate in this.) 'The Enchanted Cottage' was a series of quick changes, dematerializations, and reappearances culminating in 'A Night in Old China,' an enthralling display of fire-juggling, fire-eating, and fireworks. (Griffin wrote 'sounds dangerous – doubtful' in his notes.) Next, Carter placed a subject, usually an attractive young woman whom he selected from the audience, into an ordinary wooden chair, which rose above the stage without apparent assistance. He asked the subject humorous questions, keeping the audience enthralled while he pulled out a pistol, loaded it, and carefully shot the woman point-blank – the chair fell to the ground, but the subject disappeared into the ether. ('Absolutely not!' Griffin wrote, underlining this notation.)

After the intermission was a levitation, psychical mind reading, and prediction routine with Carter's associate, Madame Zorah.

('Possible,' Griffin wrote, 'but won't it hurt Px Harding's credibility?') He asked, 'What else is there?'

Ledocq scratched above his ear and squinted at Griffin. 'Well, there's not a lot left then. There's the Vanishing Elephant trick.'

'Would the President be in danger from the elephant?'

'Mmmm. No.' Ledocq smiled. 'But I can't imagine a Republican being happy making an elephant disappear.'

Griffin crossed out the Vanishing Elephant. 'Isn't there a third act?'

'There is. There is. It's hard to explain.'

'To tell you the truth,' Griffin sighed, 'I don't really care about every detail of every trick. Should the President be involved?'

Ledocq laughed, a dry cackle. 'Believe me, you don't want your boss anywhere near the stage when Carter beats the Devil.'

An hour later, at the Palace Hotel, Griffin produced his full report, typing it on his Remington portable and inking in the places where the keys hadn't come down hard enough to make duplicates. He went to the Mint to turn it in, and returned to his room. Twice, he picked up the phone and asked the operator if there were any calls for him. There weren't.

Just before the performance that night, the Bureau Chief met in the lobby with eighteen agents, including Griffin, to pass out programs and set up a duty roster for the evening. The Chief announced that the President would indeed go onstage – as a volunteer in the third act. When Griffin objected, he was told – lectured, actually, for the senior agents all knew about Griffin – that there would be no arguments. The President and Carter had met and concluded that the most effective use of the President's time would be in a trick called – Griffin mouthed the words as they were announced – 'Carter Beats the Devil'.

Griffin, still objecting, was dismissed, and was sent to stand at the back of the theatre, where he cursed under his breath until the lights dimmed, when he began to make small, coarse gestures toward the Bureau Chief and the other Kentucky insiders, who sat in the eight-dollar seats.

The curtains opened to a spectacularly cluttered set meant to represent Carter the Great's study. A lackey bemoaned the audience's presence. 'Eight o'clock already, the show is starting, and the master's room isn't ready yet. He'll have my hide for sure.'

The lackey dusted everywhere, with huge clouds choking him when he blew across the top of an ancient book. Most of the audience laughed, but not Griffin. He felt a lot of sympathy for the poor guy onstage. In his haste to clean everything, the lackey knocked over a suit of armor, which fell to the stage in a dozen pieces, empty.

When he put it back together again, and returned to cleaning, the suit of armor snuck up on him and kicked his backside. The audience roared. Griffin looked at them sourly, thinking, *Sophisticates.* What kind of a guy used all his smoke and mirrors to make fun of a poor egg just doing his job?

A sting of violins, then Elgar's 'Pomp and Circumstance,' and Charles Carter appeared in his white tie, tails, and trademark damask turban, to tremendous applause. The suit of armor froze. Carter lectured his servant about the shabby way his study looked, and asked why the suit of armor was standing in the middle of the floor. Trying to explain that the armor had just attacked him, the lackey gave it a shove. It toppled in pieces, empty, to the stage. No amount of pleading could convince Carter that his servant was anything but unreliable.

Griffin whispered, 'Brother, I believe you.'

Two hours later, the curtain went up on the third act. The *Examiner* of the next morning would say that 'the enthralled audience had already watched in amazement as a dozen illusions, each more magnificent than the last, unfolded before their very eyes. The President himself was heard to say, "the show could finish now and still be a thrilling spectacle."'

Here the initial newspaper account ended, following Carter's request – printed on the programs and on broadsides posted at the theatre entrance – that the third act remain a secret.

The act began on a barren stage. Carter entered and announced that as he had proven himself to be the greatest sorcerer the world had ever known, there was no reason to continue his performance, and he was prepared to send the crowd home unless a greater wizard than he should appear. Then there was a flash of lightning, a plume of dark smoke, and the infernal reek of pure brimstone: rotten eggs and gunpowder. The Devil himself had arrived onstage.

The Devil, in black tights, red cape, close-fitting mask, and a cowl capped with two sharp horns, issued a challenge to Carter: each of them would perform illusions, and only the greater sorcerer would leave the stage alive. As soon as Carter agreed, the Devil produced a newspaper, and pulled a rabbit from it. Carter responded by hurling into a floating water basin four eggs, which, the moment they hit the water, became ducklings. The Devil caused a woman to levitate; Carter made her disappear. The Devil caused her to reappear as an old hag. With a great magnesium flash, Carter had her consumed by flames.

Then the pair began doing tricks independently of each other, at opposite ends of the stage. While the Devil ushered forth a floating tambourine, a trumpet, and a violin, which played a disembodied but creditable rendition of *Night on Bald Mountain,* Carter cast a rod and reel into the audience, catching live bass from midair. The Devil did him one better, sawing a woman in half and separating her without the casket in place. Carter made hand shadows of animals on the wall that came to life and galloped across the stage.

The Devil drew a pistol, loaded it, and fired it at Carter, who deflected the bullet with a silver tea tray. Carter drew his own pistol, and fired at the Devil, who caught the projectile in his teeth.

They brought out two white-bearded, turbaned 'Hindu yoga men,' each of whom had a hole drilled through his stomach so that a stage light could shine through. The Devil thrust his fist into and all the way through one man, making a fist behind him. Carter bade the other drink a glass of water, and he caught in a wine goblet the flow that came from his stomach, as if from a spigot.

Then cannons rolled onto stage, and Carter and the Devil urged their Hindus into the cannons, each of them aimed skyward so that the projectiles' paths would intersect. Then *BANG* went the cannons, and out flew the yoga men – when they collided over the audience's head, a burst of lilies rained upon the cheering crowd.

Carter cried that this was enough, that the contest had to be settled as if between gentlemen. He proposed a game of poker, high hand declared the winner. When the Devil assented, Carter broke from the program to approach the footlights. He asked if there were a volunteer, a special volunteer who could be an impartial and upright arbiter of this contest. A spotlight found President Harding, who, with a good-natured wave, acknowledged the audience's demand for him to be the judge.

Griffin's eyes were pinwheeling like he'd been through an artillery barrage. With each volcanic burst of mayhem, he'd assured himself it was just an optical illusion, that the President wouldn't actually be exposed to harm. But there'd been fire, guns, knives, and, he could barely consider it, *cannons*. Harding walked down the aisle, shaking hands along the way, and flashing his shy but winning smile.

Onstage, it was obvious what a big man Harding was, standing several inches taller, and wider, than Carter. He looked genuinely pleased to be of service.

Carter, Harding, and the Devil retired to the poker table, where a deck of oversized cards awaited them. Harding gamely tried to shuffle the huge cards – the deck was the size of a newspaper – until one of Carter's assistants took over the duty. As the game progressed, the Devil cheated outrageously: for instance, a giant mirror floated over Carter's left shoulder until Harding pointed it out, whereupon it vanished.

Carter had been presenting his evening of magic at the Curran for two weeks. Each night had ended the same way: he would present a seemingly unbeatable hand, over which the Devil would then, by cheating, triumph. Carter would stand, knocking over his chair, saying the game between gentlemen was over, and the Devil was no gentleman, sir, and he would wave a scimitar at the Devil. The Devil would ride an uncoiling rope like an elevator cable up to the rafters, out of the audience's sight. A moment later, Carter, scimitar clenched between his teeth, would conjure his own rope and follow. And then, with a chorus of off-stage shrieks and moans, Carter would quite vividly, and bloodily, show the audience what it meant to truly beat the Devil.

Carter's programs advertised the presence of a nurse should anyone in the audience faint while he took his revenge.

This night, as a courtesy, Carter offered that President Harding play a third hand in their contest. Just barely getting hold of his giant cards, the President joined the game. When it came time to present their hands, Carter had four aces and a ten. The Devil had four kings and a nine. The audience cheered: Carter had beaten the Devil.

'Mister President,' Carter cried, 'pray tell, show us your hand!'

A rather sheepish Harding turned his cards toward the crowd: A royal flush! Further applause from the audience until Carter hushed them.

'Sir, may I ask how you have a royal flush when all four kings and all four aces have already been spoken for?' Before Harding could reply, Carter continued: 'This game between gentlemen is over, and you, sir, are no gentleman!'

Carter and the Devil each drew scimitars, and brought them crashing down on the card table, which collapsed. Harding fell back in his chair, and, uprighting himself, dashed to a rope that was uncoiling toward the rafters. Harding rose with it. Carter and the Devil, on their own ropes, followed.

In the back of the theatre, Griffin frantically looked for fellow agents to confirm what he thought he'd seen. During the past two weeks of the trip, President Harding had been stooped as if carrying a ferryload of baggage. In Portland, he'd canceled his speeches and stayed in bed. The sudden acrobatics – where had a fifty-seven-year-old man found the energy?

The whole audience was just as unsure – the lighting was brilliant in some places, poor in others, causing figures to blur and focus within the same second. It forced the mind to stall as it processed what the eye could have seen. This was a crucial element of what was to come. For though the visual details fringed upon the impressionistic, the acoustics were ruthlessly exact: as the audience clamored for more, there came the sound of scimitars being put to use.

Then, with a thump, the first limb fell to the stage.

The crowd's cheers faded to murmurs, which took a moment to fade away. An unholy silence filled the Curran. Had that been something covered in black wool? Bent at the – the knee? Had that been the hard slap of black rubber heel? A woman's voice finally broke the stillness. 'His leg!' she shrieked. 'The President's leg!'

The one leg was followed by the other, then an arm, part of the body's trunk, part of the torso; soon the stage was raining body parts hitting the boards in wet clumps. Griffin unholstered his Colt and took careful steps forward, telling himself this was just a magic trick, and not the joke of a madman: to invite the President onstage, and kill him in front of his wife, the Service, newspaper reporters, and an audience of one thousand paying spectators.

Chaos took the audience; some were standing and calling out to their neighbors, others were comforting women about to faint. Just then, the voice of Carter came from somewhere over the stage. 'Ladies and Gentlemen, I give you the head of state.' And then, falling from a great height, a vision of grey, matted hair, and a blur of jowls atop a jagged gash, President Harding's head tumbled down to the stage apron, striking it with a muted smack.

Screams filled the air. Some brave audience members rushed past Griffin, toward the stage, but everyone halted in their tracks when a deep, echoing roar filled the theatre, and a lion catapulted from the wings onto the apron, where he gorged himself on the corpse's remains.

'He is all right! I know he must be all right,' an hysterical Mrs Harding wailed above the din.

Suddenly, a single shot rang out. The echo reported across the theatre. Carter strode from the wings to the midpoint of the stage, a pith helmet drawn down over his turban. He carried a rifle. The lion now lay on its side, limbs twitching.

'Ladies and Gentlemen, if I may have your indulgence for one last moment.' Carter spoke with gravitas, utter restraint, as if he were the only calm man in the house. Using a handheld electric saw, he carved up the lion's belly, and pried it open, and out stepped President Harding, who positively radiated good health. Griffin sat down in the aisle, gripping his chest and shaking his head.

As the crowd gradually realized that they had witnessed an illusion, the applause grew in intensity to a solid wave of admiration for Carter's wizardry, and especially Harding's good sportsmanship. It ended in a standing ovation. In the midst of it, Harding stepped to the footlights and called out to his wife, 'I'm fit, Duchess, I'm fit and ready to go fishing!'

Two hours later, he was dead.

* * *

Four days later, Monday, August sixth, Harding's remains were on their way to their final resting place in Marion, Ohio. At the same time, the *Hercules,* still under surveillance for signs of Charles Carter, was in a storm south of the tropic of Cancer. At noon on that day, Jack Griffin and a superior, Colonel Edmund Starling, ferried from San Francisco to Oakland. They took a cab to Hilgirt Circle, at the top of Lake Merritt, where some of the wealthier families had relocated after the great earthquake. One Hilgirt Circle was a salmon-colored Mediterranean villa that rambled up the steep slope of China Hill. There were seven stories, each recessed above the last, like steps. Whereas its neighbors were hooded Arts and Crafts fortresses, One Hilgirt Circle was a rococo circus of arch-ways, terra-cotta putti, gargoyles, and trellises strung with passion vines. Its builder couldn't be accused of restraint.

Griffin looked at the one hundred stairs leading to the villa entrance with dismay, then hitched his trousers over his paunch and struggled up until short of breath. He had recently started a program of exercise, but this was a bit much. Starling, thirteen years younger, went at a brisk trot.

Starling was handsome and gracious, a golden boy, one of the Kentucky insiders, quickly promoted and used to having his opin-ions acknowledged. He arose each morning at five to read a chapter of the Bible, exercise with Bureau Chief Foster, and eat a tidy break-fast before attacking that day's work. When enthusiastic about life (all too often, Griffin thought), he whistled the tunes of Stephen Foster. The hardest part for Griffin to bear was Starling's relent-less, honest humility. Griffin hated himself for hating him.

Reaching the top landing of Hilgirt Circle, the agents had a magnificent view of the lake, downtown Oakland, and, behind a milky veil of fog, the San Francisco skyline, which Griffin pretended to appreciate while he rested.

Starling whistled. 'Oh, for my rifle at this instant.'

'You think we're gonna need it?'

'No, Mr Griffin. The mallards on the lake. And I think I see some canvasbacks, though that would be peculiar, this time of year.'

Griffin nodded, dying to look knowledgeable, or intelligent, or *something* besides useless around the Colonel. He'd had a rough few days (guilt, depression, a fistfight, a vow to redeem himself) and had spent hours researching Charles Carter's shadowy past. He had reported his suspicions – he had many suspicions – to Starling, who had said nothing except, 'Good work,' which could have meant anything.

Out came Starling's watch. 'If I'm not mistaken, at this very moment, the *Hercules* is approaching the Panama Canal, in heavy seas. This should be most interesting.'

Then Griffin knocked at the door of One Hilgirt Circle. It was answered, almost instantly, by Charles Carter.

Carter was still in his stocking feet and wore black trousers and a shirt to which no collar was yet attached. He looked amused to see them. Glancing back into his foyer, he then stepped out into the day, pulling the door closed behind him.

Griffin said, 'Good morning. Charles Carter?'

'Yes?'

'Agents Griffin and Starling of the Secret Service.' Griffin handed Carter his badge. Carter held it in his left hand. Griffin pointed at Carter's right hand, which was still extended backward, keeping the door shut. 'Are you concealing anyone or anything inside?'

'I'm just trying to keep the cat from getting out.'

'Okay. We'd like to ask you some questions about events of August second.'

'Certainly.'

'May we come in?'

Carter frowned. 'I don't think that's such a good idea.'

Griffin looked toward Starling, who gave a nod; obviously, they had caught the magician up to no good. Griffin continued, 'Mr Carter, please step aside.'

Carter ushered the agents past him.

Carter's foyer led to a three-bedroom pied-á-terre with fireplaces in the parlor and dining room. Since he had collected curios and Orientalia from every corner of the globe during his five world tours, it was a room where – save for one pressing detail – the eye hardly knew what to consider first. There were aboriginal sculptures, magic rain sticks from Sumatra, geodes on dusty silver stands, and more of the same, but, most important, Griffin put his hand on the butt of his pistol, for he saw, sitting on a large Persian rug that covered most of the front room, an enormous African lion.

The lion's shoulders were dropping to the floor, ready to pounce. Griffin touched Starling's shoulder, and Starling, too, stared at it without saying a word. Griffin could see its stomach flutter as it breathed, its tail thumping against the carpet.

'I said I didn't want to let the cat out,' Carter said.

Griffin swallowed. 'Does that thing bite?'

'Well,' Carter said thoughtfully, 'if he does, go limp. It's less fun for him that way, and he'll drop you sooner or later.'

'Mr Carter,' Starling said in his slow Kentucky drawl, 'I would appreciate you locking your pet in a side room for just a few minutes.'

'Certainly. Baby, come.' Carter whistled between his teeth, clicked his tongue, and Baby reluctantly looked away from the agents and followed his master out of the room.

'Jesus wept,' Griffin sighed. He straightened his tie. 'Why does everything have to be so difficult?'

'There are other occupations, Mr Griffin.'

A moment later, Carter returned, a silk robe around his shoulders. 'May I offer you something to drink?'

Starling asked, 'Are you going to make it yourself?'

Carter's pale blue eyes flickered, and then, tightening the cinch around his robe, he bowed. 'Yes, Mr Starling, I've had to squeeze my own oranges for the last few days.'

Griffin looked back and forth between them with confusion.

Carter continued, 'Bishop has always wanted to see Greece. He sketches, you know. Landmarks and such.'

Griffin tried to catch Starling's eye. Bishop? Bishop who? Once again, Griffin had been passed by.

Starling looked for a good spot to sit on a seven-foot leather couch that was occupied by open volumes of the 1911 *Encyclopædia Brittanica*. 'Mr Griffin, please make a note: it's Alexander Bishop, Carter's servant, who's on the boat.' Then, to Carter, 'The chinchilla coat was a nice touch.'

'He's always liked it. I am quite serious, would you like refreshments?'

'No, thank you, sir.'

'But you, Mr Griffin, I'm sure you're game for a muffin or two.' Carter gestured grandly toward the kitchen as if eggs, bacon, and

14

a raft of toast might dance out on his command. Griffin glared at him.

Starling, looking as comfortable as if he'd been sitting on fine leather couches for years, glanced at his notepad. 'Mr Carter, did you speak to the late President alone on the night of his death?'

'I did.'

Starling asked, 'What did you talk about?'

'Before the performance, we met backstage with the Secret Service in attendance, and then alone for, what, five minutes perhaps. I described the various illusions. He wanted to be in the final act. That was all.'

'How was his demeanor?'

'He seemed depressed at first.'

'Did you ask what was wrong?'

'In my years on tour I've learned that with the powerful, it's wise not to ask such questions.'

'Was there anything at all unusual about your conversation?'

'Only that . . . I'm unsure how to describe it, but his mood was weary. Yet, when I told him his duties onstage would involve being torn to pieces and fed to wild animals, he brightened considerably.' Carter shook his head. 'That defies reason, don't you think?'

Starling cleared his throat. 'Actually, sir, the President had been under some stress.'

'For a stocky man, he seemed fragile.'

Starling looked past Carter, to an *ukiyo-e* woodcut of a Kabuki player. 'Did he happen to mention a woman named Nan Britton?'

'He did not.'

'A woman named Carrie Phillips?'

'He did not.'

'Did he mention anyone else?'

Carter looked to the ceiling. 'He mentioned my elephant, approvingly, his dogs, also approvingly, my lion, with some lesser approval, and though we covered the animal kingdom, I believe that no one human was mentioned.' Carter smiled like a child finishing a piano recital.

Griffin snarled, 'Look, Carter, this might be a game to you, but the President's death is a matter of national security.'

'How did the President die, exactly?'

A glance between the agents, then Starling spoke. 'The cause is undetermined. Three physicians say brain apoplexy, but no autopsy was performed.'

Carter asked, 'Why not?'

Griffin said, 'We're asking the questions here. It might have something to do with an exhausted man being forced to do acrobatics up and down a rope all night long.'

Carter's face cleared. 'Mr Griffin, this *isn't* a game to me. I'm able to make a living because I don't explain how my effects are performed. But if it helps you: from the moment the President left the card table, his stunts were performed by one of my men in disguise. The President hid until after I gave Baby the signal to play dead. There was no exertion on the President's part, and I had nothing to do with his death, I assure you.'

'Then why'd you run away, Carter?' asked Griffin.

'But, as you know, I didn't. The feint with the *Hercules* was to keep the general public from stringing me up. I thought the Secret Service would find me. And so you have,' he concluded warmly, like they'd made him proud. 'Is there more to this interrogation?'

'We'll tell you when it's over, pal.' Griffin squinted menacingly at Carter, but saw that Starling was already folding up his notebook. 'Okay,' Griffin said, deflating, 'it's over.' He pointed at Carter. 'Keep yourself available. We might have more questions.'

Carter nodded, as if admitting that into every life a little rain must fall, which made Griffin want to pop him one.

Carter showed the two agents to the door. Griffin began to take the stairs back down. When he got to the first landing, he heard, behind him, the Colonel asking if he wouldn't mind waiting. Griffin paused. He looked back up fifty or so feet of staircase, where his superior and the suspect stood and watched him in turn. He patted his hand against the railing, feeling the vibrations pinging back and forth, and then, resigning himself to a life out of earshot, he looked at the view of the lake.

At first, Starling said nothing to Carter. He simply let a few moments play out in silence. 'I wish I knew more about gardens.'

There were flowers in tiered planters on either side of the stairs, and trellises of jasmine and honeysuckle. Carter indicated a few stalks that were growing almost as high as his fingertips. 'This is Thai basil, and that was supposed to be cilantro, but it's turned to coriander. Whenever I'm overseas, I pick up a few herbs. It makes my cook happy.'

'The photograph in your drawing room, is that your wife?'

'She was my wife. I'm a widower.' He said this flatly.

'I'm sorry.' Starling massaged a mint leaf and brought his fingertips to his nose, closing his eyes.

Carter spoke. 'Was the President in trouble?'

'That depends,' Starling said, opening his eyes again. 'Is there anything else I should know?'

Carter shrugged. 'I had but five minutes with the President.' He watched a pelican fly in a lazy circle by the lake. 'Being a magician is an odd thing. I've met presidents, kings, prime ministers, and a few despots. Most of them want to know how I do my tricks, or to show me a card trick they learned, as a child, and I have to smile and say, "Oh, how nice." Still, it's not a bad profession if you can get away from all the bickering among your peers about who created what illusion.'

Starling had very small eyes. When they fixed on something, a person, for instance, it was like positioning two steel ball bearings. 'I see. You put on a thrilling show yourself, sir.'

'Thank you.'

'Now, I'm just an admirer here, and I hope this question isn't rude, but have I seen some of those tricks before?'

'Those effects? Not the way I do them, no.'

'So you are the creator of all of those tricks.'

Carter found something interesting to look at, over Colonel Starling's shoulder: a very, very large sunflower.

Starling continued: 'Because Thurston – I've had the pleasure of seeing Thurston – does that trick with the ropes as well. Doesn't he? And I saw Goldin several years ago, and he had two Hindu yoga men, as well. Is there any part of your act—'

'No, there isn't,' Carter replied briskly. 'The fact of the matter is, Colonel Starling, there are few illusions that are truly original. It's a matter of presentation.'

Starling said nothing; saying nothing often led to gold.

'In other words, I didn't invent sugar or flour, but I bake a mean apple pie.'

'So you're just as respected in the business for the quality of your presentation as the magicians who actually *create* illusions,' Starling said sincerely, as if looking for confirmation.

Carter folded his arms, and a smile spread to his eyes, which twinkled. 'At some point this stopped being about President Harding.'

'My fault. I'm intrigued by all forms of misdirection.' Starling reached into his vest pocket, then withdrew his business card, which he looked at for a moment before handing to Carter. 'If you think of anything else—'

'I'll call you.'

Starling joined Griffin. They walked several steps before Starling turned around. 'Oh, Mr Carter?'

'Yes?'

'Did the President say anything about a secret?'

'A secret? What sort of secret?'

'A few people told us that in his last weeks, the late President asked them . . .' Starling opened a notepad, and read, 'What would you do if you knew an awful secret?'

Carter blinked. His eyes flashed in excitement. 'How dramatic. What on earth could that be?'

'We'll find out. Thank you.'

Carter watched them walk all the way down the stairs to their cab, which had waited for them. A half mile away, the pelican above the lake had been joined by a half dozen others. The day was turning out calm and fair, giving Carter a perfect excuse to visit his friend Borax, or to stroll in the park, or to take coffee and dessert at one of the Italian cafés downtown. For now, he watched the Secret Service agents depart, their cab lurching down Grand Avenue in traffic. There were a dozen houses under construction in Adams Point, and so Carter watched the cab alongside panel trucks owned by carpenters and plumbers and bricklayers until it turned a corner and vanished.

And then he tore Starling's card into pieces and scattered them across the stairs.

With age, the world falls into two camps: those who have seen much of the world, and those who have seen *too* much. Charles

Carter was a young man, just thirty-five, but at some point after his wife's death, he had seen too much. Every six months or so he tried to retire, a futile gesture, as he knew nothing except how to be a magician. But a magician who has lost the spark of life is not a careful magician, and is not a magician for long. Ledocq had chastised him so often Carter could do the lectures himself, including digressions in French and Yiddish. 'Make a commitment, Charlie. Go with life or go with death, but quit the kvetching. Don't keep us all in suspense.'

Sometimes, Carter walked in the military cemetery in the Presidio. After the Spanish-American War, if a soldier were a suicide, his tombstone was engraved with an angel whose face was tucked under his left wing. But in less enlightened times, there was no headstone: suicides were simply buried facedown.

Six nights a week, sometimes twice a night, Carter gave the illusion of cheating death. The great irony, in his eyes, was that he did not wish to cheat it. He spent the occasional hour imagining himself facedown for eternity. Since the war, he had learned how to recognize a whole class of comrades, men who had seen too much: even at parties, they had a certain hollowing around the eyes, as if a glance in the mirror would show them only a fool having a good time. The most telling trait was the attempted smile, a smile aware of being borrowed.

An hour before the final Curran Theatre show, he had been supervising the final placement of the props, smiling his half smile when called upon to be friendly. Suddenly a retinue of Secret Service agents appeared, all exceptionally clean-looking young men in a uniform Carter committed to memory: deep blue wool jackets, black trousers, and highly polished shoes, a human shell around President Harding.

The President was still beloved by most of the country. Word had only just begun to trickle down from Washington that the administration was in trouble. Harding had made no secret of his intent to hire people whom he liked. And he liked people who flattered him. He innocently told the Washington press corps, 'I'm glad I'm not a woman. I'd always be pregnant, for I cannot say no.'

Though significantly overweight, with a high stomach that seemed to pressure his breastbone, Harding was still an impressive man, olive-skinned and with wiry grey hair, caterpillar eyebrows, and the sculpted nose of a Roman senator. Yet in a glance, shrewd men noted his legendary weak nature: his several chins, too-wet mouth, and his gentle, eager eyes. More than one person who saw him during his last week on earth commented on his apparent deterioration. Even if they did not know of the extraordinary pressure he was under, they could see it reflected in his slack-skinned complexion.

Carter, who frequently had to size up a man in an instant, saw something more dismal. He remembered an unfortunate creature he'd seen in New Zealand: a parrot that had evolved with no natural enemies. Happy, colorful, it had lost the ability to fly and instead walked on the ground, fat and waddling slowly, with no sense that anyone could mean it ill. When humans arrived and shot into a flock of them, the survivors would stand still, confused and trusting that a mistake had been made, actually letting people pick them up and dash their brains out against the ground.

Harding approached Carter with his right hand extended. 'I am so very, very pleased to meet you, sir.'

'Mr President.' When they shook hands, Harding jumped back shocked: he now held a bouquet of tuberoses.

'For Mrs Harding,' Carter said softly.

Harding looked around, as if checking with his company to see whether it was dignified to show delight. Then he cried, 'Yes, these are the Duchess's favorites. Wonderful! You're quite good. Isn't he good?'

They were a standard gift from Carter to potentates, fresh flowers – from his own garden, if possible, and in midsummer, his tuberoses were beautiful and fragrant.

'Now,' said Harding, 'I'm supposed to talk with you man-to-man about my perhaps going onstage tonight. I have an idea.'

'Yes?'

'You might not know this, but when I was a boy, I did a lot of magic tricks.'

'No!'

'Let me tell you a couple I know pretty well,' the President said slyly.

Carter fixed a smile on his face. While Harding spoke, he focused on his ability to hold his breath and listen to his own heartbeat.

As soon as Harding finished, Carter said, 'Let us think about that.'

Harding leaned in close, whispering. 'I understand you have an elephant tonight. Do you think I could see him?'

Carter hesitated. 'I can take you. But not your aides. She's in a small space, and a crowd would frighten her.'

Harding turned to a pair of Secret Service agents, who shook their heads – no, they would not let him out of their sight. Harding's lower lip went out. 'There, you see, Carter? So much for being a great man.' He wagged his finger at the agents. 'Now, listen here, I'm going to see the elephant. Take me to him, Carter.'

Puffed up like he'd negotiated a tariff, Harding passed through a curtain Carter pulled back. The two men walked side by side down a narrow corridor toward the rear wall of the backstage area.

They passed the solitary figure of Ledocq, who nodded politely at Harding, and made sure Carter saw him tapping on his watch. 'Not much time, Charlie.'

'Thank you.'

'You have your wallet?'

Carter touched his trouser pocket. 'Yes.'

'Good. Always take your wallet onstage.'

Harding produced a hearty chuckle. He seemed uncomfortable with silence, so, as he and Carter continued walking, he admitted he had never seen an elephant up close, though at his recent trip to Yellowstone, he had hand-fed gingersnaps to a black bear and her cub. He was elaborating on his poorly scheduled trip to a llama farm when Carter drew back a tall velvet curtain.

'My God.' They were in a small but high-ceilinged area closed off from the rest of the theatre with screens and soundproofing. There were two cages: one for the elephant, one for the lion. There were no handlers. The animals were quite alone. The elephant, eating hay, stomped twice on the floor when she saw Carter, who rubbed her trunk in response. She was wearing a jeweled headdress and sequins glittered by her eyes in the half-light. Harding cast but a brief glance at Baby, the lion, before approaching the elephant's cage. 'Is it safe?'

'Oh yes. Here.' Carter handed the President a peanut. With deliberation, Harding showed the peanut to the elephant, who took it with her trunk and put it into her mouth.

'It tickled when she touched my palm. Do you have more peanuts?'

Carter handed Harding a whole bag, which Harding had to keep away from the elephant's probing trunk.

'What is her name?'

'I call her Tug.'

'I like her. She's very quiet. You always think of elephants trumpeting and stampeding and so forth. But you don't act naughty, do you, Tug?' Harding touched Tug's trunk as it found more peanuts. 'Do you always need to keep her chained up?'

'Luckily, no. Tug lives on a farm about a hundred miles south. When we go on tour, she is cramped up, but not much more so than the rest of us.'

Harding brought his eye near Tug's, so they could look at each other. 'I wish she could always be on her farm.'

'Have you met Baby?'

Harding shrugged. 'Not much of a cat man. Allergic, you know. I have a dog.'

'Of course. Laddie Boy.'

Harding beamed, looking surprised. 'You know him?' Then his face fell. 'How foolish of me. Mr Carter, for a moment I forgot I was President.' He fell silent, and directed himself to feeding the rest of the bag of peanuts to Tug. When he spoke again, it was to mutter, 'I've been counting dogs these last few minutes. I've owned many dogs. People are so cruel to dogs, aren't they? When I was a lad, I had Jumbo, who was a great big Irish setter. He was poisoned. And then Hub, a pug. Someone poisoned him, I'm sure it was the boy next door, who never liked him. Laddie Boy is lucky, if anyone poisoned him, it would be national headlines. Quite a scandal.' Tug's trunk ran against his hands, which he held forth, palms out. 'Sorry, sweetheart, all gone. You've eaten all the peanuts.'

'Mr President, we should discuss what part of the act you might appear in.'

'Mmm? I was just thinking how tremendous it would be to have a pet elephant. It would be like a dream, wouldn't it? If I had an elephant, I would walk him down to the shops on F Street, and, Lord, imagine the expression on the grocer's face when the Duchess went for her produce!' Harding tilted his head toward the rafters.

Even in the dimness, his face looked ravaged. 'A pet elephant!' He smiled as if cheerful, and in that moment, Carter saw that the President of the United States had that awful, borrowed smile of a man who has seen too much.

'Mr President—'

'I have a sister in Burma. She's a missionary. One of the natives had an elephant who was old and dying. He tried to run off and die alone. I think the keeper couldn't bear that, so he put his elephant in a cage. As long as the elephant could see his keeper by his side, he was calm, but if he left even for a moment, he became distraught. And when the elephant's eyesight failed, he would feel for the keeper with his trunk. That's how he finally died, you know, with his trunk wrapped around his best friend's hand.'

Harding stood away from the cage, turning his back and bringing his big hands over his face. His shoulders quaked, and the floorboards creaked as he shifted his weight. Carter was aware of motorcars passing outside, people laughing over dinner, bankers and factory workers and phone operators and ditchdiggers and chorus girls and attorneys speeding right now through their lives, gay and so very far beyond the four walls of this soundproof stage.

Harding faced him. He sniffed, bringing his voice under control. 'Carter, if you knew of a great and terrible secret, would you for the good of the country expose it or bury it?'

Carter could see dire need in Harding's face. It lit him up like electricity. As was Carter's way since Sarah had died, he withdrew. He looked at his sleeve, inspecting his jacket for flaws. 'I don't know if I'm qualified to answer such a question.'

'Please just tell me what to do.'

He brought his stage voice into play. It was like a stiff arm holding Harding at a careful distance. 'You are asking a professional magician. One of my oaths is to never reveal a secret. Intellectually—'

'Oh, hang "intellectually." This is not a secret like how a trick works. It is concealed to harm, not to entertain.'

'Then perhaps you already know the answer, Mr President.'

Harding put both hands to his face and moaned through them. 'I wish this trip were over. I wish I weren't so burdened by all this. I wish, I wish . . .'

And here, for Carter, the ice cracked. Behind his sangfroid voice, he had the soul of someone who truly wanted to help. He had a glimmer of how he might best serve the President. He said, slowly, 'I know of a way you might take your mind off this problem. Do you know of the Grand Guignol theatre in France?'

Harding shook his head, face buried in his fleshy hands.

'In any case, I know which part of my act you might enjoy the most.' Carter smiled his half-smile. 'It involves being butchered with knives and eaten by a wild animal.'

Harding let his hands down a little, and peeked his face around them. It was very quiet for just a moment, and then the two men, president and magician, began a discussion. As time was short, they couldn't speak at length, but they did manage to speak in depth.

Harding's casket stood at the west end of the lobby of the Palace Hotel on Friday, August third. There was some embarrassment at first, as the only American flag anyone could find to drape over it was the one that had flown in front of the Palace since 1913, and weathering and soot made it a shabby tribute indeed. Eventually, a new flag was found, and wreaths from local, national, and world leaders began to arrive, and by dusk, the lobby was overflowing with floral arrangements, so the hotel had to start stacking them outside the front door. By the next morning, there were flowers, singly, or in bouquets, or in expensive vases lining the entire block. It was said that to breathe deeply by the Palace Hotel was to smell heaven, and for several weeks in downtown San Francisco, when foggy, the faint, sweet aroma of roses came in hints, then vanished.

The train that had carried Harding through his now abandoned Voyage of Understanding was converted to a funeral train. Black bunting draped down the sides of the locomotive and the three cars. The casket was placed just above the level of the windows so all of the pedestrians who stood by the platform at Third and Townsend could take off their hats and have a final moment with Harding's remains.

Soon, Harding would become the most reviled of American politicians, his name synonymous with the worst kind of fraud and egotism, but for now, as the train left the platform, boys ran after it, trying to touch the side panels, to tag the Presidential Seal, to get a souvenir of his passing.

The plan had been to fly across the rails at full speed, to arrive in Washington, D.C., for official mourning, then to have the remains interred in Marion, Ohio, Harding's birthplace. But even before the train reached the city limits of San Francisco, it became apparent that America would not let him go so fast. Crowds lined the tracks, holding candles, calling out to the Widow Harding, singing 'Nearer My God to Thee,' and the Duchess ordered the train to slow down so everyone might see the coffin, touch the train, wave to her, so she might hear the hymn again and again.

As news of the train spread around the country, families who lived far from the tracks drove all night in all weather to reach them, so they, too, could watch it passing. An eighty-six-year-old man in Illinois told everyone he knew that five presidents had died since he was born, and this was his last chance to see such a thing.

Soon boys began putting wheatback pennies on the tracks, retrieving shiny flattened ellipses once the train had passed over them. Someone discovered that putting two tenpenny nails in an X would fuse them together like a Spanish cross, and word spread by telephone and radio and telegraph, and in every town, while farmers changed into their Sunday best, and miners scrubbed their faces and washed their hair, and church choirs lined up on either side of the tracks and rehearsed 'Nearer My God to Thee,' hardware store owners ran barrels of their nails to the tracks, to make more crosses.

But before the train had even left California, it traveled through Carmel, where it crossed a railway trestle over the Borges Gorge. The engineer blew the whistle, and on a hilltop not so far away, Tug the elephant answered briefly before returning to search her favorite eucalyptus tree for celery and oranges and other treats Carter had hidden there.

ACT ONE

Metamorphosis
1888–1911

I have often sat at the table with Unthan the legless wonder, who would pass me the sugar, and the fat lady, Big Katie, would obligingly sit at the edge of the table, so as to give poor Emma Shaffer, the ossified girl, plenty of room.

— HARRY HOUDINI

It is well known that a magician feels no suffering while on the stage; a species of exaltation suspends all feelings foreign to his part, and hunger, thirst, cold, or heat, even illness itself, is forced to retreat in the presence of this excitement, though it takes revenge afterwards.

— ROBERT-HOUDIN

Chapter 1

He wasn't always a great magician. Sometimes he said he was the seventh magician in his family, the great-great-great-great-grandson of Celtic sorcerers. Sometimes he claimed years of training at the feet of Oriental wizards. But his press releases never told the truth, that from the moment Charles Carter the Fourth first learned it, magic was not an amusement, but a means of survival.

All magicians had boyhood stories. Kellar, Houdini, Thurston, and many of the best found inspiration during periods of illness and bed rest, when a relative would bring them a magic set to while away their days. But not Carter. Instead, his first performance took place in a deserted house in the dead of winter, when he was nine years old.

At first, the house was full. He grew up in San Francisco, Pacific Heights, specifically Presidio Heights, 3638 Washington Street between Spruce and Locust. This was a three-story Italianate built in 1874 to house the Russian consulate. But after a decade of poor fur-trapping seasons, the Russians could no longer pay the mortgage. Mr and Mrs Charles Carter III, newlyweds, moved in.

On the ground floor was the foyer, then the parlor and the drawing room, with chairs and tables from Gump's and window boxes around the fireplace where the ladies sat for tea in winter. The grand piano was in the parlor, and there Charles was forced to sit upright twice a week, pecking note by note through 'Twinkle Twinkle Little Star' and other tunes from *Instructive Melodies,* the worn cloth songbook his humorless teacher pointed to with bony fingers.

Running from the parlor to the back dining room were forty-five feet of freedom, in the form of a hallway with rugs that always slipped, and when they were being cleaned, Charles tiptoed from room to room, looking for every adult – mother, father, nurse, cook, valet, maids – and if all of them were upstairs, he kicked off his shoes and skidded down the floors in his stocking feet. Then he was the lookout while his brother James had a go. James, younger than Charles and devoted as a duckling, never instigated, and was brilliant at behaving innocently when called upon. They never pushed their luck. Just two or three transits down the floorboards, enough to find exactly the right posture to carry them farthest and fastest – they were racehorses, freight trains, comets – then Charles would crouch in the breakfast nook, retying his shoelaces, and James's, and putting on his sweetest face to ask Cook for a glass of milk.

The house was paid for, as were most houses in Pacific Heights, on the trading of stocks, bonds, and notes. Their father was an investment banker, and better than most in his character and intuition, riding out the occasional panic and run on gold with good humor. Further, Mr Carter was blessed with a hobby to which he could apply his imagination: he collected. When it was fashionable to collect European artwork, he did so, and when fashions shifted to Japan, the Carter house was home to three – but what three! – scrolls mounted behind glass that showed the cast of Genji Monogatari. Though the Japan mania caused many of the Pacific Heights social set to fill room after room with woodcuts of every single one of the 53 Stages of the Tokaido, Mr Carter believed that to have three of anything was a collection. Then it was time to move on.

Charles's mother, Lillian, was a complexity: she had grown up in a house of New England Transcendentalists and passionately pursued the riches of interior life. A robust woman who could argue the politics of suffrage for three hours straight, Mrs Carter also suffered fainting spells, allergies, and the overaccumulation of nervous energy. In one year, she received a neurologist, who said she had a depletion of phosphorous so that her nerve cells conducted electricity improperly; a somatic hygienist, who prescribed bed rest to replenish nutritional energies lost to excessive thinking and feeling; a psycho-analyst, who wanted to explore her girlhood conflicts with her parents; a hypnotist, who put her into trances to relieve her overstimulated emotions; and a spirit medium, who led a séance to rid her of abnormal spirit clusters.

'I have many, many neuroses,' she declared at a parlor room tea to which Charles and James had been invited as long as they were quiet.

30

'I have them, too,' said Mrs Owens, who was competitive.

'But I've been invited to Boston for a study,' Mrs Carter said, which defeated Mrs Owens and caused many of Mrs Carter's other friends to ask questions: was she following the theosophists? Or a more traditional field?

Mrs Carter was in fact to be a patient of Dr James Jackson Putnam, a psycho-analyst and Harvard professor. 'He recommended this book,' she explained, displaying with pride her inscribed copy of *Psychic Treatment of Nervous Disorders*.

'Oh, psychic treatment,' Mrs Owens said. 'That was popular . . . several years ago.' Her lip curled with sympathy.

'No, no, this is quite new. Honestly.' Mrs Carter looked to her husband for support.

'It's . . .' Mr Carter met his wife's eye and he charted another course. 'It can't be dismissed.'

Charles, almost nine years old, followed the conversation with an interest that deepened as he realized his mother was considering a trip to Boston. How long would she be away? Could he go with her? He glanced at James, who was just six years old, and who turned the pages of a stiff-backed *Famous Men and Famous Deeds*, humming quietly to himself. He almost whispered, 'James, pay attention,' but he didn't want to be dismissed from the room. The topic was abandoned, but Charles listened for the rest of the afternoon for clues: was his mother actually going away?

A few nights later, she sat at the end of his bed and explained that he and his brother wouldn't be left alone: there was his father, and Fräulein Reinhardt, and of course the rest of the servants.

'I need you to have a stiff upper lip,' she continued. 'James will look to you for guidance. You can't let him down.' Charles watched her twist her necklace between her fingers. 'He's so young he'll wonder why he can't come with me.'

Charles considered, then, a different question to ask her. 'When are you coming back?'

'That's a tremendous question, Charles. There are circles within circles. In fact, Dr Putnam compares the experience to the *Divine Comedy*. You know.' His mother nodded at him, and he nodded back, to show he understood. At bedtime, she had a habit of talking as if they were allies sharing a confidence. 'First, you descend into your emotional life with a doctor as your guide, and then the repressed memories are washed away in the Lethe.'

When she spoke – she was adept at speaking and annoyed at those who merely talked – his mother drew on many dramatic gestures whose source Charles could hardly guess at, as she shunned the theatre itself. Describing her progress through psycho-analysis, she flamboyantly waved her fingers and winced as if in pain. 'You pass the moaning souls in the lake of fire, but you must push on past that despair' – she displayed a faraway gaze of contemplation – 'till you come to' – with a sigh of release – 'inner resourcefulness.'

Charles followed the gestures and the sound of her voice, but little else. She was going to have an adventure, and when she came back, she would be more experienced and in better mental health. But there was no way to know how long it would take.

His last sight of her that night was in the doorway, her hand on the wall as she dimmed the light, her face illuminated by the dying orange cast of the gas jet. Lillian Carter knew how to leave a room with a flourish, and Charles loved the pauses before she left. She whispered, eyebrows arching, 'The next time we see each other, we'll both have changed so much!' She put her fingers to her lips as if she'd just told him a secret. As she closed the door, slowly, stepping backward into the hall, Charles memorized the look of promise on her half-shadowed face, the way she anticipated a great mystery. It would be his last sight of her for two years.

Chapter 2

Immediately after his mother left, Charles became his father's shadow. On long Sunday afternoons, Mr Carter could barely walk from his bookshelves to the ledgers on his desk without becoming entangled with his elder child.

On the longest wall of Mr Carter's study were woodcuts set behind beveled glass, matted with hand-cut linen, and placed, because the wall had so many other pieces of art on it, at a child's eye level. All three woodcuts depicted instruments of torture: the bilboes and the pillory and the brank.

The bilboes looked like handcuffs that went around the ankles. The prisoner lay flat on his back, in the dirt, his feet suspended in the air by a length of iron bar to which the bilboes were fastened. The penitent faced a jeering crowd of angry faces and fists raised high over buckled hats.

Charles couldn't quite understand the punishment. His father explained it: it was humiliating to lie in the bilboes, to be restrained against your will in front of all those people. Your reputation was forever ruined.

Running a finger around the frame's edges, Charles repeated this. 'Your reputation.'

'Please don't get your fingers on that, Charles,' his father said, and to close the matter, he reiterated, 'The bilboes disgrace you.'

Now Charles understood. 'Oh, yes. Because you don't know how to get out.'

'No,' his father sighed, 'that certainly isn't it.'

Charles was no closer to understanding why he was so interested. That night he lay in bed long after he was supposed to be asleep, wondering what it was like to be clapped into the leg cuffs and pelted with rocks by the crowd. His legs up in the air so that coins might fall from his pockets – they would be Sommer Islands tuppence and sixpence, Willow Tree shillings from the coin collecting books

33

his father read with him. Yes, it would be humiliating not to know how to escape from the bilboes.

When his nurse, Fräulein Reinhardt, woke Charles in the morning, she pinched his cheek and hissed, 'No, no, beds are for sleeping the other way,' because she found him with his feet jammed into the cutout fleurs-de-lis of his headboard.

The illustration of the pillory was less enticing to him. Standing with his head and wrists pinned with a makeshift stocks was tiresome, so he never pretended to be pilloried.

However, according to a Boston Settlement Court record that his father had copied and displayed on the wall, in 1659, a certain Thomas Carter – almost certainly an ancestor – had been 'nayled by both eares to the pillory, 3 nailes in each ear.' His crime was being 'an incorrigible forestaller.'

'They nailed him to the pillory?'

'Yes,' his father sighed, for these conversations were becoming more frequent.

'Put nails through his ears?'

'Yes.'

Charles asked his father, eagerly, if the woodcut above the court record showed their ancestor himself being punished. But no, to his disappointment, it just depicted a 'typical' prisoner. Still, he was rather excited by all this, so he looked from the ledger to the picture. 'What is a forestaller?'

With this question, Mr Carter put down his reports. 'Just before a French ship carrying sailcloth was about to dock, he bought the whole inventory and arranged to sell it at retail.' For the first time in his life, Charles saw his father's eyes probing his own for interest. 'He bought low and sold high and he was punished for it.'

The clocks in the study ticked, and one of them purred, as it was about to chime the half hour. Charles knew he was supposed to have a response, and he didn't want his father to dismiss him. 'If he wasn't just locked in . . . but if he was *nailed* to the pillory,' he said slowly, 'it would be much, much harder to get out.'

'Yes?' His father's lips pursed as if he would continue, but only if Charles earned it.

Charles looked away from his father. He could think of nothing further to say. He pretended new interest in the pictures on the wall until his father returned to his financials. Though he didn't want to look at it – he never wanted to look at it – Charles was staring directly at the depiction of the brank.

Once, he had been on a train that had hit a team of horses. His mother covered his eyes. He fought to see between his mother's fingers, and simultaneously wanted to be protected from seeing. This is how it was with the brank.

One afternoon in October, Charles and James came home from school and saw, as if it were St Nick's sleigh, a cab waiting in front of their house. They ran as fast as they could, shouting to each other that their mother was returning.

But the driver was carrying trunks out of the house. They belonged to the valet, and to one of the maids. In Mrs Carter's absence, they had broken into the liquor supplies, and Mr Carter had immediately sacked them.

Fräulein Reinhardt was the next to go. In November, she received a transatlantic cable, from Mölln, where her father had suffered a stroke, and by that afternoon, she was crying – something Charles couldn't have imagined her doing – when she hugged him and James good-bye.

Because it was impossible to hire domestics with references during the holiday season, Mr Carter told his sons they would muddle through with just Cook and Patsy until after the first of the year. Charles felt nervous about this, but hoped it would at least mean their father would forget certain rituals, like washing behind the ears (he didn't) and piano lessons (he did). James asked their father if he would read them stories at bedtime, and, to Charles's surprise, Mr Carter said he would be delighted.

Mr Carter turned out to be a terrible reader, but Charles was so pleased to hear any voice at all he didn't complain. He didn't even mind that to make things more efficient, Mr Carter made James's bedtime the same as Charles's and that the brothers had to share a bed.

After the first night's reading, a Brothers Grimm tale, Mr Carter wished his sons good night, and departed. Charles waited a moment, until he heard his father's door close, and then whispered, 'James, remember how Fräulein Reinhardt reads? How she does all the voices?' When James made no response, Charles shook him, but James was already asleep.

His father read to them every night for two weeks and, every night, James drifted off quickly and Charles was left awake. It was worse, it turned out, to lie awake with company than to do so alone. He would wait until he heard the clock strike midnight, then he would crawl out of bed and slip into the hallway, listening for his father, or Cook, or Patsy.

The house was larger at night, swollen with dark shadows and strange creaks that terrified him, and yet Charles could not help exploring it. Sometimes he prowled into his father's study and took out the coin collection, which he wasn't allowed to touch, pointing to each drachma, each half-cent, and whispering its story aloud, 'Only six hundred experimental proofs were made that year, and the designer was Christian Gobrecht, a master craftsman.' Sometimes he imagined there were fairies in other rooms, wicked imps, urging him to discover them. Come look at the brank, they said. If he concentrated hard enough, maybe his mother would hear him wandering and would come back.

At the rear of the house, by the kitchen and the pantry, was the dark and formal dining room, where Charles would push under the curtains, and surface on the other side, his breath making half-dollar-sized clouds on the window, to watch the wild back garden and listen for the faint wheeze of an accordion.

The Carters' garden was a menacing place, with vines and nettles and bushes that were more thorn than rose. But still Charles would have played there were it not for their gardener, the deformed and hostile Mr Jenks. Jenks gardened mostly at night, rarely visiting the daylight, except to growl at children or animals who mistakenly came too close. He lived in a cottage on the far side of the garden, past the cloaking row of elms, where Charles wasn't allowed to go alone.

In the middle of the night, Charles sat in the velvet folds of the curtains, and felt afraid. He was afraid of losing the rest of his family. When James was fresh-born, his mother had put Charles's hand on top of his bald head, and said, 'Feel that movement? The bones of his skull haven't grown together yet,' and from then on, he feared for James's fragility.

He made himself small there in the window, imagining all the things that frightened him. Bullies. Falling down the stairs. Wolves. Mr Jenks. The clothes mangler. How the orphans in the stories his mother's club read aloud to make each other weep forgot their parents' voices. He hadn't forgotten how his mother spoke, nor would he, and some nights he crept into her closet to smell her remaining clothes. 'The souls in the lake of fire,' he whispered, grimacing and waving his arms in a way that wasn't quite right.

In the middle of the night, with his father and brother asleep, and his mother having an adventure, he felt fits of longing for places he'd never been, places he couldn't describe, and he wondered if there were anyone else like him in the world, awake and catching glimpses of the unknown. He wondered if he were truly related to his family, or if instead he had dropped in among them, a changeling.

Mr Carter was not immune to the house's atmosphere, as it was hard to ignore two anxious boys in a household of slowly dwindling numbers. Further, in December, holiday wreaths began to appear on neighbors' doors, and letters from Mrs Carter began to hint at presents to come, which made both his sons now follow him from room to room.

One day, he arose early and announced he had a treat for them. He had outfitted the spider phaeton carriage for a trip, which struck Charles as treat enough already – whereas their mother always made them take the surrey, which was slow and safe, the spider was slight and spry and jumped excitingly over cobblestones.

'We're going to a fair,' his father said, clapping his hands. 'It's all the way in the wilds of Berkeley.' Charles's face fell. He had been to fairs before, and suspected that this would be as much of a treat as a trip to the grocer's. Fairs were for women to display quilts and merchants to gaze fondly at displays of new cotton batting. At best, he might get pie.

But on the ferry to Berkeley, with the three of them huddled in the spider phaeton's seat, and salt spray rising bracingly in their faces, Mr Carter explained that this was different. The old fairs they knew were things of the past, stale and dead, and, he noted with disdain, unprofitable. Now they'd been revitalized by capitalists who had added amusements and frivolities. 'Since we're coming out of a depression, the country needs a little diversion,' he said, holding out a broadside so that James could see it over one shoulder and Charles the other. Mr Carter drew a finger down what looked like a diagram of a village square. 'The Midway Plaisance.'

'The what?' asked James.

'It's like a town, but the only business is pleasure. Here's the Moorish palace, and the Egyptian Theatre, a shooting gallery, and, oh, here's the Merry-Go-Round with Parker's Famous Military Band Organ.' Charles had drawn so close his cheek scratched against his father's overcoat. He didn't know what a Merry-Go-Round was, but it sounded exotic, and as his father listed off the other attractions – the Volcano of Kilauea, Vienna bakeries, a model of St Peter's of Rome, the world's tallest man, 'amazing oddities of the vegetable and animal world' – Charles began to fidget.

After they arrived in Berkeley and took the horse to the livery, Mr Carter walked them onto the fairgrounds. James and Charles immediately began to bicker about which attraction they would see first. Their father didn't notice, as he was perusing a broadside for a cattle auction.

'Boys,' he said, digging into his trousers for coins, 'you each get thirty cents. I have an appointment.' In the hours he'd been promoting the fair, he hadn't mentioned an appointment, but the Carter brothers asked nothing, as they were distracted by the sight of silver dimes hitting their palms. Their father explained that the tax benefits of owning a small herd of livestock had led to waves of *fin-de-siècle* 'urban farming' and he was determined to come away from the fair with exactly three fine animals.

So Mr Carter went left, to the auction, and his sons were sent right, toward the heart of the action. This was their first adventure out of the house since their mother had left, and Charles was excited and nervous about the possibility of getting lost, or even stolen by brutes who were said to prowl around the edges of parks. Yet there was music from a steam calliope, and the sounds of games being played, and when Charles saw children escorted by both parents, he tried to feel free rather than lonely. James was quick to spot the sweets table, and so, gorging themselves on cotton candy and taffy and coconut crisps, the boys took their remaining coins toward the midway.

38

To their disappointment, regardless of the broadside's promises, there was no shooting gallery, nor was there a Merry-Go-Round, and they had to walk carefully, or they would trip, as the ground along the Midway Plaisance was a nightmare of fossilized wheel ruts from heavy wagons that had passed during a rainstorm. Still, Charles looked at the tents with their gaily painted promises – the Wonders of Germany! – the Vistas of Venice! – and he began to feel at ease in a way he never had before.

They paused outside a tent whose yellow sign announced The World's Smallest Horse, with arabesques and filigree designs suggesting the idea was most attractive indeed. The boys were in complete agreement that they had to see the world's smallest horse.

They handed their nickels over. Inside the tent was a corral. A small black horse knelt in a bed of dirty hay beside a bowl of dirty water. The brothers watched the horse pant for a moment.

'He isn't that small,' Charles said.

'He's a little bit small,' James agreed, 'but not that small.'

They left. Carter felt irritated, as he'd been keen on seeing a much smaller horse. The next tent promised Dangerous Reptiles, which made his heart jump with anticipation, but when they entered, there were simply three boa constrictor snakes, each – or so the man who took their nickels said – diabolical, though it was hard to tell, since they wouldn't come out from under the rocks on the other side of the glass.

As this exhibit had been a gyp, the brothers avoided the next two tents: the Florida alligator and the Fat Lady. Charles was unsure of what to do next – he wanted more badly than ever to be taken over by genuine wonder, and he felt that *some* tent *somewhere* would provide what he wanted, but still he decided to avoid the entire pavilion of oddly shaped fruits and vegetables. He was in fact prepared not to enter another tent all afternoon. However, James insisted they see the world's tallest man.

The sign outside the tent declared: Stretch Sullivan: 8 Foot 5 Inches of Fighting Irish.

'It might be a gyp,' Charles cautioned. But since they still had time before the cattle auction was over, Charles agreed to enter. They paid and they walked together past the canvas flap, into the mildewing tent.

It was gloomy inside. Where the tent's seams had given way, shafts of light made faint ovals on patches of dead grass. There was a tent pole in the center and leaning against it was Joe Sullivan. He was reading a newspaper. He glanced at the boys, then went back to his paper, licking a thumb and turning a page.

James reached out and held his brother's hand. At the touch, Charles, who'd been staring for several long seconds, realized he had neither blinked nor breathed since entering. He inhaled quietly. Sullivan's black and scuffed shoes were the length of shotguns. He could pick up a mature pumpkin one-handed. As Charles tilted his head back he felt like he was in the nave of a church; Sullivan's head nearly touched the ribbed vaulting of the canvas tent.

Charles walked a few paces back and forth, bumping into James as they each toed an imaginary line. They kept their distance not from respect, but from a vague fear of being eaten. In fairy tales, giants ate little boys. Charles was old enough to know that these were only stories, but not old enough to dismiss the possibility completely.

Sullivan was dressed in a black wool suit, a bolo tie and a huge tan Stetson. His grim expression – hooded eyes, a mouth as straight and plain as a ruler – looked less like flesh than a waxy kind of stone. He didn't seem in a fighting mood. Still, Charles's unease began to outweigh the wonder he felt.

'Well, we've seen him,' Charles said, taking his brother's hand. James, however, wouldn't budge.

'How tall are you?' James asked.

Without looking away from his newspaper, Sullivan jerked his thumb at the pole he was leaning against. 'Like it says there,' he murmured. He had a soft voice, as if the air were thinner up where it came from. The pole's hashmarks indicated feet. There was an exclamation mark at 8 feet 5 inches, which, because he was slouching, Sullivan did not quite meet.

Charles said, 'Well, we've seen him,' again, but James still had his stubborn look.

James put his hands on his hips. 'Why don't you have a chair?'

'What'd you say?' Sullivan continued reading.

'Why don't you have a chair?'

'No one wants to see me sitting down.'

'Oh. What's your name?'

'Joe Sullivan.'

'Oh. I'm James Carter.'

'Uh-huh.'

'How old are you?'

'Twenty-two.'

'Oh. I'm almost seven.'

'That's dandy.' Sullivan flipped his paper over.

Because James never talked to strangers, Charles was unsure what he, the older brother, should do. For some reason, James started a story – about a friend of his who had his own bicycle – that had so many false starts that Sullivan finally put his newspaper down and stared, hard, at James. Charles wasn't sure why, but he felt growing embarrassment for himself and his brother, as if they'd seen someone naked in the bath, and, even worse, they'd paid to do it. He began to take James by the hand. But then he glanced at Sullivan's gloomy face once again, to tell him good-bye, and faltered.

'Excuse me,' Charles said. He tried to be polite, but excitement began to make him dizzy.

'We must be going,' James added. 'Good-bye,' and he extended his hand to shake.

Sullivan squatted down. He slowly went onto one knee, his joints cracking as loud as pencils snapping, and put his massive hand out and gently curled it around James's. James turned to his brother and said, with an angelic smile, 'See, he ain't gonna eat us.'

Sullivan looked at each brother slowly and carefully. Finally, he muttered, 'Don't say "ain't."' Crouching, he was still the size of an average, standing adult. He smelled like cough medicine. His lumpy white face, which Charles had to look up into, hadn't changed expression, and perhaps couldn't change. Charles still wanted to run away. But the decoration in the center of Sullivan's bolo tie rooted him to the spot.

'Excuse me,' he said, trying to sound casual and mature, 'is that a Gobrecht dollar?'

Sullivan touched his bolo tie with his fingers. 'What?'

'If it's from 1838, it's worth over three hundred dollars.'

'This thing?' Sullivan struggled with the coin. 'What are you talking about?'

'I collect coins,' Charles announced. 'American coins, actually.'

He continued, repeating something he'd heard his father say. 'I know more about things of value than most ever will.'

He did not understand the look Sullivan gave him, but it wasn't a respectful sort of look. Sullivan stuck the newspaper under his arm, loosened his bolo, and held it out so Charles could examine it. 'What's it say there, Elijah?'

'Oh.' Charles looked at the date carefully, disappointed. 'It's an 1850. And it's scratched up.'

'Is it worth three hundred smackers or not?'

'It's worth about five dollars.' Charles colored again.

'Well, why ain't it worth three hundred?' Sullivan barked.

'In 1838 they only made thirty-one silver dollars, total, for the whole United States. But in 1850, they made forty-seven thousand five hundred. If you had an 1851 dollar, you'd be luckier, because then they made only one thousand three hundred of them, and so it's worth—'

'Okay.'

'—worth about a hundred and fifty.'

'I get it, I get it,' Sullivan said, straightening so that the boys were eye level with the grass stains on his knees.

Charles pulled a coin from a fold in his cap. 'Do you know what this is?'

'Some kinda five-dollar gold piece?' Sullivan shrugged.

Charles smiled. 'You fell into the trap,' he said, as he'd said to a dozen adults. 'This is an 1883 five-cent nickel in brilliant un-circulated condition. See, it says "five" in Roman numerals on the back, but they forgot to say "five cents," and a racketeer dipped it in gold solution. And people who weren't all that smart believed it was a five-dollar gold piece.'

'Huh.' Sullivan tapped his rolled-up newspaper against the leg of his trousers, and poked his tongue into his cheek. 'Can I see that thing?'

It was the most valuable piece in the collection that Charles was allowed to handle himself. He wasn't sure what it was worth, but he had never let anyone else touch it. Feeling triumphant, he handed it over.

Sullivan examined it, murmuring, 'Well, whaddya know. Thanks.' He brought his hand down toward Charles, the gold coin braced

42

between his finger and his thumb. As Charles reached for it, Sullivan grabbed it with his other hand, and made a fist, which he opened. It was empty. The coin was gone.

'Hey,' Charles said feebly. Sullivan tipped his hat and returned to the tent pole.

'Give it back,' Charles said.

'Give what back?'

'My nickel.'

Sullivan's face showed it could indeed change expression: he smirked. Then he opened up his newspaper.

Charles looked at James, who was shaking his head gravely. 'Daddy said never show anyone the coin. You're in trouble.'

'Give it back,' Charles yelled. 'That's not fair.'

Sullivan murmured, 'Get used to it, squirt.'

'I want it back!'

It had happened so fast Charles couldn't believe it. His stomach hurt. He stood there, speechless, as the simplicity of having lost his coin – having given it away with no possibility of return – welled up in him. He burst forward and pounded on the giant's leg. 'Give it! Give it!'

He felt a snag on the back of his collar and suddenly he was propelled into the air; Sullivan had picked him up and heaved him close to the dirty yellow cloth of the carnival tent. Charles could feel his shirt buttons straining, and the huge, rough fingers against the flesh at the back of his neck as Sullivan turned him so he was but inches from his mouth.

And then Sullivan whispered into Charles's ear, 'I should make you disappear, too, brat.' Sullivan's hand flapped open and then closed into a fist the size of a turkey and Charles remembered a picture in *Tales for Tots* of a pearl diver engulfed by a deep-sea clam. He blubbered, and let out a low, awful moan, which seemed to startle the giant.

'Shhhh.' Sullivan looked toward the tent flap quickly. 'I said "Shhhh."' But Charles could not stop his crying. As if weighing several poor decisions, Sullivan lowered Charles a couple of feet, and then casually tossed him toward his brother like he was a soft-ball. Charles hit the ground hard, and broke into a run, pulling James out of the tent.

Charles's first impulse was to run to their father for help, but as they got closer to the auction, James's chant of 'You're in trouble, you're in trouble' began to get to him.

They stopped a hundred yards from the livestock pavilion. Charles felt his face, which was hot and stiff in places with dried tears. There was no way he could tell their father what had happened. So he attended to his brother, brushing at his clothing, rubbing the hand he'd pulled on so hard. 'Do you want more taffy?'

'No!' James cried.

'Are you sure?'

James coughed, fingers by his mouth. 'No.'

They found the taffy booth. Having something to do, someone to take care of, calmed Charles. He'd never heard of anyone disappearing, and he began to get mad at the giant. But where had the coin gone? There was no one he could ask. The adult world refused to give straight answers to so many questions, and this was sure to be one of them.

Charles didn't know if James could actually keep a secret, and was convinced he would eventually have to thrash him for telling. But when they saw their father, James said nothing about the coin, and he was just as silent on the ferry ride. Charles, too, was quiet, as he was feeling awful. For a few brief moments, he'd felt the Midway Plaisance was going to welcome him, and then he'd been tricked. He spent the remainder of the carriage ride home imagining a gold coin tumbling in space, alone.

Their father, however, was bubbling with an excitement he didn't explain.

Reins in hand, he exclaimed, 'I shouldn't jinx it,' which was so unusual for him to say that Charles remembered it on Christmas day, when his father explained what he meant.

Chapter 3

It was a gloomy sort of Christmas. There were the usual laurel wreaths lining the walls, and candles burning in the front window, and bowls of penny candy left out for St Nick, and James and Charles dutifully joined their father on the front stoop with brooms they used to sweep out the old year. But the atmosphere around the house was so still and ascetic that no amount of presents, and this year there were even more presents than usual, could fool James or Charles into believing they were having fun.

There were many parcels from Boston, with elaborate labels and ornaments from their mother. New catcher's mitts. Sheet music ('Oh yes, you boys were supposed to be continuing your piano lessons,' Mr Carter muttered. 'I'll catch whatfor from your mother. What's next?'). Next was clothing for them to rough and tumble in. A kaleidoscope. A magic kit. Charles moped through the gifts, though, as he still felt guilty for having lost the nickel, and he tried several times to hug his father, who shooed him away so that the present opening could continue.

Mr Carter was increasingly distracted, handing out presents quickly, saying 'lovely' or 'that's a keeper' even as he reached for the next one. Charles wished he could arrest his father's attention, even for a moment. He knew his mother had a reflective side, and she, even in her letters from Boston, was forever asking him questions about his inner self. Yet Charles had so far not found his father's inner self. He wanted on Christmas morning to unlock the gates to that secret place, whatever it was, and in the process to be forgiven minor sins, such as losing a certain coin.

When the boys finished, Mr Carter leaned forward in his chair. 'Charles, James, do you know what a land forfeiture is?'

Charles shook his head, but James, admiring the gloss on a tin soldier he was turning end over end, nodded absently. Charles was about to punch him in the arm but then James said, 'It's when property goes up for auction before the end of the year.'

James was not yet seven years old. 'It is not!' Charles shouted.

'Actually, that's very close. Someone's been paying attention,' Mr Carter smiled. And then he explained it to them. 'Boys, there's a land forfeiture in Sonoma this Friday. A vineyard. Usually, the bank posts notices at ninety days and sixty days before any auction to give prospective bidders time to prepare. But this land is owned by a down-at-their-heels family, and they're considered a flight risk.' As he talked, he became more and more passionate, and Charles realized that unlike when he told their bedtime stories, if he cared about the subject matter, Mr Carter could be a very good reader indeed.

In short, an incredible financial opportunity awaited him, but he had to travel to Sacramento immediately. He would be back in forty-eight hours, possibly as the owner of four thousand acres of prime vineyard land. They would all celebrate together when he came back, and until then they had Cook and Patsy to depend on, and it would be a great adventure for the boys, a maturing experience.

When the boys awoke the next morning, their father was gone. James, who seemed privy to areas of his father's life that Charles couldn't understand, was tranquil, and sure that all was right with the world.

For two days, Cook and Patsy, the laundress, were their caretakers in name. But Cook was given to hectoring them with stories she said were true that always ended with little boys going to hell, and Patsy was jittery and brittle, worried at every moment the boys would break like china, so the boys spent as little time as possible in the servants' presence. They washed themselves and dressed for bed themselves and presented their fingernails for inspection to Patsy, who was so eager to be done with them she didn't even rub their forearms to see if they squeaked with cleanliness.

Mr Carter was due back at dusk on the twenty-eighth of December. That afternoon, Charles and James sat on the floor of the playroom to play Stealing Bundles with a deck of cards they'd fished out of one of their toy chests. It was frightfully cold; the boys were done up in layers of wool like Eskimos. Charles played with one eye on the clock, and an ear cocked for the sound of an approaching cab. James, who usually liked card games that he had a fair chance of winning, plummeted into a snit.

'You're cheating!' he cried.

'I am not.'

'You aren't playing fair.'

'James,' Charles said, 'you can't cheat at Stealing Bundles. That's why it's a game for babies.'

'Patsy!' James yelled. He stood up.

'We're not supposed to bother Patsy. James!' Charles followed his brother as he raced out of the room.

'He's cheating! Patsy, Charles is cheating!' With Charles in close pursuit, James ran up the back stairs, not even holding onto the banister.

The third floor, the servants' quarters, was a narrow hallway lined with doors, all of which were closed. The amber lights of the wall sconces flickered gloomily. Charles felt uneasy. This was unfamiliar territory – the boys weren't supposed to disturb the domestics in their private rooms.

James banged on Patsy's door; Charles tried to restrain him, but James lurched away and banged again, yelling, 'He's a liar!'

'Fine,' Charles declared. 'Let the baby cry, then!' He folded his arms and pretended interest in the wall, where there was an etching of a European city.

It was cold in the hallway. Charles tried to see his breath, but it wasn't that cold. Still, he wondered why no one had thought to build a fire. Heavy clouds swelled outside the tiny window at the end of the hallway.

James went quiet. Biting at his knuckle, he looked up just as Charles frowned and looked down at him. They both knew how long they could carry on before someone, somewhere, hushed them. That time had passed.

James removed his finger from his mouth. 'Cook! Cook!' And he bolted past Charles, to the stairs.

But there was no one in the kitchen, or the pantry, or even in Cook's ready room, where she always sat and read while her stews simmered. In the parlor, they found a note from Cook, printed in her block lettering. She and Patsy had gone to a very important revival meeting and picnic just across the bay, and would be back before dark.

Charles pushed the buzzers on the wall, all of them, at once: they rang all the rooms on the third floor. When there was no response, he looked at the note again.

'They left?' James asked.

'Yes, they left,' Charles nodded. 'They'll get in trouble for that.'

'Why did they leave?'

'Religion,' Charles said, with the same sour expression their parents used when saying the word. 'Please tell your father dinner will be ready by seven o'clock. If you have any trouble this afternoon, don't worry, Mr Jenks will look after you.' Charles shuddered.

'We're all alone,' James said. Charles could see James wasn't sure what this meant: was it exciting? Or a nightmare?

'It's the first time they've left us alone,' Charles said. He looked out the window; the sky was gloomy, darkening. 'They'll be back any minute.' He put his hand on James's shoulder. 'Where does Cook keep the Fry's chocolate?'

The sky was dark for a remarkable reason. San Francisco was about to be blanketed with snow. When the first flakes fell, at 3:30, the Carter boys bolted out the front door and onto the street, where they twirled in a circle together, heads back, feeling for the first time ever snow on their faces.

It was like feathers on their skin, for the first minute, and then there was a violent shift in the winds. 'Ouch!' Charles winced, for he had just discovered what hail felt like.

'Look!' James shouted, as he caught a pellet of hail on his hand. 'It melts! It melts on you!'

The hailstones scattered as they hit the streets. It sounded like it was raining pennies. The boys ran inside and stood in the open doorway, watching in safety until the hail switched again to snow.

'It's not melting anymore,' Charles cried. Before they knew it, there was an inch of snow on Washington Street. James dashed back into eddies of powder, kicking it around with his boots.

Charles was about to join, but held back. He needed to watch for just one moment – his brother, dancing a jig, scarf flying, in the white, as snow caught and stuck in the oak trees. There was no one else around. No children sharing in this miracle. Up and down Washington Street, all the families were gone for the holiday week, and servants were taking their leave. James was the only sign of life.

By dusk, there was almost a foot of snow on the ground. Charles and James had spent the afternoon in the parlor, noses pressed to the window, mostly delighted. But every hour, when the clocks chimed, they fell quiet, and Charles suddenly felt the need to be brave.

Patsy and Cook didn't return that night. Nor did Mr Carter. The boys silently ate cereal with milk for dinner, with more chocolate tablets for dessert.

'The snow is keeping them from coming back, right?' James asked.

Charles nodded. He had a better command of geography and transportation than James. 'Daddy comes back from Sacramento on a train, and Cook and Patsy take the ferry, and it's storming over the bay, so maybe they're staying overnight in Oakland.'

They decided everyone would return the next day, and their only problem was staying warm until then. Neither one of them was allowed to touch the gas or the fireplaces.

'We could ask Mr Jenks for help,' James said.

'That's not a good idea,' Charles replied, folding his arms tightly around himself. In his universe of things to fear, Jenks outranked the wolves, the mangler, and even Sullivan, whom Charles recognized as simply a bully. Jenks was something different, something unknowable.

They looked in all the fireplaces, discovering that each had already been prepared with wood. The one in their father's study seemed most inviting, as it also contained kindling and old pieces of mail. Charles sent James to fill a bucket with water, in case there was a mishap, and then, after making sure the vent was open, he touched a match to the paper in the fireplace. The wood caught easily. 'We're explorers,' Charles said. 'We're on an island and we've gathered all the wreckage from our boat.'

'And we're making a fire. So they can find us.'

'Right.'

Soon they had a splendid fire, which popped excitingly, and which they fed with extra wood stored in the benches that flanked the fireplace. James dashed to the windows of the study and waved his arms back and forth.

'What are you doing?'

'Signaling.'

Charles let his brother signal to their rescuers while he laid out some blankets for them to sleep on.

'It's still snowing,' James announced.

Charles joined him. Pellets of snow made a kind of lace curtain through which they could see a light coming from Jenks's cabin window. There was a single slender wire running from their house to Jenks's; all Charles had to do was ring for him, and Jenks would come. It was a terrible idea, and Charles imagined going to the kitchen, pushing the button, opening the door, and waiting. He had the sudden urge to draw the blinds. 'The snow is beautiful,' he said woodenly.

'When is everyone coming back?'

'By daylight, for sure.'

'But if it's still snowing now, how will they get back?'

'They just will. They know we're alone, they'll come back.'

'Who knows we're alone?' James looked at Charles, who normally would have smacked him for being so stubborn.

Charles said, coolly, 'Daddy knows—'

'He thinks Cook and Patsy are here.'

Charles shrugged. 'Cook and Patsy know that we're—'

'No, Charlie, they think Daddy's back now.'

'Oh, be quiet!'

'Does Mr Jenks know we're alone?' James drew a face on the window, right where his breath had made a spot. He tended to trust the world and had never noticed, when they played outside, the way Jenks loomed at the periphery of the garden, blotting out the sun.

'I don't know.'

'I think he knows,' James said. 'And Daddy was supposed to pay him today.'

'What are you talking about?'

'Daddy and I go over the accounts sometimes,' James said.

Charles and Mr Carter had never gone over the accounts. He didn't even know what the accounts were. James continued to sketch on the window, making a fat body under the smiling face. Charles felt himself shrinking.

'When do you look at the accounts?'

'We'll see Mr Jenks soon. Today was his payday.'

But Jenks did not show himself, and it continued to snow long into the next day.

Chapter 4

For almost ten years, the blizzard of 1897 stood as the worst natural disaster to hit San Francisco. Telegraph wires snapped. Water mains burst so that awkward ice sculptures dotted Market Street. Some buildings under construction, like the new civic library, partially collapsed under the weight of the snow. Transportation halted – the streetcars wouldn't run, and even though horse and buggies could make emergency trips, few knew how to drive in the snow, and there were many accidents. San Francisco's cobblers, it was said, produced fine shoes for walking, but not for skiing. So pedestrians stayed indoors, waiting out the storm.

Though Jenks was accustomed to snow, he preferred to stay in his cottage, far out of the eye of strangers he might startle.

Years ago, he had looked all over the country for a fortune, and Alaska was supposed to be the last stop. He had prospected for gold, losing three fingers and all of his toes to frostbite. Finally, a stick of dynamite had blown a brass ingot through his cheek.

He sold his claim at a loss, and came to San Francisco, where the Carters took pity on him. Officially, he was the gardener, but he was excused from any sort of adequacy in that regard. He also was available if anything heavy needed to be lifted.

His cottage overflowed with the Carters' old newspapers, which he burnt without reading, for reading reminded him of how hard it was to think. But the day of the blizzard, when he rolled and bound a hundred pounds of newsprint into dozens of tight logs, a headline caught his eye. How could he miss it – it took up half the front page: GOLD STRIKE! Beneath it, a map of Alaska, showing exactly where the Klondike was.

Involuntarily, Jenks made a small sound, like fabric tearing. Tears welled up in his eyes.

* * *

By the morning of the thirty-first, it had stopped snowing, and had begun to thaw. Across the city, people were taking the first tentative steps back into life. But there was still no sign of Mr Carter, or Cook, or Patsy.

That day, their third in solitude, was the first that Charles hadn't performed a hygienic inspection for himself and James. If their faces looked a bit grey, Charles wasn't sure if he cared anymore.

He began to trespass. He wasn't listening for imps; he felt instead like a detective looking for clues with which he could punish the guilty for having left him alone. His first area of ingress, his mother's dressing room, was also his last, for he found something truly baffling there.

It was a wooden box about the size of a dictionary, with twin latches that opened easily. Inside was a metal object with a round head and long nose, and a hand grip. It could almost have been a pistol but for its immense weight – further, it had a cord and an electrical plug. Charles had seen but one object in his life that had an electrical plug: the toaster. His father had explained that one day, there would be an electrical refrigerator and an electrical oven, and that Patsy had an electrical sewing machine upstairs that eased her chores. 'Electricity is a marvel,' Mr Carter said. 'It starts here, in the kitchen, and one day will be in every room.'

Charles wondered if this odd appliance was related to sewing somehow. There were a half dozen attachments, which he quickly determined fit over the ball-shaped nose: cones, grids, planes with raised bumps.

Then he found the brochure:

VIBRATION IS LIFE

What woman hasn't lost her fair share of life to the mysterious ailments that incapacitate her zest and zeal? Feminine complaints can constrict the flow of the vital humors, leading to restlessness, furtive amativeness, a corruption of morals and the downfall of her happy home.

Treat yourself to an invigorative cure! Lindstrom Smith White Cross Electric Vibrators provide 15,000 pulsations per minute, relieving pain, stiffness and weakness. Just five to ten minutes with the Electric Vibrator, and all the pleasures of youth will throb within you. Steady and frequent application treats hysteria, chlorosis, greensickness, neurasthenia and all manner of hysteroneurasthenic disorders, and even simple fatigue and melancholy.

Apply to the area that feels the most congestion, and let the Lindstrom Smith White Cross Electric Vibrator relieve you with its thrilling, penetrating, scientifically-proven action. The application, when pursued for five to ten minutes (time will indeed fly!), leads inevitably to a convulsion of the affected region, followed by blissful relaxation and sometimes a tranquil slumber.

Can be used in the privacy of the dressing room or the boudoir.

The text didn't help – he still hadn't a clue what he'd found. Feminine complaints? Corruption? The diseases would no doubt be listed in the dictionary, but he suspected the definitions would, in the maddening way of dictionaries, lead back to themselves with the practiced evasiveness that excluded children.

Then his eyes fell on an electrical outlet. He would have been less surprised to find a zebra grazing off the makeup table. That his mother had an electrical outlet in her dressing room made him breathe shallowly, as he'd stumbled across yet another adult mystery.

Without further thought, he sat on his mother's fainting couch and plugged the device in. An illustration showed a woman holding it to her cheek. This Charles did, and the sensation was indeed pleasant. He pretended to have come home from a hard day at work.

Gradually, however – in truth rather quickly – he grew bored. After five minutes of studious application to the cheek and forehead had passed, he looked at the brochure again, for he hadn't proceeded through any convulsions; nor did he wish to slumber. He gave it another minute about his head and neck, and then turned the vibrator off, for his face was beginning to go numb.

A strangely incomplete feeling nagged him as he wound the cord around the appliance and packed it back up just as he found it. The light against the walls felt different, as if he'd peeled back a curtain on the world and found there only more curtains and drapes and odd masking. He wondered how Joe Sullivan had made the nickel vanish.

That afternoon, James read a book and Charles visited the attic, where he was not allowed. It was a well-organized place, free of dust, and illuminated by windows on all sides that today showed friendly slices of blue sky. In one corner, under a bell-shaped glass, was a small marble figurine, a nude that had once been on top of their piano. It was very delicate and cold to the touch. Charles inspected it carefully, running the tips of his fingers around its breasts.

He was proud of how responsibly he held this piece. Admiring it in the light, turning it to better see the details. 'This one,' he said to himself, 'comes from Italy. It is an Italian woman – note the texture.'

And then, without even seeming to slip, it dropped through his fingers. It hit the floor and shattered.

He gasped. He stooped to see if he could somehow patch it, explain the noise. He paused. Who was going to scold him?

It was New Year's Eve. Every year, he had been put to bed early and told that when he was old enough, he could stay up to ring in the New Year. And now, he was allowed to do whatever he wanted. As if they had a life of their own, his arms reached out and held a brick over the statue. *This was an Italian sculpture*, he thought, dropping the brick.

He lifted his brick up, then dropped it, then again, and when the statue was reduced like broken bits of seashell, Charles crushed them under his shoe.

In the back of his throat, he felt a miserable longing for someone, anyone, so he could hit them with all of his might. It had stopped snowing; the snow was melting now, and there were people out on the street: still, both his mother and his father were gone. It dawned on him that there was no one coming, no one to stop him from destroying the world.

Charles miserably joined his brother in his father's study, where their fire was still going. They had dragged in wood from other rooms and thrown in logs whenever it had threatened to die. Since they had fought that morning over who got to look through the kaleidoscope, and were not speaking now, Charles looked out the bay window. In many different places the color white capped a hundred shades of green: snow on the far ivy cliffs of the headlands, rough water on the bay, frosted branches in the nearby Presidio. Right below him, snow on the eaves of Jenks's cottage.

The wire connecting their houses had survived the snows and a finch sat on it, head twitching, wings fluttering.

James, who lay on top of the tangled blankets on the leather couch, had a huge old book from their father's shelves propped on his stomach. He said, 'Well, well, what do you know?'

Charles didn't answer him.

'Well, what *do* you know?' James said, louder, eyes popping at his book.

'I'm not interested in whatever baby book you're reading.'

'I'm not talking to you. Well, what *do you know*?'

'I'm coming over there and I'm going to hit you.'

James opened his hands. 'Ala-ka-ZAM,' he cried. A quarter dropped out of his hand. It rolled in circles on the carpet.

'What's that book?'

'It's mine.' But James had to retrieve his quarter from under the carpet and he left the book open on the couch.

Charles stared at it. It had illustrations, like a child's book, but it also had dense text. The page James had opened to showed a series of diagrams: a hand with a coin in its palm; the hand closing; the hand opening with the coin gone.

Charles had only to take one step toward the book before James slammed it against his chest. 'I'm not done,' he said.

'All right,' Charles said, so calmly it surprised him. He felt such a crushing ache to see the book, he was weirdly willing to wait for it.

Making a coin vanish was difficult for James, even when weighed against the promise of annoying his older brother. Charles sat quietly, looking out the window at nothing in particular, until he heard James cry, 'This is stupid,' and throw the book to the floor.

Charles didn't move until he heard the door to the toilet slam shut. Then he picked the book up. It was cloth-bound, with splits in the seams; the pages were yellowed around the edges. The title, *The Practician's Manual of Legerdemain*, by Prof. Ottawa Keyes, was embossed in metallic gold on the spine.

This book would explain how the giant had taken his Racketeer nickel. He let it fall open randomly, reasoning that he could guide it, magically, to the right page.

He read the line his finger pointed to. 'If you purchase used equipment, varnished surfaces may be made to look like new with a pound of wheat bran boiled in a gallon of water.'

Wheat bran? No sentence had ever disappointed him more, not even those in the Electric Vibrator brochure. He flipped a few pages, to a drawing of a candle.

To produce a lighted candle from the pocket, one of the illusions most pleasing to the eye, prepare the candle using a wax match as the wick. The best waxes are tropical in nature. . . .

He shook his head. This was an awful kind of book. But he wasn't ready to let it beat him, for he had started to sense that the world was at its best moments a place for crafty men to explore. The book had no apparent organization, Professor Keyes inter-mixing methods for specific illusions with his general philosophy.

A master conjurer must have spirit and will-power. Above all, he is in *control*. How else can he command an audience's attention?

He read that twice. It sounded better than wheat bran.

When performing the coffin illusion, and you are in that confined space, do not panic, as no magician has ever escaped by panicking.

He held his arms rigidly at his sides. He breathed though his nose, slowly. He decided he would be good at not panicking.

The rarest need in life is the one met suddenly and completely. This is how it was with Charles Carter and the art of magic. Had he easily found the diagrams showing how to vanish a coin, he might have just examined the method, confirmed that it could be done, and moved back to looking out the window. However, looking for an index – there was none – Charles found a page in the back of the book that changed his life.

The page was bordered with a lovely tangle of roses, flags, doves, and decks of cards. Unlike the rest of the book, it was printed with red highlights so that the flowers, the diamonds, and the hearts glowed. At the top, written in tiny cloister text, was a colophon:

If you have diligently worked through this humble tome, perhaps you have the disposition to be indoctrinated into the mystery. Here are the rules – seven positive commands, seven negative – that each master conjurer should follow.

Below were two columns of commands. Carter was sure he could obey if not improve on each rule. But Professor Ottawa Keyes had outsmarted him, for the rules were written in French.

Adding to the torture, Carter knew a little French, enough to see that the first column, headed 'toujours,' showed what he should always do, and 'jamais' everything that was not allowed.

Frustration rose in his throat, but then he remembered he was good at not panicking. He understood why the Professor put the rules in French. Of course he wouldn't hand out secrets like caramels – you had to work at them, pry them loose.

His father had a French dictionary and so, with a pen and a little patience, Carter began a translation. For long minutes, he was absolutely silent, because he was already practicing discipline. He allowed himself, when particularly excited by making an entire rule give up its meaning, to raise his eyebrows. James came in once, causing Carter to look up, then immediately look down again. Whatever James wanted, it would wait, for, upon seeing his brother's expression, he turned around and left.

By the time the clock chimed 6 P.M., he had put most of the page into English:

ALWAYS!!!

- BEFRIEND OTHER MAGICIANS
- MAINTAIN A CALM DISPOSITION
- PUNISH MEDDLERS
- THINK ON YOUR FEET
- IRON YOUR SILK HANDKER-CHIEFS AND POLISH YOUR SHOES
- RESPECT YOUR AUDIENCE
- If volunteers have joined you onstage, politely bid them au-revoir and TAKE YOUR FINAL BOW ALONE

NEVER!!!

- EXPLAIN OR REPEAT A TRICK
- GAZE WHERE THE AUDIENCE SHOULDN'T
- MISTAKE OBNOXIOUSNESS FOR AUDACITY
- STEAL ANOTHER MAGICIAN'S EQUIPMENT, PATTER, OR PAPER
- CALL YOURSELF '_____ THE MARVELOUS' IF YOU ARE NOT YET MARVELOUS
- SHOW FEAR
- FAIL

58

He translated until the phrases made sense, but he paid no attention to what they meant. And though he returned to it repeatedly, he had to leave his work incomplete for the night. There was a final note, alone, bold, and in a monkish font, that he couldn't translate. 'Puisque toutes les créatures sont au fond des frères, il faut traiter vos bêtes comme vous traitez vos amis.' It was something about animals and brothers and friends, but the specifics eluded him and so he put it aside.

He put more wood on the fire. James appeared several times, once with food, but Carter paid him no attention.

When he felt it was exactly the right moment, Carter, by the light of the fireplace, opened the book to the beginning. He fanned a deck of cards.

Chapter 5

'Look, James. Is that your card?'

'No!' James whined.

'You aren't even looking. Now, we have to start over.'

'I'm tired. What time is it?'

Their plan had been to toast in the New Year with cider, but James had complained at ten o'clock, three hours ago, that it was already too late, so Carter had stopped all the clocks in the room. 'It's ten-thirty. Now, pick a card.' He fanned the deck.

'I can't stay up until twelve o'clock,' James moaned.

'You can go to sleep when I've done this right.'

'When is that?'

'When I guess your card.'

James looked at the card and put it back in the deck.

Carter shuffled the cards. 'Tap on the deck twice.'

'Why?'

'Just do as you're told, and stop complaining.'

James reached out and touched the deck with his finger as if it weighed a thousand pounds. 'There.'

Carter revealed the top card. 'Was it the six of spades?'

James shrugged, 'I don't remember.'

'James!' A good pinch to James's cheek would wake him up no doubt, but then he remembered: James was a volunteer and should be treated *grandly*. He took a deep breath. 'I'm sorry. We need to make this trick work. We'll do it once, and then – then I'll give you a surprise.'

'What kind of surprise?'

Carter hadn't expected this question, and had no ready answer. 'It's a surprise.'

'You aren't going to hit me again, are you?'

'No, it's a good kind of surprise.' Carter shuffled the cards and fanned them. 'This time, concentrate on your card. We'll both

60

concentrate.' After James had selected and replaced the card, Carter shuffled.

'I'm concentrating,' James said quietly.

'So am I. Tap on the deck.'

James did so. Carter turned over the top card, a nine of diamonds.

'Hey!' James picked up the card. His back straightened. 'How about that?'

'That was a good one, eh?'

'Do that again.'

'All right, I—' His hands froze as he was about to scoop up the deck. 'I can't do that.'

'Why not?'

'It's one of the rules.'

Since Carter had been referring to the rules for hours now, James nodded sagely. 'And you can't tell me how you did it.' He picked at the edges of the cards. 'Like when you cut the rope and put it back together again.'

For a moment, James had seemed excited; he was now on the verge of becoming cranky again, and Carter did not want to lose him. 'But there's the surprise.'

'What is it?'

Carter wished he knew how to bend people to his will, like a master conjurer. He gathered what natural gravity he had and said, 'I don't know if you really want it—'

'Charlie!'

'No, honest. You might hate it. But you could know how all the tricks work. You could never tell anyone, but *you'd* know. The surprise is, I want you to be my assistant.'

'What assistant? Assistant for what?'

'For the magic shows I'm going to do.'

'That's not a good present. Why can't I be the magician and you be the assistant?'

Carter bit his lower lip. That would never do. But James had asked a very good question, one that demanded respect. 'I'll be your assistant sometimes. We'll switch.'

James considered this. 'That sounds fair.'

'Do you want to practice now?'

'I'm going to sleep. Tell me when it's 1898.'

Soon after, James's eyes closed.

Professor Keyes, it turned out, had advice about assistants. 'If you can, select a man who looks so stupid that a hundred magicians working for a hundred years could not teach him the simplest French drop.'

Carter appraised James and concluded, sadly, that his brother was far too intelligent looking to make a good assistant. On the other hand, he was unbeatable at being stubborn, and that would have to be an asset.

When Carter was finished for the night, he nudged his brother to tell him it was the New Year. James only murmured, 'That's lovely,' and continued to sleep.

Each morning started with James running outside to see if the snow was still there. Periodically during the day, he would say he thought he heard horses or even a motorcar, and he would run outside again, returning discouraged. The snow grew gritty and brown, receding into shadows. By the fifth morning, January second, the snow was gone, and wagons and carriages passed their house ten times a day, but James no longer raced to see them.

'We mustn't attempt tricks publicly if we haven't mastered them privately,' Carter said, holding the Keyes book on his lap.

There were seven types of tricks: the antiscientific demonstration, the disappearance, the mentalist demonstration, the penetration, the production, the transformation, the transportation. Some of these involved special apparatus – collapsing birdcages, carpets with trapdoors – that had to be ordered from Europe, and so the Carter boys simply pretended to levitate each other, or to produce doves on command.

They could do none of the advanced tricks correctly. When James grew tired of trying to hold a card by its edge, just so, his brother asked him to find in their parents' rooms a suitable costume for their impersonations of Phillippe the Court Conjurer.

While he was gone, Carter tried and failed to get the proper knuckle grip on the playing card. Keyes's book had a rhyme that went straight to the point:

You must practice and practice and again till sore

Only then are you ready to practice once more

So he continued to practice for long minutes.

Because adversaries will challenge him outside the theatre just as much as inside, a master conjurer shall always carry each and every one of his trinkets with him, lest he otherwise be ashamed.

Carter laid out on the table a length of cored rope, two torn-up aces of hearts, the rock that stood in for the egg, and crumpled-up red tissue mounted on a stiff wire that he would pretend was a rose.

'James?' he called. He listened carefully, as his brother had been quiet in the other room for too long. He walked down the hallway to their parents' bedroom. The doors to an armoire stood open, several of their father's suits and mother's dresses heaped on the floor. James sat among them.

'It smells like them,' he whispered.

'It's going to be all right. They'll be back.'

'When? It's been five days. Everyone forgot us.'

'They didn't forget us.'

'How do you know?'

'We have to put on our show when they come back, so they'll see.'

James rubbed his nose. 'See what?'

'That . . . that we survived.'

After a moment, James sniffled, 'We have to practice for them.'

'That's the spirit.'

'We need an audience. The book says we should have an audience before the really important shows.'

'And who—' Carter stopped. He knew exactly who his brother meant. Carter knew better, but could not bring himself to crush James when his wings were already so close to broken. With a strange thrill, he knew it was an awful idea, and irresistible. Mechanically, he nodded. 'Yes. We'll get good and ready. And we'll perform for Jenks.'

Jenks slept in the half-light of his cottage, heavy and awkward as if thrown on his bed by the sea. He was dreaming of splitting timbers and collapsing mine shafts. An incessant ringing in his ears.

He grunted, pulling himself up from sleep. The ringing continued. His mouth hurt. He touched the puckered edges of his cheeks. He was awake: the main house was ringing for him.

He slapped at the wall until he found the switch that stopped the buzzer. Dizzily he straightened all the bottles that made a half-circle around his bed, as if expecting company.

But no – he would be seeing people outside, in the main house. He dipped his fingers into a washbasin to finger-comb his hair. His clothes smelled of mildew. He couldn't go to the main house that way. So he struggled into his better shirt and trousers carefully; they were worn in many places but not split.

For the first time in days, he opened the front door to his cottage. His eyes stung in the sun. He was out of food and liquor and his head pulsed with each heartbeat. But that didn't matter. The buzzer meant Mr Carter had returned, and had his pay ready.

The kitchen door was open. Jenks wiped his feet. He nervously ran his fingers through his hair again, tucking his chin down to better throw his face into shadow.

He found a place to knock on the edge of the door frame. There was no response. He knocked again. Speaking required a great deal of concentration; Jenks started to form a word, and then a figure flew toward him so fast he jerked backward.

It was Charles Carter sliding down the hardwood in his stocking feet. 'Preee-senting James! The Mystic Apprentice!'

James tottered out from behind the pantry door. He wore a conical paper hat with a long ostrich feather, his father's pinned-up nightshirt, and a collection of silk scarves around his waist.

Jenks covered the most ruined part of his face with his good hand. 'Boys,' he managed. What were they doing? Where was Mr Carter?

'Take a seat,' Charles cried, 'for the Wonder Show!' He reached out toward Jenks, who, not wanting trouble, met Charles's hand with the stumps of his fingers. Charles flinched.

'Welcome, Mr Jenks.' James grinned. 'For my first trick!'

'Wait, James, wait for me to . . .' Charles put his hands on Jenks's shoulders, easing him into a kitchen chair.

James pulled the paper rose from his sleeve.

'James!' Charles slapped his palm against his forehead. 'Misdirection, James! You're supposed to—'

'Here you are, Mr Jenks.' James handed over the paper rose. Jenks took it between his thumb and forefinger. Sitting stiffly, he was ready, at any moment, to be teased or worse. He watched James, who pretended to twirl a mustache applied with charcoal that would have been more effective had he been less dirty elsewhere. Charles, too, looked filthy, like he hadn't been groomed in weeks.

'Annnd my second trick for Mr Jenks.' James waved a scarf in the air, then wrapped it around his fist. When he unwrapped it, there was a white rock in his hand. 'Behold the egg!' He handed the rock to his brother. 'Now, Mr Jenks, just you wait for the third trick, the great card trick.'

'No, James, do the coin palm.'

'It's the card trick. Get the deck of cards, assistant.'

'You're supposed to – oh, you're hopeless.' Charles handed James the deck of cards.

'Now, pick a card, any card, Mr Jenks.'

While staring at the fan of cards, Jenks realized he wasn't getting paid. He wanted to leave, but he was sitting, and they were standing between him and the door. He was somehow overmatched. He picked a card.

James tilted his head back and forth, smiling. 'Look at the card carefully.' Charles, who stood next to James, smiled until he grimaced. It was very hard for him to be the assistant, but he wasn't the one who would have otherwise thrown a tantrum. He watched his brother misapply the overhand grip.

'James—'

'I'm doing it right. Now, Mr Jenks, put it back in the deck. Right. Is this your card?'

Jenks nodded, hoping that was all. He needed to leave.

'A-La-Ka-Zam!' James cried. 'Good work, Mr Jenks!'

'Now, the coin palm,' Charles added.

'Oh, that's later. Oh, Mr Jenks, no, don't leave yet, stay here, there's more. Please.' James gently put his hand on Jenks's knee, which seemed to keep him in place.

Charles wasn't about to let his brother change the act. 'If you don't do the coin vanish—'

'No. I have another trick. It's the . . . Chinese Mystery. A-La-Ka-Zam,' he murmured, spinning on his heels.

'What Chinese mystery?' Charles squinted. Since Jenks had sat still through the card trick, Charles tried to treat him the way James would – a kind soul who'd done them no wrong. But as James twisted and swirled the scarves, beads of sweat appeared on Jenks's brow. Having Jenks there was like standing too close to a guard dog.

'The Chiii-neeeese Mysss-tery,' James sang out. 'Mr Jenks, watch me!' He flapped his arms so that the scarves made curlicues in the air.

Jenks choked out a slow message. 'Gotta. Go back.'

'No, stay,' said James in a rush. 'It's not over.'

'We'll be very cross if you go now,' Charles added. 'There's just one trick left.' It was easy now to look beyond the torn flesh and into his eyes; Jenks was an audience member, and he had to be shown a good time. Charles had outfitted himself for tricks like James, with a duplicate wire-and-tissue flower and cards and his own rock, just in case he had to take over the act.

Carter whispered to Jenks, 'The next trick requires a coin from the audience.'

Grimly, Jenks reached into his pocket and pulled out his last quarter dollar until payday.

Carter said, '1896, San Francisco mint mark.'

'Look, look how they move now,' James called from behind Jenks, spinning the scarves in corkscrews.

'There is nothing up my sleeve,' Carter said quietly. He willed Jenks to look away from his brother, and toward his hand. It worked. He had Jenks's full attention. The quarter dollar was supported by Carter's right thumb and forefinger. He grasped at it with his left hand, closing it into his fist. He pointed at his left hand, opening it slowly, and, remarkably – even he was stunned – in his first attempt in front of an audience, Charles Carter performed a successful magic trick: the coin was gone. Beautifully done. He smiled, full of wonder.

It was like being hit by a locomotive. He slammed against the wall of the kitchen so fast, he had no time to react, so fast James was still singing 'The Chinese Mystery' to himself. Jenks's hand, at

Charles's throat, had picked him up and carried him there in three strides, all in one second.

Choking, Charles stared into a face apoplectic with rage. Jenks's grip made it impossible to plead or explain that the coin hadn't really vanished. James gasped in midsong, and then he, too, was smashed against the wall.

Charles planted both his hands on Jenks's arm, to no purpose. The quarter dollar bounced to the floor audibly, but Jenks didn't seem to care. Looking into those black, watering eyes, Charles saw hatred. If magic was a great force for Charles, then it was great, too, for Jenks.

When he could breathe a little, Charles let out a sob, just one. James cried furiously.

Jenks barked, 'Little! Rich! Rats!' Charles hoped that yelling was the worst, that he would put them down, but instead, Jenks readjusted, tucking one of them under each arm.

He began to walk.

Charles's mind went blank; it was as if a plug had been pulled and he drained away with the bathwater. Wedged under Jenks's arm, smelling the stale liquor and dirt on him as he found the flight of stairs, going down to the basement. Jenks knew where they were going, even in the dark, and he didn't care when one or the other of the boys collided with stored furniture as he took them deeper and deeper under the house. The sound of James crying filled Charles's brain, as if occupying where Charles himself had once been.

He could hear James crying because he, himself, was not. He was no longer panicking. He was maintaining a calm disposition.

A jangling of keys. They were at the deepest end of the basement, by a padlocked door Charles had never seen open. Jenks took the two boys into a room that was illuminated only by small, smeared windows high on the wall. It was small and unfinished, with a concrete foundation that extended halfway across; the rest was earth.

For the first time, Charles saw his father's other collections. The room housed what Mr Carter thought wise and decent to exclude from the house: a blunderbuss, a flintlock, a musket; erotic engravings from *Les Mémoires de Saturnin*; first editions of books from the Index Librorum Prohibitorum; stereoscopic cards from Paris, France. There was a magic lantern and drawers of forbidden slides in cabinets marked 'Not for young eyes.' It was here that Mr Carter had Jenks carry the items too disquieting to display in the home, such as the instruments of punishment from Colonial America.

Jenks lowered James to the ground, slowly, and Charles noted the care he took, and he felt relief, for this meant he would treat them gently.

Then Jenks devoted his attention to Charles.

Jenks flipped him upside-down and smashed him against the wall. Charles's shirt fell over his face; he could hear but not see what was going on. He wanted to call out, but was also curious about what was being done to him. If he listened, perhaps he'd have a clue. Something hard grasped around his ankles; there was a clatter of chains, and then a final-sounding click, and then he jerked toward but not against the ground. He pulled his shirt away from his face.

The light coming from the windows showed him he'd been clapped into the bilboes. There was a pole attached to the wall and soldered to the pole was a pair of foot cuffs, from which he dangled, upside-down, so that the blood was rushing to his head. Something in his pocket, probably the tissue rose's wire stem, was jabbing him in the leg. He let his arms go limp.

James whimpered. He looked like a wreck, nightshirt and scarves askew. He'd lost his hat and shoes. Jenks picked him up and fastened him into the pillory. As the heavy oak top beam fell against the lower plate, James was pinned between the two, his head and hands sticking through the portholes. He shrieked.

'Don't be afraid!' Charles called. 'Don't be afraid!'

Jenks padlocked the pillory into place. Red-faced, James was silent, but also trembling, because he was drawing in another breath with which to shriek again.

Jenks slapped him across the face.

Charles flinched with the sound. 'Don't!'

James looked at Jenks with astonishment. He was waiting for a misunderstanding to be made right.

Jenks yelled, 'Shut up! Punk!' And then James started crying again.

'Don't cry, James!' Charles thrashed in the bilboes.

'Shut up!' Jenks backhanded James so hard the pillory shook.

'James!' Charles looked at his brother, whose face was losing definition. His charcoal mustache was half consumed by sweat and a small trickle of blood. 'Jenks! I'm going to kill you!' Charles bucked against the wall, arms reaching up achingly toward the foot cuffs to see if he could pull them apart. 'Jenks, when our father gets home, you're in big trouble!'

Jenks was silent now. Slumped with fatigue, he regarded the boys: James was shivering, but finally quiet; Charles wasn't about to shut up. So Jenks walked to a dark corner and returned with a heavy iron device in his hand that caused Charles's blood to freeze. It was a brank.

The woodcut on his father's wall had frightened him enough. Seeing it now was far worse. The brank, 'the crown of the curste,' was a set of iron bands that made up a slatted cage into which the head was placed. A strong adult needed two hands to carry it. Beneath the space for the nose was 'the Devil's bit,' a spiked plate of adjustable length that was inserted, spikes down, into the victim's mouth. A second set of spikes fit just under the chin. The penitent, as long as his jaw remained still, would be uninjured, but a single attempt at speech would puncture his mouth in a dozen places.

It was used on women who scolded, or men who spoke blasphemy, or debtors who claimed to be wealthy. It promised not only suffocating confinement, but also an unknowable kind of blistering pain. Now, Jenks fell to his knees and methodically tugged at the bit so that it came all the way free of the brank. He inserted a key into a lock, turned it once, and the device fell open. Charles watched like this was happening to someone else, all feeling squeezed out of him, displaced by leaden terror. Jenks brought it over his face and locked it again behind him. There were slits for his eyes and his nose showed through, just where it was supposed to.

Jenks grabbed Charles's nostrils, pinning them shut. This forced him to open his mouth, and the rusty bit was shoved in. A coppery-tasting lump filled his mouth. While Jenks secured the spiked chin strap, Charles swallowed carefully, knowing that the wrong motion would send a spike into some soft part of him, the side of his cheek, behind his jaw, the meat of his tongue.

With a grunt, Jenks stood, pocketing the key. A second later, Charles heard the door shut, and lock.

With Jenks gone, Charles's first reaction was, 'I am good at not panicking,' but his second, at gut level, was pure panic. Upside-down, stomach churning. The taste in his mouth of rust and iron, and the force of the spikes against his chin, the weight of the cage pulling on his neck, his head filling with blood like it was about to burst. But, somehow, the panic felt like a ripple across deeper water, as it was so very interesting to have something terrifying happen. He was still sure they were about to be rescued.

James was silent. Charles saw him, ravaged and small, shivering. He wished he could reassure him.

At some point, fifteen minutes, an hour later, no one was there to count, something poisonous rose in Charles's mind. How exactly were they going to be rescued? When someone found them? When their father, or someone, finally came home?

If he had learned but one thing recently, it was that no one would come, no one would rescue them. A great sob jolted his sternum, and his jaw fluttered. This made the spikes jab him and he sobbed again. Now it was his tongue that suffered. He couldn't tell whether he was bleeding. He cried, choking, overcome by exhaustion. Nothing mattered and no one cared about him.

He had failed poor James, the shadowy boy who was pale and fading, silent in the pillory.

He had a list of all the people who had disappointed him, from his mother and father to his nurse and everyone else who had fled. He saved for last the most recent and crippling failure: Professor Ottawa Keyes. Never fail. Always punish meddlers. How naive, how cruel it was to extend that hope. The world was never so simple as the promise extended by that book – how could you possibly never fail and always be calm?

His jaw cramped, and he accidentally flexed it, causing a stabbing pain under his chin, which made him sob again in despair. The adult world promised so many wonders and delivered only horrors to those who wanted a place to belong.

Then his watering eyes sprang wide open. The brank was causing him such pain he had ignored the jabbing in his leg.

He reached deep into his trouser pocket: here were the rock, the cards, the rose. Carefully, he pulled out the rose, separating the tissue from the wire stem. The wire was flexible but very strong. It could be curled in a hoop for easy concealment up the sleeve. Charles felt around the brank, for the keyhole locking its back hinge into place. The wire slipped in. Keyes suggested that when escaping from a coffin, one should, instead of focusing on the unseen lock, take the pulse at the carotid artery. This was said to soothe the nerves. So Charles put his left index finger against his neck, and counted, while his right hand worked the lock.

The wire was thin; the lock was made of heavyweight iron. He had to work upside-down. There was no reason he could make it spring open, save one: it was inconceivable to the ironworkers of Colonial times that a penitent would try to escape from it.

At the ninetieth beat of Charles's heart, the rear lock parted, and the back of the brank swung open. His elation was cut short by gravity: he had undone the wrong lock first. Now the full weight of the iron cage pulled against his face, where the spiked strap still held his chin.

Iron dug into his mouth and under his jaw. Grimacing, he fit the wire into the chinstrap lock, twisting and tugging until it, too, fell open. Then the whole brank, devil's tongue and all, fell off his face and clattered to the foundation.

Charles spat out the foul taste from his mouth. He felt heavy scratches on his face, but the spikes hadn't penetrated his tongue or chin. He was by no means through – the bilboes would be next. But he felt raw exhilaration as he never had before. 'Ahoy, James!' he cried.

Unmoving in the pillory, James managed a weak 'Hello.'

It took only a few seconds to undo the bilboes, but during his labor, Charles noticed that the light from the windows had dimmed. More bad weather, perhaps.

'I see wheels. Carriage wheels,' James observed.

'Jenks is escaping. He's probably taking our surrey. Oh, he's in trouble.' Charles rubbed at his ankles. He limped across the room, to work on the ancient lock that kept James in place. 'I'm rescuing you,' he said flatly.

'Thank you,' James replied, weakly, but no longer crying.

71

'We're going to get Jenks,' Charles declared.

James rubbed one foot against another. 'We don't have to.'

The lock fell open, and Charles lifted the top beam wide. James pulled his head and hands out, and then sat down in a chair by the wall. Charles crouched before him, outlining a plan for revenge. James looked everywhere but at his brother, and when Charles finished talking, James said, 'I want to go home.'

Charles stared at him. 'We are home.'

The carriage's wheels were on the driveway side of the house. Charles pried open a window on the opposite side, boosted James out first, and slipped through himself next. They raced around the back of the house, to the kitchen door, to better spy on the carriage to see if Jenks had escaped yet.

'Papa!' James cried.

'What are you—' Then Charles saw what his brother had already seen. Their father, in his impeccable cravat, vest, and coat, stood by the spider phaeton, one hand lifting his leather satchel from the luggage rack, the other waving at them. He was clean, and smiling, and as impossible as a mirage. But here he was! The boys raced toward him, half tackling him, and he responded with delight.

'Hello, little men! I hear you've had an adventure.'

He went down on one knee while James and Charles fell on top of him, explaining everything all at once. Mr Carter put on a concerned face when listening to the most awful parts, but his underlying smile told Charles his father in no way understood what they were saying.

'Jenks tried to kill us. Where were you?' Charles asked, and the heat of his tone made his father stare at him.

'I was surveying our new vineyard,' Mr Carter explained. He had more to say: the purchase had been phenomenal, far more complex than he'd anticipated, they would appreciate it when they were older, there was nothing wrong with the servants' watching · them for a few days.

'But Cook and Patsy—' Charles started.

'Did you know they're heroes?' Mr Carter interrupted. 'The tent at their revival meeting collapsed in the snow, and they've been tending the injured. It even made the newspaper.'

'Why didn't they come back for us?' Charles asked.

Mr Carter looked disappointed. 'These were poor people. The most wretched. You boys had Mr Jenks to look after you.'

'You have to let Jenks go,' Charles said. 'He put us—'

'He already told me and I gave him a piece of my mind.'

'You have to let him go!' Charles touched his face, where the deep scratches from the brank ached.

'He shouldn't have taken you into my collections room.' Mr Carter wet his thumb and rubbed roughly at Charles's cheek. 'That place isn't for young eyes, and you could have damaged some valuable pieces.'

Charles quaked, choking against his father's misunderstanding. 'No, he put me into the brank, and—'

'He put you in your place, didn't he?' The corners of Mr Carter's mouth turned up.

'He hit James and put him in the pillory—'

'You teased him, and you know you're not supposed to.'

'We didn't!' Charles cried, nudging James. 'Tell him.'

But James only held on to their father's hand silently. He was staring beyond their father, and Charles followed his eyes; Jenks was approaching.

'You're in trouble,' Charles hissed. Jenks ignored him.

'Mr Jenks, I apologize for the boys' behavior,' Mr Carter said, taking out an envelope. 'Boys, before you wash up, I think you have something to say.'

Charles teared up. His father wasn't listening.

James whispered, 'I'm sorry, Mr Jenks.'

Jenks didn't move. His eyes were on Mr Carter's envelope.

Mr Carter said, 'You're a big boy, James. Now go wash up. And take care with my nightshirt.'

James limped up the back stairs and into the house.

Charles spat it out: 'I'm not apologizing.'

His father grabbed him by the collar. 'Young man, you live a life of privilege and when called upon, you will behave with respect and humility and self-control.'

It was in the words his father used that Charles found a swell of unexpected freedom. He wasn't just a rich man's son; he was a master conjurer. Though it made his mouth tremble, he forced himself to say it. 'Mr Jenks, I apologize to you.'

He awaited acknowledgment, but there was none. Jenks watched Mr Carter pull bills from the envelope. Mr Carter said, 'The storm caused a run on gold, I'm afraid. So I hope silver certificates will be all right.'

Jenks nodded. Mr Carter passed a one-dollar bill to his son. 'Look what the Treasury is up to. They call this the Educational Series.' There was a movement to edify the masses, to promote classical civilization in all governmental pursuits. 'So the architecture from now on will be Greek Revival, and the greenbacks, the ones, twos, and fives, they'll depict important scenes from historical, scientific, and mythological viewpoints, the creation of the steam engine, and so forth.'

For once, Charles didn't listen. He didn't even bother to look at the bill between his fingertips. Instead, he focused on his father: the brilliantly polished surface of his shoes, the neat pressing and starch to his shirt, the easy smile on his face as he counted a stack of five-dollar bills into Jenks's palm.

'And here, just for watching the boys,' Mr Carter dropped a final bill onto the stack.

When he became aware that Charles was still there, Mr Carter waggled his fingers at him. 'Go wash up,' he said.

Charles watched the money slip into Jenks's pocket. He wished he could vanish it. Instead, he entered the house. He walked up the staircase, holding the banister tightly, feeling that he was more tired than he had ever been.

In the bathroom, steam was rising, clouding the windows. James sat on the rim of the bathtub as it filled with water. The remains of his costume were on the floor, including their father's soiled nightshirt. Charles removed his own clothing; when he was done, he saw that James was holding the white rock, the egg rock, between his fingers.

'Here,' James said. 'You can be the magician.'

Charles took the rock, and covering it with his fingertips, made it disappear. James made no response, so Charles pulled the rock out from behind James's ear. 'Father was right, you are dirty,' Charles said.

James snorted. Then he was quiet.

'I'll need an assistant sometimes.'

74

Their eyes met, and James's watered. He looked away.

'It's all right,' Charles added. 'I can do it alone.'

James slipped into the tub, under the water, and then resurfaced.

Later, Charles, too, would get into the tub, but for now he stood alone and held the rock in his hand, because it had already started for him: his hands felt naked without something in them – a card, a coin, a rope – and whenever they held something secretly, they felt educated.

Chapter 6

Mrs Carter returned to San Francisco after two years of therapy, glowing with the wonders of psycho-analysis. In her first months back, she encouraged her boys to lie eyes closed on the chaise longues in the parlor, her hands extended to their foreheads, and tell her how they'd felt about her while she was gone, and how they felt about her now that she was back. She declared aloud 'that's a breakthrough' so many times that James and Charles often asked to be excused early to go to bed.

She encouraged her husband to write down and interpret his dreams. She was disappointed – so much so that she secretly considered divorcing him – that they were almost always about stock market hunches.

But the Carters were allies, regardless, and Mr Carter took seriously his wife's suggestion that their elder son was in the grip of an interesting passion; they should let Charles find his way in the world.

He passed quite unexpectedly from amateur to professional magician when he was a fifteen-year-old student at the Thacher School, a private academy in Ojai, California. Thacher was both rural and academically challenging: in addition to the regular slate of courses to prepare for Yale – all Thacherites went to Yale – the boys were each given a horse to care for, as Sherman Day Thacher had declared there was something about the outside of a horse that was good for the inside of a boy.

Carter later claimed he had entered Thacher on a 'wizardry' scholarship. There was of course no such thing. Thacher was a cradle for future politicians and captains of industry. As a lower lower, or *smut*, the term used for boys who were so hopelessly green they came back from camping trips covered in soot, he practiced his card effects in his room in the hour between supper and study hall.

He was an indifferent student, excited by Shakespeare, better than anyone expected at physical sciences, hopeless at economics, mediocre in debate, and excellent (as was any Pacific Heights boy raised under the influence of stocks, bonds, and notes) in the areas of deportment and social hygiene. That Thacher was a gateway to Yale meant little to him, for college meant preparation for banking, and Carter, unlike his classmates, lacked the soul of a banker. He made no lasting friends. His horse, a gelding he spoiled on apples and licorice, loved him very much.

Instead of burning the midnight oil with other students, Carter romanced the arcanae of physiology and self-improvement. He filched anatomy books from the library and studied the architecture of his palms, the bones like irregular cobblestones packed together under sheaths of muscle and fibrous ligaments. He was hypnotized by certain etchings, such as the bands of muscles around the thumb: the abductors, the adductors, the saintly flexor ossis metacarpi pollicis, the muscle of the opposable thumb, which separated man from the animals and, when exercised, the magician from his fellow man.

Success, it was said in Ottawa Keyes, and in many other books (he now learned), hinged upon the application of will against the physical body. Great challenges to his willpower would come soon enough – more immediately, Carter learned about the tools he had: skin, muscles, tendons, ligaments, bones.

The palm bones were named in times that respected mysteries: here was the cuneiform bone, the unciform, the semilunar, the pisiform, which sounded as if they'd been discovered by candlelight and recorded on papyrus by hooded men with long-quilled pens. The fingers radiated action, intelligence, deviousness. 'This is no longer the shaft of my thumb,' Carter thought, 'but my abductor pollicis, and my fingertips are flexor sublimi capped by flexor profundi.' He felt like he could shoot sparks off them.

One night in the spring of his sophomore year, there was a lecture on moral instruction that no one wanted to miss. The speaker was Borax Smith, whose wealth, it was said, exceeded even the imaginations of boys who'd had their own fair taste of money.

Smith took the podium in the faculty chapel, looking as old and plump and simple and kindly as a grandfather. Born and quickly abandoned near the Erie Canal sometime around 1840 (he never knew how old he was or where his parents went), Francis M. Smith matured into a hoodlum, but not a very good one. After many abominable exploits – he admitted he'd stolen linen from churches, forged cheques, rolled the intoxicated, and poured spiked drinks in a thieves' den – he drifted to Nevada, with a mule and a stake of fifty acres of worthless land – Teel's Marsh. Here he prospected hopelessly for gold. He dug alone in the blazing sun for many days, and then saw a single raincloud, which he prayed would cross over him. In the midst of a downpour that lasted only seconds, he heard the voice of God, which commanded him: *'Be good.'*

When Borax reached this part of his lecture, there were suppressed snickers all around, as the voice of God was a silly old chestnut. But the rest of the story left the boys silent, for that cloudburst had pounded away the sand at Borax's feet, revealing the top layer of a white vein of a curious substance, a scouring agent that could clean glass or metal. Smith told them he was disappointed – gold or silver would have been nice – but still he thanked God.

As it turned out, Teel's Marsh contained 98 percent of the world's supply of borax. Smith started a company, Twenty Mule Team Borax; within a year, he became a millionaire, and within ten years, wealthy beyond calculation, for he allowed the women of America to drive away dirt and grime, achieving a domestic sheen their mothers could never dream of.

Carter, who had arrived late to the lecture, was unimpressed with the speaker – the idea of the richest man in the America reminded him, faintly, of the tallest man in the world, and the only other prospector he'd known was Jenks. He spent the lecture practicing looking attentive; in fact he was thinking about cryptic shuffling illustrations deep in Professor Hoffman's *Modern Magic*.

Borax told the boys that he still listened daily for the voice of God, which had told him to *be good,* and that was why he had come to live in Oakland. He had built there, on the grounds of his great estate, a first-class home for unfortunate women. His theory was that with the feeling of luxury under their feet, these women would go forth and *be good* themselves, and not abandon their fatherless children. Borax slowed down here, explaining that a man could have a thousand interesting investments but what counted in this life and the next was good works: his was the rehabilitation of lost women.

He asked for questions. Immediately a dozen boys in succession asked him in various ways how rich, exactly, he was. He admitted he didn't know, no, he was sure he didn't know, and they asked, well, compared to Morgan, for instance, are you richer than he is, and he had to admit he didn't know that, either, nor compared to Hearst, nor Rockefeller, and gradually his answers grew shorter, and then he said 'Thank you,' and there was some applause.

The boys disbanded, most striding immediately to the dormitory for tea and debates of how much Borax must have netted in his lifetime. Carter, however, did not follow; he hesitated on the patio outside the chapel, under the pepper tree. After a moment of consideration, he opened a deck of cards and squinted at them as if they were ill-behaved children. He might have found an avenue for bottom-dealing Professor Hoffman had inadequately explored. He couldn't tell if the effect would be transparent to an audience, and he was cursing himself for not having brought a mirror as he flexed his thumb – which was over the deck – and at the same time fired cards out with his ring finger.

He realized he was being observed. Borax Smith watched him with lucid brown eyes. Carter looked around; they were alone on the patio.

'I have been watching you for two, three minutes,' Borax said, raising his bushy eyebrows. 'You been involved.'

Carter put the cards away. His ability to dismiss Borax as yet another prospector vanished. Man-to-man, he felt intimidated to be alone with him. 'I'm sorry. I . . . I wasn't gambling, sir.'

'That's all right. I done worse things.' Borax dug in his pocket and pulled out a quarter dollar. 'Show me what else you do.'

Carter looked blankly at the coin, making no connection between it and what he'd been doing. Borax misunderstood, and with a deep sigh of 'Thacher boys,' pulled out a dime. 'There,' he said, 'thirty-five cents. I want to see a private show for thirty-five cents.'

'Oh!' He almost handed the money back, for he had no routine and no particular idea of constructing one. But it was late in the month and he'd torn through his allowance, and thirty-five cents would carry him through nicely. So he did a series of fans and ruffles, then asked to borrow Borax's handkerchief, which he vanished and then found wrapped around a deck of cards in his pocket. He had recently heard much about the coin techniques of T. Nelson Downs, and so he pretended to double and triple and quadruple the thirty-five cents Borax had given him. Finally, he grew bolder, shaking money out from under Borax's shabby straw hat.

When he was through, he took a shallow bow, and Borax applauded thoughtfully. He asked if Carter had considered taking his act on the road. Carter hadn't, but he knew the right thing to do was nod. 'You can meet plenty interesting folk out there,' Borax continued. 'Play on the same bill as the Barrymores, or the divine Sarah Bernhardt, or la Loie Fuller. There are plenty magicians in vaudeville who aren't half as good as what you could do.'

Carter had been brought up well, and so he said 'Thank you, sir,' and he timidly accepted Borax's card, and promised to keep him posted as to how his career advanced.

He had no plan to perform onstage, but a seed had been planted. By that night, shoots and leaves and flowers erupted: he could be *paid money*, night after night, to do his *magic*. This was far superior to tallying numbers in a ledger. If he did well enough onstage, he needn't go to college at all.

But the thought of performing for an audience unnerved him. Though he preferred being alone, on some Sunday afternoons, when the rest of the fellows had ridden their horses into town, Carter often felt a desire to be among a population of people who were like him. Being onstage would be a grand way to meet people. The thought was a tremendous attraction, like an open window.

He wrote a letter to his parents, mentioning to his mother what an adventure it might be and to his father the financial possibilities and asking them both if they knew how one joined a vaudeville troupe.

The idea of Charles touring as a magician for a summer amused his parents, who imagined it like packing off to sea as a cabin boy, though safer, landlocked, and temporary. Mr Carter was actually well equipped to help: a man from Albee's Keith-Orpheum circuit, the best of all vaudeville shows, had recently solicited his aid in securing a loan to build the San Francisco Port, a small, refined theatre that would feature European performers only.

So, rather quickly, Charles Carter was given an audition at the Keith-Orpheum's United Booking Office, where he sweated through a ten-minute scarf-and-coin act cobbled together with bits and pieces of patter from his magic books. It failed to impress the United Booking Office much. They gave him a letter of recommendation to the lesser circuits, the dustier venues that were more desperate for acts. Three auditions and three rungs down the ladder later, he had his first paying job.

During the summer break of 1906, between his junior and senior years at Thacher, Carter toured the shoddy Lyceum circuit, and played halls in the Deep South, where the playbills shaved five years off his age and claimed he was 'nature's prodigy.' On what the troupers called Lyceum time, Carter was devoured by fleas, his earnings were regularly stolen, and he returned to California smelling like a smoldering cheroot. He loved every moment of it.

His senior portrait in the 1906 *Highwayman*, the Thacher yearbook, showed him in school tweeds standing on the same riverbank where all senior portraits were taken. Below his name was written 'Destination Yale,' as was written below all the senior names that year. However, close inspection revealed his true destination. Though some of his classmates distinguished themselves in their photographs by affecting a pipe or consulting a railway watch, Carter simply fanned a deck of cards in each hand, all of them aces.

Contrary to vaudeville's claims, he wasn't a prodigy. He had a workman's undistinguished face, lacking all suggestion of precocious brilliance. In the sepia tone of the *Highwayman* photograph, the full effect of his ice-blue eyes was muted. His hair was a midnight black, and his features had not sharpened yet. His contemporaries had trouble describing him, and he was difficult to pick out in group photographs.

His anonymity appealed to him. 'Because I am so plain faced, the audience at first expects little of me,' he wrote to James. 'Were I handsome, I should not be so much in control, as they would expect such great things.'

* * *

The summer of 1906, Charles Carter, age eighteen, moved up in rank to the nine-week Redpath Chautauqua Circuit, which had been founded by revivalists. Though the circuit no longer had a religious slant, its reputation remained, and the crowds were well behaved and the shows exuded an air of moral order. He made twenty a week, which was standard. He did well enough with his cards, coins, scarves, and paper flowers that a scout for the Keith-Orpheum circuit asked if he might join their circuit at, say, twenty-five a week.

Now that his physiological abilities had been appreciated, just a little, Carter began to work on his application of willpower. At a welcome-home dinner, he broke the news to his parents carefully, phrasing it as not just a tremendous opportunity but a financial advancement. He told them he was postponing Yale, but just for a year, to build 'character.' He'd read that Pierpont Morgan valued this above all else. His father protested, but hesitantly, for he, too, had read what Morgan valued.

'But just for a year,' his father confirmed.

'Of course,' Carter nodded, delivering his most rational smile. 'Just a year.'

A year later, at the next welcome-home dinner, the conversation was repeated, more or less as before, the element most changed being Mr Carter's squint when his son said he was postponing college for just another year.

At successive annual dinners, 1908 and 1909, Carter was increasingly declarative about his intentions: some performers, he said, made five thousand a week. None of them had gone to college, not one of them. Even if he did only a tenth as well, five hundred a week, which he could manage with enough experience, he could establish a profitable career.

In September 1910, when Carter was twenty-two and his fifth annual tour was about to leave San Francisco, his rhetoric began to fall apart. His father invited him to the study for a glass of wine, a Semillon grown from grapes harvested at their Napa property. Then: 'How is your progress toward that five hundred a week going, Charles?'

'It's coming along,' Carter said. In fact, it was: he was making thirty-five a week, up from the previous year by four dollars.

Conversation foundered, as it often did, and then his father produced from his jacket a letter from one of Carter's former teachers at Thacher. For long minutes, Mr Carter read aloud, as the chatty missive described how many young men from the class of '06 had already made senior clerk or junior auditor. This recitation became a lecture, then an argument, then, rather abruptly, silence, for, though he would rather die than admit it aloud, Charles Carter was starting to agree with his father. Magic could be a career for certain talented men, but its potential was passing Charles Carter IV by.

After a dispirited dinner with his parents, Carter walked through the city alone late that night. He was almost twenty-three years old. He had worked his way up to thirty weeks of continuous employment on the Keith-Orpheum, almost respectable for show business. But he had stalled. For four years, he had been Karter the Kard and Koin Man. His billing was mediocre – he appeared smack in the middle of the program, presenting his eighteen minutes of effects between Laszlo and His Yankee Hussars, a musical group who imitated famous band conductors, and Fun in Hi Skule, antic sketch comedy with jokes stolen from better acts.

He ached to be better than he was, but he didn't know how. Though he had ideas for spectacular illusions, he had no chance to implement them, as his contract specified that he would stick with small tricks – close-up magic. When he met other magicians, or when his parents inquired as to his progress, he had to say that he was still performing in-one, on the apron of the stage, curtain down, no large-scale work.

Mysterioso would change that.

Carter had been walking aimlessly for an hour or two before the noises from a carnival attracted him. Though it was late, the midway was still open, and he was pulled toward the familiar smell of kerosene burning in the pan lamps that lighted the grounds. As when viewing any entertainment, he tried to notice everything in hopes of improving himself. He quietly watched a shell gamer work the suckers. There was a Find the Lady booth and a dozen gaffed pitch-till-you-win contests for men to compete for stuffed animals while a steam calliope played 'Turkey in the Straw' and 'Waltz Me Around Again, Willie.' Finally, he took his place in line for the palm reader, Madame Zinka, who complimented his Head and

Heart lines, tutted at his rascettes, and told him he worked with his hands, he was about to take a long journey, and he was a fool not to get into his father's business.

He produced a dollar bill for her; when she reached for it, he vanished it with a frown.

She put her hand on her forehead, sighing. 'Oy! Every rich kid knows a magic trick. Next!'

'No, wait. You felt my palm, so you could tell I worked with my hands, and you saw my suit and realized I couldn't afford this myself. You're right about the long journey, but what's the gimmick?' He handed her a dollar, and another when her expression didn't change. Finally, he added, 'I'm on the Keith-Orpheum time. A magic act, in-one. It's not like I'm going to Europe on my father's nickel.'

'Everyone wants a long journey, kid. That's all. Next!'

'That's it?'

'What did I just say?'

Carter left her tent, hands in pockets, as the next person in line sat down at Madame Zinka's table. A dozen paces away, he heard her voice over the calliope music.

'Hey!' Madame Zinka had pushed aside a tent flap, and leaned out. 'You're gonna get married this year. Her name is Sarah.'

'Excuse me?'

But the tent flap dropped down, and Carter knew he would get nothing more. He continued alone across the grass, and out of the gates, and to the streets, where he wondered what in heaven's name was going on.

Over the last five years, while investigating all types of performance, he had also had a dozen Gypsy women read his palm, give him tarot card readings, look into crystal balls. He learned he would take long journeys, make huge sums of money, should avoid rough seas, and was desperately interested in contacting the spirit world, which could be done, it turned out, for a modest fee. He also learned the trick was to hold his hand, look him right in the eye, and see how he reacted to information, with a twitch or raised eyebrows. This was fantastic for forcing cards on people.

There was a complication he could not explain. Among generalities and flatly wrong guesses, more than one prophecy had said that when he was twenty-three years old, he would marry a woman named Sarah.

Returning to his parents' house, he didn't sleep. He could never sleep the night before a tour, but this night was particularly hard. James was enrolled at Yale and no longer lived at home, so there was no one to talk to now. He wanted to ask someone why he was so different than anyone he knew, and why he wasn't in some essential way different enough. Why were some people headliners and others rather forgettable? And, most importantly, was he about to marry someone? He wrote in his journal, 'It could be: the laws of chance; a cabal among fortune-tellers; that there is more to this physical world than I yet understand.' As he was approaching twenty-three (his birthday was in November), he believed all of these, sometimes simultaneously.

He opened his palm. Head line, Heart line, the mount of Venus and the four fingers that Gypsies – real Gypsies – called Mercury, Apollo, Saturn, Jupiter. He ran a finger over his skin and imagined beneath this romance and mystery the hard anatomy, just as romantic: the deep palmar fascia that could clutch silver dollars, the adductor obliquus pollicis that allowed the thumb's flexion away from the hand, small in most people but growing each day he shuffled cards past it.

About four in the morning, he brought out a new trunk, and transferred all of his props into it. The old Kard and Koin stencil seemed like an admission of failure, but he wasn't yet ready to add 'the Amazing' or 'the King' to his name. He stencil-cut a new title – simple, direct – and painted it on the side of the trunk: Charles Carter, Magician.

Chapter 7

The next morning, his parents took Carter to the train station. His father asked him no questions and his mother made no encouraging comments. It was only when they presented him with going-away presents – *Capital Thoughts*, the latest pamphlet attributed to J. Pierpont Morgan, from his mother, and Freud's *The Interpretation of Dreams,* from his father – he realized that other than a white flag, there was no clearer sign they had reached some compromise about him.

'So, dear, your weekly salary is what, now?' his mother asked sweetly.

'Thirty-five.' Carter halted the porter, who had his single trunk on a rack. 'I'll take that.' It was unwise to start a tour by having the company see a porter carrying your luggage. He wished he'd thought to distress his new trunk.

'How do you make out on that?' His father showed some teeth.

'It's just right, if I'm thrifty.' In fact, his mother sent him a secret extra fifteen a month, allowing him to break even.

'That's – nice,' his father said. 'Listen, Son, I know we've had some words, but I realize you have to follow your heart, too.' He spoke the way an actor might read a text for the first time.

'But we hope you make some progress,' Mrs Carter added, looking back at Mr Carter, who nodded appreciatively, as if he hadn't thought of that himself.

'Of course,' Carter said quickly, having survived this implied threat for several years now. He stepped up his pace, toward the farthest platform, where trains for performers always ran.

'In other words,' his mother continued, 'I think this should be your last tour.'

That it was she saying it stopped him in his tracks. He could see the other performers ahead, some women with boas, men struggling with heavy bags. He looked from them to his parents, who were, he saw, united in a way they never had been before. He heard the click of a purse snapping shut.

'We love you,' she added.

Carter nodded nervously. The turnover from his parents to his fellow vaudevillians was never easy, and the added pressure today made it worse. 'Yes,' he said, 'I understand. The train – let's go to the train.'

But when he saw the train, his heart sank – caked in last season's grime, it promised a smell in the compartments that would fade only after three weeks of citronella. His parents regarded the car with the painted-on smiles they'd had all morning.

The train hand, in battered derby and garters on his sleeves, waved his unlit cigar stub at Carter. 'Name?'

'Carter. I'm the magician.'

The train hand straightened up. 'The magician? Right away, sir.' He snapped his fingers and an assistant took Carter's trunk from him. 'Is this all you're carrying? We'll handle this, sir.'

Carter took a step toward the company train, but a gentle hand fell to his shoulder. It was a smartly dressed redcap, who said with a laugh, 'Oh, no, sir. Come this way.'

'Well, this is pleasant,' Mrs Carter said.

'Were you expecting this, Charles?'

Carter made a sweeping gesture to cover his surprise. 'Well, I do have a new contract, and magicians are being shown more respect these days.'

The redcap led them down the platform, where they stood alone in front of a polished four-car train. The engine, which sighed a plume of smoke, was painted a royal purple.

'Your train, sir.'

'My – train?'

'It's the magician's train, sir. As per your contract.' The redcap's buttons flashed in the sunlight.

'Mother, father . . . would you like to see my train?'

The first car was dark; the only light came from the front and rear doors, which stood open. Carter, praying his parents would see this as a clear sign of financial advancement, cautioned them to step carefully. There was a narrow aisle down the center; on either side of them were flats and scrim, props and scenery, trunks and packing crates, five tons at least, Carter thought. He saw markings stenciled on one box, 'Property of MYSTERIOSO!!!' He'd never heard the name. As they walked out the back of the car, Carter noticed a cage draped with blankets; something was moving inside, an animal of some sort.

'The next car probably has my sleeper,' he said. But he was mistaken: the car contained a dozen strangers who seemed to know each other. They were all dressed as if for church, and regarded him with suspicion.

'Hello,' he said.

They did not respond. He wondered if he were for some reason traveling with the Russo-Chinese acrobats. He smiled and nodded at them awkwardly as he passed through their quarters – but none of the sleepers had his card posted.

'That's odd,' he said.

'Maybe it's the next car,' his father said.

'That must be it.' The third car had a gold plate on its door: DOMUS MAGII, Home of the Magician. This was a sweet touch; Carter was deeply impressed by management's consideration. He opened the door, expecting a set of sleepers. But what he saw as he stepped in took his breath away. Most of the car had been converted to a single open room. The walls were done over in velvet, and the ceiling draped with silk tapestries. He stood in the most opulent traveling quarters he had ever seen: Louis Quatorze furniture, including a divan and writing desk; a great four-poster bed with angels carved into the headboard; a lounge stocked with pillows and fat candles straight from a Turkish seraglio.

'My goodness!' his father exclaimed.

His mother added, 'This will be very comfortable for you.'

Carter almost wanted to give it back – surely, he didn't deserve such splendor. And then the rear door opened, and in walked a tall man in a dazzling damask vest and shirtsleeves.

'Yes?' he said.

'I'm Carter. The magician?' Carter replied quickly.

The man's eyebrows raised. 'The – the magician.'

'Yes. Charles Carter. And these are my parents.' Carter extended his hand.

The man walked toward them. He was huge, well over six feet

tall, had glossy black hair, and a mustache waxed to its tips. By the time they were face-to-face, Carter realized the mistake he'd made, but his brain hadn't yet caught up with his mouth, and so he waited silently for the handshake that never came.

Instead, the man glared at him with the blackest eyes he'd seen. Carter felt an oceanic contempt swell against him, and then, finding him unworthy, it slipped away. Now, the man acknowledged his parents. 'You must be so . . . proud of your card and coin man,' he said.

'Oh, we are,' said Mrs Carter. She added, proudly, 'He performs in-one.'

Having put two and two together, Carter jumped in. 'Are you Mysterioso?'

'So few people ever have to ask that question.'

'Are you a magician, too?'

Together, Carter and his new enemy listened to that word, *too*, echo in the splendid train car. 'Mr and Mrs Carter, why don't you be Samaritans and help your son find his place in' – Mysterioso waved toward the far tracks – 'the other train?'

He ushered them out, politely.

Carter walked in silence, wishing for a distraction, an earthquake, say. He hoped his parents would say nothing.

'The other performers' train is this way?' his mother asked a redcap.

The redcap nodded.

'All the way at the end?'

'Mother.'

'Where they're loading the chickens?'

'Mom!' Carter angled his hat down farther over his eyes.

'So. Do they usually book two magicians on the same tour?' his father asked.

Carter shook his head. 'My act is just close-up, so he must be a large-scale illusionist.'

'Then you two will be friends,' his mother declared.

Carter glanced at his father, who sucked in his cheeks in the way that showed he'd learned never to disagree.

'I'll be going,' Carter said. 'But I'll be back—'

'Six months, one week,' his mother replied. 'We already have our tickets for the Orpheum that night.'

'Well, the following show would be better rehearsed—'

'We're looking forward to whatever wonders you dream up,' his father said, a hand on his shoulder, gazing at his son with genuine fondness. 'I know you'll be good with your cards and so on.'

As Carter hugged his mother good-bye, he heard Mysterioso, leaning out of his train, cry out across the platform. 'Carter! They've loaded your trunk onto my train. Don't worry. I'll have it sent to you.'

As the performers' train limped out of the station, it paused so that Mysterioso's regal locomotive could pull ahead of them. Carter watched, his dirty window open as far as it could be to start relieving the smell of mildew, straw, and last season's desperation. The first, second, and third of Mysterioso's cars – all painted a purple so rich it seemed enameled – passed him. Then he saw the last car of the train. The decorations on the outside of this final car were so bizarre, they caused much discussion among the other performers. By the time the tour had reached its first destination, Sacramento, Carter had overheard the whole story.

It turned out the fourth train car was the domain of Mysterioso's rare Chinese crested dog, a palm-sized animal with bulbous, wet eyes like suspicious marbles and an enormous tuft of white hair that made it look like he was raising cotton on top of his flat head. He yapped and shivered and bit people. His name was Handsome.

Handsome's train car had a featherbed, a gold-plated dish from which he ate steak, and a four-by-six-foot planter overflowing with tall grass imported from China – a place for Handsome to hide his bones. The side of the car was painted with Handsome's portrait over a phrase written in Latin: 'The more I know of people, the more I love my dog.'

The first show was in Sacramento. An hour before his act, Carter asked the road manager, again, if Mysterioso had returned his trunk; word came back, in the form of a sorrowful, handwritten card, that Mysterioso hadn't yet found it, suggesting that perhaps it had gotten mixed up with Mysterioso's five tons of equipment.

Carter, who was not so easily defeated, improvised a show with coins borrowed from the audience. He added a watch-destroy-and-restoration that worked especially well. When he returned to the boardinghouse after his act, he found his trunk waiting for him. Every piece had been examined thoroughly and replaced.

Removing his makeup, he was angry, but more than that, curious: why did this particular ratfink merit forty-five minutes on the stage? He returned to the theatre to find out.

Mysterioso had come from the hell of the five-show-a-day grind, and, before that, according to his program, from India, where he had studied at the feet of holy men whose names could not be revealed for fear of thuggee retribution. He had a buccaneer's laugh, especially when he knew people were listening. He seemed to find pleasure in taking up as much space as possible, standing in the cramped backstage, arms akimbo, legs spread. Onstage, he spoke with a British inflection, but Carter guessed from the atonal twang he heard leaking through that Mysterioso was a Cornhusker or a Hoosier.

Carter moved to the back of the house when Mysterioso's end-of-the-bill program began. After much to-do by stilt-walkers and fire-eaters, a trio of bloodthirsty Indians rushed from the wings with hatchets. Just as the performers looked as if they would be scalped, Mysterioso appeared on horseback, waving the American flag and crying, 'This is for Custer! This is for the Alamo!' He swung his cavalry saber, beheading one man and, using a rope that seemed to defy gravity, stringing another up from the rafters. The third Indian managed to manacle Mysterioso and escape with a beautiful woman. A volunteer was called onstage to check the handcuffs and see if it were possible for the magician to escape from them. But regardless of how the volunteer tugged or twisted, the network of handcuffs and chains was seemingly impossible to escape. Seconds later, however, the magician managed to shrug off the bonds, mount his horse, and swear revenge.

After a quick change of scenery, during which the company displayed alacrity and panache with fire-eating (again), the maiden was seen tied to a stake in an Indian camp. The braves showed their gymnastic and juggling skills, much levity occurring when one Indian, in pink warpaint, showed less interest in her than in a fellow brave, who chased him off the stage. The maiden refused to relinquish herself to any of them. Finally, an enraged chief revealed her fate: she was to be married to the lion.

A great cage was rolled onstage, and in it an agitated, pacing young lion. The chief addressed the beast, 'Will you have her as your bride?'

In response, the lion let out a terrifying roar.

With seven braves juggling lit torches, tossing them from man to man in a hypnotic pattern, the woman was led to the cage and thrown in; the lion gathered on his haunches to pounce as she cowered against the bars in helplessness. And then, after terrible seconds elapsed, the lion flung himself forward – revealing himself to be Mysterioso in costume.

As the rescuer hugged the woman, a bugle call sounded, and the cavalry, in a spectacular ending, burned the village to the ground, to tremendous applause and standing ovations. .

By the second show in Sacramento, Carter understood how all the illusions were accomplished. Had he the assistants and the money, he could have done them better. He could see exactly the moment the lion and the magician switched places – when the torch juggling was at its most furious, a revolving platform spun around. But try as he might, Carter couldn't figure out how the lion was made to roar on cue. The roar was what proved it was a real lion, and its timing, in response to the chief's question, was critical.

What a gulf Carter saw between Mysterioso's huge production and his own modest tricks. He swore to himself that when it was time for the week twenty-seven pay negotiations, he would have something new and grand-scale, something of his own.

How to swap secrets? Mysterioso was clearly a louse, but some member of his company might like to know variants on cup-and-balls that Carter had discovered. When he approached that night to invite someone out for whiskey, a juggler stopped him. Mysterioso had a special rider on his contract: neither he nor his company was to be 'molested' by other acts. This meant any form of conversation whatsoever.

Carter didn't much care for Mysterioso's attitude. Still, he wanted to know exactly how the Lion's Bride effects were achieved; more importantly, the young woman who was rescued every night was the most beautiful woman he'd ever seen. Her name was Miss Sarah O'Leary.

Chapter 8

In the next two weeks the tour stopped in Auburn, Reno, and Carson City. With times tough all over, the threat of being shut and sent home was even worse than last season. The Elko Palladium had a sign backstage that read: 'Performers: Do Not Send Out Your Laundry Until the Manager Has Seen Your Act.'

Carter was in no danger. Western towns loved magic. Really, the only troupe on the program that had to worry was the most pathetic act Carter had ever seen: Karl and Evelyn Kowaleski.

The Kowaleskis were Polish immigrants who traveled with a piano, a guitar, a cow, a rooster, a sheep, and two pigs. They called their act The Funny Farm. Programs described it as 'musical moos, boisterous baaas and oinks to tickle your funny bone.' While Karl played folk tunes on the guitar, Evelyn milked the cow in time with the music. Then Evelyn played chords on the piano – she had never learned melodies – while her husband shook the different animals to get them to make funny noises.

Carter watched their every performance before silent audiences, feeling queasy when he saw the sincere effort the Kowaleskis put into their miserable act. He frequently arrived early, just in case he had to wish them good-bye. In Salt Lake, as The Funny Farm performed, Carter stood in the wings next to Minnie Palmer, who stage-managed Fun in Hi Skule, which starred several of her sons. Carter didn't need to ask why Minnie was there; her fingers were crossed, and she seemed to hold her breath until the curtain closed on Karl and Evelyn. Then she let out a sigh, and patted Carter on the shoulder. The Funny Farm had made it through another performance.

After he had performed each night and locked his act away, he talked to Chase the monologist and fed Karl and Evelyn's animals, and then took a short walk through town to buy postcards or a newspaper, returning just in time for the entrance of Mysterioso's company. Sarah always walked with the men, but never any one man in particular. She wore the same silk scarf, turbanlike, and wool coat, until they hit Denver, when she switched to a rabbit wrap.

If it was nice enough weather, and if the theatre had a large back patio, the company warmed up outside. The men did standing somersaults and cartwheels and, to make each other laugh, struck fitness poses like they were lifting weights with Eugene Sandow. Sarah danced.

By Mysterioso's rules, Carter was not allowed to talk to her. So, he talked to himself. He told himself he didn't know her. He said there were many Sarahs in the world. He asked what kind of rube is smitten by a woman just because of a fortune-teller's – several fortune-tellers' – guesses? But Sarah O'Leary was beautiful; Carter wanted very much to know her.

Vaudeville, for a young man with a scruple or two, was a lonely business. It had taken Carter all these tours to realize his most fragile prop was his heart. No wonder so many men found sweethearts whose lockets they wore, and whose photos they studied late at night. Carter, a veteran now of cold showers and mental exercises to curb his desire, had always held out the slim hope he could find a sweet companion, but so far it had been impossible. Good girls in the towns they visited were prohibited from talking to actors. And there were few types of women to choose from in the show: stocky matrons, highly religious girls, suffering wives chained to alcoholic men, and the adventurous sort whose touch required a liberal dose of salvarsan. But in a heartbeat, Carter could tell that Sarah was none of these.

It was in Denver, with dusk falling, that Carter sat on a dusty carousel horse in the storage area backstage, on the second floor of the Metropole, and knew he was just seconds away from falling in love. Though it had been a dry summer, the theatre had watered their back lawn well, so the troupe had a nice green field for their warm-up. Carter positioned himself by a tiny window smudged with years of grime. He cleaned it using his handkerchief, and saw the lawn, the sycamore trees, and then the show-offs: the men in warpaint, one standing on another's shoulders, two more helping each other stretch, another tumbling backward across the lawn.

Sarah danced alone. Her white antebellum dress was hanging

from a tree. She wore a black leotard, black toe shoes, a tiny silver cross. Her blond hair was pulled back to show off delicate features. Going en pointe, in the grass no less, she was obviously trained in ballet.

He wanted to tell her she was pretty. But she had never disobeyed the dictum that she couldn't communicate with other acts. He had never even heard her voice. Ultimately, leaning on the carousel horse, Carter felt a sickening hopelessness – that she hadn't found anything good enough in him to break the rules. And so he watched as she danced in and out of his field of vision.

By the next night, his room in the boardinghouse seemed awfully small and quiet. He didn't feel like reading. He didn't feel like practicing card tricks or creating new illusions.

He looked for his fellow performers, knocking gently on the pasteboard doors of the rooming house, but none of them were in. He supposed they were at bars or brothels. Mysterioso's crew were staying in a real hotel – Carter wasn't sure where.

The cast of Fun in Hi Skule played a rowdy game of poker in the parlor. They were all around Carter's age, and generally friendly enough. Carter said hello to them, but received in response only tepid greetings. Magicians were never asked to play poker. Hat in hand, Carter hovered as their game started again. It was played with both laughter and insults.

Leonard won a hand; his brother Adolph whooped 'Back to the kitty with it!' and good-naturedly tried to wrestle the pot out of his arms, and Carter wondered what James was doing right now. James was terrific at poker. Perhaps he was making friends at Yale. The longer Carter thought about that, the more he wanted to find Sarah.

Minnie Palmer might know the name of her hotel. Carter spied her through the lace curtains, on the porch, under the lights. He opened the door and walked outside. Minnie was holding hands with Evelyn Kowaleski, who openly sobbed. Not wanting to interrupt, he turned on his heel to duck back into the house, but Minnie saw him.

'Mr Carter,' she said. She had a heavy German accent. When she was lecturing her sons, she sometimes slipped into Plattdeutsch or Yiddish. 'Can we have a word with you?'

'Surely,' he said, cautious because even the nicest people in vaudeville could try to run scams. Minnie was in her fifties, wearing a red wig and a corset to pass for thirty in her sons' act in case one of the girls was sick. Evelyn was fleshy and red-cheeked, especially in the light of the kerosene porchlamp.

'Mr and Mrs Kowaleski are having career problems,' Minnie began. Then she exploded, 'Oh, he's being completely unfair.'

'What exactly is the problem?' Carter asked.

Between sobs, Evelyn explained: the manager had seen their act, and told them that they were shut. Evelyn had begged for a second chance. 'I told him. I told him that tomorrow we could make it good. He said okay, but . . .' and here she broke down completely while Minnie patted her shoulder.

'I think your act is very nice,' Minnie said. 'I think that manager is just insensitive.' She looked at Carter.

'Yes,' Carter said. 'Your act is very sweet.'

'All it needs is some oomph,' Minnie said. 'A little razzle-dazzle.'

Carter knew nothing could make the act better. He said, 'I'm sure you can think of something.'

'I wish Karl was like his brother. His brother was a sailor. He looked so handsome.' Evelyn, her face pressed into Minnie's shoulder, wept. 'I don't know why it's so bad here. We did so good in Krakow. There was royalty there sometimes. We played in castles, private shows.'

'Maybe learning more songs,' Carter said.

Like it was the most natural thing in the world, Minnie added, 'Or a little hocus-pocus.'

Carter unthinkingly agreed, 'Hocus-pocus,' then glared at Minnie.

'What do you mean "hocus-pocus"?' Evelyn sniffed. She looked at Minnie, then at Carter, who could not for the life of him think of a reason to go along with this idea.

'Boy,' Minnie exclaimed. 'No one would expect card tricks in The Funny Farm, would they? That would be something.'

No matter how bad he felt for them, he wouldn't teach anyone the tricks his paycheck counted on. 'Mrs Palmer, I'm taking a brief constitutional. Do you know the name of the hotel where Mysterioso's company is staying?'

'I do, it's . . . it's where that lovely girl Sarah is staying, isn't it?'

'I think so – perhaps.'

When she smiled in response, Carter understood how this little woman in the red wig had done so well for her sons on the circuit. She said, 'I have it written down somewhere. Why don't you and I see what you can do to help out the Kowaleskis and then we'll go look for it?'

As Carter accompanied Mrs Palmer and Mrs Kowaleski to the barn, the women spoke excitedly about how things might be looking up, maybe this was just the ticket. Carter, who had brought a small bag of supplies, was mentally running through the possibilities. There were card tricks. Coin tricks. But those were what he performed. Cup-and-balls was, literally, the oldest trick in the book, but to be good at it involved weeks of training, and they had only a day. A two-person team could perform a black bag disappearance quite easily. Perhaps an animal could be pulled out of a hat.

But these thoughts seemed naive once Carter saw Karl. He was lying in the hay under a pile of horse blankets, humming to himself, a whiskey bottle upside-down next to him. His plump face was even redder than usual, and there was barley in his hair.

Carter picked up the bottle, which had been stuffed with straw. He looked around the barn: there was the cow, haltered to a post, the sheep and two pigs in a pen, and the rooster in a wooden crate. After a moment of rooting through the hay with his shoe, he found a wet box of matches.

While the women tried to rouse Karl, Carter scratched one of the pigs under her chin, whispering, 'Puisque toutes les créatures sont au fond des frères, il faut traiter vos bêtes comme vous traitez vos amis.'

Minnie said, 'That's French. Should Karl learn that?'

'No. That's from the first magic book I ever read. "Since all animals are brothers under the skin, we must treat our beasts like we do our friends." Mrs Kowaleski, you will have to learn the trick.'

'What? I don't know how. Karl is the one.'

'Karl is soused. There's no time to sober him up.'

Carter brought out two black bags and a length of rope and there, in the chill air under the lanterns in the barn, explained an old and simple trick. As an adolescent, he had learned it in five minutes, adding his own flourishes within the hour.

The trick was basic: a person climbed into a bag, which the magician knotted shut with a rope, as witnessed by two volunteers who held on to each end of the rope, pulling it taut to keep the bag from opening. A screen was put up to hide the bag and on the count of three, the volunteers pulled with all their might, and the bag – now empty! – flew over the screen.

Because the illusion involved minor participation by Karl, Carter asked Minnie to bring coffee. She brought with her a folded piece of paper on which she'd written 'The King Edward Hotel.' Carter folded it, put it in his pocket, and saw by his watch that it was already very late.

Karl and Minnie acted as the volunteers while Carter made Evelyn vanish, using a saddle blanket to cover the necessary manipulations. This worked perfectly the first time, but never again. When Karl sobered up a little, he was promoted from volunteer to assistant, and this was a disaster. He just wanted to sing sea shanties.

'She likes sailors better than me. It's okay, it's okay.' And then, with great happiness, he started singing again.

No matter how many times Carter explained the simple motions he had to make, Karl botched them, and ended up at the count of three still under the saddle blanket, with a bashful smile on his face that enraged Evelyn beyond all comforting.

Finally, they performed it once, adequately. There was nothing to do but wish them good luck.

It was long after midnight when Carter, ragged and a little dirty under the fingernails, finally ran to the King Edward. It was far too late to inquire at the desk about a lady, and, after several hours in the barn (the Kowaleskis' pig had taken an almost amatory shine to him), no amount of grooming could entirely mask Carter's smell. So he had thought ahead, wrapping a half dozen of his landlady's white roses in tissue paper, taking off his celluloid collar and wearing his rattiest hat.

As he approached the hotel's front desk, the night manager dozed on his stool, thumbs hooked in his pin-striped vest, until Carter cleared his throat.

'Mmm? Yes, what?'

'Maybe it's a wild goose chase,' Carter sighed. 'Is there a bunch of actors staying here?'

The manager blinked. 'Does this look like the type of establishment that would allow actors?'

'That's just what I said when my boss told me the King Edward. There's supposed to be a guy named Mysterioso?'

'Mysterioso, who is staying here, is not an actor. He is a magician, like Houdini.'

'Okay. Is there a Sarah O'Leary here?'

'No.'

''Cause these actors keep strange—' He squinted. 'Pardon?'

'She's no longer here.'

'What hotel is she staying in, then?'

He chortled. 'You'll have to work hard for your tip, boy. Mr Mysterioso put her on a train back home.'

'What? Why?'

'How should I know?' He settled back on his stool.

'But where . . . when . . .' Carter couldn't think of a whole question to ask. The manager closed his eyes, leaning against the wall and rehooking his thumbs in his vest pockets.

Carter took his flowers and card and crossed the lobby. He thought of asking if some mistake had been made, but knew in his heart that there hadn't. He had been an idiot for believing that he should woo Sarah. He walked most of the mile back to the boardinghouse before he realized he still had the flowers.

So he simply arranged them nicely and left them leaning against the Kowaleskis' door.

The next morning, while shaving, Carter had a thought: no matter what town Sarah had returned to, he would eventually tour through it. In fact, the difficulty and distance would only make their eventual reunion sweeter. He was almost humming to himself by the time he got to the theatre.

Carter sat in one of the many empty seats, listening to a woozy-looking Karl playing 'Three Blind Mice' on guitar while Evelyn milked the cow. He could just barely hear them over the shouts and screams of the children of miners, who fought gangs of ranchers' kids in the aisles. There was a large group backstage watching The

Funny Farm's performance. Word had gotten out that Carter had tried to help the Kowaleskis and therefore almost anything might happen.

When the musical section of the program was over, Evelyn stood up and said, grimly, 'This is a special part of our program. It is a little hocus-pocus.'

Carter watched their attempt at the illusion with his fingertips pressed to his forehead, ready to cover his eyes if necessary. Evelyn called for two volunteers to come onstage, and, as she hadn't specified that it would be a magic trick (Carter, who *knew* she was saying 'hocus-pocus,' still had trouble understanding her through the glottal stops of her accent), two farmhands, in overalls and work boots, came up, probably assuming the Kowaleskis needed some help with the animals.

'Oh,' said Evelyn, 'no, it's a magic trick. Not a farm trick. Maybe there's someone else.' Carter furrowed his brow: farmhands were fine volunteers – why wasn't Evelyn using them? She shaded her eyes and looked into the audience. Carter followed her gaze and saw, to his horror, two sailors sitting in the second row. Why were sailors in Denver? He prayed that Evelyn wouldn't choose them. Onstage, she gestured toward them. 'I see two patriotic boys. You come up onstage.'

Carter raised his hands, trying to signal Evelyn, trying to stop this from happening. He hadn't mentioned a cardinal rule behind this trick because the possibility had seemed so absurd, but here it was unfolding before his very eyes: when you're an escape artist, never choose sailors to tie your knots.

It was too late. The swabs had joined Evelyn as Karl, squinting evilly, went into the black bag. Evelyn held the bag shut while the sailors tied their knots.

In the audience, Carter murmured, 'No, Evelyn, you were supposed to tie the knots while they watched you.'

The two young men were having a good time. Even from the sixth row, Carter recognized a goose neck knot topped by a Spanish bowline, with a sloppy but impressive-looking manharness knot finishing off the slack in the rope. Evelyn, too ignorant to be worried, handed an end of the rope to each of the men, and told them to pull taut. She put up a screen she'd borrowed from the

Chinese dance number, hiding the bag Karl was in. The sailors stood on either end of the stage, and began pulling.

'One! Two! Three!' Evelyn clapped her hands. The sheep bleated. Nothing else happened. 'Four?' The audience, who had been paying little attention, perceived something unusual was happening, and the children in the aisles slowed down and focused onstage. The sailors redoubled their tugging efforts.

'Five? Karl?'

The bag launched over the screen, empty, weightless and with the sudden slack, the sailors tumbled to the floorboards. There was a short burst of laughter from the audience. Evelyn looked at the bag in amazement. Carter looked at the bag in astonishment. The trick had worked!

Then Evelyn remembered to have the sailors inspect the knots. When they had dusted themselves off, with some grumbling about not getting warned that they'd fall on their cans, the sailors admitted their knots were still good. Evelyn collapsed the screen. Karl was gone.

'Where is Karl?' she asked the sailors. 'Does anyone in the house know where Karl is?'

Carter sensed confusion in the audience – Evelyn was so concerned-looking that no one could tell if Karl going missing was part of the act. Then Karl walked onto stage from the wings. He waved at everyone. No one in the audience applauded.

'Thank you,' Evelyn said, bowing. 'That was our trick.'

Carter scanned the crowd, seeing them fanning out their programs, trying to decide whether to stay for the soft-shoe number or to get a taffy apple now and come back later. But gradually, something happened that Carter had never heard before in vaudeville: from the wings, from the flies, starting slowly, but building, genuine applause as fellow performers gave The Funny Farm the ovation it deserved.

A few minutes later, Carter was backstage, and there was Chase the dramatic monologist, and Reilly and Schultz, the singers, and Minnie, with Julius and Adolph, two of her sons, and the wan-looking girl who danced in the Chinese number, and band conductor Laszlo with most of his brass section. They clapped Evelyn on the back. Evelyn was showing off the black bags to everyone, and explaining how the trick worked, '. . . see, so simple.' Carter, pushing through the crowd, wanted both to congratulate her and keep her from revealing more. She hugged Karl, who shut his bloodshot eyes when someone yelled encouragement into his ear. Evelyn saw Carter and extended her arms to hug him.

Mysterioso, who had never come so early before, was drifting like a black cloud near the exit doors. Carter saw him approach the stage manager, a man with a mustache and thin toupee. While Carter was being hugged by Evelyn, he watched Mysterioso pointedly take out a legal-sized document and direct the manager's attention to it.

A moment later, the manager approached the troupe. He jerked his chin to Karl and Evelyn. 'Yer shut,' he said.

The crowd, as one, gasped, for no one could believe what the manager had said.

'Can't have three magic acts on the same bill. It's in the contract, I seen it. Getcher stuff, scram!'

The buzz began: what had he said? They were shut? That was awful! But as Minnie first comforted Evelyn, then ran after the manager to give him a piece of her mind, the other acts began to disperse, the flats pushed toward the stage for the comedy number, and everyone withdrew back to their own lives. Another act shut – best keep your distance.

Carter didn't leave. He stood perfectly still, close to the darkest corner of the backstage area. When the final person was gone, he concentrated, knowing he wasn't really alone. Almost completely concealed by a papier-mâché shield and sword used in the tableaux vivants act, Mysterioso stood still, holding his little dog. The moment Carter perceived him, the other magician gave a slight bow, turned on his heel, and left.

That evening, Carter performed his act with particular skill and grace. He was furious. Whenever he glanced to the wings, in either direction, there was Mysterioso again. This was the first time he was aware of Mysterioso watching his act, but the timing of his appearances in the wings suggested he knew exactly when Carter would be facing stage left or stage right. Mysterioso wore a faint smile and, as Carter went through the tricks he'd been performing for years, he gave nods and shakes of his head, as if impressed. Carter was adding up numbers while he was waterfalling decks of cards: they had been on tour five weeks. In twenty-two weeks, in San Francisco, at the Orpheum, he would need to perform spectacularly. Twenty-two weeks was a great deal of time, enough to perfect a new illusion or two.

There was a problem. According to Minnie, Sarah had returned home to Bristol Bay, Alaska. The tour would not pass near her hometown, and it was unlikely any professional engagement would ever pass within eight hundred snowbound miles of her. Furthermore, she had left because she was returning to her first great love, the church. She was joining a convent. She had quit when Mysterioso would not let her perform a dance solo based on Lamentations.

Some people, Carter mused as he flicked a scarf in the air, turning it into the American flag, would be embarrassed to have fallen in love from afar without getting to know the girl first. But he had no time for that; Mysterioso had shut down The Funny Farm. Ever since the days of Jenks, Carter had felt a sour kind of hatred for triumphant bullies.

Now was the time in his act when he brought in a volunteer for his big finish. Robert-Houdin had written, 'It is easier to dupe a clever man than an ignorant one' and Carter had taken that to heart.

'Will the smartest man in the house please come onstage?'

The line always got a laugh; and this time, accompanied by hoots and applause, a prosperous-looking man ambled up the aisle. He wore a European black wool suit with two side vents, and he was one of those types not willing to be fooled.

'What is your profession, sir?' Carter asked.

'I am an investment banker, sir.'

An investment banker. Perhaps someone who admired the Carter family name, as it was known to the legitimate, nonmagical world. Carter's sangfroid voice chilled another five degrees. 'I imagine you know how to judge a man's worth by looking at him.'

'I do.'

'And character counts as much as anything, doesn't it?'

'So Morgan says.'

Knowing the answer, Carter asked, 'If I walked into your bank, would you give me credit?'

'No, sir, I wouldn't.'

There was a little laughter from the audience, and, from the corner of his left eye, Carter sensed Mysterioso having a chuckle. 'Perhaps we can change that situation.' Carter had him unseal a deck, shuffle it, and pick a card, placing it in an envelope. 'Now, sir, would you please sign the card, then seal the envelope and sign your name across it?' As the man wrote his name, Carter said, 'Is that the signature you'll use when I come into your bank tomorrow morning?'

'It's the signature I use when signing all documents.'

Carter put the envelope into the man's jacket pocket. All he had to do was toss a deck of cards into the air and catch the right card. But Carter had reached a point he'd never reached before: he opened the deck distractedly.

A four of spades.

'Is this your card?'

'No, it is not.'

Carter looked at the four of spades. 'Really?'

'Really.'

In the wings, Mysterioso approached the very edge of the stage. He leaned, arms crossed, against the back of some scenery painted with devils and wizards.

For a horrible moment, audience member turned to audience member, the whispers just beginning. Carter felt time slowing down for him. But thinking onstage was becoming second nature: unseen, he located the correct card and an idea for a good finish sprang as full-blown as Athena.

He shook a throwing knife down his sleeve, drew his arm back, and threw it directly at the flat his rival was leaning against. The blade cracked the wood three inches from Mysterioso's head.

Returning his attention to his volunteer, Carter heard the offstage sound of Mysterioso stumbling over his boots and falling to the floor. 'Now then,' Carter said calmly, 'is that your card?'

The investment banker frowned. 'Is *what* my card?'

Carter tilted his head toward the flat. The six of hearts – signed by the banker – was impaled there. The knife blade had skewered it neatly. The banker looked disappointed. 'Why – yes. That is my signature.'

'Thank you.' Carter showed him offstage. He took a bow and approached the footlights. 'Ladies and Gentlemen, let us all learn how to give credit where credit is due.'

Carter then left the stage, repacking his kit and locking it away in the train's cargo hold. He hurried to Karl's and Evelyn's rooms, but they'd already been vacated. No chance to say good-bye.

That night he ate the landlady's salt horse stew, and later he lay in bed, staring upward at the peeling paint on yet another dirty ceiling, while cats howled outside his window. He tried to think of respectable illusions, ways to stand out from the ranks. Something involving fire, perhaps, or a new twist on spirit mediums. His thoughts kept drifting to Karl and Evelyn, to them sitting on a train, them not waving good-bye, for there was no one to see them off. And Sarah, gone, too. And Mysterioso, the headliner. Outside, two tomcats cried out, their voices raising like sirens.

Suddenly, Carter threw the covers off, opened the window, and howled back at them.

They fell silent. He imagined them stunned. He closed the window and went back to bed, but did not sleep.

Chapter 9

Carter turned twenty-three in November in Wichita. Borax Smith sent him a fountain pen, along with an invitation to write him as often as he liked. He also received a package from his family – books, long underwear, a trick photograph taken at Woodward Gardens in which James seemed to be playing a hand of cards with himself. Besides these gifts, Carter's celebration consisted of climbing to the roof of the boardinghouse, drinking a single shot of whiskey, and making a frame with his fingertips that he swept around the sky until he found a constellation he recognized, but could not name. He wondered if it were also visible from Alaska. He'd heard nothing from Sarah, but imagined her frozen in time there, waiting for him though she didn't even know it.

The last two nights of week twenty-seven were a grand show at San Francisco, the Orpheum, the gem of the circuit. With a fifty-piece orchestra and velvet seats for two thousand patrons, the Orpheum was where the finest performers in the world – Houdini, Sarah Bernhardt, the Barrymores – played for five thousand dollars a week. The thirty-week players, who averaged perhaps $110 a month, were allowed two nights at the Orpheum so that management could watch their acts and renegotiate contracts for the following season. These were the shows where they were expected to add twists, nuances, and improvements.

Carter's old ideas for illusions seemed vulgar, and lately, his imagination dwelt on tricks involving beheadings or electrocutions or the brank, and he did not trust his judgment. He wrote to the brothers Martinka, the great illusion builders, to inquire about the costs of fabricating a levitation effect. They wrote back with steep quotations for an aga levitation and steeper still for what he really wanted, an asrah, in which the subject not only floated but vanished. He could hardly afford even the former without touching his trust fund and alerting his father.

By the twelfth week, 'purchased' word of mouth was in full swing. This meant that when the tour was about to hit a smaller town, just a single night on the schedule – Okmulgee, Oklahoma; Nacogdoches, Texas; Plaquemine, Louisiana – advance men went to taverns and churches, speaking to each other loudly about the many marvels the next Keith-Orpheum circuit show held. In church, they clucked their tongues when considering their poor wives, who had missed the show, and hadn't seen handsome Chase Wiley, the poetic monologist. In the taverns, they laughed about the antics of Fun in Hi Skule and murmured to each other about the risqué dance set in the opium den. Why, they wondered, had so much of the girl's flesh been allowed to show? The tactics worked – seats were filled close to capacity.

But as the tour progressed, a genuine swell of public opinion greeted them, based on a new member of Mysterioso's act: Annabelle, the woman who replaced Sarah O'Leary after three other girls had filled in and were dismissed.

Carter had little interest in her. Before his attempt with Sarah, he had never been one to fling woo at girls. And in Sarah's absence, he kept a noble sort of detachment from Annabelle for almost three days. Two days, nineteen hours after she joined the troupe, they were both backstage, Annabelle stretching in her black leotard, one leg propped up on a ballet bar. While he checked the band of his top hat for extra aces, he saw her to be awkward-looking and red-faced, with her brow wrinkled as if in complaint.

But as he popped his top hat on his head and swirled his cape in anticipation of his entrance, he glanced her way again, and saw that Annabelle had silky, fine hair, henna red, that fell in curls on either side of her heart-shaped face. How large her hands were, how chipped her nails. The blue ribbon in her red hair was sad and frayed. But, just as he started to feel sorry for her, he saw, in her shifting weight from foot to foot, the play of muscles in her back.

She caught his eye. He said nothing. Neither did she. They both turned away, successfully. He moved to the apron of the stage as the orchestra played 'Pomp and Circumstance,' and he bowed to the audience. He performed perfectly well onstage, but while he was pulling hard-boiled eggs out of the ear of a small boy, he was recalling what terrible qualities he'd just seen in Annabelle's eyes.

He would not talk to her. He was too afraid of the very quality he'd seen in her green and gold-flecked eyes, the quality that made her an asset to Mysterioso's company. Her eyes reflected volcanic anger.

Her first night onstage, in Topeka, she had fought – truly fought – the men approaching her, throwing one aside and kicking another in the stomach and knocking the wind out of him. Then, as if it had been a passing summer cloudburst, she lost interest and let herself be kidnapped. The crowd had never seen a woman who could fight before. They went wild. At the closing curtain, unbidden by anyone, she took her own bow, getting a glare from her employer, and even more applause.

Word trickled down from Mysterioso's camp that after the first performance he had actually fired her, but that a dozen women of Topeka had lined up at the stage door to bless Mysterioso for showing the world that they could fight Indians, too. The women said they were telling all of their neighbors to come to the next evening's show, and they told him 'God bless you' so many times he rehired Annabelle and made her performance part of the act. When his men complained, he chuckled, and said he was now doubly sure he was making the right decision. He told them to choreograph a mock fight.

Had Carter been interested in watching her (he wasn't – his position on this was so strong he wrote it down), he could have stood in the vacant lots behind the theatres and seen Annabelle and the men rehearsing an increasingly athletic and complex battle. The men were reluctant, but as Annabelle bought drinks for any man she knocked unconscious, they became firm supporters of her place in the act.

Whenever the tour intersected with another vaudeville circuit's show, Carter watched performances by other magicians, usually taking notes. He saw full-length shows at the legitimate theatre: the Great Raymond (in his journal, Carter wrote, 'he was good'); Adelaide Herrmann, last of the great Herrmann family ('good'); Thurston, successor to Kellar, and named by his peers as the world's greatest magician ('not bad,' Carter wrote); T. Nelson Downs, the

King of Koins (Carter made no mention of Downs's act, but wrote a page defending his own act, concluding, miserably, that he had to find a new effect).

The only performance that he considered at length was at the Boston Keith's theatre. Houdini. 'Last night,' Carter wrote James, 'I saw the most famous man in the world give what I suppose is a typical performance. It is now three A.M. and I am still trying to comprehend what I saw: a short, muscular man with a precise way of speaking, like a Dutchman who speaks the Queen's English, in a dirty tuxedo – I was in Row S, and I could see soot on him – botching ten minutes of card tricks before tossing the deck aside and getting to the real business: being Houdini. Have I mentioned that he is the most famous man in the world? He did, for ten minutes. "Ladies and Gentlemen, George Bernard Shaw said that the three most famous men in the history of the world are Jesus Christ, Sherlock Holmes, and Houdini. Only one of us could be here tonight. . . ." He listed all of the things he has escaped from in the last twelvemonth: handcuffs, straitjacket, sea bag, jail cell, convict ship, crazy crib, coffin, glass box, padlocked case, giant football, witch's chair, chains, ropes, etc. Then he explained, for another ten minutes, all the old stories of how many foolish imitators he has destroyed. "If you are a handcuff king, beware of me," he said, "for I am unveiling a new weapon." Then he showed a motion picture show of him jumping manacled into the Mississippi River and escaping and then construction crews roping him to a girder of the Heidelberg Tower in Manhattan; he escaped that, too.

'Then the lights went up and he proceeded to perform the most amazing stunt I have ever seen in my life.'

Two hot-water boilers were brought onstage, one empty and the other full of warm water. Men from the Albert Mann Boiler Works shackled Houdini with chains and handcuffs they'd brought themselves. Houdini walked up a platform and stepped into the empty boiler, which came up to his neck. Then the men began draining the warm water into the boiler Houdini stood in. This took quite a long time, an interim that Houdini filled with jokes: 'It's not even Saturday night,' and 'If I escape, this will be a good trick. If not, buy an Albert Mann Boiler tomorrow – I vouch for its integrity.'

When the water was level with the top – spilling over, in fact

– two men carried the boiler cap across the stage, and Houdini took a great gulp of breath and ducked under the surface as the cap was placed on top and the bolts tightened. Immediately, the orchestra struck up 'Asleep in the Deep.'

Carter, who had been impressed with the beginning of this illusion, was suddenly let down: of course the cap could screw off. But then two more workmen came out of the wings holding menacing-looking rivet guns. With the snap and retort of metal piercing metal, the boiler cap was riveted shut in twenty places. The men walked off and the curtain swung shut on the sight of the boiler trembling slightly from whatever motion the entrapped Houdini was making inside.

The audience began talking excitedly. The man to Carter's left was holding a watch. 'It has been two minutes since he held his breath,' he said quietly.

'That long already?'

'Yes. Do you think there was air between the surface of the boiler and the cap?'

'I think so, but not much.'

'The cap looked concave.' The man stared at his watch.

Behind Carter, women were discussing with their husbands how they had seen Houdini escape from nested automobile tires and snow chains.

'I hear he can undo locks with his toes,' one woman said.

'He keeps a full set of tools down his throat. He can bring them up at will,' her husband answered with the authority of one who has heard a rumor.

'It's been four minutes,' the man with the watch said.

'He escaped from a paddy wagon in Russia, and he was nude then, so the only way was if he had the keys down his throat.'

At five minutes, the orchestra finished playing 'Asleep in the Deep.' There was brief consulting between the conductor and a stagehand, then they struck the song up again, from the beginning. Carter sensed that something had gone wrong.

Conversations dried up as the rest of the audience began to catch the same sense, the sense that the disaster awaiting Houdini, the one he tempted with every escape, might have finally caught up with him.

Carter thought Houdini must be taking precautions – there was no way he could actually be risking death – and yet, as the seconds ticked away, his concern grew and he rolled and rerolled his program between his hands. He consulted his watch. He thought about the date. He could tell his grandchildren that he was in the audience the night Houdini failed to escape. How long could someone hold his breath? Three minutes? Four? It had been eight minutes – the musicians in the orchestra looked worried.

A tremble of red velvet, the curtain parted slightly, and Houdini, soaking wet, his shirt torn, staggered toward the footlights. His hands were bloody. The crowd burst into applause and cheers as the orchestra shifted into 'My Country 'Tis of Thee.'

'Eight minutes, forty seconds.' The man put his watch away.

Houdini held his arms up for a moment, as if about to speak, but then he shuddered and sank to one knee. With the audience gasping, nurses draped a blanket over Houdini's shoulders. They helped him to his feet. The rounds of applause were overpowering. Carter, shaking his head, clapped till his hands stung as a hunched-over Houdini made a supreme effort, threw the blanket off, and raised his arms in victory. And the whole house, as if with one voice, screamed his name, 'Houdini!' Houdini's hand went to his brow, and the nurses came to his aid, taking him into the wings.

The curtain was raised and the boiler was shown still to be riveted shut. Applause continued throughout the demonstration, with calls for Houdini finally answered when the manager announced that Houdini had been taken to the hospital due to the exertions of the escape. If people wanted to see him again, he would be escaping from a giant lightbulb, provided by the Edison Power Company, at noon the next day.

Carter left the theatre feeling exhilarated, caught in the great flood of people who all chattered about the spectacle, the suffering, the triumph. Houdini had escaped, somehow, at great personal sacrifice. As Carter filed through the double glass doors, he felt a hand at his elbow.

'You were very impressed, Carter.'

That voice. He stopped, regarded the fingers locked around his elbow, and then looked up into a grinning, unpleasant face. Mysterioso wore a black silk suit, wool overcoat, and black silk scarf. He was about six inches taller than Carter. He stood so close that Carter had to turn his head back uncomfortably to meet his eyes. 'You were applauding.' It was a condemnation.

Carter freed his elbow. 'It was a fine show.'

'The man risked nothing. He is the worst sort of charlatan,' Mysterioso boomed, ignoring the dirty looks of patrons, 'getting a houseful of people to pay for his bleating like an egomaniac before that phony stunt with the boiler.'

'I respect the serious danger—'

'Oh, please: those men fired phony rivets—'

Carter, whose cheeks were burning, tried to hush him. 'You know the walls have ears.'

'I don't care who hears this – Houdini is a fake.' Mysterioso looked down on the hats of other patrons as they filed around him, and announced, 'He got out of that nice bathtub in five seconds, and sat backstage reading a newspaper while children like you sweated and prayed and felt tremendous sympathy for the third-most-famous man in the world as he painted up his hands with fake blood and counted up the house receipts.'

The angrier Carter became, the calmer and more observant he was. He noticed Mysterioso had a fresh bruise just under his eye.

Carter had learned the signs of Annabelle's presence on the tour: Leonard, Minnie Palmer's eldest son, had been found knocked unconscious backstage; Walter Huston, who usually did a soft-shoe and sang 'I Ain't Got the Do-Re-Mi,' was, after making a play for Annabelle, reduced for a week to shuffling across stage on his one good foot. It was astonishing to Carter that men didn't know some women just didn't like them. The bruise on Mysterioso's face was exactly the size of Annabelle Bernhardt's fist.

'You know,' Carter murmured, 'raw beefsteak is a wonder—'

'You mind your business,' Mysterioso hissed. He narrowed his eyes, rubbing the lapel of Carter's topcoat between his fingertips. 'Did your father buy you this coat?'

'I've been buying my own clothes for several years now.' Carter knocked the fingertips away, wishing for a baseball bat to do the job effectively. 'As for Houdini, it happened as you say. He had all of us feeling pleased with ourselves, just because he fooled us. If I think about it, I suppose he's well enough to escape from a lightbulb tomorrow. But I don't want to think about it.' Mysterioso smirked and Carter continued. 'That's right, that's right – that's the magic of it.'

'Oh,' Mysterioso moaned, clutching at his heart as if Carter had shot him there. 'Magic. Of course,' He shook his head. 'I'd been wondering exactly what kind of idiot you are, rich boy.'

The crowd had tapered a bit. Mysterioso gave one last sad shake of his head and walked away.

Carter called after him, 'Mysterioso,' but got no response, so he continued, 'how do you make the lion roar?'

Mysterioso called over his shoulder, 'Magic, you moron,' as he turned his collar up and merged with the crowd.

Chapter 10

The tour looped the northeastern states in early spring. The New England crowds, as if leaving their houses for the first time since fall, seemed the most grateful in the country. The circuit traveled west along the Highline, crossing back and forth into Canada, where the crowds were reserved and polite, which was never a good combination for a magician. Far better to tour the northern climes in winter, when the audience applauded anything and everything just to stay warm. As they entered rougher territories – Montana, the Dakotas – Carter noticed a change in Mysterioso's behavior.

When they set up in a new town, acts from the program would give a free demonstration, a ballyhoo, in the largest public square. Mysterioso would give a brief speech decrying his skills, passing behind a curtain to show how quickly he could change uniforms – a fifth of a second! This, followed by throwing handfuls of his copper 'Mysterioso' tokens into the mob. In Butte, an astonishing thing happened. After Mysterioso changed from buck private to colonel, there was a unified call from a group of cowpokes: 'Annabelle!'

Carter watched as Colonel Mysterioso stared daggers at them. 'Yes,' he said 'Annabelle Bernhardt will be at the theatre tonight. She is the most fantastic furious female fighter ever to be tamed. Bring your wives!'

The men, who were leaning against a gate at the edge of the square, called again, 'Annabelle!'

Whenever Carter thought of this moment, and he thought about it often, he put himself in Mysterioso's place. Carter would have encouraged the calls for another member of his company. But, instead, Mysterioso ignored the men and barked out an order to an assistant. A moment later, a pile of chains and handcuffs clanked onto the stage.

'Watch,' Mysterioso cried, 'and learn!' This was a new moment in Mysterioso's public repertoire. He was bound with a dozen pairs of handcuffs, inviting as many people to examine him as the stage could hold. When he shrugged once, twice, three times, the cuffs fell off of him.

The crowd cheered. Mysterioso, surveying his subjects, called out: 'I am the master!' There were hollers for more, and Carter could almost see the magician weighing his words as he said them. 'I am the king of escapes!'

The crowd continued their clapping, someone yelling, 'Down with Houdini,' and Mysterioso, pumping his hands in the air, seemed to realize the heavens had not darkened. He laughed. 'Yes, down with Houdini!'

This was suicidal behavior, akin to spitting on the Cross, but with the threat of more immediate retribution.

For the next week, Carter waited cautiously for reports of reaction from Houdini, who had been known to appear unannounced at a rival's show and embarrass him onstage. Other times, Houdini, a born scrapper, simply ambushed other magicians in alleyways and beat the tar out of them.

It turned out, however, that Houdini had just undergone one of his periodic transformations, and was touring under a banner that read 'No Handcuffs.' Because of their sheer number, he was no longer able to assassinate the characters of the dozens of self-proclaimed Handcuff Emperors, Kings, and Wizards one by one. So, instead, Houdini had lobbed a bomb into their midst, a book called *Handcuff Secrets*, which explained in detail exactly how everyone else's tricks were accomplished. From now on, the world was welcome to the monkeys who monkeyed with shackles, he proclaimed. Houdini would escape exclusively from devices of his own creation, such as the padlocked Milk-Can and Chinese Water Torture Cabinet.

So it seemed after all that Mysterioso had risked nothing that day in Butte. But on a Monday afternoon in Vancouver, most of the performers were lazing and dozing in a park, enjoying a rare clear and cloudless day. August Schultz, who had his arm in a sling – Annabelle's work – was playing pinochle with Leonard from Fun in Hi Skule. Carter sat on the grass a few yards away, sketching illusions and crossing them out. A signature effect, something for the public to identify a magician with, was a direct reflection of personality. He asked himself, *Am I the type of magician who would like to be known for . . . pulling a rabbit out of a hat? Escaping from handcuffs? Turning into a lion?*

There was just a slight breeze and then an odd sputtering sound came from above the treetops. Carter spotted an airplane on the horizon. Aware of the distance between himself and everyone else, he cleared his throat.

'Look, everyone,' he said, 'an airplane.'

An airplane was such an uncommon sight that people stirred from their naps, put down backgammon boards and guitars, to stare at the strange machine. Carter knew a little about airplanes because, only months beforehand, Houdini had become the first man to fly one in all of Australia. As this one approached, a hollowed-out rectangular box for the wings and a square box for the tail with what looked like a ladder connecting them, it looked exactly like the one Houdini had flown: a Voisin, made in France, with an English engine. These were so expensive and unusual that the sight of it made Carter's heart beat faster – could it be Houdini himself? Of course! A dramatic entrance en route to confronting Mysterioso! The engine sputtered and droned, the plane not fifty feet off the ground. August Schultz yelled, 'That plane – it looks like Houdini's.'

Carter wished he'd said that, for the whole company jumped to their feet, waving their hats, and calling out encouragement to this daring aviator. As it circled clockwise, a great, disappointed groan arose from the crowd. Painted on the rear assembly was one huge word: MYSTERIOSO! The magician continued circling long after the troupe had gotten the message, and then he disappeared over some trees.

Two weeks passed, and the company began the final leg of the tour, the trek down the West Coast. In Portland, a package arrived for Carter from the brothers Martinka: the apparatus for the aga levitation he had settled on. It was simple and almost impressive.

The tour played the Portland Galaxy, a small, dreary stone theatre that had once been a Lutheran church. Just after dawn on the morning before the first show, Carter stood onstage and unpacked the materials, consulting the instructions the Martinkas had included. Within an hour, he had levitated a waxworks Beefeater he'd taken from the property room. He swung a hoop down from its tall black hat, over its body, to its scuffed black boots, and addressed himself to the empty seats: 'You see? No wires. The rational mind exclaims – there must be strings! Wires! And I would have to agree, Ladies and Gentlemen, but . . .' He fell silent. Dreadful. Boring. He might as well shoot himself.

He took from his pocket one of Mysterioso's throw-out tokens. Baby was on the back, and the legend below him read: 'Will You Have Her As Your Bride?' He looked up, then left, then right. The backstage storage area for Mysterioso's property was mere feet away. Every night, the lion was put back into its cage and left alone.

He made sure the theatre was absolutely empty, and to ensure privacy, he jammed the locks from the inside with some picks and putty. Mysterioso's storage area was accessible only by one door, steel plate, with a two-key locking mechanism that would stump most thieves. Carter opened it, went inside, and closed and locked it quietly.

For long moments, he let his eyes adjust to the dark. There was a single window about twenty feet up, with bars over it. All of Mysterioso's props were stored in crates stacked chest high to make aisles one could walk up and down. The lion's cage was straight ahead, but crates obscured Carter's vision as he approached on tiptoe. He didn't want to startle the animal, though he suspected it was difficult to sneak up on a lion.

When he was but five feet from the cage there was no time for him to process the ramifications of an unassailable fact: the cage was empty and the door stood open. He did, however, have enough time to think, *They must keep the lion somewhere else at night*, before he heard a cough behind him. It wasn't a human cough.

The door to the storage unit was fifteen feet away, three or four strides. In theory, it was possible to make it that far, but Carter had locked himself in. He had heard that lions could smell fear. He had heard that if a lion charges you, you should punch him in the nose as hard as you can. Make sure you don't accidentally find your hand in his mouth.

He couldn't see the lion, which was no doubt crouching some-where in one of the aisles made by all the boxes. There was a light whipping sound, which was probably his tail flicking against a crate. He measured his heartbeat: eighty, no, ninety, no, one hundred twenty beats a minute. He thought, *Puisque toutes les créatures sont au fond des frères* . . . knowing that nothing in that friendly thought guaranteed the lion would respond in kind. He turned from the waist to look 360 degrees for a sign of him. He took one step backward.

He's seen something on the floor, poking out of the aisle closest to him: a pair of feet. Someone lying on the ground? Yes, there were legs, and beside them, a pair of shoes. He leaned forward to look farther down the aisle. Annabelle, on her side, lying half up against the wall among scattered packing materials.

The lion was crouched by her head. Carter recognized the posture: his father had once owned a hunting dog that didn't like to be approached when it was about to gnaw on a soupbone. He took one step back, and the lion followed with one step forward, huge ropes of muscle trembling and flexing under his gold coat.

As the lion stepped over her body, paws the width of her face, the punching-the-lion-in-the-nose advice struck Carter as woefully inadequate.

'Annabelle?' hissed Carter. She didn't stir. 'Annabelle?' In his life, he had heard few noises so low and deep they were felt before they were heard: the first rumbles of an earthquake, the full throttle of an express train, and now the roar of the lion, a raw bellow with an underlying ticking sound, like a metronome counting down seconds. The lion was going to kill him. The lion crouched, gathered on his haunches, and propelled himself forward, up, in a perfect parabola, falling toward Carter, jolting strangely in midair. Annabelle stood behind the lion, holding his tail with both hands and delivering with all the force in her body a hard, swift jerk so that the lion's momentum carried him to the floor, where he toppled a stack of crates.

There was a moment of quiet while the three of them gathered their wits.

'Miss Bernhardt!' Carter exclaimed. 'Are you all right?'

'Yeah,' she swallowed. 'You aren't.'

'What?'

'Don't move.'

The lion's eyes were fixed on Carter's throat, and his shoulders were rapidly falling toward the floor.

'Oh, for godsake,' Annabelle muttered. She barked, 'Baby!'

Carter looked toward her; the lion did not.

With an air of disgust, Annabelle hissed, 'Don't make me come after you.' The lion's tail thumped against the floor. Then Annabelle made one simple motion: she put her hands on her hips. At once, all tension seemed to drain out of the lion, who licked his lips. 'That's better. You know it ain't worth it.' She put a hand under his collar and towed him to his cage.

When she returned to where Carter was still frozen, she gave him the once-over. 'What the hell you doing here?'

'I could ask the same of you.'

'I was sleeping.'

'Why aren't you at the hotel with Mysterioso?'

'You sleep at the hotel with Mysterioso.' She took out a cigarette. 'What time is it?'

'Maybe seven-thirty.'

She put the cigarette back. 'What are you doing here at the crack of dawn, anyway?'

'I'm . . . trespassing.' Carter felt a bit ill. When he realized he could move, he righted a crate that Baby had knocked over. 'I was hoping to find out how the lion roars on command.'

Annabelle finally lit the cigarette. Her dirty red hair hung down in her face. She looked over her shoulder, at the cage. 'Hey, Baby, how do they make you roar?' She glanced back at Carter. 'He ain't cooperating. Maybe you should get rough with him.'

Carter squared his shoulders, approached the cage, and pointed his finger, the way the Indian Chief did, and replicated his tone. 'Will you have her as your bride?' But nothing happened. Carter looked at Annabelle. 'Aren't you curious?'

She shrugged. 'It's not my act.'

'Why was his cage open?'

'I let him out so we could play. Me and him are friends.'

'I see. Then you fell asleep?'

Annabelle nodded. 'Did you think you were rescuing me?'

'No,' Carter said, 'but I would have punched the lion in the nose if I had to.'

'What?'

'You know, the way you're supposed to when . . .'

Annabelle seemed to be wrestling with a smile, and the smile lost. She gathered up her hair, binding it with the frayed ribbon he'd often seen her wear. Between lips that held her cigarette, her voice came out low and raspy like an oboe under a wool blanket. 'You haven't thanked me for saving your life.'

Carter frowned. 'Well . . .'

'Well' what?'

'The lion seems fairly docile. All you had to do was look at him right, and he put his tail between his legs.'

She stood up so fast that Carter actually flinched. 'No, pal, all I had to do was look at him. You coulda looked at him all day long, sooner or later from inside his rib cage. He took one look at you and saw meat. Easy meat.' Grinding out her cigarette, she sat back down in the aisle where he'd found her. 'Exactly what Mysterioso sees.'

He bowed. 'I'm sorry to have disturbed you.'

Her eyes were closed and she put her hand over her mouth as if yawning. 'Try and pick the lock quietly on your way out.'

Throughout the day, it rained, and Carter paced in his room, thinking of pithy things he should have said to Annabelle.

When he went back to the theatre, he discovered, with a certainty that made his stomach turn, that someone had opened, then repacked, his new Martinka devices. It had been a careful burglary; had he not been so concerned with how he would customize his aga levitation, he might not even have noticed the way the spool had been repackaged, just to the left of where he'd put it. Had Annabelle done this? Unlikely. There was a very short list of people capable of opening the lock Carter used.

Because he sometimes thought best while walking, he walked in the rain, eventually finding a small carnival set up near the Lewis and Clark statue in Three Bridges Park. Most of the attractions had been canceled. The rides were closed, and the animals were penned off at the wettest corner of a leaky, sour-smelling tent where a few jugglers unhappily tossed batons back and forth, marching in place to keep warm. Carter gave a quarter to a fortune-teller, a beautiful, young Chinese woman with a terrible cold. She threw a fistful of twigs onto a folding table and looked at them, dabbing at her nose with a handkerchief, and announced that, very soon, he would marry a woman named Sarah.

Carter folded his hands in his lap. He looked away from her, to a place in the grass that the rain was trampling. There had to be a handbook of prophecies, somewhere. 'What if I told you Sarah had already moved away? Am I supposed to follow her?'

She blew her nose. 'I don't know.'

'Or something else?'

'I don't know.'

Carter leaned back, letting his jacket open slightly, so that his pin from the Society of American Magicians showed. Rain pelted the roof as the woman took a lingering look at the pin, and nodded to show she'd seen it. She could, if she wanted, speak freely about whether she was simply following a handbook.

She shrugged. 'I just have a gift, mostly.'

'Of course,' he sighed, 'a gift. Wonderful.'

In bed that night, he fell into a restless sleep, waking at 4 A.M. with a disappointed, fading feeling: he'd dreamed of a new illusion Annabelle had performed. Unfortunately, it was a variation on a Robert-Houdin device, hardly original. Worse, it was a spiteful kind of trick, unworthy of consideration. Nonetheless, he sketched it in his notes and returned to bed.

And yet he did not sleep. He mentally turned the pages of Robert-Houdin's *Confidences d'un Prestidigitateur*, then *Les Tricheries des Grecs Déviolées*, then *Les Secrets de la Prestidigitation et de la Magie*, then *Magie et Physique Amusante*; Annabelle's trick wasn't in any of them. His eyes snapped open.

He looked at his notes again by lamplight, drawing the bedsheets to his neck. He had just dreamed a completely original illusion. The device would be sloppy, ugly, and expensive, and would require several assistants, and only a fiend would use it. He almost was ashamed of dreaming it. Almost. With clear, bold letters, Carter wrote down a name for his new device: BLACKMAIL.

At 5 A.M. Carter dashed to the telegraph office, waking the operator in order to send a wire to the Martinkas. An emergency order.

Three more optical mirrors. Another winch and pulley. Black magic, yards and yards of it. A flash pot. A table with a steel trap built in. A platform, hinged. And modify the aga to an asrah, hang the expense.

An hour later, there was a return wire. Francis Martinka said it would cost five hundred dollars and take at least a month. Carter said he needed everything in two weeks. He dictated to the operator: AM ON THIRTY-WEEK KEITH-ORPHEUM TIME.

He thought that would settle it, but there was another wire from Martinka: ARE YOU HEADLINING?

Finally, Carter realized he had to do something to impress Francis Martinka. Digging into the money his mother had sent him for emergencies, he placed a telephone call, all the way across the country, for twenty-two dollars. It took fifteen minutes to arrange, and then there was hiss and static and ghost voices from other calls, fading in and out, and he had to shout to be heard. 'One of my men will hand you a cash deposit whenever you think fair, and the balance upon receipt.' Actually, it would be one of his father's men, and Carter would face all the circles of hell for ponying up this kind of money, but he wasn't going to stop now.

'In the past weeks, you have ordered some modest equipment from us, monsieur, but . . . this is five hundred dollars.'

'I need this for the last show of week twenty-seven.'

A pause. 'The San Francisco Orpheum? Albee?'

'Albee will be there.'

Brightly, Francis Martinka declared, 'So will my devices.'

Chapter 11

Carter, away at Thacher in spring 1906, had missed the earthquake and fire. But he'd read the newspapers, and received letters from his parents describing the rebuilding efforts that followed. The San Francisco city fathers invited E. F. Albee, head of the Keith circuit, to help make San Francisco truly world-class again by building the Orpheum, a mighty theatre at Fifth and Mission. The lobby had a million-dollar Tiffany glass barrel-vaulted ceiling depicting peacocks in top hats courting peahens in ball gowns among Elysian fields. The walls were mosaics and frescoes improving on Pompeii's finest discoveries (Pompeii's art, after all, was not trimmed with real Russian gold); the counters of the sixteen full-service bars were made of Italian marble inlaid with Spanish silver. Every seat in the house was crushed velvet. When construction was complete, Albee stood on the stage and said, of the impeccable acoustics, 'This is where we can hear the Lord himself whisper.'

One unfortunate quirk to the theatre was the set of murals donated by the forty families on Greenway's social registry. Each family sponsored a different mythological scene of their own choosing. As San Francisco was founded on gold dust and sin, however, the execution was problematic. Mrs Mark Hopkins, for instance, dismissed all local artisans, claiming that she wanted to deal only with the 'old masters, personally,' and sending to Europe for an unscrupulous Venetian who claimed to be a direct descendent of Raphael. His mural was gaudy enough to impress the other families, who consequently hired his friends, who by striking coincidence were related to Bronzino and Titian. The results embarrassed Albee's managers, but so as not to offend the rough-and-tumble millionaires, nothing was said about the well-muscled men in sandals rescuing undraped women from giant snakes, and society scribes pretended great appreciation for such little-known and suspiciously spelled adventures as *Herculese and the*

Sabine Women and *The Flagelation of Artimus.*

The Carters, seeking to be discreet, had donated to a general fund for maintenance.

The Orpheum was thus sparkling and clean on the opening evening of week twenty-seven, when the tour came into town. When Carter entered the dressing room at 5 P.M. he found an envelope at his dressing table. His name and the theatre address were written on the outside in a wispy and sweet hand, and inside was a photograph, rather small, the size of a trade card. On the back, in the same blue ink as on the envelope: 'Good luck, Mr Carter.' It was signed Sarah O'Leary.

There was no time for him to consider what this might mean, for moments later, his mother and father were almost on top of him, along with James and a school chum. All performers, save the headliner, shared a large room, and on this night it was overflowing with jolly well-wishers. However, when Carter's eye fell on his father, he knew there was trouble.

'Charles,' his father said, while his mother was still hugging him, 'I understand that you drew a staggering amount from your trusts.'

'I think of it as a healthy amount, but—'

'A thousand dollars?'

'Yes.'

'Because?'

Carter's eyes went to the ceiling. Then they looked for help from James, who was engaged in quiet discussion with his pal. Carter tried to sound as sure of himself as he did when his father was not in the room. 'I needed a new finale for the act,' he finally answered.

Mr Carter was taller, broader, fleshier than his elder son. Like James, Mr Carter had brown eyes, a stout build, and curly hair. Sometimes Charles Carter wondered if he had been found on the doorstep. 'So,' his father said, 'you spent everything you made this year?'

'I had the money, Father.'

'Not exactly.'

'It's a loan from my trust.'

His father said nothing.

'It's an investment for my future,' Carter added.

His father poked his tongue into his cheek, another bad sign, and his eyes stole toward Mrs Carter, who was sorting through the postcards Carter had collected from around the country. Mr Carter said, 'You and I will talk after the show.'

'Of course,' Carter nodded. 'But I also have to renegotiate my contract after the show, and as I have this new illusion to end with, I'm sure it will pay for itself.'

'It has to, Charles.'

'I understand,' nodding again, 'you're not in the business of bailing me out. And I will renegotiate for next season with that in mind.' He was nodding so much his collar had cut into his neck.

'I'm sorry? For next – for *next* season?'

'I have to pay back the loan somehow.'

Mr Carter's eyes narrowed like he smelled a stable nearby.

'When you're finished tonight, Charles,' Mrs Carter said, eyes sparkling, 'you must come home and take a small quiz my women's group has devised.' She whispered, 'It concerns the Oedipus complex.'

'That sounds very relaxing, Mother.'

'Well, this *is* your big night,' she said.

Her interruption was just long enough to make Mr Carter regard his son in the spirit of grudging armistice. Mr Carter even tried to smile. 'So. Negotiations.' His interest was piqued. 'Do you meet with Albee?'

'No, Murdoch.' Murdoch, Albee's assistant, was a sour man who kept pots of honey on his desk, ladling it onto soda crackers during negotiations. Only headliners met with Albee.

'Oh,' his father said. Carter wished that he at least slightly impressed his father. Then it was one of those moments when all parties simultaneously exclaimed 'is that the time!' and, bidding his parents good-bye, Carter returned to his makeup mirror. His blue eyes looked back at his evening clothes, his thin frame, his scrupulously brushed black hair, as if at an unlucky stranger. On one side of him was Laszlo, who spoke in Czech to someone who had brought an immense summer sausage; on the other side was Chase the dramatic monologist, whistling, and arranging a bouquet sent by the girls at 46 Anna Lane.

Carter counted to ten, clearing all thoughts of his father from his head. He approached his brother, interrupting the conversation he was having with his friend Tom. 'James, I need an assistant.' James rolled his eyes. Since their imprisonment by Mr Jenks, James's opinion of magic had been tentative at best. He would occasionally help his brother, but only when pushed. Carter continued, 'You needn't assist me in my act for the rest of your life, but tonight I need you, very badly.'

James rolled his eyes again, and Tom punched him in the shoulder. Tom, broad-chested, blue-eyed, was a varsity football player. Carter had seen his photo in a football program that James had sent him. The caption had been 'Tom-Tom Crandall: Gritty, debonair, battling.' Tom said, 'Hey, be nice to him, he's your brother,' and Carter was grateful.

'Okay, Charlie, what's your pleasure?'

Carter explained their duties. When he was finished, James said, 'He's a madman. Charlie, if anyone says you aren't a madman, they're lying.'

Carter peered through the curtains at 6:30. For the only time on the circuit, the entire audience was seated before the first act, Colonel Munson's Russo-Chinese Flyers, began their acrobatic feats. No one wanted to miss a tradition at the San Francisco Orpheum: the late arrivals of Jessie Hayman and Tessie Wall. The center sections of rows G and H had been set aside, ushers turning back the few nitwits who tried to take the seats.

Carter avoided looking at his props, taking in the performance instead, but also absently glancing toward Tom, whom he'd stationed as a lookout. Tom scratched the back of his head, meaning no one had touched the levitation device. James stood nearby, in the prop storage area, with two local artisans from the Golden Gate Assembly of the S.A.M., whom Carter had paid five hundred dollars to style and modify the large Martinka device, the Blackmail illusion. It was wrapped securely under tarps and sheets, and anyone who asked was informed that it was the new set for the opium den number.

When the acrobats finished their athletics, to respectable applause, the curtains closed and stagehands immediately began maneuvering flats into place for the tableaux vivants production, in which actors struck poses from famous paintings. Carter heard whispers, laughter, and there was a group pushing toward the curtain, looking out at the audience, excited, for someone with friends in the orchestra pit had been tipped off, and Carter followed half the program to the wings, where they clustered and looked through the curtains, into the house.

The orchestra struck up 'Ain't She a Beauty,' and Jessie Hayman, leading twenty of the most beautiful women San Francisco had ever seen, took a leisurely stroll down the aisle. Jessie had a stately pace, her smile was perfectly controlled, and the only suggestion of a wilder character was her fiery orange hair, piled under a tall Arlington hat.

Chase, who could by no means afford Jessie's girls, muttered, 'I will take the black-haired one. No, the plump blonde.'

Carter looked at the women, and then remembered the photograph he'd received. Had Sarah signed it 'fond wishes'? No, she had simply wished him luck. Perhaps she wasn't thinking of him that way, but only as a friend in spirit. He watched the girls again. They wore muted colors, and small hats with real roses on the brims. Jessie led them to their seats slowly, casually, none of them behaving as if they were being watched by every eye in the house, but each girl careful to wave at Mayor Rolph, who sat with the Chief of Police.

When Carter laughed aloud, Chase gave him a cold look.

'What's so funny?'

'Nothing, really. That whole time, not one of them so much as looked at a married man.'

'How do you know who's married?'

'I was born here. I know almost everyone in the audience.'

Chase whistled. 'That's some pressure.'

Carter frowned. He left the curtain, considering the group that would be watching him. He'd worried so long about the mechanics of his illusion he hadn't even thought about the fact that he was debuting it before friends and family. Was Blackmail an admirable trick? This was a swamp he didn't want to enter, but there it was. He was a native son indulging in his half-respectable, no, one-tenth-respectable profession. He turned around; Tom frantically spun his cap in his hand.

Carter straightened his tie to show that he understood. Mysterioso had used the girls' entrance as a distraction. And had tampered with the levitation device. The swamp immediately dried up, the coast was clear, and Carter felt a transparent thrill of pleasure, knowing what he was about to do.

When Jessie and her girls were seated, the orchestra struck up a Debussy étude, and the curtains parted to show architectural vistas and a dozen figures frozen in the attitude of Raphael's *The School of Athens*. The audience murmured faint appreciation, and then Monsignor Dilatorio, who stood stage left in mortarboard and red-piped academic robes, announced, 'Ladies and Gentlemen, *The School of Athens*. By Raphael Sanzio.' Then there was a wave of applause.

It was 7:15. Carter had exactly an hour before he had to be onstage, and a task that would take about twenty minutes, if he hurried.

Onstage, the performers were moving through biblical images. They performed St Matthew and the Angel, from the *Book of Lindesfarne*, then moved to selections from the Sistine Chapel, panel by panel. Then Giotto, then Mantegna, then a few secular images, such as Jan van Eyck's pious-looking study of *Giovanni Arnolfini and His Bride*.

The performers built to a crowd-pleasing finale, with an astonishing modification that San Francisco would talk about for weeks. As usual, one painting became another: from *The Raft of the Medusa,* complete with panicked sailors, billowing sails, and flats painted to look like waves, to Delacroix's *Liberty Leading the People*. But tonight Liberty seemed ominously true to the painting, meaning bare-breasted, and when the stage shifted to a seashore scene, Liberty dropped her clothes entirely, stepping onto a seashell as angels with flowing robes floated toward her, the Monsignor announcing, '*The Birth of Venus*!'

There were outraged cries from the audience, with an enraged Jessie Hayman yelling, 'Cheap! Cheap!' because Venus, in what turned out to be a flesh-colored body stocking, was Tessie Wall.

Then, from each wing of the stage, came her girls. Accompanied by a great, brassy fanfare from the orchestra, each woman posed by the footlights in her rustling Paris finery before moving offstage. Last was Tessie herself, thick-waisted and blond, now dressed in a gown, using the tip of her pink feather boa to wave at all her friends. She took her time finding her seat, and afterward, while the intermission music played, the only topic of conversation was the daring Tessie Wall, and how Jessie Hayman would have to get even next year with an even grander entrance.

Chase had the misfortune of going on at 7:40. Though he'd worked hard on his program of Shakespearean monologues – he even added a wickedly insightful Henry Irving parody – he was but politely acknowledged. It was apparent he would be offered just a standard contract for next season.

At three minutes till eight, Laszlo and His Yankee Hussars set up onstage. While the band played their Sousa medley, Carter thoroughly checked his kit, stuffing his pockets with scarves, examining the seals on decks of cards. He glanced toward his levitation device.

'Good luck, Carter.' The voice was quiet. It was Mysterioso, looking deeply concerned.

'Will I need it?' Carter asked.

'That depends on how good a magician you are. Are you nervous?'

'No.'

'Then why are you sweating?'

Carter had had enough and declared, surprising himself with how good it felt to say, 'Because I had to run to the train station and back.'

Mysterioso's eyes checked Carter's. 'No, you didn't.'

'Maybe something distracted you.' They continued to glare at each other, 'Stars and Stripes Forever' playing at full fever pitch, until Carter whispered, 'I don't want to be late to work.' And he returned to hiding a garter snake in his inner coat.

Mysterioso turned on his heel. When he was out of sight, Carter plucked at the wires feeding into the platform's pulley system. Instead of going taut, they went slack; if he tried to levitate someone now, the subject would fall. It was time for Blackmail.

Chapter 12

At 8:15, the orchestra played Carter's theme, 'Pomp and Circumstance,' and Carter went onstage to prolonged applause. He focused on his breathing, in and out, fifteen times a minute, standing in front of his trusty flats decorated with demons and flying cards. The main curtain was behind him, and a set of Chinese screens surrounded the levitation device. He thanked the audience, saying, 'It is a great joy to return to the old neighborhood,' which led, of course, to a second round of applause. He breathed deeply through his nose, smelling the curls of smoke coming off the fresh gels on the footlights. Though the overhead lights hurt his eyes, he could see unusually far into the house tonight, from the elegance of the men and women in the orchestra pit to the third balcony, where men who wore their hats indoors and women in 1908 Sears, Roebuck catalogue finery fanned themselves with programs. Carter did not look toward his parents' box. He thought about the card Sarah had sent, and wondered if she might be in the house, watching him.

'First,' he said, 'as a native son, there are such high expectations of me tonight, I should get one item out of the way.' He flipped off his top hat, dug into it with a gloved hand, and gripped a pair of long white furry ears that, as he pulled on them, turned out to be – not a rabbit – but a white teddy bear, with absurdly long ears.

When the audience laughed, Carter wryly apologized, and then brought out, in quick succession, a turtle and a garter snake, each with long white ears attached, before finally pulling out a real rabbit, to pleasant applause. Albee, second row center, flanked by Murdoch and an old man wearing a white carnation, and holding a cane, was clapping as heartily as anyone else. Good.

Carter followed this with a series of card tricks, which he performed easily, pulling volunteers from the dignitaries in the first few rows. His tricks located cards in increasingly difficult-looking ways, culminating with the knife-throwing that he'd kept in the act since Denver.

As in Denver, Mysterioso was watching from the wings (he had chosen to stand in the wing opposite from the direction Carter threw his stiletto). Now, with the finale upon him, Carter faced Mysterioso for one moment; Mysterioso turned his hand palm upward, as if begging him to continue his act.

Carter turned to the house. 'Ladies and Gentlemen, I have a modest finale tonight: levitation! I need a volunteer. Will the smartest man in the audience please come onstage? I see some hands here toward the front of the house.' Carter put his finger to his lips and held his elbow in his palm, watching his audience. Laughter, encouragement, suggestions of who was the smartest man in the house. The Mayor! Tessie Wall! He could just vaguely smell citronella incense burning in the air. 'Come to think of it, there are so many smart men here. I'm going to break a cardinal rule, and *choose* a volunteer, a most unwilling participant. Will you all please show what San Francisco thinks of Mysterioso!'

In the wings, Mysterioso lowered his eyebrows. Carter gestured toward him, applause building, beckoning him to come out onstage. In fact, Mysterioso took a step away from the flats, bumping directly into the muscular and persuasive Tom, who politely pointed him toward Carter.

When Mysterioso finally came out, he bowed toward the audience, and shook Carter's hand.

'I know what's on your minds, dear friends,' Carter said. 'It seems to be a terrible idea to have one magician assist another.' Carter clapped his hands, James stealing onstage to remove the Chinese screens. This showed off a simple-looking board suspended across the backs of two upright chairs. It was the levitation device as ordered from the Martinka catalogue, but with one addition below it: a bed of eighteen-inch railway spikes that had been sharpened until they gleamed.

Carter turned to Mysterioso. 'Now, then, Mysterioso, will you be a good fellow and lie on that board so that I may remove the chairs and demonstrate the art of levitation?'

'I think not.' He examined his fingernails.

'Because we're co-conspirators?'

'I'm certainly not your co-conspirator.'

'And will you tell our audience why not?'

'Because I'm unconvinced of your abilities.'

'Meaning that—'

'Your cheap piece of machinery might fail, causing injury.'

'I see.' Carter frowned. 'You see – Ladies and Gentlemen, he *is* the smartest man in the audience. However, I submit to you that even though he is a poor sport, Mysterioso has failed to prove there's no conspiracy between us.'

The rear curtain went up, and the levitation machinery was dwarfed and absorbed, all of its hidden apparatus exposed as part of a monstrous larger entity: the stage housed a network of fulcrums, pulleys, giant gears, spindles and cams, the child of a combustion engine mated with a giant clockworks. Little of it was functional, but Carter, who'd had two weeks to make sketches of what he wanted, knew the importance of appearance. No one had ever seen anything like this before; even the rubes in the third balcony were quiet. The mechanism was perfectly still.

'What – is – that?' Mysterioso finally managed.

With pride, Carter answered. 'I call it Blackmail. Pick a card,' Carter said.

'What?' For a moment, Mysterioso seemed to have forgotten where he was.

Carter fanned a deck of cards. 'Pick a card.'

'Oh, I'll pick a card, all right.' Mysterioso reached for the deck, and before he touched it, a single card began to extend and wiggle attractively. The audience laughed. Mysterioso slapped the card out of his way. 'I can't be forced to pick the card you want me to.'

'I'm desolated,' Carter said. 'Do I have to ask a third time?'

Mysterioso jerked the whole deck from Carter's hands, cut it, flipped half the cards around, reshuffled, ran his fingers up and down the edges, fanned the deck himself, plucked out a card, and handed the remainder of the deck back to Carter.

'You've made it exceedingly difficult for me,' Carter said, fingering the cards. 'Perhaps beyond my capacity. In fact, I must confess, I have no idea what card you've chosen.' He took a step toward the footlights. 'Mayor Rolph – do you know what card he's chosen? No? Mister Albee? No?' Carter put one hand on his chin.

'Well, my rival magician, you've stumped us all. Luckily, we live in an age of technical marvels. Blackmail will tell which card you chose.'

Carter placed the deck – minus the card Mysterioso still held – in a brass tray, which he set into a toy coal car on a miniature set of railroad tracks. 'Scoot!' he said, and the tray raced up the tracks to a ledge, where the coal car dumped it onto a set of scales with a loud clank.

'Very clever,' Mysterioso muttered. Carter knew that no matter what card the machine produced, Mysterioso would simply show off a different one from the one he had chosen: Carter's fingers told him the card was the three of diamonds.

The scales tipped in the direction of the deck, causing the other side to rise and collide with a flint, which ignited with a great flash, sparks shooting up filaments toward two balloons that exploded, freeing two white pigeons. Simultaneously, a small wooden packing crate was released from a bracket, sliding gently down a set of rollers onto the empty side of the scales, and then setting them level again.

Carter approached the scales carefully. The packing crate was locked with an oversized Yale padlock. He produced a key and started to open it. Then he stopped and turned to Mysterioso. 'Is your card by any chance the three of diamonds?'

Mysterioso barked at the audience, 'Should he be asking me or telling me?'

There were some catcalls from the upper balconies. Carter saw that with a flick of his wrist, Mysterioso now held between his index and ring fingers, behind his hand, just by its corner, an eight of clubs. The audience hadn't seen it yet. It was from the wrong deck, but that hardly mattered – he would still spoil everything unless he was stopped.

Carter said, sternly, 'I'm giving you one last chance, Mysterioso. Is your card the three of diamonds?'

'Carter, with a grave, grave heart, I must—'

That was as far as Mysterioso got, for Carter had by then flipped open the packing crate. Inside was a metal birdcage. Inside the birdcage was Handsome.

'Is this your dog?' Carter asked.

133

Mysterioso drew an awkward breath. His hands fluttered in front of him like moths. He exploded, 'Do not touch him! Do not touch him!' He lunged for the cage, panicked, stopping only when Carter drew a gun.

The audience went wild with laughter. 'Catch the bullet,' someone cried, causing more hilarity.

Carter blinked a few times. He counted out heartbeats. He was feeling pleased. 'Our distinguished guests have the right idea, my friend. Why don't you try to catch a bullet?'

'You're bluffing.'

'Of course I am. But you now have two questions to answer. First, is this your dog?'

'Yes, yes, that's Handsome. Don't you dare harm him.'

'Second, is Handsome a good liar?'

'What?'

Carter waved the barrel of the gun at the cage. Handsome, who was yipping and screeching like a tortured rooster, wore tucked into his collar a three of diamonds. Carter took care to cover the hole in the back of his glove, where he'd been bitten while securing the card on the evil little dog. Focusing on Mysterioso's every move, he could nonetheless sense in the wings a huge gathering of his fellow performers.

Carter addressed the house. 'San Francisco, have you ever seen a poor magician work so hard on a simple card trick?' A smattering of applause, mostly from the orchestra. That was not so good. 'Since you won't answer me, Mysterioso, I must take one more drastic step.' With his free hand, Carter draped his cloak over the birdcage. Removing it, the birdcage – and Handsome – vanished. Applause again, fuller, but not as generous as Carter would have wished.

'Of course, a de Kolta,' Mysterioso said. 'Where is he?'

A flash, a puff of smoke, and Handsome, howling, reappeared on the board suspended between the two chairs – on the faulty levitation device! Handsome and his prison were much lighter than a human being, but, nonetheless, ominously, the device began to creak.

'No!' Mysterioso cried.

'It gets better,' Carter said. 'Look.' Directly over the cage, hanging

134

on a chain from the rafters, was an anvil. 'Now, is your card—'

'The three of diamonds! Here, yes, the three of diamonds!' Mysterioso showed Carter, the audience, everyone, the three of diamonds.

'Thank you.' Carter bowed, finally accepting an avalanche of applause. And he took a full accounting of it: the balconies had gone wild, as had the loges and the orchestra. Albee, Murdoch, and especially the carnation-wearing old man who sat with them, all were thrilled. Carter holstered his revolver, thanking the audience, adding, 'That ends our demonstration for this evening.'

It was not exactly the end. Mysterioso brushed past him, aiming to get his dog, and was in midstrut, turning toward the audience with a smirk, about to address some final, crushing comment to the house. When he was no more than ten feet from the cage, there was a cry of dismay from the catwalk over the stage, and the chain went slack – heavy iron links suspended in the air, taking for one second the shape of a question mark – and the anvil crashed right through the birdcage, then the board, splintering the chairs and hitting the spikes and sending up a shower of sparks.

Mysterioso lurched like he'd been gutshot. He fell to his knees. His mouth opened, but there was only silence, the intake of breath, and then a horrible wail of anguish. Two of the optical mirrors had shattered, so he knelt in shards of glass and silver backing.

Gasps from the audience – hands clutching armrests as thousands of backs went rigid, and then silence, except for cries from Mysterioso. Carter noted that the next time he performed his Blackmail illusion, he would reposition the mirrors to keep them from breaking. And perhaps he would shoot out the chain instead of making it look like an accident.

He met James in the wings, just off of the stage.

'That was extreme,' said James.

'We'll discuss it later. May I?' Carter took from James the cage, intact, with tiny Handsome, unharmed and just as hostile as ever. Whistling as he returned to the stage, he caused Mysterioso to look up.

'Is this your dog?'

Mysterioso made an inarticulate reply, standing so that pieces of mirror dropped from his shins to the stage, crossing at a trot and wrestling the cage from Carter's hands.

'You know,' Carter said, so that only his rival could hear, 'I love animals. As did Karl and Evelyn Kowaleski. Handsome was never in danger.' He paused, as he'd rehearsed. 'As you said of Houdini.'

Mysterioso said nothing. The curtain fell, cutting them off from the audience. At once, performers closed around Carter, tousling his hair and telling him 'good show.' Carter left the stage as his scenery was broken down and the schoolroom props wheeled into place for the next act. Leonard, Adolph, and the rest clapped him on the back. But each time he was pounded, he felt hollow and dull, and slightly ashamed of his trick.

Murdoch's office was on the fourth floor of the Orpheum, with windows that opened onto Market Street so he could see how far the ticket holders' line extended. To be called to Murdoch's during a performance was referred to as 'a visit to St Peter,' for only very very good or very very bad things happened there.

Murdoch was ninety-nine percent ruthless, but also one percent conscious of opinion, and so he had workmen build him a wide chimney whose throat was studded with hand grips. During the Yuletide season, he had a man dressed as St Nick distribute bonuses this way, and, regardless of the month, and regardless of the terrible news he might be receiving, a performer sitting in the hard-backed chair always looked toward the chimney for a ray of hope.

When Carter was told to come up, he tried to put bounce in his step, but he pictured Mysterioso's anguish, and no matter how much he thought about having avenged the Kowaleskis, he felt a sense of foreboding.

Murdoch seemed even more sour than usual. All the honey in the world couldn't sweeten his brittle monotone. 'Got no choice here, kid. Yer shut.'

'What? What do you mean?'

Murdoch pulled out a legal-sized sheet of boilerplate and put on his reading glasses. 'Says here in Mysterioso's contract, no member of his company will be molested. Seems that includes his damn dog.'

'But that's ridiculous.' He gripped the arms of his chair and crossed his legs quickly, trying to look above it all.

'Agreed.' Murdoch shook his head. 'But he's the headliner. Holds us hostage.'

'Mr Murdoch, the dog was never in danger. It was just smoke and mirrors, literally. The dog only seemed to be under the anvil because of—'

'Yeah, yeah. How'd you get the dog, anyway? Wasn't he in a train car or something?'

Carter pursed his lips. His stomach sank. 'Well.'

'Breaking and entering. Of course, it's your town, so . . .'

Carter cleared his throat. He wouldn't go so easily. 'It was a prank that got—'

'The audience didn't like it much.'

'They applauded,' Carter said.

'Eh.' Murdoch held his hand out and turned it like a rudder. 'Too confusing at the end.'

'They liked it! I saw them applaud.'

'Not the end.'

'I know, I should have shot out the chain.'

'Naw, that's not it. Just seemed cruel.'

'Well, the name of the trick was Blackmail, it's not supposed to be uplifting.' He reddened with anger but also dawning embarrassment.

'Bad idea for a magic act. And how could you do it again?'

'Well, as I said, I'd shoot out the chain, and also, move the mirrors so—'

'Naw, naw. So you got a guy you don't like onstage. And you got his dog. Could happen once. Maybe twice. But every night? Not likely.'

Carter had no response. He suddenly remembered a day at Thacher when he'd saddled his horse and forgotten to cinch her up; when he mounted her, the saddle spun 180 degrees and Carter, who'd expected to see the world from the top of his horse, was seeing it from underneath. A rival, a dog . . . every night . . . he hadn't actually worked that angle out.

'Wish there was something I could do. Could put in a word for you with Shubert.'

The kiss of death. Carter had just been shot through the forehead. Blackballed from the thirty-week circuit meant the only place to go was down, and the Shuberts were the five-a-day grind, where the audience spat tobacco on you. Once you agreed to play the Shuberts, no one else would ever touch you again.

'Mr Murdoch, for six months,' Carter said, with a touch of desperation, 'that man has run rampant over everyone else. He had another act shut for no reason—'

'His prerogative, Carter.'

'He tried to sabotage my act!'

Murdoch nodded his head quickly, almost like he was palsied, for several seconds. 'Serious. Very serious. Got any proof?'

Proof? Carter, desperation growing, mind going blank, did what a thousand men before him had done: he stared at the chimney now, wishing that a jolly, red-faced man would drop down and hand him a fat check.

'If we believed every accusation against a headliner, we'd be in bad shape.'

'But Mysterioso – he deserves to – Mr Murdoch, Mysterioso does *not* respect magic!'

The words – foolish words! – hung in the air until Murdoch hunched forward. He reached for his honey pot. He spooned a dollop onto a soda cracker, and chewed thoughtfully. Carter wished he hadn't said anything about magic. 'You aren't gonna starve,' Murdoch rasped.

So there it was. 'Well, Mr Murdoch.' Carter stood, and extended his hand like a gentleman. 'The Shuberts. If that's where I have to go to perform, I'll go.' They shook hands.

The interview was over. Carter descended the four flights of stairs – it seemed like thirty – knowing all the way that with this disaster his fall was greater than Murdoch knew: he had wasted one thousand dollars on an illusion he would never perform again – even if they'd rehired him. He would never be able to save money on the Shubert circuit. And when he defaulted on the loan – and his father *would* let him sink – he would lose the remainder of his trust fund.

He passed Annabelle in the wings; she gave him a nod, but he was in no mood to talk. He reached the backstage area, staring blankly at the current performance. The opium den number was on, the poor addict girl slithering across the stage in search of a fix while her evil coolie master tormented her, pulling the pipe just out of her reach.

Watching the dance, Carter leaned his head against a wall, wondering how hard he would need to hit his head against it to knock himself unconscious. When your profession depends on the power of perception, there is a difficult line between illusion and reality, and Carter realized he had gotten confused. There was some nobility in being poor, but absolutely none in being poor because you were an idiot.

James, Tom, his parents, were all in the private box, waiting to hear good news, but Carter could not move. He imagined the conversation, the end of the road, the confirmation of everything his father suspected about him. Carter the Magician. Carter the Broke. Carter the Banker. He found an old, empty pickle barrel tucked away in a secluded corner, hiked himself up on it, and sat, chin in hand, wondering what on earth he would do with himself.

A few minutes later, as Whipple and Huston did their soft-shoe on stage, Julius, of Fun in Hi Skule, found him. Of the brothers, Adolph played the idiot Patsy Brannigan, Leonard the wop, Milton the juvenile, and Julius the fast-talking Hebrew, or rigid German, depending on the town. Julius read books, and was clever, but he and Carter had never gotten along for Julius was a griper. Every comment led to a punch line, which was tiresome. 'So,' Julius said now, 'I hear you got canned.'

'News travels.'

'That character Einstein had it wrong: gossip travels faster than the speed of light,' he growled in his East Ninety-Third Street accent. 'Here.' He handed Carter a pint of whiskey.

Carter, taking a swig, murmured, 'I heard you got a fifteen percent increase for next year. Congratulations.'

'If they raise it much further, we'll finally be able to starve to death.'

'I see.' Carter offered him the bottle.

'Keep it. This is a lousy racket. If I had half an ounce of integrity, I'd be a writer. And if I had an ounce, I'd be a doctor.' When he warmed up, jokes poured out of Julius with unfortunate effortlessness. 'And if I had two ounces, I'd sell one to Leonard, only he'd lose it in a crap game. Speaking of lacking a shred of integrity, I hear that rat Mysterioso is gonna demand a fifty percent increase. Looks like Albee can't turn him down, or he'll just go to the legit theatres. There's a dozen producers who'd back an evening-long show for him.' Hearing Carter sigh, Julius continued, 'It's a dirty shame what that Mysterioso cretin did to you. I knew he was a fink ever since he fired that first girl, that – what was her name – '

Carter was about to supply it, but noted Julius digging in his coat pocket, pulling out a small rectangular photograph that, heart sinking, Carter recognized.

'Right, Sarah O'Leary,' Julius read.

'She sent you a photograph, did she?'

Julius nodded. 'Nice girl. She sent them to everyone on the program. Part of her good works for the penguins she's living with.'

'Oh,' Carter sighed, so nakedly that Julius immediately understood.

'I see . . . You had a passion for that girl.'

'Thank you for your sympathy.'

Hearing 'sympathy,' Julius's eyebrows shot up. It had been the wrong word to use. The fusillade began. 'Well, you're twice the man Mysterioso is, and that ain't saying much. How a couple of grown men make a living pulling dumb animals out of evening wear is beyond me. But listen, now that you're the only thing worse than a magician – and by that I mean an unemployed magician – my brothers and I are going to visit a couple of friendly girls after the show, and thought you might want to talk to some fellow creatures who know a thing or two about tricks, so to speak, and maybe if you can pick yourself up off this pickle barrel, you could walk abreast with us, if you know what I mean, and if you're half the swine I think you are, you probably do.' The eyebrows flexed, causing Carter to laugh. In the barrage of insults, he'd momentarily forgotten he'd been fired. He promised Julius he would join them, but he didn't mean it. He preferred to sit on his pickle barrel all night. Now at least he had a bottle of whiskey.

Chapter 13

At ten o'clock, the kettle drums began their thrilling, tribal beat, and the stage filled with Mysterioso's stilt-walkers and fire-eaters. A half dozen Indians swooped down on them, whooping and hollering, out for blood. Carter dropped, one by one, his coins, cards, scarves, bouquets, and hard rubber balls into the barrel. He brought his thumb before his face, and whispered, 'My flexor longus pollicis and its so-very-important terminal phalange.' He cleaned his nails with his lock picks.

There was the sound of pitched combat onstage, and martial music coming from the pit to accompany what was surely Annabelle beating the men within an inch of their lives. Carter touched his head to the wall, his eyes closed. He only opened them when he heard, with extra volume tonight, the bellow, 'This is for Custer! This is for the Alamo!' and saw Mysterioso mangling the other performers.

Carter mouthed 'the Alamo,' shaking his head, and tossing back a shot from the bottle.

A few moments later, Mysterioso was shackled, weighed down with a dozen handcuffs and sturdy chains. Because it was a special evening, they called not just one person but a committee onstage to check the restraints. Carter was thoroughly bored to see Albee and, fresh from firing a certain earlier act, Murdoch. Between them walked the carnation-wearing old man, who had wild grey hair, thick round glasses, and who used a cane to support himself. No doubt Albee's father.

The examination took longer than usual. Carter noted how slowly the old man bent over, how nimbly his hands flew up and down Mysterioso's back.

Carter first registered that something could be wrong when he heard a brief grunt from the stage. He saw Mysterioso bucking and bowing, trying to put distance between himself and the fingers feeling his locks. Then the old man stood slowly, retrieved his cane, and flipped its tip toward the audience. In a creaky voice that nonetheless carried to the back of the house, the old man said, 'Yes, I'm satisfied these locks are good and tight!'

As Albee and Murdoch led the old man offstage, Carter saw Mysterioso thrashing around onstage like a netted bear, howling, 'No! No!' At first, Carter suspected he was in real trouble, but then remembered, with another slug of whiskey, that the world didn't work so easily.

On a normal night, his chains were usually in a heap, and Mysterioso boasting about it, en route to the saddle. Tonight, as usual, an assistant led his horse onto the stage. But there was Mysterioso, still lying on his stomach, trussed up like a turkey, a hundred pounds of chains weighing him down. He twisted, face red with effort, but could not even turn over. Carter sat forward, folding his arms around his knees. He felt a ray of hope so faint he hardly wanted to jinx it.

The assistant, reins in hand, announced, 'Master, I'm sure you're just about to swear revenge on those redskin devils!'

'Yes! Yes!' Mysterioso cried from the stage. 'Revenge!'

If this was part of the act, it was a terrible idea, Carter mused. When the curtains swung closed for the scenery change, a dozen men rushed to Mysterioso's aid. One held his lock picks, another a bolt cutter. Carter was sitting at a wonderful vantage point, able to see the fire-eaters at the apron entertaining the audience, and, just behind the curtain, the drama of Mysterioso's rescue in progress.

For Mysterioso, the bad news came in waves. First, it turned out the locks were not the ones he normally used, but were substitutions. Further, they appeared to be unpickable. The holes were crammed with tiny, greased iron balls, and forged of some kind of tempered alloy that made them impermeable to bolt cutters. No one in his company had ever seen their design.

'Who was that man with Albee?' someone asked.

'He was no one! Just get me out of here!'

There was still worse news: Mysterioso was not just a prisoner of the cuffs, but somehow he'd been bolted to the stage itself through tiny but murderously effective eyelets set into the floorboards. There was no way to move him. Mysterioso declared that he wouldn't be forced to stop the show now – one of the dancers could wear the lion skin in which Mysterioso usually burst forth from underneath the cage – anything to finish out the performance.

When the curtain went up, a single flute played, a peaceful-sounding solo evoking the dignity of the noble savage. The audience saw an Indian camp, with mountain scenery in the background. Annabelle was tied to a stake, struggling, and all the men of the village were fixed in their positions, ready to impress her with their athletic skills. Center stage, a stack of colorful saddle blankets undulated of its own accord, emitting occasional muffled clanks and groans. Carter chuckled.

The entire orchestra now fired up the tempo, signaling an end to tranquility: it was time for dancing and juggling. Just then, the blanket closest to the audience rolled off the pile, revealing Mysterioso's shackled ankles. There were howls of laughter – Mysterioso was so clearly in the way that dancers had to strut awkwardly around him, as their toes stubbed against his chains. The company did their best until Annabelle finally cried out, sounding fed up, 'Stop right here! I will *not* marry any one of you!'

The blankets gave a mighty shiver, which the performers tried to ignore. The chubby man playing the chief remembered his cue, and said, doubtfully, 'Then the die is cast, worthy maiden. You will be married. To the lion.'

Two stagehands rolled the cage onto the apron, and Carter hopped off his barrel, getting as close to the stage as he could without the audience seeing him. The orchestra played quietly, just the strings, and light percussion, like a heartbeat. In the cage, Baby paced back and forth, nose brushing against the bars. The chief looked at Annabelle, who gave an almost imperceptible shrug, and then he addressed the lion with all the power of his actor's training: 'Will you have her as your bride?'

There was a long pause. Baby paced up and down, his mane brushing against the bars. He did not roar.

'Will you have her as your bride?'

The pile of blankets rocked a little, the orchestra continued the same hushed eight bars of anticipatory light drumming, but otherwise, there was nothing. The lion hadn't roared. Carter was utterly intrigued.

'Excuse me, young man.'

Carter stepped back quietly, then registered the carnation, the cane – the old man had returned from the audience, and now stood with him. He faced Carter with bright eyes.

'I liked your finale. Very creative,' he creaked.

'Thank you.'

He sniffed, looking at Carter with some concern. 'Bourbon?'

'Whiskey.'

'You'll have to give that up.' And then the old man, leaning on his cane, looked back toward the stage.

What was going on here? Could it be – ? No – Carter had been drinking, but he wasn't *that* drunk. Despite the lion's failure to roar, the music had struck up again, full blast. Braves juggled fire, leading Annabelle toward the still-pacing Baby. But she dug in her heels, bringing them to a full stop. 'Hold it, fellahs,' she said. 'Let's call it a night. Baby don't look so well.'

The old man turned to Carter and said, 'Stay right here.' He limped onto the stage, and became surprisingly agile, dodging between dancers, then holding a hand out and waving it in the air. 'Stop it now here, stop. Stop!' he yelled. One by one, the dancers stopped, looking at him in confusion. Then he called, 'Maestro, please,' bringing the orchestra to a halt. With the point of his cane, he knocked the rest of the blankets aside to reveal the sweating, tormented, disheveled magician, who hadn't yet dislodged a single cuff. As the audience began to rumble, the old man leaned on his cane, then rocked to and fro on his heels, clicking his tongue. 'Handcuff king, my eye,' he whispered. Pins and needles began to prick Carter's face. Goose bumps rose on his skin.

'Lay-dies and Gen-tile-men,' the old man cried, with a clear stentorian tone that caused the entire audience – from the Mayor to the Carters to the madams and their girls, to every customer in the balconies, the stagehands who hung from the catwalks and flies, every musician in the orchestra pit, all the performers who were massed in the wings like moths around the world's most inviting campfire – the voice caused everyone, absolutely everyone, to freeze. It was a voice that had never been disobeyed. 'This man here, this man who is pinned to the floor, helpless, promised you, in his program, that he would show you, tonight, the greatest of all escape artists.' With this, the man tossed his cane aside. Then he took off his glasses. 'And so he has.' Off came the wig, revealing a tangle of kinky brown hair. The shoulders went back, the arms folded over the mighty chest, and the feet spread in a wrestler's stance. 'I give you – Houdini!'

The next day's *Examiner* had a one-word headline: *Bedlam*! For once, Hearst was guilty of understatement. The San Francisco Orpheum was the scene of frenzy, of men standing and pointing, shouting out the name 'Houdini!' while others ran from their seats and up and down the aisles.

Carter said, in a small voice, just to himself, '1905. He hasn't done this since 1905.'

Houdini was talking onstage, but no one could hear him. Had he announced the second coming, he would have been drowned out by the pandemonium he'd already created. Tessie Wall had apparently fainted, and men rushed to her side, while a suspicious Jessie Hayman poked her with the tip of her parasol. Carter was possibly the only person in the theatre who was listening carefully, and even he heard just phrases, 'hooligan' and 'never be fooled by the cheap and insidious.' Now and again the lecture paused, and Houdini went once more to cross-examine Mysterioso, asking if he wanted to be free, not listening to his answer, and then resuming his lecture.

Six years ago, that was the last time Houdini had ruined a rival's show. Why return? Why embarrass this one magician here and now? Yes, Mysterioso was obnoxious, and deserved punishment for getting nice people shut, and for defaming Houdini, and for being untrue to the spirit of magic. All of these were excellent reasons for Houdini, if he knew about them, to appear. And, if anyone were to ask Carter, he would list all of those reasons, and say, 'Mysterioso was begging to be destroyed.' But Carter also knew what was more likely the true reason: a word from Albee to Houdini was a cost-effective way to handle Mysterioso's demand for a fifty percent raise.

Houdini held up both hands as if to beg the audience's indulgence. He walked around Mysterioso, and approached Carter, who still stood just offstage, in the wings.

Houdini leaned in toward Carter, put one hand on his shoulder, and spoke conspiratorially. 'Your name is Charles Carter?' He was shorter than Carter, square, with an unbelievably powerful frame. His eyes were grey and challenging and fiercely intelligent.

'Yes, Mr Houdini.'

Houdini laughed. 'Oh, you needn't call me Mr Houdini. Call me Houdini.' They shook hands. Houdini's grip felt like a leather-lined vise. 'Are you sober enough to join me onstage?'

'Yes. You know, I only had a few sips—'

Houdini waved his hand, shushing Carter. 'We'll discuss that later. It's a disgusting habit, and it causes weak men to make strong excuses. Come.'

It was no use trying to contradict Houdini, so he followed. He wasn't exactly sure what Houdini had in mind. He had a naive, childish feeling that Houdini would announce that Mysterioso was out, and Carter was in. A miracle: an hour after being fired, he would be anointed by the most famous man in the world. He and Houdini – Houdini! – stood by the still-trussed-up Mysterioso, who had finally succumbed to exhaustion, and lay still on the stage. The air smelled of smoke from the jugglers' torches, and Carter wasn't sure whether to make eye contact with any of Mysterioso's crew. Houdini patted Carter on the back, hailing the audience with his other hand. Some people watched the stage, but most of the audience was conversing with each other, and, Carter noted, a few young men had recovered themselves enough to exchange calling cards with the girls in rows G and H.

'Maestro, "Pomp and Circumstance" again,' Houdini said, 'but *sotto, sotto.*'

Carter was fairly sure he meant *pianissimo*, but nonetheless, the orchestra struck up the theme, quietly, and gradually the audience began to pay attention again.

'Lay-dies and Gen-tile-men,' Houdini cried. 'I bring to your attention Carter! Carter the Great!' A few people cheered and there was some applause, which Houdini impatiently interrupted. 'He is a *very good* magician.' Houdini shook Carter's hand again. Carter tried to press this moment permanently in his mind's eye, from the firm and sweaty pressure of their palms and fingers together, to how the clear gelatin Houdini had painted on his face to wrinkle it was now beginning to peel; he registered the expectant gaze of his fellow performers in the wings, as well as his own excitement. For the first time all evening, he even allowed himself to look up to his parents' box high above stage right: his mother and father and James and Tom were standing, applauding, waving to him – what pride Carter felt! what a moment in his life! 'Thank you all for coming,' Houdini said. 'Good night. Curtain, please.'

The curtain dropped in front of them with the speed of a falling tree. Houdini broke their grip, patting Carter on the arm. 'Really, Carter, you are a fine magician.'

'Thank you.'

Houdini nodded and walked off. Carter stared after him, drawing a slow and steady breath, and then, as though he had added up a long column of figures, he realized the sum of what had happened: Houdini had praised him. The curtain had dropped. Nothing more. He was still fired.

A stagehand found Carter: his family was waiting for him by the orchestra pit, and anxious to meet Houdini.

The dancers filed offstage to remove their paint, except for Annabelle, who was still in her frilly white dress. She settled down by the lion's cage to roll a smoke. Stagehands tore down the scenery, and a crowd formed around Houdini, who had already taken out a stack of cream-colored calling cards, which he had presigned, 'Best – Houdini!!!' As people approached him, he passed them the cards instead of engaging in conversation. He tossed a set of keys to some of Mysterioso's men, and told them that if they wanted to free their boss before midnight, they should start now.

Then Houdini approached Carter again. 'Blackmail was an extravagant illusion,' Houdini said. Carter prepared a 'thank you,' but was suddenly unsure of how to take the word *extravagant*. Houdini continued, 'It was wonderful how you humiliated that scoundrel, but it's not as if you can find new enemies with dogs night after night.'

That concept. It sounded familiar. 'So I've heard.' Clearly, Houdini had talked with Murdoch. He knew, then, that Carter had been fired.

'On the other hand, Houdini has enemies.' Houdini stroked his chin, approximating thoughtfulness.

'I'm not sure I follow.'

'Are you familiar with my brother Hardeen?'

Carter had seen Theo Hardeen perform twice, but wasn't sure if he should admit it. Hardeen was notorious for his deeply felt appreciation of his brother's act, meaning he stealthily used copies of Houdini's illusions six months after Houdini had debuted them. The brothers frequently, and vehemently, denounced each other.

Houdini took Carter by the arm and led him far from the rest of the crowd. He spoke quickly, but with perfect enunciation. 'He and I have an arrangement and it's good to escalate it from time to time. If he were to get a dog and parade it around for a few months, I could use your Blackmail effect at the Hippodrome, and it would certainly up the ante. Six thousand people would see it, every night.' Houdini spoke as if he'd planned this out months beforehand, and Carter was free to be amazed. 'I'll pay you well for the illusion. How much did it cost you?'

Carter didn't blink. 'It cost me two thousand dollars.'

'Two thousand—' Houdini pursed his lips. Then, smiling, he admonished Carter with a fingertip. 'That will never do, you must come clean with me, Carter. I'll pay you eight hundred dollars for it, right now.'

Carter looked at the barrel-vaulted ceiling far, far in the shadows. Houdini was swooping in with a lowball offer. Prolonged exposure to one's heroes wasn't necessarily a treat. 'No,' he finally said, pursing his lips.

'No?' It was as if Houdini had never heard the word before.

From across the stage, cutting through the stagehands chattering as they struck the set, Baby suddenly cried out. It wasn't a mighty or fearsome sound – it was a weak, frustrated complaint.

'Excuse me,' Carter said.

'Of course,' Houdini said, bowing slightly.

Carter pushed through the crowd. The word *no* had exhausted him. He needed a moment to think. What kind of an idiot turned down money when he needed it so badly? His father would kill him.

He met Annabelle, who looked with concern into Baby's cage.

'I don't get it,' she said. 'I was just talking to him, trying to get him to stop pacing. Something's really killing him.'

Baby gave his anguished moan again, closing his eyes in what looked like a wince, pacing two body lengths in one direction, turning, toenails clacking against the iron floor. Carter walked around the cage, which was divided in half by a false wall. There was a turntable built into the bottom so Mysterioso, in a lion skin, could replace Baby. Carter saw the lion skin heaped in the hidden side of the cage, the side Mysterioso usually crouched in.

First making sure there was no way Baby could get around the false wall, Carter climbed into the cage.

'Hey,' Annabelle said. She climbed in after him, holding up the hem of her dress with one hand. 'What are you doing?'

'I want to know how he's made to roar.' He rolled the lion skin up – it was real, and smelled of paint and formaldehyde – and looked where the wall met the cage's rubber-matted floor.

Annabelle crouched next to Carter. 'I liked your trick.'

'Thank you. It got me fired.'

'Yeah, but you gotta admit, it was worth it. Did you like doing it?'

Carter looked at her with surprise. 'I never thought about that. Yes, very much, except the guilt afterward.' Annabelle said nothing, no 'easy meat' comments, so Carter continued. 'Do you like scrapping every night?'

'Yeah. Why's Houdini still here, anyway?'

'He wants to buy Blackmail.'

Annabelle gazed at Houdini, who was now approaching. She whispered, 'Don't let him get it too easy.'

Carter's fingers brushed against the rubber matting, and he simply said, unhappily, 'Oh, no.'

'What's your problem?'

Carter listened carefully. Baby was pacing in the other side of the cage, *click-click-click* of his toenails. Carter didn't need to look any further. He'd figured out what made Baby roar. He sat down. Here came Houdini.

Houdini gripped the cage's bars. 'Carter, walking off won't get me to raise my price. In fact, I think seven hundred fifty makes a fine offer, too.'

'You might be interested in this, Houdini.'

'In what?'

Carter explained that there was a mystery he'd just solved: every night, as Mysterioso crouched in this cage, in his lion skin, behind his false wall, the lion, just on the other side of the cage, was made to roar.

Houdini chuckled, 'Not much of a mystery, Carter, either a voice or visual command—'

'It's not.'

'Or it's . . .' Houdini stood back, comparing the two sides of the cage. 'Good heavens,' he muttered. He looked under the cage. He looked back at Carter, mouth forming words, color coming to his face. Then Houdini turned away, shouting at the stagehands, 'Get him loose! Get Mysterioso loose right now!'

Then, Annabelle noticed it herself. 'There's something different about this side. Hey, there's rubber on this side. The floor of the other side is iron—'

Amazingly, Annabelle had an eye even keener than Carter's, and found, now that she knew what she was looking for, that two sets of wires were sticking out through the floor. All one had to do was touch one set of wires to the other, and—

Annabelle said, 'He shocks Baby. He shocks him. Every single goddamned night. That son of a bitch!'

She shot out of the cage while Carter added it up: the lion was pacing because he knew that when he was rolled onstage, he would be shocked, and tonight, he thought his torture was being prolonged.

Mysterioso, finally freed, now wobbled to his feet, rubbing his bleeding wrists. The dozen workers onstage had put their backs to him the way schoolchildren ignore the dunce the teacher has punished. Houdini, a full head shorter than he, reached up to his lapels and shook him.

'This is the end of you, Mysterioso! Do you hear me!' Houdini had more to say – when dressing someone down, Houdini always had more to say – and Carter was amazed to hear what it was. With a blunt force French accent, Houdini intoned: 'Puisque toutes les créatures sont—' but got no further; a red-headed blur ripped Mysterioso from his grasp and pinned him onto the stage.

'Coward!' Annabelle shouted, righting herself, pinning Mysterioso's arms down with her knees. 'Coward!' She punched his face, knocking his head from side to side, alternating blows with her left and right fists, then changing to open-handed slaps.

Carter stood near Houdini, each of them poised to stop her, but neither quite willing to intervene.

'Coward!' she cried again. She grabbed his ears and banged his head against the floorboards.

From a distance, Houdini called out to Mysterioso, 'Yes, you're a coward. You've broken a cardinal rule, you may no longer perform as a magician, I'm having you barred from the Society of American Magicians,' and continued in that vein. Carter had never heard another magician refer to Keyes's rules as cardinal, but now wasn't the time to ask about it.

Carter approached Annabelle. 'Annabelle,' he whispered.

She looked up with Mysterioso's head still in her hands. Her green and gold eyes were awake with anger. Then she stood, kicking a toe against Mysterioso. 'He's alive,' she said, sounding disappointed. She shook her right hand out, and sucked on a finger. 'I need some ice.' And she walked away, breathing hard.

'Well, she's spirited,' Houdini declared, as soon as she had left the stage. 'Is she your sweetheart?'

'No.' As Carter said it, he felt regret. 'When men get fresh, she tends to punch them.'

'I see. Have you been punched?'

'No.'

Houdini clapped him on the back. 'Good man! If you can keep the drinking under control, you'll be a fine magician until you're a hundred and one. Now, Carter, about Blackmail—'

'I can't sell it outright.' Aware that it didn't pay to rankle Houdini, Carter continued. 'I'm flattered, of course.'

Houdini smiled grimly. 'One doesn't get offers every day from Houdini.'

'But without an income in the future,' he said carefully, 'it's my only asset and I should consider licensing it instead. If I had five or six or seven magicians using it—'

'Five or six with enemies?' Houdini's eyebrows arched.

'It could become the new trend in magic. It could become quite common, Houdini.'

'That's a *terrible* idea,' Houdini said, grimacing as if he'd just tasted spoiled milk. Carter, who had concocted a full-scale plan by now, was gazing over Houdini's shoulder. Houdini turned and saw that Carter was looking at the lion, who, as if satisfied by the sight of Mysterioso's beating, now sat quietly, tip of tongue sticking out, his paws between the bars of the cage. Houdini looked at the stage. He looked at the lion again. He looked at Carter, who was regarding the props remaining onstage with proprietary interest, and Carter thought as loudly as he could: *Make me the headliner. Let me do the job I was born for.*

Houdini said, 'I see. I see. Yes. Perhaps I can help you. But tell me honestly – we will work something out on this Blackmail illusion? You'll be fair about it?'

Carter nodded.

'So then. Where are you from?' Houdini asked. The question sounded innocuous and sly at the same time; it wasn't what he actually wished to discuss.

'San Francisco.'

'I see. And is your mother still with us?'

'She is.'

Houdini took in a great breath. '*Is she a wonderful woman?*'

Carter responded forcefully: 'Oh, yes.'

'And you love her?'

'I love her. She gets hooked on the latest fashions in psychology, but—' Carter paused. Houdini obviously hadn't been after a critique.

'Can you swear an oath by your sainted mother to be loyal to me?'

'Of course.'

'Swear it, then.' Houdini took Carter's hands between his. 'Swear loyalty to me in your mother's name.'

The conversation had turned bizarre, but this was not altogether surprising. Houdini, Carter had long heard rumors, was fixated on such oaths among magicians; Carter felt dizzy with pride – he was worthy of an oath. 'I swear on my mother's, on my mother's life—'

'Good! Excellent!'

'—loyalty to Houdini.' Carter finished.

Houdini broke their grip. 'Have you had your supper yet?'

Carter shook his head.

'Let's go find Albee. He knows the best restaurants in San Francisco.'

Chapter 14

Back in the dressing room, Carter introduced Houdini to his parents, to James and Tom. Houdini took special care with Mrs Carter, praising her for raising such a fine young man. Mr Carter asked once, and only once, about what would happen next season. Carter was prepared to tell him that they would need to wait and see, but Houdini said, 'I will make Charles Carter the next headliner – all he needs is to follow my lead!' With that, Houdini turned on his heel, beckoning Carter over his shoulder, and striding masterfully out of the dressing room.

Carter looked behind him. His family was ecstatic, James and Tom exchanging 'can-you-top-that' type comments, his parents holding hands. He'd never seen them excited like this before, and his *career* had certainly never caused them this kind of reaction. The sight was thrilling and yet oddly melancholy, like it promised him some kind of loss. But he didn't know why. 'Dad,' Carter said.

'I know.' His father nodded. 'Go on with him.'

He had so much to say. He wanted to describe how hard he had worked to engineer an escape from an ordinary life. But Houdini came back in, looking cross. 'Where are you, Carter? We have an appointment.'

They left together, Carter nodding as Houdini outlined their strategy, but inwardly wondering if by winning, he'd left his parents, particularly his father, behind somehow.

At dinner – Wallach's, on Hyde and Ellis, the French restaurant with duck à l'orange so fine homesick Parisians were known to weep after one bite – Carter declined Albee's offer to have his kard-and-koin contract reinstated for the three weeks of the tour. Instead, he expressed an interest in the legitimate theatre and shared his ideas for an evening-length performance. He said, as if he needn't explain further, that as the son of a rich man, he could get funding for a show immediately. Houdini asked if perhaps there might be some compromise: Carter would agree to play for Albee for the remainder of the tour, but in Mysterioso's place, testing out a selection of illusions before moving up. Carter expressed his uncertainty – after all, there was the matter of having been fired earlier in the evening. With a wave of his hand, Albee said that had been entirely Murdoch's decision. He, Albee, hadn't known a thing about it. Albee added that he was thinking of backing other kinds of shows, as it seemed the nickelodeon was eating into vaudeville's profits.

This led to an animated discussion of the merits of the picture show; the consensus among them was that even if it were just a passing fancy, a wise man should investigate purchasing a theatre or two, perhaps even producing entertainment for them. Within moments, Houdini had an oral agreement that Albee would finance a half dozen shorts featuring Houdini, in exchange for a percentage of the profits.

When Carter sensed that he had lost their attention, he declared that, anyway, there had to be other magicians on the circuit who were skilled and imaginative enough to take over the headliner act. Houdini confessed that he didn't know of any. He added that in fact, the legitimate theatre had taken all of them – if Albee didn't do something to keep Carter around, vaudeville would lose its best chance for wholesome, high-class mystery.

'You think he's that good?' Albee asked.

Houdini sent an eagle's gaze across the table. 'Albee, it takes me a heartbeat to know if a man is poor, fair, or in the middle somewhere. Our Mr Carter – is—' His eyes lit up. 'Yes, Carter is *great*.'

At the end of dinner, Houdini had sewn up Carter's Blackmail act, Albee had extracted a reluctant promise from Carter to headline for a year, and Carter had been granted a salary of a thousand dollars a week – the sum Albee paid most first-time headliners – from which he had to pay his staff.

'Is that the time?' Houdini asked, pushing away from the table. 'I must go and call Bess, tell her about defeating that scoundrel Mystico, and so forth.'

'Mysteri—' Carter coughed into his palm. 'Yes, thank you for defeating Mystico. May I have a word?'

Carter walked Houdini from the back room of Wallach's through the great oak front door and to the sidewalk, where they shook hands. Carter said, 'Houdini, I wanted to ask you—'

'Yes?' Houdini flailed his arm toward a taxi.

'Puisque toutes les créatures sont au fond des frères . . .' Carter let his voice trail off. 'Ottawa Keyes was the first magic authority I ever read.'

Houdini had no visible reaction to this – he continued to wave for cabs. With a beep of its horn, a taxi finally cut across traffic toward the curb. 'You know,' Houdini said, 'I've researched it – Keyes stole every one of those rules of his.'

'Oh,' Carter said, sinking.

'But they're good rules, they're good rules.' Houdini had one hand on the door of the taxi; the other he directed toward Carter, not to shake, but as if pointing him out in a crowd. 'Carter, you *are* loyal to me, aren't you?'

That again? 'I'm as loyal as—'

'Yes, yes. You can break many rules in that book and still be a great conjurer. I, for instance,' Houdini paused; Carter was sure he would admit to never ironing his silks. 'I find that pretending to show fear is most effective. And I'd argue if you were to take your last bow with others onstage—'

'Hey, Mack, you getting in the cab?' the driver yelled.

Houdini looked hurt. Carter exclaimed, 'Excuse me – this is *Houdini*.'

'Oh.' The driver thought about it, and turned on the meter.

Houdini gestured at Carter again. 'I could add a great many rules myself. But tonight highlights an excellent rule: one should always treat one's animals well. All else will follow. Good night.'

They shook hands yet again, and Houdini settled into the cab. As it pulled away from the curb, Carter waved, and Houdini rolled the window down, yelling, 'And remember – from now on, you're Carter the Great!'

Back in the restaurant, Albee had Carter sign a napkin – they would have proper contracts drawn up tomorrow – and then Carter made a list of all his new responsibilities. He had a messenger (he now had access to the Keith-Orpheum messenger service) run to the Ferry building, where the troupe was housed, to alert them to a special 8 A.M. meeting to discuss the show. There were a thousand other details to deal with, but for now, his mood remained happy disbelief.

Monsieur Wallach gave Albee his beaver hat and Carter his derby, and the two men ambled outside, where Albee patted his flat belly with pleasure. Albee was a salty man, with tufts of hair in his ears, and a completely bald head that he had his manicurist rub with rosewater twice a day, to stimulate the mind. Carter watched him reach into his pocket and pull out a square leather jewel box, which he hefted as if to assure himself he wanted to hand it over. Decision made, he passed it to Carter. 'Open it,' Albee said.

Inside the box, an Edward Koehn watch sat like a metal on a velvet cushion. The hunting case, which bore the enameled masks of comedy and tragedy, was machine-turned eighteen-karat gold, with a frosted texture that reminded Carter of a fine dessert.

'It's from Geneva,' Albee said. 'Geneva, Switzerland.' Before Carter could touch it, Albee had used his short fingers to pull it out, pop open the back, and reveal the works, which all but hummed under their exhibition backing. He turned the watch back and forth so its innards sparkled. 'Thirty-one sapphires,' he said. 'It's a minute repeater.'

Carter nodded. 'So it chimes?'

'Does it chime?' he chuckled. 'Even the *hammers* are jeweled. The bells sound like angels playing them.'

'I'm overwhelmed,' Carter said, for he had never seen so fine a watch.

'Look at the dial,' Albee continued. His smile went boyish and proud.

Carter held it at an angle, to better see under the streetlights. The dial was inlaid with porcelain and abalone shell, and where the maker's insignia was usually found, there was instead, in gold script, the name *Jessie Hayman*.

'All you have to do, Carter, is show her butler the watch. You'll have the run of her house.'

Carter thanked him. He added he was very tired, and said that since his parents lived in the city, he would be going home straightway. But Albee wouldn't hear of it. He put Carter in a cab, and told the driver to take him to 44 Mason, no ifs, ands, or buts.

Before the cab left, Albee leaned in, to say, 'Just ask yourself, Carter – in fifty years, do you want to remember that on the night you made headliner, you went home to your parents and then had a glass of warm milk and took a nap?' Albee laughed.

The question was good enough to bring Carter as far as the front stairs of 44 Mason, Jessie Hayman's Georgian mansion. The first time Carter looked at the watch, it was one-thirty in the morning. The night air was warm. He could hear girlish laughter and piano music. Someone was playing 'Waltz Me Around Again, Willie' at dizzying speed. He weighed whether he should go in or catch a taxi home. He was not the type of man to visit a parlorhouse girl. But he was wide awake, and felt perfectly capable of having just one drink and leaving.

Jessie's butler took Carter's hat and topcoat and led him to the parlor, which bubbled with piano music. Others from the program had already paired off with girls they liked and gone upstairs, but he still found two colleagues, Adolph and Leonard, at the piano bench, playing a merry four-handed waltz. Surrounding them were about a dozen of Jessie's girls. Their preferred late-evening attire was long silk dresses. By the way their bodies were silhouetted before the amber electric lights, Carter could see they no longer wore their corsets. He folded his arms then unfolded them, feeling like the clumsiest man on earth. Was it more polite to stare or to not stare?

Leonard shoved Adolph in the chest, and Adolph shoved back – one of them or the other changed the tune to 'Peasie Weasie,' and at once Julius leapt up from a leather sofa (Carter hadn't even seen him) and did an awkward little dance, which made the girls laugh. Then he sang:

My mother called Sister downstairs the other day.
'I'm taking a bath,' my sister did say.
'Well, slip on something quick, here comes Parson Brown.'
She slipped on the top step and then came on down.

Everyone in the room, except Carter and Jessie Hayman herself, joined in on the chorus as Julius continued his dance, crossing his arms like a Russian sailor and kicking his legs in the air. It was at this moment that Jessie noticed Carter, and welcomed him in. She stopped the music, calling for another round of champagne, and toasting Carter, the headliner.

'News travels quickly, doesn't it?' Carter said to the group.

'Einstein has it all wrong,' Julius said. 'Gossip travels faster than light does.' There were a couple of chuckles, Carter (who was thankful he wasn't a comedian) among them, then Julius added, 'And if any of you girls are faster than gossip, you know where to find me.'

Because of the grape blight in France, champagne was almost impossible to find, yet Jessie had an abundance of bottles. Julius sang 'The Boy in the Boat' and 'Pick Me a Flower,' and when his repertoire of naughty songs ran out, he made up dirty lyrics to the most innocent tunes, while his brothers fought over the piano.

Carter was happy he'd come, happy he'd had a free glass of champagne, and was ready to leave. As he was looking around for his hostess, Jessie freshened his glass.

'Mr Carter,' she said.

'I was just looking for you,' he replied.

'I would like you to meet your greatest admirers,' Jessie said. She presented two petite women in royal blue silk gowns. They had dark skin, long, straight black hair, and almond-shaped eyes. 'Marissa and Lupe Juarez, of Brazil. I'll get all of you more champagne.'

'My name is Marissa,' said the slightly taller girl. She had a small pockmark by her hairline, but otherwise her bronze skin was flawless. She spoke with no accent. 'This is my younger sister, Lupe. She's rather shy.'

Carter shook Lupe's hand, then Marissa's. Each was small and soft. It was impossible to tell how old they were, eighteen, perhaps nineteen, but Carter guessed they were younger than that. They had been trained to speak like debutantes. A servant poured them champagne and they toasted Carter's success.

'You're a wonderful magician, Mr Carter,' Marissa said.

'Charles, really. But thank you. It's been quite an evening for me.'

'I understand. Your fortunes went up, they went down, they went up again.'

'Well, I hope to stay up,' Carter said too quickly, tipping up his glass to disguise his reddening face. But Marissa and Lupe simply laughed. Their laughter was a beautifully polished performance.

'I rather enjoyed the Blackmail part,' Lupe said. Her ability with cotillion discourse was slightly less agile than her sister's. 'Everyone around us was rather amazed.'

'Thank you.' Carter knew better than to rely on this particular review, but still, he was charmed. 'I thought people might not have liked it.'

Lupe said, 'If people didn't like it, well, they're wrong.' Then Carter saw something he didn't understand: Lupe's dark eyes were tearing up. 'Thank you for what you did to that horrible man,' she said. Then she excused herself and vanished from the room.

Carter looked to Marissa for an explanation. Marissa, who was also on the verge of tears, took a sip of champagne.

'Excuse me,' she said, also departing.

Carter stared after them. He finished his champagne, then gingerly opened his Edward Koehn watch. He'd been here half an hour, and had made two beautiful girls run away in tears. He wanted to leave.

At the piano, Leonard played the first eight bars of Brahms's Hungarian Dance in F minor, and then, with a flourish, shifted into 'The Maple Leaf Rag,' which he played maniacally, shooting the keys with his fingers. Then Adolph played yet again the only song he knew, 'Waltz Me Around Again, Willie.' Some of the girls were dancing together, doing the most energetic of steps: the Texas Tommy, the Bunny Hug.

Carter, drunk, watched from the couch, where Julius sat with a thick-waisted blond German girl on his lap. Somehow he found himself trying to explain to Julius, who couldn't have been less interested, that no matter how many different ways he came at it, he could only say that he knew less today than he had yesterday.

'What, did you think you knew something yesterday?' Julius asked.

'Do you follow psychology? I'm embarrassed to be thinking this way, but I think that today I replaced my father with a father figure,' he mused. 'Or perhaps I started that when I met Borax Smith.'

'You're a complicated little weasel, I'll give you that.'

'You know, you go from wanting your parents to love you to something else when you're onstage, and . . .' Julius was staring at him uncertainly, and Carter remembered he was speaking to a man whose manager was his mother.

Julius managed to break the awkward silence, as was his gift. 'You know what life is? One damned thing after another. No, wait, that's love. Life is a tale told by an idiot, signifying nothing.'

Carter looked at all the women. The champagne had not made them any less beautiful. And yet wasn't there a chaste girl in a Yukon convent perhaps waiting for him? He couldn't imagine two more different kinds of lives than those in this parlor and what Sarah's was. 'The one problem is, I just don't have this love business worked out,' he concluded, almost to himself.

'I told you, love is a tale told by an idiot,' Julius said. The German girl kissed him, and pulled him upward with her strong arms. 'Of course,' he said, 'I may be wrong about that.'

When some hours had passed, Carter pulled back the lever at the bottom of his watch. It chimed. It was the first time he'd heard it, melodious, rich, surprisingly full: four bells, a pause, then three airy bells, sounding, yes, just like angels playing them. How had it gotten to be 4:03 in the morning? He was still on the couch. Julius had gone upstairs long ago. Leonard had disappeared briefly three times, each time with a different girl, but an hour ago he'd left for the evening with Gladys, who had chestnut hair down to her waist. Adolph had made a comic scene of being unable to decide among the women who remained, gnashing his teeth and making faces, finally scooping up a small blond Russian girl, and, hollering like a wildman, dashing up the stairs with her.

This left Carter. It was four o'clock in the morning, he hadn't had a drink in over an hour, and he felt like the evening had wound down around him. He was the only man in a room of ten women. He noticed their yawns, their smiles when he met their eyes, their occasional glances toward the window – Jessie didn't allow clocks in her house, but, from certain angles, you could see the clocktower across the square. Someone cranked up the gramophone, and two tall girls danced together to the second movement of a Vivaldi lute concerto.

Jessie, smiling, appeared at Carter's side. 'Mr Carter, you've been a very thoughtful guest tonight.'

'Thank you,' then he realized the implied second meaning. 'Lost in thought?' He laughed. 'Yes, that, too.'

'If any of our girls can help you sort it all out, just say the word. If you'll do us the honor of staying overnight, we'll wash and press your shirt and shine your shoes, and we have a lovely chef who comes in to make breakfast.'

'Thank you.'

'*Au revoir*,' she said, and stood. As she left the room, she said a few quiet words to the Juarez girls, who left with her.

The remaining girls, one by one, wished Carter a good night, and let him know, each in her own way, he was welcome to join any of them if he so desired.

And then he was alone.

Light footsteps going up creaking stairs. The satin wallpaper had a red floral pattern embossed in it, and the air smelled of French perfume. From the couch, Carter could see out the big bay window that faced a small side garden where honeysuckle vines and oak trees grew.

In the silence, Carter could hear himself think. In the transition to headliner, he might have changed already in ways he didn't yet know, but he had brought with him this solitude. Parts of him were built to be awake before dawn and yearning to be both absolutely still and moving everywhere at once.

Suddenly, a scrappy little terrier ran into the room. She was followed closely by Marissa and Lupe.

'Ginger!' Marissa called. 'I apologize, Mr Carter. We were going to take her for a walk.'

'We wanted you to meet a most excellent dog,' Lupe added.

'Hello, Ginger,' Carter said, letting the dog scrutinize his fingers. 'Does Ginger know any tricks?'

Lupe shook her head. 'She might roll over, but only if she wants to.'

'Ginger! Roll over!' Carter commanded. He made encouraging motions with his fingers, but Ginger paid no attention. The Juarez girls laughed. 'Roll over!' he barked. It was like addressing a friendly and puzzled wall. Ginger sniffed at his shoes, and licked Marissa on the chin as she tucked her legs under her and sat on the rug.

'You aren't particularly a dog trainer,' Marissa observed.

'If you think that's bad, in just a few hours, I have to make friends with a lion.'

Lupe said something to Marissa, covering her mouth.

Carter asked, 'Is that Portuguese?'

'Pardon me?' Marissa asked.

'The language you were just speaking? Portuguese?'

'No,' Marissa said.

'What other languages do they speak in Brazil?' Carter asked with honest curiosity, but as the words left his mouth, he knew that neither girl had the first idea what Brazilians spoke.

'They speak many languages,' Lupe said, looking at her older sister. 'All kinds. French and German, for example.' Lupe looked at Marissa. 'May I tell?'

'No. Well, I'm unsure.' Marissa looked toward the staircase, as if someone might be listening. Then she whispered to Carter, 'We aren't actually from Brazil.'

Carter nodded. 'Where are you from?'

'We were raised in Texas.'

'I've played Texas,' he said.

Marissa looked at Carter. 'We're—' She hesitated long enough to see if she could trust him. 'We're Comanches.'

'That's why we dislike that Mysterioso. That warpaint!' Lupe exclaimed.

'And the Alamo?' Marissa looked disgusted.

'There weren't *Indians* at the *Alamo*,' Lupe declared with the indignation of a girl who had recently learned this herself.

'Please don't tell Jessie we told you about us,' Marissa whispered. She took Carter's hand. 'Thank you for taking over as headliner.' She kissed him softly on the cheek, her breath smelling of peppermints.

Lupe kissed Carter on the other cheek, and also said, 'Thank you.'

'When I take over the act, we won't have that Indian business,' Carter said. 'It lacks dramatic unity.' Marissa was looking into his eyes, and she put her hand on the back of his head. 'Illusions must have dramatic unity,' Carter continued stupidly as Lupe kissed his hands.

'You have rather strong hands,' Lupe whispered.

Marissa opened her mouth. Her lips were full, and the moment they parted, they commanded Carter's complete attention. 'My sister and I,' she said, kissing Carter again, 'are grateful to you.' Her teeth grazed his earlobe.

'Yes . . . you're welcome . . .' He could have jumped through his skin. His arms were full of two girls. They laughed as they pushed him down on the couch. His act seemed a hundred thousand miles away. He was drowning in their smells, silk and peppermint and perfumes distilled in France, smells of berries and apricots and tangerines.

Marissa put Carter's left hand at the top of her stocking; Lupe did the same for his right. He could barely breathe.

'Maybe you should join us upstairs,' Lupe said, and then each of them took a stride backward, almost in unison, like it was a new dance step, and Carter's hands held only the air.

Carter found his voice. 'Yes,' he said.

The girls, holding hands, raced out of the room in excitement, and a second later, he could hear them trot up the stairs. He righted himself on the couch. He wasn't sure he could stand.

Then, in excitement, he found his legs and bolted out of the room. He was at the foot of the stairs, one hand on the banister, when he heard a deep sigh from back in the living room. Ginger was stretching on the carpet. She waved a paw toward him.

He hesitated.

He went back to the couch and sat down, not entirely sure what he was doing. He watched the staircase as if it might roll up at any minute. Ginger jumped up onto the couch. She put her chin on his knee. He was getting hair on his trousers. The shirt he could have pressed. The shoes he could have shined. They thought of everything here. He remembered how, after his father had taken overnight business trips to Oakland, his mother had always gravely examined his shirts and his shoes. He lay back on the couch, next to Ginger, and tried to imagine sprinting up the stairs. He could hold on to the railing, taking the steps two at a time. He thought of what their room must look like, the fresh pastel stalk in a porcelain vase, erotic etchings from Paris in tasteful frames, a bed, brass, no, four-poster and of oak. They would be waiting for him in the bed, or perhaps there would be a game, an ambush as he went in. Before he went up, he had to remember the sensations, the fingers against pliant skin. Lupe, the younger sister, stepping back, saying, 'Maybe you should join us upstairs?' Something was familiar about that, it had a hollow ring to it, and then he remembered, yes, it made perfect sense, it was the same intonation, exactly, as 'Will you have her as your bride?' An act. Everything here, in this house, even sincerity, was an act, and sweetly performed.

He fell asleep there, on the couch. His dreams were unfocused and pleasant. Relief. Someone was playing Franz Liszt's gentle *Bénédiction de Dieu dans la solitude*. It was the type of aching solo piano music that spoke of sitting by the edge of a lake in summer at night, looking for comets.

When he opened his eyes, he was still on the couch and Ginger was gone. Across the room, Annabelle Bernhardt was playing the Liszt harmonies on Jessie Hayman's grand piano. Her eyes were closed, her lips slightly parted.

When waking to something unlikely, the mind usually tries to make excuses – that it's just a dream. But Carter knew, even as he was still half asleep, that this was real. Annabelle sat near him, in this parlor, and she could play the piano beautifully. It was quiet music that built to great passion slowly, then faded back to reflective states, then charged again into full tempests and whirlpools. The *Bénédiction* was a long piece, with many asides along the way, and when Carter closed his eyes, he had dreamy, pleasant thoughts, and when he opened them, he saw Annabelle, dressed in a man's work shirt, Levi's dungarees, and her tall harness boots.

He had no idea she could play the piano, or when she rehearsed. He knew nothing about her offstage life. For example: what exactly was she doing at 44 Mason?

Annabelle breezed through a difficult stretch, but on the *diminuendo*, missed a chord change. She tensed, let out a deep sigh, then flipped the keyboard shut.

She looked over her shoulder at Carter.

Carter said, 'That was beautiful.'

'It stunk. Shut up.'

Carter walked over and sat next to her on the bench. She shifted, putting more distance between them. Carter looked toward the window. The sky was purple. It was almost dawn.

'I was thinking about it,' she said carefully, looking at her hands, 'and I realized you're the only man on the program I haven't had to punch in the mouth.'

He ran his fingers through his hair. 'So you're here to finish the job?'

She shook her head. She seemed sad.

'You know, you play the piano very well.'

'Stop,' she said. 'Don't even start with that. I was icing my hand after I decked Mysterioso, and I just started thinking.'

She didn't say what she was thinking about. Carter said, 'If you have talent that involves your hands, you shouldn't risk it by punching people. You saw how Houdini and I didn't touch you when you were beating Mysterioso.'

'Yeah. You guys are pansies.'

'We are not—' Carter stopped. He folded his arms, and realized he was smiling.

She picked at a chipped nail. 'I was at the Ferry building, and I couldn't sleep. Everyone was talking about you taking over the act and I wasn't sure it was a good thing.'

'No?'

'You've gotta take over an act tomorrow morning. How the hell you gonna do that?'

'I have no idea.'

'Well, anyway, I was thinking of quitting.'

Carter shook his head. 'I won't allow it.'

'Yeah, right. So, I heard you were here, and I thought, *Just what I need, another whoring, leering kind of boss*, and so I came over and I sat in a tree right out there . . .' She pointed out the bay window, to the yard Carter could now just faintly see. 'And I watched you . . . *for hours!*' She looked mad when she said this. 'I kept thinking, any minute now, Charlie Carter's gonna prove himself a chicken chaser, but no.' She glared at him.

He said, 'They're very accommodating here – they would have brought you a pillow.'

'If you had gone upstairs with those two little girls . . .' Annabelle said, and Carter wondered what the threat would be. Finally, she murmured, 'But you didn't. So I can't quit right now, and so I thought I'd come in. Plus I was getting cramps in my legs.'

Carter went to the window, looked out into the yard. There was the tree, a magnolia whose leaves were becoming distinct as the night sky around it was, by the minute, fading into blue. 'Why did you play the piano just now? It seemed to mean something to you.'

'Sometimes,' she said, 'I play the piano.'

'But not usually.'

'How the hell do you know?'

He crossed to the window that faced the street, and he pulled back the draperies, which were damask, and smelled of burnt wood. Outside, it was silent and the rarest of San Francisco dawns: no fog. He could see, between the rooftops, just one spire of St Boniface's Cathedral. It was lovely. He and Annabelle were alone together. It was 5:30 in the morning. 'Would you take a walk with me?' he asked.

'What'd you have in mind?' she responded quickly.

'A walk. Nothing that would rate a punch in the nose.'

Chapter 15

It was warm. They didn't even need overcoats. They didn't pass a single person on Mason, and when they hit Market, Carter realized he wanted to take Annabelle to the foot of Powell. 'Listen,' he said. The trolley cars weren't running yet, but there was the whine of a turbine under the red bricks of the street. 'They put all the cable cars in a barn for the night, but the system runs anyway. See all the metal plates? There's a cable underneath them, and it goes for miles, over the hill there, and it moves all night long in a tremendous loop.'

She told him she was from Lawrenceville, Kansas, which was flat, so she was unimpressed with all the uphill hiking required in San Francisco. As they went up Columbus, he pointed out the new buildings, and the gaping, vacant lots awaiting new structures. He described all the beautiful things now gone: parks, monuments, ramshackle houses, playgrounds, amusement parks, all destroyed five years ago. But Carter remembered them. 'When I was ten and eleven, I often couldn't sleep. I would wake at four in the morning and I'd be so excited I had to go for a walk. So I left the house and walked miles and miles in a straight line, down Washington Street, right to the Barbary Coast.'

Annabelle groaned. 'That wasn't smart.'

'*I* wasn't smart, just restless. Boys like me were usually kidnapped and sold to seamen at Shanghai Kelly's. I don't know how I managed, but I did, back home before sunrise, maybe twice a week, and no one ever bothered me.'

'What did your folks think?'

'They never knew. They were asleep. I used to tell my brother, James, about it, but he didn't understand what I was getting into any better than I did. I always wished I had a friend I could take with me.'

'You could have taken James.'

'He was always sleeping.' To their left was the Winged Victory statue, to the right, a vacant lot that had once been a row of houses. 'Did you have brothers and sisters?'

'No.'

'I wish I'd known you.'

Annabelle snorted, shook her head. 'No you don't.'

Columbus led to Filbert Street, and Carter indicated that they would have to walk up a hill, in fact, the steepest hill in the world. All the way up, Annabelle moaned that all this walking uphill was no good for people from Kansas. When they got to the top, they were in a small park. Carter pointed toward the bay, where there were ships at anchor: schooners, ferries, square-riggers, Chinese junks heading back, already, from that morning's shrimping.

'Once, I stood here just before dawn, and there was a huge ship at that dock, that one there, and she was listing to her side. Not listing, nearly capsized – all of her masts were tied to the dock, and there were dozens of men on a raft, with lanterns, and her hull was exposed down to her keel. I'd never seen all the parts of a ship that are usually underwater. They were just recoppering her, but I thought I'd stumbled onto a terrific secret. I ran most of the way home, looking at everything. I was sure I'd see all kinds of things in the middle of the night that adults were hiding.'

'And that's when you decided to become a magician.'

'Oh, no,' Carter said. 'That started when the world's tallest man stole my lucky nickel.' And he told her the whole story. She laughed throughout. He liked many small things about her, even the things that anyone would do, like how she shielded her face as the sun was coming up. There were times that he completely forgot what he was saying, and she had to prompt him.

They bought biscuits and honey and milk, and walked to the top of Telegraph Hill (Annabelle called it Telegraph Mountain). On the way up the spiraling path, which took them through overgrowth heavy with dew, he told her about the eccentrics of San Francisco. He told her about Lillian Hitchcock, who as a little girl had been rescued from a burning house by firemen, and who grew up obsessed with the Knickerbocker Number Five fire company. Because she was wild, her parents sent her away to France, where she attended an imperial ball dressed as a fireman. She sang songs about firemen, in French, to Napoleon III, which horrified her parents, who summoned her home. They were determined to marry her off, and over the next year, fifteen men claimed to be her fiancé, but she never married any of them.

'I like her,' Annabelle said.

Carter told her how Lillian came into her trust when she was twenty-one, built a mansion in Pacific Heights, and threw parties for everyone in society. Carter's parents had attended one at which Lillian had put down canvas and roped off the parlor and, all evening long, staged boxing matches between professional fighters.

'Did she ever marry?'

'No.'

'Someone that good shouldn't be alone,' Annabelle said.

'She had a companion. A very lovely woman named Irene. They said she was a Russian countess.'

They were passing a vegetable garden where tomatoes, still green, hung wet in the sun. Annabelle made no further comments about the story of Lillian Hitchcock. Carter was disappointed. He had hoped the story would invite some kind of confession. But they came to the top of Telegraph Hill. The park here was vaguely municipal, in that there were benches for admiring the view, but there were also herb gardens and goat pens belonging to local families, and, at the distant end, patches of dense overgrown weeds surrounding an illegal quarrying operation where bruisers from the Barbary Coast slept the night off.

Carter and Annabelle sat on a bench nearest the bay, and here they finished their biscuits. The waters were green in some patches, or grey, or blue, but calm everywhere.

Carter told her more stories of things once here now vanished: an old castle, a trolley car line, terrific and wonderful houses the size of cathedrals. When he asked her questions directly, she found ways not to answer them.

He asked, 'How long did you train before you went onstage?'

She shrugged.

'Have you thought of playing piano onstage?'

'That's a bad idea. I like fighting.'

'I mean, in addition to fighting.'

Annabelle said nothing. She was looking at her hands.

'You have an evocative style of playing,' Carter said.

'What?' Annabelle looked like he'd stabbed her.

'I mean it as a compliment.'

'Carter, you dope, be quiet.' Annabelle stepped away from the bench. She stood with her back to him. Annabelle, with all of the colors of San Francisco Bay behind her. Finally, she groaned, 'Aw, nuts,' deflating like some army inside her had raised a white flag. She sat back down on their bench. 'What a revolting development this is.' And quiet again. Then, 'Before I say anything else, I gotta let you know one thing. I hate you.' She looked at the bench, then back at Carter. 'No, two things. You have beautiful eyes. And I hate you.' They looked at each other for a long time, until she finally said, 'What?'

'Are you about to hit me?'

'No.' When she spoke again, her voice slowed, as if she weren't sure she could finish her sentences. 'I was a prodigy. When I was four or five years old, you could play anything for me, once, and I could play it back, only better.'

'That's incredible.'

'It's terrible. It was the only thing I knew how to do. And when I was twelve . . . I am not *gonna* cry.' She looked at the bay for a moment and, true to her word, she didn't cry. 'It was like fog rolling in. One day I had it, the next day, I didn't. People thought I sounded good, but *I* knew. I lost it.'

'You sounded excellent tonight—'

'Can you imagine being the best in the world, you feel music like it's another one of your senses, and one day, you wake up, and you're only excellent?'

Carter shook his head.

'You're supposed to get better. And I didn't. When I found you tonight, I was . . .' She swallowed. 'Oh, I was proud of you. You did good tonight, with the Blackmail bit, and Mysterioso, and Houdini, and the girls, and everything. You're just a real straight-up guy. I thought maybe I could show you something without getting screwed, and there was the piano, so.' Her voice, which was still woolly, rose and fell almost musically, Carter realized. From calm to passionate, and now, slumped over, elbows on her knees, she went full bore again. 'Why did I follow you? I am such an idiot.' She put her head in her hands. 'I am *stuck* on you, Charlie. I can't stand it.'

'You like me?'

'God! I can't even be *mad* at anyone right now. Do you know what that's like for me?' She kicked the ground, hard. 'God!'

Carter watched everything: her limp red hair hanging around her face, the anguish she wore, her insistence that there had to be something in the bay worth looking at, the fists she had pressed into her knees. And the dew on their bench, the grass beside them, the smells of rosemary and basil and sage in the Italian gardens all around.

She would not meet his eye. 'It is *torture* to be with you. You've been teasing me all night long.'

'No, I haven't,' he said, 'really.' And he was overwhelmed. 'I didn't know you liked me. I thought the only joy you took in men was violent.'

And then she looked at him. The backs of her hands were swollen and knotted, her palms rough like burl, and he took her head in his hands, and her lips touched his, chapped, but sweet. They kissed long enough for Carter to feel all the tender possibilities of contact: kissing! touching! feeling! and then, with a flood of happiness, he realized he was kissing Annabelle Bernhardt, and she was exactly the right person to kiss.

'I could look at you all day, I think,' Carter said. He shook his head, smiling. Around them was the city and the world and the universe in all its known and as-yet-unexplored parts, and with them, the future.

Astonishingly, the meeting with the performers would start in just half an hour; Carter and Annabelle had to rush. He took her down side streets and through alleys, until they found a cable car. Inside, crushed together in the crowd, they had trouble taking their eyes off each other.

He was a headliner, he had stood side by side with Houdini, who had named him Carter the Great, and he was holding hands with a woman who thrilled him.

Annabelle said, 'Is your name really Carter?'

'Yes.' They pushed together as the car lurched to a stop.

'Charles Carter is your real name?' They had to draw even closer together, the workaday crowd pushing in on either side of them, as the trolley resumed up the hill.

'Charles Carter the Fourth. Who would make up such a dull name?'

'Well, my last boss's name was Mysterioso, and you were just talking to Houdini tonight, and that's not his real name—'

'True.'

'And Minnie Palmer changed her last name from Marx so she wouldn't seem related to her act, and I bet those parlor girls all have different real names, so it's just in the air.'

'No, my name is just Charles Carter. Is your name Annabelle Bernhardt?' The trolley jerked to a stop, then picked up again. The cab man rang the trolley's bells in double time.

'No.'

Carter said, 'No?'

She shook her head. Her red hair rustled, flowed, calmed down again. 'Well, Bernhardt is. Annabelle's my middle name. But I could never perform under my first name, because it's the name of someone famous, and I might get sued.'

She stopped here. Carter stared at her dumbfounded. He felt chills like someone was running a fingernail up the back of his neck. Even as he began to suspect the answer, he asked the question. 'Your first name—'

'It's Sarah.'

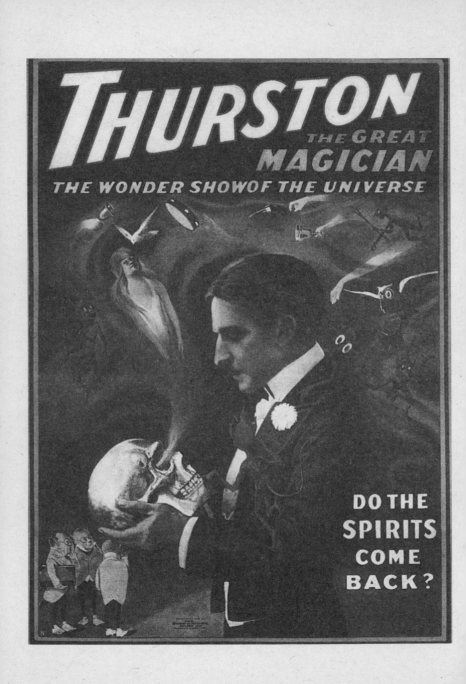

ACT TWO

An Inquiry into the Spirit World

1923

Long experience has taught me that the crux of my fortunes is whether I can radiate good will toward my audience. There is only one way to do it and that is to feel it. You can fool the eyes and minds of the audience, but you cannot fool their hearts.

— HOWARD THURSTON

When it comes to the requirements for pleasing an audience, all the knowledge and instruction and apparatus in the world is worth less than one ounce of soul.

— OTTAWA KEYES

Chapter 1

Once upon a time, Jack Griffin had been lean and hungry enough to slither down a chimney, and had in fact done so in 1901 on his first assignment, in Mochnacz Flats, Cleveland. It was a terrible area, home to the dregs of the melting pot, dangerous even in midday, and he went there alone, at midnight. His mission was to eavesdrop on a meeting held on the top floor of a boardinghouse on the corner of Broadway and Fleet.

He was a twenty-two-year-old Treasury agent, serving the first year of his Secret Service duties. So far, he had attended classes in counterfeiting and pension fraud (dull to him, deathly dull), the use of fisticuffs and armaments (far more gripping), and information gathering and interrogation. His scores in the last areas were so dizzying that Chief Wilkie had pulled him aside to ask if he would perhaps enjoy a special assignment.

Griffin had heard rumors of these assignments; they were why he had joined the Service in the first place. When Chief Wilkie's hand fell on his shoulder, and the twinkling black eyes looked up into his, Griffin stood straight, as if ready to salute an unseen flag. 'Sport,' Wilkie creaked, for all green agents were 'Sport' to him, 'I have a plan. It ain't in the budget yet. But one day, it will be. Especially if you do good.' Wilkie had a vision that only a fool or a politician, he was fond of saying, couldn't see: the Secret Service would one day protect the Commander in Chief. For years, he'd lobbied Congress, which didn't believe the threat of assassination was real. 'High-and-mighty, primrose-picking, harp-playing bastards on the hill,' Wilkie moaned, voice popping from the excitement.

There would be no pay for it, Wilkie explained to Griffin, and the duties would be hazardous and thankless. Griffin was to follow all leads, especially foreigners, and a very good lead was what brought him to Mochnacz Flats, where anarchists would gather in less than an hour.

His plan was to climb the fire escape, to sit outside the window, and listen carefully for incriminating schemes. But as he circled the building twice, he discovered there was no fire escape. He had never in his life seen a boardinghouse without a fire escape. He felt sorry for the people of Mochnacz Flats, but not sorry enough to excuse plots to overthrow the government. Then he saw it: a broken clothesline hanging off a spool anchored into the bricks. He tested it for strength. It held. Scaling two stories to the roof was as easy and quick as the ropes at the Treasury's obstacle course.

But once on the roof, he realized the lack of a fire escape meant there was no place from which he could watch the anarchists' meeting. The roof itself was almost featureless – very few places to hide in case someone came up the stairway: only the chimney, which he could crouch behind, and the hooded accessway to the stairs. Without a noise, Griffin stepped around the perimeter of the roof, looking out and over the edge. One top-floor room glowed, lights on. The windows were closed. Voices carried upward faintly, but he couldn't hear much.

How could he listen to the meeting? He leaned back against the chimney, and chewed on the ends of his mustache. He ran his tongue across the back of his teeth, and counted off the ways to infiltrate a cell: disguise; paid informants; listening from a common wall; secretion within the room. All of these required preparation he no longer had time for. He butted the back of his head against the red bricks as if the proper ploy could be dislodged like the last bean in a frying pan.

The chimney. Low, squat, wide. Wider than his shoulders? Removing his jacket, he went in, feet first. His clothes would be ruined, and there were men at the Treasury, the sons of rich men, for whom that would be no consideration. Griffin could in no way afford a new pair of trousers, and yet that very thought propelled him into the chimney. Let it be a sacrifice.

Arms over his head, he slithered, he squirmed until his whole body was stuffed snugly like a rag into bottle. He had one moment of panic, but only one, the moment he lost sight of the roof. The walls were tight around his chest, and he couldn't breathe deeply. He thought, *I wouldn't want to breathe deeply here anyway.*

The descent, once he created a system for it, required that he stretch out the points of his shoes, find a rough piece of mortar, hook into it, then, simultaneously, push down from above with his hands. Two, three inches at a time. When he was done with this assignment, he would be covered in soot, and his clothes would be tattered. He would report to Chief Wilkie like that, just to see what the old man said.

If his fellow agents asked what had happened, Griffin would dummy up. He knew how to play it. There were already a dozen stories circulating about Griffin and the first was true: when he was just four months old, he had become an orphan. He and his parents, crossing the usually tranquil Appleton Ridge in their wagon, had been caught in a freak summer storm. The wagon tumbled off the trail and into a ditch, instantly killing the horses, and pinning his parents underneath. The afternoon turned to evening, and the rains continued, bringing flash floods. When a search party arrived the next morning, they saw the wagon wheels turning as the muddy river rushed past. There was no immediate sign of survivors.

But they soon saw a sight the whole county would discuss for the next ten years: upstream, beyond the islands made by the drowned snouts and broken legs of the two geldings, baby Jack was suspended in the air, dirty and asleep, exhausted and safe.

They thought he had come to rest in the branches of a tree. It wasn't until they waded to the middle of the river to rescue him that they saw he was held in his drowned mother's hands.

Griffin, when joining the Service, said that he admired beyond all other qualities the following: sacrifice, tenacity, and the application of will against overwhelming odds. He was no stranger to performing the impossible. Tonight, he would climb down a chimney. Tomorrow, he would do something new: find counterfeit money secreted in a hive of bees, perhaps, or disarm a man with a bomb.

His eyes stung with dust and grit; he had kept them closed most of the way down, as the only sight was the increasingly distant opening to the evening sky. His hands ached where he'd cut them. To keep the pain away, he imagined bringing flowers to Lucy, Senator Hartley's daughter – caught in the act, he would confront the Senator, who might chide the lovers at first, but be so impressed with Griffin's tenacity, he would give their union his blessing, and then agree with Griffin's sudden and inspired soliloquy: 'By gum, you're right, pension fraud and counterfeiting are important, but the Service should also be allowed to protect the President.'

Griffin's feet found empty air: he was at the bottom of the chimney. The chamber belled out a little. He lowered himself into the firebox, where he could crouch and catch his breath without being seen by the room's occupants. His eyes, caked and clogged with soot, were almost useless; blinking made them worse. He willed them to fill with tears, to wash them out.

He could hear women, two of them, speaking in a foreign language, but haltingly, with long pauses, as if each found her companion terribly dull. Griffin chanced dipping his head down for a moment. Sitting in chairs with their backs to him were two stout women, hair up, in widow wear. They faced the door to the room. One of them talked glumly, showing off the backs of her hands. *Age spots*, Griffin thought. *She's complaining.*

Two informants had promised him there would be a meeting tonight. What kind of a meeting was this?

The women stopped talking. Footsteps in the hall, then three quick knocks on the door and, a heartbeat later, a fourth knock. A code! When the door opened, Griffin let his head hang down again. A group of dirty-looking men filled the hallway.

'Thank you for coming,' one woman said, in English, like it was a phrase she'd been forced to memorize. Then she added, 'Go downstairs.'

Griffin couldn't hear the response, but apparently there was one, for she continued.

'Leon said up here was maybe a bad thing. People listening here. Maybe. Something. So, in basement.' She shut the door, and addressed her companion. '*Schmucks.*'

Griffin noticed the Colt Peacemaker the other woman cradled in her lap. It was an old gun, and she looked ill trained in its use, but that was hardly a comfort. Griffin had to get to the basement, and a frightened woman with a gun was harder to predict than a trained killer.

Somewhere below him, the meeting of anarchists had begun. If he dropped to the floor, he would probably be shot before he said a word, and if not, the women undoubtedly had a way to send an alarm.

Up, he thought. Back up the chimney. He regarded the flue wearily, the way a logger who has just felled a mighty oak might size up the long mile to the sawmill.

The ascent was where Griffin, tugging with his hands, inching up, then securing footholds, pushing from there, repeating, began to tire. When the placket of his shirt gave way, the stones tore freely into the skin on his chest and back, and he no longer imagined Lucy Hartley enjoying his guitar serenades – he wondered if he would get to the roof alive. He started to hope the meeting would be over before he could find it.

His hands found the opening; he thought he could pull himself up seconds later, but his muscles were so depleted he had to stay in the chimney, arms over his head, feet braced just so, until he had the energy to push, stagger, and then actually fall out, landing on the roof hand-first.

He squawked like a bird. His wrist! He pulled his arm close to his chest, rocking back and forth.

Then he remembered there was no fire escape.

His wrist meant he couldn't use the clothesline. He walked around the edges of the roof, shuffling, really – one leg seemed to be asleep. Then, without even knowing he'd done it, he was sitting down.

The roof access stairs – they led inside the building. He lurched to the stairhouse, and threw the door open. It banged against the wall, ringing in his ears. Too loud! He half ran, half tripped down three flights of boardinghouse stairs, expecting doors to be thrown open, women to start yelling, or firing on him.

When he thudded to the street, light glowed from the basement windows, partially eclipsed by rotting wooden boards nailed over them. Griffin couldn't stay in plain view – he was shirtless, and where he wasn't blackened with soot, he was bleeding.

Then he saw the coal chute. A little reluctantly, he opened the hatch, and peered inside. It was empty, free and clear all the way to the bottom. Another cramped passageway tonight.

One last time, he cast aside all physical complaints, and began the part of his mission that would make him famous to a generation of Secret Service agents: he climbed into the coal chute. He slid on his own perspiration down to the bottom.

His luck had turned. The moment his shoes hit the door in the basement, the sound was muffled by applause coming from within. The coal chute, though chilly, was a far more comfortable spot for eavesdropping; Griffin could in fact huddle with his ear against the door and relax.

He was there for no more than twenty minutes. He heard a voice, Griffin's age, maybe, declaiming in Midwestern English. Griffin heard some ideological talk. He'd been trained in such talk, but this speech still made no sense to him. He heard the sounds of a pointer hitting a corkboard, and he imagined there were diagrams showing the masses, the bourgeoisie, the wealthy, the merchants. The usual. At some point, Griffin began to pay more attention to the twinging in his wrist. The assignment seemed like a wash.

But the lecturer changed topics. In words Griffin was never able to accurately reconstruct, he began to present a plan to assassinate President McKinley.

Later, Griffin said that made him sit up and take notice, but the truth was, he so disbelieved his own ears, he had to hear it twice before he understood what he'd heard. Luckily, the speaker was poorly organized, and given to repeating every point he made: Gaetano Bresci had murdered King Umberto of Italy in the name of anarchy, and this deeply impressed the American anarchists, who'd been too often accused of enjoying the *glamour* of anarchy, but not the hard work. So, to show the Italians and the rest of the world, it was time to kill the President of the United States. At the agreed-upon spot. Griffin heard the sound of the pointer hitting the board. What spot? Where? He brought all his powers of investigation into focus and away went the aches and pains.

'The President will be in the crowd,' the lecturer said slowly, and Griffin moved, very slightly, to hear better. The coal chute creaked.

The voice stopped.

Griffin froze.

'Was there a noise?'

Griffin heard other voices he hadn't heard before. There were five or six of them. He opened his mouth to breathe orally. He would not move. If they opened the chute, he would burst out and the door would knock the first man down. There had to be chairs in the room, and they made fine weapons.

'I heard a noise from the coal chute,' the lecturer said, and Griffin could imagine him, wild-eyed, suspicious, ready to shoot. And then something happened that made Griffin feel like he was on a ship swamped by a monstrous wave: the coal chute creaked again, though he hadn't moved a muscle. More creaking, and then the sight of the evening sky as someone threw open the street-level hatch.

At the same time someone in the basement set the lecturer's mind at ease.

'Don't worry, Leon,' Griffin heard, 'it's the coal man.'

'At this time of night?' a second man asked.

'He steals it for us,' answered a third.

'Ahh,' said Leon – Griffin's last bit of inductive reasoning that night told him the anarchist's name was Leon – 'then let us return to the matter. A man with a bandaged right hand will approach the President—'

A rumble, the sound of an approaching landslide, as the coal man made his delivery. Griffin threw his hands over his head and then a hundredweight of coal fell down the shaft, crashing into him like a steam engine, forty freight cars, and caboose.

He did not hear the rest of the plan.

When Griffin regained consciousness, the pain was indescribable. In a fetal position, he pressed against the metal door of the coal chute; all it took was a little shouldering, and he spilled onto the floor, registering the daylight outside, then landing, again, on his broken wrist.

He eventually limped away from the boardinghouse, and somehow found his way to Wilkie to make his report – in tatters, though that no longer seemed so heroic. He had learned much that night, but he had not learned everything, for he still believed he understood how the world worked. He believed in struggle, setback, reward, as if that process were as immutable a law as gravity.

Wilkie did not react as Griffin had expected. Because Griffin was the greenest of all agents, his story was not believed. Griffin swore he would prove himself, and would keep a steady eye out for a man with a bandaged right hand.

Less than a week later, at the Pan-American Exposition in Buffalo, New York, President McKinley greeted a large crowd at the Temple of Music. Griffin, guarding him, noticed the President shaking a swarthy man's left hand – his right hand was bandaged. At once, Griffin dove for the man, knocking him down, and putting the President into a direct line of sight, at point-blank range, with Leon Czolgosz, who assassinated him.

Soon after, the Secret Service received its charter to begin protecting the Commander in Chief from all enemies foreign and domestic. Griffin received a commendation, at a nearly silent ceremony that no other agents chose to attend. There are few sights from which the world turns its head faster than a golden boy who has died. The old stories about Griffin ceased; the new ones he never heard to his face.

He began a twenty-year cycle of drinking, and probation, and menial duties, still trying to understand what lesson – for he persisted in believing that life was a series of lessons – he had learned in the coal chute. Be more ambitious? Surely he'd been ambitious enough, leaping from roof to chimney to basement in an evening. Show caution? No amount of caution could have caused the coal to arrive an hour later. He had similar problems believing the lesson related to piety, intelligence, stamina, courage, fortitude, or even developing a philosophy.

And yet, as he grew older, he did not leave the Service. When asked why he stayed – and some agents did indeed ask this – his answers 'Why not?' or 'They'll have to drag me out by my blue, blue heels' were not the whole story. He was still an agent because he held out *hope*.

His notes, which usually spelled out duty rosters and expenses, also speculated about sacrifice. There were lists of assassination methods (poison, bombs, a sabotaged boat) matched with lists of fates that would befall the dedicated agent (coma, mutilation, drowning). The opportunity to die justly gave him a reason to live. No matter how hard he was hammered at, Agent Griffin still felt this small, flickering hope.

Chapter 2

WEDNESDAY AUGUST 2, 1923 – FINAL REPORT – EYES ONLY (cont'd)

16:00   Px Harding rests (headache) – aspirin prescribed by Palace Hotel MD Midvale; unsupervised mtg w/MD
17:30   Px / Mrs dinner in hotel room (room service). (Px: salmon, fried potatoes, asparagus, dinner rolls, butter, chocolate cake, water; Mrs: lamb, rice, asparagus, water.)
18:30   Px rests (headache, sour stomach)
19:15   Px departs for Curran Theatre
19:45   Unsupervised mtg btw Px, Carter (magician)
20:00   Performance by Carter (magician)
23:00   Px, Mrs return to hotel.
23:15   Px meal in hotel room (room service): chocolate cake, soda water.
23:30   Photographers from Examiner in hotel room; supervised mtg. Discusses fishing plans, etc.
23:45   All dismissed

THURSDAY AUGUST 3, 1923 – FINAL REPORT – EYES ONLY
01:02   Mrs telephones Starling: emergency physician needed
01:20   Arrival Dr J.T. Boone; Dr Ray Lyman Wilbur
01:22   Arrival Dr C.M. Cooper
01:33   President Warren Gamaliel Harding declared deceased.

HERE ENDS REPORT –

                                    (signed)
                                    Jack Griffin,
                                    Investigating Agent

When President Harding's funeral train departed from San Francisco, Griffin was left behind. His official duty was to keep the presidential suite sealed to discourage souvenir hunters. Immediately after Harding's body was removed, and the Duchess escorted to a new room, Griffin sealed the doors of room 8064 with wax, stamping them with the scales-over-key Treasury Department seal. The maids weren't even allowed to take away the sheets.

On Saturday, as Coolidge was sworn in by lamplight in Vermont and dignitaries began to arrive in Washington for the funeral, and the search for Charles Carter aboard the *Hercules* continued, other agents were removed from San Francisco. But with each roster, the same letters were posted by Griffin's name: 'MPP' – Maintain prior position.

To show he was game, Griffin took extra four-hour shifts, but still had nothing to do for most of each day. Other agents frequented the diners and speakeasies of the Tenderloin, so Griffin frequently walked instead to North Beach, where he could be anonymous as he sat in a hash house, reading the newspaper, doing the crossword puzzle, or reading and rereading the front pages for any slip of information that he didn't already know. His old boss had died; the new boss hadn't yet requested his services. Griffin read stories about President Coolidge over lunch, filling in each *o* with blue ink, and looking at photos of the new President with some compassion. If he, Griffin, were President, he wouldn't want a two-time loser guarding him either.

No one talked to him about it directly, but no one had to. He knew that in the classrooms and train cars, older agents befriended the new ones by telling them legends of the Service. He'd learned to intercept the glance of the rookie – at an organizational meeting, they saw his fringe of reddish-grey hair grown long and combed over his bald spot, his trim, underfed mustache, his two gold teeth, his bulbous nose, his awkward posture (the joke was that he walked like a man hit by a ton of coal), and they knew who he was: bad luck.

As of Saturday, the President's death was still, to him, inadequately explained. He asked if he might investigate the departure of Charles Carter – who was at that time still thought to be bound for Greece. (Griffin was still several days – and a vicious beating – away from Starling's invitation to find Carter in Oakland.) Each roster, with its 'MPP,' was a kind of rebuke. He was to keep Harding's room sealed, and that was all. It was unclear to him whether his guard duty was designed to wear his spirit out.

He played solitaire on his bed. He used a deck he'd bought intending to play poker or hearts, but so far there was only solitaire. At some point he began to use the game to bargain against doing his duties. Cracking open the deck, he told himself he could play only until he had a complete game, or had reached a certain number of points. When he exceeded that limit, he set a new one. His eyes began to hurt, and when he closed them, he saw cards flashing by, red and black, until he felt vertigo.

His room was oppressively dark. His only personal effect was a tinted photograph of his daughter, now grown, whom he hadn't spoken to in months. It was an old photo, back when she still hunted; rifle in one hand, she kneeled next to a deer she'd shot and dressed. He had it set up in a frame but during one especially bad spell of solitaire, he put the frame facedown on the table.

Late in the evening of Sunday, August fifth, Griffin was on his bed in his undershirt, suspenders hanging in loops by his sides, when he heard a clatter in the other room of his suite. He had been playing solitaire, about to start his midnight-to-4-A.M. shift at Room 8064, and he held a card face up, suddenly unable to recall what play he'd just made. Had he only imagined the noise? Perhaps a new agent had shipped in or, more likely, one of the men knew the room next door was empty, and had elected to take an unauthorized nap. Griffin threw down the cards. He wasn't going to let someone slack off.

He turned off the lights in his room, and quietly leaned against the suite door, listening for, and hearing, faint creaking sounds – someone sitting on the bed, possibly. He tested the doorknob and found that it was unlocked. Easing the door open, he breathed through his mouth, feeling his heels slide across the thick Palace carpets, and then he was in the next room, advancing slowly toward the bed in the dark. The shades down, blinds drawn, the room felt closed in, too warm and too musty, a curious pressure in the air as if it were full of stored furniture. Too late, Griffin heard a rustling by his side, and suddenly arms wrapped around him. He was being searched and he tried to cry out but strong hands found and clamped over his mouth and he was pulled again to his feet and a voice he recognized whispered, 'Shut up, Griffin.'

Another voice, louder, 'He didn't bring his gun.' It sounded like Agent Stutz.

A third voice which he also knew. Wheeler. 'Okay, lights. Get those lights on.'

One by one, the room lamps went on and Griffin saw, with a sinking heart, that the bed, armoire, and dresser had been pushed back to the walls to accommodate a group of his peers, and without even counting them, he felt sick in his craw: there had to be seven of them, plus one to appear. Eight Righteous Men.

Four of them stood in a loose line by the far side of the room. Two held him steady. Wheeler sat in a wooden-backed chair with a leather-bound book in his lap. Glancing up at Griffin, he adjusted his spectacles, smoothed back the thinning hair that he wore parted down the middle and slicked back in a style twenty years too young for him, and, picking up the book to read better by the lamplight, coughed into his hand.

'I know what you louses are up to,' Griffin said.

Wheeler read in measured tones, as if from a legal document. 'To serve your government is a privilege few men will ever know. Only the elite are chosen for the Treasury's law enforcement divisions. Only one percent of those who apply are accepted into any division of the Secret Service.'

'Get on with it,' Griffin spat. 'Where's the eighth man?'

Wheeler continued to read. 'Only the quintessence of that crop is allowed to guard the life of the President. To serve is to admit the imperfections of democracy. For with education and the love of God in his heart, every man should have only goodwill toward the President and the Service should not be needed. Yet the urge for anarchy lives in men's souls.'

'Hollis, Stutz,' Griffin barked at the men holding him, 'are you two idiots with Wheeler?'

Stutz growled, 'We're here, aren't we?'

Wheeler held up a hand for silence, and Griffin sighed. 'I know the rest of this part. I was handling this kind of thing before any of you. Bring out your eighth man.'

Wheeler said, 'For a Secret Service agent to be effective, he must show facility with deportment, foreign language, athletics, the pistol, the machine gun, observation, tactics, strategy, special investigative work, psychology, boxing and wrestling. To fail at any of these is to fail the Service, the President and the Country.'

'Therefore,' Griffin strained his arms which were now cramping; sitting in the pool of lamplight, Wheeler echoed him.

'Therefore the Service will never let a fellow Service member grow weak or infirm or shameful. If an enclave of eight righteous men says so, then an agent shall be called on to defend himself. If he fails, he does so honorably, and men will not speak ill of him and the Service need not know why he has chosen to voluntarily retire. If he succeeds, the stigma is removed in his triumph.' Wheeler closed the book and again pushed up his glasses. When he spoke now, his eyes were averted from Griffin. 'We eight feel you, Jack Griffin, have behaved in a manner unbecoming. Francis O'Brien has issued the challenge.'

The door to the bathroom opened, and O'Brien lumbered out. Six foot four, 220 pounds, O'Brien had played left tackle for Notre Dame before the War. He was stripped to the waist, showing that he carried his weight gracefully.

'Why can't you look me in the eye, O'Brien?' Griffin called. As O'Brien approached, the restraining hands fell away, and he was half released, half shoved into the room. 'You guys think Harding was my fault? How do you figure that?'

Wheeler said, 'You need to save your breath, mister.'

O'Brien began to circle Griffin, his meaty hands making small windmills in front of his chest. A slow and tenacious agent, he was known less for intelligence than ambition. Bitterly, Griffin thought that O'Brien would of course be the one to challenge him. It would be an easy win over a tired old man, but it would also be a dirty job that someone had to do, the type of scut work O'Brien had built his reputation on.

He squinted as if Griffin were an oddly shaped box he was required to lift. Griffin faced him reluctantly, arms hanging at his sides. O'Brien was six inches taller and forty pounds heavier. The only way out of this was his brain. 'Is this your idea, O'Brien?' he asked. 'You think you can hit a superior?'

'If I beat you, you won't be my superior anymore.' His right fist flew just short of Griffin's jaw and a quick left grazed his mouth, Griffin feeling a dull rap against his teeth. Griffin stepped back, allowing O'Brien to come forward, and, feet screwed into the floor, Griffin drove the heel of his hand straight up into O'Brien's chin. O'Brien's head snapped back, but that was all, and instead of falling, he used his arms to lift Griffin off the ground and squeeze him. Trying fruitlessly to move his pinned arms and grunting with exertion, Griffin could barely breathe, sweat already stinging his eyes. He thought, as the breath was crushed out of him, how O'Brien smelled like pickles and beer. The larger man enveloped him completely, Griffin's legs uselessly flailing, arms losing strength, the only thing he could move was his head, from side to side, or just a little forward and Griffin dropped his head fully as if he'd lost all of the muscles in his neck, then, with every ounce of his strength, he threw his head back, driving the back of his skull, full force, into O'Brien's nose.

It sounded like a walnut cracking. O'Brien dropped him in a heap on the floor, where Griffin scrambled into a kneeling position, gagging, holding his ribs. O'Brien slowly came toward him, one hand outstretched, the other clutching his bloody nose, and Griffin realized O'Brien was bringing his foot toward his groin. With a grace he hadn't known in years, Griffin threw himself head over heels backward; O'Brien missed him.

A kick in the nards! If he wanted to play that way, Griffin knew how to do that. With a glow on his face – freedom! – he grabbed O'Brien's slippery neck from behind and slammed him face first into the armoire, O'Brien's arms and elbows blocking most of the impact. Griffin pounded him repeatedly into the heavy oak piece with little leverage, until a three-foot length of oak brocade crashed to the floor. As O'Brien stumbled and searched for balance, Griffin grabbed the brocade plank and hefted it for weight like it was a baseball bat. Turning away from the armoire, O'Brien walked directly into the swinging oak bat that Griffin, starting from a full, roundhouse swing, brought directly into his solar plexus.

There was a great outrush of air, a mild squeak, then O'Brien tumbled to the floor, where he curled up like a cooked shrimp.

The other agents looked at each other, but none of them moved to help either fighter. Griffin, sucking in air, looked around the room as if sizing up other comers. He tossed the bat in Wheeler's general direction; Wheeler flinched.

Griffin leaned over the wheezing O'Brien. He patted his shoulder, and muttered, 'Don't worry. You'll get to be a Kentucky man one day.' Then he stood straight, catching his breath and straightening his clothing. At once he realized his tongue was slipping around his teeth unnaturally. One of his gold teeth had fallen to the floor.

Wheeler fidgeted with his book. 'You've come through, Agent Griffin.' He offered his hand to shake. Griffin looked him over, trembling as the adrenaline left his body, nausea and pain spreading in its place. He took Wheeler's hand and, instead of shaking it, turned it palm up and dropped his gold tooth into it.

Griffin spoke. 'Courtesy of Agent Bell. A Righteous Man. Twenty-two years ago. I paid for the dentist last time. This time, I'm billing you. You have a problem with that?'

Wheeler shook his head.

Griffin stared down the others, who stood, uneasy and awkward, in the suite. 'You should put the furniture back in place. I'm going to bed.'

Returning to his room, he shut the door behind him and collapsed against it. He did not move for several minutes. Then, weakly, he scooped up the half-finished game of solitaire and threw the playing cards into the Palace's carved oak wastepaper basket.

His mouth ached. He reached for his flask, but thought better of it. Instead, he called Room Service for a bucket of ice, which they left in his room while he took a short, cold shower and gathered his thoughts. Once he heard an inquiring knock at his front door, but when he barked 'Get out of here,' feet padded away on the thick hall carpeting.

He shimmered between anger and self-pity. He considered typing up his resignation and having it on the Director's desk by morning. The Pinkertons were hiring, even losers, if he didn't mind the pay cut. But that was surrendering and Griffin wasn't about to surrender.

Even if he'd survived just now, he knew he was clear in name only. Nothing about his reputation had really changed. He couldn't redeem himself through the usual channels. With his distance from President Coolidge, he couldn't take a bullet or a bomb or knock poison out of his hands.

Jack Griffin had been blamed for too much in his life. He held ice to his gums, and when it came away bloody, he began leafing through his notes and telegrams about Harding's Voyage of Understanding.

Chapter 3

The next morning, they broke the seal on Harding's room at the Palace. Griffin doubted it was a coincidence that as soon as they realized they couldn't get rid of him that easily, it was suddenly time to turn the last administration over to posterity. Told to catalogue all of the late President's belongings, he responded with a seven-page memo that described, down to the carpet lint, the condition and disposition of every item as it was examined and packed for storage. He stood in Wheeler's office on the second floor of the Mint while Wheeler flipped through documentation Griffin had prepared.

Wheeler murmured, '. . . five packs playing cards, all Bicycle decks, two decks unwrapped; one box cigars, three cigars missing; one Krazy Kat comic strip from 7/18/23, from *San Francisco Examiner*, glued to note on W. R. Hearst letterhead. Note reads: "Thought you'd get a chuckle over that meany Ignatz – Bill."'

Griffin noted how Wheeler read now. It was nothing like the way he'd read the Eight Righteous Men charges. Right now, in his office, Griffin sensed no respect from Wheeler, no forgiveness – just fear.

The list went on. The remains of dinner and the chocolate cake Harding had eaten for dessert, all of which tested out clean. Harding's suits of clothing, shoes, programs, and souvenirs from the Voyage of Understanding, the text of his speeches, newspaper and magazine clippings about himself. Harding had died while the Duchess was reading aloud a *Saturday Evening Post* article about the charitable work Harding had done. His last words had been, 'Excellent. A happy description. May I have a glass of water?'

There were bottles of homeopathic medicine to fight infection, tongue depressors Griffin had found in the trash can, and two oxygen tanks that had been used in the futile attempt to revive Harding. There was even the final glass of water the Duchess had brought him.

Wheeler cleared his throat, which Griffin had long ago noted was his way of preparing to tell a joke. 'Your memo doesn't say whether the glass is half empty or half full.'

'Look at the appendix, sir.'

'Oh.' Halfheartedly, Wheeler flipped a few pages and read aloud. 'Glass was completely empty, but was apparently, based on trace mineral residue, approximately one-fourth full of water upon Harding's death.'

'And the lab says it was just normal San Francisco tap water.'

'Thank you, Agent Griffin.' Wheeler considered the papers in front of him, and then, with great effort, for the first time, looked at Griffin carefully.

'How's the tooth, Jack?'

'Fine. Sir. You should be getting the bill soon.'

His embarrassed attempt at human contact now over, Wheeler returned to the memo. Its last page, marked Eyes Only, described several items Griffin had tucked away, separately. He'd found them in the false bottom of Harding's toilet case: two letters from Nan Britton, asking for money for support of their child; notes from women in Chicago, Helena, and Seattle suggesting rendezvous; three tins of prophylactics.

Wheeler sighed. 'Where is this separate package?'

Griffin placed it on his desk. Wheeler peered in, and pulled out one of the tins of Ramses. Following the King Tut craze, it was decorated with Egyptian hieroglyphs.

'All three tins were unused, sir. Their conditions suggest President Harding bought them over a year ago. As I note in my memo, I concluded that they don't indicate new mistresses.'

'Very good.' Wheeler put the package under his desk. 'I understand the crew at the White House found a few more of these in the Oval Office. None of them were used. I guess he just liked having them around.'

Griffin made no response.

'This is a commendable job, Agent Griffin. We have another assignment for you. More of a top priority.'

'For President Coolidge, sir?'

'Indirectly, indirectly,' which was a way of saying no. 'We need a background check on Charles Carter, the magician that Harding met on the night of his death.'

'Will I be trying to locate him, sir?'

'On that damned boat? No. Colonel Starling thinks Carter might actually be hiding out in one of the other local properties he owns. He's narrowing down the possibilities.'

Griffin bit down on his disappointment. 'The President died of natural causes, sir.'

'Yes.'

'So Charles Carter is not considered a suspect?'

'No. But since he's fled, he's considered a security risk. He's probably just a publicity nut, but we need to know, for our own peace of mind, that he's clean.'

Wheeler said more, but Griffin only half listened, bowing out when Wheeler dismissed him.

The assignment, as he thought about it, was probably important, but the reasons given struck him as bogus. In short, he smelled a rat. Which was okay, because Griffin had begun to like the smell of rats.

In the hallway, Griffin looked at his notes, where he read the name that was supposed to unravel Carter's past: Olive White, of the San Francisco Public Library newspaper morgue. Another job for him that required sitting in a room and flipping papers. He found a pay phone and called her number. A woman, friendly to the point of near frenzy, told him the library was officially closed for renovations, but as long as he didn't mind a little dust and noise, he could literally have the library to himself beginning at, say, two o'clock? He told her that would be fine.

He found an Automat on Geary, away from the crowds, and bought a newspaper that was filled with terrible things. An actress he'd never heard of had taken dope and driven her car into a tree. Sometimes he was amazed there were any actresses left. And there was a frightening article at the bottom of the front page that Griffin read three times: a nanny in Boston had just put her young charges to bed when the telephone rang, and a spectral voice asked her if she'd checked the children. She received the same call three times in total, 'Have you checked the children?' and then, terrified, she called the police, who told her the phantom caller was in her very household! Agents of the law kicked in the door in the nick of time: a huge man was about to chop the babies up with an ax.

Everyone was safe now, and the parents were giving the nanny a week of paid vacation. Griffin shook his head. Just when he'd thought he'd heard everything, something new and terrible came along to raise the hairs on the back of his neck.

Right below that article was another: federal narcotics agents in Chicago had confessed to stealing thousands of pounds of cocaine during raids, and selling it back to dope fiends on the streets. Griffin wasn't surprised and he felt sick at his own cynicism.

President Harding had died, somehow. Griffin had heard the following causes: heart attack, bad fish, brain apoplexy, even, and this had been said in surprisingly jovial whispers, that Mrs Harding, tired of Nan Britton and all the others, had poisoned him. According to Griffin's notes, Harding had muttered in the last weeks of his life about a scandal that would tear the country apart. But Griffin had heard of so many scandals in the past year: fake oil leases; border agents running guns to Abd-el-Krim in exchange for gin; the Reds' plans to infiltrate the American Legion; the Jews and their banking conspiracy; senators taking kickbacks from bootleggers; moneys diverted from the post office and the veterans' fund. Which of them was Harding talking about? In Washington, scandals had always been like mosquito bites – sometimes you had a couple, sometimes dozens. But they had never been fatal.

The rules were changing. Griffin watched the men and women ambling past the Automat, and he wondered what was happening to the world. O'Brien trying to kick him where it counted. Some fiend threatening children with an ax. And murdering the President? Maybe drawing a line now was just an invitation to cross it.

It was close to two o'clock, and he was suddenly aware of the onions in the meat loaf he'd eaten. He had in his breast pocket a tin of German peppermints, 'PEZ – for the relief of toothache, tobacco breath, and fatigue,' and as he left the Automat, he sucked on one, concerned whether it was the right thing to do. PEZ had shipped a crate of peppermints to every military camp and Secret Service office, *gratis*, explaining it in an accompanying pamphlet as 'our way to new friend making.' The company added that 'if soldiers and police put our product to use, the rest of America will show for us much respect.' So there were boxes of PEZ everywhere, but they made Griffin, who knew nothing was free, uneasy. If Wilson had still been

President, he would have ordered the candy shipped back to Germany. Everything, when you scratched the surface, could end up being a conspiracy, maybe malicious, maybe just to turn a profit.

At the library door, he showed his credentials to the guard, who gave him a hard hat and pointed him to the stairs. The newspaper morgue was on the fourth floor. Its swinging oak doors had been taken off their hinges, and Griffin had to pass under scaffolding underlit by arc lamps to enter. The room was huge and drafty, mostly in darkness, with sunlight hitting the drop cloths on the worn concrete floor. Because the city was installing skylights, large panels of the roof were missing; looking up, Griffin could see, among exposed wiring and cracked moldings, blue sky. It was lunchtime, the workers were gone, and for a moment, Griffin thought he was completely alone.

'Mr Griffin?' An energetic voice called him from a gloomy spot in the corner of the room. 'Is that you?'

'Mrs White?' As his eyes adjusted, Griffin could see a woman behind an oak table piled high with newspapers, among vague and bulky fixtures covered with protective sheeting. She was a tall woman, and as she walked quickly around her table, Griffin noted the contrast of her porch dress and her galoshes.

'It's Miss,' she said, and because her hand was extended, Griffin shook it. 'I'm so happy to help you, Agent Griffin.' Her eyes were bright and welcoming. 'What kind of case are you working on? Or shouldn't I ask? Would you like a drink of water?'

'I'm just doing a background check, that's all, ma'am.'

'Miss.' Miss White hurried away, gesturing that Griffin should follow. 'Isn't this construction dreadful?' As she talked, her hands moved like excitable pets. 'They were supposed to be done six months ago and we're lucky it hasn't rained lately, though the weatherman says it might anytime, and that would spoil all those nice August weddings coming up. You should see the announcements. Don't you hate it when they say "bridges and grooms" by accident? It always makes me laugh.' And she laughed, gay and clipped. 'So. Agent Griffin. You being a Secret Service agent, you must be very observant. What have you observed about *me*?' She looked over her shoulder, beaming at him. 'Are you wondering about my galoshes?'

Before Griffin could answer, Miss White explained that she didn't want to get her good shoes dirty during the renovations. He'd guessed that, but didn't get a chance to say it: she had more to tell him about what an honor it was for her to serve the Service, as it were, and how her father had fought the Spanish. And how she had already noticed so many things about Griffin, no wedding ring, but surely such a handsome man had once had a wife, but it wasn't her business to ask, now was it? The walk to the clipping file was just a matter of yards, but by the time Miss White had set Griffin up at a study carrel, he felt dizzy. He was better at handling criminals than a helpful citizen.

'Thank you for your help, Miss White.' Griffin nodded at her civilly, but she didn't move.

'I'll leave you alone, but I do have one little question.' Her eyes were on the ceiling, then on him. 'Agent Griffin, do you carry a gun?'

'Yes, Miss White, I do.'

Her face erupted into a terrific smile. Then she turned on the heel of one galosh, and strode away, humming a tune Griffin didn't recognize. Finally alone, Griffin rubbed the bridge of his nose, clearing his mind. On the study table was a large bound journal labeled 'Carter, Charles, 1888–' Griffin adjusted his hard hat. The first clipping, wheat pasted onto stiff brown paper, was from the September 12, 1912 *Examiner*:

CARTER THE GENIUS CAPTIVATES, PROMISES TO ENTERTAIN, DELIGHT

In an exclusive interview with the *Examiner*, favorite son Charles Carter, the magician who at age twenty-three has already been seen by tens of thousands in the four corners of the globe, reveals that there are still places that the ever-inquisitive microscopes and theodolites of scientists have neither examined nor explained. Carter tells his wide-eyed audience of a moment in Ceylon where his life itself was imperiled. 'I had just performed my act for the sultan, and in exchange for my method of levitation, his vizier taught me the secret of running a knife through my body without causing me harm. I'm of course sworn to secrecy on the topic, but it involves hypnotism. One of the sultan's underlings, a rascal who'd been after the secret himself for years, came after me with a loaded pistol. If it weren't for my friend Baby and the quick thinking of my assistant, Annabelle, I wouldn't be here today.' In fact, 'The Sultan and the Sorcerer,' the final act of his current show, now playing for a two-week run at the Majestic, re-creates this incident for the benefit of—

Griffin frowned as he scanned the rest of the article. He wrote 'Ceylon. Hypnotism. Confederates: Annabelle.' The next article was from January 14, 1913.

LAST PERFORMANCE OF SPECTACULAR ILLUSION
CARTER RETREATS TO WIZARD'S DEN

Charles Carter has announced that near the town of Grindu, in the Carpathian Mountains, the mage from whom he learned all of his occult arts lies near death. Carter must travel 8,000 miles to his side, bringing the plans for 'The Sultan and the Sorcerer,' the spectacular illusion that ends his program, so that the great master may be burned with them. 'Thus the show will never be performed again, and I positively must leave next Thursday.'

The next clipping, just a squib one sentence long, was dated a week later, 'Carter the Mysterious magic show at Fox is extended three more weeks.' Griffin, wondering why so many people paid money to be fooled, wrote 'Grindu. Carpathian Mountains.' Something about that struck him as suspicious.

The following item was concrete enough: an application to Sacramento to start a charitable organization for retired performing animals. There was a folder of supporting documentation: a deed, transatlantic cables, and some documents written in spaghetti script with bizarre wax seals. Where was this organization, anyway?

In the folder was a letter written on the stationery of the Raffles Hotel in Singapore.

10/1/13

My Dear James:

We are off to Japan next (I have an idea for a Japanese cannon illusion, by the way). I know you wanted me to bring you something ornate from Siam. How about a Rococo kind of story? It sounds like something from a pitch book, but it's true, I swear!

Another hand – though it was bold, Griffin recognized it as feminine – added, 'And I'm here to make sure he tells it right.'

With various asides, the letter described how Carter had performed 'The Sultan and the Sorcerer' for two nights at the Chetachuk Showcase in Bangkok. Afterward, Rama VI, Vajiravudh, the King of Siam, had invited him and Annabelle for an informal performance at his weekend palace and there, at the banquet table, Carter had performed the 'Royal Mystery,' in the style of Robert-Houdin. Carter wrote, 'At a French royal command performance, Robert-Houdin vanished a bundle of handkerchiefs, giving his King, Louis the Something or Other, three choices of where they should reappear. The first problem for me was that the King of Siam doesn't wear a handkerchief.'

Annabelle added, 'No, the first problem for Charlie is that they don't allow women at the banquet table, so while he was eating his franks and beans with royalty, they exiled me with the rest of the dames, their loss.'

Carter reported that he'd borrowed the wristwatch, a Hamilton, of which the King was most proud. He'd put it inside a smoked glass jar, had the King tap it for extra magical power, and revealed it had vanished. 'Applause, applause, along with glaring from Rama VI, who understandably felt I'd helped myself to his watch.' Carter passed out slips of paper and had everyone at the table write places, anywhere in the country, they wanted the watch to reappear. He shuffled them, and had the King choose three.

The King, whom Carter liked, for he was a man who truly enjoyed magic, moved slowly. He tried to behave in a canny manner as he read the first suggestion: under his chair ('Too easy for you, I think!'); then the second, the end of the fruit seller's boat at the Proha market-place. Finally, after fixing Carter with an intelligent eye for the longest time, the King chose the third location, under the reclining Buddha in the garden about a half mile away. He sent his men to dig.

While a string quartet played Bach, and pastries were served, the King and Carter talked pleasantly, the King looking at his guest for signs of stress or concern ('but did I show them? Well, yes I did').

Finally, the men returned with a box so heavy it took two of them to lift it. It was sealed by an impressive-looking wax stamp. Prying it open, they found not only the watch, but an ancient note written in archaic Thai script. It was quite crabby, but it generally approved of the methods used by the foreigner Charles Carter.

The King was so pleased, he gave Carter an island. It was called Koh Pheung Thawng, in the Andaman Sea, at the end of an archipelago known best for its rocky cliffs and leeward beaches.

Carter wrote James that he had no reason to be suspicious of the honor; however, a day later, he was presented with a tax bill, and learned that Thurston had already given up and leased *his* island back to the King.

But the idea of that prickles at me, so while I visit Japan I want to turn you loose in the realm of international property law. I have an idea about a charitable organization . . .

The rest of the file set up the paperwork for the Home for Retired Performing Animals. Griffin wrote the co-ordinates of the island down on his notepad. He wrote 'Annabelle, again' next to that.

In May 1914, there were several small articles from the *Call* and the *Examiner*.

CARTER THE MYSTERIOUS RETURNS
FROM JAPAN SECLUSION

World traveling sorcerer supreme Charles Carter, yclept Carter the Mysterious, has made a startling discovery that makes the news from Europe seem mild indeed. The Japanese have a horrifying secret weapon: a means of propelling their infantry through solid matter. It is apparently how they achieved victory over both China and Russia.

Griffin frowned. He'd attended the Naval Weapons Treaty negotiations with Japan and he hadn't heard anything about a secret weapon. He kept reading.

Carter promises that in his show a person is put into a special armament, a modified cannon, and is launched through a brick wall, landing in a net on the other side of the stage. 'I have leased this equipment from the Japanese military for a brief time, and I'm very concerned about safety. In showing me its use, the Japanese misadjusted the controls, and they accidentally killed three of their own men!'

Griffin, overcome by revulsion for the Japanese, wrote 'secret Japanese weapon,' but even as the last word was drying on the page, he was suddenly unsure. Sending someone through a brick wall? That sounded ridiculous. But then again, so did radio waves. The Black Chamber had decoded all of Japan's secret documents, and something this big couldn't have escaped notice. And what had happened to Carter's voyage to the Carpathian Mountains?

He turned the page, expecting to see reviews of the show, perhaps another indication that the run had been extended, sure proof that this limited lease of military equipment – and why would the Japanese let any foreigner use it? – was just a ruse.

But the next clipping, in sequence, was from October 1917, three years later. Griffin checked: there was the May 1914 clipping, then, two blank pages later, the 1917 clipping. Facing the latter clipping was a rectangular piece of paper, light blue, heavy stock, embossed with the library seal, and stamped with the words 'For other articles, consult special collections.' He considered asking Miss White about the special collections. The *excited* Miss White. He concluded he would rather read the rest of this volume first.

The 1917 clipping was a review of a benefit at the Hippodrome in New York for the families of the men of the *Antilles*, which had been torpedoed by a German U-boat. Griffin scanned the article three times with growing puzzlement.

> . . . the largest gathering of professional magicians ever to occur. When the cause is just, and the organizer is Harry Houdini, no one dares be a spoilsport. Most notable, Kellar, King of all American magicians, was lured from retirement for the first time since 1908, and after his show, women dashed onstage to shower the old magician with baskets of red and yellow chrysanthemums. The 125-piece Hippodrome orchestra played Auld Lang Syne as 6000 spectators sang along and Kellar was carried offstage in a sedan chair by the greatest magicians currently performing: Houdini, Thurston, Jansen, Nicola, Raymond and Goldin.

Near the bottom was this paragraph:

> Also, Charles Carter, a San Francisco magician, came out of the
> retirement enforced by an incident. But there were no hard feel-
> ings among these men of magic and he was welcomed with open
> arms . . .

Retirement? What incident? Griffin flipped through the remainder
of the book, and found nothing to explain what had happened
between 1914 and 1917.

The articles after the Hippodrome benefit were all dry: reviews
of shows, promises of spectaculars that sounded interchangeable.
There were no mentions of Annabelle.

He brought the blue 'special collections' card to Miss White, who
was sitting at her table and reading under a small, bright desk lamp.

'Oh, you startled me,' she said, hands jumping to her chest.

'I'm sorry, Miss—'

'I was just reading a dreadful article about a nanny. A man kept
calling her to ask if she'd checked the children.'

'Yeah, I read that.'

Miss White accepted the blue Special Collections card from
Griffin. 'You know, I believe the very same thing was reported last
year, only it was in Atlanta, Georgia.' She put her hand to her
mouth. 'I wonder if it's the same man.'

Griffin shrugged. 'It's a pretty unusual m.o.'

'*Modus operandi*.' Miss White closed her eyes. 'Mr Griffin, it's
such a pleasure to hear you speak.'

Griffin quickly said, 'Can you tell me what's in the special collections?'

She stood upright, like she'd been called to the head of the class,
explaining that when recording the lives of prominent San Francisco
families, the library used discretion. 'There are so many things in
the paper that you don't want just anyone to come gawk at. Now
let's see,' she said. '1914.' As she peeled back a blanket that was
covering a locked file cabinet, she repeated the date to herself. 'I've
seen Carter a dozen times. He's such a wonderful man. I wonder
if I saw him in 1914.'

'He was exhibiting some kind of cannon from Japan.'

She sighed. 'The Phantom War Gun.'

'Yeah, I guess that's it.'

Miss White set her mouth in a silent O, and she began searching through her folders. She was so quiet that Griffin wondered what was wrong.

'Does that mean something to you?'

'Well, yes.' And she looked at Griffin with her bright eyes, eyes suddenly shiny with welled-up tears. 'Such a tragedy. Poor Mr Carter.'

Chapter 4

'It doesn't work yet,' sighed Ledocq.

'I'm certain that it does.' Carter watched the stage, where eight men were busy polishing brass hinges, touching up props with paint, and arranging mirrors with scientific precision. The cannon, such as it was, lay in a half dozen pieces.

'Carter. Postpone. Just for a week.'

'No,' Carter said with a pleasant smile.

'When you get so sure of yourself, I could kill you.' Ledocq squinted at his pocket watch. He had recently reached the age where people began to describe him as vigorous. Carter had met him in England a year before, spiriting him away from quiet days at Maskelyne & Devant and promising him a second childhood. 'Charlie, the sun goes down in an hour. I don't know how much longer I can work on it.'

'It'll be fine. Trust me.'

'I trust you, I just don't trust that *furshlugginer* hunk of junk over there.' He scratched his nose, leaving behind a grey smear of grease.

The show was divided into three acts: First was 'The Artist's Model,' in which Carter painted a portrait of a beautiful woman that came to life and fought off thieves who clubbed Carter over the head. After an interlude where she – for of course, she was Annabelle – played piano and the stage was struck, Carter launched into the second act, 'Cornucopia,' which he called a salute to American bounty. He poured from an inexhaustible blue glass bottle any drink requested by the audience – beer, Coca-Cola, water, apple juice – and then, from an empty teak cube three feet to a side, suspended in the middle of the stage and lavishly painted with fleurs-de-lis, he produced flowers, balloons, doves, and a girl dressed in red, white, and blue, holding sparklers. The third act was 'The Phantom War Gun,' which did not work, and the show would start in two hours.

Carter might have considered substituting another illusion tonight, even though he'd advertised and sold out the house based on this one. There was, however, a complication: both the Great Leon, in Philadelphia, and P. T. Selbit, in London, had their own versions of the same effect, and would have them onstage within the week. Each magician was friendly enough with the other to confirm he'd come up with his idea independently, but each was also competitive enough to want his illusion unveiled first.

All week, Ledocq had argued that Carter could wait: Leon fired a woman through a *steel* wall, and Selbit had a woman *walk* through a brick wall. Their methods were completely different from the Phantom War Gun. But Carter knew the public's mind: the first magician to pass a girl through a wall would be the winner. Carter had developed a taste for winning.

'What's wrong with it now?' Carter asked.

'What isn't wrong with it?' They approached the equipment, which Carter had designed with a few sketches on a tablecloth, and which Ledocq had spent eight months forcing to conform to the laws of physics. The gimmick, when finished, had mechanics that were ingenious but not quite ingenious enough.

If it ever worked, it would follow Carter's description in his patent application: 'A committee is called onstage to inspect the brick wall. They sign two sheets of paper, 30"×30", and one is pasted to each side of the wall. The woman is lowered into the cannon, which is brought within a foot of the wall. There is an explosive concussion, and the woman is hurled out of the cannon. She passes through the wall. She lands in a safety net on the other side of the wall. The committee is called to examine the wall again. It is solid. Both of their sheets of paper, however, have been ripped by the force of the human cannonball.'

All week, gunny sacks sixty-four inches long, filled with 122 pounds of sand, had been lowered into the gun and shot through the wall and into the net. Based on the experiments, the angle of the cannon's mouth had been altered five degrees, and the net raised six feet, and the eight-pound snap-release claws that held the net to its frame had been replaced with eighteen-pounders, for stability and strength. And all week, Toots Becker, American high-diving champion, had been waiting in her hotel room for her turn in the cannon. Sarah Annabelle Carter had never been interested in this part of the show. Being the artist's model was sweet, beating the tar out of thieves was great fun, but she would under no circumstances come out of the Cornucopia box or be fired out of a cannon.

At Carter's request, stagehands began to assemble the cannon for a dry run. Carter asked Ledocq, 'Is it a matter of safety?'

'Vibration.'

Carter clapped his hands three times; the entire theatre fell silent. 'Thank you. We'll be testing the cannon in two minutes.' At once, his workers set their tasks aside and took places in the house: some in the front row, some at the edges of the farthest rows.

As Carter ran through his patter, verbatim but without inflection, the sack of sand was lowered into the cannon, and a 'committee' of his men signed sheets of paper, which were pasted on either side of the wall. The actual committee would be civilians; for the show tonight, Carter had invited four professors of engineering from the University of California to examine the wall. As his own men retired to their positions, Carter spied his wife standing in the wings. She wore a new hat, a shopping bag in each hand. When Carter made eye contact with her, she crossed her eyes and stuck out her tongue; he continued his patter as if nothing had happened.

A dummy instrument panel glowed beside the cannon, and a single band of electric current trembled between two tall filaments. 'Because of the great forces about to be unleashed, I advise you men to stand back. On the count of three – no, hold!' Carter stopped his patter. He turned to Ledocq. 'Can we station two committee members upstage? That way they can see we aren't rolling the wall toward the backdrop.'

Ledocq agreed it was a good idea. Carter had them repositioned, and started his patter from the top. 'On the count of three, this brave woman will be fired through the wall.' The barrel of the cannon was lowered, and, as the assembly wheeled forward so that the mouth of the cannon was just a foot from the wall, Carter was distressed to see tremendous shudders coming from the wall itself. 'Hold!' He approached the footlights, and, knowing the answer, he called, 'How does that look?'

'It's . . . it's not too bad,' said a young stagehand in the middle of the house. Carter made a mental note never to ask him that question again.

'It wouldn't fool a four-year-old,' said Ledocq. 'A brick wall. A solid brick wall, moving. "Momma, why is the solid brick wall moving?" "I don't know, sweetie, but I'm sure it's not because there's a motor inside."'

After a moment of silence, Carter sighed, '*Oy vey.*'

Pressing his palm to his forehead, he continued, 'Fine. Gentlemen, back the cannon up to position one. Ledocq, will anything keep the wall from moving?'

'Sure. If you and I stood there and held it in place, it wouldn't move. But other than that, I need a week to get more juice out of a smaller motor or make the wall a little bigger.'

Carter brought out a half dollar and started walking it across the back of his fingers. Ledocq had seen Carter think before; he knew not to say anything. A moment later, there were two quarters flipping end over end, little silver tumblers, crossing Carter's hand. Then they froze. 'I am an *idiot*,' Carter hissed. 'The answer is right in front of us. We'll make the marks do our work for us. The *committee* holds it in place.'

Ledocq nodded for three seconds. 'You're worth every penny I pay you, Charlie.'

'Places!' It would take two minutes to take the sack out of the cannon and reload it. Carter walked toward his wife, speaking aloud, 'To prove to yourselves that there is no optical illusion involved, sirs, I ask that you stand on all sides of the wall, holding it in place, et cetera.'

'Et cetera,' Annabelle said.

'That would take up less time, wouldn't it?' Carter made a generous wave to the theatre. 'Ladies and Gentlemen – et cetera. Good night.'

'So, who's your wife?' Annabelle asked, pushing down the brim of her hat so it nearly obscured her eyes.

Carter put his hand to his chin. 'The most beautiful—'

'Uh-uh. Nope.'

'The strongest, fastest, smartest . . .'

But Annabelle was shaking her head, her hat's absurdly huge feather wiggling in his face, for each of these guesses. Finally, she said, as if it were obvious, 'The most resourceful woman you ever met.'

'How was I supposed to guess that?'

'Because I found out you got company tonight. Kellar.'

'No! He hasn't set foot out of Los Angeles for years.'

'He heard something about some nut that impressed him.' Annabelle took off her hat and handed it to Carter. 'Capwell's,' she said. 'I figure I deserved something with a giant, foolish feather.'

Carter tickled his palm with the feather. He didn't know whether to be happy or frightened. Kellar, a very cordial man, had made Thurston his successor, and since then had shown little interest in magic. Was the Phantom War Gun that good an illusion? 'Are you going to tell me how you found out?'

Annabelle took her hat back. 'You are so lucky you know me it's frightening.'

There was a whistle from across the stage. Ledocq, pointing at his watch.

'My man has to get to temple. Can you stay?'

'Hey,' Annabelle said quietly. She brought her lips to Carter's ear. 'What if you drop that chump Toots Becker for tonight? She's a tart if you ask me.'

'Are you proposing that I fire a sack of sand through a brick wall?'

'No, I'll go for a ride.' She took two steps onto the stage and jumped up, pawing for the safety net. 'But only once. Kellar's here. It looks fun and I figure I wouldn't mind doing it one time before I retire from this racket.'

'Are you sure?'

'Only if it's safe.'

'Of course it's safe.' Carter ushered her two steps back, to the wings.

'A lot of men would tell their wives that.'

'Yes, I wouldn't trust me if I were you.' Carter whistled. 'Ledocq! We need to change the bag.'

Annabelle was sixty-nine inches tall, and proportionately heavier than Toots Becker. There wasn't quite time to make up a new bag, but weight was a more important variable than height, so another twenty-five pounds of ballast was added as Carter consulted with the script girl for revisions to the committee business.

'Places!' Carter was thinking about Harry Kellar, the magician's magician. Houdini was better known to the outside world, but Kellar! Before he retired, all Kellar had going for him was fifty years of performing a seemingly endless array of tricks with either the simplest or most complex equipment, and an unmatched understanding of the audience's need to be mystified.

'Ladies and Gentlemen, five men died in bringing this terrifying weapon to the United States for our edification.' The committee was inspecting the wall and finding it solid. Then they were signing the sheets of paper which Carter's aides were pasting to the wall. 'This remarkable young lady will follow a trajectory into history.' As the bag was lowered into the cannon, Carter considered the word *trajectory*. He was twenty-five years old, the youngest magician ever to tour the world with an evening-length show. But this illusion, the Phantom War Gun, when he used it tonight, could – *could* – catapult him into a new category entirely, one of the top three or four magicians in the world. At age twenty-five. 'Hold!' he cried. Everyone onstage froze. 'Positions! Is everyone exactly where they should be?' From all around, behind him, below him, in the seats of the house, calls of 'clear!' from people he could or couldn't see. The committee was holding the wall. The sack of sand was in the cannon. The cannon was aimed at the wall. 'Committee – could you feel the wall vibrating?'

A chorus of *nos* in response. And then a final no from Ledocq, who had been drifting around the stage, looking for angles from which some audience member might be disappointed; at that moment, he'd been touching the wall. 'It just feels like shaking from the cannon rolling forward.'

Carter checked his watch, then looked to the wings, where Annabelle was watching and smoking. The beauty of this illusion was that the person set into flight was passive, absolutely safe, needing only a child's gymnastic skills to complete it unharmed. But there was the matter of size and weight – what if she missed the net entirely? Best to use the sack now, test carefully.

'Ready! Set!' He cleared his throat. 'Action!' Then: 'With a simple twist of these dials,' he declared, 'this woman is reduced to a stream of electrons, neutrons, protons, and is beamed like X rays through solid matter. More power! More power!' Backstage, stagehands shook pieces of tin, and a violin bow was drawn across a saw to give the eerie sound of scientific equipment overloading. 'Three!' The lights came down to bright spots on the cannon, the wall, the net. 'Two!' In the orchestra, a snare drum rattled furiously. 'One! Let the infernal device roar!'

A magnesium flare ignited, simulating a fuse, and, offstage, a shotgun blank round was fired simultaneously with the sack of sand being launched, thrown by the tension of retracting shock cords out of the mouth of the cannon, accelerating instantly to a velocity of 140 feet per second, tearing through the first sheet of paper, passing through the space now opened in the wall, then tearing through the second sheet of paper, landing almost soundlessly in the canvas netting, which gave in its frame to a surprising extent, bowing toward the floorboards. It worked, Carter thought, and What will Kellar think? and Will it work twice? all in the space of time it took for the force of the falling sack to rip one of the six support braces from the net's frame. The metal brace – fist-shaped, eighteen pounds of steel – swung like a pendulum and on the upswing made an audible crack as it hit Annabelle squarely in the forehead.

Her head snapped back; her arms flew up and she fell backward to the stage.

'Annabelle!' For one second, Carter wasn't quite worried except for the dumb wonder of how she could go onstage tonight. And then, a feeling like he'd never known: like the earth in motion under his heels, like he wasn't walking but tripping. 'No!' He ran to her, sickened and skidding, the stage was miles wide, and he fell by her side. Her skirts were twisted, arms and legs twisted. The broken brim of her hat was smashed under her head. There was no blood. Her eyes were closed. He hoped that the impact hadn't been as bad as it looked, he hoped it was a trick, but when he touched her cheek he felt nauseous. He could feel her blood rushing up from primal, buried places, blood flooding places it wasn't supposed to go, filling in pools and pressing up under her skin. It was swelling, darkening. He reached out, about to cradle her head. But if her neck were broken, was that the right thing to do? He was helpless.

He was yelling 'No!' and realized he'd been yelling it repeatedly. Then, because he didn't know what to do, he yelled, 'Help!'

The shout was feeble. Darkness. Blurs. He was on his knees, asking again and again, with diminishing voice, for help. Ledocq was by his side, yelling for people to call a doctor at once. People moved around. They were above him, around him, he wasn't sure where. Misery welled up in the pit of his throat – he could feel it taking him over as he hunched down, whispering into her ear, 'I'm sorry. I'm sorry.'

There were a half dozen articles about that terrible night. Griffin read them all, then got up from his chair and walked a full circuit of the empty reference room, sat back down and read them again. He wrote 'June 1914, Annabelle (wife) dies.' It was hard to read between the lines, to suss out what had actually happened. Drumming his fingers on the hard hat that rested on the table before him, he sent his pen to the word *dies* and hesitated for several seconds before adding, just below it, 'murdered?' and then he turned the page.

An insurance adjuster's report. He began to read it.

Chapter 5

In 1915, the world was treated to a sense of acceleration. Spools of electric, telegraph, and telephone wire were uncoiling faster than the eye could follow, and the chirps, dots, dashes, and shouted conversations were all inescapably about the War. Land, air, and ocean speed records were broken weekly and the most popular conjurer, suddenly, was Horace Goldin, who performed a new trick every minute he was onstage. When Carter returned to stage a scant two months after Sarah Annabelle's funeral, he latched on to Goldin as an inspiration.

His family and Ledocq all asked him if he should be performing again so soon, and Carter said, 'Yes.' Rather, his lungs made the intake of air, his larynx and vocal cords made the word on his exhalation. Meanwhile, his astral body floated in the clouds over-head, sending back occasional faint whispers of pain along the silver cord connected to his earthly body, which moved, and smiled, and conjured.

In May 1915, he and his entourage steamed from nine weeks of performances in Sydney, Australia, to a set of shows scheduled in Tokyo. In the Molucca Sea, the ship changed course to answer a distress call from a ship that turned out to be a perfectly functional decoy vessel. The crew was overpowered quickly, and the steamer boarded by the Indonesian pirate Tulang. Unlike his mother, Madame Darah, Tulang stayed clear of political intrigue and hostage taking. His only interest was money.

After stripping the passengers and crew of their valuables, Tulang's men began hauling cargo out of the hold. Initially excited by the tremendous weight and sturdy crating of some of the storage boxes – the pirates had learned that lately steamers carried weaponry or ammunition shown on the manifest as, for instance, farming equipment – they unloaded onto the deck all of the heavy devices and props used in Carter's act. Prying open the boxes, they were disappointed to find that beyond some fine costumes they might give to their wives, there was little they could sell on the black market.

Carter, who was held on the forecastle at gunpoint, separate from everyone else, imagined his astral self suspended over the proceedings like a kite. It was blazingly hot, yet he felt dry and cool as he looked down at the deck from a great height. Here, in the shadow of the bridge, were some pirates going through his wardrobe, there, outside the mess, were other pirates pointing their rifles at the sailors and the members of his troupe, who were hugging themselves with fear. There was Ledocq, watching everything intently, hands fluttering whenever it looked like one of the devices he'd built might get damaged. Carter wasn't worried; he was floating.The pirates used the bayonets on their brand-new rifles to root through the extravagant silks used by Miss Aurora, his young mind reader and spiritualist. While one pirate comically held up a nightgown to his own chest and wriggled his hips to make the others laugh, another, beefier man tested for hidden compartments, thumping a pole against an oak table Carter used for his levitation act.

When the last shipping box was emptied, Tulang had Carter brought to him for questioning. He knew Carter was some sort of performer who had played to a packed house for just over two months. Where were all the gross receipts?

Tulang, a small rust-colored man with hooded black eyes and long, fine black hair tied into a knot, spoke perfect English with an accent Carter couldn't place; it was in fact Dutch.

'Where were you educated?' Carter asked.

Tulang's right hand came up from his hip efficiently, slapping Carter across the face with exactly enough force to knock him down. Carter rose to one knee, feeling his face sting. He was back in his body again, unexpectedly, fetched on wings of pain. His palm, cool against his cheek, was shaking. Thirty men saw him, some of them his troupe, some sailors, and Carter wondered if he now looked to them just a little smaller. He met Ledocq's eye, and tried to wink, but couldn't.

'Where are the gross receipts?' Tulang asked again.

From the deck, Carter wondered if he could stand or if Tulang would hit him again. 'The receipts, net, were deposited in Sydney.

The bank has an arrangement with my bank in San Francisco.' He turned his palms up, empty, as if he were showing there was nothing up his sleeve.

Tulang glared at Carter's hands, then Carter's face. Carter knew how to overcome an audience's reluctance to be persuaded. But Tulang's downward gaze was something far more probing and disbelieving than he'd experienced.

'Stand up.' Tulang called for his men to bring the 'package' from belowdecks. A moment later, they brought up Aurora, who struggled against them as they pushed her up the stairs. Carter hadn't counted on this. The sight of her in danger made him suddenly feel ill. She was a foolish girl, just twenty years old, given to offstage theatrics and endless complaints about the accommodations. At Ledocq's urging, Carter had been planning to pay off her contract once the Tokyo performances were over.

Since she spent an undue amount of time reading romantic potboilers, she had dressed herself in knee pants, an oversized man's shirt, and a tweed cap, as if she could fool the pirates into thinking she was a boy.

'Take your hands off me! Take your filthy hands off me, you brutes!' No one was touching Aurora; most of the pirates had never seen an American woman before, except in advertisements, and so they stood back, shielding their eyes against the sunlight as they stared at her, unsure how to treat her until Tulang gave them direction. Tulang, who'd grown up in a brothel, and who'd watched as a toddler while his mother disposed of hostages whose ransom wasn't paid (her favorite method was to line them up tied to an anchor chain, which she pitched overboard so that one man after the other was yanked off the deck in a synchronous rhythm that had made little Tulang clap his hands), said that people were all basically the same. He would do what it took to make Carter give up his money.

Carter, cheek still smarting, did not now know his own limits. Had it been a year ago, he would have been plotting her rescue, but an angry, willful pride settled on him now like bad weather. Even though it was dangerous, he would not let Tulang humiliate him again.

'Charlie! Are you going to let them treat me like this?'

Carter ignored Aurora. Tulang lit a cigarette. At the time,

machine-made cigarettes were uncommon, and this one was a Player's Navy Cut from a shipment Tulang had just hijacked. While he smoked, he unfolded a playbill from Carter's act. 'If you played nine weeks at the Palace, you must have made about forty thousand.'

'Fifty-five.'

'Good.' Tulang laughed. 'I saw Horace Goldin last year.'

'The mile-a-minute conjurer,' Carter noted.

'A busy man.' Tulang made circles with his wrists. 'So much work. I think you sent *some* of that money to the bank, but you didn't want to pay the war tax on all of it. I think you hid fifteen, maybe twenty thousand.'

Carter said nothing. He was thinking about Goldin's posters, which mimicked the surreal portraits painted by Giuseppe Archimboldo, seventeenth-century court painter of Prague. Goldin's portrait looked like a colorful lithograph of his face and upper torso. If you looked closely, his face and dinner jacket dissolved into a collage of scarves, doves, spirits, flags, flowers, coins, cards, and imps, the bare bottom of one making up Goldin's nose. *What a genius idea*, Carter thought.

'Charlie!' Aurora stamped her foot.

Tulang waved the program at her. 'Are you the mind reader?'

Carter hoped she understood that she should say nothing.

'Yes,' she said, eyes squinting. 'I am *Aurora*.'

'What am I thinking?' Tulang took a drag on his cigarette.

'I don't care, you animal.' She started to walk away from him, but Tulang's men blocked her way.

Tulang whispered to Carter. 'I could retire on thirty thousand.'

'According to you, I'm only hiding twenty.'

'There is a place in Jakarta that would pay me thirty for her.' Tulang stretched and yawned.

'Then she'll be worth more to you than she ever was to me.'

Tulang blew a smoke ring, laughing again. 'You are a cold-blooded man. Aurora, come here.'

Because Aurora made a show of resistance, she was finally carried by two of Tulang's men until she stood, defiant, just next to Carter and the pirate. She began to speak, but Tulang quieted her by waving his hand near her face.

'Watch.'

He extended his left hand toward her, then, with his right hand, ground his cigarette into his palm until extinguished. Aurora screamed. Her legs buckled, and she slid to the deck. Tulang waved his palm at her, showing off the unharmed flesh, and the copper coin he'd hidden there.

'It was a trick,' he said, relighting the cigarette because he was not a wasteful man. Watching her cry into her hands, he muttered to Carter, 'She's easily upset. Life in Jakarta would be very hard on her.'

'As I said, I can't stop you.' Carter spoke slowly, his demeanor beginning to frighten him. He felt a stab of shame. Aurora was just a child who needed his help. With an effort, he spoke in his normal voice. 'Can you kidnap an American girl without consequence?'

Though the pirate only shrugged in response, pursuit by the United States and British navies didn't appeal to him. Nonetheless, he wasn't leaving the boat without Carter's money. He offered Aurora his hand to help her up, and when she took it, she was looking straight at Carter with an accusatory stare – as if he should have done something better to protect her – when Tulang drove the tip of the lit cigarette into the back of her hand.

Aurora was so startled she couldn't even cry out. Because she was still glaring at Carter as the pain took hold of her, he saw something few people get to witness: experience invading the gaze of an innocent.

He thought from a great distance, I'm sorry. The world inflicted pain that began to vibrate along that silver cord, bringing him closer to his body. Tulang released her and she took a step back, staring at her hand in amazement. She could not even think to faint. And Carter felt awful, as Aurora now understood what he did: to be placed in jeopardy did not mean to be rescued.

Aurora stumbled away, whimpering, and cupping her injured hand against her chest. Carter focused on Tulang and awaited the end of this game. If his hands were shaking, so be it – he clasped them behind his damp and dripping back.

Tulang said that since he and his men were leaving empty-handed (not counting, of course, the passengers' valuables), they might as well get something other people had to pay for: he wanted to see this performance that was worth fifty-five thousand dollars. At first, Carter was relieved. Tulang was leaving his own realm and entering the place where Carter ruled. Of course, in broad daylight, on the rolling deck of a rusting steamer, without makeup, without unpacking many of the props, performing at gunpoint, the act would have to be a failure. But Carter was determined to beat the odds.

At the time, his act consisted of Goldin-paced imitations of Ching Ling Foo, the Chinese magician who worked with the materialization of doves and full bowls of water. Carter had no doves here, and because of the slow pitching of the boat, he couldn't balance the water jugs – he tried a small, simple set piece, and was rewarded with a shower of water down his face and neck. He focused on his stage patter, which was excellent, but because of the poor acoustics on the boat, and because most of the pirates didn't understand English, he got no reaction.

He was allowed to set up the levitation table, with Ledocq as the volunteer to be levitated – Aurora was sitting in a daze by the matron's feet with a cold compress on her hand. Every time his gaze fell on her, he thought again, I'm sorry, the phrase ringing off-key. But just as Carter made the table fall away, the pirates chattered: they could plainly see the wires holding Ledocq up.

At a loss, he returned to the simplest tricks, close-up, relying on his own skills, not on props or machinery. He produced coin after coin well enough, but one gold piece slipped between his sweaty knuckles and rolled across the deck, to the pirates' tremendous laughter.

'I'm sorry,' he said aloud.

He tried to turn that into a joke, but he was flustered. He couldn't think of another trick to perform. And what was the point? Cards, scarves, flags – Goldin's portrait, all the imps, the coins, the flowers so carefully wedged into place – give it a good shake, and see how all the detritus of illusions would tumble away until not even the faintest outline of the magician would remain. He realized he had been relying on his skills in misdirection for six months, not to earn a living, but to prevent a dark thought from coming into focus.

It was such a surprising thought he found himself saying it aloud, just once, 'I am no one.'

He could hear voices faintly, like ghosts. They weren't real voices.

They were memories and doubts. He felt things spilling out of him, nameless and amorphous things slipping away, every precious thing he could call his own. Without magic, he was an empty screen onto which but one image fit: an iron fist put into pendulous motion, and Sarah Annabelle's head snapping back.

He walked away from the makeshift stage and sat on the edge of the deck, by the hand railing, his legs dangling over the sea. At once, he was cool, kissed by salt. At once, the heat did not bother him, and when Tulang approached, Carter looked up with dull, beaten eyes. He said that there was twelve thousand hidden in the levitation table, and then he said nothing more; he simply watched the swells as they swept past the boat.

He could hear behind him the sounds of pirates attacking the table with axes, and protests from his company as one by one all of the illusions were thrown into the Molucca Sea, where they would sink a mile or more and be covered in silt, where huge sea anemones would close around crooked decks of cards and moray eels would find a home in the brightly painted spirit cabinet.

Carter retired from magic. No performances, not even private shows, no sleight of hand for the neighborhood children. He moved back to his parents' home, and lived in his old room, and he whittled sticks into abstract shapes. If, by accident, they became too representational, he destroyed them.

His mother encouraged him to see a psycho-analyst; analysis was all the rage now, she said. And because she understood him, she added, 'Don't hold its popularity against it.' But he declined. While psychotherapy had saved her – in fact at the *very same time* it had saved her – magic had saved him. And it had also, after promising so much, been the thing that killed his wife.

For a year, there was a pattern. Carter thinking of Sarah Annabelle, Carter swamped by a wave of grief, and collapsing on the floor like he was praying to Mecca. He cried so much he ruined the rug and it was replaced.

Jenks was gone now. A drinker to the end, he had died during one of Carter's vaudeville tours. Mrs Carter recognized the excellent light in his cabin, and converted it to a painting studio, should she ever be inspired. Carter took to standing in this cottage in those beautiful afternoon hours and wondering about the nature of triumph. His old enemy was dead. How hollow the world seemed, even on balmy days when the light came in the window to illuminate particles that could only be called golden.

Jenks's gardening tools hung in a tiny, spider-infested shed. Carter planted tomatoes and herbs, and sweet-smelling flowers, and got dirty every day. Nothing pleased him more than uncovering the upper roots of a complicated weed, and following them to their terminal points and ripping them to pieces.

There was a war coming. The news was full of it. He took hikes through the Presidio hills because the vistas were said to be thrilling, but all he could look at when he'd reached one summit or the other were ships departing for Europe. Every time he saw one, he waved. 'Good luck,' he said. 'Good luck over there.'

His mother had started a hobby, photography, and had joined a women's club that took weeklong wilderness excursions to better capture unspoiled beauty. His father, too, was gone – business trips, again. But he had an apprentice: James had streaked through Yale and begun building a fortune, and for several years he supervised Chilean metallurgy interests for Carter & Company.

So Carter was alone in his childhood home. He could hardly stand it, so he went often to the picture shows. He shunned the Market Street houses, the big theatres with live orchestras. He frequented instead the neighborhood haunts, the Red Wagon or the Glitter, tiny and dirty theatres, home to single, out-of-tune upright pianos, one step more permanent than a tent show. Comedies, melodramas, it didn't matter which. It was dark, and there was entertainment going on.

For long hours he had no idea what to do. He couldn't say when he began to pay regular visits to Borax Smith, but he found himself, twice a week, taking the ferry boat to Oakland, and wandering up the long meanders that took him from the gates of Arbor Villa to the house of fallen women. Borax lived there surrounded by terrible stories, and perhaps that was what drew Carter there.

There was a massive house in the center of the property, and a dozen cottages surrounding it, all of them active with women who were expecting, or who had covered bassinets on their porches and smoke coming from their chimneys. Some set up easels for landscape painting; others, following the style of the day, took to dancing in the woods. They had classes in the arts, or useful occupations, such as secretarial work or domestic services. At all times, they wore huge bonnets with white veils, and remained silent around visitors, to protect their identities and to save them from being judged on the day that they returned to society.

When Carter began coming, the old man encouraged him to talk about his sorrows. And this was a place where Carter could talk. This house understood loss. Borax knew how to talk about the hard matters that wore people down to the bone. Carter shared stories of Annabelle while they drank tea served by silent figures cloaked like beekeepers.

'You know,' Borax finally said one summer afternoon, sitting beside Carter in their lawn chairs, 'the girls would enjoy a magic show from you. Something small. It would cheer them up.'

'Of course. Yes,' Carter said.

Summer turned to fall. Borax gently brought up the idea a second time. 'I'd enjoy it, too,' he said, stroking his long white beard. He was a patient man. He'd held on to property by the estuary for twenty-two years rather than sell at a loss.

When Carter came on Boxing Day, he had a motorcar filled with small presents, trinkets he thought the women might like. But the house and all the cottages were dark. The previous day had been the worst in Arbor Villa history, and was forever after called Black Christmas.

Eventually, Borax shuffled to the door. 'She was smart as a whip,' he told Carter immediately, without prelude. 'Ten whips.' And then he was quiet, as he knew that 'ten whips' was inadequate, but he didn't know how to say it better. Borax didn't have the gift of speech; he was more of a listener, so having to tell the story was especially difficult for him. One of his favorite women, who'd arrived in summer, newly in the delicate condition, received correspondence from the man who'd abandoned her. The man had been engaged to another, but had come to his senses, and wanted to take his first love, his true love, away. 'She tore 'em up. Every last letter,' Borax said. 'Made him grovel. Then he showed here. I seen a lot of men, and I seen the real ones, the ones that fall back in love. I swore this guy was one of 'em.' He looked at Carter. 'I told her he was sincere, go, go on with him.'

Borax told Carter this story on the front porch of the house. He paused, long enough for Carter to know the worst possible thing had happened. He felt dizzy. Wind cut through the tall, exotic trees Borax had imported from Siam, and wild birds chirped all around but the air felt silent nonetheless. Borax stood with his weight on his good leg, his knuckles white on his cane. 'He killed her, Charlie. Took her up to a cabin, locked it up, and burned it down to the ground.'

'Oh, dear God . . .'

'She woulda had the baby in two months, about.'

A sickly feeling snaked through Carter's whole body. He focused on his car, which was still filled with presents.

'That's awful,' he whispered.

'It's worser.' Borax wiped at his eyes. He started to say one thing, then said another: 'That devil, he's gone. I got some friends who know more than the coppers, and this man, he's gone. Mexico. No one's gonna make him pay.'

'It's not your fault.'

'I sent her right into his arms. I made her go.'

It could have ended there – Carter could have simply said 'I'm sorry for your loss' and left, but he didn't. Instead, he walked to his car, walked slowly, for he felt like he'd been drained of three quarts of blood. He asked Borax for help with bringing gifts into the house, for the girls. Borax held open the twenty-foot oak door, leaning against it as Carter ferried armfuls of gaily wrapped boxes inside. It felt wrong and right at the same time.

On the final trip, Carter put a hand on Borax's shoulder. 'I know you feel guilty. You shouldn't.'

Borax moved his lips for a moment before he responded. 'If I told you that about Sarah, would that make you feel better?'

Carter shook his head.

'What happened to my girl,' Borax continued, 'what he did to her, it's worse than you can imagine.'

Carter nodded. And he kept moving. He spent the day at Arbor Villa, and walked the grounds, feeding the birds, sensing mourning that had overtaken the estate, like the whole world had died on Black Christmas.

But life cannot so easily grind to a standstill. When Carter returned from an hour's contemplation by the river in the late afternoon, he listened to the sounds of babies awaking, and he smelled bacon cooking, and was suddenly ravenous.

To draw a straight line, then, from one moment to the next: on New Year's Eve, Borax put his thirty best chairs into his smaller ballroom, and before an audience of most of the unfortunate women who lived at Arbor Villa, Carter appeared in his evening clothes for the first time in over two years.

Each and every one of the women wore a black mourning dress, and some had dyed their bonnets and veils black to match. Carter had for so long depended on seeing delight or suspicion on the faces of his audience, he didn't know where to look as he nervously took the low-rise of the stage. He began with pantomime he had no idea what to say. He pulled scarves from the air, and they became doves, and some hats tilted back to see better. He heard several pleased gasps, and adapted: he would have to *listen* to his audience. How strange.

When he had exhausted all the silk tricks he could remember, he made a small bow, and measured the applause, the muffled sound of gloves patting each other. He opened his mouth to introduce his next trick. For a moment, a hollow, yearning moment, as he looked out at the sea of veils, he felt how his audience, each and every member, had survived the very worst things in the world. He wanted to say, 'As some of you may know, my wife died.' His mouth trembled.

Then: a pack of cards was in his hand. He looked at it like spoiled fruit. Still, he said cheerfully, 'This next trick requires two volunteers.' He couldn't imagine why anyone in this room would want this frivolity. 'Could I have two volunteers? Please?' The response caused him to take an involuntary step backward. Their hands went up. All of them. So many of them, two dozen or more white-gloved, slender hands, asking to be picked. And there was a sweet sound – their voices. He'd never heard any of them speak before, but he could hear them now, 'Me,' they called. 'Pick me.'

He surveyed them, with a smile breaking across his face. And there was something breaking inside of him, too, something old and titanically heavy, as he said, 'Wonderful! So many of you!'

Griffin rolled his head back, toward the ceiling. He massaged his neck muscles, which had long ago begun to cramp. The final five pages of clippings detailed Carter's several world tours. There were updates from the United States, and China and India and Ceylon. There was nothing fabulous documented here, nothing on the scale of pirate invasions or being given islands or tragic deaths. Each performance, Carter said, 'I shall give it my all tonight, as I do every night.'

There was a very small article dated July 20 of this year, promising two weeks of vaguely described delight at the Curran, and then a final piece dated July 25, 'President Harding to Attend Carter the Great Performance of Magic and Mystery.'

Griffin read this last article carefully for clues to an assassination plot spoken as if in all innocence.

♣ ♦ ♥ ♠

'Charles Carter, who couldn't care less . . . no, Charles Carter, who, had he been brought up less well, would proclaim how uneventful it is that the beloved President will attend his show . . . no, how's this—'

'Charlie,' Ledocq said, knowing he wouldn't get another word in.

'Charles Carter retires,' Carter said blankly. Then he looked at Ledocq for a reaction.

'Don't keep me in suspense.' He shrugged. 'I've said before: Pull the trigger, be done with it. What do I care?'

This particular conversation was unraveling in an East Oakland warehouse on the evening of July 24, 1923, a night off from the run at the Curran. Weeks ago, they'd planned this evening as a break from performances – 'No show on the evening of the 24th' was written on the schedule – because of an unusual fixation held by Ledocq.

Carter had grown to love his effects builder, not just because of their complementary vocations, nor what they'd so far suffered through together, but because Ledocq was, like him, an odd kind of egg. Through some bizarre alchemy, Ledocq had been born into a family of moneylenders with a mission in life unheard of in their clan: he wanted to build things. Clocks. Watches. Adding machines. Automata. He took firsts in all his physical science classes, and he wanted so badly to construct his strange and complex objects he was prepared to leave home to do it, but he needn't have bothered – no one in Belgium or its neighbors would hire a Jew to engineer anything.

Then he heard of Robert-Houdin and his mysterious toys, and he learned that since it involved deception, the world of magic was open to him. He moved to England to work for Maskelyne. 'We know how ninety-nine percent of the universe works,' he told Carter shortly after they met, 'and that's the clockworks, that's what we build with. But the other one percent makes the clockworks wind down. That's inertia. No one knows how that works, but it does. It's that one percent mystery that's the way of our maker. Put everything together, energy and inertia, the explicable and the inexplicable, and that's how you and I make our living.'

When he was building something, a spirit cabinet, a new way to spin cards, a production box, he could be awake all night, lecturing Carter while adding shellac to a surface with a fine bristle brush. He was quite the scholar on the appearances of magic in the Old Testament, and could discuss its resurgence in the Middle Ages, along with, for instance, early engineering in stone mills, but none of this philosophical stew was remotely as attractive to Ledocq as was – to the surprise of everyone who knew him – boxing.

As befit a European Jew, Ledocq cared not a fig for American sports. Baseball, football, and their ilk meant nothing to him. Yet he felt an intemperate excitement about boxing, one boxer in particular. Benny Leonard, 'The Professor,' the twenty-seven-year-old Jew from the Lower East Side of Manhattan. He had been lightweight champion, but had lost his crown and tonight, July 24, he was fighting Lew Tendler to get it back.

Ledocq had shown more interest in planning to listen to the fight than he did the latest manifestation of the Carter extravaganza. He wanted to sit with Carter in the props warehouse, drinking beer and eating sandwiches, away from the rest of the world, and no one – meaning Mrs Ledocq – would bother them. Sports had no appeal for Carter, but he enjoyed Ledocq's enthusiasm, and so the evening began to mean something to him as well.

Thus it was with disappointment that Carter received a telephone call informing him that President Harding would be attending the final show of the run. The *Examiner* was sending a reporter to meet with him the night of the fight to get his opinions on the nation's great man. It was publicity, so he couldn't avoid it.

When Carter arrived at the warehouse, it smelled of freshly hewn pine and a thrill of sawdust, as Ledocq was running boards through his lathe. Ledocq turned off his tools to hear Carter's announcement that they would be visited by some genius of the cigar-stub-and-rye variety, which quickly devolved to Carter complaining, which ended up with Ledocq staring at him.

'I'm sorry,' Carter said, 'I'm being petulant.'

'That you are.' Ledocq yawned. 'Let me show you something.' He walked to this workbench, where his radio was waiting. It was a Crosley, and just weeks ago he and Carter had used it to listen to Benny Leonard's fight with Kepler, the giant Swede.

'It's your radio.'

'Yes. And next to it, what do you see there?'

Carter saw another radio, but unlike any one he'd seen before. Whereas the old Crosley was simply a metal plate with two dials and a crystal receiver – it looked at home with the lathe and Ledocq's drill bits – this was an elegant, richly polished wooden box. It had *three* dials, all emerald green with brass trim. On the front, on a polished metal plate, it said 'Crosley' in cursive. Carter felt mildly sorry for the old radio, which looked bald and utilitarian, a combustion engine's innards side by side with a Durant touring car.

Ledocq opened the new Crosley up. Inside were vacuum tubes, which surprised Carter. 'Tubes?'

'And the reception? One thousand times better. Not only that, it has separate speakers. Six months, they changed it like that.'

Carter whistled. 'The world is changing.' And he saw it clearly enough – radios no longer belonged on a workbench but in the living room, beside the couch, like a vase of flowers or a phonograph.

'Guess what the third dial is for. Tuning,' he answered, beaming like he'd built it himself. 'Many different stations, at once.'

'Well, then. What station is Mr Benny Leonard on?'

'K-U-O,' Ledocq said, turning on his radio, and tuning it.

For a few minutes, their evening went as planned. They drew chairs up, and huddled together, talking while KUO played phonograph records. The ubiquitous and vastly annoying 'Yes! We Have No Bananas,' followed by a faceless rhumba. A summer night, crickets outside, and inside, two men, leaning in, listened to each other and the radio, under an orange light in a drafty warehouse decorated with old posters and long-disused scenery. It should have been peaceful for Carter. Ledocq explained how scientific Leonard's style was, and Carter checked his watch, for Bernie was late.

A voice on the radio said, as if not quite sure he believed it himself, 'To you fifty thousand persons now sitting in on the ether wave, the *Examiner* sends its greetings. This is your operator, Sparks Gaal. You've been listening to top music, truly top-flight music. And if you want to buy the music you've been listening to, go to Doeflinger's Music Shop, on Jackson Street. Please buy your phonograph records from them.'

'Advertising on the radio waves. Who knew?'

Carter nodded. 'It's a good gimmick.'

'And now,' Sparks Gaal said, 'The Benny Leonard–Lew Tendler fight. In progress.'

Both Ledocq and Carter groaned aloud as the fight, in its fourth round, suddenly reached them. Thrown into the mix like that, it was hard to understand what was going on, and the announcer was having trouble with his microphone, but Leonard was in the lead. Soon, they were swamped with the language of fistiana, with cheering swells and rapid-fire descriptions of a brute struggle between two cherubic assassins on cauliflower row, each landing pancake blows that knocked the gallery gods cuckoo.

At the end of the fifth round, Carter attacked his corned beef sandwich while Ledocq popped the top off another beer. 'What sportsmen! Neither of them are ham-and-eggers,' Carter said, repeating a phrase he'd heard the first time three minutes before. He was quoting an adage about Leonard, 'No one can even muss the man's hair,' when Ledocq said, 'Hello.'

Carter looked over his shoulder. Standing in the middle of the warehouse, under the main lights, was a woman. She had brunette, wavy hair in a permanent that must have cost at least four dollars. She wore a cloche hat, a tweed jacket and skirt, and a necktie. Her eyes were flicking from place to place, like she was memorizing her surroundings.

'Bernie,' she said. 'Are you Carter?'

Carter swallowed twice, successfully clearing his throat the second time. Bernadette, he thought. 'Hello,' he said. He wiped his hands on a towel. 'Pleased to meet you.'

'Nice shack,' she said, squinting all around her. She shook his hand. She had extremely dramatic brown eyes, and so the flicking and squinting effects worked much to her advantage.

Carter swept his tongue around his mouth again, feeling one hundred thousand poppy seeds in his teeth. 'Please do make yourself at home.'

'Don't mind if I do,' Bernie said. 'I saw your show last night, so I have the skeleton. I just need a few nice quotes from the mage himself, and we'll be set. How's the fight?'

'Leonard's winning,' Ledocq said.

'No one can muss his hair,' Carter added.

'Yeah, I heard you saying that.' She'd already looked somewhat amused, but now the volume of her delight increased. 'So what do you think of Harding visiting you, Mr Carter?'

'Well, it's an honor,' Carter said, 'to be visited.' He had more to say, but he was looking at his visitor. She was a modern girl, and he was thinking absently about suffrage, employment, freedom, hemlines, and how she had managed to find a gloss of lipstick that was actually hypnotic.

'Yes?' she prompted.

'Yes. Harding is a great man. It will be an honor to have him in my theatre,' Carter said. 'I've played for many heads of state, and Harding is of course one of them. It's good.'

Mercifully, Bernie nodded. She turned on her heel and approached a wall, which was draped with Carter's eight-sheet posters. Carter looked at Ledocq, who bugged out his eyes, and made small shoveling motions with his hands, which meant Go!

Carter approached slowly, preparing the way he would onstage. He had a checklist to tick through in unusual circumstances: if he felt too cold, the lanolin on his palms could cause the coins to stick;

if a stage light crashed to the boards while he was throwing a knife, he would be startled, and perhaps miss his mark. For Carter, the shorthand question was simple, *How do I feel*? And the answer came back today as it had every single day for years, *I feel fine*.

So Carter, feeling fine, feeling charming even, approached Bernie, who was apparently captivated by the nearest poster. It showed a wraithlike Carter flying out of a noose, enraging a colorful crowd of imperial Chinese who'd plainly come to see him executed.

She read aloud, 'Carter, condemned to death for witchcraft, cheats the gallows.' She chuckled.

'Yes,' Carter said, 'that's an effect we borrowed from a Goldin review. It's, well, it's not in the current show, but—'

'I like your show.'

'Thank you.'

'And I like your posters. They're romantic.'

'Ah, yes – oh, they – excuse me?'

She smiled at him, and her eyes switched back and forth across his own, taking readings of voltage. 'Romantic,' she repeated. 'You know. Like from a bygone era.'

'Oh.' He felt a thud in his chest.

She pouted, 'Ah, I'm only joshing you. I mean romantic as in the good kind of romantic.'

Relief. 'Thank you.'

'You yourself, Carter, are you the romantic sort?'

He had no response. Her demeanor was entirely too brassy. She was obvious, and had but one pathway, the confrontational. Still, she could play a man like Carter all evening long as effectively as with a rod and reel. There were ways to extricate himself. What were they again?

'Well.' She pulled out a pad of paper. 'We should get the quotes over with.'

'Yes, that would be heroic. Can I offer you, well, all we have is beer and sandwiches, but—'

'Another time.' Her tone had changed; Carter had failed a test, and now she was here to do a job. 'So what's your magic about?'

'Pardon?'

'Well, any schmoe can pull a rabbit out of a hat. I asked Thurston why he does it, and he said he does it for the kids. And Houdini says his job is to show the world that man can escape from any circumstance. So what's your take on it?'

'Well.' Her pencil was ready for him to talk. His patter, however, was missing, and what he felt in its place, the truth, was inadequate. How could he say he'd become a magician because he felt abandoned once in a lonely house? How he'd returned to soothe abandoned women? How he'd fought off loneliness so many times by picking up a deck of cards that now it was simply rote? That if he weren't a magician, he'd be nothing much at all? 'It's a way,' he murmured, 'of turning back the darkness.'

'Excuse me?' Her face contorted. 'Excuse me very much?'

'What I mean is, the world is an awful place, isn't it? Magic makes it less awful for a moment or two.' He felt like he'd torn away a bandage, and confirmed that an old wound was indeed still there. 'If I can shake the world off a man's shoulders, I feel better.'

All over Bernie Simon's features, lights were dimming and doors politely closing.

'I mean,' he rallied, 'there's joy and wonderment to be had. I love to perform. It fights back the loneliness. It's all I really know how to do anymore.'

'I see,' she said. There was no reason she should understand him. He had in his way cupped his hands around his mouth and shouted across a canyon, hoping she'd heard.

When she left, Carter waved good-bye.

'Well,' Carter said to Ledocq, smiling, 'how was that?'

'*Quelle catastrophe.*'

'What?'

Ledocq pointed both palms out to Carter, and, at a loss, slapped them to his forehead. 'I don't even know where to begin. No, not true. You have mustard on your collar. It's been there the whole time.'

'That's hardly a disaster.'

'It's highly symbolic,' Ledocq said.

'Just because I was too rusty to flirt with her—'

'Ah, Carter. You're a lost young man.'

'I thought I was very honest.'

'Exactly.' Ledocq wrestled internally for a moment, and then turned off the fight, which was in the tenth round. 'Tell me honestly, then, what do you need from this life?'

'What do I—'

'Need. Need,' he repeated, and blinked. Without the hissing excitement of the Leonard fight, the room seemed airless.

'I don't know. Nothing? I'm content,' Carter said. 'I'm fine, you know.'

'Ehhhh.' Ledocq shrugged, producing a silver dollar. 'You're content like the Kaiser. Watch this.' He held the coin by its edge, and then placed it in his palm. He squeezed his palm shut, made a pass over it, and opened his hand again. Carter stared. In Ledocq's palm was a silver dollar.

'Have I missed something?'

'Yes.' Ledocq did it again. And a third time. Finally, Carter noticed: the date on the coin changed from 1921 to 1923.

'That's a tedious sort of trick,' Carter sighed.

'That is true. But why?'

'If you do a trick that the audience doesn't notice—'

'Ah! Yes! I've got you! An audience. You need an audience.'

'Oh, that sounds awful.'

'No, not much. We all need love. When you're ready, you'll find it somewhere else, like in a pretty girl.'

'I don't need that.'

'Yes you do, I saw you a minute ago.'

'I need *Bernie*? Please!'

'No, you don't need her, she's *a nishtikeit*, a *pitsvinik*, who cares? But the truth is there's a man under all that magic somewhere, Charlie, we'll dig him out for sure.' Nodding like he'd come to the end of a geometric proof, Ledocq turned the radio back on. There was haze and static, a turbinelike whining, and then the sounds of a crowd, and announcers.

Carter listened long enough to learn that Leonard was still ahead. In fact, he became absorbed in the narrative of the fight, the rights and the lefts, the devastating uppercut that, *Oh,* Leonard dodged with intelligent footwork. And then a brutal assault by Leonard, who wasn't known for his hard hitting, but he was peppering Tendler, just peppering him with blows, and then with a gasp, 'Leonard has laid Tendler among the sweet peas!' and there was the sound of bells, and Ledocq cried, 'Yesss!' for Leonard, at the end of fifteen rounds, was the only man standing.

'You know,' Carter said, as the cheering faded, hoping this would solve everything, 'I *do* love magic. By itself, for its own sake.'

Ledocq nodded. 'So. If you do a trick and no one notices, does that satisfy? Or is it like a tree falling in the forest without anyone to hear it?'

Carter sighed. His curse in life was to be attracted to people who understood him. With a sip of beer, he said, 'I feel sorry for that tree.'

♣ ♦ ♥ ♠

. . . Though the President is said to be fatigued, there will be no worries at the Curran Theatre on the night he pays his respects to favorite son Charles Carter. For Carter the Great promises effects to confound the imagination. Quothe he, 'There's joy and wonderment to be had.' The President himself may have spent weeks on his Voyage of Understanding, but Carter has been traveling for years. Even after all his world tours, Carter says, 'I love to perform.' And if delights await our beloved Commander-in-Chief, the responsibility for such massive entertainment never for a moment affects the suave and bubbling mahatma. With a wink and a nod, he says, 'If I can shake the world off a man's shoulders, I feel better.'

– *Bernie Simon, staff*

By the time Griffin finished the holdings on Charles Carter, it was dinnertime. The workmen had come back, and their hammering and sawing sent out clouds of plaster dust. In the shafts of light that moved across the library, it almost looked like it was snowing. Miss White had brought Griffin many glasses of water, and even though he had sucked on mints almost continuously, his new tooth still hurt.

When he was done, he closed the journals, and his own notes, and sat quietly for a moment. He thanked Miss White, returned the hard hat at the door of the library, and walked outside. The rising certainty of a hunch made younger agents excited. They ran too quickly to tell their superiors about half-baked theories. But the more Griffin had to go on, the calmer he got. Carter had stolen another magician's show in vaudeville. He claimed to have consorted with the Japanese military. His wife had died in a mysterious accident. There was some kind of insurance scam in Indonesia, which he'd tried to cover up with a story about pirates. Griffin couldn't quite figure out the island for retired animals, though using it for smuggling was a possibility. They didn't have much liquor in that part of the world, but they did have opium. Maybe Carter ran dope.

Carter had performed for President Harding, who had died of causes that were being covered up. Shaking the world off a great man's shoulders. What did Carter mean by that?

Griffin sat at dinner with his findings, unmoving except to flick his tongue against his tooth, which still tasted pungent, like metal. Carter couldn't have acted alone. Someone had to have prompted him – the players behind the Veterans Bureau, maybe. Or Fall's Springs. Or the Post Office. Or even the Duchess, simply tired of her husband's affairs. And the Service had helped him, and wanted dirt on their new ally.

Or Carter was completely innocent, and they were looking for a patsy.

After he'd eaten everything on his plate, Griffin flipped through his notes. Harding had asked several people, 'If you knew a secret, would you for the good of the country expose or bury it?' No matter how he looked at it, Griffin had trouble imagining a man like Carter wanting any kind of secret exposed.

When he returned to his hotel room, there was a message from Starling. Would he, Agent Griffin, accompany him on an interview tomorrow morning? He believed he had found Charles Carter in Oakland, and would like Griffin's help in questioning him.

♣ ♦ ♥ ♠

On Monday, August 6, 1923, Carter stood on the stairs of his Oakland property, his fingers playing with the tips of his Thai basil plants, and his agile mind trying to keep up with Colonel Starling, whom he was beginning to find troublesome.

The Colonel asked, 'The photograph in your drawing room, is that your wife?'

'She was my wife. I'm a widower.' He said this in his stage voice, calmly.

'I'm sorry,' Starling responded.

While Starling massaged a mint leaf and brought his fingertips to his nose, Carter weighed another question, and found it innocuous enough. 'Was the President in trouble?'

'That depends,' Starling said. 'Is there anything else I should know?'

Carter shrugged. 'I had but five minutes with the President. Being a magician is an odd thing. I've met presidents, kings, prime ministers, and a few despots. Most of them want to know how I do my tricks, or to show me a card trick they learned as a child, and I have to smile and say, "Oh, how nice." Still, it's not a bad profession if you can get away from all the bickering among your peers about who created what illusion.' Carter ended here, satisfied that he'd in no way answered the question.

But Starling's eyes changed. Carter realized he'd somehow stepped in a bear trap, and Starling was walking around him, looking for the best place to amputate his leg. 'I see. You put on a thrilling show yourself, sir.'

'Thank you.'

'Now, I'm just an admirer here, and I hope this question isn't rude, but have I seen some of those tricks before?'

'Those effects? Not the way I do them, no.'

'So you yourself are the creator of all of those tricks. Because Thurston – I've had the pleasure of seeing Thurston – does that trick with the ropes as well. Doesn't he? And I saw Goldin several years ago, and he had two Hindu yoga men. Is there any part of your act—'

'No, there isn't,' Carter replied briskly. 'The fact of the matter is, Colonel Starling, there are few illusions that are truly original. It's a matter of presentation.' He hoped that might stop this conversation; when Starling only stared in response, Carter continued, 'In other words, I didn't invent sugar or flour, but I bake a mean apple pie.'

'So then you're just as respected in the business for the quality of your presentation as the magicians who actually *create* illusions,' Starling said.

Carter suddenly felt like Starling had knowingly drilled into a live nerve. He wanted to shout at him, 'Yes, it's true, I'm not that well respected the way I once was, I'm a fraud,' but in the heartbeat it took him to recover, he folded his arms, and smiled. He said, 'At some point this stopped being about President Harding.'

'My fault. I'm intrigued by all forms of misdirection.' Starling reached into his vest pocket, then withdrew his business card, which he looked at for a moment before handing it to Carter. 'If you think of anything else—'

'I'll call you.'

Starling joined Griffin. They walked several steps before Starling turned around. 'Oh, Mr Carter?'

'Yes?' Carter felt a wave of exhaustion, as if the finishing line of a long race had just been yanked into the distance.

'Did the President say anything about a secret?'

'A secret? What sort of secret?'

'A few people told us that in his last weeks, the late President asked them . . .' Starling opened a notepad, and read, 'What would you do if you knew an awful secret?'

'How dramatic. What on earth could that be?' He said this as great fatigue welled up on him, and Starling faced him with one of those icy stares. This time, Carter almost folded. He was that tired.

But his facade was apparently composed enough, for Starling simply said, 'We'll find out. Thank you.' Then he and his silent compatriot Griffin left Carter alone.

Chapter 6

For several seconds after agents Griffin and Starling left him, Charles Carter stood in his dressing gown, his forehead tilting against the door, one hand on the doorknob, the other hand thrown lazily over his head so that his elbow pointed toward the high beams of the ceiling.

Once he had assured himself there was no possible reason for anyone to approach his door again, he let his knees give way until he was more or less sitting on the floor with his legs bent at the knee. 'Thank God that's finally over,' he said to no one in particular. He had gotten ten hours of sleep in the last three days, so he was prepared to stay on the floor as long as was necessary.

And yet he was now face to face with – himself. Stacked against a coat rack, peeking out of half-torn-away brown paper was a bundle of fifty window cards. It was a design that lacked originality: the standard bust portrait, three-quarter profile, a turbaned-and-tuxedoed Charles Carter with imps whispering in his ears. Ever since Kellar, all magicians had adopted this poster – it told audiences, 'Come see a man to whom the Devil himself whispers advice.' Every foreign land knew the imps meant the performer was a magician, the way three balls aloft meant a pawnshop.

To Carter, the imps meant something different. They were whispering, 'You can sit here, Charles Carter, and never move again until your heart stops beating.'

To an exhausted man resting on the walnut-stained floor of his Oakland pied-à-terre, this suggestion, the voice of the devil himself, was very attractive. However, Carter straightened himself and walked forcefully to the kitchen and did dishes. As the sink filled up, he said, 'Ha!' as though the effort were the same as conquering the Alps. He was hopeless at all domestic chores, from beating the rugs to dusting his shelves, and when Bishop was gone, Carter couldn't leave a drinking glass spotless for one million dollars in gold.

Nonetheless, he now worked assiduously, making plans for many activities he would perform today and tomorrow and the next.

He washed out his orange-juice glass, telling himself, 'Mr Carter, your presentation of Goldin's trick was quite remarkable.' He imagined he was scrubbing clean a human skull and hiding it beneath the dishwater. Should anyone ask again, he would say, 'I have performed many illusions, gentlemen, which are unique and compelling. And original.'

But when, Carter the Great, did you last perform such an illusion?

Recently.

And what was it?

His eyes flared. In frustration, he actually said, 'I'm afraid I can't tell you that.' Regardless of Ledocq's advice about trees falling in the forest, Carter had performed a trick for which there had been no audience. This made Starling's needling that much worse. Not only were his recent stage illusions stale, the sole and singular *good* one had occurred after the show, offstage, as if it had never happened, and no one could ever know it had happened at all.

His internal interrogator, which knew how to ask questions more effectively than any Secret Service agent ever would, continued: *Now then – when was the last time you performed a completely original illusion, an illusion for which there was an audience, not just a tree falling in the forest, but an advancement of your vocation?*

Under the water, two hands that were extremely skillful at magic – not dishes – slowed. He said, quietly, '1914.' He did not say the rest aloud: The Phantom War Gun.

He dried his hands, realizing the rack beside him was now filled with wet dishes.

He pulled a leather-bound ledger from the shelf. Here was red ink; there was black ink. He had performed in seventy-two theatres on this last tour, in eighteen countries, and had seen beautiful and exotic lands.

And his net profits were off. Again.

His two weeks at the Curran had been marvelous, but then again he was San Francisco's native son. Ending his tour here was a present he'd given himself to help forget that, increasingly, universally, he was playing to houses in which more and more seats were empty.

Thurston was probably doing well, still, and Houdini was of course beyond any sort of decline. Nicola and Goldin debuted so many new illusions with each tour that they, too, were probably turning profits. But except for that short list, the magic business was getting harder every year. For instance, Grover George, *George el diablo*, clearly knew when he was beaten. These days, he toured overseas, in Andean terrains and remote villages that had never seen the enemy: motion pictures.

So, Mr Charles Carter, he continued silently, *have you even tried to come up with new illusions?*

But of course. And based on real life, too, which is always the best kind, he answered glibly, as if he could fool himself.

Shortly after Black Christmas, a phrase had begun to appear, usually – but not always – in a feminine hand, all over Borax's estate. It had been written on trees, on the walls of cottages, in the dust beside the pigs' feeding pens. It was something many of the unfortunate women wrote, *She Never Died*. It was a quiet cry, a reference to the nameless unfortunate woman murdered on Christmas Day, 1917. *She Never Died* was a way to say her life had not been in vain. Women tended to walk to the edges of the property and write it when they felt depressed.

But just before the election of 1920, the saying began to show up all over Oakland buildings and train yards, even once or twice in San Francisco, sometimes with a second phrase below it, *Don't waste our suffrage*. The phrase had grown into a feminist declaration that as long as one woman was still alive, then that unknown woman was indeed still alive. The *Tribune* had commented on it in the same breath as their condemnation of the Reds, the Drys, and other forces eroding the American way of life. 'Now that women have the vote, can they be trusted to use it?'

The phrase resonated, too, with Carter. He opened a second leather-lined volume, this one thick with pen-and-ink drawings, ideas for new effects. Here, in 1919, he'd begun to design an effect called She Never Died. He looked at it closely, as he hardly remembered it. He would make an assistant vanish, and when he tried to bring her back, everything else on the stage would, with each pass that he made, vanish, too. Finally, he himself would vanish. The end.

He stared at this illusion dumbly, confirming that he'd thought enough of it to record it. How exactly was that an exemplar of She Never Died? He looked at another illusion of the same title: a woman tears scarves in halves, then in quarters, and then Carter passes a cloth over her. She disappears and the scarves are shredded into tatters. The end. Another one: he calls up the spirits of the dead and they confirm that everything is just fine on the other side of the spectral veil. Then they come back to life. The end.

As he flipped through illusion after illusion, all of them equally depressed, incomplete, and joyless, and perhaps half of them called She Never Died, he finally admitted to himself something he had long denied: though he liked the name of the illusion, he couldn't trick himself into feeling the hope it expressed.

He turned to a recent page. 'If I were to perform a truly original trick,' he had written, 'it should be a metaphysical one.' He had divided the page into thirds: on the uppermost tier, he had drawn himself as a stick figure in a turban, with a wand, and written beside it, 'For my next trick, I shall, without benefit of wires or mirrors, change my mood from sour to genuinely happy.' In the middle tier, he had sketched the stick figure now stiff with concentration, beads of sweat spraying off of its body. And at the bottom of the page, there was the figure, sour mood intact, now being pelted with rotten vegetables.

When had he drawn this monstrosity? It was undated. It seemed to have appeared on its own, as if elves had done the work.

He thought, *I feel fine*.

He stood in his study, poring over his sketchbook of ridiculous ideas for illusions, feeling *fine*, and also feeling a churning dissatisfaction. It wasn't as if ideas for tremendous illusions simply dropped out of the sky, he reasoned.

Except, perhaps, now.

He looked out the bay window; the wind blew on his trellises so that green leaves and jasmine flowers shook wildly. In his study was a telescope, an Alvin Clark nautical model. It was fixed in place with verdigris, for Carter was keeping it trained on the Tribune building in downtown Oakland. During the war, in a burst of optimism, the *Tribune* had built a sixty-foot mooring mast in case dirigibles should dock there. It was quite a dream, which the newspaper had presented in a spectacularly illustrated special edition that showed off the monorails and transbay bridges and tunnels and trains and subways that the future held. Furthermore, the forward-looking newspaper had already rented rooftop space all over town, where it painted advertisements that only sky-bound passengers of the future would ever see.

The plan worked as well as most Oakland civic dreams and, to date, the mast was unused, and the advertisements mostly forgotten. But three times a day, Carter looked southward, to the top of the Tribune building, in case a zeppelin, the best of all possible worlds, had arrived in his adopted city. But typically, there was just a crow, if that.

He glanced again through the telescope. The naked mast; that was all he saw. He could stand right here at his desk and watch that mast for a very long time. Someday they would find vines wrapped around his skeleton. 'Him?' they would ask, 'wasn't he Carter, the magician who at one time performed original tricks?'

Then he picked up the telephone. The black candlestick felt clumsy in his hand.

A moment later, a sprightly voice answered. 'James Carter.'

'Is this Carter the Great's little brother?'

'Charlie! Say, this doesn't sound like a ship-to-shore call.'

'I performed a small substitution illusion. James—'

'Where are you?'

'Oakland.'

'Tom and I came back from four months in Europe, ready to see you, and we thought you were hightailing it for Greece.'

'I know. James, look out your front window. Is there anyone standing on the street, trying like a saint to look inconspicuous?'

A moment passed. 'There's a pious young man looking right at my window. Shall I ask him in for coffee?'

'He's from the Secret Service, and hasn't gotten the all clear yet.'

'What's all this in the papers about you and the President?'

'James, I need to see you.'

'Tremendous. I picked up some trinkets for you in Europe, and, anyway, we have accounts to settle, with the tour over. Madame Zorah, for instance—' And James said something about her salary demands, profit shares, interest on a note coming due. But Carter was paying less than strict attention. His eye was caught by the imps portrait again; he crouched before the package and, holding the receiver between his ear and shoulder, he tore away the brown wrapping paper. Finally, he interrupted his brother.

'Excuse me, James. You know my imps portrait?'

'The Otis? We paid eight and a half cents each for them, and you believe one of the imps is telling you to kill yourself. Is that the one?'

'I think one of the imps has started whispering to me about a new illusion.'

'I'm sure he is. One of Selbit's?'

'I have a new illusion in mind. My own.'

Silence on the telephone, made rougher by the static and yawning of a call across the bay.

'I mean it. An original effect. Completely original.'

'Is this another version of those "She Never Died" kinds—'

'No, no, and I think I need to apologize for making you listen to all of those. No, a good illusion. Finally.'

A pause. Then, carefully, 'Come over and talk to me, Charlie. Tomorrow at eight. No, nine. Bring me panettone.'

They hung up. Carter looked again at the docking tower atop the Tribune building, and reached for a necktie that was draped around his telescope. At some point, his younger brother had started acting disturbingly like an older brother. He knotted the tie with one hand and used the other to dial his second telephone, the new one, with the separate base, and combination ear and mouthpiece. Most importantly, it had its own dial: no operator to connect you.

'Yes?'

'Is this the florist? This is Charles Carter.'

The voice on the other end – which in no way belonged to a florist – was chipper. 'We're looking into your order, Mr Carter. We haven't found the flowers you're looking for.'

'Have you looked everywhere?'

'Every possible place in San Francisco and Alameda Counties. We actually completed the search this morning. No flowers by that name, anywhere. We've checked with all the florists.'

Carter wondered if the person he was looking for might go to a boardinghouse rather than a hotel. 'What about nurseries?'

'Those, too. And Mr Carter?'

'Yes.'

'You have esoteric tastes in flowers – no one else has been asking for that type.'

That was excellent news. 'Thank you. Keep looking.'

Minutes after that phone call, Carter put some utensils, magazine clippings, and a light meal into a leather bag. He rode the trolley to the top of Piedmont Avenue. To his left was a stonecutter's, and to the right, an actual florist, industries for the dead. Straight ahead was the Mountain View Cemetery.

Mountain View was large, green, and uncrowded, with sections set aside near the entrance, by the flatlands, for the poor, the Jews, the Chinese, the Portuguese. There were foothills thereafter, and pathways that snaked around reflecting pools and fountains. A quiet knoll planted with lilies, representing innocence, was reserved for the unbaptized babies, and a U-shaped valley for the Spaniards who wanted to be buried facing their ancestral home. There were rows of eucalyptus and sycamores placed so the wind would produce a soft rustling noise designed to aid contemplation.

Carter walked briskly, eyes to the pathway. Around him, resting on marble benches or stepping from tombstone to tombstone, or standing with eyes downcast in contemplation, were dozens of young men and women. Perhaps one in ten was actually acquainted with someone buried here. The rest had come to meet members of the opposite sex.

Carter had chosen Mountain View because it was out of the eye of people. That had changed with the war and the flu pandemic. There had been so many burials at Mountain View that services were scheduled around the clock, and families had to wait, sometimes for hours, sometimes in the pitch of night, for mourners from the previous funeral to disband. And because there were weekly trips to remember the war dead, young people learned that it was a way to meet without their parents' chaperoning them. A boy laying flowers at a gravestone was obviously of high moral standing,

242

and if he were honoring a hero, the girl could tell her family that he was a patriot.

Carter counted many young women sporting the same Sears, Roebuck catalogue silk mourning dress, with decorative belts, sashes, and tassels. When worn with a flirty hat and vamp button boots, the dress looked just playful enough to show that the mourner might receive company.

Carter tried to come to Mountain View at times when it was not a playing field for courtship. Though today was Monday, it was summer, and so it was crowded with youth. He walked briskly to the top of the cemetery, the highest hill with the best view of the bay, the site of Millionaires Row, where the crypts and mausoleums were in the shape of Gothic cathedrals or Masons' pyramids. Passing the monuments to Crocker and Ghiradelli, he took a shortcut through some underbrush and approached the monuments one row below, those of slightly lesser ostentation. He scrambled up an oak, and dropped from a low branch onto a tomb whose granite flagstones had one word spelled out in obsidian chips: CARTER.

From the front, it looked like a small Greek temple, with a pitched roof to show off a pediment. It had once held a marble frieze of the gods at rest, until vandals had taken it. One name, with space below it for another, was engraved in marble: SARAH ANNABELLE CARTER, 1888–1914.

The roof behind the facade was flat. Using the triangular form of the facade as a windbreak, a sunscreen, and a backrest, Carter cored an apple with a penknife, then wiped the blade with his handkerchief.

The sky overhead was a rich blue, and the apple was good, and when he had last been here, ten days ago, he had lain on his back and reported all the good stories from his tour. Mishaps. Close calls. Small pleasures. His parents' travels. Of late they were in South America. The Carters all seemed attracted to that continent, though they never managed to visit each other there. In fact, Carter hadn't seen his parents in several years, but he wasn't thinking much about them today. Today, he was exhausted but still his mind was firing on all eight cylinders.

Piano recitals, gossip. 'I have a letter here where Mom says . . .' or 'James is very . . .' The animals – how was Baby feeling? Old.

And Tug was a sweetheart, and he had recently discovered she liked apple butter, and that was a story he could tell. Instead, he said, with a thrill, like confessing a crime, 'I need to tell you. I have an idea for an illusion.' He paused. He could feel her already granting him permission to pursue it.

He held his breath. Had it been that simple? Of course she would want him to do it. He could see how her eyes would close to slits as she barked, 'Don't be a dope, Charlie!'

Now he felt something so strange it took him several tries to identify it. Because it was neither pain nor melancholy he distrusted this new feeling, yet here it was, a feeling like he had been given tickets to the circus.

He pulled a cigar tube from his pocket. He tossed it skyward, catching it a moment later by its tip, and tossing it again. 'So. If you knew of a great and terrible secret, would you, for the good of the country, expose it or bury it?'

Footsteps below him, and voices. He palmed the cigar tube, and peered over the edge of the monument. A young couple crouched in the shade of a willow. He couldn't make out the words, but the tone was apparent: a lovers' spat, fueled by the flask tucked into her Russian boot. The young woman's hands went to the hips of her sailor dress, then one finger jabbed the air – she was clearly outraged. The young man hung his head, ran his hand through his gleaming hair, and said something, then the woman declared, with great feeling, 'You can go cook a radish!'

She stomped between the tombstones with the indignation only an irate flirt could muster, and the young man leapt off the bench to pursue her. 'But, baby! I was just fooling!' he cried.

Good luck to you, Carter thought, easing down onto his slab. He loved that couple, and all couples like them who were walking down sweet roads everywhere. It was an avuncular sort of love, the sort a retired boxer would have for the ring.

If you knew of a secret, what would you do, Sarah Ann? She would milk it. Every drop. He had some ideas. First –

Another interruption: 'You are my baby vamp.' The boy's voice. Carter, flat on his crypt, looked down the road at the girl and her beau returning, arms around each other already, the girl accepting the flask as they took to the bench. Carter should have looked away then, but the boy was making love like a madman, falling to one knee to declare something iambic, and the girl's eyes softened. They were drunk and in love. And then the boy, reaching a crescendo, showed the girl a ring. The girl threw her head back and screamed, 'Billy! Baby! Yes!'

Carter sank back down behind the cornice. The true love of the drunk. He hadn't really wanted to see that. In five years, a messy railway flat, father at the speakeasy, mother breaking table legs over the behinds of her crying children.

On the other hand, here he was, having a rational conversation with his dead wife. The couple was petting, so he looked up at the sky.

He drummed his fingers against the tube in a jazzy syncopation. The world was vast. He couldn't remember the last time he'd known that but it seemed like a fresh idea: the world was vast, and he was equal to it. He had a wonderful secret in his hands and all he needed was unfettered time to focus.

When the chapel bell chimed five o'clock, he dropped from the crypt to the grass and joined the rest of the mourners in leaving the grounds, which were closing for the night.

He was not expecting, and did not notice, the two men who followed him.

♣ ♦ ♥ ♠

As the sun began to set over Oakland, citizens in a metropolitan area two thousand miles east were lodging complaints for the third night in a row.

The skies of Marion, Ohio, were choked with ashes. The Marion *Star*, which President Harding had once owned, did not publish an account of events, but the *Press-Telegram,* its rival, noted that on the first night, Marion authorities professed to be baffled by homeowners' charges that their houses, their lawns, and their automobiles were blanketed by cinders and ash. On the second night, the police responded with 'no comment,' and the *Press-Telegram* itself stopped reporting the evenings' 'black rains.'

There was more. The skies over the warehouse district of Alexandria, Virginia, a time zone away, were also afflicted. Since it was not a residential neighborhood, the only complaints came from the wholesale produce market, where buyers backed their trucks into stalls before dawn, only to find, hours later, their fruits and vegetables smudged with ash.

A. J. Vaughn, who owned the market, took a few of his cronies to find the source of the pollution. It came from a four-story public storage facility with a six-story brick smokestack at its eastern end. Attempting to enter, Vaughn and his crowd were turned away by policemen who appeared from within the warehouse.

Vaughn knew when he was licked, and so he returned to his business, and erected a canvas awning to keep away the ashes, which continued in the predawn hours for just over a week.

Fires also burned at the White House. The Duchess had started burning Warren Harding's personal papers. In the Oval Office were two steel filing cabinets, with a separate key for each drawer. On the first night, the Duchess burned all of the papers and all of the hanging file folders.

It was no longer her home, and yet the current residents made no moves to stop her. Calvin Coolidge was a silent man who took long naps and whose favorite phrase was 'steady as she goes.' The rest of the White House took his lead.

So, while a pair of assistants tended the fireplace in the Lincoln Bedroom, the Duchess appeared with a full, locked suitcase. She made the others in the room turn their backs, then added items from the suitcase into the fire.

The next day, strong boxes stamped with U.S. Army stenciled letters stood in the center of the Oval Office. The Duchess sat on the floor with a glazed expression, sorting papers into two piles. Ultimately, she burned both of them. She allowed no one to see the papers or to aid her in destroying them.

The Duchess asked to have a pit dug in the garden behind the White House. Here she made an enormous bonfire of files and boxes and personal effects, and as it burned, she muttered to herself, 'It's all for the best, Wurr'n, it's all for the best.'

She had to rest in her old dressing room frequently. A great many public men visited, to pay their respects: Secretary of the Interior Albert Fall, who expressed his condolences, staying until he managed to communicate to the Duchess his innocence of all charges relative to the leasing of the naval oil reserves. She told him, 'that's all behind us,' and with a sigh of what could only be construed as relief, he left. Next were Edward Doheny and Harry Sinclair, oilmen, who wanted the Duchess to know – after paying their respects – they had only accidentally profited from certain deals her late husband had known about, that there was nothing scandalous involved, and she assured them that she knew this.

An hour later, Charles Forbes, a man known to perspire under pressure, burst into the room already talking, saying that it was his poor memory and bookkeeping that made it appear he had defrauded the Veterans Bureau. The Duchess said, quietly, that he had already shown his forgetfulness this very day, as he'd forgotten to tell her how sorry he was that her Warren – who had known every effort he'd made in his bookkeeping – was no longer among the living. With that, Forbes fell silent, mopped his brow, and took the Duchess's hand. 'Thank you,' he said.

Last was Harry Daugherty, who was intoxicated. He truly missed Warren, he said, like a brother, and with him gone, who was left on Earth to dispel all the ugly rumors about selling liquor permits to bootleggers, and taking kickbacks for fixing trials, and about the Post Office confiscating checks sent through the mail to Democratic opposition campaigns, and he went on at such length that finally the Duchess stopped him. 'Harry,' she said bluntly, raising up her veil, 'Warren is dead. You're still Attorney General. The man overseeing you is Mr Coolidge.' With that, she dropped her veil back into place, and Daugherty brightened like a man who has just discovered he's in love.

And so it went, all conspirators great and small realizing that the only man with a conscience was no longer about to spill the beans. The Duchess went back to her duties, and when she was finished with her tires, she left the White House with blisters on her hands, never to return.

Paddock's Storage House, a block-long facility abutting the waste disposal incinerator in Marion, Ohio, had over two hundred rental units, the largest of which – thirty thousand square feet – was paid for in perpetuity by a trust set up early in Harding's political career. When federal investigators finally were issued a subpoena to enter the unit, it was completely empty.

The Alexandria warehouse had contained at least four thousand boxes ten feet long, a foot wide, a foot deep, each tightly packed with documents. When the National Archives called for documents pertaining to the political and personal life of Warren G. Harding, they received two boxes, with generous space for more boxes, should they appear.

Chapter 7

When the sun had been down for an hour and the street lamps had come to life, Carter took the winding circular stairs from his living quarters to his garage. There was just enough space between the Pierce-Arrow and the Bentley for Baby to pass between them, stopping, as he always did, to sniff at the wheels for interesting smells. And then master and cat walked onto the streets of Oakland.

Carter walked Baby without a leash. There was no real point to having one. Instead, he used voice commands to keep the lion in sight. They had walked together for twelve years, all over the world, in cities and villages, on seashores and over mountain trails. In the last two years, Baby had increasingly preferred to stroll, and sit, and listen to the wind coming through the woods rather than stalk squirrels or race after shadows. He was almost thirteen, his mane was thinning, and he had lost nearly seventy pounds. He had an arthritic hip. As Carter watched him negotiate the narrow stairway down to the park, he considered that the performance with President Harding might have been Baby's last.

Carter lived near the entrance to Lakeside Park, which surrounded Lake Merritt. This small smudge on the map was the pitiful evidence that Oakland had once tried to compete against Central Park and Golden Gate Park in the City Beautiful movement. Its maintenance budget resulted in a seedy and unkempt wilderness of overgrown trees and cracked paths interrupted by bandshells and pergolas that, even upon their dedication, looked to have been discarded by other cites. Further, it was said to be haunted, so there were few visitors after dusk except robbers and dope addicts. In short, it was a perfect place to walk Baby.

Baby trotted between the two weathered stone lions that flanked the entrance, paying them no attention (though Carter was always hoping for some kind of recognition). Instead, Baby was intent, as ever, on trotting to the lake's nearest lip and peering over the edge, opening his jaws slightly to better smell the night herons who flocked on the water, far out of reach. A breeze caught the water, and ripples played against the reflection of thousands of tiny outdoor lights that hung between the street lamps, making what the Chamber of Commerce called the Necklace of Lights. The kidney shape of Lake Merritt was outlined like a theatre marquee. It provided a small amount of illumination and, perhaps, safety, for the lights, now celebrated as yet another way that would surely make Oakland a landmark city, had originally been installed because of complaints about the ghosts.

Carter, who'd never seen a ghost, nonetheless found the idea of them wonderful. Who wouldn't want to see a ghost? Whenever he visited the park at night, he saw nothing. On weekend afternoons, he detoured through its rambles on his way to the ferry, watching the boaters, the Sunday painters, the wild and frantic children, and he thought how odd it was that the same joyful places, minus sunlight, became frightening.

Which brought him back to the ghosts, as his first fresh idea in nine years was a type of highly realistic spirit manifestation. Twenty-five minutes of his recent show, 'The Levitation of Madame Zorah,' had involved a séance with disembodied moans, a rapping spirit hand, and the floating medium who made predictions and answered the audience's intimate questions about loved ones on 'the other side.' Carter had never been comfortable with this act, but all of his peers presented such illusions – they were popular. He insisted that his programs also include the disclaimer that he would provide five thousand dollars in gold to the person who could produce a genuine spiritual effect that he himself could not replicate.

He hoped this would show that his spiritualism was just a gag and yet, inevitably, each performance resulted in several letters reaching Carter's hotel, desperately worded petitions to bring a loved one back from the grave. On some days, these letters depressed Carter – their authors were never clever – but on others they simply broke his heart.

He sympathized. There was a thin line between pulling rabbits out of hats and turning water into wine. And when one dealt in wonders, the temptation to pretend divinity, especially when people so *wanted* divinity, was extreme. Even *Scientific American* was beginning to evaluate the machines spirit mediums used in hopes of advancing realms of knowledge. As the world now had odorless gasses that ate away flesh and molds that prevented disease, why not a device to speak with the dead? No one really knew what was possible anymore, and further, whether the means to a given miracle were technical or a mystery. Carter had noted how strictly physical explanations, like X rays showing the skeleton within, were ultimately a disappointment. What the public wanted was to marvel twice, once at what they'd seen, and then again at how progress, in which they had faith, could still be trumped by the hand of God.

How could his new effect be as spectacular as he imagined, and yet not be cruel to the believers in his audience? He would throw out all the trappings of spiritualism – the tambourines, the moans, the ectoplasm – and simplify. Capture a ghost onstage, show it off, make it answer questions, dismiss it into the ether. Ledocq and James would help him make it real.

He and Baby walked through the pergola, toward the bird sanctuary. At this time of night, most of the herons and geese were nesting on the offshore islands, and the rest would scatter when Baby's scent was in the air. Baby had never caught an animal in his life, and Carter was sure that he'd have no idea what to do with a captured goose. Still, he liked to chase and to pounce sometimes, to remind the birds that he was a lion.

Is the ghost here? Carter said to himself, pointing stage right, and imagining a quick manifestation within a crystal ball, *or here?* Stage left, the ghost transporting into another crystal, instantly. The idea of it promising answers to those in need troubled him. Perhaps he wouldn't call it a ghost, but an imp. A pixie. Or what? Now, doubt erupted from fertile ground. The same doubt he'd had since the days of blackmail: was this an admirable illusion?

Baby trotted ahead. His body went rigid, golden teardrop at the end of his tail flicking, and he was off like a shot, disappearing into the undergrowth.

Carter clicked his tongue disapprovingly. He could hear the crunch of breaking twigs. If somewhere in those three hundred pounds Baby had an ounce of catlike grace, it was unapparent. He whistled, and the sounds stopped. The lion did not return.

Baby had left the shoreline and gone deeper into the park. No feral animals there. If Baby were after a robber, his master would not mind – and might even enjoy it a little. He stood silently by the edge of the lake, peering in toward the woods, hoping for a sound to give Baby's game away. There was a brief outline of the lion as he ducked, belly to the ground, out of one bush and into another. But where was he going? The necklace of lights was not bright enough to see clearly. A quick gust of wind jangled the lights and brought the smell of guano and creosote, and in horror, Carter saw, outlined under a street lamp, the wide hat and slender figure of a solitary woman sitting on a park bench. Baby was hunting her.

There was no time for Carter to cry out; in less than a second, Baby had vaulted the back of the bench, and landed with a thud, paws outstretched, back arched, teeth bared. Carter ran toward the scene with his heart in his mouth, reciting all the things he'd said to street urchins in London and customs officers at the Port of San Francisco: Baby was just playing, Carter would say. He couldn't hurt a fly.

Then he saw something that stopped him dead: the woman was passing Baby a bite from her sandwich.

The lion took the meat and lapped it up noisily. The woman tugged out another strip of meat, unimpressed that a lion was nuzzling the ground by her ankles.

With Carter a dozen yards behind her, the woman said, loudly, over her shoulder, 'I hope it's all right that I feed him roast beef.'

After clearing the rocks from his throat, he answered, 'Yes. Yes, he likes roast beef.' What a cool customer.

'Good. I am wondering what sort of dog he is, exactly.'

Carter laughed. A *very* cool customer. 'He's a schnauzer.'

'You're teasing me,' she said. She had a clear voice, enunciation like a schoolteacher. As Carter drew close, he could see that she wore a simple wool dress that was out of fashion by many years, and too lightweight for evening wear. Her back was to him. She had faced him for just a second. He had the impression of sizable red lips and a flash of eyeglasses. Her age, her complexion, her hair color were masked by the huge brim of her hat. She seemed completely out of place. 'I happen to know that schnauzers are much smaller. What's his name?'

'Baby.'

'And what kind of a dog is he?'

'All right, if he isn't a schnauzer, then he's a lion.'

'Now I know you're teasing me,' she said, tossing another piece of roast beef to Baby, who gulped it down.

'He's not a mountain lion, either. He's a lion from Africa.'

She said nothing, and Carter was disappointed. When she held out the next piece of roast beef, and Baby advanced toward it, she slowly pulled it out of reach, making Baby pass by her. She ran her hands from his mane to the bulb of hair at the end of his tail.

'My God!' she shrieked, stumbling from the bench and turning, and there, under the lights, Carter saw her face, now a bloodless white, her lips obscured as she brought both hands to her mouth. She was shaking. Her glasses were painted black, matte black, across both lenses.

'Oh,' he said without thinking, 'you're blind.'

'It's a lion!' she cried.

'I'm sorry, I thought you knew. I thought – please, don't worry. He's tame.'

'You have a *lion*!'

'Please don't be scared. He won't hurt you. I think he only came after you because he smelled your roast beef.' Carter glanced at Baby, who was now snuffling at the wax paper. 'You're safe. But he's eaten your sandwich.'

She walked backwards until she touched the street lamp, and she grasped at it with both hands.

'My name is Charles Carter. I'm a magician,' he said, in the soothing voice he used on volunteers onstage. 'I live nearby and I walk my lion when it's dark so we don't run into people. I'm sorry we frightened you. He and I will be on our way.' He clicked his tongue. Baby reluctantly came to his heel. Carter touched his fingers to the brim of his hat, etiquette perhaps idiotic when leaving a blind woman, but he was thrown off, and he needed to leave.

He was only a few feet away when the woman said, 'The suave and bubbling mahatma.'

'Excuse me?'

'The paper called you the "suave and bubbling mahatma."'

'Oh, yes.' He frowned, 'They should have said "suave and lion-owning mahatma."'

She folded her arms across her stomach, shivering still, and remaining several paces away from Carter. 'Maybe.' She added, 'Did they leave anything out? Black widow spiders?'

'I've had a few assistants who could have moonlighted as black widow spiders.'

'What about your friends?'

'Excuse me?'

'I think there are several men in the woods near us.'

Carter turned toward the maze of trees and bushes. 'If there are men in the woods, they are no one's friends.' He wasn't about to leave a blind woman alone with unseen muggers. Still, he didn't understand why she wouldn't ask for his help.

'And this is the lion that ate President Harding?'

'He's still full.' No reaction from her, not even a smile. Torn between teasing her and being helpful, he added, 'He never really ate the President, you know. It was a trick.'

'There were rumors.'

'I know.'

She drew a deep sigh, arms still crossed. She seemed capable of arctic silence.

'I apologize for not making your acquaintance.'

'My name is Phoebe Kyle.'

'What brings you to Lakeside Park, Miss Kyle?'

'I was . . . walking. Thank you.'

'Do you know where you are?'

'Certainly,' she said. 'The lake is right there, the bird sanctuary over there, and the Home is' – her hand fluttered in a general direction – 'there. And yes, I know there are many dope fiends between here and there.'

Of course. She was too proud to ask for help. 'Would you take the escort of a man and a lion back toward the Home?'

'I'm not lost.'

'I know.'

She patted her palm against her collar. Carter wondered what options she was weighing. Finally, she extended her hand. He expected a tentative grip, but there was steel in her fingers. 'The problem is, I live at Telegraph and Thirty-Sixth. I can't ask you to walk all that way with me.'

'We'll sort it out.' Carter could feel each of her fingers, distinct and strong, on his arm. They seemed to pulse, as if she couldn't keep still. As they walked, he made several attempts, but could not successfully see her face.

She said, 'Do you know about the ghosts?'

'Did you think I was a ghost?'

With great authority, she shook her head. 'No.'

'Are you sure you aren't cold?'

'Just a slight chill.'

Carter draped his jacket around her shoulders.

'You're too kind, Mr Carter.'

'It's nothing.'

'No, you are too kind. If people saw us walking like this, they would think we're sweethearts.' They walked slowly, while Miss Kyle stroked the fabric of his jacket.

Carter said, 'If people already think I killed the President, other gossip lacks a certain amount of scandal.'

Since she didn't respond, he looked away from her, and focused on the muscles of Baby's back as he walked, how one shoulder, then the other, rose with each step. Carter could not tell if Miss Kyle ever smiled, but as they walked, her tone had became more inviting to conversation. He had been so misled by her casual feeding of Baby that he still didn't know what she was like. He decided to listen rather than speak. Perhaps she was more the serious sort.

'I make brooms,' she announced.

'Pardon?'

'Not day and night, but several hours a day. All the girls at the Home. We all make brooms.'

'I have a broom. Perhaps I could get an autograph.' He immediately regretted it. He remembered boyhood attempts, before he learned self-control, at throwing darts and trying to will them toward the target, and knowing, even as they left his hand, that they would go wide. He asked, 'Is it much of a life, making brooms?'

'It's a fine life,' she declared. 'I have many acquaintances among the women at the Home. We listen to the gramophone while we work. We are supposed to get a radio. Sometimes the matron reads to us. I make enough money to buy dresses and sweets. When my prefect retires, I could take over her job making cane-back chairs.'

Carter had a cane-back chair, too, but he caught himself before commenting on it. 'Is that a promotion?'

'It requires more skill. If I had the patience I should be a necklace maker, but I don't have the mind for it.' She explained that several of the girls had wonderful brains, and could make fabulously complicated strings of multicolored beads that never clashed, keeping the whole design in their heads while they worked. They were the most clever girls, and all the men were most impressed with them. 'The men have it far worse than the women. There is much competition, and all the girls quickly have sweethearts.' She hesitated. 'You must have many women who want to become your sweetheart.'

He said, 'That sort is identified with ease.'

'This jacket is from London,' she said, so artlessly it sounded like a response. 'The weave is different than domestic jackets. Sears says theirs are just like the imports, but you can always tell.' She quickly said, 'Not that I spend a great deal of time feeling men's jackets.'

They continued walking the path between the old oak trees.

'Do you have a gentleman friend, Miss Kyle?'

The dirt path joined the pavement, and Miss Kyle took the opportunity to lengthen her stride. 'It's difficult for girls at the Home. You cannot really go out unless you're in a man's company, so it's . . . to say . . . of a man's . . . if he knows how to explore the city without getting lost . . .'

Carter said, 'I hope he at least got a slap in the face.'

'Who?'

'The man who left you in your predicament.'

'Is this Grand Avenue already?' she asked. 'I could catch a taxicab from here.'

'We are close to the avenue,' he admitted, 'but taxis tend not to stop for people accompanied by lions.' Baby padded past them, along a stone path that branched away from the one they stood on.

Miss Kyle looked confused. 'Has he gone ahead?'

'There's a fountain. During the day, he's frightened of the noise, but at night, they turn it off.' Carter paused. 'Just listen.'

They listened together, and then came great, sloppy sounds of a huge tongue lapping. Baby stood with his rear legs on the ground, front legs on the fountain's stone edge, and his face almost kissing the skin of the water. Phoebe Kyle might be smiling, but it was hard to see her in the poor light. He was trying to form an offer without sounding like a masher: to take her to his house – to get his car and drive back to the home.

'Mr Carter,' she said, 'do you follow fashion?'

'I'm not much of a clotheshorse.'

'I mean ladies' fashions. I hear there's a new fad for girls, the flapper sort. Knee-painting.'

'Excuse me?'

'I've heard that girls paint pictures of their sweethearts on their knees, and walk around town that way. Is that true?'

'I'm sorry – I don't look much at ladies' knees.'

'You'll have to pay better attention.'

'Miss Kyle?'

'Just tell them you're allowed on account of a blind girl.'

'Miss Kyle?'

'Phoebe.'

'Phoebe.' He watched Baby ambling toward them, blinking and moving his tongue around his whiskers. 'Let's walk to my garage, and I'll put Baby away for the night, and then I'll drive you to your home. Unless that would cause talk.'

'Well. Some parties could benefit from talk.' When they continued walking, she said, 'Thank you.'

They took a path paralleling the avenue, a few feet into the woods so that Baby wouldn't startle other pedestrians. Their conversation was sporadic, and throughout, he could neither get her to reveal information nor be relaxed and gracious himself.

As she surmised, many women wanted to make his acquaintance. Several times since the War, he'd half considered assignations he couldn't quite explain, with a chorus girl or an heiress, and it always ended badly before it had even begun. He'd concluded that he was quite clumsy when it came to love, and for the past several years had flirted out of politeness, but nothing more.

When they were climbing the final hill that met the base of the public stairs next to One Hilgirt Circle, they stopped to let Baby into the garage entrance, and she said, 'You are a suave man, but you are not bubbling.'

Closing and locking the door to Baby's lair, Carter said, 'Wasn't I bubbling just now?'

'No. No, you tell jokes, but they're not bubbling. Your voice, your posture, and I suspect your face, too, all suggest you are a suave and sad mahatma, I think. Why is that?'

'Carter! Carter!' Amanda and Amy Chong, the ten-year-old twins who lived next door, were on his stairs, descending in great excitement. It was after nine o'clock, and they were in their nightgowns.

'You're about to meet some children.' Carter turned to Miss Kyle, quickly, too quickly, colliding with her – she let out a gasp as her glasses slipped off her nose. He caught them in midair. 'I have them,' he said.

'Carter!' He was used to hearing his name shrilled from all sides on weekend afternoons, when the neighborhood children wanted him to do tricks. His time in the limelight would last until the bells from the ice cream wagon sounded.

But tonight there were no other children, and the Chongs weren't asking him to do tricks. They grabbed for his hands, the better to pull him up the staircase. Carter began to say something apologetic to Miss Kyle as she took her spectacles back. And then, before the perfectly round lenses found their place again, he caught a glance of her face in distress, her green eyes wide. He wanted a second glance.

'Carter . . .'

'. . . men came . . . Carter, come on . . .'

'Two fat men . . . come on.'

'. . . see the rope, it's still hanging, Carter . . .'

He followed the two girls, who ran with their hands holding on to the hems of their nightgowns. When they got to his front door, they simultaneously told their story to him. '. . . just went to bed, and we were looking out the window, looking for Baby . . . over there . . . they didn't see us . . .'

Carter had excellent home defenses. Otherwise rival magicians might break in to steal his notes (most of which were in a safety deposit box) or his illusions (all of which were dismantled after a tour, the key mechanisms kept under Ledocq's supervision). Also, society pages inevitably announced Carter's departures overseas and his triumphant returns, with speculations as to what treasures he had accumulated. Carter knew that if *he* were a burglar, he would read the society pages, and so his houses in San Francisco and Oakland were fortified.

A rope with a frayed end was hanging down in front of his front door. When he looked for them, he found black heel marks, showing one man had ultimately dragged the other away.

'They didn't get in,' Amanda said.

'I see,' Carter replied. 'Did one of the men try to force the door open?'

'Yeah, one of them did, and then . . .'

'And when the trap went off, did the other man have to cut him down?'

'Right . . . and then . . .'

'One of them touched the doorknob. Then what happened?'

Amy said, 'Boom!' And she and her sister danced from foot to foot and shook their arms and legs, giggling.

Phoebe Kyle had come up the stairs, and stood near the girls. 'Boom?'

Amy sang out, 'Everyone knows you don't touch Carter's door!'

'Not on a dare!' Amanda added.

'Or else – Boom!' Amy did her little dance. The girls told Carter how the man who touched the door had to be carried away by the other man, and how they hadn't come back. When they had told the story a few times to each other, and had each gotten an opportunity to say 'Boom!' again and perform terpsichorean dramatics and collapse, and had begun to digress about how they were taking swimming lessons, and had already gotten their dolphin badges, Carter thanked them, and gave them each a dime, and they raced off home, to get back into bed before their parents found out.

'Children. So *cheerful*,' Miss Kyle said, as if she'd heard the word used successfully.

'They're sweet girls. Children are a terrible audience for magicians. It's very hard to make them look where they're supposed to. So they also make—'

'Good neighbors?'

'Oh, yes.'

Carter deactivated his defense system and entered his house. He led Miss Kyle to a chair, and then walked from room to room. Everything was the way he'd left it.

When he returned to the foyer, Miss Kyle's chair was empty – she was standing, her fingertips darting in and around an ornate vase.

'Miss Kyle, I should get you home as soon as possible. You could be in great danger if you stay.'

'Really?' she said, curious and perhaps even delighted.

'I'm serious. You might dislike your life in the Home, but the truth is, there are desperate people in the world.'

She continued to explore the foyer with her hands, then stepped left carefully, following the wall: hands on the table, then on to the shelves in his living room, then to his desk, where she found his telescope. She seemed to linger here.

'It's pointing upward, I assure you.'

Still, she felt around its base, and on the reeded edge of its eyepiece. 'It's pointing toward the Tribune building.'

'What a remarkable guess,' Carter said, as astonished as if she'd produced a bouquet of flowers. 'How—'

'I wasn't guessing,' she interrupted. 'So tell me how you feel about all this.'

'All what?'

'Thugs. Desperate men.'

His heartbeat was at eighty, his breathing was normal. 'I feel fine.'

'I see. Mr Carter, how do you feel about strange men being electrocuted on your doorstep?' Because he was sure he'd just answered that question, he stared at her until she continued, 'While you think about it, I'll look at your books.'

'Good luck.' It came out of his mouth before he'd even considered what he was saying. Miss Kyle turned slowly, very slowly from the bookshelf; it seemed to take an hour and a half for him to see her face. And what a radiant face it was. She was smiling, wonderful red lips parting to show off dazzling white teeth, the first smile she had directed at him.

Then back to the shelves. She picked up and felt and replaced an ivory letter opener. She had him at sixes and sevens – and without even seeming to pay full attention to him. The letter opener back on the shelf, then fingers darting over and around a set of gimmicked cups. She could be here all night.

And so Carter put his mind to it: besides fine, how did he feel about being pursued by thugs? If he had a new challenge on his hands, it was one for which he was remarkably prepared. He had evaded the Secret Service once, and had just put some idiots down without effort. He knew he had something they wanted – but they couldn't be sure he had it, for he was outwitting them at every moment in ways they hadn't even discovered – misdirection! The truth was: he didn't just feel fine.

'Excuse me,' he said, and then brought two glasses from the kitchen. He passed one to Phoebe, who had pulled out the oldest book on the shelf – incunabula – spells the Inquisition suspected were used to conjure up demons.

'What on earth is this binding made of?'

He took it from her. 'Human skin. Listen carefully. I would like to toast something.'

She smelled the glass. 'Oh, water. I can drink water, I suppose. What sort of thing are we toasting?'

'The unknown.'

She considered this, and then held out her glass. He gently tapped his against it.

'To the unknown.' She sipped from her glass. 'And how, Mr Carter, do you feel about the unknown?'

'I feel very, very good about it.'

When he said that, she extended her glass again, for a second toast.

Chapter 8

Man cannot survive by bread and water alone, but bread and water and *hate*? It was time for afternoon prayers in Cairo, and the mosque across the street from the Ezbekieh Theatre broadcast the call from a newly installed gramophone, with speakers situated on the second story. There was one bitter man waiting outside the theatre for Bechara Hemaidan, the promoter. The man hated the sun-baked day and the shrill singing of Arabic.

Until prayers were over, he could not see Hemaidan, so he looked at the plain lobby cards that were mounted in the dusty old windows. 'Prescott!' The cards were printed in two colors, red and blue, and were not illustrated because the man who called himself Prescott could no longer afford it. They did not say he was a magician because he was convinced he could not risk being found, even here, eight thousand miles from nowhere.

He smoked. He wore a new fedora and a cream-colored silk suit with a bow tie. His head was shaved every morning and every evening, and he bleached his Vandyke blond. He wore two types of cologne, one for morning, one for evening. Even so, with the wind beginning to pick up, he could smell the stench of human excrement, and he winced as a small dust devil in the street collapsed nearby, sending detritus tumbling toward him. He ducked into an alcove behind the ticket taker's booth to protect the $100 python-skin shoes that he had taken from an unlucky man in Rhodesia.

He noted with disdain the waxed canvas dropcloths that were pitched over the top stories of the unfinished office buildings on either side of the mosque. A stagehand had explained all the incomplete buildings to him, in the formal-sounding market English spoken among Arab entertainers. When the construction boom had hit Cairo, the government levied a property tax on completed buildings – only completed buildings – so in the downtown area, four out of five structures stood with bare girders, unfinished walls, entire stories naked to the elements.

Presently, the prayers ended, and there was silence on the street and then the people of the city began to spill out again into the scorching sunlight. The shade over Hemaidan's window rustled and spun up on its roller.

Prescott rapped on the frosted glass immediately. He was here to extend his run for another two weeks.

Hemaidan, short and thick around the middle, showed no sign of emotion when he let Prescott into his office. Seeing what Prescott cradled in his arms, he murmured, knowing the answer already, 'Would you leave your animal outside?'

'I think not.' Prescott found and sat in one of the two leather chairs on the visitors' side of Hemaidan's desk. Like promoters' offices around the world, this one was deliberately shabby, decorated with posters of long-forgotten acts and furnished with hand-me-downs from defunct productions that could not finish out their contracts. The message sent was that Hemaidan had no money to spare, and furthermore would not hesitate to take your livelihood should you fail him.

Hemaidan eased into his own chair, making eye contact with the dog that shivered in Prescott's lap. 'You are lucky I understand the pleasure pets bring to their owners.'

'Handsome is not a pet,' Prescott said. When he showed no signs of elaborating, Hemaidan cleared his throat and continued.

'We need to discuss this note you have passed on to me. I'm afraid that what you have asked for is not possible.'

Prescott blinked. It was standard procedure to be put through torture, to be told you were not needed, before the real offer was on the table. He stroked his dog's back and haunches.

But then Hemaidan told him something he hadn't expected. 'I have booked a new act into the theatre beginning tomorrow night. It is a man and a woman. Acrobats and comedians.'

'And the attraction of their act?'

'My brother-in-law in Carthage wrote me about them. The man acts drunkenly and the woman throws many, many dishes at him. The crowds find it hilarious.'

'Of course.' Prescott looked at his nails. They were perfect. His

263

voice, while always smooth, like a woodwind, became more consonant, as he added, 'But you still have an obligation to me that you'll be no doubt fulfilling.'

'What obligation is that?'

'Payment for the next week, as that is how long I had been scheduled to perform.'

Hemaidan folded his hands over his belly. 'Your contract says you are on a night-to-night basis, and can be fired at my discretion, immediately. It is quite standard. I'm allowing you an extra twenty-four hours because I feel sorry for you.'

Prescott fixed Hemaidan with eyes that, for only one second, widened. 'My goodness. Sorry for me. That's generous, Mr Hemaidan. Why, may I ask, are you sorry for me?'

'Your show is a mess. I'm not even sure it's magic. I do not understand it. Your audience does not understand it.'

'Perhaps you should be finding a better class of audience.'

'I do not think so. You perform tricks, if that's what they are, that make no sense. You talk to invisible people. I thought it would be spiritualism when I booked you, but it seems to be invisible people.' Hemaidan leaned forward and, with his hands, described the shape of a hat. 'And when you take a man's hat from the audience and put the milk and the eggs and the flour into it – you're supposed to make a cake. What kind of magic is it when you leave that mess, and slap it back onto his head?'

'It's the magic of teaching people not to trust anyone.'

'I do not find this amusing, Mr Prescott. You have several interesting tricks. I would even write you a letter of introduction referring to them. Like the card throwing. Throwing a playing card through a candle, and then an orange, and then bamboo – that is impressive. But this is a family theatre and I do not like when you abuse that mannequin.'

'It's not a mannequin. It's a dummy.'

'It makes people confused to see you yelling at it and pretending to dash its brains out on the stage. It is not family entertainment when you saw it in half. No one cares to see such a weird thing. Here.' Hemaidan reached behind him and brought Prescott's dummy onto his desk, its limbs scattershot, its outfit of evening clothes in disarray. Prescott made no move to take it. Instead, he scratched his dog behind the ears and regarded the dirty black yarn that was the dummy's hair, the faded blue buttons that were its eyes, and he smiled with the air of a man who has heard he is about to be crowned king.

'You should cancel your comedians,' Prescott said. 'Once word of mouth spreads about my act, your theatre will be overflowing with crowds as they did in Tangiers.'

'You haven't sold out one of the performances. The last two days, I've been begging all of my wife's relatives to come, but none of them want to anymore.' Hemaidan halted here, and then, by speaking again, made a mistake. 'You know, you have a stage presence and those few good tricks. You just need to study more, follow the important magicians—'

'Important – I'm sorry. I interrupted you. Which magicians are important?'

Hemaidan looked toward the low ceiling of his office. 'You've heard of them. Houdini. Thurston. Nicola. My brother-in-law saw Carter the Great last year, and said he was marvelous.' He nodded with enthusiasm.

Prescott said, 'Your brother-in-law, he certainly has all the luck in the family.'

'I'm sorry I cannot book you for another night, Prescott, but be a good fellow and get your things. My men have already put them together backstage.' Hemaidan looked down at his desk and began to shuffle papers around.

Prescott, holding Handsome tightly, stood but did not leave.

'I suggest on your way out you leave me your card.'

Prescott said, 'Excuse me?'

Hemaidan looked up. 'Leave me your card.'

'As you wish.'

There was no taxi to meet Olian and Bugeau, the acrobatic husband and wife, when they arrived at the train station that evening. Their contract had stipulated there would be a taxi, and its absence triggered an argument. They bickered as they loaded their luggage into a cab, which they paid for out of their own grouch bag, and went to the Ezbekieh Theatre, where their pounding on the promoter's door went unanswered.

It wasn't until the stage manager appeared that the door was unlocked, and that was how Bechara Hemaidan's body was found. He had not died easily; chairs and bookshelves were knocked over, playing cards were scattered across the floor, blood was everywhere. Someone had slashed his throat and his wrists and had stabbed him dozens of times in the stomach.

The police were unable to identify the murder weapon, as none was apparent, and the wounds were inconsistent with either a sharp knife, like a stiletto, a blunt one like an ice pick, or a triangular shape, like a bayonet. As the body was examined, and scores of wounds were uncovered, the task of counting the punctures seemed impossible. But then, suddenly, before the count had even begun, the Chief Inspector said, with authority, 'There are fifty-two wounds.'

The roomful of police murmured in response. The Chief's hunches were often correct, but how had he determined this?

In reply, he gently tugged an obstruction out of the slash across Hemaidan's throat: it was an ace of spades.

Chapter 9

'You've gotta be kidding, Sam.'

'I kid you not. I saw him. With my own eyes.'

Tuesday morning, Secret Service agents sat at a corner booth in the Automat on Market and Seventh. The Service's numbers in San Francisco had diminished, and of the Eight Righteous Men, there were but four left locally – three in the booth, one in line to get food – all junior, all cut from the same blond cloth. Their names were Hollis, Stutz, Samuelson, and O'Brien, the latter nursing a broken nose and a black eye that beefsteak had been unable to address. Since their superiors were eating lunch at the press club, they felt free to smoke cigarettes, and to use poor grammar.

'What did he look like?' Stutz asked.

Samuelson, who was a ladies' man, withheld what he was about to say, as Hollis was returning from the cashier. Hollis, cowlicked, face still red from his twice-weekly shave, was the youngest agent assigned to the San Francisco office, and his tray was crowded with everyone's pie and coffee. 'Turn it over, Hollis,' said Samuelson. 'Pie in the morning.'

'What'd I miss? You gents were just laughing.'

'Sam here saw a damned mermaid this morning.' O'Brien spoke gingerly because of the beating Griffin had administered.

Samuelson shook his head. 'I'm not saying that. I'm not saying that.' Samuelson had learned the knack of telling stories, leaving out key details that begged for questions.

Hollis pulled up a chair. 'What was it you saw?'

Samuelson said, 'I was walking through the Presidio about five this morning, and I was just about at the Marina Green when I saw, in the bay—'

'Hold on.' Stutz poked Samuelson's arm. 'You haven't told us why you were out at five A.M. in the morning.'

'I was just . . . taking in the bounty of nature.'

'I bet you were,' Stutz cried. 'Who was she?'

'What did you see in the bay?' asked Hollis.

Samuelson gave him an annoyed look.

O'Brien grinned. 'You were in the Presidio all night, weren't you? The Major's daughter. Right?'

Samuelson blew smoke toward the table as the others chimed in with encouragement. 'All I'm saying is you gents should take the trouble to get to know this fair city a little better.'

Stutz prompted: 'A bit of nocturnal surveillance, Sam?'

'Men, men, men,' Samuelson clicked his tongue. 'A gentleman never tells these sorts of things. The important thing is, five A.M. in the morning, and what do I see in the bay but Senior Officer Jack Griffin?' The others laughed, so Samuelson continued. 'Jack Griffin, Grumpy Griffin, swimming. In the bay at five A.M. in the morning.'

'Stinking up the bay,' O'Brien muttered.

'Now, O'Brien' – Samuelson grinned – 'you did your best.'

Stutz said, 'I wonder what he was doing in there?'

O'Brien said, 'I bet he was drunk.'

'Did he look happy?' Stutz asked.

'Well, you know how he looks,' Samuelson said, which caused more laughter.

'Maybe he was getting ready for his calisthenics,' Hollis said, taking another bite of pie. More merriment followed, and Hollis looked up. 'What?'

Stutz said, 'That's rich. Really rich.'

O'Brien added, 'And then maybe putting on his skirt to go ice skating.'

'No, really,' Hollis said. 'Because I saw him doing calisthenics at six yesterday.'

'Where was he doing calisthenics? What was he doing?' Stutz growled. 'High kicks?'

'Yes, there were some high kicks involved, actually.' Hollis spoke as if accuracy might count toward popularity. 'He did sprints and stretches. And I saw him do twenty-five chin-ups and a hundred push-ups. I left while he was doing sit-ups.'

'And where exactly was this?' No one noted the frost in Samuelson's voice.

'The Green, around six yesterday morning.'

Stutz whistled. 'That's not the Griffin I've heard about.'

Samuelson said, 'Well, beating the bejesus out of O'Brien here must make him feel ten feet tall.'

Teasing O'Brien was an excellent sport, with Stutz and Samuelson taking turns as the matador. When they were done, they considered aloud – now that they noticed it – the change in Griffin's demeanor. Then, with a squint, Stutz said, 'Hollis. What were you doing on the green at six o'clock in the morning?'

Hollis blushed. He brought his napkin to his mouth. 'Well, nothing. It's just that there's this girl.' And the rest of his comments throughout lunch were covered by gales of laughter and increasingly jealous comments from Samuelson.

Chapter 10

Early Tuesday morning, Carter walked down Lake Shore Avenue. He couldn't remember having seen better weather in poor old Oakland: the air smelled fresh and sweet like someone nearby was baking bread. On the lake were tight flocks of coots, and in the grass nearby, Canadian geese and canvasbacks and egrets pecking at seeds. Carter crossed the avenue to see them better. It was a long walk to the ferry, but today it felt invigorating. It was a day when, had he been a singing type of man, he would have burst into song.

Ferrying into San Francisco, he stood with his hands balled into his pockets, tapping the cigar tube, and attempting to conquer the concept of money, which he in no way comprehended. To launch a new tour, he needed capital, and to develop his illusion he also needed capital – this much he understood. And he made money by performing. But the specifics, the way a week of receipts from the Broadway Showcase in Buenos Aires was pared into a pocketful of silver dollars, was for him as elusive as how water flowed from reservoir pipes and aquifers into his bathtub.

According to his posters, Thurston had spent $50,000 on his vanishing horse illusion. Carter would probably need to spend at least that to create what he had in mind and considering this, his imagination flew from the responsibilities of money to how fun it would be to spend it. He moved his lips around the words, *Ladies and gentlemen, I introduce a clever pixie, an imp from the netherworld.*

He tipped his boater back, observing the deck of the *Charlie Mae*. A sparse group of passengers, any of whom could be members of his audience. There were bachelors and families with schoolchildren and, now that he thought about it, each of them had paid their nickel for the ferry, which had cost money to build. Where, if money were a finite resource, did it come from in the first place?

He noticed a pair of girls, flappers, in last night's rumpled clothing, sitting on a wooden bench, leaning against each other and looking unhappily out at the horizon. He glanced at their knees, which were bare and sweetheart free.

Soon they docked, and Carter walked to North Beach. Delighted to see shops open so early, he ducked under the salamis hanging in the doorway of the New Union Grocery. This was James's favorite emporium, as it was so overpacked with imported and homemade culinary fancies, it was less a shop than a thieves' repository, like Ali Baba's cave. Carter puttered among cheeses and candied fruits until he'd located an excellent panettone, and flanked it with assorted rich pastries.

A few minutes later, bearing a pink box, Carter entered the Ferry building. This was the Columbus Avenue rooming house equidistant from the theatre district and the pier where the passenger boats docked. Carter had first come here early one morning in 1911 to announce he was taking over Mysterioso's show. Today, he pressed the button by the engraved brass 'J. Carter/T. Crandall' name plate and was immediately buzzed in.

James Carter had taken over the building in 1920. He had turned the top floor into a penthouse, where he lived and entertained and, when he so wished, phoned the office to see how his investments were playing out.

James had been managing the World Famous Carter the Great Paragon of Mystery Show since his return to stage in late 1917. This meant that to finance his new illusion, Carter was coming, hat in hand, to ask his younger brother for an advance. He rang the bell decisively, now wishing he'd brought flowers instead of pastries, which had become somewhat controversial.

Immediately, James threw the door open. His tousled golden curls were thinning but still bright. He wore royal blue silk pajamas under a monogrammed bathrobe Carter had given him. 'Charlie!' James cried, and then he cried, 'Panettone!' and then he hugged his brother.

Carter put his arms around James, which had become slightly more difficult in the last two years. His oceanic travels had obviously been eased with many pastries.

James looked at him with pride. 'I've become opulent.'

'You're a pasha!'

The penthouse of the Ferry building had panoramic views of San Francisco and the bay, and the morning sunlight flooded into every window. James had knocked out most of the walls, save for a small suite for living quarters, and the result was a backward-L shape of an open room.

James had never been a collector, but he had inherited their father's taste. His home was like an inviting series of tableaux to be appreciated first, then to be inhabited. Whenever Carter visited his brother, he first pitied how meager James's furnishings were, but always ended up wanting to purge his own houses and re-organize his rooms.

While slicing the panettone, and arranging the other pastries so they flanked it, James ran down the list of people who'd told him to say hello, and how well their mother was faring with her photography, and how Dad actually seemed *interested* in her work. Though presented with benevolence, the topics were also a checklist of small talk. 'And how are your animals?'

'Baby is slowing down a bit. Tug has developed an odd craving for apple butter.'

'You don't say.'

Carter said, 'Where's Tom?'

'If you can believe it, he's at church.'

'No, I can't believe it.'

'It's about the only place his family will see him. Here we go. We won't stand on further ceremony, you're a man of the world, you've seen how coffee is made. It's Red Gate, mocha java.' James took the percolator off the stove, and carried it to a table by the fireplace.

Carter settled in a fine armchair nearby, and felt that James had purchased the most comfortable armchair in the world. He didn't want to move. 'Anything else about Europe?'

'Paris was beautiful. London was beautiful. Berlin was depressing. You'd like Berlin.'

There it was, the segue from small talk, performed with one raised eyebrow, something James could do with admirable efficiency. In spite of himself, Carter laughed aloud.

'Are you all right? What's that you're doing?'

Carter wasn't aware he'd been doing anything. 'Laughing?'

'Good for you. Listen, I'm glad you're in such a fine mood – we have some problems here.' He glanced at a notepad. James had many notepads, all excruciatingly well organized.

He crossed the room, returning with a fourteen-by-twenty-two window card, which he handed over to his brother, who let out a gasp. It was like looking into the face of a dear friend who had been worked over with brass knuckles. It was his poster: the horned, crazy-eyed Devil holding four kings, and the turbaned, triumphant magician holding four aces. But the magician also had a monocle and pencil-thin mustache, and the title at the bottom made Carter's skin freeze.

'*Dalton* Beats the Devil,' he whispered. '*Dalton*? Who the hell is *Dalton*?'

'He's a very foolish Englishman who's going to be spending his every waking hour in court for the next five years. Not an issue, really. The actual problem – this isn't a silk screen.'

Carter looked carefully at the details and highlights of the poster. They were perfect. 'You mean it was struck off stone plates?'

'It was struck off *your* stone plates. I just checked. Your plates are missing.'

He breathed slowly. He willed his heart to behave. 'We have a weasel in the company.' It happened from time to time. He'd had his patter stolen, gimmicks copied, and it usually meant cleaning house. 'Carlo.'

Carlo had many lady friends around the world, whom he kept happy with puzzlingly expensive pearls and silver trinkets. James had his Waterman pen suspended over Carlo's name on the yellow pad. 'It's the end of the season. We'll let everyone go and start afresh in the fall, only there won't be room for Carlo.'

'Yes, that's an excellent – no, no. Wait.'

'We'll give him a hearty raise?'

'Not that,' Carter said. 'If you have Dalton subdued, we'll go on as everything was before. I like having an informant on staff. We'll tell Carlo the fall tour is of Antarctica, and watch Dalton and George and all the rest in an absolute flurry to charter fishing boats to beat me to it. James, I like this news very much indeed. Thank you.'

'You're *welcome*?' James eyed his brother as if he were mildly insane. 'Final problem. I received a wire. That's it, on the tray there.'

The telegram, addressed to 'James L. Carter, Business Manager for Carter the Great,' was from 'Thomas Bryson, Esq., representing Madame Zorah.' Carter had never heard of Thomas Bryson, but, given that his mind reader's real name was Thelma Brysonski, and that she was a notorious cheapskate, he suspected she was getting cut-rate legal advice.

After reading the telegram, Carter said, 'James, why does she think we'll be doubling her salary?'

'She claims that on the night Harding attended, she predicted his death.'

'She certainly didn't. I'd have fired her on the spot.'

'The trades are backing her up.'

'They can pay her salary.' Carter tossed the telegram into a pile of mail that was in the cold fireplace, and put on his Ledocq voice. 'Her, the tramp, we fire.'

'You'll need a new mind reader, then.'

Carter wondered about that, what sort of person to hire and train – for on top of his spirit illusion, he had plans for a mind-reading effect. How very convincing it would be if the new mind reader were a blind woman.

'Did you just go somewhere for a moment?'

'I'm having ideas.'

James finished off a cruller. He didn't ask what sort of ideas. Even as an adult, James was stubborn.

'I was thinking . . . James, I just want you to know that I'm very open to profit.' It was like climbing up a mile of ladder to a tree house and hoping the boys inside would let him join. 'I know in the past, I haven't paid enough attention to my finances, but I'd like to know how to manage my funds. Manage them well.'

'That's good. That's perfect. I have something else to show you.' He went to his desk, returning with a poster that he unrolled on the carpet. 'A contact at Otis Lithograph gave me this proof. Your friend is onto something.'

The poster advertised Thurston's Wonder Show of the Universe, a show Thurston had presented for the last fifteen seasons. His posters had inevitably featured Thurston's famous Vanishing Fire Engine illusion. But this year Thurston had outdone himself: the poster now showed a dozen wraith-like girls in diaphanous gowns surrounding an impeccably rendered, floating automobile that struck Carter as far less dramatic than a vanishing fire engine, until he began to read the text aloud. 'Thurston's greatest mystery: The Vanishing Willys Whippet Six-Cylinder Luxury Car. See this fine sedan with hand-tooled leather seats and oiled rosewood dash . . .' He read the small print. 'How helpful, it lists financing terms.'

'I can set something like that up for you.'

'Not unless I can put Madame Zorah in the rumble seat and materialize it underneath Tug's foot.'

'They're paying him fifteen thousand just to use their automobile next season.'

'I've made four world tours, I've played every thousand-seat venue in the world, I've never signed a product endorsement—'

'And another season of wild success and you'll be lucky to do three-card monte blow-offs for sailors.' James pulled the sash of his robe together. 'Charlie, I thought you were open to profitable plans.'

'Shilling for Henry Ford isn't a plan, it's a suicide pact.'

'What did you have in mind, then?'

'A whole new show. Something that will really pack them in!' Though he said it forcefully, it sounded weak in this penthouse. He remembered The Funny Farm, his personal barometer of awful showmanship.

James located a small cinnamon roll and had it halfway into his mouth before seeing his brother's appraising stare. Then he pushed the entire thing past his lips, and cocked his head as if to ask whether someone in the room had a problem with how simply he pleased himself. Carter felt a twinge of jealousy. Faintly, in his mind's eye, he saw a seven-year-old James slipping into the bathtub, forever finished with Carter's avocation. Did magic always have to separate them?

'James – about your suggestion. I'll keep an open mind.'

'Splendid. Now tell me everything I need to know about these adventures of yours, and hold nothing back.'

Carter said, 'Where to begin?' He told James of his performance for President Harding, of his bogus flight from the country, of his interrogation by Griffin and Starling, and of the attempted break-in.

The entire story took ten minutes, during which James ate a final two slices of panettone. Afterward, James was silent for a few moments, during which he finished his mocha java, eyes gazing at the ceiling.

'So,' he finally said, looking at Carter, 'what does this girl look like?'

'Who?'

'Phoebe Kyle. She sounds wonderful.'

'I'm sorry, perhaps you missed the point of my story.'

'I don't think so.'

'Did you hear the part about the President?

James shrugged. 'Did you like her?'

'You're impossible,' Carter murmured. He turned his eyes toward the ceiling, then the Persian rug, then out the window, then back, looking for something to stare at. He finally settled on a rich blue and gold Klimt watercolor – not a major Klimt, a square golden landscape, golden and autumnal – Carter at the moment disliked how its colors matched the single orchid in the vase before it, and how the painting and the flower and the vase and the table all made perfect harmonious sense. He sensed that if he tried the same in his own home, it simply wouldn't work.

'I don't know what I should do.' Carter leaned forward, his hands flexing and releasing.

'About Miss Kyle?'

'No. But she's—' Carter made a steeple of his fingers, and glared at them. 'She seems to be a nice young woman. I didn't get to know her.'

'Will you see her again?'

'She left her gloves at my apartment. I didn't even realize she'd taken them off.'

James laughed. 'Clever girl.'

'You don't understand. She's so fresh. Not in the sense of being brazen—'

'I know what you mean. Like a breath of fresh air.'

'Yes.'

'That does sound horrible, Charlie.'

'I'm not so fresh. I don't want to poison her.'

James nodded. 'I have no idea what you mean.' When his brother began to explain, he interrupted, 'You know why people like your act?'

'Yes.' Then Carter muttered, 'All right, why?'

'Because it's fun. You give the audience hours of fun, and when they think about it later, they have fun all over again.'

'I like that,' he said, as though asking James whether he should in fact like it.

'So you should have fun, too.'

Carter fished for a witty rebuttal until James finally continued:

'I really do appreciate entertainers and artists. It's why Tom and I live here instead of Pacific Heights. There's so much more vitality to be had over dinner with a mezzo-soprano than with a bank president. But honestly, why does this cloud follow you offstage and down the alley and all over the world? I know what happened with Sarah destroyed you. But that's almost ten years now. I think you love the idea of being wounded like you're St Sebastian. Which is all well and good, because it keeps you from pursuing nice young blind girls.'

Carter steepled his fingers again. He was troubled that his younger, richer, unimpressed-by-his-famous-sibling brother had more insight into him than the reverse. The Klimt painting, trees half hidden in a golden and copper tunnel of leaves, was just visible out of the corner of his eye. He began to think of an illusion: a valuable painting is found cut out of its frame, slashed to ribbons and vandalized with rude graffiti. It has been ruined; restoration cannot fix it. Carter would appear, cover the frame with a cloth, and remove it, showing the painting miraculously restored. Applause. It could be done.

Carter cleared his throat. 'I'm becoming, by the hour . . . by the minute, awake to possibility.'

'That's wonderful. That's the spirit.' James threw something at him, a key, which Carter caught without looking.

'What is this?'

'It's a key.'

'One day, I will in fact murder you.'

'The Bayerische Motoren-Werke is a small company in Germany. They used to make aircraft engines, but the Treaty of Versailles prevents them from doing that anymore. Lovely man runs it, Max

277

Friz, the jowly, *sour* Herr Max Friz. They're trying desperately to export something, anything, and so they've built a motor vehicle. See if you can use it.'

'I won't use it in the act.'

'Don't. Whatever idea you say you have is probably better.'

'I'm not really ready to discuss it. It will cost money to develop, so I need—'

'I'm sorry, did I ask you what it was? I'm not interested in the slightest. Go to the docks, there's a present waiting for you from Germany, drive it around in the open air, and that should inspire you to come up with a new trick.'

'Okay. All right.' He took a deep breath. 'It's a spirit illusion,' he said as flatly as possible. 'A new method. I think it can be used for mind reading, too, and transportations, and productions. Vanishes, of course. And if Ledocq can make all the mechanics of it work, it might even allow me to do close-up for the whole house.'

They sat, James flicking pastry crumbs into the fireplace. 'So, after nine years, you have a new method that will revolutionize every type of magic there is.' He sounded like he was trying to talk his brother down off a high ledge.

'It has no impact on penetration or immolation illusions.'

'Charlie, did you come up with this out of nowhere? Was it trial and error? Or inspiration?'

'No.'

'No?'

'No.'

Annoyed, James asked, 'So a man came up and handed you a piece of paper with the idea written on it?'

'Yes.' Carter snapped his fingers. The cigar tube was now between the thumb and forefinger of his right hand. He placed it on the table. It was white all over, except for a crest: a formal-looking eagle holding arrows in its talons.

James stared at it. 'Please tell me that design isn't the Presidential Seal.'

'President Harding gave me this on the night of the performance. It's undoubtedly what the thugs are searching for.'

For a full fifteen seconds, James was silent. 'Can't they get their own cigars?' he asked weakly.

Carter pushed the cigar tube toward James.

'What's inside?'

'Open it.'

James covered his eyes. 'Why couldn't we have one of those distant, spiteful relationships? Just so I'm firing on all sixes here – am I to understand the President gave you a magic trick worth murdering him for?'

'Open the cigar tube. It should explain everything.'

James sniffed at it, eyes troubled, as if it were a dubious piece of fish. He popped the top off the cigar tube and shook out its contents – eight sheets of onionskin paper. They were covered in script, diagrams, and equations stacked with Greek letters. He looked at them for a moment. Then at his brother. Then back at the sheets, which he turned upside-down, and back upright. 'I have absolutely no idea what this is.'

'To tell the truth, I need it explained, too.'

'So?'

'If you aren't busy, we have an appointment this evening with a certain Belgian, Benny Leonard-loving Jew.'

Chapter 11

At dusk, the Carter brothers took James's Ford roadster along a route that avoided hills (James was positive he would stall on them; Carter, eager at first to encourage him to take a chance, quickly remembered what a timid driver James was, and agreed to the most sober path). They took Bay Street (absolutely flat) through North Beach, then went up Van Ness (a moderate hill during which James refused to let his car, in Carter's words, 'see what she can do'), and then straight along Ellis (flat again) until they hit the Jewish section of town, which this pleasant evening, as the electric streetlights were coming on with audible pops, seemed to be populated entirely by families ambling from one of many kosher restaurants to one of many soda fountains.

Mr and Mrs Ledocq's house sat on a narrow slice of property on Byington, a block-long tree-lined street just off Fillmore. It was a railroad-style three-story museum of reconstructed automatons, old newspapers in four languages, and a dozen rooms that were half-workshop, half-living quarters, custody of which Ledocq had wrestled from his wife, who valiantly tried to keep things clean. The backyard fared little better, home to a kiln, a crucible furnace, an annealing oven, and three or four incomplete sets of bocce balls that made interesting dents in the garden of weeds. Ledocq was the master of the 'It's Around Here Somewhere' school of mechanical engineering. Carter had once found a set of screwdrivers in the icebox.

This evening, Carter sipped iced tea and looked at the mementos of their tours Ledocq had tacked or taped to his walls: postcards and photographs, banners and reviews clipped from *Billboard*. He looked at the testimonials to the Phantom War Gun, the rights to which they had licensed to other magicians. Nine years had passed, but seeing its name still made him turn away.

Carter, Ledocq, and a fidgeting James stood in a playroom

completely taken over by miles of track for model trains that ran from floor to ceiling. A half-dozen trains at a time could hustle through tiny alpine villages and industrial towns with real smoke-stacks.

'The President asked me what I would do if I knew of a secret, I told him that I was a magician, and I'd taken a vow, but he wasn't impressed by that. He wanted to *do* something about his secret.' Carter stirred his tea so the lemon wedge danced around. 'Eventually, we settled on how he would participate in the show, and then he returned to the topic. What would I do if I knew of a terrible secret?'

Ledocq squinted. 'Why did he keep asking this?'

'That's exactly what I asked,' James murmured. He was examining a silver O-gauge sleeper car Ledocq had populated with hand-painted wooden passengers.

'He was desperate. He thought someone was going to be murdered.'

'And then he died,' James added.

'What was his problem, Charlie? Did he tell you?' Ledocq took the train car from James and put it on the tracks.

'He listed off a great many scandals, something to do with the Post Office, and oil leases, and so forth, I rather stopped paying attention. He was a nice man, but it was like being cornered by a drunk in a barroom. They all sounded the same to me – stealing public money, profiting on secret information, the usual business. And they didn't much bother him, it was just boys being boys, except for one. A scientist had invented something that Harding thought was quite wonderful, and had brought it to the White House at one of those meet-the-public Sundays Harding was so fond of.'

'Oh,' Ledocq said with disappointment. 'That's it? Another mad scientist.'

'No – a nice scientist. Harding said he was very sweet.'

'So he was a sweet mad scientist.'

'That's just what I said. We're on the same pathway here,' James added. 'Poor Harding was never the most acute judge of anything. Have you done anything new, Ledocq?'

'Have you seen the mirror tunnel?' When James shook his head,

Ledocq flicked on his transformer. 'Send a train right here,' he pointed to a trestle suspended between two snowcapped peaks about eight feet off the floor. James settled in at the controls. Carter watched a train leave the yard, heading for the mountains. He was nonplussed at how Ledocq was taking this, for it was his way to concentrate on the matter at hand by looking everywhere else.

When the train had traveled for a while, Carter added, 'Harding went to his friends and told them about the invention and the sweet man who had the idea, looking for investors, and that's where the scandal comes in.'

'I've heard about this kind of thing,' Ledocq said, eyes still on the trains. 'They were going to buy out his patent and sit on it?'

'That would be a normal scandal,' Carter said. 'Harding told me they were going to steal his idea and then kill the inventor.'

Ledocq squinted at Carter. 'Kill the inventor?' he frowned. 'What are you talking about?'

'I mean killing the inventor.'

Ledocq fumbled with his glasses, and wiped them on his shirt. 'Killing? As government policy? That can't be so.'

'I'd like to tell Harding that, but he seems to have died.'

James asked, 'Are you saying you think he was murdered, too?'

Carter watched the train. 'He was ill from bad fish, that much I know. But have you ever looked his wife in the eye?'

Ledocq took off his glasses and polished them on his shirttails. '*Degoutant*. This is exactly why I voted for Cox.'

'Harding said the invention was so clever it seemed like a magic trick, and he begged me to hear about it. So I did. From what I could understand, it seems highly sophisticated, quite raw, but it has possibilities. With some imagination, we could refine and use it onstage, if we could get exclusive licensing rights. What do you think?'

Ledocq said, 'It's hard to evaluate without a technical—'

'Here you go.' Carter extended the cigar tube toward him.

Ledocq stared at the tube, then at Carter. 'You can't just let an old man play with his trains? Oh, boy.' He took the tube from Carter and shook out the pages of onionskin, shiny and slippery. James switched the tracks in several places, and the train continued its climb through alpine meadows where pigtailed maidens were milking wooden cows.

'Where is that magnifying glass?' Ledocq approached his workbench.

'Where it's always been,' Carter observed.

'I knew that.' It was hinged; Ledocq pulled on it so it extended and its lightbulb flickered to life. 'What kind of tumult do we have here, my friends?' The first page was a letter, handwritten. Ledocq read its opening aloud. 'Dear Mr President: As we discussed, my name is Philo Farnsworth. I have invented a device . . .' blah blah blah. Everyone has an invention.' He squinted at the next page. He turned it upside down, then back up. It was a diagram covered in notations. The remaining pages were also diagrams and figures, showing parts of a device at rest and in use. Ledocq thumbed through them slowly, his face betraying little but concentration.

Carter said, 'This is the only place this is written down.'

'Excuse me?' Ledocq asked.

'The inventor was afraid of writing it down.'

'So why did he give it to a schnook like Harding?'

'Read the letter.'

Ledocq recited, 'Who can you trust if you can't trust the President of the United States?' He shook his head. 'Oh boy. Oh boy. Now there's a judge of character. So Harding sees magic, you're a magician, he gives you this.' Ledocq nodded.

James, guiding the train cars, was chewing on a thought. 'Has anyone else noticed how things have changed recently? Since the war, perhaps. Every time we come back from abroad, I try to read the atmosphere, and it's gotten very odd.' Ledocq continued reading, and Carter stood, stretching his legs. It was warm and misty; the curtains were drawn, and he knew enough not to pull them back, for he would be outlined very well, and he thought, *Yes, things have changed*. So he leaned against one of Ledocq's workbenches – this one for glass-blowing – and with his fingernails he tapped out a metallic *ting-ting-ting* melody on the various pontils, gathering irons, pucellas, jacks, and tongs.

'What I mean is this,' James continued. 'You read the newspapers and maybe it began with mustard gas, you know? No one could believe anyone would do something so awful, and then there were more terrible gasses unleashed every day. Ever since, it's become a daily contest for people to behave terribly, and then other people say, "Ah, yes, I knew that would happen." There's a jaded feeling in the world, so why not kill the President? Why not kill an inventor?'

'But that's not all of it,' Carter said. 'People are also wonderfully naive.'

'Maybe in 1910 they were naive,' James replied.

'When was the last time someone at a dinner party sat you and Tom across from two delightful young ladies?'

James sighed. 'Point taken. But I stick by what I said, too. I suppose it's a paradox.'

'It's your national character,' Ledocq said, putting the papers down for a moment.

'Ours?' Carter asked, raising his eyebrows.

'Belgians believe in idling and progress, no more, no less. But Americans, everyone here, they all say, "I seen everything, you can't pull one on me, I'm a real wise guy," and then two minutes later, we show them a chess-playing automaton, and they lose every ounce of savoir faire. "Hey, that automaton is marvelous, what's that?" and the truth is, they *really* don't want to know how it works.' He flattened out the papers again. 'The naive and the knowing, that's our audience, boys, that's how we make a living.'

Carter smiled. 'I thought it was the explicable and the inexplicable that—'

'Same difference, exactly. Now pipe down for five minutes.'

Carter watched Ledocq pore over the diagrams. He was a rarity, a bona-fide genius in that he made simplicity out of the complicated. There was a gramophone in the corner, now silent, that sometimes played one of the most terrific recordings Carter had ever heard: Ledocq had cut it himself, and it consisted of him sawing and hammering and muttering. He played it some nights because otherwise Mrs Ledocq would knock suspiciously and ask him to fix the leaky sink.

Ledocq said, 'Manipulation of electrons,' I see,' and, 'magnetic coils in proximity to . . . the anode finger's *aperture*'? *Jamais*,' and then he was quieter.

'Ah! Very nice!' James cried. When the train went over the trestle, a set of mirrors made it seem to disappear. Better still, a pair of Tyrolean hikers in lederhosen performed a simultaneous double take.

Then Ledocq said 'dissector tube'. He looked up at the Carter brothers as if they might share his worries. 'A cathode ray gun that bombards . . .' He pushed back the magnifying glass. 'This is monstrous. Truly monstrous.'

James, looking impressed, made a beckoning gesture, and Ledocq passed him the notes. 'Is it a death ray?'

Ledocq straightened his glasses, tugged at his beard. He cleared his throat. 'No. This is not a death ray.'

'Can we use it?'

'Where's Farnsworth?' Ledocq asked.

'He's here, somewhere,' Carter murmured.

'Where?' asked James.

'Might I use your telephone?'

Ledocq's eyes popped open. 'Yes!' He started rummaging through his junk. 'Look what I have.' He produced a heavy black telephone with a separate mouth and ear piece, beaming, 'Brand new.'

Since it was important that Ledocq have the newest gadget, Carter didn't mention that even his Oakland apartment had been blessed with a new telephone during their eighteen-month absence. 'Quite spiffy,' he said, dialing. And then, when the line connected, he said, 'Hello, is this the florist? Charles Carter, checking on my order.'

He spoke on the phone for less than a minute, half words of assent, then hung up.

Folding his arms, he said, 'Perhaps he isn't here. I've had my sources check every hotel, every boardinghouse, every storage unit, every scientific instruments dealer. He's not to be found.' He looked up. 'But at least no one else has even been looking for him. Harding told me he'd never given up the name to anyone else, and now I believe him. If there are bad men out there, I'm ahead of them.' Carter put his hands into his pockets. Outside, finally, the sound of a foghorn in the night, sweet and lonely. 'I'll find him.'

'What else, Charles?' James looked slightly worried.

'Harding set up a meeting for young Farnsworth. With the only capitalist whose advice he would trust. They're to meet tomorrow at noon.'

285

James clapped his hands. 'Splendid – you know where he'll be, and when, so—'

He stopped when he saw his brother rubbing his chin, which stubble had brought to the consistency of sandpaper. 'It's not going to be so easy . . .' Ledocq and James, who were hard to hold captive, hung now on his every word, though he wasn't exactly enjoying it. 'It's Borax.'

Chapter 12

Pem Farnsworth lay next to her husband under the imported cotton sheets of their suite at the Palace, listening to the sounds of late-night traffic outside the open window. The velvet bedspread was in a crumpled heap at the foot of the bed. The air in the room felt heavy with the August humidity, and, Pem thought, there was something about the fog that made the air smell like roses tonight. She had never been so happy in her life.

'Keep talking,' she said.

'I thought I was boring you, Pem.'

'I adore your voice, husband.'

'Wife.' He kissed her and they called each other 'husband' and 'wife' several more times. They had been married four days before in Provo, Utah.

'Okay.' His left arm was around her shoulders, and with his right arm he gestured. 'What you see when you look around in the dark, those are called retinal flashes.'

'They look like little fireflies.'

'It's got to do with the rods and cones,' and as she listened, she stopped paying attention to what exactly he was saying, but his passion pleased her. She could just barely make out, in the dark, his Adam's apple rising and falling, and she conjured up in her mind his skinny arms and legs, how they looked almost hairless, how she could only feel the blond hair there but not see it, and how quickly his brain worked, so quietly she thought steam might funnel out of his ears. On the train to San Francisco from Provo, he'd made sketches of devices called 'captive balloons' that he said would soon float a hundred miles over the earth and replace telegraph wires.

'I just know,' she finally murmured, when he had finished, 'that when I looked up in the dark, I saw all those little flashes, and I thought they were mine. They were a private show just for me.'

'I like that. I love that.' And a moment later he propped his head up on his fist and turned on the bright bedside lamp.

'And I want to stop time,' she said. He laughed, for they'd had this conversation often. She was so happy she wanted to make time freeze, and the first time she said it, he'd given her the whole relativistic lecture on the possibilities of altering time's path, only stopping when he realized what she actually meant, and now it was one of their jokes.

'Honey, if that's what you want to do, I'll build you something,' was his response now.

'Make it something that goes with my bob,' she said.

He touched her cheek. 'I wanted to see your face when I told you this.' He had blond, unruly hair, light grey eyes, a pork chop of a nose. They had met two years ago in sophomore chemistry – she was taking it, and even though Philo was only fifteen then, he was teaching it. Back then, his parents wouldn't let them meet after school because Philo had chores. So he stayed up all night, three nights in a row, and built a motor for an automatic clothes washer and a vacuum-sealed pump that milked the cows twice as quickly. For a week, he and Pem held hands and talked, but then a load of laundry caught fire, and Philo had to do the wash by hand again. But now he was older: seventeen. His voice still broke when he was excited. They were so young they couldn't even register for their room at the Palace – they'd had to sign in with a notarized permission from her mother, and even then the hotel had them registered under her folks' names. 'Are you enjoying your honeymoon?'

'Oh, Phil, of course. This is so wonderful.'

'Would you like Paris, France, better? Or London?'

She laughed, touching his face. 'This is just swell. We don't have the money to go those places.'

'Actually, Pem, to tell you the truth, we don't have the money for this place either.'

'What do you mean?' Her voice dropped. 'You didn't get the money from your parents, did you?'

'Oh, gosh, no! I wouldn't do anything to upset you. We're a little leveraged, to tell the truth. I just figured there might be more investors in San Francisco, so I picked San Francisco. But, heck, if you'd wanted to go to Paris, we could have gone there instead.'

Pem sat up in bed, drawing the sheets around her. She and Philo had never argued, and she didn't want to start now, but something in his tone troubled her. 'What investors? For what?'

He did not answer immediately. Philo had a way of being crafty that she was still getting used to. Sightseeing in San Francisco, they had been suckered once for three dollars, but Philo hadn't let it happen again. They even had a joke about how he learned so quickly: 'You can't fool me twice. I haven't seen the world, but I *have* been to Boise.'

Philo left the bed and took a key off of his dressing table. 'I'll show you.' He extended his hand. 'You'll like this.'

Pem put her bare feet to the floor. 'Where are we going?'

'You don't need your robe, honey. It's just in the other room of the suite.'

'I didn't know we had the other room, too.'

'Well, that's the least of the surprises. Come on. Don't be bashful.'

Pem had wondered if she would be able to simply walk around naked with a man in the room. And days into their marriage, she felt as comfortable with Philo as she did alone. Tonight she still hesitated as Philo put a protective arm around her, unlocked the door, and walked her into the next room, which was dark.

He whispered. 'You know, there's another woman in my life.'

Her jaw tightened. When she was able to breathe again, she would sock him in the mouth.

'And I'd like you to meet her.' He flicked on a small light and she saw the room was overrun with his laboratory equipment.

'Oh.' She put her hands to her sides. 'An invention.'

'Yeah, honey. Oh, you didn't think—' He looked at her wide-eyed. 'Honey! Golly!'

Amazed by the equipment, but still feeling a little angry, she settled for saying, 'Philo, you have to learn to express yourself better.'

'Oh, honey!' He kissed her. 'Don't be mad. I shipped it all out from Salt Lake.' He threw the sheets off of stacks of condensers and transmitters, and started flicking switches and connecting ground wires. As he talked, his voice rose until it cracked. 'I never told anyone exactly what all this stuff could do if I got it right, except poor

President Harding, and now you, of course, and I decided I wouldn't tell you till I had to. It's kind of embarrassing to be tinkering all the time when you don't have anything to show for it, and, well, maybe now I can show you a little something. Cover yourself up for a second, honey.' Philo pulled back the curtains and connected a couple of wires. 'And I figure I should show you now since I've got some big plans to show this off,' he added. 'Okay. Stand right here.' He put both hands square on her shoulders and faced her toward a cherry wood cabinet that was about four feet tall. Inset toward the top was a perfectly round, milk-colored, four-inch piece of glass that looked like a dinner plate.

'What is it?'

'You'll see.' Philo stood behind her, arms around her shoulders, and he handed her a long cord that had a switch mounted at the end. 'Whenever you're ready, flick the switch from off to on.'

Pem looked up at him, and when he nodded, she looked back at the box. She flicked the switch. At once, a humming sound came from the equipment around her. A spark flew from one connection to another, and she jumped, but Philo held her tight. 'Look straight ahead.'

The glass glowed, changing from a milky white to an electric blue, a dozen parallel strands of electric blue with thin royal blue strips between. She heard the sound of hoofbeats.

'What's that?'

'Mmm. Sounds like a horse to me, Pem. Look.'

The strips of blue were beginning to refract and pull into – Pem gasped – the image of a man on horseback. Galloping. She could see the horse's hooves moving, the rider's arms holding the reins rising and falling. Philo was explaining – this was kind of a cheat, it wasn't really what he had in mind, but it was okay for now, a six-second loop, the sound wasn't really hooves, a simulation made with something or other – Pem stood amazed. It looked like having your own piece of the world under glass. For a long moment, Philo and Pem Farnsworth held each other. Their bodies were bathed in the blue light of the screen.

'Pem, I'd like you to meet television.'

Chapter 13

Carter awoke just before dawn on Wednesday. To his surprise, he was curled up under a blanket on James's couch; his dreams had all been set in Oakland.

Even when Ledocq said 'television' aloud, James looked at him blankly, as well he should, for only a handful of people, engineers mostly, had heard of it. Radio with pictures, Ledocq had explained, like listening to the Leonard fight – only being able to *see* it, too, he said, eyes almost popping. Like having your own movie palace in your living room, only with sound. He dug through a stack of journals, eventually finding a couple of highly technical articles he'd seen years ago, first theoretical discussions by brilliant men about the possibilities of transmitting moving pictures through the ether, followed by crackpot experiments that never went anywhere. Mechanical television – shining a light through a spinning disk – had been attempted in England, but the image, about as precise as hand shadows, was never sharp enough to be exciting. What Farnsworth was thinking, it wasn't just innovative, it was a revolution. Electronic television, it was crazy, no one had ever considered it. But the plans just might work.

This was too theoretical for the Carter brothers, so Ledocq brought out his radio and put a fishbowl on top of it, and started swapping in and out photographs, wriggling them. In went Helen Willis, tennis racket aloft. 'You see? You might watch Forest Hills, and not only could you see the players, but you could hear them, too, and when you get bored' – out came Helen Willis, in went Leopold Stokowski – 'you can watch the symphony, and hear it, too.'

'Yes,' James sighed. 'Yes, you can hear them, too, and you can't hear movies, that's true, you've mentioned that.'

'And it's not on film – the audience would be experiencing all of this while it was happening. They would *feel* like spectators, just

291

like being there, without the artificial nature that film has, no editing, no schmaltz, just real life. It's fantastic, I tell you boys.' He seemed positively giddy.

Carter in the meantime had located a supply of photographs and amused himself with popping them into the fishbowl randomly. 'Can they see, too, then?'

Ledocq squinted. 'Pardon?'

He reddened, as he wondered if the question were foolish. 'If I'm looking at Pola Negri through this, and she's . . . well, can she see me in return?'

'No,' Ledocq said, but then continued, 'no? You'd need . . . well, I think—'

'Ledocq,' James said, 'please build my brother a device through which he can watch Pola Negri without her seeing him. You do that, and I guarantee you a fortune.'

This degenerated into teasing, and trying to imagine all the events one might watch ('and hear,' Ledocq kept adding) on the television: political debates, artists at work, theatrical productions, perhaps one could follow Treasury agents on their beat – the concepts were stunning. But as his brother and Ledocq continued to punctuate the discussion with new ideas, Carter was increasingly quiet, wondering how to use this odd little device on his stage. His instincts told him that as he'd suspected all along, television was magic.

So Carter had lain down on James's couch that night to return to scheming about Mr Philo Farnsworth. How to approach him, and what sort might he be, and was he the sort to license his invention to a magician? Carter had specific plans that went vague in places, so thinking about them late at night had left him nervous. Around 2 A.M., he began flipping through the latest several numbers of the *Sphinx* – never a good idea for relaxing, as the gossip columns usually detailed who was ahead of him, and who was fast approaching from below.

He had read cautiously this time, assuring himself no one else had television. Augustus Rapp had contributed more atrocious patter. The Society of American Magicians Golden Gate assembly had met in a waffle house and afterward, 'dancing was attempted'. Page ten was a full-page advertisement that had nothing whatever to do with his situation – E. F. Rybolt, a distant acquaintance, was selling off his magical literature library for $10,000. The list of available volumes seemed quite exciting, so Carter thought about writing him, then wondered if he had $10,000 to spare.

He tried to calculate his net worth, so difficult a task he had to close his eyes, which led to various disappointed dreams, and when he awoke, he made coffee and stared out of James's window to watch all the boats on the bay. He had several bank accounts that James had set up, and drafts seemed to go in and out like the tide. During the War, he'd taken over the old Martinka magic shop, but he was hopeless at all the work involved, and he ultimately sold it to Houdini. He still had the Oakland property, the Napa property, and had purchased James's half of their parents' old house in Presidio Heights, but what meant the most to him was technically his most worthless holding: his island, Koh Pheung Thawng in the Andaman Sea, a gift from the Siamese King.

There was a photograph, tinted, thirty inches by eight inches, framed on the wall of James's study. Taken with a military camera that rotated on its axis, the photo depicted a line of tethered animals on the beach: zebras, llamas, horses, even a cat and two dogs (Mooch! Earl! Noodles!) that had performed in a Sells brothers high-wire act. Carter looked up and down the line, mentally adding Tug, who would retire within the year.

At the center of the photograph, waving awkwardly – they had frozen in position for five minutes – were the managers Carter had chosen to rule the roost. Karl and Evelyn Kowaleski. Though they had disappeared after their disastrous vaudeville closure, they'd seen the notice in *Billboard*, and had sent a short note of condolence when Sarah died. They were cooks at a fraternity in Middletown, Connecticut, but Evelyn wrote that they were rehearsing and, any day now, they would be back in the game.

In the photo, they looked proud and anxious that at any moment someone might take this little paradise away from them. Carter waved 'hello' back to them. No matter where he went, there was a small dot in the Andaman Sea where he had made someone happy. It was very hard to rescue people and the older he became, the more impossible it seemed. Today, he was going to find Philo Farnsworth and, if necessary, rescue him.

But now it was time for his morning exercises. He poured milk into a saucepan and set it on the stove on a low flame. Then he took a small wooden chest off a shelf in James's study and returned to the kitchen. With one eye on the milk – it had to warm but not boil – he angled a mirror over the table in the breakfast nook. Removing items from the chest, he arranged and rearranged, until he was satisfied, ten silver dollars, a twenty-dollar gold piece, two decks of cards, three foam balls, three billiard balls, a candle, and a pack of cigarettes.

He took the saucepan off the flame, poured the milk into two bowls, and stirred a few tablespoons of olive oil into each. When he was satisfied with the proportions, he submerged his hands. He flexed them, eyes closed, visualizing his skin becoming more supple and his ulnar, median, and radial nerves more sensitive.

After five minutes soaking, then patting his hands dry on Egyptian cotton, Carter performed the Downs coin roll, right hand first, then left hand, then coins rolling down each hand, fingers tucked in so it looked like the dollars were riding a street carousel. Then fifty French drops with each hand, then pinch drops, then it was an exercise in palming stacks of coins in either hand. He had a small cut on his right forefinger, from Baby's playful swiping, and it made his finger just stiff enough that the finger palm vanishes from that hand looked mechanical. He tilted the mirror from all angles, to see what an audience stage left, or stage right, would see.

His feelings about close-up magic were especially acute now. If magic were a channel he'd been digging his entire life as a way of linking himself to others, television would infinitely expand it. He could bring images of his hands to the farthest reaches of the house. He imagined the third gallery of a performance, where there was a dirty-collared, cloth-hatted man forever squinting at performers, suddenly able to see every flourish of a coin vanish. The best audience member was one who felt informed and baffled at the same time.

He heard footsteps in the hallway, and looked up. Excellent! Entering the room was Tom Crandall. The moment Tom saw who was sitting at the table, he froze, as if prepared to disbelieve the next ten things out of Charles Carter's mouth.

'Good morning,' said Carter, brightly.

Tom glanced out the window, confirmed that it was indeed morning, and then grumbled 'Hello.'

'I've made coffee.'

'Mmmm.' Tom looked into the pot, took a mug, and slowly poured, sniffing at the curls of steam. It was rare for Carter to get a chance to practice in front of someone, and he now desperately wanted Tom to come over and sit down near him. But Tom was a hard sell. He'd lost a great deal of patience and enthusiasm since helping with the Blackmail illusion in 1911. Like many college athletes, Tom had found his thirties a continuous disappointment. He had bags under his eyes and usually behaved in Carter's presence as if he were about four hundred years old.

'Come over here, Tom, and pick a card.'

'I'd rather have a nail driven through my forehead.'

'Oh, now! How are you?'

'Tired.'

'And how was seeing your family?'

He shook his head. 'Mmm . . . a lot like having a nail driven through my forehead.' As he sipped coffee, Tom began to complain, and the longer his list of discomforts (sitting in the church pew with his bad back, how the train compartment two nights ago had caused his circulation to rebel, etc.), the more he seemed to perk up and by the end he was even smiling somewhat.

Carter looked at him appraisingly. 'Gritty, debonair, battling,' he said.

'That was a long time ago.'

'In your own way, you're still gritty, debonair, and battling.'

Tom looked himself over in Carter's hand mirror, then shook his head.

Carter took a chance. 'You know, I'd be honored if you'd watch this card routine.'

Silence. A sip of coffee. Then Tom *did* nod, so Carter shot three cards, facedown, out of the deck. 'Tell me which one is the queen of hearts?'

'Oh, God.'

'Just guess.'

Tom pointed. Carter turned over the card: the queen of hearts. He looked at Tom, who had absolutely nothing written on his face. 'That was amazing. Let's eat breakfast.'

Carter was a little hurt by that, and must have shown it, for Tom apologized in his own way. 'All right, all right, do some more.'

Carter fanned a deck in each hand, spread them on the table like ribbons, turned them over, waterfalled them from hand to hand, and vanished them, just like that. Then he produced card after card until he had two decks, complete, and then he did every trick he could think of using a Hindoo Shuffle.

'Well, I'm exhausted,' Tom said, just as James was coming into the room.

'Morning, Charlie.' James touched both men lightly on their backs. 'Tom, did you ask him yet?'

'What were you going to ask me, Tom?'

'Nothing.'

'Ask me anything. I made you sit through a magic show, I apologize, ask me anything.'

Tom looked at James, who gave him an encouraging look. Tom leaned in closely. 'All right. *Ramon Novarro?*' He raised his eyebrows.

'Ahh, Ramon Novarro,' Carter sighed. 'I'm sorry to disappoint you, but I do believe he's married.'

'Like that makes a world of difference!'

'No, I mean really married, as in happily.'

'That man is such a tease,' James declared while pouring coffee.

'He definitely courts a certain kind of fan,' Tom said, crossing to his desk. 'Look at this.'

He produced for Carter an eight-by-ten photo that had been tinted. It showed Ramon Novarro, eyebrows cocked, holding a cigarette at a jaunty angle. It was signed, 'To my supporter Tom Crandell, sincerely, Ramon Novarro.'

Tom was incensed. 'See?'

'The way he's holding his cigarette?'

'No! The tie!' Tom jabbed his finger at the offending neckwear. 'He's wearing a red tie.'

As always when faced with a secret code, Carter tried to make no sign whatever, silently bringing his coffee cup to the sink, but curiosity got the best of him. 'You mean a red tie . . .'

'What kind of a man wears a red tie, but someone who's *that way?*' Tom made a swishing gesture with his wrist.

Carter glanced at his brother's tie – it was red. Carter, for whom good days began when he realized he had much to learn, whispered, 'Holy mackerel.' Red ties. Who knew?

A few minutes later, the three men were set up with bacon and eggs and cereal and toast and Carter used the Thurston and Dalton posters as kindling for a marvelous fire.

James watched his brother's rivals go up in flames. 'I'm trying to determine what Mom would say about your little fire.'

'How sad for us all she's in Brazil. James, I need to ask you a serious question.'

'Mother would say that burning posters shows aggressive tendencies. You're getting ready for glorious—'

'How much money do I have?'

The question hung over the breakfast table, and Carter felt like he'd appeared at the opera in his union suit, trap door flapping open, until James asked, 'Why?'

'I want to pursue television as part of the act. Thurston spent fifty thousand on Beauty, and I want to spend at least that.' When there was no response, he added, 'If possible.'

James said, 'Howard spent three thousand on Beauty. What made you think he spent fifty?'

'His posters claimed—' He stopped dead. And felt like the worst kind of rube.

'Yes, they did. He spent three thousand. I have no idea how much it would cost to use television onstage. Do we even know if there's a working system anywhere? Or is this all in Farnsworth's head?'

'I don't know if there's a system. But we have the only set of plans. And Farnsworth is trying to get investors, so licensing shouldn't be a problem, as it's free exposure for him. So how much money do I have?'

Tom cleared his throat. 'I think I'll go through the mail. I'll be in the other room.'

After Tom had closed the door, Carter looked wistful. 'Odd how you can talk about sex in modern company these days, but money is still taboo.'

James put his hands together and addressed his thumbs. 'Charlie, you don't have any money.'

'I know I have property, but don't I have some sort of income that—'

'You have the properties, and you have a very good income from your magic shows, all of which goes out immediately. You have a small savings fund that generally lasts you through the off-season. Are you really serious about becoming financially responsible?'

'Absolutely.'

James went to his writing desk, from which he withdrew a small journal. 'This is an expense book.'

'I've seen one before.'

'Max Friz of Germany is going to give you $7,500 today. Write that amount here, on this line. No, no, here. Good. And below that, put another $2,500.'

'What's that for?'

'That's the amount I always reserve for you to develop your show each season. It generally pays for new flats and scrim, and for you and Ledocq to put your stamp on all the fine effects available out there. So—'

'I add the two figures together and get ten thousand. This is easy, James.'

James gave him a look that was difficult to interpret, but that gradually became a patient smile. 'That's your budget.'

'For the show.'

'For everything. Your life, including the show. Write all of your personal expenses right here, and everything you spend on the show over there.'

Carter nodded. 'Now what other money do I have?'

'What do you mean?'

There had to be some obvious description, but he didn't know the words. 'I mean remember how I once had money tied up in Martinka's shop and then I cashed out, correct? What sort of old War Bonds, or stocks, or—'

James shook his head. 'Nothing.'

'Because there was an advertisement in the *Sphinx* for a magic library I'd love to acquire.'

'Charlie, really. Nothing.'

'But I have a Pierce-Arrow and a Bentley and—'

'Exactly.'

Comprehension arrived: a cold tingling that settled in like influenza. 'I see. My new zest for this comes when my back's to the wall?'

James nodded.

Carter nodded back at him. 'Good. There's something good about that.' And he actually felt pleased, as if he'd counted all the bottles of wine in his cellar. *This is what I own.* He checked his watch. It was just after nine o'clock. He stood, and brushed imaginary lint off his lapels. 'It's going to be a busy day. Max Friz first. And I'm going to pay Borax a visit around noon, and—'

'Aren't you worried about being followed by thugs?'

His hands in his pockets, a big smile on his face, Carter shook his head.

'Oh, you think you can handle them?'

'I *know* I can handle them, but what I mean is, they're about to realize that I don't have what they're looking for.'

'But you *do*.'

'Oh, speaking of that, here's Harding's cigar tube.' Carter tried to pass it to him, but when his brother kept his arms folded, he placed it on an end table next to a vase of stargazers.

James shook his head. 'I know it's not safe here. I don't want the plans here.'

'It's just the tube. Empty.' Carter showed off another cigar tube, plain and silver. 'The plans are in this one. Lovely way to keep them, actually. They're safe with me.'

'And what about the thugs who know you have them?'

'They *used to* know. They don't know anymore.'

The beaming blue eyes and tight smile were just too much for James, who rubbed his face quietly, knowing it was no use asking for clarification. He led his brother to the door, muttering, 'You have the straight and narrow nature of a Borgia Pope.' He gave Carter a hug. 'Might I at least remind you to return Miss Kyle's gloves?'

'Of course.'

'You know,' James said, not letting him go yet, 'it's a new world out there. You can go to bed with a girl and not marry her.'

'James, I've managed an assignation or two, thank you.' Carter reached for the doorknob.

'Yes? With whom?'

'I'm a gentleman.'

'Exactly. With whom?'

'No one you know.'

'I believe *part* of that. Charlie, girls are allowed—'

'Thank you.'

'To not only discuss sex, but—'

'Thank you.'

Carter had the door open and was half out of it, James coming after him, exclaiming, 'And have fun!' Carter was down two flights of stairs by the time James, leaning over the banister, had shouted, 'And don't spend any money!'

Chapter 14

Colonel Starling was the linchpin of many efforts to be coordinated on each coast, no easy task, but one he fulfilled gracefully. He traveled from San Francisco to the East Coast in less than forty-eight hours, and when he arrived in Washington, before attending to any other pressing matter, he made an appointment with an odd little man with singular talents.

At the time, the entirety of the U.S. espionage effort was housed on the third floor of a shabby rooming house in one of the marshiest areas outside of Washington, D.C. Their landlady, a pious and shrill widow, had started eviction proceedings against them for nonpayment of rent. If nothing changed, the Black Chamber, the only bureau to handle cryptography, domestic and international surveillance, and communications monitoring, would close on September first.

The agency consisted of Herbert Yardley, and his assistants, all women, all of whom were on the verge of quitting because he hadn't paid them in two weeks.

Yardley had spent his adult life trying to live down his childhood nickname: Bunion Head. True, his head was slightly lopsided, and, worse, he had a cowlick, and he had been unable to find a sweetheart in high school or a wife during his international travels, but he wasn't going to let personal problems stand in the way of destiny.

He had an angry letter from former Secretary of War Stimson, framed and mounted by his work desk. After two paragraphs of fire-and-brimstone, the letter concluded, 'And I remind you, Mr Yardley, that gentlemen do not read each other's mail.' Yardley kept the letter to remind him of the mentality he had to fight against.

He had just lost two more cryptographers. One, who'd been decoding messages for a year, was finally let go after she accused

Yardley of letting an invisible bulldog loose at her desk. The other girl, who'd clung to the job for fourteen months, had dreamed nightly about walking along a lonely beach, weighed down by an enormous sackful of pebbles, and searching for more pebbles that matched those in the bag. When she burst into tears at the office, Yardley had no choice but to fire her.

This left three junior girls who were still getting the hang of codes and ciphers. It was a far cry from the glory days of Versailles and the Japanese Naval Treaty, when the Black Chamber had not only a dozen doctoral candidates and missionaries fluent in all the allied and enemy languages working around the clock, but also a pipeline to the President's ear. Yardley had gone to Paris, had decrypted foreign cables all day and all night, had ordered champagne on the War Department's tab, and even though he hadn't found a sweetheart in France, he had set up an office that he called *La Chambre Noire*.

Now all that was gone, and there was still room to plummet. Yardley wasn't alone in this – with Harding gone, the whole of Washington was operating at peak efficiency, trying to convince the new administration that their jobs mattered. As Colonel Starling was about to arrive, Yardley wondered if it would be better to look like he was on top of things or overwhelmed?

He left a stack of monographs on the corner of his desk, next to the three encrypted messages the Colonel had asked him to look at. Yardley bit his thumb. Were Starling's messages a trap? If the Colonel were of the antique opinion that gentlemen did not read gentlemen's mail, then perhaps Yardley had walked straight into his own doom. Two of the messages were innocuous enough, but the final one made him bite his thumb harder, until his false teeth left marks.

Also: he had an ace. Something the Colonel didn't know about.

An hour later, when the Colonel himself was seated, smiling faintly and scanning a budgetary request form, Yardley's breathing was quiet but irregular. His discomfort had erupted the moment the Colonel had spoken, and Yardley had heard his relaxed Kentucky accent. The Colonel was a gentleman, through and through, and gentlemen had no use for Yardley's services. Yardley's eyes shifted around, and he ran his fingers over his tooth-marked thumb, preparing to fire off reasons the Black Chamber should not be disbanded.

'So,' Yardley said, 'what *is* our new President like, hmm?'

'He's a fine man,' the Colonel murmured.

'Mmm-hmm. I've heard he enjoys cheese. Vermont cheddar.'

The Colonel nodded. He still hadn't looked up from the budget request.

'Mmm-hmm. And naps in the afternoon. And he's very thrifty. I understand he borrowed ten cents from you already. Ha ha ha.' Yardley was almost vibrating from nerves.

The Colonel looked up. 'Where did you hear that?'

'Word gets around.' He froze. It was a saying of his, but obviously Starling didn't appreciate it. 'Gathering information, it's what we do. You know.' With the Colonel's cool gaze on him, he felt his entire body itching. 'Maybe I should show you the samples?'

They had appeared on Yardley's desk that morning, three messages, with a request from Starling that he 'decode' them. In fact, only one of the messages was in code; the other two were ciphers, and Yardley was annoyed when people didn't know the difference. 'Well, the first message that I *deciphered*,' he cleared his throat, 'I'm guessing came from a gin-rummy. An amateur, someone from Canada, am I right?'

'You're correct, Mr Yardley.'

'He's strictly small potatoes. No threat to the Volstead Act, but I don't need to tell you your business, now do I? Ha ha.' He passed the original message and the deciphered version to Starling. It read:

Got your loving letter last night, and am glad that I heard from my girl. I know you still wear his ring, but that is temprary, and at least when you lay your head down you isn't loansome. Trapping this weekend was tough – only 30 rats, only $35, and you know how I will use $8. I wish you were here to trap with me. I do want to see you aful bad. A kiss to you

'I think "trapping rats" is what they call transporting gin, and I'm sure the sums he mentions are severely deflated. Otherwise, it's all straightforward.'

'Treasury agents found the note with a shipment of gin heading for Chicago,' Starling said, putting it aside.

'And think of it, a criminal vagabond and he can't even get his own sweetheart.'

'I was struck by the pathos, too, Mr Yardley.'

'He had another man's wife as his girlfriend! Ha ha.'

Starling put on a smile. 'What about the next message?'

'Oh, yes. That was coded. State-of-the-art code for someone. But I licked it in fifteen minutes. It's from Standard Oil and Petroleum, a chemical analysis of their holdings in Oklahoma, with percentages of methane, butane, crude oil, and so forth. They encoded it since they were sending it by telegram.'

'What about the third message?'

'Oh. Yes. Mmm-hmm.' He laid out a leather-bound journal on his desk. He placed three typewritten sheets of paper next to it. As Starling picked up the translation, Yardley spoke in a way he hoped was circumspect. 'Now this one . . . this was a joke, of course. Yes. Very clever.'

'A joke?'

His skin itched again. 'I thought someone in the Service . . . Well, it claims of course to be a journal kept by the late President, but I thought it had a *wicked*, ha ha ha ha, Menckenesque quality.' He found his mouth moving automatically. He explained: not only were the journal entries for the most part banal (the scores from gin games, who owed him what amount, attempts at love poetry for women who were certainly not the Duchess), but the cipher used was, well, moronic.

'Moronic,' Starling said.

'*A* equals *1*; *B* equals *2* and, well, it should be obvious after that . . . but he even copied it out on the last page, as if he couldn't remember it otherwise. And he *still* made mistakes.' Yardley shook his head. 'That's not, that's not possible, that can't be Harding, not really. I just thought it was a funny joke, that's all.' He shrugged, twice, for effect.

The journal ended with a one-paragraph note.

Saw a wonderful magic show. The elephant's name was Tug. I got to be eaten by a lion, but it was all in good fun. An excellent mood was created. Magician wanted to know about secrets but I would not tell. Tonight, felt resolve. Excused myself to powder room and burned all notes relating to T.V.

'I mean,' Yardley said. 'You see what I mean. I don't know what

"T.V." is supposed to be, maybe he got confused or tired.'

Starling nodded. He had a thousand-yard stare, and Yardley wondered what that meant. Had he failed somehow? 'You've been very helpful, Mr Yardley, and I'll explain that to the President as he is establishing his priorities.' Yardley didn't know what *that* meant either. 'I'm afraid, however, we can't promise any sort of funding. It's up to Congress, of course—'

'Here.' Yardley had a good, solid justification for the Black Chamber's existence. He had it memorized. But right now, he couldn't think, and talk would just bounce off the Colonel. And so, Yardley simply reached into his jacket pocket and produced his trump: a stack of telegrams, decrypted. 'We've trapped a murderer.'

'What do you mean?'

'The Black Chamber . . . we are an important agency for our country's future.' No, that was the midpoint of his argument. He tried to make sense, but it was hopeless. 'It's not like it used to be. People laugh in your face when you're civil. When children are brought up by the Reds—'

'I respect your passion, sir, but I don't follow you.'

Yardley tapped the telegrams. 'We monitor everything. All communication. There's only me and the girls now, but we do the best we can. And we have friends and accomplices – sometimes the international cables find their way to us.'

Starling picked up the stack of wires and put it on his knee. Then he scanned the translations.

Yardley spoke: 'They thought it was a card game. People play bridge by mail, though I don't know how that works. It seemed to be taking up months, and one of the operators plays bridge and said the bidding didn't make sense and so they sent the wires to the Black Chamber and . . .' he paused. 'Every one of them is sent to the same theatrical agency in New York. And the person sending them was in Tangiers, then Rhodesia, then Cairo, all within the same week as those murders.'

'What murders?'

'Oh, I didn't know about them either, not at first. But I've been tracking this man for a while now, just as a hobby, on my off-hours. I liked his code – it's very devious. I wondered if I could determine his real name. No luck on that front, but the English newspapers from those countries report murders, unusual ones, occurring where this man has just been. The last one was a man in Cairo, killed with a deck of cards.'

'Cards? Playing cards?'

'Thrown – like—' Yardley flicked his wrist. 'So when I read the last cable, it was very short, but I thought you might want to pass it on to the police.'

Starling regarded the final message carefully.

MUST KNOW NOW STOP IS IT SAFE
TO RETURN TO AMERICA STOP

Smiling faintly, Starling nodded at Yardley. Yardley's heart jumped. He could tell there had been a sea change in the man.

'This is very interesting, Mr Yardley. Very interesting work indeed. Thank you. May I keep this?'

Chapter 15

The San Francisco branch of the Secret Service taught classes in interrogation ('Never question a female suspect alone'; 'Use proper grammar when questioning the highest or lowest members of society'), logical syllogisms, and other methods of assessing information. Until the War, one of the graduation exercises had been Satan's Stirrup, a tangle of metal chains and horseshoes that could be separated into three simple components, but only if the student knew when to apply inductive and deductive skills. In short, one had to follow the knot from one side, then the other, use force, then finesse.

Griffin had done well with Satan's Stirrup when he was a young man. He was disappointed that the agency no longer had patience for metaphors, and so the new generation went out instead with logbooks and highly advanced scientific methods to expose criminals.

When Griffin could no longer follow Carter's trail forward, he looked at its more recent end and began to tug.

After the performance of Thursday, August second, Carter had supervised the dismantling of the show. Dozens of people had seen him, beginning with members of his troupe (of whose testimony Griffin was suspect), continuing with San Francisco police, and the train yard crew, who had helped load the elephant onto a railcar bound for Carmel. Carter was literally surrounded by people at all times but, Griffin noted by looking at a street map, the train yard and the Palace Hotel were only a half-mile apart. So Griffin tried the route himself, checking the results on his stopwatch. Carter could have slipped away for twenty minutes, poisoned the President, then returned before anyone questioned his absence.

He had to have accomplices. But who? Someone powerful. Harding, for instance, hadn't been autopsied. Was it the Duchess? The attending physicians? The Ohio Gang? Someone in the Service?

When, to his own satisfaction, he had locked down opportunity, he looked at motive and more or less threw up his hands. Carter was a magician and in their interview had made little sense. He probably disrespected authority, and thrived on half-baked ideas borrowed from Madame Blavatsky and the Satanists. All that was left was means, and this Griffin pursued next. He wasn't nearly powerful enough to order an autopsy on Harding, and he was unsure which of his superiors he could trust enough to put those wheels in motion.

The quietest possible way to investigate was walk several blocks, to a Western Union that had no Secret Service account, where he used his own money to telegraph the staff at Pineview Cemetery in Marion, Ohio. He inquired gently about Harding's burial. Harding, he learned, hadn't been buried – he'd been entombed, and even then, his remains were interred in the columbarium. Harding had been cremated.

Griffin telegraphed back: When had Pineview cremated Harding and under whose approval?

When he read the response, Satan's Stirrup appeared in his mind.

DECEASED'S ASHES RECEIVED IN MARION STOP
CREMATION SITE UNKNOWN STOP

Civilians had knelt around the funeral train, linking hands and singing hymns, every time it had stopped – no one had hustled the body into a crematorium in, say, Winnemucca. Griffin consulted the city directory, finding that because of earthquake concerns, there were no crematoria within San Francisco. The closest was in Oakland. In the same cemetery where Charles Carter's wife was buried.

At roughly the same moment that Colonel Starling was reading the translation of Harding's sad, final diary entry, and seeing that the plans for television had been destroyed and that Carter couldn't possibly have them, Griffin telephoned the Chapel of the Chimes, in Oakland, to request an interview.

The interview, alas, was never to occur, for when Griffin returned to his room, he found taped to the door a new duty roster, signed by Colonel Starling. The investigation into Charles

Carter was closed. President Coolidge was planning a trip to the southwest oilfields; in forty-eight hours, Griffin was to report for advance detail duty in Albuquerque.

He read and reread his packing papers for implications and found, to his own satisfaction, plenty of them. Seemingly polite orders from the Colonel. A tug, too hard, on Satan's Stirrup, and Griffin was suddenly thrown off this horse. For just a few moments, he mentally packed his toilet kit and cardboard suitcase, stopping when he reached the photo of his daughter on his night table. What would she think of him? She had inherited his stubborn gruffness – or perhaps his wife's – but she tended to melt when he performed heroics.

He had to phone the Bureau Chief to acknowledge receipt of his orders. What else would he do? Mechanically, he picked up the candlestick.

When the switchboard picked up, he gave his name, and began placing the call to the Treasury Department.

'You have a message, Mr Griffin,' the hotel operator said. 'The San Francisco Public Library called.' Here, the woman's voice tightened as if holding on to laughter. 'You have an overdue book.'

'What? A what?'

The operator held her fingertips over her mouthpiece, though unsuccessfully; Griffin could hear her saying to the other girls, 'He's playing dumb,' and laughter. Then, clearing her throat, she said, 'The Sherlock Holmes mystery you checked out. *A View of the Poisoned Duke.*'

Griffin said nothing. Duke. Duchess.

'Is that sounding a little familiar?'

'Maybe.'

'You have to see Miss White at the library today.'

'I'll do that.'

'Can I place a call for you?'

'No, I think that can wait.' He hung up the telephone and replaced the candlestick in its alcove. There were thousands of interlocking patterns in the rug.

Moments later, he was out the door and down the hall. But just before he left, he slapped on a little cologne.

Chapter 16

Unlike San Francisco, the Port of Oakland was just far enough from the Golden Gate to be protected from the worst weather, its depth was perfect for cargo-bearing ships, and, best of all, Oakland was the terminus of the transcontinental railway. Given its location, it should have been the most powerful and profitable harbor in North America and, when he visited it, Mayor Davie promised that this would one day be so. But the port had been managed the same way as the rest of Oakland, and so it was deserted and dirty, San Francisco's poor relation.

Still, ships from Germany and other defeated nations docked here. Carter ferried in from San Francisco (*five cents*, he wrote in his journal), and took a cab (*thirty-five cents*, with tip) to the farthest pier. The air was terrible: the waste from the sardine cannery was dumped nearby, along with sludge from the dredging machines.

The *Hermione* was docked at the farthest berth, beside a one-room structure that was too large to be called a shack and too rickety to be a warehouse. This was the primitive living area for overseas crews who needed to wait for local connections. Because of its high screen windows, a constant wind sucked air toward its ceiling, and so the building was called a loft.

Carter felt thrilled this morning, for he was launching a new show. Being pinched made him feel younger, hungrier. There were crates and tarpaulins throughout the loft; in a way, Carter felt at home.

Max Friz, who was pacing inside, threw down a cigarette and weakly took Carter's hand between both of his, looking him in the chin. 'Max Friz,' he said. 'Welcome. Welcome. Good.' Friz was hollow-cheeked, with a drooping mustache and grey beard stubble. Carter saw in him unimaginable sorrow, as if he, Max Friz, had single-handedly lost the War.

Friz had a speech prepared, something welcoming the great magician on behalf of international relations, but he was too nervous, and his English left him, and so Carter spoke a few words of German, telling him everything would be okay. He added, in English, 'My brother tells me you have something for my show.'

Friz looked down. He said he was using his factory to make tool-boxes. But Germany no longer wanted anything with his company's name on it. 'No good, no good, Bay-Emm-Vay.'

It was more than Carter could stand. 'Really, it *will* be okay. If I can, I'd like to help you. Show me your automobile.'

Friz looked stricken. 'You want an automobile?'

'Yes. Don't I?'

'*Gott.*' With a moan, he put his hand in his jacket, quite obviously stalling. He pulled out a tin of mints. He popped a couple into his mouth and extended the tin. 'PEZ?' he asked.

Carter accepted a mint.

'Take the tin,' Friz said. 'Crates of them are here.' Throwing back a tarpaulin, he began to apologize for not having an automobile, and he said he understood if Carter wanted to cancel the contract.

It was a motorcycle. Black, angular, and sleek, unmistakably European, it was the most beautiful object Carter had ever seen. He wanted it. He would fight anyone who tried to take it away from him. How soon could he ride it? He didn't want to interrupt the depressed Max Friz, who explained that he hated motorcycles, but at least they were closer to airplanes than toolboxes. He under-lined the technical features like he was naming cuts of horse meat: a horizontally opposed twin, transversely mounted with completely enclosed valve gear; dual brakes (hardwood for dry weather; soft-wood for the rainy season); revolutionary three-speed shifter. If Ledocq were here, he would have understood – Carter was more interested in its fine appearance: the matte silver finish of the engine housed in a polished black frame, the white double pinstripe piping on the gas tank and fenders. American motorcycles came flanked with two ugly metal boxes for storage; this bike, the R32, had a pair of clamshell-shaped packing kits, black, set off with the signature double white pinstripes, and gently sloped as if leaning into the wind. They were stamped with Max Friz's logo: a circle divided into blue and white quarters. This single patch of color was a clever touch; it looked quite sporty.

'How fast will it go?'

Max wrinkled his nose. 'One hundred ten, one hundred twenty kilometers, in Germany. In Germany, there are roads, long paved roads for good drives. Here, one mile, two miles, then *pfft*.'

'I know some roads,' Carter murmured, picturing them.

'Fourteen-liter tank,' Max declared. 'Ah, petcock. You turn this from auf to zu, and, trickle trickle trickle. This mark is for reserve. Leader hose, make sure the clamp is good, otherwise, the fuel the ground to soak. You get it?'

'May I ride it now? I've ridden motorcycles before.'

'American?' he snorted. He showed off the ignition switch, how to kick the bike over, how to adjust the revolutionary headlamp.

'Oh?' Carter murmured, amused, easing into the saddle. 'The headlamp is revolutionary, too?'

'Yah. It's on the *battery*. Six volt. Electric, not acetylene. Not so much burning the hands.'

'What type of fuel should I use?'

'Anything, aviation fuel.'

There were papers for him to sign; Friz had customs reports and contracts that James and Tom had already approved. Carter would devise an illusion showcasing the Bayerische Motoren-Werke R32 in exchange for $7,500 American. In exchange, BMW would use a likeness of Carter the Great in their print advertising at the October 1923 Paris Motor Show.

Max sank down to one knee with a pigsticker of a knife, which he used to pry up a floorboard. He pulled out three cotton sacks tied shut and sealed with wax, and stamped with the San Francisco Mint stencil. 'Heavy,' he said, unnecessarily.

Carter took them, and tried not to show the exertion as he walked them to the bike's panniers. When he returned to the loft, he asked, if only to make James proud of him, 'Now, the R32 – how much will it retail for?'

Friz sucked on his peppermint loudly. 'The mark is difficult . . .' His grim tone became funereal. 'This will be the most expensive motorcycle in the world.'

Carter was quiet. Motorbikes were for sportsmen, for college men, and for those who couldn't afford automobiles. Carter put himself in Friz's shoes. To come from unthinkable poverty with such a dream, all hopes riding on an expensive motorbike – that was clearly unrealistic.

Which of course made Max Friz so much more endearing to him.

Carter stalled twice on his motorcycle, each time a chance to learn the interplay of clutch and throttle. It was hard to fully enjoy the ride, as he wasn't prepared for it. So he returned to his house, lugged most of the gold into his garage for safekeeping (he kept some on him, for fun's sake), and went to his apartment to change into appropriate riding attire: a fitted canvas jacket and trousers that tucked into a pair of brand-new ten-eyelet lace-ups. While Baby gnawed on a steak on the kitchen floor, Carter ensured his jacket, which he hadn't worn in years, was properly outfitted. He had a checklist of items that came in handy when out and about.

A few minutes later, he sat on his motorcycle again, wearing a pair of tinted goggles, and now quite ready to ride. It was two miles from his apartment to Borax's estates, by the most direct way. But this was a utilitarian route, so Carter found a way that took him over twelve miles of bayfront, railroad crossings, Lake Merritt vistas, and winding hillside roads. The BMW was unexpectedly quiet, its engine making just a *chuff-chuff-chuff* sound that increased in tempo, but not volume, as he sped down the straightaways.

The first time he found third gear, on a long, flat stretch of Grand Avenue, and opened the throttle, the bike leaped forward, snapping his head back with acceleration to the unbelievable speed of sixty miles an hour in less than fifteen seconds.

At the next intersection, a four-way stop, he simply muttered to himself, 'My God,' until an image came to mind: the same speedy trip, with Phoebe Kyle on the little leather pill that was the passenger seat. 'My God,' he whispered again.

Trestle Creek, a trickle in the summer months, wound from the Oakland hills to the mouth of Lake Merritt, with Fourth Avenue its companion the whole way. Carter had never noticed what an excellent and well-paved boulevard Fourth was, with tree-lined curves and ever-broadening glimpses of the bay. Coming to see Borax, he was excited and nervous anyway, the way he was supposed to feel when visiting kings and princes, and he wished his ride could last a little longer. But he had to arrive before Philo did – if he did – and so, at three minutes till noon, he arrived at the gates of Arbor Villa.

He sat on his motorcycle under the shade of a pepper tree. He produced a cigarette and smoked it until he heard a weak pop, like a distant champagne cork – the Arbor Villa noon cannon. He was pleased that his friend could still afford that small luxury, for Francis Marion 'Borax' Smith, octogenarian master of Arbor Villa, had gone from untold wealth to being perhaps the poorest man in the world.

Carter cautiously rode through the ruins of his estate. There were missing letters in the wrought-iron gate so that it spelled ARB V LL .

Borax had made a grisly mistake after the great San Francisco disaster of 1906. Seeing how the survivors recuperated in Oakland, he leveraged every penny of his worth in a massive land purchase, the largest since the days of the Spanish. He purchased almost the entirety of Contra Costa and Alameda counties, every available scrap of land from Mount Diablo to the Oakland waterfront, thousands of acres of city land zoned for industry, business, shopping, theatres, houses, and apartments; further, in the countryside, hundreds of thousands of acres of farms and ranches for the breadbasket.

After a year, the population had not increased and so Borax decided that what Oakland's populace-to-come needed was easy transportation, so he bought all of the streetcar companies, merging them into a single system, the Key Route, and he kept the drivers sober, a first for public trains. He placed interesting sights at the end of every line: Idora, an amusement park; Stolzer Gardens, a botanical exhibitory; a public theatre; Neptune Beach; Lake Anza.

An early Key Route car was on his property. Choking ivy had crawled up its sides and into its broken cabin where, for a brief time after his collapse, Borax had kept his troupe of spider monkeys. Carter walked past – he'd parked his BMW by an impassable section of road, where a palm tree six feet thick had long ago fallen down.

Two events, almost simultaneous, turned Borax from a visionary into a folk hero: first, a restless class of San Franciscans discovered the charms of Oakland and trickled into the neighborhoods he'd set aside for them – and the money started to come in. Second: in Mexicali, in 1918, Branson Chemical Exploration found a richer, purer, cheaper vein of borax. In a snap of the fingers, Borax, whose ownership of all that wonderful land was heavily leveraged, went from owning to *owing* several hundred million dollars.

This should have been fatal, and perhaps in time it would be. Now he was flush at one moment with real estate sales and, an hour later, at the mercy of promissory note payments. His position was a mystery, and deliberately so, for there were men whose families could retire for the next three generations if they knew when best to hold him hostage.

So when Carter rang the door at the big house, he didn't know whether it would be a day that caviar would be served or gravy and hard tack. He was escorted from the door to the arboretum, where Borax was taking lunch. Patches of warm sun illuminated the dwarf palms growing in planters. Carter noted a shadow moving on the floor and, glancing up, saw the outline of a woman on the roof, dressed in trousers and the huge white bonnet, wiping down the skylights with soap and water. He waved and she waved back at him enthusiastically.

Borax himself reclined in a wicker chair, surrounded by the day's newspaper, open to the public notices page of the financial section. He was rarely out of his chair these days unless carried. His body, once swollen up with a prosperous belly, had become as shapeless as an old balloon, and his face had shrunken into crags and wrinkles visible through a white beard so thin it looked like it could be washed off. 'Charlie Carter,' he said. 'How's tricks?' It was a question he never tired of asking.

'Tricks are looking up, you coot,' Carter replied. He pulled up a chair and found it too rickety for sitting. Searching for a second chair, his eyes fell on something tall, wood and metal, perhaps the last object in the world he could imagine in Borax's conservatory. 'What *is* that?'

Borax followed his gaze. 'It's a guillotine.'

'Where did you get it?' Carter asked with a pang of jealousy.

'I dunno, France? Are you staying for lunch? The girls can make you a sandwich.'

Carter approached the guillotine and found the veneer smooth and lustrous. The blade, locked in the down position, was engraved with roses and thorns and cloister text that in some places was worn smooth. 'This must be eighteenth century.'

'That's what the man from Sotheby's said yesterday.'

'You don't mean you're selling it?'

'He was here for hours, poking around. I had a first edition of *Gulliver's Travels*, too, seemed to interest him. He wrote down a whole pile of stuff I can't remember buying in the first place.'

'Does this work?'

'Ain't tried it out. But that don't matter – seems this is an original, Monsieur Guillotin himself built it.'

'If the man from Sotheby's told me that, I'd have thrown him out of the house.'

'Why are you here, Charlie?'

'Well, now I'm here to protect you from Sotheby's. They'll tell you anything to get a piece in their auction.' He crouched by the frame of the guillotine, unlatched the blade, and felt for resistance. 'The first fifty-three guillotines were built in April 1792 by a harpsichord maker named Tobias Schmidt. The public executioner had been complaining about how hard it was to chop off people's heads with a sword. Guillotin did make a pretty speech, though, and so they named it after him. Ah.' He pulled the blade up a few inches. 'See? The chop mark? Swiss.'

'Um-hmm.' Borax blinked at him.

'It's a valuable piece, but . . .' And here Carter paused. He wanted it. It was completely unfair that he, who knew what it was, didn't own it yet. He didn't know how to pretend otherwise. 'It's rusty,' he said, fooling exactly no one. 'You'd have to give it a good cleaning—'

'Sotheby's says it's worth about a thousand.'

'I'll give you seven-fifty.'

'Sold! Make sure you give me cash. And wipe that grin off your face.'

Carter stood with one arm around the frame, imagining all the wonderful things he could do with a guillotine. Then he remembered he'd promised James he would stop spending money. And how he'd felt quite good about swearing off purchases. Perhaps he would omit this expense from his new journal.

Patting the device once more, he squatted by Borax's chair. 'Well, then. I need your help to sort something out.'

'Information? Teach me a magic trick, I'll tell you what you need to know.'

316

'No, those secrets are my livelihood.' Considering how to explain it better, he added, 'They're how I make money.'

'Sounds right. If I could get out of this chair, first thing I'd do is hit you over the head, steal all your tricks, and make me the *real* moolah.' Borax dissolved into laughter.

Carter looked again among the indoor plants and shrubs, sculptures and gardening tools for a proper chair. He found one, and sat backward in it.

Recovering, Borax said, 'Secrets are my livelihood too.'

'Well, then. I need to find something out from you, and you can find out something equal from me.'

Borax considered the tray of sandwiches. 'That's square.'

'Tell me who's involved in this television business.'

A breeze had come from somewhere around the rafters, something warm that made the date palms shake and, seen against them, Borax seemed to stop chewing. 'Okay,' he finally said, swallowing, 'how do you make the elephant disappear?'

'Is it that big a deal?'

'Have a sandwich.' Borax looked at Carter. It was a sizing-up kind of look. In the twenty years they'd known each other, Borax had looked at him many ways, but this was the first time Carter was aware of what a troublesome adversary he would make. While Carter looked among the rounds, selecting with some hesitation a low-grade meat spread, Borax asked, 'Did you get the guy's name?'

'I heard he would be here around now.'

'He ain't coming. Whoever he is.' With annoyance, Borax explained: he'd received a call two days ago from the inventor himself in which he politely canceled their appointment. Borax had tried to make him reconsider, but the man was adamant. 'I told him there was a load of people out there, ready to steal it, and he said he knew, he could handle it. You ready for this; he says, "I ain't seen the whole world, but I have been to Boise," he says.'

'Some people would tell that story even if they'd arranged to meet with Mr Inventor a day earlier.'

'You gonna lie to me about how Tug disappears?'

Carter shook his head.

'Well, all righty, then. I figure it's mirrors, right?'

Carter blinked. 'No, not mirrors. Who's after television?'

'What's in the bag by your feet? The white cloth bag. Yeah, pick that up.' Borax struggled to swing a gumwood desk tray in front of him, and patted it to indicate Carter should upend the sack there. He did so, and with a dirty clunking sound, several dozen lead soldiers painted with colors of the Revolutionary and British armies fell out. 'I had some like these at the orphanage,' Borax said, seeming half-lost. 'They were mine, fair and square, but they were hard to keep, and when I was about fifty, I was in London, and I saw this toy shop . . .' He began to set the soldiers up into ranks, silently, and when Carter began to wonder how much age had crept up on him, Borax added, 'One day, there'll be a bunch of rich men who want the toys what got taken away when they were little, and they'll pay real money for 'em. So what did Harding say the guy's name was?'

Carter chuckled. 'If I had his name, would I be here?'

Borax said, 'That's two times you haven't answered the question. So, these guys, over here, the dirty, sloppy ones,' he indicated the Continental Army, 'this is RCA, Westinghouse, some other guys. Basically the corporations who control radio.'

'Oh!' Carter said, in spite of himself.

'Yeah. Makes sense, huh? Lordy, one day I hope Oakland gets more than KJWR playing psalms. King Jesus Will Return my left eye.'

'I heard the Leonard fight last week.'

'Yeah? With the new frequencies coming, I have applications for eight stations, and I put a transmitter on Capwell's about a month ago, figure I'll have a boy in there, put an ad in the *Tribune* saying you can hear jazz records every day, and see if anyone buys themselves a radio to hear it.'

'That's a great idea.'

'It's an experiment. Won't make me a dime, directly. No, the money is with making radios, and there's probably more money than that, maybe, selling advertising space on it, maybe. And since television is radio with pictures, RCA figures they better own it and keep it secret until they've made their dollar back on selling everyone a radio or two. So that's who told those goons to break into your house.'

'You knew about that?'

Borax looked up at Carter like a boy caught soaping windows. 'Heard about it. Figured they'd try it once. Anyway, look here.' He touched the steeply ridged lead hats of the Redcoats. 'These guys are soldiers. The army.'

'Yes,' Carter said, 'and who do they represent?'

Borax looked at him. 'The army. Really. The War Department. General Pershing, he sees it like this: you put cameras under the bellies of all the planes, or on the tanks, and that way the officers back at camp can see what the enemy's up to. So they're pulling the more official strings, like the Secret Service, the coppers, anything with a uniform, it ain't your friend right now.' He held the sack to the edge of the table and began sweeping soldiers into it. 'RCA. War Department. Neither of 'em wants the other to have television, and they probably figure God wouldn't mind if they stepped on a neck or two.' He paused. 'That's why the Secret Service guys got those orders to investigate you. They figured you know something, and that's why you headed out.'

'Ah.'

'That and you maybe killing the President.'

Carter reached for the sack. 'I seem to have gotten away with the murder part far too easily,' he sighed, dropping the soldiers into the bag one by one.

'Charlie, you ain't up to murder, so don't pretend. Hey, forget the guy's name – why do they want to kill him?'

'I don't know.'

'It don't make sense. Why not just buy it for a couple mil and sit on it? They got billions at stake. Maybe U.S. Steel–type money. That's on one side. And changing the way we fight wars on the other. It's huge.'

The house around them felt lonely now. No women were in the room, or making noises from adjoining rooms. Even the skylight was empty.

'What's your angle?' Borax took a sip of tea.

'Well,' Carter cleared his throat. 'I thought it would be nice to use in my card tricks.'

Borax laughed so hard he choked. 'All the capitalists and all the armed forces on one side, and Charlie Carter on the other. Now I know where to put my money.'

'You don't have faith in me?'

'I didn't say that. I just think you're too sweet to go up against murderers. They're out of your league.'

Carter met his friend's eye for a long moment. Then he dropped the last soldier in, cinched the bag shut, and said to him, 'When you have faith, there's always a payoff,' making small circles over the bag, then upending it so that a bushel of ten-dollar gold pieces came pouring out. He carefully turned the bag inside out; there wasn't a single soldier inside of it.

Borax casually ran his callused hands through the ten-dollar gold pieces as if debts were always paid to him this way. 'Feels like seventy-five of 'em. What's the guy's name?'

Carter sighed – Borax was certainly not charmed by magic when in the presence of a business deal. 'Harding explained television and told me the name. I've been trying to locate him, to no success. I don't think anyone else has found him.'

'Think that since Harding died, he packed up and went home?'

'Anyone sensible enough to invent something so interesting, and then not give his name away, would take his benefactor's unexplained death as a kick in the pants. He's regrouping somewhere. I know I would. Frankly, I'd like to save him.'

Borax shook his head. 'You can't really save people.'

Borax, of all people, saying this? Carter felt like a curtain had, unfortunately, been drawn back for him. 'You have to try,' he responded, but without much force. He looked around the room for concrete evidence, a photograph of an unfortunate woman, or a *real* one, but all he could see were the palms and their planters and, of course, the guillotine. He took the white sack, turned it inside out again, and said, 'Look, I saved some people just now.' Out tumbled Borax's lead soldiers.

With that bit of magic, something in Borax melted. His shoulders drooped. 'Even if you can find him,' he spoke haltingly, as if the mechanism by which he gave up financial advice were rusty, 'you wanting to license it for your magic show . . . well, I bet he'd have some other mighty attractive offers you'd have to ace out.'

Carter shrugged. 'I have the knack.' He stood.

'I mean, including my own.'

'Which side do you favor?'

'Whatever way turns out most profitable.'

'You're free to back my magic show.' Carter knew by Borax's blank stare that he looked like a child who'd wandered into a boxing ring.

'What about that elephant?' Borax asked.

'Oh, yes. Here.' He sat back down. 'Now, promise me—'

'I won't tell a soul.'

'No, no. Promise that you won't be disappointed.'

'How can I be disappointed? I'm gonna see how you make a ten-ton elephant disappear!' He clapped.

Carter made a series of sketches that explained the way Tug walked onto the platform, then was surrounded on all four sides by a screen for exactly two seconds. Then it opened, empty. The gimmick was one the audience never noticed – the platform was the depth of two elephants. 'So, Tug walks up, and we close the four sides of the screen so it makes a box around her, only it has an extra wall between her and the audience. When we open the doors, the false wall looks exactly like the actual rear wall of the box, very ornate, spells out some impressive Hindi words, actually the text of an advertisement for cough drops.' Carter looked up from his sketches to see Borax ruminating.

'You mean I told you about television for *this*?'

'Didn't I say you shouldn't be disappointed?'

'Yeah, but . . .' Borax folded his arms. 'Yeah.'

'We've stumbled onto something here. I think having secrets protects the audience, not the magician.'

They exchanged a few more social comments after that, Carter mentioning his motorcycle, Borax suggesting he use the vehicle and the fine weather they'd been having to impress a lady or two, and Carter agreed that this was a fine idea.

As Carter left the house, his spirits fell. In twenty years, he'd never rubbed against Borax. He felt like they'd gone into in the forest and lost something on the way.

A hundred yards from the house, he saw a familiar graffito in red paint, lowercase letters across a turned-over wheelbarrow. *she never died*, it read. Such a phrase, beaten down and yet hopeful.

she never died put Carter, stepping over the fallen trees, finding his BMW, into a contemplative mood. You can't save anyone, Borax had said. He did his good works, but no longer fully believed in the spirit his unfortunate women showed every time they wrote that phrase in paint or ink or with a stick in the dirt. Now, finding his motorcycle, turning it around, ready to return a pair of gloves, Carter knew exactly what made him so sad: when faith is gone, what always takes its place is profit.

Chapter 17

Carter & Company took up one impressive-looking floor of 333 Pine Street. Here, behind frosted glass doors, or in the wide-open bullpen, clerks fed contracts and cables and bids and quotes into tubes that, by pneumatic means, shot across the floor to be cross-examined under green eyeshades, then executed or returned or filed in great mahogany cabinets. Teams of men read the ticker tape quotes aloud to those manning the broad electric page tape machine, which brought financial stories via teletype and, together, they rushed facts and strong hunches to apron-wearing boys who marked the great chalkboards with net changes in the Dow Jones Industrial Average, which stood today at a strong-as-a-dollar eighty-eight.

But the real work occurred in two small offices toward the back, fiercely plain in design, save for personal photographs and, in James's case, one framed Carter the Great poster he rather liked, an early one celebrating 'A Masterful Escape from a Locked Pillory.'

As was their custom when returning after months abroad, James went from person to person, from the receptionist to the senior-most auditor, ensuring that business was on course. Tom opened mail, the way he had at home, as his demeanor was unsuited for motivational pep talks and chats.

At 12:30 the office was mostly at lunch. Thus James, regarding the trail of paper pumping from their stock ticker, was alone when he heard Tom yell 'Sweet Jesus!' from the back office.

Tom was prone to such exaltations, so James hardly looked up until he saw Tom standing in front of him, his face ashen, even more ashen than usual. He had in his hand a letter. 'So, this arrived this morning, meaning it was at the bottom of the pile, thank you. We don't need this.'

James saw it was addressed to him, and to Tom, at Carter & Company, and had spelled their names correctly, thus clearing the first hurdle for solicitations.

'Dear Messrs Crandall and Carter: I understand you occasionally finance individual corporate development if you judge it worthy. I cannot make any promises as to its worthiness, but I have a working model for a device,' James got to this point, and whispered, '*oh no*' before continuing, 'that combines radio and pictures. It is called television.'

James looked at Tom, the blood beginning to drain from his face. Tom said, 'Keep reading.'

I will be publicly demonstrating television this afternoon at 5:00 P.M. at Wheeler Auditorium, on the University of California campus. I have invited many local financiers, in hopes of better understanding what backing, if any, my device will receive.

I apologize for the short notice, but the brief lead time will discourage copycats.

Philo T. Farnsworth

'It gets worse,' Tom said.

'You always think that,' James returned, and then Tom handed him the financial section of the Examiner. On page three was a public advertisement for Farnsworth's demonstration, at the University, at five. 'We're going,' James said grimly. 'Call out our messenger boys. We need to make sure Charlie's there, too.'

♣ ♦ ♥ ♠

In summer 1771, a courier galloping away from Frankfurt-on-the-Main was struck dead by a single bolt of lightning that came from an otherwise clear blue sky. Witnesses – not just simple farmers, but a doctor and a landowner – noted that the body was cooked through to its center, but a leather satchel escaped unharmed. Inside the satchel was a tract, 'Original Shift in Days of Illuminations,' a plan to manipulate world events in the name of the previously unknown organization the Illuminati. It was an age where reason and tactical planning was beginning to influence the masses, and the discovery of this secret society horrified the populace, which wondered if spreading secular doctrines – such as democracy – was inherently evil.

If the tract was a theoretical monstrosity, something more concrete and far more troubling was also found on the body: a silk purse containing a dozen tiny ivory skulls, each with a three-digit gilt number embossed on its jaw.

The numbers were in sequence, skipping 322, which had been sent to an agent in the rebellious American colonies 'so the agents in place there too may contribute to the new world order.'

When the Skull and Bones society appeared at Yale University, in Lodge Room 322, the connection was ambiguous, perhaps deliberately so, as Bonesmen were devoted to world domination (or so it was said) through secrecy and ambiguity.

At the noon hour, while Carter sat with Borax, and Tom Crandall was just uncovering Farnsworth's solicitation, Agent Samuelson was having the telephone conversation of his life with a man three levels his superior. Samuelson sat at a phone booth by a luncheon counter, taking notes furiously. Cologned, hair slicked back with exactly the acceptable amount of cream, a Yale man who made quite the show of never seeming to mention he was a Yale man, Samuelson had been waiting for his entire life for this conversation. He played with his watch fob: ivory, carved in the shape of a human skull engraved with gilt numbers – 322.

The first three minutes of the conversation were a blur to him. He said 'Thank you, sir,' so many times he had to stop himself. He could only remember certain phrases the Colonel had used in the beginning, 'How is the weather?' and 'This requires discretion and flexibility' and 'With Agent Griffin's invaluable assistance, we've put together a profile . . .' and, finally, 'We could of course continue to use Agent Griffin in this matter, as he's one of our finest veterans,' and then the slightest hesitation, 'but the situation is quite dynamic.'

Colonel Starling cut to the chase then and there. Though he was no longer suspected of withholding evidence, Charles Carter would probably try to interfere in Treasury Department business being conducted at the University of California at seventeen hundred hours. As a personal favor, would Samuelson mind giving him a *nudge*? Just *detain* him at sixteen thirty?

Samuelson accepted, of course. On its face, it was just a step higher than taking a bootlegger for a ride. But Samuelson was ambitious, and understood what the Colonel meant when he added,

'And off the record here, son, the magician has evaded capture that relied on accepted methods.' A pause. 'We'd like him off the field for a couple hours, minimum, and, frankly, there is no maximum. Do you follow?'

'I do, sir. Thank you, sir, for trusting me.'

The mistake they'd made trying to detain him before was in not treating him like a magician. Samuelson had seen magic shows, like anyone, and knew the protocol whereby magicians bested volunteers. He spent the better part of an hour revising a plan that was just clever enough to get himself promoted. He rehearsed saying 'It was nothing, really,' when other agents would ask him about it. 'Ultimately we showed Mr Carter who the best men were.' Said solemnly, like a Skull and Bonesman.

And fifteen minutes later, in a small room at the Palace, Samuelson was addressing O'Brien, Hollis, and Stutz rationally, laying out every step of the plan. At the end, he added, 'We'll show him who the best men are.'

Nods all around. Stutz, whose froggy voice had been silent, muttered, 'Think we'd have to knock him unconscious?'

'Well, that could be part of it,' Samuelson admitted.

Stutz swallowed. 'I'll handle it.'

Samuelson continued talking, fielding questions with a precision that he had always known was his great, untested skill.

♣ ♦ ♥ ♠

Walking to the library, Griffin whistled to himself as if careless. He stopped and bought a newspaper; at intersections, he waved at policemen. He was also catching reflections in windows, on parked cars, and looking for faces to show themselves in the afternoon crowd more than twice.

He had no way of knowing that no one was watching him, and no one much cared how he occupied himself today. But his senses were on alert, and even a simple bureaucratic motion – an assignment in Albuquerque, for instance – seemed tinged with sinister meaning. Would he be met on the train by another agent, taken between cars for a smoke, and then would he, Jack Griffin, career washout, be found the next day on the tracks, a suicide?

He showed identification to the construction crew at the library and put on his hardhat. When he entered the gloomy newspaper room, Miss White waved gaily.

'Yoo-hoo!'

Griffin took a book from his pocket: *Anderson's Fly Fishing*. It was his only book, but at least he'd had something in his hand when walking to the library. 'Miss White.'

'It's so, *so* good of you to return the book.' She took the book from him and examined the spine. 'Ah, Doyle, Doyle, Doyle.' Her voice fell to a whisper, perhaps the loudest whisper Griffin had ever heard. 'Follow me.'

She took him to a small, glassed-in office at the corner of the room. When she turned on the lights, the glare caused Griffin to wince. The walls of the room were covered, floor to ceiling, in newspaper headlines from around the world.

She beamed at him – downward – for even slouching, she still stood an inch taller than Griffin. 'Mr Griffin, you are so clever to actually bring a book, but then again, that's your job, isn't it?'

There was a certain type of woman who liked the Secret Service; warnings were posted about them everywhere. But Miss White was far more intelligent than those women who, Griffin had to admit, never gave him the time of day anyway.

'The job's more boring than you'd think.'

'I can't imagine anything that you do would be boring.' She said this innocently, her eyes the size of pie plates. 'But what happened to you?' She pointed a desk lamp at him. 'Were you in a fight? A few days ago? It's plain as day under these lights – when I saw you the first time, you must have just been in a fight and you didn't even talk about it.'

He had no business explaining Eight Righteous Men to an outsider, so he just swallowed roughly. 'Did you have something to tell me, Miss White?'

'Olive. Oh, I do.' Unlocking a deep file drawer, she asked, 'How goes your research into Mr Carter?'

'We don't talk—'

'Oh, of course. I understand. I do understand. Here, this is what I wanted to show you.' It was a bound journal, like the one devoted to Charles Carter. The label read 'Warren Harding in San Francisco, Summer, 1923.'

Griffin opened it. First were headlines proclaiming San Francisco as a stop on the Voyage of Understanding; then updates on his itinerary; then notices about the President's ill health; photographs of the mayors of Oakland, San Francisco, and Sacramento greeting Harding; an article listing all the canceled appointments due to illness; an interview with J. Phillip Roemer, head chef of the Palace Hotel, promising that only the most healthful of vitals would reach the President ('"'Twill be no fault of mine," he added, wagging his head over shining copper kettles, "if the President's appetite does not improve"').

'You've probably seen this,' Miss White whispered. Under the thirty-six-point headline was the final photograph of a waxy-looking Harding, propped up in his hotel bed in his dressing gown and pajamas. He wore a shadow of his famous smile and waved as if his arm were made of stone blocks. The Duchess sat in a chair next to him, looking either concerned or sour. The caption: 'Though he knows it not, Warren Harding here bids us farewell.'

Griffin nodded. 'I've seen this.'

'But you haven't seen these.' She opened a large yellow folder and shook out a score of photographs. 'The *Examiner* sends us the negatives and rejected photos of all major events in the city. This leads to problems that you wouldn't believe – when the photographers found that the newspaper morgue was run by a woman—' Miss White shut her eyes and shook her head. 'Those men have a scandalous sense of what photos to send.'

But Griffin wasn't listening. Instead, he began sorting though the photographs. Twenty of them, numbered from the negatives. None missing. He arranged them in order; the third and the eighteenth photograph both showed the clock in the corner. The photographs were all taken between 11:35 and 11:42 in the evening of August second.

The resolution of the *Examiner*'s printed image was terrible – the original photo had excellent depth of field so that the room was alive with details: in the foreground, Griffin could see the vials of medication, and on the bureau, the playing cards. There, on the dresser, a note, from the size of the letterhead, probably from Hearst, the one about the funny papers.

'Did you say something about Hearst, Agent Griffin?'

'What?' He didn't know he'd been talking aloud. 'I know this room pretty well. I'm just looking for . . .'

When he hadn't spoken for fifteen seconds, Miss White gently asked him what he saw.

'Nothing, Miss White.'

'Olive.' She hummed to herself, adding, 'I see you're looking at the very, very photo I found so interesting.' The photo printed under the headline was the same as the photo he held, but the edges had been cropped. 'It's hard to think of poor President Harding being so ill without wondering why he died. I heard he'd eaten bad fish. But look, here's his last meal, only they cropped it: not fish, but *chocolate cake*.'

'Is that why you called me?'

'Any irregularity like that suggests foul play, don't you think?' Her eyes sparkled. The idea was like a mink wrap.

'The President had fish early, around five thirty.'

'Oh.' Until now, she'd been smiling every second he'd known her. 'I had so hoped I was being helpful.'

'That's okay . . . Olive. You're being helpful.'

'Why did you stop at that photo yourself?'

'This'll be a good photo for the archives.'

She looked at him suspiciously. 'I think you're fibbing to a civilian. What is it that you see?' Griffin should have confiscated the photo then and there, but he also was trying to remember the last time a woman had enjoyed his company, and he moved too slowly. Her hand came out to hold his wrist in place. 'Something odd, I'll bet you.'

'I should really take this,' he said weakly.

She gasped. 'Oh, Mr Griffin. Mr Griffin.' Her eyes were watering. 'Look at my skin!' She showed off goose bumps. 'Ever since I read Keats, I've waited for a moment of wild surmise; isn't that exactly what you'd call this?'

'I dunno.' He tugged at the photo. 'I should go.'

'*Wild surmise*,' she whispered. 'The wine bottle means something to you, doesn't it?'

'I don't think there's a wine bottle in this photograph.'

She pointed at other photos. 'Oh, it's here. And here.'

While he gathered the twenty photographs back into their envelope, Miss White bit the end of her fingernail.

'What is it about a wine bottle? Aha! Poisoned wine!'

'Hey, quiet down a little.' He glared at her. Immediately, she obeyed. And if before she had seemed fascinated, now she radiated something Griffin had never seen in his whole life: complete infatuation. Not with the job, but with *him*. It almost made him drop the envelope. 'Listen,' he whispered, 'I'm glad you found this. Is there anything else?'

'Oh, no. This is everything.'

'Have you told anyone about this?'

'Certainly not, Mr Griffin.'

'Have any other agents asked?'

'Is there a cabal formed against you? There is,' she gasped. 'The fight you were in!'

'No.'

'Does this have something to do with Charles Carter?'

'I don't know. I'm leaving now.' Griffin moved toward the door. Their eyes met.

'Agent Griffin? I have to warn you,' she said carefully, 'that I'm falling under your spell.'

'Okay,' he nodded. He reached to tip his hat, and was surprised to feel his hardhat's cold ridges. 'I'll come back around, when, y'know.' His legs felt like breadsticks.

He kept walking, did it successfully, one foot in front of the other. Halfway across the room, he scratched an itch on the back of his neck with the envelope. He had a favor to ask Miss White, but he wasn't sure if he needed it or if it was an excuse to speak to her again.

While he was making up his mind, he saw her coming out of her office. She looked hypnotized with fondness.

'Olive, how long would it take you to find the five, maybe the ten rabbis closest to the Palace Hotel? The ones with big, I mean, you know, really big congregations?'

'Rabbis?' she asked, putting her large thumb to her lower lip. He watched her for signs of puzzlement. She seemed like she led a sheltered life, and he didn't want to bring her into the world of the gutter, so he didn't explain further. Finally, her eyes twinkled.

'You are such a delight. Rabbis,' she shook her head, 'of course. Wait right here.' She disappeared into her office, laughing 'rabbis' to herself, and Griffin tugged at his collar, for she'd succeeded in making him uncomfortably warm.

Chapter 18

When Carter left Borax's, his plan was to go home and telephone James, but as the trees flashed past him, he realized all he had to report was that he'd spent $750 and Farnsworth was nowhere to be found, neither of which he looked forward to discussing. Further, James would tease him about Phoebe Kyle.

As Carter approached the Industrial Home for the Adult Blind, his mind's eye replayed that smug look on James's face – the 'Have fun!' as if he were urging Ledocq to go and try the shellfish for once. So Carter resolved that today he would launch on a light-hearted affair with a pretty girl. They would share banter and kisses and revel in mutual entertainment.

However, since that approach suited him about as well as bib overalls, his plans were in a shambles before he even turned into the well-manicured circular drive on Telegraph. Dismounting, slapping the dust off his thighs, he approached the Home with an awkward smile and several tactful remarks he would employ in case she turned him away, for Carter carried with him the same thought as many decent men: that it was unlikely a woman he liked could actually like him back.

The main house, set back at the end of the drive, looked like it had once been a private home. It had high gables, arched windows, and several irregularly spaced cupolas on the second floor, and a wide, airy porch running all around the sides as far as one could see. It looked like a place where band concerts had been held long ago. Flanking it were two hulking, utilitarian-looking dormitories, separated by a brick wall.

There were people walking slowly, mostly in pairs, about the grounds. Carter nodded to them all, unsure of which, if any, were blind. He wondered where she was or if she was expecting him. He had several things he wanted to say, and all of them sounded idiotic, but at least he had stolen a rose from Borax's, and secreted it in a pocket. As Borax had served him some repellent liverwurst, he popped open his PEZ tin and dropped two of them into his mouth.

The front door to the Home flew open with a bang, and three women ran out. They held Bibles. One of them was crying, and the other two comforted her.

'That was terrible!' cried the most visibly upset woman, who dabbed tears off her chin.

'I'm sorry,' Carter said, but at the same time, on the porch, a woman in a white uniform cupped her hands around her mouth to yell, 'I'm very sorry,' which drowned him out.

'That was terrible!' the woman repeated. Then she burst into tears again, her two friends holding her upright as they shuffled toward a small bus parked nearby. Carter looked from them to the nurse, who was shaking her head.

'Good afternoon,' he said, puzzled.

'Excuse me.' She put her hand up, which stopped him, and then yelled back into the house, her voice broken with fatigue, for it had obviously been used in exactly this tone a thousand times before, 'Phoebe!' And then, to Carter, 'May I help you?'

'I'm – actually I'm here to see Miss Kyle.'

'Lord, what has she done now?' she asked.

'Nothing. Honestly.'

Her head tilted back as if to see better down her nose. He remembered his mother at the butcher's, picking and choosing among game hens. Carter joined her on the porch nonetheless, and glanced into the house and down the main hall from where he stood. There was a braided cord on the wall, a handhold, at about hip level.

'Are you Carter?' the nurse finally asked.

'Yes, ma'am.'

'So you actually exist.'

The way she said it, he was unsure whether she approved, so Carter simply tipped his hat.

'You know she tells lies,' she continued.

'I was unaware.'

'I love her to bits and pieces, but she tells lies.'

'All right,' he replied, because she seemed grave. 'I'll be careful.'

'No you won't.'

'I—'

'Phoebe,' she said again, this time quietly, as Phoebe had appeared at the door, one hand on the braided cord. She wore her gingham frock. Her black hair was tousled like she'd just fallen out of bed.

'Mr Carter,' she said. 'How nice of you to come. Have you met Jan?' Phoebe patted Jan on the shoulder, found the crook of her elbow, and linked her arms around it. 'I've disappointed her.'

'You have to apologize, Phoebe.'

'I know, I feel terrible,' she said pleasantly. 'Mr Carter, thank you. Thank you so much, isn't he nice?' She extended her arms, palms up, which mystified Carter. It looked like she was ready to receive a gift.

'Oh!' The rose in his jacket. So much for hiding it. Why hadn't it dawned on him that sleight-of-hand, which he had used for small flirtations, would be utterly useless? He felt naked. Gently, he slipped the rose into her hands, which she brought to her nose. She touched her fingertips to the rose's petals, tracing out tiny veins Carter hadn't noticed. 'I love this,' she whispered, brushing it against her white cheek, as if she could take the afternoon to fully appreciate it.

'I was hoping to see you,' he said with such an attempt at gaiety he sounded demented.

'You'll have to wait your turn,' Jan said. 'Phoebe—'

'Oh, all right. Where are they?' She put the rose over her ear and secured it with a small clip. She held her hand out to be escorted. Carter surprised Jan by taking it before she could.

When she touched him, he smelled a hint of a familiar scent – D'Orsay's La Renommee, all vanilla and almonds, something several of the women in his troupe wore, but never so memorably.

Carefully, they descended the stairs and walked toward the parking lot. He put her gloves into her free hand. She cleared her throat. 'Transparent of me, I guess.'

'I understand you tell lies,' he said.

'I used to tell lies, when I was still drinking.'

'Drinking.'

'Pickled like a herring.' She clutched at his forearm twice, quickly, as if it were Morse code. 'Do you promise not to eavesdrop right now?'

'No, not really.'

The women were already inside their bus, and their driver had started the engine. He had to turn it off to hear Phoebe, who stood nearby and rather tonelessly began her apology. Apparently, the women were Christian Scientists. They came twice a month, and this time had lectured that blindness was all in the mind, that if the inmates' faith was strong enough, they would certainly see immediately. Two of the men who'd had horrible industrial accidents stood, declared they could see, and started walking into furniture and walls, causing a great commotion. Finally, they threw off their glasses and brought the pits of their eye sockets close to the women's faces, and asked to be told if faith had brought their missing eyes back.

This had led to tremendous, chaotic laughter among the blind, and shouts of congratulations to Phoebe, who had orchestrated it. Standing by the bus, listening to her detail all the reasons she'd been so bad, Carter wished desperately he'd arrived ten minutes earlier to witness it.

She was concluding, '. . . really, honestly, terribly sorry. Truly.' She smiled.

'Start the bus,' the eldest ordered. And to Phoebe, she said, 'We'll come back.'

'Please do.'

After the bus pulled away, and they'd been alone for several seconds, Phoebe said, 'Mr Carter, do you know Helen Keller?' Her tone was brisk, as if she hadn't been enjoying herself a moment ago.

'She and her caretaker—'

'Anne Sullivan,' she said.

'Yes. They came to a show once. Afterward, Helen came backstage to tell me how much she enjoyed it. She was quite inspirational.' As he spoke, he was thinking of taking Phoebe to the motorcycle now, for it seemed like a rebellious thing she might enjoy, but she seemed rooted to this patch of gravel.

'Helen is so *cheerful*,' Phoebe said, with exactly the same tone she'd used when describing the Chong girls. 'She makes a girl who's only blind feel so inadequate.'

'May I show you something?'

'Please tell me it's scotch.'

He took her hand. 'I thought you no longer drank.'

'I want it,' she said grimly. 'I want it every day.'

They walked toward the motorcycle, feet crunching across the ground. 'Here. Feel this.'

The moment her hands touched the handlebars, she lit up, head to toe, seeming to burn off whatever blue clouds had been gathering. 'Well, this is a fine beast.' Hands running down the tank, finding the two separate seats.

'Would you like to go for a ride?'

'A ride on a motorcycle?' She stood up, seeming dizzy with the thought. 'Is that how you go courting girls?'

'My rollerskates are in the shop.'

'Bubbly, bubbly mahatma. Hmm.' She put both hands on the leather saddle, and leaned against it. Eased away. Her hands, brushing from one side of it to the other, finding the stitching around the edges. 'No,' she murmured. 'You never took her on a motorcycle.'

'Excuse me?'

'You've never given a girl a ride on a motorcycle.'

'Yes, that's true, but how—'

'Mr Carter, I'm awful company today. You should be riding your motorbike, dodging thugs, catching bullets in your teeth and sawing women in half, all sorts of things, but you shouldn't be here with me.' She found his arm and began towing him toward the main house. 'Not today. Thank you for my flower and my gloves.'

He dragged his feet, and searched for something to say. 'I don't saw women in half,' he murmured. 'My mother won't let me.'

Full stop on the pathway. Phoebe turned her head toward him. 'You jest,' she said.

'Oh, no, I certainly don't jest. My mother, God help us all, never much liked the idea of sawing women in half. She is a lifelong student of *psychology*.' On this word, Carter sighed, which made Phoebe laugh with a single, coarse bark that sounded like a bat hitting a ball. He continued, 'Are you sure you want to hear this?'

'I have a moment free.'

Carter told her, in a few not altogether clever sentences, how his mother had been convinced for years that P. T. Selbit, the magician who invented Sawing Through a Girl, secretly hated women. Each time she heard of a new Selbit illusion, she reported to Carter that her intuition was confirmed. The list of illusions was in fact quite awful: Stretching a Girl; Destroying a Girl; Crushing a Girl; the Stick Rack Girl; the Pincushion Lady; the Indestructible Girl, the last illusion actually proving that the girl *could* be destroyed if only the magician tried hard enough. Carter told Phoebe, 'I thought Percy was simply reusing a profitable idea, but my mother made *transatlantic* phone calls, and learned that before he patented his first effect—'

Without hesitation, Phoebe exclaimed, 'His wife left him, didn't she?'

'Yes. His wife left him, and six months later, he destroyed his first girl.'

'Your mother is wonderful.'

'That would be the consensus.'

She laughed again, and then she was quiet. They had stopped walking toward the house some time ago. He could look unabashedly at how beautiful she was. Years of being inside had left her skin translucent. He could see every kind of cloud passing through it: pleasure, sorrow, anger. Carter understood why women powdered their faces: it made great sense to try to look like Phoebe Kyle. She said, 'I've been thinking about how I would saw someone in half. It seems to me, you'd have a secret compartment, and two girls—'

'Oh, no, don't ruin it for me,' Carter exclaimed.

'If I'm riding on your motorcycle, I need to change into trousers,' she announced. And there was her smile, her beautiful smile.

Fifteen minutes later, the East Bay was swarming with activity. Samuelson and his team had secured the matériel they needed, including a truck, and were surveying the route they would take when Carter was their captive. Moving vans on the University of California campus were unloading crates stamped 'Ogden, Utah' by the science lecture halls. One of James's messenger boys was leaving Borax's, and another was on his way to the Blind Home, and others were fanning out past the cafés, parks, and amusements Carter was known to haunt.

No one, however, was paying attention to Jack Griffin, who still moved as if unseen eyes were plotting misfortune for him. At two o'clock, he had an experience that was unmatched in his career, in that it was easy and bore instant results.

He had returned to the Palace Hotel, to the basement, where management provided kips for service people who'd earned enough seniority. These were small rooms with cots and lockers, and tiny slit windows that could open several inches on a chain. One room belonged to Tony Alhino, whom Griffin had interviewed once before. Twenty-seven years old, Portuguese, Alhino ran the Palace beverage service and had brought Harding his last glass of water.

He came on duty at four, so there was no reason for him to be at his kip when Griffin knocked. And yet he was. He was dark, with a full mustache, and acne-scarred cheeks, and the moment he saw Griffin, he looked guilty of every crime committed in the State of California.

'Tony Alhino?'

'Ehhh . . .'

'Griffin, with the Service. We talked earlier.'

'*Macacos me mordam,*' he responded. He'd been shocked into speaking Portuguese, but as the words came out, he'd found a kind of power in them, and he finished with a grin, as if a second language gave him an edge over Griffin.

So Griffin said the first thing that came to mind. 'I don't give a rat's ass where monkeys are biting you.'

Which shut Alhino down, completely. Griffin decided to press.

'Listen, pal, let's talk about a wine bottle.'

'Oh, no.' Alhino sat on his cot. He put his face into his hands. 'I have eight brothers and sisters. My dad, he's a barber, but he's getting the shakes.'

'Where's the wine bottle?'

'I can't lose my job!' he wailed.

Griffin had seen a few kinds of whiners in his life. He actually felt sorry for this one, in his small room with grimy windows. The cot was too small for him to sit down, too, so he crouched, and said, gently, '*É muita areia para a seu camioneta.*' It was an old, folksy saying that adults used when telling children they were in over their heads.

'Where'd you learn to speak Portuguese?' Alhino sniffed.

'My ex-wife.' He rubbed his chin. 'I liked to know what she was yelling when she was throwing chairs at me.'

The younger man chuckled. Griffin offered him a smoke, which he accepted.

'You have kids?' Alhino asked after a moment.

'Daughter.'

'I got a daughter. Is she sweet or fresh?'

Griffin thought about it. 'Both.'

'Yeah. Ai!' Alhino stubbed out his cigarette, stood, and opened his locker. Inside, wrapped in a dish towel, was a wine bottle. With a sigh, he passed it to Griffin.

This is the way it must be for guys like Starling, Griffin thought. *Easy.*

Alhino explained: he took this out of the room around twelve forty-five, a quarter-hour before Harding died. He took it, in fact, the moment he saw it, because he didn't want to be blamed for allowing liquor into the hotel. And he kept it as a souvenir. 'You have to believe me. I didn't bring it in the first place. You couldn't, I don't care if you're the President, you couldn't pay me to move hootch inside this hotel. I get fired, and you know who comes after me? My wife.' His brown eyes met Griffin's. They understood each other.

Griffin glanced at the bottle. Its label, a light beige, was typical of domestic wines: a bizarre cabalistic symbol. And the legend 'For sacramental use only.' It was empty.

'Who brought it?'

Griffin hadn't expected an answer, so his eyebrows shot up when Alhino said, 'The guy from the speakeasy.'

'What guy?'

'The guy,' he said, as if that explained things. Elaborating, he said he'd passed a guy in the hallway just before all the reporters arrived. He was carrying a paper sack, and when Alhino was about to ask him what he was doing, the guy gave him the high sign. 'Like this,' he said, making an 'a-okay' with his right hand, and sweeping it left to right. 'I didn't tell about him because I didn't want to lose my job. My wife—'

'What's this guy look like?'

'*Madre*,' he said. 'This is weeks ago.' He stumbled through a description that left Griffin fuming: average height, average build, dressed like any guy.

'Did he have blue eyes?'

'Phew,' he sighed. 'Oh. He was wearing a hat,' he said with conviction.

'Did he have black hair?'

'Yeah,' Alhino brightened. 'Yeah. Or blond. The hallway lights, not so good.'

The returns on this rapidly diminishing, Griffin wrapped the wine bottle in its towel. 'You'll keep your job if you stay quiet,' he said.

'Thank you. I don't want trouble.'

Griffin opened the door. He slowed. 'Hey. Which speakeasy uses that high sign?'

'Across the street.' Alhino waved toward the window. 'It's the big one.'

'Where, exactly?'

'The big one. Jossie's, right under the police department.'

Chapter 19

North on Telegraph, bearing west on Shattuck, following Shattuck until it became Henry, Carter chose exactly the route that allowed him to keep the bike in second gear and above, and then, finally, the road took on interesting serpentine shapes that demanded leaning, acceleration, and speed. Phoebe held on to him tightly. After the first set of curves, he asked if she was all right, and she responded, 'More, please.'

Beyond that exchange, they made little conversation, so Carter chose a destination: Neptune Beach, by the Alameda shoreline. He slowed down outside the entrance gate, a hulking Moorish tower through which people passed in their bathing suits, some holding towels and goggles. There was a pavilion just inside the gate, where a jazz band played for those who knew the new dance steps, and, beyond that, saltwater wading pools for the children, and a bathhouse, and a lengthy stretch of beach, seemingly packed solid.

With the bike halted, Phoebe loosened her hands from around his waist. She took a deep breath, smelling the air. 'The beach? I'm afraid I'm not much good in crowds.'

He hadn't thought of that. 'Do you like the motorcycle?'

'The speed is terrific. It's great for such a smelly contraption. Say, wouldn't that be a tremendous slogan!'

'I'd like to find a place we can talk.'

'I want to – how do you drive it? You do something with your wrists that accelerates, am I right?'

'You really want to know?'

'Of course.'

He helped her off, and then put the bike on its centerstand so Phoebe could sit on the main seat. 'Excellent!' she cried, hunching over with her hands on the bars. She squeezed the front brake several times. 'Are you ready to take a chance?' she called.

'Mmmm. No. But you can start it up.' She followed his hands, turning the petcock on. 'Careful of that feeder tube below it, or the fuel runs straight out. Good, now, put your foot here, and just push down.'

She managed to turn it over on the third try, which caused her to jump up with both fists in the air. 'Idora Park! We'll go there. I know, it's an odd place for a conversation, but there won't be crowds, at least.'

Carter admitted that she had a point, and so they got back on the bike. He merged into traffic, without looking backward, and since there was no rearview mirror, he couldn't see the messenger boy running after him, then falling back, waving, beside the roadway.

They rode by the train tracks for miles, and then Carter pulled up to Idora's northern entrance, admiring its great sign carved from panels of oak, each letter a different color of the rainbow: 'Idora Park,' then, 'Amusements for the Family,' and, in very small letters below, 'Borax Smith, Proprietor.'

Carter held his arms out to help Phoebe balance as she dismounted, a careful task for a blind woman. He looked about, and saw no line at the box office, which simultaneously pleased and distressed him. He and Phoebe would have little company, but here was yet another failed investment by Borax.

He purchased their tickets (*thirty-five cents* for two people, he wrote in his journal), and walked her inside the park. A series of trails was flanked by shrubs and tall trees on which signs were nailed that pointed the way to the concession stands, the wooden opera house, the huge swimming tanks, the zoo, or the orchards where families could pick their own apples and peaches.

They passed the largest skating rink in the west. As today was Tuesday, the theme was *Jardin de Danse*, and all ladies were given handmade silk flowers scented with real French perfume. It sounded grand, but in large block letters was the necessary addendum: 'No rough skating, shoving of ladies, or vile attentions.'

It was still a sunny day, a little humid and breezy, and Phoebe walked with her head tilted slightly upward, as if to catch both the sun and every scent. She had lost her rose somewhere on the motorcycle ride. Carter closed his eyes, too. He heard calliope music and shouts from distant rides, and he smelled popcorn and burned sugar.

'There's something . . .' she said, and her voice trailed off.

'Yes?'

'At the Home, we get to know people by feeling their faces. It's a queer thing to do, I know, but will you . . .'

'Of course.'

'Perhaps we could stand off the main path, then?' They walked into the shade of an elm, where there was a wide bench, and they sat. She tugged off her gloves, one finger at a time, and tucked them into the pocket of her work trousers. 'It's just a way of saying hello. Sometimes we say hello instead by saluting each other with pistols, but they frown on that indoors.'

She began at his crown, and if he'd expected a featherlight reading, the way she'd traced the rose's veins, he was surprised that it felt more like being sculpted. 'Your hair is very thick.'

'It's a toupee.'

'You have to be quiet. Jan told me you're handsome, and I have to see whether she was trying to make me feel better.' Her fingertips went over his forehead, lightly now, repeatedly, like rainwater trailing down a window pane. Over his eyebrows, his cheekbones, behind his ears, then both hands meeting at his nose, brushing over his upper lip, his lower lip, his chin, and his neck. Then the whole process in reverse, this time forcing him to close his eyes so she could feel his eyelashes.

She cupped his cheeks in her palms and didn't move them. He could smell dust on her hands, and lanolin, and her vanilla and almonds. Her right thumb was stroking an inch-long scar on his lower lip. He looked directly into her face, and read a deep concentration that he'd seen mind readers imitate. Though she had porcelain skin, she was in no way delicate. Nothing was ever quite still on her – her lips bowing, or her eyebrows darting above her glasses for a moment, as if she were powered by a hidden turbine. Under the black hair, kinky and knotted by the wind, and behind the glasses, he sensed a keen mind analyzing intimacies his face had blatantly shown.

He was suddenly uncomfortable.

'What's the verdict?'

'Jan and I will remain on speaking terms,' she allowed. 'Are you famished?'

'Yes.'

They walked to a grab stand a few steps away. After she finished her hot dog in about three seconds, she asked Carter to read her the list of attractions that were open. They had missed the balloon ascension and the diving horses, but the daytime fireworks were scheduled for three-thirty. In a way, nothing had changed since Carter's first visit to a midway, in that only a handful of the promised attractions were actually available. The Helter-Skelter was closed, as was the Electric Studio, but the Haunted Swing, the Circle Wave, the Merry-Go-Round and, best of all, the Thunderbolt were open.

Phoebe said, 'The Thunderbolt, definitely, we shall go there first, and second, and third.' As they walked, she said that even though Idora was but a mile away from the Home, she rarely got to make the trip, as it was frowned upon as a distraction. 'Everything we do needs to be spiritually uplifting,' she said. 'You'd think the Home was populated by smugglers and second-story men.'

'How did you end up there?'

'I went blind. I can hear the Thunderbolt. Can you?'

Of course he could – it was a gigantic roller coaster, with two-story drops, and it was currently making grown men scream.

The Thunderbolt was the only attraction in the park that had a line. They stood in the shade of the roller coaster's great wooden frame while they waited.

'You know, at some point, I'll ask you a question about yourself that you might accidentally answer,' he said.

She reined in a grin, and, lips parting, also fought back a quick response. Eventually, she said, 'How did you get that scar on your lip?'

'Well, I was being held captive by pirates in Indonesia—'

Phoebe covered a theatrical yawn. 'I'm sorry,' she said, 'is this going to be one of those long stories?'

'As I was saying, a pirate had taken over the steamer I was on. And, after slapping me, and threatening to sell my mind reader into slavery, he forced me to do my magic act.' Carter continued

344

with many details, though skipping the part in which he lost all hope.

'Was it the slap in the face that left the scar?'

'Oh, no,' he replied. 'About an hour later, the Captain offered to show me how to throw a boomerang. I did it extremely well the first time, but the second, I was arrogant, and caught it on my lower lip.'

'So you could have said "I hit myself in the face with a boomerang."'

'Yes, but then where would we be? In the time I took to tell that story, we've moved up an extra ten places in the line.'

'No, no, I'm sorry, that whole story you told me about the pirate had absolutely nothing to do with your scar.'

'It added color?'

'It added color. I'm going to find a boomerang and hit you with it and that should add all kinds of color. You were overreaching and trying to impress me.'

'It rather comes with the conjuring business. I'm simply going to boast until you tell me about yourself.'

He and Phoebe were now at the head of the line, and he sensed a million nimble calculations being made before she spoke again. 'I don't trust you.'

He'd been expecting more banter, not that serious stare, that flat voice. Not being able to take direction from a woman's eyes was a serious handicap. 'I *am* trustworthy, though. Ploddingly.'

She shook her head. The toboggan clattered to a stop just beyond them, and four young people, giggling and wobbly as if leaving a petting party, launched out of the car. An attendant helped Phoebe into her seat, and Carter joined her as the safety bar held them in place.

They had to wait for the couple behind them to be secured. Carter felt awkward, as if he and Phoebe had just argued. She worked her mouth around a phrase, finally saying, 'What I mean is, when you told me about that adventure with Tulang, I didn't believe it.'

'But it happened,' and he began to understand what this might be about. 'Are you concerned about people lying to you?'

'No. I believe the events you described happened,' she said

345

carefully. 'I just think there was more to them.'

The attendant hit the safety pedal, and pulled down the long ratchet that sent them on their way onto the tracks. Phoebe made a startled noise and grabbed Carter's hands. The toboggan creaked and shook as it found the chain taking them up the first incline.

'Oh, dear,' Phoebe cried. 'This is good.'

Up and up they went, and Carter closed his eyes to know what the ride was like without seeing the ground fall away. Why didn't she trust him? He wanted more than anything else to be trusted. The wind increased as they climbed, and, unmistakably, the sounds of the orchestra that played in the skating rink echoed differently, as if the players were left behind in a distant alpine meadow.

When he opened his eyes, they were at the end of the chain and suspended, for one blood-curdling moment, at the precipice. They were so high he could see the bay. There were sailboats, and they looked so calm out there on the water. The pause before the fall was always the most terrifying for him. He looked at Phoebe, who was grinning, teeth showing, holding her breath.

'Wait. I didn't tell you the pirate's name,' Carter had enough time to say, and then they fell.

Soon after, they were helped off the ride, and Phoebe hung on his arm. She was laughing. 'I feel like a big, overcooked macaroni!'

They went down the metal stairs to the ground level, where they stood again in the shadow of the great roller coaster.

'Shall we do that again?'

'You'd heard that story before,' he said.

Her face, which had been supporting one of those wonderful smiles, fell in. 'Are you sure you didn't tell me his name?'

'I don't say his name much.'

'Why not?'

'Why not?' He really had no idea, except that he always skipped over it. Tulang, filed away along with other parts of the story that didn't sound so sporty or amusing. 'Where did you hear the story?'

'My sad mahatma,' she whispered. 'Is there a more secluded place?' He took her arm to lead her to another bench, this one near a seedy attraction called Europe by Auto. 'It's hard to have fun and be serious at the same time, isn't it?' she sighed.

346

When they'd been sitting for a moment, Carter said, 'How did you know his name?'

'You're like a terrier,' she replied. 'Charles?'

'Yes.' Though he liked how she said his name, he also expected that something awful was about to happen.

'Here's what I see. Tell me if I'm wrong. I see a big, rusty old tramp steamer. And there's pirates, and captives, and way off on the edge of the boat, there's you, with your legs dangling over the edge. And you're broken and wracked with guilt. I see that.' She reached for his face, perhaps to touch his scar, but Carter grabbed her hand.

'What's the gag,' he asked sharply.

'You're hurting me.'

'I'm . . . I'm sorry.' He relaxed his grip. 'I've never told anyone that part.' His mind raced through the passenger manifest. 'Were you friends with Aurora?'

Phoebe shook her head. She seemed very small, as if he were seeing her from atop the roller coaster. 'You're the one I know.'

The winds shifted, picking up, and a wispy cloud drifted across the sun. He dropped her hand and folded his fists across his chest.

'You're breathing like you just put armor on,' she said, rubbing her thumbs together. 'I shouldn't have said anything.'

'What's next? Can you put me in touch with my dead wife for a small fee?'

'I think you should take me home.'

'Blind girl sees all, knows all, tells all. Quite the con.'

'Stop it.' Her jaw set. 'It's not like that.'

'You know, I did fire my psychic, you could—'

'Stop punishing me for knowing you.' This came out quietly. It was like throwing a net around Carter and bringing him down from a dead run. Leaning forward, she whispered, 'I can't help knowing that you've been hurt. Don't hurt me back. Please.'

Behind them, the Europe by Auto ride now had paying customers, a family of four, the children just toddlers. They settled into the Durant touring car, which was on rollers, and it rocked gently to simulate the continental roadways, as a painted backdrop on a continuous loop began to scroll past. Here was a castle, then a cathedral, then London Bridge, then the Parthenon, all of them cracked and worn.

'You know the booth with the milk bottles?' Phoebe asked. 'You get three baseballs for a nickel?'

'Yes,' he said, clipped.

'Well, about three months ago,' she continued, 'I went to that booth, and paid my nickel, and I don't know what they thought, but I could tell the man behind the counter was very curious how I thought I'd win the stuffed bear. So you know what I did? I threw wherever the heck I felt like.' She ran her fingers up under her glasses, wiping below her eyes. 'I threw right down the midway, and where the man was standing, and then I put fifty cents down and asked for thirty more balls. He wouldn't take my money, he immediately gave me the teddy bear I wanted.'

Carter nodded. It was a story both funny and painful. He could imagine her doing just that.

She said, 'I was hoping we'd have something good today, not me being roasted here on a bench.'

'In my profession, there are many scams, many spiritualists. They prey on hope, Phoebe. I don't like that.'

'Oh. You said my name.' She grinned. 'That was nice.'

'I have an orderly mind when it comes to this sort of thing. I need to know . . . Do I know you?'

She shook her head.

'Did someone else tell you that story?'

Again, she shook her head. 'Are we going to miss the fireworks?'

'No, we have some time.' He continued down a checklist he'd half-prepared long ago in case he ever ran into something like this. 'Do you feel you have a gift that—'

'It's certainly not a gift. If I try to touch you are you going to stop me again? I didn't like that.'

He took her hands. He was going to say something – he had many more items on that checklist – but found instead that his fingers were moving on their own, exploring palms that were as tough and complicated as his had become. Then her hands were back on his jawline, light as smoke.

'You used to be open to the possibility of real magic,' she declared. 'But that was a long time ago.'

He stiffened. 'That's exactly what palm readers say, they make these statements that are just broad enough—'

'Oh, be quiet.'

Her hands continued across his face, brushing on his beard like she was testing him for resilience. 'You even pursued girls named Sarah because you were so open. And then you found the right one.'

Above them, the sound of metal wheels screeching across wood. The Thunderbolt toboggan swooped down low, and passed, children inside screaming, then pulled away into the sky that was now clotted with clouds.

'Who are you?' Chills, like someone was applying a cube of ice to the back of his neck. 'Are you . . .' He spoke so slowly he no longer knew how to finish that question.

'I just know things about you.'

'Are you . . .'

'I didn't mean for you to think I was anything. That was an accident. I know – you have an orderly mind, but you also love a mystery. Can you let me be a mystery?'

When he found his voice, he was saying, 'You are so beautiful.'

'What?'

He reached for her glasses and made it as far as having a hand on each earpiece before she stopped him.

She cleared her throat. 'I'm thirty-one years old.'

'All right,' he said, pulling away.

'I'd rather tell you that embarrassing fact than have you see me without my glasses.'

'I see.' He knitted his hands into hers, again. 'Have you ever been married?'

'No. I've . . .'

He was getting better at reading these pauses. 'Love 'em and leave 'em?'

'Well, I've always been good at the leaving part.'

'Do you have brothers or sisters?'

'I'm very worried about missing the fireworks.'

'Have you always been blind?'

'No.' She brought her hands in front of her glasses, and made sweeping gestures. 'I ran through burning poison oak.'

'Oh, that's terrible. When did . . .' He felt now the fine balance between order and mystery. He stopped his pursuit. 'I think the best place to see the fireworks is the Ferris wheel.'

She grinned. He felt a flicker, a disconcerting shadow, like the ghost dodging between headstones that you see out of the corner of your eye: hope.

She linked her arms around his elbow, and they walked a deserted path toward the Ferris wheel, which had once been surrounded by palms, long ago dead. Now it stood by itself, at the edge of the park, a white elephant five stories high. Though the ride itself was fine, there was so much space around it, the approach through scrub was desolate. So Carter and Phoebe had the wheel to themselves. As they boarded, the ticket taker checked his pocket watch.

'I'll leave you folks at the top at the stroke of half-past three,' he said.

They thanked him. Seated, there was the gentle but persuasive lift, the separation from the ground, and then the wide vista, which Carter didn't know what to make of. Idora, in all its tatters and attempted cheer, and then Oakland – much the same – and the world, much the same again.

'Charles?'

'Yes.'

'When you said I was beautiful, you meant it?'

'Of course. You're very beautiful.'

'I haven't heard that for a long time. In the Home, no one tells you you're beautiful except the nurses, and that's usually just after I've been a good girl or made a broom.'

They had made a complete circuit, and were on their way up again. When they reached the top, they stuttered to a stop. It was half-past three.

'This is going to be great,' she said, and put her hands around the metal bar that crossed their seat.

There was a chill in the air. Carter gave up his jacket to her. She threaded her arms into it and waited.

Daytime fireworks were peculiar to Oakland. Everyone, hearing of such a thing, wanted to see them, once. But rarely more than that, for they were just crackles and dim sparks that left behind them shredded, burning newsprint and colored smoke.

On the ground, crowds were forming – if 'crowds' were

clots of three or four or five pedestrians who had folded their arms and cocked their heads skyward – and the orchestra's brass section stood at the edge of the fruit orchards, playing Handel.

But in spite of all contrary evidence, the park made quite a lovely show of putting on a good time for all.

'You know what the hardest thing is?' Phoebe said, as the first pair of fireworks went up. 'The hardest thing is to know everything you know so far and still have faith.'

A sizzling sound, as a ratty-looking brownish smoke trail ignited, and bits of carbonized paper rained down. And then two purple ones, twisting like a pair of snakes, and a *boom* as sparks made a brief, flickering halo.

It would be easy to pretend to feel faith this moment, suspended over Oakland, with fireworks bursting. Carter closed his eyes. To hear them was to notice that no matter how bright, they were all launched with dull thumps.

But then the people. The cries from the ground, the exclamations.

He opened his eyes. He saw Phoebe, listening to pops and whizzing above. He wasn't lonely. Faith was a choice. So, it followed, was wonder.

By the finale of the display, a half-dozen rose-colored smoke trails dusted with glitter that caught the sunlight like diamonds, he'd found a voice in himself, calling 'bravo' with the rest of the crowd. It was unbelievable – he was actually disappointed when they ended.

About a half-hour later, he took her to the gate of the Home, and after they dismounted, they stood on the gravel path. There was a huge Italian cypress between them and the house and a brick pillar, to which the gate was attached, between them and the street. She still wore his jacket and he was in shirtsleeves. 'That was swell,' she said.

'Rocky at first, but yes, ultimately swell.'

She put her fists into the jacket pockets and pushed outward, like she had wings. 'So.'

'So.'

'Sew buttons, we've got enough thread,' she said quickly. She buckled at the knee, then straightened.

'Have you ever noticed how foolish two people begin to sound right before they kiss?'

'No. Never.' She shook her head.

'What if we took off your glasses?'

'There are *so many* possibilities.'

Gently, he eased off her glasses. Her eyes were clenched shut. When he put a hand on each shoulder, she suddenly relaxed and opened her eyes wide. They were bottle green, like a chemist's belladonna tincture. The pupils, which did not fix, shivered from point to point like hummingbirds.

'Here I am,' she said.

She looked helpless like this. Carter could sense delicate veins alive beneath the skin. 'You're shaking.'

'I don't like having my glasses off.'

'Phoebe.' He tried to read her face the way she had used her hands to read his. He imagined he saw things he couldn't quite place, as if they were words in a language in which he had never been fluent.

'I'm going to think you're cruel,' she whispered.

'Who hurt you?'

'May I put my glasses back on?'

'No.'

'How about a bag over my head?'

'I want to look at you still.'

'There's a one-way street.' She made a grab for them, and on went the glasses, and with them, she regained some composure. 'Charles, if you don't kiss me in five seconds, I'm going to run.'

He kissed her on the mouth, lightly, and in return she put her hands around his neck and kissed him until he remembered he needed to breathe. He started to pull up for air, but she protested.

'You can breathe with me,' she whispered, returning her open mouth to his. And with her hands on his face, and his against the small of her back, where her shirt had come untucked, they shared a breath, and another.

She broke their embrace, her shoulders bowed so that he caught a glimpse of her collarbone and then, in shadow below it, the flicker of an undergarment.

'Was that enough?' she whispered.

'No.'

She patted him on the chest. She stepped carefully away from the pillar they'd been leaning against, finding the gravel on the road, and then walking the well-practiced path away from him, back toward the home. Slowly, he closed his mouth. He could not take his eyes off her. What was that sound in his ears, echoing with her footsteps? His heartbeat.

Chapter 20

Jossie Dover's speakeasy had no formal name. She'd come back from Paris in 1920, an early complainer about all the Americans who'd 'roont the joint,' and opened her own private club the day Prohibition started. It was known universally as 'the Lips,' for if the police had really wanted to find it, all they had to do was look right under their nose.

Griffin approached the steel-plated door. He knocked briskly, and a small plate in the door opened up. Behind it, a pair of serious eyes looked down on him. Unless the guy was standing on a stool, he had to be almost seven feet tall.

Griffin made an 'a-okay' sign and waved it left-to-right. There was the sound of a bolt being thrown, and the door opened.

The guy was in fact almost seven feet tall and handsome as a movie star. The rest of the place was nothing special. It was like every speakeasy he'd seen: dark, choking with fumes, walls draped with velvet curtains to give it a classy sheen. Since it was after lunch, but before dark, business was light: a few men at a long zinc bar, a few more in the candlelit corners, several of whom had young women in their laps: amateurs.

Griffin approached the bar with four one-dollar bills. 'Two rolls of nickels, please.'

The bartender didn't take his money. She was short, grey-haired, and wore a nubby man's suit. 'I don't believe we've met,' she said, with a hint of an English accent. 'I'm Jossie.'

'My pleasure.' They shook hands. 'Jack Griffin, Treasury Department. Two rolls of nickels, please.'

She inclined her head toward the nearest barstool. 'Have you met Captain Morgan?' Morgan grimaced at the mention of his name, but made no other motions. 'As you're a federal agent you might not be familiar with our Chief of Police, but here he is.'

'This isn't a shakedown,' Griffin said. 'If it makes you feel better, get me two rolls of nickels and a beer, you can tell anyone who asks I got loaded. I just want to see the rabbi.'

'Oh!' She slapped the bar. 'Mr Griffin, pardon me for being a poor hostess.' Drawing a long draft for him, she expertly minimized the head. 'When the late President was in town, every two-bit Federale thought he could help himself to my cash register.' She took his money and passed him the rolls of nickels. 'Rabbi Golod is at the last table on your left.'

Griffin thanked her, and she went off to help other patrons. Sipping at the beer – his first alcohol in more than a week – he took out the list of rabbis Olive White had prepared for him. Golod was near the top. According to his registration under the Volstead Act, Rabbi Golod was allowed sacramental wine shipments to fulfill the religious needs of the fifteen thousand Jews who worshipped at his synagogue. Given that there were only two thousand Jews within fifty miles of San Francisco, Golod was either optimistic about increasing his flock or as crooked as the eight other local rabbis who claimed congregations of more than five thousand.

'Rabbi Golod?' Griffin stood by a table in the very back. The rabbi was hard to see, as he had a flapper in his lap. She was drinking gin, straight.

'Yeah?' The voice came from behind her. 'Excuse me, honey.' Rabbi Golod peeked around her narrow shoulders. Bearded, he had a dreamy smile and benevolent eyes.

Griffin showed his badge. 'My name's Jack Griffin. I'm with the Secret Service.'

The rabbi bodily lifted the girl from his lap. 'Baby, this is business.' He gave her a swat on the rump. 'G'wan, scoot!' He kept his eyes on her rear as she left, and then he said to Griffin, 'There's documentation on file for me. Each and every one of those names will check out.'

Griffin looked at him as innocent as a sun-dappled fawn. 'What names?'

'My congregation,' he said, with a rising inflection, like he was asking a question.

'Good,' said Griffin. 'I'd like to convert.'

'Pardon me?'

'I'd like to convert.' He leaned forward, and dropped both rolls of nickels so they banged against the table.

'You . . . want to what? Be Jewish?'

'Yeah. I had enough of being Presbyterian. It doesn't satisfy me. I want to be a Jew.' He picked up one roll of nickels, then the other, making fists around them.

'That's noble.' Rabbi Golod's eyes set on Griffin's fists.

'So what exactly do I need to do to convert?'

'You have to do many things. It's a long process.'

Griffin arched his neck, looking him over. 'Don't rabbis wear those fringes? What are they called?'

'Hey, I *am* a rabbi, see? You got nothing on me.'

It was beautiful watching him crack. Griffin wished he'd come up with this strategy himself, but it had been pioneered by Izzy Einstein, one of the only honest Prohibition Agents. 'So how do I start getting converted? Do I study the Bible, or—'

'That's a good idea. You should eat kosher foods, and study the Bible for . . . forty days, that's how it starts.'

'Thank you, Rabbi Golod.' Griffin unwrapped his hand from the roll of nickels. He took out a piece of paper.

'What are you writing?'

'I'm writing your name down. See, I'm writing a letter to the, uh, how do you say this?' He pointed at the name he'd copied out from Izzy Einstein's memo. 'The B'nai B'rith. I'm going to tell them you were very helpful in telling me I needed to study the Bible for forty days.' The B'nai B'rith Hillel Foundation had sprung up recently and, among other duties, ferreted out wet rabbis who'd recently found religion.

'Okay!' Rabbi Golod slammed his hand onto the table. 'What? What do you want?'

Griffin could have prolonged this – it was actually fun. Instead, he opened his satchel and passed him the wine bottle. 'Where'd this come from?'

'Huh!' He grabbed it and looked at it under the dim light. He looked at the dimple in the bottom and at the label again. 'Home brew. Could of come from anywhere.'

Griffin silently picked up his two rolls of nickels again.

'Honest,' Golod exclaimed. 'I'm really not anxious to get worked over. I have a book in the back, has every label I ever carried, and one example of every bottle I ever saw. This one isn't in there. Believe me.'

'How often you make deliveries to the Palace?'

'Whew. Ten times a minute, maybe. You serious?'

'Any of the guys about average height, average—'

'Girls. Jossie only uses girls. Anything I run to the Palace goes through her, she takes a cut.'

Griffin was ready to fold up his cards and go home, but he had a sudden, faint memory. 'Any of your parishioners named Ledocq? Jewish, works for a magician.'

Golod frowned. 'He works for a magician? Ledocq? We don't get many Jews in here.'

Griffin noted this. Home brew. Much harder to trace. He'd hit a dead end, his time in San Francisco was over, and he wasn't sure where to go next. He sipped his beer. '*Mikvah*,' he said.

'Excuse me?'

'Next guy comes in here looking to convert, just drop the word *mikvah* in there somewhere. That should shake him.' Golod glared at him for the whole time it took him to drain his beer. Griffin didn't even know why he was being so generous lately.

Outside again, he checked his watch. In a couple hours, he had to catch the train that would take him to New Mexico. He could try to harass Carter. He could bring the bottle to his superiors. He took about three steps toward his hotel, but then in a maneuver he could never quite explain to himself, turned 180 degrees and walked to the public library.

Chapter 21

There was no feeling that deserved more to be bottled and reapplied at leisure than having recently been kissed by a pretty girl. Waiting at an intersection, Carter touched his fingers to the scar on his lip and thought, *She felt this*, until a Model T behind him honked.

He took the curve onto Grand Avenue, a mild curve, with a deeper lean than he needed to, but he felt at every moment like a daredevil. *What a smelly contraption!* Opening the throttle, he felt air rush up his shirtsleeves, and the engine make a slight flutter and gasp, a strange draw like he was pulling against elastic, which meant trouble. He was low on fuel. He turned the petcock to reserve and the R32's power returned.

The top of Lake Merritt was home to two gasoline filling stations: a Standard and a Shell. Though Standard was papered with banners trumpeting their ethyl no-knock premium, Carter chose the Shell – he always chose the Shell – because it sported a fine view of the lake, the attendants' uniforms were the more regal, and especially because the stationhouse was molded into a thirty-foot yellow stucco clamshell.

When he pulled in, he was greeted by a swarm of attendants, six of them, each about eighteen years old, all gawking at his BMW. They had a patter about their fine products and were required to recite it for every customer, but all that blew away in the warm summer winds – no one had ever seen a motorcycle like Carter's.

'Mr Carter, this is the bee's knees,' said Jimmy, a young man whom Carter particularly liked. Jimmy's father was a haberdasher, but Jimmy was mechanically inclined.

'It's the cat's meow,' another one cried. 'What's she take?'

'Aviation fuel,' Carter responded, which caused a babble of appreciation, and then one boy who hadn't spoken yet concluded, 'It's the cat's pajamas.' That was a new one to Carter.

'You do have aviation fuel, don't you?'

'Do we ever!'

Carter reached for his expense journal and remembered it was in the pocket of his jacket. An excuse to visit her again. He unscrewed the gasoline cap and then the six boys did a ro-sham-bo to win the privilege of pushing the bike to the aviation-grade pump. Jimmy was an early loser of the contest, and ended up walking, head down and hands in pockets, to the farthest pump, where a matte black bread truck was parked.

'Good afternoon, sir,' he said in a monotone, 'would you like to try our tetraethyl-leaded Blue Stripe gasoline, with a higher specific gravity than any other premium brand?'

'Yes,' said the well-groomed man behind the wheel. Jimmy filled the tank, checked the oil, and wiped the windows of the truck, remembering to smile cheerfully at each and every passenger even though his friends were getting to see the motorcycle. Keeping one eye on the tank, he also watched the aviation fuel pump, from which joy and laughter seemed to radiate.

'Jeez, this is the worst day of my life,' he moaned. He tabulated the bill on his chit of yellow paper and said to the driver, 'Forty cents.'

The driver handed him a dollar, eyes focused elsewhere. Jimmy followed his gaze.

'Yeah,' he shook his head, making change, 'that's some swell motorcycle.'

'Right, son.'

Son? The driver and all his passengers weren't that much older than he was. And why were four men wearing Brooks Brothers suits all riding in a bread truck, anyway?

Then he heard a hypnotic sound – the BMW starting up. 'Wow,' he said. Carter rode in a wide circle around the whole station, waving at the boys, who turned with him as if he were magnetic north, and then he merged into the Lake Shore traffic; seconds later, the bread truck followed.

One of James's messengers slumped on the staircase to Carter's Hillgirt Circle apartment. Though he'd been prepared for an exciting afternoon – delivering an urgent message to a magician! – he had long ago gotten bored enough to take out his Jew's harp and lean against the masonry.

His afternoon had almost become interesting to a degree he wouldn't have liked, as Samuelson and Stutz had debated whether to detain him and replace him with Hollis, who would deliver a bogus message to Carter – 'Meet me at the docks, urgent, James.' Though Stutz found excellent reasons for replacing the boy – several times he mentioned, as if making a rhetorically perfect argument, that he had enough chloroform – Samuelson stuck to his guns: even proposing a kidnapping was illegal, and his vision of the Service did *not* include illegal activities. He didn't add the more accurate dictum that suggestions that were not his own stood little chance of adoption.

The plan was to intercept the magician at his apartment garage, but when Carter left the gasoline station, he turned right on Lake Shore – he *should* have turned left – and the men followed him as he rode to the Fourteenth Street Bridge, then right on Harrison, and into Lakeside Park, then out on Grand again, in other words making a complete loop around the lake.

'He's onto us,' Stutz growled. 'He's trying to shake us,' later adding, 'He's making monkeys out of us,' and so forth until Samuelson ordered him to be quiet.

On their third circuit around the lake, when conversation had otherwise fallen into a confused rut, Hollis made a valuable observation: if they parked the truck at the eastern end of Lakeside Park, they could watch Carter's entire route without having to follow him and risk detection.

'He'll get away,' said Stutz, and Samuelson, who'd been expecting Stutz to make that prediction, set the parking brake, folded his arms, and announced it was better not to be toyed with. If Carter made a break for it, they'd catch him somehow.

For a full fifteen minutes, the men watched Carter whiz around the lake, and when the air was just right, they could hear the chuffing sound of his motor accelerating. They discussed whether he was in fact making fools of them, with emphasis placed (by Samuelson) that since he was a magician, he was likely up to *something*. 'Luckily, we have all of *that*,' he said, pointing a thumb toward the back of the truck, where O'Brien, the final member of their team, dozed among the sundry equipment they had rounded up that morning from the Treasury, the Postal Authority, and other San Francisco federal offices.

Just as it seemed Carter could ride in circles forever, he broke the pattern: entering the park and passing the truck, as he had a dozen times before, he rounded the bend in front of them and slowed. He disappeared behind a clutch of oak trees.

A moment later, he was in plain sight again. On a rise behind a hillock planted with daffodils, he had turned and was puttering back toward them. He put the bike on its stand and killed the engine.

'He sees us,' said Samuelson, for Carter was now walking directly toward the truck.

'No, hold on,' Stutz waved that suggestion away, 'we might have a shot here.'

'Well, aren't you the blankety-blank optimist,' Samuelson snapped, and Stutz shrugged his narrow shoulders.

A word about Agent Stutz: he owned a sap and had among his belongings wherever he traveled a small bottle of chloroform, as well as a Skinner mask, for in all of the lectures he'd attended in the academy, the only one that had appealed to him was 'abduction procedure'. He frequented news-stands to purchase the weekly adventures of the Yarrow Twins, one of whom was always 'going under the cloth' after gloved hands darted from behind Egyptian pilasters. That he could actually get to use his anesthetic in the course of duty thrilled him in ways he could hardly contain, and so Carter's slow approach – it was really sort of an amble – toward their van seemed like a gift from heaven that he wasn't quite willing to dismiss.

Carter had turned, and was now on the dirt pathway that ringed the lake. He stood with one arm against a eucalyptus tree, leaning into it, as if he were holding it up, and he regarded a pair of geese that waddled past him.

'What's he doing?' Hollis jockeyed between his peers. 'His mouth is moving.'

'Is he singing?' A frowning Stutz rolled the window down, listened, and then whispered, 'He's singing.'

Carter was indeed singing, for he was overcome with how he

361

felt for Miss Phoebe Kyle, and he was using his voice – so well trained for speaking in large theatres – to attempt the popular ballad, 'Oh That Brown-Eyed Girl.' It was a difficult song for even the most skilled singer, and Carter, no matter how sweet he might have been on Phoebe, had an awful relationship with melody.

Ahead was the bench where they'd met, and longing, an *ache*, had brought him here again. How she wouldn't ask his help. How she'd said 'the suave and sad mahatma.' He remembered a song he'd heard in his vaudeville days, but never since, 'Mysterious Melanie,' which had high praise for the curve of a woman's throat, an area he'd not previously considered fascinating.

The humidity was increasing, the sky thickening with the Midwestern-style summer storm clouds that never seemed to trouble San Francisco. Carter welcomed the idea of warm rain. He sat on the bench, which looked out over the eastern arm of Lake Merritt, a hundred feet of dirty water, ducks swimming through tendrils of widgeon grass, and as he looked into the ripples, what he saw with anxious clarity was Phoebe Kyle, leaning forward, and how she had shown off her collarbone. What an amazing display of light and shadow gathered in that hollow.

'Excuse me?'

'Yes?' Carter looked over his right shoulder. His head exploded in pain as something collided against it.

'O'Brien!'

It was a voice to his left this time. Carter lurched up and backward by instinct, trying to avoid whatever had hit him, his hands at his head, eyes tearing with pain. Something large stepped up and clouted him in the head a second time, then punched him in the stomach, dropping him as neatly as clipping the head off a rose.

'Stop it, O'Brien, stop it!' A third voice.

'What?'

He was on all fours. Someone rushed to his side, he knew no friendly aid was coming his way, that he had to move, but his body wouldn't obey. He couldn't breathe, the wind was knocked out of him, he couldn't even grunt. His stomach had collapsed, it felt like a vacuum, how could he ever fill his lungs again? Something papery with leather straps went over his head, and now he realized he could move a little, but what his body wanted more than anything was to turn and see, stupidly, what was going on behind him. But everything was pointillistic and dissolving into flashes.

'It's over his ear,' he heard, and then, 'I'll fix it, I'll fix it,' and then hands went past his face.

'He's not breathing.'

'You punched him in the stomach, you moron!'

'You said to ace him.'

'I told you to *distract* him.' Samuelson threw his hands up.

Stutz, in the meantime, crouched near Carter, his hands darting around the Skinner mask like he was trying to keep a vase from falling off a shelf. Carter tried to sit up on his heels then he sprawled sideways into the dirt. Stutz noted how the impact pulled the mask half off, so he replaced it and watched.

'Is he out?'

'When do you take that thing off him? Stutz?'

Stutz had never actually seen someone chloroformed before, and if Carter were indeed unconscious, the results disappointed him. Carter looked relaxed, half-smiling like he was getting forty winks. Stutz had expected to see him collapse 'like a marionette with cut strings,' then 'lay as helpless as a fish in a net' as was frequently the case for the freckle-faced Yarrows.

Stutz unbuckled the mask and pinched Carter's cheek, hard enough to leave a mark.

'He must be out,' O'Brien said.

'Let's load him.' Hollis looked around the park anxiously.

'He might be faking,' Stutz said. He removed the sewing needle he kept in the leather case with his chloroform.

'What are you doing?' Samuelson checked for pedestrians. A pair of kids riding bicycles were on a distant path.

'Testing,' Stutz replied, rolling up Carter's sleeve. He jabbed the needle in and removed it. There was no reaction, unless one counted bleeding.

'Is he out?'

'I guess he's out,' Stutz said. He shook Carter's shoulder; the magician's head lolled, and his arm fell down, wrist out, smashing his watch crystal in the dirt. 'Hmm. I should put the mask back on him.'

The rest of the men, who had no patience for Stutz, voted to gather Carter up and throw him in the back of their truck, where the equipment awaited.

While Hollis drove them over the trolley tracks, and down Broadway, and through downtown, toward the estuary, and Stutz hovered in case more chloroform was needed (twice, he reapplied a rag to Carter's nose, 'just in case'), Samuelson and O'Brien began to wrap up the unconscious magician, with much arguing and second-guessing by all four agents.

The first issue over which they disagreed was the four pairs of handcuffs – three standard-issue plug eights, and the fourth an interesting pair Samuelson had brought back from his trip to England. Whereas Stutz felt they should be applied immediately, Hollis yelled, from the driver's seat, that they should strip him down, in case he had tools hidden on his person.

Once Hollis said it, the idea was clearly a clever one, but since he was their junior, he was told to keep his yap shut and keep driving. Carter's shirt was removed, and his belt, and his many trouser pockets were thoroughly searched, and all items removed, from the obvious tools (keys and picks) to objects probably designed to *look* innocuous (a cigar tube, for instance). There were no hidden aids sewn anywhere into his clothing.

While awaiting crosstown traffic on Fourteenth Street, much debate occurred about removing his boots before cuffing his ankles together. Barefoot, the manacles would go on much tighter, but the prevailing wisdom was that he could probably undo knots with his toes, and so his boots stayed on, with the English cuffs around them. Two pairs went around his wrists, and the final set was used to link the wrist and ankle cuffs so that Carter was doubled-over.

Then it was time for the seventy-five feet of rope. Samuelson had heard about Houdini escaping from seventy-five feet of rope, which sounded impossible, and he wished to attempt the feat properly, with a team of trained professionals. But they ran into problems almost immediately. Traffic was terrible on Broadway, and the stop-and-start progress of the bread truck caused the men standing in the back to frequently jostle each other. Carter's dead weight was difficult to turn over in such a cramped space, and as the coils began to surround him, it occurred to Samuelson first, then O'Brien, that if bound, he would no longer fit in the sack, which was next.

Samuelson said, 'We have to untie him.'

'We can skip the sack.' O'Brien had already invested tremendous sweat in the ropes.

'No, the sack,' Hollis called. 'I vote for the sack. It's impressive.'

This brought on another round of arguing – which would be more impressive, the sack or the rope, culminating in a cursing O'Brien bringing out his Bowie knife to cut through the fifteen or so feet of cord they'd managed to tie around Carter. He finished just as they passed under the ionic columns that marked the entrance to the Port of Oakland.

It had begun to rain. The truck's windshield wipers went on, and in the back, Stutz held the mouth of the mail sack open while Samuelson and O'Brien banged into each other and yelled repeatedly in the process of securing Carter inside of it. First, his heels kept catching on the mouth, then the handcuffs, and finally there were problems getting his head fully past all the eyelets at top.

'Make sure you seal it right,' Samuelson said. The top of the mail bag was like a cold and stiff mouth – its lower lip was a metal bar with buckles, and its upper was a perforated metal plate. When Samuelson closed the two sides together, O'Brien fed a leather strap through all the buckles, securing it with the U.S. Postal Service Regulation Rotary padlock.

'Hey,' Stutz called out, 'he flinched.'

'What are you doing down there?' Samuelson gave him a shove. 'Why did he flinch?'

'He just – jerked.'

Samuelson could hardly believe Stutz hadn't provoked that somehow, but there was no time to investigate. They were at the docks. 'Into the crate, quickly.'

It was a standard sixty-four-cubic-foot U.S. Customs crate in which gin rummies had once smuggled Canadian Club. It lay atop a pair of chains that crossed exactly under its center. Once they dropped the sack in, they began nailing the three narrow planks on top of it. The sound of hammers put to use in the truck's payload was as deafening as rifle shots.

Finally, as they backed to the end of the last pier, the one farthest from the mouth of the bay, they threw the truck doors open, and fastened the chains together with a ratcheting band, which Hollis connected to a dockside winch.

The rain made their labor that much more difficult. With great shouts of excitement, they sent the winch to work, careful that nothing slipped, and soon the crate went up overhead, and then outward, over the choppy green waters. Upstream were the marshlands of the slough, and downstream, dozens of piers with loading docks and men at work. The crate spun on its chain, which quickly beaded with raindrops.

'Let 'er go,' said Samuelson, and then the grappling hooks were removed, and the box plunged into the saltwater, a ring of spray blossoming as it broke the surface. It bobbed, gradually listing to the side.

The four men stood on the dock, all grinning madly, waiting for something interesting to happen. Samuelson had brought his umbrella, but the other three didn't mind standing in the warm rain.

'I thought it was going to sink,' Hollis said.

'Customs crate,' Stutz responded. 'Guess it's airtight.'

Samuelson took out his revolver. He put a corner of the crate into his sites and fired one round that immediately sent splinters into the air.

'Sam!' O'Brien yelled, holding his ears.

'Holy cow, Sam!' Stutz's jaw dropped.

'Well, it's sinking now.'

'What if you hit him?'

'What if I did?'

Gradual, ascending laughter, the sounds of disbelief.

Carter hadn't been hit. The bullet had simply clipped out an inch or so at the very corner of the crate. The port had recently been dredged, so the waters were deep but muddy. The tide was waning, the estuary emptying into the great San Francisco Bay, and as early pelicans dropped like meteorites, looking for fish, the crate began to find the current and drift into the channel. It was a slow drift, perhaps ten feet a minute. As the crate eased away, the men followed it.

When nothing had happened for enough time that they began to get bored, O'Brien remembered that as they were all members of the Legal Tenors, the Treasury Choir, he could start a round robin.

Oh what do we do with a drunken sailor
What shall we do with a drunken sailor
What shall we do with a drunken sailor
Ear-lie in the mor-ning?

Chapter 22

Until noon, the Berkeley campus was quiet, as it was summer session. The intensive language workshops had ended a week ago, and so the only early morning activity was in the agricultural studies department, where goats and lambs and cows were fed their breakfast, then taken to the Oxford Street pasture.

But after the campanile chimed twelve, trucks drove up Telegraph, through Sather Gate, and pulled up to the loading docks behind Wheeler Hall. Crews unloaded crates and sent them on their way to the classrooms and auditoriums, where they were unpacked for the poor soul who had rented his share of space.

Since the War, summers had been lucrative for the University of California, as its lecture halls were excellent venues for inventors to meet with investors. The university neither judged nor encouraged the men who sent in their twenty-five-dollar reservations, but did require a brief description of the marvel to be demonstrated. Occasionally, a clerk might feel genuine pity when yet another eager man was to display yet another perpetual motion machine, but the 1922 brochures proclaimed that 'the University of California is committed to excellent thought, even the heterodox.' As this phrase encouraged checks to rain down like manna, the 1923 brochures highlighted it. Inventors were a paranoid lot, so the university published no schedules, and distributed no publicity, and every communication was stamped 'confidential' in red ink, which seemed to please everyone.

That such precautions inevitably led to small audiences never seemed to bother the inventors, who relied exclusively on their own bizarre invitations. 'Dear William Randolph Hearst,' one such read, 'I am going to make you a fortune. How, you ask, well, I will tell you how. Euphonics!'

This afternoon, Wheeler Hall's dozen classrooms hosted an engine powered by seawater, a grain harvester, a new type of newspaper printing press, several poorly designed automobile accessories, and a number of other production methods and devices, most of which had been presented in summer 1922 and the summer before that.

The inventors stood outside on Wheeler's wide stone staircase. During the 4 P.M. to 5 P.M. break, they smoked cigarettes and feigned enthusiasm at seeing their colleagues again. Mostly, each wanted to know if anyone had stolen his mailing list of widows and relatives, and each in turn wanted to know if he himself were suspected of stealing anything.

While they talked, university workers carried in crate after crate stenciled with Ogden, Utah, shipping marks. This caused great mirth, as these belonged to a 'newbie', who had made all the mistakes they had once made: he brought far too much equipment, which meant paying extra workmen; he had made a stab at camaraderie early that morning by asking them what their inventions were; he had volunteered, in front of all of them, that he had a fine invention called television; most amusingly, he had rented the *large* lecture hall, no doubt ready to fill it to the rafters with capitalists who would shower him with money.

The man with the grain harvester, who was a great wit, blew a smoke ring, and said, 'Television? What a terrible thing to call it – the word's half-Greek, half-Latin!' During the ensuing laughter, he went pale. 'My God! Is that James Carter?'

To a man, the inventors turned to see, indeed, James Carter, vest stretched over his stomach, sauntering up the stairs in step with his partner Tom Crandall. They trailed a bespectacled Hebrew man who breezed past the group without a word.

'Which one of you got James Carter to come? And . . . that's Grossman.' Passing through Sather Gate, Aggie Grossman of Bank of Italy, right-hand man of A. P. Giannini, waved an envelope before his sweating face.

To say that the small group fell into silence wouldn't give proper respect to the rapid mental calculations each man made – who was worth the time of Grossman and Carter and . . . wasn't that James Fagan from W. W. Crocker, and how many men from Borax Smith's firm? – who were all these businessmen now coming up the steps? The man with the seawater engine recognized scientists from RCA's

San Francisco labs, but why was Colonel French from the Presidio here with two lieutenants?

Tiny raindrops began to fall, making dusty marks on the stairs. The inventors ground out their cigarettes and, as an afternoon downpour began, they followed the crowd and found to their horror that the lecture hall was filled to standing-room only.

In short, Farnsworth had rented exactly the right-sized venue to give his public lecture on television. By the time the campanile chimed five o'clock, Pem counted 110 people, which caused her to jump up and down behind the side curtain until she regained her composure. Philo for his part looked glum and pale. Few people in the world had ever heard Philo Farnsworth present his ideas, but those who had all made similar comments: before he spoke, he seemed bright, obviously, but nervous and ill-prepared, ready to be judged poorly.

He had lain the groundwork for this day a year ago, sitting in public libraries with issues of *Forbes* and the *Wall Street Journal*, copying out addresses of men who aided inventors. On a family trip to Washington, he had on a Sunday excused himself after church and traveled to the White House. Sunday was Harding's afternoon to answer the door there himself. Philo had vowed he would remember every detail of the visit, but all he could remember was a wilting bunch of daisies on the low, scuffed coffee table in front of the couch Harding had him sit in. Philo soon enough identified with those daisies – in high spirits, he had revealed his design to the President, who had reacted badly – he seemed to want the boy to limit the number of people who knew about it. Where was the glory in that? Philo had left the White House drooping, stoically accepting Harding's proposed meeting with Borax Smith, but had all along wanted to debut television before as impressive an audience as possible. Harding's death, shocking as it had been, freed him in good conscience to use the lecture hall he had reserved so long ago.

Still, he had delivered his invitations only this morning. He didn't want anyone to get ahead of his research.

The worst of it, he thought, would be defending his theories to RCA's men, who sat in the front row in a line, scowling. Also, his unorthodox ideas about television would take the military some time, he felt, to agree with.

However, there was actually something worse awaiting Philo. Two rows back sat a man in a white lab coat, a wild-eyed spectator who'd taken a seat early. He was not a scientist, but a Russian anarchist. He had been given a simple instruction: when Farnsworth had revealed enough about television, the anarchist was to shoot Farnsworth through the forehead, several times if he were so moved.

His presence was a coup for the military, in that foreign anarchists, like captive gorillas, were more discussed than actually seen. The anarchist's name was unclear – currently, he preferred to be called 'the Spider' – but he'd been a violent Luddite since the chlorine gas had killed his four brothers in the Brusilov Offensive. He'd come to the United States in 1920, as it was the center of a new kind of industrial behavior, consumption promoted as the road to happiness, that he found especially galling.

He expected to be arrested and tried for venomous letters he'd sent in summer of 1921, targeting Westinghouse, General Electric, and President Harding (whom he rather liked, but still, he was a symbol). The only result had been a visit from a dignified man who discussed philosophy with the Spider in a slow way of speaking he'd learned was called 'Kentucky.' There were many people who felt the same way as the Spider did, the man explained. They should help each other.

They remained in touch and then, three weeks ago, the Kentucky man brought him to San Francisco and asked him to wait, as a terrible madman was going to meet Harding here. When the Spider was told about television, he prepared to write a blistering letter, but then the Kentucky man showed him blueprints. Aeroplanes, with cameras in their bellies, could cruise over battlefields, sending images back to home bases, where generals could relax with their whiskeys.

So now the Spider sat, knee bouncing in anticipation, awaiting a single nod from his contacts at the other side of the room. Simultaneously, some of the corporate attendees, who had been caught unaware by Philo's letter of invitation, looked at their watches uncomfortably. They, too, planned to steal television and patent it – that is, if television actually worked, which their researchers disputed. They had no specific interests in rubbing Farnsworth out. However, since so many RCA executives played tennis with officers high in the War Department, they gossiped like washerwomen. Not wanting to be left behind, they had tried all day long to arrange for some sort of frightening man, perhaps an associate of bootleggers, to attend the lecture, but they'd come up empty-handed.

The room buzzed with conversations. James, Tom, and Ledocq had seats toward the center of the lecture hall, and Ledocq kept switching his glasses to better see the audience or the space behind the podium. Ledocq asked, 'Do you know anyone here?'

'I know most of these people. Rare to see them all in one room,' James replied.

'We are such small fry,' Tom said. Several rows down, someone waved at him. Tom waved back, smiling. 'Is that John Cannell? I hate that man, he's a total cretin.' He kept waving and smiling. 'Looks like Charlie won't make it.'

'He might be here,' James sighed. 'Behind a pillar or with a false mustache or something.'

♣ ♦ ♥ ♠

When Carter was five years old, his father had taken him to a vaudeville show, one act of which was an a cappella group of bullies who sang 'Blow the Man Down' and 'Pell Mell' and who would pick a boy out of the audience and toss him back and forth, miming the actions of the song. The boy they chose that afternoon had soiled himself with fright. Carter barely remembered this event, but he was always courteous to children whom he invited onstage. Also: he hated sea shanties.

So when he awoke in the packing crate, his ears rang, and he had the vague sense of a gun having been shot nearby. He heard muffled sounds of a quartet singing, 'Tie him to the taffrail when she's yard-arm under,' and he worked his mouth to tell them to stop it immediately. But his mouth was dry, and he had trouble making his eyes focus, then he realized he was awake, but in absolute pitch darkness. Excruciatingly twisted up, he tried to straighten.

Simultaneous with his fingers touching the handcuffs on his wrists, he remembered being clocked in the head. A smell like turpentine had brought him down. His cheek was pressed against some fabric. Sailcloth. He moved his face along the cloth until he found the metal lip he expected. A mail sack. He took a deep breath though his nose. He smelled saltwater, the grimy sack, his own sweat. He was damp.

Now he listened to the singing voices again. None of the Golden Gate Assembly of the Society of American Magicians could sing that well. 'Dante, you bastard,' he muttered, for Dante was the only magician he knew who could sing, and magicians were fond of ambushing each other.

But he'd been chloroformed, or ethered, he didn't know which, and no magician would do that. Faintly, he remembered crouching among four young men who wore their matching dark wool suits like uniforms. A high gloss to their boots, all of them exactly the same style. A familiar style. When had he last seen – the night the President had attended his show.

The Secret Service.

Way-hey up she rises
Way-hey up she rises
Way-hey up she rises
Ear-lie in the morning

They dissolved into laughter at the same time as Carter became aware of something inflating the sailcloth against his cheek. He pushed against it; it gave way, then filled up again. Water. He turned slightly, and the whole sack went with him, sickeningly, throwing his equilibrium off. The report of hammers, hammering shut . . . a crate?

More singing. They were having fun with him. Some magicians welcomed impromptu escape challenges, but Carter, who had never made peace with Mr Jenks for trapping him in the bilboes and the brank, was not among them. He hated escapes. It went beyond fear or the urge for self-preservation. The few times he'd had audience members bring their restraints onstage, he'd had to fight back a growing black, dumb anger. It obliterated his better judgment and, sometimes, his abilities.

Still, he'd studied cuffs and crates in an academic kind of way, the way he looked at diagrams of automata he didn't love enough to own. In addition to the regular picks, which he kept in his pockets – kept them there so they'd be found – he traveled with a concealed tool kit, as per the instructions of Ottawa Keyes. Wires, hooks, passkeys, magnets, odd objects that he'd made himself that had functions but no names, all cunningly hidden such that no one would ever find them. He turned his left wrist upward to reach his right sleeve and found only skin.

The tool kit, all of its lovely various parts, was sewn into the fine coat he'd draped around Phoebe Kyle's shoulders.

'Fuck!'

Shouting an obscenity in a small canvas sack drifting somewhere in the bay suddenly made him feel quite small. He added, 'Fudge,' as if that would make things better. The sailcloth now pressed insistently against his cheek. He realized that he was sinking.

'My mouth is dry, my pulse is eighty-five, my feet are asleep, I'm cramped and can't see, but I'm fine. *Fine.*' Actually, there was a strange, shooting pain in his right calf, but since he was cuffed, he couldn't touch it to see what it was.

The handcuffs around his wrists felt like Bean-pattern plug 8s, the kind issued to law enforcement, the easiest kind to open. All he needed to do was strike them once, firmly, against a concrete floor or a metal plate, best kept under the trousers, on the shins, and they would spring open. It was devastatingly simple, he remembered a young man from an annual Society of American Magicians picnic saying, what did he call himself, Lotharini, a man of no experience, talking around a sausage dismissively, 'If someone can't escape from plug 8's, he's a dunderhead,' and looking around to see if he'd made points. Since Carter was cuffed hand-to-foot, there was no way to get leverage. That devastatingly simple method did him no good.

There was another way. He'd heard it worked. His fingers were quite literally pressed against his boots. The shoes he normally wore – the ones now standing on his living room rug – had false heels in which he had a few useful items. The ones on his feet, however, were simple, Sears-issued lace-ups. He reached out, left hand to left boot, right hand to right boot, and started undoing both laces, which were standard-issue black bootlaces, cotton weave wrapped around narrow cotton core that made the knots stand up to a fashionable height.

He had to work the laces under the leg cuffs without tearing the woven cloth, which required him to be nimble.

His hands felt stiff and half-asleep, but almost thirty years of practice allowed him to make movements so subtle they seemed impossible. Out came the left lace. Carter tied a simple slipknot in it and worked the loop, by touch, into the keyhole of the first pair of cuffs. He breathed shallowly, through his nose, counting out his heartbeat, and gingerly twisting counterclockwise. Regardless of how careful he was being, he still felt the fabric support give way. *That is completely unfair*, he thought. He continued putting fine, continuous pressure on the lace until he heard a click, which relieved him more than he had expected.

Working quickly, Carter freed himself from the first three pairs of handcuffs, feeling clever for using a shoelace to defeat iron. Take that, Lotharini. The last pair, on his ankles, resisted this method. They felt different, nonregulation cuffs, and he couldn't be bothered with them anyway, as water was filling up the crate. He was protected from it for now by the waterproof mail sack, but once he escaped it – if he escaped – he would have to figure a way out of the packing crate, and he needed to examine it while there was air left.

Blue skies, he thought, *wide open spaces*, and sweat dripped into his eyes as he maneuvered into a sitting position, knees to his chest. Escaping a mail sack required skill, and a patience he was rapidly losing. He tapped along the canvas until he felt something hard that swung back against his fingertips. The padlock. If he had a knife, he would simply cut his way though the cloth, but he didn't (there was one in his blessed jacket), so he tested the canvas's flexibility. It was as supple as flannel; he could hold the lock steady with one hand. All he needed was the key to the sack and opening it would be simple. It was getting stuffier; he was running out of air.

The rain came down pleasantly on the dock, and the men there went through 'Blow the Man Down' and 'Sugar in the Hold.' Hollis asked if anyone else knew one he'd heard, 'The Dead Horse Shanty,' but when no one else joined in, they sang 'Good-Bye Fare Thee Well.' On the Alameda side of the channel, a fishing boat was returning from its morning by the Farallons, and Stutz was the first to speculate that its wake would pass over the crate.

Carter's leg still hurt. Irritated, he touched the sore spot and found, to his surprise, a needle stuck an inch deep into his calf. He was instantly aware of several other sore spots, and as he touched them, sticky with blood, he knew that someone had jabbed him while he was unconscious. Coldly, he bent the needle. He was picturing the lock, what kind of tumblers the standard U.S. Postal issue had, while in a deep, primitive place, he recalled hanging upside down in the bilboes, and how his fake rose had jabbed him in the leg, ultimately freeing him.

Suddenly, crazily, the packing crate dropped a foot, bobbed up two feet, wobbled onto its side, and Carter tumbled against the pile of discarded handcuffs, water percolating around him, as some watercraft passed him. *Just riding its wake*, he told himself.

He'd dropped the needle.

It was no use trying to find it in the pitch black; it was somewhere at the bottom of the bag. Frustration tightened the muscles in his neck, even in the blackness he began to see red. He needed a perfect coil shape.

His watch. When he touched it, he realized the crystal was already broken. 'Fine,' he murmured, as it was that much easier to pull out the mainspring.

He punctured the sailcloth with the sharper end of the spring, and with a corkscrew motion he worked most of it through, leaving a sliver for him to grip. The padlock he held steady with his left hand. With his right hand holding the tiny spring between thumb and forefinger, he worked blindly, imagining the scene from outside the bag: here was the padlock, and poking out of the cloth, a coiled lockpick, drawing closer. Gently, he turned his hands inward; the supple cloth just allowed the lock to face the pick directly, and there was something slightly wrong about the resistance he felt, something too slow. It was water. The lock and pick were now working underwater, he realized, which meant the crate was nearly empty of air. He twisted the coil, trying not to breathe, feeling it bump against the metal surface of the lock. Probing left, right, up, down, he still couldn't find the lock hole. He saw, for a moment, a roomful of blind women threading multicolored beads on a string, making complex patterns and never making a mistake.

The coil found the lock. Carter squinted, trying to feel for the tumbling mechanism, imagining vibrations traveling up the watch spring. Though the heat made his face perspire, his palms were dry.

The packing crate lifted a little. Carter could feel a swell beginning. The drone of another ship engine. No, not another wake, not now! He held on to the lock and spring for dear life as he was tossed up, then down, all violence, head banging against the crate, then flat calm. His hands were empty. No lock, no spring, and frantically he searched for them, hands stroking the sailcloth in total darkness. But it was no good. He felt along the canvas and could tell where he'd been holding it by the impression of his nail marks, and the lock was no longer there. He tapped. Nothing. Which didn't make sense, unless . . . With dim hope, he pushed at the mouth of the mail sack, and it opened wide. The last twist of the spring had popped the lock off, he'd succeeded, complete success! – which he could hardly celebrate as a flood of muddy water poured down on him, in a second filling up his bag, backwashing into his eyes and mouth, all widgeon grass and silt choking him so he bilked it up again.

He shucked the bag like dead skin, half-stepped, half-floated out of it, gagging on the acrid taste of salt. There was less than a foot of air left. The packing crate was just tall enough to crouch in, but he couldn't stand up. He touched its rough surfaces and knew, heart sinking, that it was in no way gimmicked or prepared. A couple of splinters lodged under his fingernails, which made him angry all over again.

There were wonderful devices, collapsible jacks and such, and clever devices like sliding panels that made packing crate escapes quite easy. Carter had a jack on his desk at the Washington Street house. But unlike handcuffs and mail sacks, there was no way to escape from an unprepared packing crate.

Soon, Samuelson's knowledge of shanties, from the short-haul shanties to the capstans, was exhausted. To his surprise, Hollis knew more and was singing them alone as all four men watched the slowly sinking crate, which had drifted between the arms of one of the larger berths. It rocked gently, but was no longer in danger of drifting into the bay at large.

'He is going to get out of there, right?' O'Brien asked.

Samuelson shrugged. 'That's his problem.'

'If he doesn't get out, we'll have to get him.' Stutz looked at the crate nervously. 'Right?'

They stood on a dock about ten feet above the water, which roiled in patches below their shoes, as the planks had eight-inch gaps every several feet. This was supposed to (but never did) discourage drunks from fishing here at night. The crate was in the slip between docks.

A moment later, Hollis said, 'Maybe I should go to the truck, and bring the crowbars back.'

Samuelson looked at the crate, and then at the horizon. A boat of some sort was pointing at them, prow forward. It was fairly close, but the odds of it trying to dock at the one berth in which the crate floated were quite slender indeed.

'If you want.'

Carter pushed the sack to the back of the crate, its mouth on the floor and its end floating on the water like an onion. He was on his hands and knees, soaked to the skin, his trousers ballooning around him, his ankles still shackled together and he supposed he had less than two minutes of air left. He went into a crouch, feet braced against the floor, his shoulders and neck pressed to the top planks, and he pushed, reasoning that brute force was his only option. He strained for several seconds, visualizing nails popping from the boards. No. Nothing.

He was breathing faster. Less efficiently. Getting dizzy. Though the water hadn't yet reached the top of the crate, the air left was filling with his own exhalation – little oxygen, too much carbon dioxide. He took another breath and pushed harder than before, feeling stronger than the boards, feeling only triumph, anger, and then, a creeping despondency, weakness, floaters in his eyes.

Houdini, who never revealed a specific method unless he was done with it, never shut up about the general philosophy of escape. 'Were I ever in trouble,' he assured Carter, as if Carter had been asking him about this very topic, 'I would think of my loved ones and feel their strength filling me.' Houdini had never actually been in trouble, to Carter's knowledge, but he had pretty thoughts about the situation, and seemed to fantasize about it often. 'For instance, if I were in the milk can, and I became stuck, with my dying breath, I would think of my mother. And Bess, of course. Or if I were buried alive,' continuing, eyes wide like describing paradise.

Now, his head feeling uncomfortably light, nothing left to lose, Carter thought of his loved ones. His dead wife. He felt guilt. He felt like a failure. He thought of his animals, whom he loved, and yet having Baby and Tug in his mind simply made him realize how he would miss them. He imagined his mother and father and James standing on the dockside, waving to him broadly, loving him from a distance, the way you love an odd pet, and he choked. His knees gave way. He brought his hands against his face, water pouring all around him, a mess, and lonely. *Hello, folks, hello, James.* Which, after a heartbeat, became *Good-bye.* The human heart was a terrible thing. His family would mourn him, and then they would survive. The essential resilience of human nature made his throat contract. Here, in his horrible crate, he admitted something he hadn't before: he no longer mourned Sarah. But he just couldn't bear to be one of the ones who forgot.

And then he said, 'I am *not* fine. I'm a goddamned *wreck*,' with a burst of laughter that became tears, saltwater joining saltwater. The crate shook, and water rushed into his face until he didn't care.

He almost gulped down the sea that was now rising over his chin. There was a continuous grinding noise outside, an engine close by, a seafaring vessel that made the waters vibrate. Then he thought: *Phoebe.*

It surprised him so much he tossed his head back from the water, banging it against the crate with a curse. He rubbed his head. Phoebe, with whom he'd spent a few quiet hours, and that was all. She knew him. Somehow. And wasn't that quite marvelous? He didn't know her yet, as much as he felt her. He guessed she, too, would survive if he died. But the thought did not weaken him. It lit a candle somewhere in a distant corridor. He couldn't stand forcing her to be resilient.

When had that engine become so cripplingly loud? The crate bumped against something, stalled there. Carter winced, covered his ears. There was a small pocket of exhausted air left. *Phoebe*, he thought again. And the word was enough. He inhaled slowly, as if sucking in only the oxygen, and held on to it, and dipped below the surface. He slid to the end of the crate, put himself squarely in place, feet underwater, ready to push, his shoulder, his back, his upper thighs burning, ready. All he needed to do was force his body to stand straight, and the crate would burst.

Hollis returned in the truck and brought an armload of crowbars with him. Samuelson directed him to dump them on the dock. He'd been silent the past few moments, as the distant boat was now much closer, its bow still dead-on. He extinguished his pipe.

The others were quiet, too, until O'Brien said, 'There's a hundred places for that boat to dock. You don't think . . .'

Balls of his feet against the planks, back ready to topple temple columns, Carter didn't count off as he held his breath, there was no point, for he didn't need to know when his limit was approaching. Humming in his ears, the crate shaking, the last pocket of air was gone in a flash, fully consumed by the bay, no time to think about that, his heels were made of iron, his back and shoulders made a fine jack for which nails and boards were no match, he could hear Ledocq telling him to move it, and James, who stood with Tom, and even Tom was cheering him, C'mon, get those bastards, they're annoying me, and there was Borax telling him to give it the old heave-ho, the strain on his thighs was unspeakable, that sound, was that nails beginning to give way, his head was about to burst, he went beyond his limits, to where he smelled gunpowder, and saw a crowd of thousands out there in the Palace, some worried, others chanting 'push push push,' and beside him, quietly, there was a woman. She was beautiful.

I'm sorry you've been hurt. She touched his scar. *Breathe with me.*

He said something, he didn't even know what, and with a strength he didn't actually possess he pushed. There was a horrible wrenching sound.

Chapter 23

With the rain pounding down on the windows of the great Wheeler Hall, Ledocq pointed at a mass of cotton sheets covering a table at the front of the room. 'There is what you call tons of ponderous impedimenta.' He scratched his beard. 'He has something there. I wonder if it's a working system, or a mock-up.' Under the clock, which showed 5:05, was a set of chalkboards, also covered with cloth. A girl came from the wings, looked at the clock, and disappeared back into the wings. She reappeared with a pitcher of water and a glass, which she put on a table by the podium.

'This is a little bit exciting,' Tom allowed. The girl stood beside the chalkboards, holding a long pole to pull the cloth away when cued to do so.

A boy joined her, and they quietly exchanged words. He wore a white laboratory jacket, slightly too big for him. He reached for a pair of rimless spectacles and slid them onto his nose. He walked to the center of the lecture area and coughed into his fist.

'Hello,' he said, sounding exactly seventeen years old.

'Oh, my Lord,' Tom whispered. 'Is that him?'

'Thank you all for coming. My name is Philo Farnsworth.' He was not helped by this fact. In the crowd, neighbor turned to neighbor, checking to see if they had all heard correctly.

He rocked from leg to leg. 'Yes, I know,' he said. 'I apologize for being so young, it's my fault for being born so recently.' He said this in a rush, and listened carefully.

Tom leaned in toward James's ear. 'That was his little joke.'

'Yes, I know. *Shhh.*'

Farnsworth glanced around gravely. 'Let's start with something we can agree on. Pem, board one, please?'

Using her pole, Pem bared the lower left-hand chalkboard, which had a drawing of a circle; within it, a spiral of diminishing holes, like on an abalone shell. At once, twenty people in the audience groaned; these were the scientists.

'The Nipkow disk,' Farnsworth pointed at it. He spoke, but it was hard to hear him, as several of RCA's men were packing up their notes. The rest of the crowd had no idea what was going on. The Nipkow disk was the basis of mechanical television, an arcane idea that had been investigated by John Logie Baird of England. No matter how huge the disk or small the screen, the only images that appeared were blurry silhouettes. Farnsworth looked at them, and said, almost trilling, 'All I'm going to say about that idea is it isn't mine. Really, honest. I'm not trying to sell you mechanical television.' He turned to Pem. 'The only way to go is electronic. Board two, please.'

When this board was uncovered, it was half-filled with diagrams and equations. 'Twelve years ago,' Farnsworth said, 'Swinton said something interesting, that if you put together a mosaic of cubes of rubidium, you could turn light into electric current, and, well, he's right, and we know that because of Zworykin.' He pointed at a diagram, seven or eight improbable geometric shapes connected with squiggly lines. This made James squint, for he had no idea what it was, but it did hold Ledocq's attention. Farnsworth continued, 'So Zworykin, he said, well, let's put a photoelectric surface, like this, on a plate, and then, here, a layer of aluminum oxide, like so, for insulation. So the light takes away these electrons and leaves positively charged atoms, see they still have their protons here, and that made sense to me, but I was thinking that even if he had a million, say, yeah, a million potassium hydride droplets, and each of those droplets electrically separate so the charge wouldn't dissipate, see, even if he did that, it just wouldn't do the job.'

'And why is that?'

Philo had been speaking with increasing conviction, and the interruption seemed to knock him offtrack. He searched the auditorium until he saw a hand waving. It belonged to RCA's West Coast laboratory chief, who looked as if he'd eaten a bad sandwich for lunch. Philo said, 'You aren't Dr Zworykin, are you?' which caused a small ripple of laughter.

'No, I'm Dr Talbot. I'm familiar with his work.'

Philo went back to his chalkboard and pointed. 'Here's his

mechanical scanner and his cathode ray tube. And the beam goes here, on a fluorescent screen, I'm guessing. I mean, gosh, he hasn't published anything about it, but it has to be that way, and the idea is, the image would be reproduced there. Like I said, maybe that works. Sir, maybe, but—'

'What do *you* suggest?' Dr Talbot accompanied that 'you' with a grand spread of his palms.

Philo took a drink of water, red patches blossoming on his cheeks.

'Or hadn't you thought of that,' Dr Talbot continued.

'Okay, all righty.' He seemed to be gathering up his nerves. 'Board three, Pem.' Pem pulled up the cloth and revealed a fresh chalk-board, this one tightly packed with small diagrams of triangular and oblong shapes, surmounted with function and integral signs, Greek letters, and scientific symbols.

All around the room, men who had notepads out froze. What was this mishmash? Suddenly, Philo began to speak, and as he did so, he gestured at the board precisely, but he never took his eyes off Talbot. 'It's called an anode finger. It has a small aperture and the electrical image formed on the cathode end is emitted here and sent across the tube, toward the anode. Erase, please.'

Pem erased it.

'Hey!' someone called out involuntarily.

'I'm sorry,' Farnsworth said. 'I'm sure you all understand.' He pointed to another diagram and spoke clearly, enunciating each word, enjoying the way it sounded, but also quickly, like there were even better things to come. 'The magnetic coils here move the elec-tric image over the anode finger's aperture, left to right, line by line, so a picture forms just like the original source image. Erase, please.'

Pem erased this diagram, too, to the sound of a dozen pencils slamming against desks. Talbot looked at H. J. Peterson, the War Department's top electronics man, who also shook his head. Neither of them had gotten it.

Farnsworth continued, his voice seeming smoother, more controlled, with each word. 'The output current creates a corre-sponding current in another cathode ray tube, which creates an electron beam that causes a fluorescent surface on the end of the tube to glow. Erase, please.'

The board was now blank, dripping wet where Pem had erased it especially hard. She looked out into the audience with a smile that looked ready to burst, as she watched all the heads shaking, beards being pulled, frustrated white-jacket sleeves moving hopelessly along graph paper.

'Questions?' Philo asked. Unlike Pem, he seemed to take no pleasure in his audience's reaction. Instead, he was ready to continue his fight. He recognized an enemy in Dr Talbot and knew, simply knew with the objectivity that made him a scientist, he could convert the man to his way of thinking.

For much of the room, there was disbelief, of course, but overall an air of suspended judgment. They were businessmen, mostly, and until they saw something with their own eyes all they had to go on was how well Farnsworth handled himself against an informed heckler. So they welcomed Talbot clearing his throat.

'What about magnetic focusing?' Talbot fired back. 'Signal amplification?'

'Well, at first we thought we could use an Audion tube, or of course, a series to amplify the signal—'

'That would motorboat the whole system until it was out of control!'

'You're right! You're absolutely right! So we built what I call a tetrode, a shielded grid tube, and then I switched from potassium to cesium oxide.'

'You haven't explained to me the focusing.'

'We use willemite – zinc silicate – as a photoelectric surface, as a coating for a tube, and bombard it with an oscillating beam of electrons from an electron gun.'

'That can't function?' Talbot spat, but with the slightest inflection in his voice.

'We're working on it. And we're working on—'

'Synchronizing the scanning coils?'

'Precisely.'

Talbot folded his arms, unconvinced. Philo touched the board Pem had erased and found it just dry enough to draw on.

He was doing a sketch of his Multipactor tube, and answering more questions from Talbot, when he sensed that he was losing his audience. He wasn't sure why – wasn't he being informative enough?

Finally he heard someone yell, 'Hey, Farnsworth, when are we going to see some money in this?'

James hung his head, for it had of course been an impatient Tom yelling this.

Chalk between his thumb and forefinger, Philo asked, 'Is five minutes good?'

Some laughter, then rustling as the attendees struggled to become comfortable. The Spider, for the tenth time, looked at his contact to see if he could shoot Farnsworth yet, but he received a stern shake of the head. So he sank down into his chair, sulking.

'I had the idea for electronic television a long time ago. I was thirteen, and I was plowing a field, and I looked back at the furrows, and I thought, *Gee, if I could make electrons behave that way magnetically, that would be something.* So I bought most of the material I needed to make a working system, and made everything else, but what completely defeated me was the tube. All I needed was an optically clear Pyrex vacuum tube, with one end completely flat.'

This caused those in the white coats to snicker, some of them sounding nasty, but most compassionate, as this was like admitting all you needed to do was reverse Niagara Falls.

Someone, not Talbot, yelled out, 'That's impossible.'

'They told us that, too,' Farnsworth said in a conversational tone, 'but we needed it, so we just went ahead and made it. Look.' He reached behind the podium and pulled out exactly what he was talking about: a vacuum tube with a flat end.

There were gasps everywhere. Even Ledocq gasped.

'What?' asked James.

'How did he do that?'

'Do you smell a scam?' James whispered.

'No. How did he do that?' he repeated, leaning forward and putting his chin on his fists.

At the front of the room, Philo and Pem worked together to uncover their bulky apparatus. Philo spoke nonstop, listing off the components without giving away enough detail for someone else to copy him. He mentioned nichrome wire, radio tubes, resistors, transformers, the crystal that provided polarized light. He had used a manually operated coil-winding machine, and shellac, and heavy paper strips.

Beside the banks of equipment was a nickel-alloy Kerr light, which he tilted backward, uncapping a small bottle over it. 'The slightest humidity causes this to smoke,' he explained, using an eyedropper to coat the surface. 'So this is 240-proof alcohol.'

A voice from the audience, 'Is that registered?'

'Yes,' he said without smiling, 'I certainly am not going to violate the Volstead Act. Even for science.'

His calm, humorless response began to tilt the scales for Farnsworth. It struck the literal-minded financiers that once the equipment was unveiled, they would perhaps see something interesting. As Philo checked all the connections, he flicked on switches to the condensers, and remarked so that only Pem could hear that he was fairly sure the fuses on the university could handle the power his television would draw. 'There's a small possibility that this could go up in flames,' he whispered.

'Yes,' she smiled, 'I guess maybe you could be a complete charlatan.'

He smiled at her. He touched her on the wrist. It was a sweet gesture, one even the Spider had trouble hating, but hate it he did. He touched the butt of his pistol.

Philo turned the wooden cabinet that held the body of his working television box toward the audience. It was a flat-matte white.

'This will take several seconds to warm up,' he announced. 'Can we turn off the lights?'

This command caused the Spider to sit upright, as he could no longer see his contact, or his target. His fingers closed around the handle of the pistol, in its leather holster.

With the lights out, the audience rustled and adjusted. Ledocq closed his eyes. James listened to the sound of rain pelleting against the skylights far above. He called out, 'Mr Farnsworth?'

'Yes?'

'What uses do you project for television?'

'Yes, good question.' His voice came through the darkened auditorium while the screen began to turn a deep blue. 'First and foremost, it will be a medium of education. I suppose it could be used for entertainment, as well, but primarily, it will bring the world closer together, I believe.'

'Thank you,' James said, and sat back.

No one asked further questions as the screen glowed brighter, and when Philo spoke again, James anticipated he would describe what they were going to see. He was wrong. Perhaps it was the dark, and the sound of rain, and the attendant feeling of safety, or perhaps the excitement of having more than a hundred people hear for the first time what he had only hinted to President Harding, but Philo continued answering the question in a way he hadn't intended on revealing. 'It will end war.' He said this shyly. It was as if he hadn't spoken at all until a phantom voice from the front said, coarsely, 'Say that again.'

Philo squinted. 'Did someone just ask me to repeat that?'

'Yes,' said the Spider, who couldn't believe his ears.

'This is about keeping world peace. Forever. We set up captive balloons to carry the transmission signals around the globe,' he said with conviction. 'And if someone in Berkeley, California, could sit in his house and see a man from Berlin, Germany, and how he eats his breakfast,' he swallowed, 'how could they kill each other, then?'

There was no direct response, just an elaborate, embarrassed silence, as if he'd cut his promising presentation short to give a speech on the virtues of temperance. Ledocq leaned over to James. 'It's becoming clear,' he hissed.

'How much will you charge licensees to use it?' Someone else yelled out.

'Oh, that's the beauty of it. It's going to be free.'

Had there been crickets in the auditorium, crickets would have been heard. 'Did you say *free*?'

'Oh, yes. Yes. I'm not going to sell television. Something like this should be given away, like schooling.'

The sounds of a hundred necks rubbing against a hundred collars as people turned to their neighbors to check if they'd heard correctly. 'But if you're not selling it '

'It should be in the public domain. I'm asking for your help, so corporations can split the cost of development. It will be a boon—' he hesitated.

The room found its voice then, a discontented rumble that seemed to build to laughter. James could hear the words *charity case* echoing around.

'Clearer and clearer,' Ledocq said into James's ear. James nodded.

An idealist with a device that he believed could end war? One that he wouldn't sell, but would only give away? Reason enough to kill him. However, ten rows ahead, the Spider, who was also an idealist, and intelligent, had mentally unloaded the bullets from his revolver. He began to look with awful eyes for his contact, with whom he wished to have a violent quarrel.

'People will settle their differences around a conference table instead of—' And then Philo heard gasps. He turned around and saw the television screen, where the first image he'd prepared, the horse, was frozen. He hadn't been able to get a moving image since the evening with Pem, the gadget was still that finicky, but still, a horse that didn't move was at least something. He hadn't finished his sentence, but no one asked him to continue.

He wondered if that was because they all were ready to leave, but as he surveyed the crowd, he began to feel something prickly and wonderful happening to his skin. Horripilation. The mood had shifted, just like that, to sheer awe.

But was that enough to get funding? Was the beauty of television such that it could make capitalists want to help the public and the poor? He looked at the audience, row after row of dark shapes bathed in a blue light. They were a group of kin in a cave around something that glowed warm while, outside, the storm beat down like kettledrums. He remembered Pem saying she was so happy she wanted to stop time, and how he'd foolishly given her all the reasons you couldn't do that. Now he knew what she meant.

Two seconds, three seconds.

He had a good gag prepared precisely for the type of man who'd asked when they would see money in all this. It was a slide with a picture of a dollar bill.

'Pem,' he said. He decided to introduce her, 'Pem is Mrs Farnsworth. Pem, would you change the image, please?'

Five seconds, six.

Off came the horse. The screen went white.

'Philo, is this—' she said, then 'Oh!'

He turned, feeling annoyed that he might miss the audience's reaction to the next slide. He saw an arc, a jagged blue arc of electricity over the anode finger, that wasn't supposed to happen, and a flash so bright it turned everything in Philo's view black and white. Pem contorted, her hair on end. Then spots before his eyes. A heavy thump, like a flour sack hitting the floor. His eyes smarted. It had gone as fast as the flash of a photographer's lightbulb, and it left a similar smell of ignited resins. His television apparatus was on fire.

'Pem?'

And now everything went so slowly he wondered if he were dreaming. Shouts. His eyes dazzled, he felt around the floor in perfect blackness for his wife.

'Pem?'

That awful smell of things burning, he looked on the tabletop to confirm it was only his invention, then back to the floor, the lights went on. People rushed up to help him.

'Put out the fire,' someone yelled, and someone else was reaching for the pitcher of water. Philo was crouched over Pem, patting her hand. She was looking at him through singed eyebrows, before he realized he had to turn and scream, 'No!'

But it was too late. Whoever it was meant well, pouring the water on the flames, but since they were fed by potassium and sodium, what had been a small sizzle of wires and rubber roared into a conflagration that consumed every scrap of metal, every hand-wound coil, and forced people to leap backward as others, thinking quickly, used the cotton sheets to bat at the showers of sparks. A faint popping sound, then the collapse of broken glass as the vacuum tube went out. Impossible to build, and now it was gone.

More things happened to him in those early minutes – people fetching help, a blanket covering Pem, anonymous trouser legs surrounding him, awkward stares, whispers. He hardly noticed. Instead, one image was forever etched into his memory: the flash, with Pem in agony. He had wanted time to stop, and there it was.

In all, Philo's television had been demonstrated for eight seconds, and burned for thirty.

He huddled by his fallen wife.

Finally, her lips moved. 'Philo,' she said silently. He nodded. He held her hand. And he sat like that, legs folded under himself, returning the feeble squeezes she gave with her hand, barely even blinking himself, until the ambulance came.

Chapter 24

Hollis, O'Brien, and Stutz were singing a different kind of harmony now, all of them yelling frantically, jumping and waving at the boat that was settling into the berth, regardless of their screaming, as if it belonged there. Samuelson, however, stood back – Carter was either going to drown or be crushed to death – he couldn't decide whether it mattered which way he went. The tuna boat, as it approached, slowed, and two mates jumped off its sides, ropes in hand.

'Back off!' O'Brien yelled.

'You back off, chum!' returned one of the fishermen.

As the boat continued to ease inward, the crate bounced off its bow and then rolled along its side, corners catching as it spun lazily toward the starboard side.

'There's a man in the crate!' Stutz yelled.

'Eh, piss off,' said a sailor.

The agents gathered together, Hollis carrying crowbars in his arms, all of them watching helplessly as the crate was scraped between the concrete pilings and the tuna boat's hull. It was like a pair of jaws coming down on a peanut shell. The crate burst, sending up splinters and beads of water.

'No!' Stutz yelled.

'Did he get out?' O'Brien craned his neck.

Samuelson shook his head, curiously pleased, watching air bubbles and movement where the crate had been, then he said, 'He's right there,' and pointed, heart thumping, to something drifting up to the surface.

It was the mail sack, a hump of air making it float like a dead jellyfish. Samuelson couldn't tell if Carter were still in it, and if so, if he were alive. The boat's crew had unloaded their haul, using the port side, so the agents were unmolested as they gathered around the sack.

Hollis had the idea of poking it with a crowbar, but the dock was a good ten feet above the water's surface. There was a rope ladder, though.

'Go check,' Samuelson directed.

The rain continued, and Hollis looked at the sack, the rope ladder, and his still-dry group leader, for just long enough to appear sullen. He stepped off the side of the dock, found the upper rungs of the ladder, and began to descend toward the white canvas. He had the crowbar tucked under his belt.

The three men remaining on the dock crouched carefully, as the planks felt dangerous and wobbly. In addition to the deliberately missing slats, some were broken or ready to yield; when Oakland successfully collected port fees, they never wasted money on upkeep.

Hollis went down to the end of the ladder. The sack was too far away to touch. He pulled the crowbar from his belt.

Above, Samuelson yelled, 'What do you see, Hollis?'

'I don't see anything down here. I'm going to see if I can get it.'

'Hollis?' The three men were all crowded together, shoulder to shoulder, trying to see over the edge of the dock. A gust of wind made Samuelson's hand clench around the shaft of his umbrella.

'Hollis, where are you?' O'Brien sounded annoyed.

'Hey, get off,' Stutz said faintly, further complaint dying on his lips as he realized none of his companions had touched him. His gaze traveled from the edge of the dock to his shoe, where he saw unlikely movement: a hand between the dock slats. 'Hey!' He leapt backward, constricted by something, and in a blind panic leaped again, landing on his tailbone and bowling over O'Brien, whom he hadn't touched.

He saw fat water droplets gathering on the links that cuffed his right leg to O'Brien's left.

'Sam!' he yelled, pointing. O'Brien was struggling upright and Stutz, too, hurried to his feet. Stutz pointed at the cuffs in a panic, 'I saw a hand! I saw a hand!'

And, indeed, Carter was just below them, clinging to the dock's rotting underside, on the kneebrace where the wooden joints came together. His clothes were ruined with mud and bay dreck. He had kicked out the underside of the crate seconds before it was crushed, and, propelled past a point where he could count the ways in which he hurt, he moved primally now, feeling the anger he had never in his life followed as far as he could.

He'd never punched anyone in his life. His hands were too valuable for that. But now he wanted to hit them all, hit them hard. He expected them to run, which they did, but their panic was so complete they wasted several seconds choosing a direction, and Carter saw the chain above him flashing within reach. If he grabbed it, he could cuff it to one of the iron rings sticking out from the dock itself. With them held still, he would beat them senseless using whatever was handy.

He grabbed the chain and jumped off his shelf so his full weight brought the links down with him, like a conductor signaling a freight train's full stop; above him his plan went awry immediately, for Stutz and O'Brien crashed against each other, and then the plank beneath them gave way and they fell through the dock.

Carter let out a gargling sound as the chain flew from his hands, and he fell backward into the water again and disappeared almost without leaving a ripple. The men who were cuffed together had the misfortune of falling several feet apart, among broken lumber and nails, on either side of a cross-beam that was unusually sturdy, and so their bodies no longer fell *down* but swung *inward* in an arc terminating when the backs of their skulls collided.

Samuelson walked backward two steps from the huge gash where his men had been pulled through. Walking backward was a terrible idea, as the magician could drop him, so he turned around and walked into the rain, toward the truck. He was alone. Hollis? Under the pier somewhere. The wind had kicked up, so he brought his umbrella down. This obscured his vision, which seemed like another bad idea, so he brought it back up again, behind him, and kept walking stubbornly over the gaps between planks. He expected hands to come out, or Carter to leap over the side, or to come up behind him, so as he walked he made full 360-degree twirls.

The umbrella was holding him back. He dropped it and ran, batting his pockets for the truck keys. He was just steps away from where Hollis had parked it. Missing Hollis. Who had the keys.

So he reached for his holster at the same time that he saw something drop behind the truck, landing with a clatter. Crowbar. His fingers made it to the leather strap buttoned over his pistol butt. Then he was tapped on the shoulder. He turned, drawing his gun, and something huge flared in his face. His umbrella, unfolding, made him stumble and, more quickly than Samuelson's eye could follow, the umbrella retracted, showing off Carter, who ran the hook end down his gun arm like scraping ice off a window. The gun dropped to the dock, clattered across a plank, then into the bay. Samuelson looked up as the umbrella handle swung into his face.

Metallic sounds in his ears as he was clouted. He noticed Carter's bare feet were still cuffed so he swung a fist to make him step back or duck or go off-balance. But Carter stepped inward, under his arm, and then he was behind him, where he quickly peeled Samuelson's jacket down off the shoulders, pinning his arms, and ripped open his vest so the buttons popped off. He knotted the vest over the now-reversed jacket before the last button had bounced into the water. A makeshift straitjacket. Samuelson couldn't move his arms. He fell over.

From the horizontal position, Samuelson's world became more disappointing by the minute. First, Carter took a single step so that his feet were on opposite sides of his neck, bringing the ankle chain flush to his trachea. Samuelson twisted helplessly, seeing out of the corner of his eye a flashing movement – Hollis, now on the dock. He was saved!

Hollis crouched by the edge of the dock, seemingly torn between impulses. Carter watched him impassively, shifting his weight to better choke his victim.

'Yes?' he finally asked.

Hollis looked at Carter. He looked at Samuelson. He ran. He ran to the truck, and as Samuelson began to pass out, his penultimate sight was the bread truck stripping gears to get away.

The final sight was Carter bending over to his wayward watch pocket, then straightening. 'What have we here?' he asked, holding the ivory skull between his finger tips. Then Samuelson blacked out.

'Agent Samuelson.'

The rain was steady and warm; on a more chipper sort of day, it would be wonderful to walk in. But Samuelson wasn't able to go anywhere. He was reclining on a pile of rubber tires through which heavy ropes were wound. His arms, which he couldn't quite see, were secured to something behind his head. He could move his legs a little, but when he did so, they made clanking noises. Somewhere, muffled, echoing, he heard someone shouting. Stutz?

To his left, sitting on a weathered bollard that looked like a mushroom cap, was Carter. His face was cut, and rainwater streamed from the black hair plastered to his head, down his torn shirt, past his trousers, which had gaping holes in them. His legs were crossed so that one bare ankle touched the opposite knee. Somehow, he managed to keep a cigarette going in the rain.

'What are you doing?' Samuelson heard himself ask.

'I'm having the time of my life.' He French-inhaled smoke and blew rings in between raindrops. 'Look over your head. Ah, my mistake – you can't. Listen, then. Your arms are manacled to a bollard just like the one I'm sitting on.' He paused. Then, using his cigarette to get Samuelson's attention, he directed him to look just beyond his wingtips. There was an incredible tangle of chains and ropes, and at the edge of the dock were three anchors: two Danforths, the other a close-stowing model made for larger vessels. Samuelson recognized them from his childhood, when he'd crewed on his father's boat.

Cocking his head to listen to vague shouts – O'Brien this time – Carter addressed Samuelson. 'Your friends are trapped under the dock, by the way. I had an extra pair of cuffs, and I took some mooring swivels from that ferry boat, and – listen, do you know three-card monte? It's also called "find the lady."'

Samuelson, bewildered, made no motions at all.

'You have three blind cards, and one of them is the right one. It's a sucker's game. Anyway, one of those anchors is secured to the pair of cuffs that's around your ankles. The other two are not. Are you following me?'

'I'm not telling you anything. The Service has a code—'

'That's fine,' Carter interrupted. 'I understand codes.' It was impossible to read his blue eyes. They seemed as quiet as Sunday streets. 'I'm going to drop each of these anchors one by one off the dock. I don't know what's going to happen when the one attached to you goes over. If you weren't also manacled to the dock, you'd simply be pulled under and drown, but since you *are* manacled to the dock—'

'I told you, I'm not telling you anything.'

'Either the anchor will rip your hipbones and shoulders out of their sockets, or you'll actually be torn in half.' He took another drag on his cigarette. 'I actually *have* seen a man torn in half before, in India. They used elephants. So,' he patted Samuelson's shoulder and asked, conversationally, 'which anchor do you pick first?'

In the distance, O'Brien was bellowing for help.

'I'm a Secret Service agent,' Samuelson said. 'You can't get away with this.'

'How about the Danforth that's on the left?' Carter stood and stretched his legs. He yawned widely and ambled to the edge of the dock. Samuelson watched him, but also watched to his left and his right. There was a ferry boat. Someone would see, eventually. And if there were three anchors, of course Carter would knock the first two off the dock before choosing the one actually connected to his legs. There would be time for someone to see them. Samuelson knew this, and clung to it.

Carter's palms were both on the Danforth. He looked over his shoulder at Samuelson. 'By the way, I didn't want to cheat. So I mixed all those chains and ropes quite a bit, and I have no idea which one of these is connected to you.'

'What?'

'Allez-oop!' he cried, and sent the Danforth over the side, thirty feet of wide-gauge chain snaking with it.

Samuelson made an inarticulate cry as something snapped against his legs, but it was just the end of the chain passing him by on its way into the bay.

Carter looked over the edge. 'That was very interesting. Would you like to play again?'

'We were only told to detain you! That's all I know!'

Carter squatted next to Samuelson. 'Along with the keys to the cuffs, and your identification and so forth, you had notes in your pocket. Detain me at such and such a time. Keep me off the field forever, which isn't so very cryptic. You also had twelve dollars in your wallet. Which anchor shall I throw over next?'

'I don't!' It sounded like a full sentence to Samuelson; he'd meant it as such, but he realized it made little sense. 'What do you want?'

'Honestly, what I want is to throw the remaining anchors over

395

the side and see what happens. Why did you put me in the bay, you round-heeled ham-and-egger?'

'You're a magician.'

'I'm a magician,' he replied blankly.

'I figured it served you right.'

'You figured . . .' he hesitated. 'You really thought that?'

'I figured you'd either get out or you wouldn't, and it would serve you right.'

'For what?' He looked disarmed, and newly hurt.

Samuelson blinked. He didn't know how to explain what had seemed so obvious just hours ago. Shuffle the deck yourself. See that this spirit cabinet is totally normal and free of wires or platforms. How the magician dared the audience to find a way he couldn't trick them. Samuelson simply thought every magician he'd ever seen had been antagonistic, daring – *begging* – to be shown up.

Finally, Carter asked, 'Which one of you drugged me?'

He had no trouble giving this information up. 'Stutz.'

'The one who ran way?'

'No. That was Hollis,' a fact that he also felt fine revealing. When he saw Hollis again, he was going to thrash him.

'Hmm. So Stutz is one of the two hanging down there?'

'Stutz is . . . I shouldn't say what he is. He stabbed you with a needle. That's not protocol.' Samuelson bit down on his lips, looking to Carter for some sign of understanding.

'He's a pervert. Wonderful.' In a perfect world, Carter would have worked suitable revenge on him, but as he realized what sort of men he was up against his passion for this sort of thing was draining away. Still, he wasn't done.

'Hey!' The voice came from the left, and above. The deck of the ferryboat. In yellow slicker and peaked hat, it was the ship's captain.

'Help me!' Samuelson cried. 'I'm a federal agent—'

Carter shielded his face from the rain. 'Is that Captain Willow?'

'Charlie Carter!' Said with delight. 'How are you?'

'Tremendous.'

'Good!'

'Actually, I'm ravenous, too. I could eat a horse.'

'This man is assaulting a federal agent,' Samuelson cried. 'Call the police immediately.'

Captain Willow folded his arms. 'Is that so?'

'Yes!'

He chuckled and slapped the rail with his fingertips. 'That's awful. Rehearsing one of your magic acts, Charlie?'

'No,' Carter replied blandly. 'He's telling the truth.'

The Captain wagged his finger at Carter. 'Always pulling my good leg. Send me and the missus tickets when your show goes up. I'll keep the passengers away.' And then he was gone.

Samuelson looked at the now-empty deck like he'd missed the last train home.

'Excuse me,' Carter said, leaving Samuelson's side. He approached the edge of the dock a second time, and without fanfare, shoved the other Danforth off the dock.

Samuelson screamed, retracting into a ball as yards of chain slithered around him, followed by a soft splash.

He was intact.

Carter was again leaning into his face. 'I'm sorry for deceiving you, Samuelson. It's in my blood. I knew all along which one was tied to you, so let's cut to the chase. There was a cigar tube in my pocket. Where is it?'

'I—' Carter's hand went over his mouth.

'The first thing you want to tell me is "I don't know what you're talking about." Let's you and I pretend you've said that already. You've said it several times, with great sincerity. If you stick with that story, I will kick that last anchor off the dock and *boldly*. Do you follow?'

Samuelson nodded. Carter took his hand away. Several times, Samuelson made as if to speak, and his eyes darted away, half-focused, like he was recalling all the steps in assembling a machine gun.

'All right. Okay. Everything in your pocket,' he said carefully, 'was in the truck.'

'So Agent Hollis has it?'

'That makes sense.' He broke into a relieved smile, as if now that he and Carter had put this puzzle together, they could be friends. And when Carter joined in, making a grin himself, Samuelson relaxed.

'I suppose I should let you go then. There's just one problem,' he said, producing the ivory skull with '322' on its crown. 'And this would be it.' He made it vanish. Then reappear. Then vanish. 'I'm just trying to determine what exactly this signifies.'

'It's a good luck charm.'

'And how has it been working for you, then?'

Samuelson stared at it. There were levels, and levels, to which he was a loyal man. The skull, and all it represented, was something so vital to him, he actually *would* die before he gave anything up to Carter. He braced himself.

Carter looked upward, and intoned, '*Wer war der Thor, wer Weiser, Bettler oder Kaiser?*'

Samuelson's heart nearly burst from his chest. He finished: '*Ob Arm, ob Reich, im Tode gleich.*' He laughed. He couldn't stop, the relief actually made him dizzy. 'You're a bonesman!'

'Lodge Room 322,' Carter whispered, and as if painting the image before him, he gestured, 'here's the slab, with the coxcomb and bells, and the beggar's scrip, and the crown, and the four old human skulls. Wonderful room,' he said.

'The best days of my life,' Samuelson replied, desperate to be released.

'All that time at college, learning about business and wealth and such,' he added.

'Yes. Yes!'

'Too bad the room doesn't exist.' Carter arched his eyebrows and tossed the skull up, caught it.

'It – what?'

Carter's eyes were flat – endlessly blue, like the horizon.

'That's just . . . nonsense.' But Samuelson could barely commit to this last word.

'You know my brother went to Yale.' Sounding kind, Carter explained, 'This is called a numbskull. Bonesmen are instructed to occasionally lose them in poker games or to use them to pay off debts to men who always wanted to join, but whose character didn't quite make the cut.'

'But—'

'So your quadmate, or someone, lost this to you, made a big deal over it, and taught you that German poem, which is also hogwash if you think about it, as the password. You could pretend you belonged.'

'But,' Samuelson looked quite miserable now. In a child's voice, he asked, 'But are you a bonesman?'

'Actually I didn't go to college. But I *was* in vaudeville.' And then, languidly, he kicked the shaft of the last anchor.

'No!' Samuelson shrieked. The remaining chains shot over the side, scuttling, striking his legs as they went. 'No!' he cried again, braced for a crippling jolt that never came.

He opened his eyes. He was still on the dock. Nothing had happened to him. None of the anchors had actually been attached. It was all a trick. Though he tried to laugh derisively, it came out instead as tears.

Carter stepped away, limping, and then impulsively turned. He crouched down and held Samuelson's head between his hands. Samuelson looked up miserably into a face that was frighteningly merry to its core.

'Thank you,' Carter whispered. He kissed Samuelson on the forehead, making a theatrical smacking noise. 'Really, this has been the time of my life. Thank you.'

Carter took one last glance at the caved-in dock, from which came weak and diminishing calls for help. And at the soggy man he'd lashed to a bollard. He accounted for himself, bruised, cut, torn, robbed of his tools, his shoes, and the cigar tube.

He limped down the thoroughfare beside the docks. In a few minutes, the pain from his cuts and bruises would catch up with him, as would his conscience. Until then, he wanted pie, and to kiss Phoebe Kyle, and he wanted television and a thousand other new illusions, and great piles of cash, and new enemies to face. In short, some new pipeline of desire had opened in him, and he wanted *more*.

There was a taxistand where the port met the city streets. Though a line of people was waiting, they parted to make way for this bleeding, crazed-looking man. He was smiling and then scowling as his mind skipped from moment to moment. He had never thought of life as a scorecard of assets and debits, but today – having kissed a girl, ridden a motorcycle, shown up a snotty Yale boy and his crew, and purchased a fine guillotine, but also having been knocked unconscious, been put on a budget, and having lost the plans to television – he began to see the point.

There was so much life here in the spirit world. One could hardly keep track. He reached into his pockets and found the numbskull, which he would eventually return to James – it would bring back old, amusing times for him and Tom. He also located cash for a taxicab. When he recovered his expense journal, he would write 'Rec'd from Agent Samuelson, *twelve dollars*' in the asset column, which pleased him to no end.

He looked toward the city of Oakland, to what he could see of the deepening orange skyline, from the new homes at Adams Point to the ferryboats, from the dark lake – there, the necklace of lights flicked on, just now! – to the underfed downtown, with its empty offices and buildings constructed awkwardly and cheaply due to graft and ambition. As a taxi arrived for him, he regarded the tall and straight Tribune Tower, pointed at it, made a dirigible in his mind, and placed it there.

♣ ♦ ♥ ♠

Across the bay, the rain caught San Francisco – which pretended it had no rain except when picturesque – by surprise. At the end of the workday, people bought the morning *Examiner* only for its ability to keep away the wetness.

Griffin stood on the steps of the public library, which had closed moments before he got there. Finally, Olive White – who had a mauve umbrella today, one that matched her galoshes – came out. She was, to say the least, stunned to see him.

'Mr Griffin, you're soaked through.'

'It's nothing. Look, Olive, I've been assigned to Albuquerque. I have to leave right now.'

'Oh, Mr Griffin!' She covered her mouth as if he'd said he'd been shot.

'No, it's okay. But I have something I need to keep researching, and I don't know if I can do it from there. If—'

'Anything you say. Anything.'

He unwrapped the wine bottle and showed it to her. She held it to the rainy afternoon sky, and he looked up and down the street – no one seemed to be watching them.

'I've never seen this brand before,' adding, as she colored, 'I have a prescription from my doctor for my high blood—'

'Okay, yeah, look, just keep your eyes open. If you see anything like this, let me know.'

'May I keep the bottle?'

'Evidence. Sorry.'

'I wish I could commit this label to memory. I'd sketch it if that were possible, but . . . it's so odd.'

The graphic to which she alluded was almost impossible to describe or reproduce; a clever bootlegger always wanted such a logo. This one was as follows:

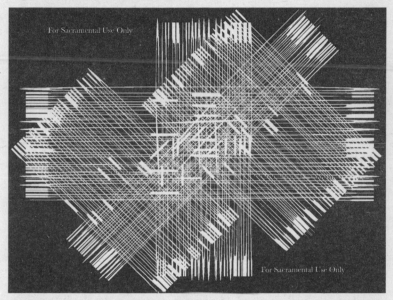

Finally, Griffin had to leave. He put the bottle back in his satchel. He offered Olive his hand, and she shook it. She didn't seem to want to let go, and when she spoke, it was to ask if she could have a hug. Griffin nodded. She wrapped her arms around him for a moment, and he gave her a peck on the cheek.

Then, because duty called him, Jack Griffin turned up his collar, and walked into the rainstorm. Olive watched him from under her umbrella, and even though he didn't look back, she kept one hand up, preparing to wave, until he was lost from her sight.

Chapter 25

A week later, Carter drove his Pierce-Arrow onto the grounds of Arbor Villa. He wasn't using the BMW much, as his ribs had been taped and his wrists were sprained. He limped to the front door slowly, even more slowly than his injuries would allow, as this was a trip he couldn't believe he was making.

Borax was outside today, in his chair, reading a book. Beside him was a table on which there was a pitcher of lemonade.

'Hey, Charlie,' he called. 'How's tricks?'

Carter didn't answer. He took the book from Borax's hands and closed it, and then dropped it on the grass.

Borax drew a heavy sigh. 'I'm sorry. I really am.'

'Twenty years ago, I heard a rumor from someone that God told you to be good. Who told me that?'

'Guilty.' He raised his hand. 'I ain't gonna ask for forgiveness, because that's not yours to grant.'

'I don't want to forgive you anything. I want the plans to television back.'

Borax fanned himself with his hat. 'You gonna tell me how you figured out it was me?'

'I'm not playing.'

Borax's eyes fixed on an unknowable point among the trees. 'You watched Hollis, I figure. And you got friends in the bank business, so you see he's making twice as much as everyone else. Darn it, I thought no one could trace those transfers back this way. You know some smart guys, Charlie.'

'I want it back.'

'That Hollis is a mover.'

'They drugged me and threw me in the bay, Borax.'

'I feel real bad about this one. It's eating me down to my guts. But I had the word out, anything that looked fishy that had to do with Harding, bring it right to me. And there it was. Didn't mean for you to be the middle man.'

'Middle man? Harding gave that to me, not you.'

'Like I say, it's eating me, Charlie. But it's too big to leave alone. Just one investment in the right place could get me straight out of hock. You don't know what that feels like.'

Carter said nothing. He simply stared at Borax with such ill-contained rage that the older man had to look away.

'Okay, here it is. I look at this as a trade.' Borax folded his arms. 'That's the only way—'

'A trade?'

'Yeah, a trade.'

Carter said, 'I know I'm not a financial genius, but wouldn't a trade involve me *getting* something besides drugged and dropped in the bay?'

'Sure.' He sounded calm when he said it. 'I figure it has to be a good trade. You gave me television, whether you meant to or not, and I give you something you like even more.'

Carter looked over his shoulder as if he were looking for what on earth Borax meant. 'And?'

'You'll get it eventually.'

'I'm sorry, are we being metaphorical here? You're going to give me the gift of going bankrupt in a few more seasons?'

'No . . .'

'Peace of mind? Good health? Tell me if I'm getting warm.'

'Charlie, it ain't anything like that. I'll give you a tangible asset. Trust me on this.'

Carter put his hands in his pockets. He stretched to his full height. 'Somewhere down the line, you became a bastard.'

A week after that sorry meeting, Pem Farnsworth was discharged from Cowell Hospital. She had a slight palsy that was expected to clear up as long as she had enough bed rest. She was sent home by special train to Utah. The tab for the train, and for the hospital bill, was picked up by a few men who had attended Philo's demonstration. When Philo heard this news, he brightened, but only until he found the group had also paid for a second-class ticket for him to leave town.

His failed experiment hadn't made the front page of any paper, but several recorded it in their local sections. Consensus was that he was a gifted crackpot who had tampered with forces he didn't quite know how to control. Dr Talbot, from RCA, was quoted as saying that when the precocious boy learned the rudiments of physics, there might be a place for him at the table. Television was just another dream whose specifics were written on a cloud.

Philo boarded the train in downtown San Francisco, escorted there by two lieutenants from the Presidio, and a slouch-hatted man who didn't speak, but whose general demeanor Philo had seen a lot of recently – he was there to make sure Philo didn't get any cockamamie ideas.

The man needn't have worried. When the train pulled away, Philo sat absolutely still, alone in his compartment, focusing on the boater that he kept perfectly level in his lap. He watched the straw for its interlocked patterns: zigzags, or, if he looked at them differently, arrows pointing left and right, or herringbones. When he looked up at the windows, he saw grime and soot, so he looked back down again.

When the train stopped in Sacramento, he was joined in his compartment by the most nondescript man he'd ever seen. The man dressed and behaved as if he were trying with his boater and his sunglasses to blend in seamlessly, but as there were only two of them in the compartment, Philo gave a deadly laugh.

'Yes?'

'You don't have to worry,' Philo said. His throat was dry from having not talked in hours. 'I'm going home.' The man didn't reply, so Philo said, 'I know you're one of them, checking up on me.' Briefly, he fumbled, as it was possible he wasn't one of them at all, and now Philo had embarrassed himself in front of a total stranger, yet another indignity.

But then the man said, 'I hope you don't mind me checking up on you.'

'Well, frankly, sir, I *do* mind.' He could be sure of himself now, and with that came indignity.

'I see. Let's talk until the Auburn stop. That's less than an hour. Perhaps by then we'll have an understanding.'

'Oh, I understand already. I'm not going to tinker with television anymore. It's done with. For the last two weeks . . .' his lower lip shook, and he looked down. 'For the last two weeks, I have been in agony. I have been in agony. You don't know what I mean.'

'Maybe I do.'

'You can't.' He leaned forward, and with the same articulate intensity he had once found in front of a chalkboard, he declared, 'I'm giving it up. Hang the idea. Kill it. My vocation, my passion, what was going to be my career almost killed my wife. No one can know what that's like.'

At this the man pursed his lips. 'I think I can.' He removed his boater and put it on the seat beside him. He took off his sunglasses, revealing bright blue eyes. He extended his hand for Philo to shake. And he said, 'My name is Charles Carter. I very much admire your television idea. And I think I do know what you've been through.'

CHUNG LING SOO

HAS REACHED THE HIGHEST PINNACLE OF FAME

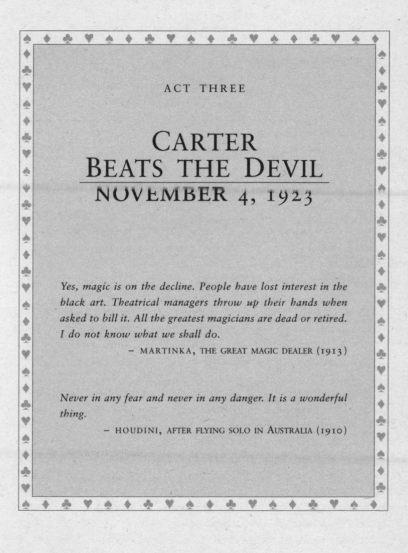

ACT THREE

CARTER
BEATS THE DEVIL
NOVEMBER 4, 1923

Yes, magic is on the decline. People have lost interest in the black art. Theatrical managers throw up their hands when asked to bill it. All the greatest magicians are dead or retired. I do not know what we shall do.

                   — MARTINKA, THE GREAT MAGIC DEALER (1913)

Never in any fear and never in any danger. It is a wonderful thing.

                   — HOUDINI, AFTER FLYING SOLO IN AUSTRALIA (1910)

Chapter 1

In San Francisco, where misdemeanors were mostly forgiven, if not welcomed, the penalty for posting bills on the sides of buildings was a startling thirty dollars. A boy paperhanger could never pay this; nor would his employers. With eight large theatres and dozens of smaller venues all booking acts and motion pictures and exhibitions, however, the paper, legal or not, had to be hung. From midnight until dawn, Tally's Gulch and Market Street and the Tenderloin and North Beach were overrun with boys whose best qualifications were quick wits and stealth. Working in trios, one holding the heavy paste pot, another the sheet rolls, and a third working the brushes and hangers, they could cover a block in a few short minutes.

However: a poster put to the glue at midnight would undoubtedly be covered by another put up at 3 A.M., so the game was to wait as long as possible – but not long enough to be caught by the sun or the occasional predawn raid of the paddy wagon.

The first week of October 1923 marked the opening of fall season, so the streets were especially crowded. Touring companies of *Elagabalo* and *Carmen* were in town, the Sells Brothers Circus was setting up in Golden Gate Park, *I'll Say She Is,* featuring the Marx Brothers, would open for two weeks at the Tower, and a dozen film companies were rushing out product to compete with the new Chaplin, a drama set in Paris. Even the grand lady herself, the Orpheum, which had fallen into disuse, a victim of the movies, had been booked for the first time in three years, though for what, no one was quite certain.

As it was the season, competition had a certain edge, for the police had raids nightly. The raids were inevitably scheduled for 4 A.M., as the local bakeries opened their doors to the constabulary shortly thereafter. Woe to the slow boy who was still on the streets after 3:45 A.M.

Thursday night's performance of *Elagabalo* was the final one for the Italian company featuring the great tenor Cavelli, and though the performance ended at 11 P.M., the audience demanded encores, and when the opera house shut down for the night, the stage door entrance was packed with admirers who forcibly whisked members of the company to their homes or to speakeasies to hear them sing more. The boys on the sidewalk pasting up eight sheets of lion-tamers shared the streets with women in gowns and men in evening wear surrounding confused but happy Italians who sang like canaries as they ambled from the Lamplighter to the Four Sins Café.

Shortly before four, the streets were emptied of boys and the last stragglers from the opera, throats sore, had fallen into beds or behind sofas, and for a few short minutes, the theatre district of downtown San Francisco was absolutely silent.

At four o'clock exactly, a dozen policemen, including the chief himself, piled into the department's newest wagons, excited and talking among themselves. They raced past the construction site at Geary and Hyde, the tremendously inviting south side brick wall of the Edison building, the planks and boards around the main library – in short the most attractive sites for bills to be posted. And at every site, working diligently, were fresh trios of boys who waved at them.

There were no arrests made.

At ten minutes past four, the wagons pulled up in front of the Olympic Club's Doric columns, and the police, all in black tie, ran together – or as 'together' as they could, for they were quite snockered – into the club, where they were treated to a light French meal, a brief and humorous message of appreciation from their host, Mister James Carter, and then a private concert by the finest tenor in all of Europe, Cavelli.

He began with 'Oh, Lola,' a deft tune from Caruso's songbook, and from there launched the police into the realms of joy via 'Lunge Da Lei . . . De' Miei Bollenti Spiriti' before an impassioned 'Celeste Aida' that caused several grown men to bring out their handkerchiefs. Throwing back his shoulders, he rallied, getting them to clap in time as he sang 'Evviva! Beviam! Beviam!' which he turned into a medley ending with the current Ziegfeld favorite, 'I Love My Wife, But Oh You Kid!'

410

When the sun came up, the police spilled out of the club and onto the stairs, elated, in love with Cavelli, and Captain Morgan lit a cigar and said 'It's good to be alive.' They elected to visit a waffle house for breakfast and as they walked, the men noticed how their shoes made a kind of rhythm on the sidewalk, and two officers began to sing together, for they recognized exactly the time signature that echoed down the warming late-summer streets: the Anvil Chorus, from *Il Trovatore*.

Soon, the rest caught the tune, and even if they didn't know the words, they could shout along enthusiastically. It was a song sung by gypsies at work in the early morning, and the feeling of cama-raderie was infectious. A lamppost made an excellent substitute for an anvil; one cop calmly removed the bullets from his revolver and used its butt as a hammer.

> *Chi del gitano i giorni abbella*
> *Chi del gitano i giorni abbella*
> *Chi? Chi i giorni abbella?*

By now, they were just outside the Edison building, with its great brick wall now completely covered not with Chaplin posters, nor the circus, nor the work of anyone who'd come out before 4 A.M. Instead, every square inch of space was covered with three sheets and eight sheets and even one spectacular twenty-four sheet, all of them showing in various sizes exactly the same image: on a deep blue background, so blue it was almost black, a warmly colored man in turban and tails, his smile dazzlingly white, his right palm extended, and in it a box that displayed a futuristic-looking clear globe capped with a yellow and orange halo of flames. At the top of each poster, it said, 'Carter the Great,' and at the bottom, 'EVERYWHERE!'

The policemen were walking in several rows, with their arms around one another's shoulder. When they passed the posters, they, to a man, stopped in their tracks, and they were dazzled. Immediately, they started addressing their song directly to the posters, gesturing to the giant figures of Carter, at once their bene-factor and their best audience, some of them choking on laughter as they changed the lyrics to 'Car-ter-is-ev'ry-where, Car-TER-the GREAT-is-ev'RY-where.'

Across the street, sipping from a paper cup of coffee, the real Charles Carter, who'd come to see the first public display of his posters for himself, went unrecognized. He watched the group of cops singing to his image and, as they disbanded, he felt a swell of pride. Such a good first reception felt like an omen and a blessing.

The cops noticed him and, using their billy clubs for emphasis, told him to move along. So Carter touched the brim of his hat and ambled down the street, humming the Anvil Chorus himself. There wasn't much time left and there was a show to put on.

The posters were well noticed. Tickets sold with fair briskness for an act that had played the city but three months before. Also: more than one representative of the military (there was quite the permanent garrison at the Presidio) recognized in Carter's hand something that looked peculiar, very much resembling a device they'd been told to look out for. Letters were written and cables sent, and soon after, Col Edmund Starling had in his office a man he'd been keeping on call for several weeks, the way he once had kept the Spider on call. But this man was of more specialized talents, which he was happy to put to use in America after his extended journey through the African continent.

Chapter 2

CARTER SHOW REQUIREMENTS

Mister Carter and his Company will provide all equipment, security, personnel, promotional materials, etc, as per requirements of contract. In response, the ORPHEUM THEATRE will provide the following:

SCENERY DEPARTMENT

Five spot lines, one over center of each trap, other two explained.
Fifteen battons, one with eye arms.
Use house traveler in one. Three men on scenery.

ELECTRIC DEPARTMENT

Reds and whites in foots and borders – Replaces *all* blues with whites. *No blues used. No side lights used.* Display City permit for new wiring. One man on electric.

PROP DEPARTMENT

Runway over pit – 36 inches wide, steps to floor, steps painted white or covered with white cloth.
Platform under stage, 5 feet wide, 14 feet long, 7 feet below stage floor. This platform placed directly under center traps, reinforced for weight of elephant and equipment.
One bag sawdust.
For 500-gallon water tank: access to drain from stage to associated or main sewage line. Three mops and one mop wringer. One practical carpet sweeper.
Two men on props.

ORCHESTRA DEPARTMENT

Piano as near center of pit as possible with keyboard facing audience. It is essential we have drums and brass.

COMPANY COMFORTS
Three kitchen tables for props.
Changing room on each side of stage.
Seven hall trees and three chairs for change room.
One gallon springwater in Mr Carter's room.
(Pillow?)

James Carter
Company manager

The morning of November 4, standing in the wings of the Orpheum
Theatre, James Carter stared at the 'comforts' section, pen poised
over the word *pillow,* which he had added not twenty seconds
beforehand. Did Charlie want a pillow for his dressing room chair,
and if so, what sort?

Though the sound was slightly muffled by the draperies, James
could hear the opening monologue. He knew it by heart. He had
memorized the act as it would actually occur, as it was written
down, as it had been explained to the press, and as disseminated
to certain members of the company who couldn't quite be trusted
– in short, it was a layer cake frosted with levels of truth and
deception. It was a measure of his exhaustion that while he stared
at the stage, witnessing the opening salvo of card tricks, he almost
called out, 'Are you sure you want a pillow?'

Rather than contribute to the nightmare this show was
becoming, James walked quietly through the double side doors,
past security, and into the massive house. Two thousand seats in
crushed velvet had been recently cleaned and the aisles vacuumed
and scrubbed. Cinnamon-scented incense from Chinatown burned
in urns scattered about the house. The expenses had only begun
there: along with programs and posters, they'd printed decks of
promotional playing cards. Carter had outdone himself in coming
up with new effects on his limited budget – at least, James
suspected he'd remained close to budget, but as soon as the final
invoices rolled in, he was prepared to yell at his brother for going
somewhat over. He prayed it was only 'somewhat,' as every penny
counted, and every seat for the next two weeks had to be sold to
avert disaster. At the moment, with the magician onstage, exactly
twelve seats were occupied.

This would have been catastrophic had it been showtime, but it was still early morning, a rehearsal, and the man onstage was not Carter, but Carlo, his stand-in, and his delivery of the patter sounded, as usual, awful. James grimaced as Carlo hammed up the end of a small bit, rhythm all wrong, 'How do I *know* then that you are *not* my con-fed-er-ate?' All around Carlo, men performed eleventh-hour repairs, down to restitching the grand drapery, the velvet teaser at the top of the stage, and the tormentors at its sides.

By the time James found the third gallery, a sheen of perspiration had broken out on his forehead. 'I'm beginning to understand,' he gasped, dropping into a seat next to his brother, 'why you respect the paying audience that has to sit up here.'

Carter brought a finger to his lips. He squared his shoulders toward the stage, his arms crossed. He wore a mask of concentration. 'Carlo isn't projecting well.'

'That's because Carlo is an idiot.'

Carter mused, 'He's probably memorizing the patter so he can sell it tomorrow morning to the highest bidder.'

'I'm glad you realize that, Charles.'

'You know, I'm imagining the man who will be sitting right here in seat 3C42 tonight, a paying man, disinterested but ready for entertainment,' he whispered, 'and I hope that the five-foot-nine-inch idiot he'll see onstage will be engrossing. More engrossing than the five-foot-nine-inch idiot I'm seeing right now.'

'We're down to the absolute final preparations—'

'So we are.'

'Do you want a pillow for the chair in your dressing room?'

Carter looked away from the stage, where the monologue continued with strange Italian inflections. 'A pillow?'

'Thurston's rider requires a pillow.'

'Find out how big it is, and get me a larger one.'

'Excellent. Silk tassels?'

'Let's not – *Hold!*' Onstage, Carlo froze in position. Carter walked from one end of the balcony to the other, patting the railing. Finally, he called out, 'Lighting! Bring up the spot on the stage, and we'll sweep the audience with it. Can you get the axis to rotate this high? The people back here should have a chance to raise their hands and be seen.'

When it was arranged that, yes, the spotlight could indeed swivel to the third gallery, Carter returned to sit next to James, who was writing that Carter wanted a large, tassel-less pillow in an attractive but not over-wrought fabric, perhaps velvet, but not to bother with imported silk.

This took a great deal of time to write. He was aware that his brother was watching him.

'You've gone mad,' Carter said quietly.

'Why do you think Thurston needs a pillow so badly he puts it in his contract?'

'Are you suggesting a medical condition that requires the use of *unguents*?'

As Carlo droned on, James and Carter were reduced to holding back snickers like children during a sermon.

'I am so tired,' James said, wiping his eyes. 'Unguents.'

Carter half-sang, 'Un-guents,' imitating the awful Carlo.

'Well,' James took a cleansing breath, 'now the pillow business is settled, I believe the show is ready.'

'Hmmm,' Carter said after a moment. 'Well . . .'

Carlo had gone silent; the opening was over.

Carter clapped his hands. 'Thank you. I'm coming down. Men, please rehearse the scenery changes in act one, and I'll be there shortly.' Carter took James by the shoulder. 'Join me, I need to address the company about a detail.'

'Oh?' James ran through a list he had long ago filled with checkmarks: costumes, orchestration, the lion, the elephant, all the motorcycle licensing, briefing the ushers. 'I thought we had everything in hand except for final rehearsals.'

'Yes and no.' He showed James the way to the main stairs and took them himself two at a time. 'There's one last thing.'

'The permit for the water tank? We got it last night.'

Carter was now a dozen steps ahead of his brother, and he swung around the next set of stairs, disappearing. James slowed to an irritated stop. Carter popped his head back into view. 'The posters. They show me with a television box in my hand?'

'Yes . . .'

'We have neither the plans nor the equipment to produce that particular illusion,' he said, as if discussing how mild the weather was.

James could feel heat rise in his chest. 'We don't have . . .'

'Not exactly.'

'The single most important illusion?'

'Yes, that one. It's a minor detail,' Carter smiled. 'But thank you for the pillow.'

Five minutes later, Carter trotted onstage in a newly pressed shirt. He clapped his hands and directed everyone assembled to pay him attention. 'Ladies and Gentlemen, we're going to put on a show this evening,' he said, without breaking stride. Behind him, a fidgeting James stopped at the act curtain, beside a little table with a pitcher and six water glasses. He poured himself some ice water and waited. His brother never referred to note cards during these preshow rallies, he never stammered, he spoke in complete sentences as if he'd rehearsed (James never saw him rehearsing), and he could, if needed, discuss thirty items that wanted improvement without skipping or repeating. It was an odd group of forty that he addressed – centermost was Carlo, who lay on the stage, feet in front of him, resting on one elbow as if a dryad would soon feed him grapes. To his left was the stone-faced Willie, shy and frequently cast as the villain, as he had mottled red skin and a turned-in eye.

Also: Albert and Esperanza, a married couple of acrobats, both of them lithe and handsome; then Scott, an apprentice magician whom Carter hoped to promote one day to an in-one interval performer. To the back was Cleo, a statuesque woman who was for some odd reason wearing her Egyptian costume hours before she needed to, and four other box jumpers whom Carter had drafted from the Golden Gate assembly. And then there were electricians, grips, stage runners, the conductor and the lead orchestra players, six men clothed in black, Ledocq (who spent the whole time doing a crossword), prop men, carpenters, the box office crew, ushers, and crafty men whose job was to look nondescript as they sat in the audience.

After a general praising of all the talents he saw before him, Carter said he would make no hyperbolic predictions of how well the show would be received; understatement, he hinted, was the code word – the less promised, the more astonished the audience would be at what was actually delivered. He had instructions, and he dismissed groups as he spoke, for there was no reason for ticket takers to know more about the show than that it would start promptly; there would be no late seating; mind that no one swiped the window cards.

Soon, he was down to the core of his company, the ones who appeared onstage or worked the effects behind it. With the departure of each group, Carter had drawn closer, and spoken more quietly, causing those who'd hugged the edge of the stage to approach so they could hear his increasingly hoarse instructions. The air grew intimate, as they all had high hopes and, James knew, a slim chance of solvency. Surveying them, he had a vision of a group of shipwreck survivors drawing around a campfire.

'Friends,' Carter said. He cleared his throat. 'You are the only people in the world who know the entire performance. You're all going to be quite marvelous.' He looked from face to face. 'Frankly, I need to ask for some help. To discourage some of my more ambitious competitors, I've allowed the plans for the "Everywhere" illusion to be stored in a location that needs to be visited, oh, *immediately*.' He smiled, 'And tactfully.'

Eyes began to shift within the company. Small murmurs. Intrigue was always welcome on opening night.

'Act three, the opening.' He directed all attention to the stage left apron, where he would begin that act by announcing he was the greatest conjurer the world had ever known. 'Now, traditionally, we've had the Devil appear onstage in a puff of brimstone. There's a new device that will allow me to summon him in a crystal ball. I've been a bit vague with you about how that works. Well, this afternoon, I need to pay a visit to an office safe, and I need a volunteer upon whom I can rely. The qualifications are simply keeping the eyes and ears open. Hands, please?'

Because they loved Carter, and adventure, and because some of them were crooked, all of them – from Madame Cleo to taciturn Willie – extended their hands, straight up.

'Thank you,' Carter said. 'I'm honestly touched. Carlo, thank you, you're my man. Please come with me.'

There was a crash from the edge of the stage. All eyes looked there; even Ledocq looked up from his crossword. James had knocked over the table, shattering the water pitcher.

'Are you all right, James?'

'I'm excellent, Charles,' James called from that great distance. 'And yourself?' He began to pick up shards of glass.

Carlo, looking woozy with pleasure, joined Carter at center stage. Carter patted him on the shoulder. 'Excellent. Everyone, please remain on call throughout the day. We'll only have time to rehearse the sticky parts before curtain.'

He made a baroque wave at them, a sultan's *au revoir,* and the group disbanded. The last to depart was Ledocq, ambling away with the newspaper held out before him, his pen to his lips. James tried to catch his eye, but Ledocq walked into the shadows, exclaiming 'Ah, b-a-u-b-l-e! Six letters!' as he disappeared. Carter, James, and Carlo were left together.

'Carlo.' Carter looked directly into his immense brown eyes. 'Do you have an automobile?'

'Yes.' He smoothed his hair. 'Well, I can get one from my girl.'

'Go and get it, and change into street clothes. I'll pack the kit. Meet me back here in thirty minutes. *Ciao!*' Carter slapped him vigorously on the back.

When the stage doors closed, they sent echoes across the theatre. Carter and James were alone. 'So, dinner at your flat at four?'

'Are you *fully* insane?' James yelled.

'Come with me, my voice is tired.'

They walked to the dressing area, where Carter filled a kettle with water and James began speaking quickly.

'Why bring Carlo into this? I thought you and Ledocq had been talking to Philo for weeks now. I thought he'd told you everything.'

Carter played with the gas flame under the kettle, running his finger through it a few times. 'Philo hasn't told us much.'

'Secretive?'

'No, worse. He comes to the workshop, and he and I talk about this and that, or he and Ledocq talk about physics, and he's fine for a moment, but when we ask him to think about his invention, he goes south. It's hard to see him like that. I've been feeling just grand, and I've got more new illusions than I know what to do with, and I'd hoped that some of that would rub off on him.'

James considered the complex mass of machinery he'd seen

demonstrated unsuccessfully at Berkeley, and he looked at his watch. 'Given that it's all been destroyed . . .'

'Oh, things aren't that grim. Ledocq saw the plans that night at his house. And he saw the demonstration, and from that he was able to piece together everything. What we're missing is how you make the flat-end vacuum tube, where the image goes. The description in Borax's safe includes that information.'

James looked at his watch again, confirming there were only hours left before the performance. 'Why leave it there for so long?'

'If we have weasels in the company, the moment anything showed up, the thugs would just snatch it back again. Borax isn't doing anything with it – he's used to waiting people out for years. So why not leave it there?' He threw tea strainers into two cups.

'Hmmph.' The idea of keeping the illusion safe by leaving it in enemy territory had a certain elegance. Nonetheless, James was angry, and he remembered why: 'Weren't we concerned that Carlo is a weasel? The very people you want to avoid are being notified.'

'You know, in the center of downtown, two weeks ago, I put up a twenty-four-sheet poster of myself holding a television box in my hand. I expect *that* alerted all necessary authorities quite effectively. Tea?'

'Oh, dear God, you don't actually have a brain, do you, it's more a filigreed spiderweb, with little chambers in it where trained monkeys play the pipe organ.'

But when James was finished with that, he saw Carter wasn't wearing his battle face. Instead, he sank to the dressing room chair with a sigh. 'I'm so sorry,' he said. 'I'm maintaining a great many things right now, and . . . are you sure you don't want tea? I seem to have poured two cups. And we are having dinner together at four, correct? Something nice and quiet?'

James nodded. He took a cup quietly, and when he'd had a moment to control his breath, he blew puffs of steam across the cup's mouth.

Carter winced. 'This is an awful chair.' He stood and thumped on the seat. 'I think it was designed by Germans. It needs a pillow.'

'Please go on.'

He sat on the makeup table, cradling his teacup. 'So, Ledocq says when he has the plans, it should take him a few minutes to make a flat-end tube, and there's the annealing process and it should have an hour or so to cool before we use it, or,' he continued, dismissively, 'it catches fire. My point is—'

'Excuse me—'

'My point is, at first, I'd wanted to use the television box for a spirit cabinet, but I don't know, I've had a sea change. I'm tired of spirit gags. Television is much more interesting than that. So I thought of using it all night long, for various effects. But that quite overdoes it – people would get used to it. So instead, I've been inspired lately, positively swimming in it,' he snapped his fingers in quick rhythm, 'one after the other, creating illusions for tonight.'

'Yes, there are some interesting effects.'

'So, television – we'll build up to it. Use it to summon the Devil. I can't think of a better way to make Philo's case.'

James, who'd been thinking about evading thugs, felt like he'd been following the wrong ace. 'Make Philo's case.'

'It should cheer him up.'

'A public demonstration,' James said, and it was like he'd lifted a blanket off his head. 'Yes. Right, yes. One that works. But Carlo will rat you out – the army will send someone.'

'Good.'

'Good?'

'James, you weren't drugged and thrown into the estuary. Let Carlo report to them. It's my theatre. I can handle them.' Carter folded his hands around the steaming hot cup and opened them to show it, contents and all, had vanished. In its place was a dove, which flew from his palms and fluttered around the dressing room until it perched on a coatrack. James looked at the dove, which was grooming under its wing, then back to his brother, who was sipping the tea that had apparently never left his hands.

James knew reasoning with him wouldn't work. He'd long ago resigned himself to his brother, and his brother's magic, being a bit unknowable. 'All right then. Take care when you're with Carlo.' He placed his teacup and saucer on the drain board.

'I have very specific plans for Carlo.' Carter glanced at the coatrack. 'You might want to fetch your hat.'

'Thank you.'

As James took his hat, careful not to startle the dove standing over it, he looked at his brother as if trying to see him for the first time. He had a faint memory of being about seven years old, and Charlie seeming like a great hero. But details were scarce, not exactly retrievable – as they dimmed, he was left with a feeling of respect that he couldn't quite place. 'I do believe you'll be okay,' he said, 'but still, do take care.'

The Orpheum box office opened at noon. What had been Murdoch's office in 1911 was now a deep storage area for props. His famed window, from which he could see how far the line extended, was nailed shut and covered with two-by-fours.

The line for the opening night of Carter's show was healthy, but not outstanding. A few pedestrians stood and read the publicity blowups that rested on easels by the sidewalk. The afternoon papers contained a charming article hinting at how wonderful this favorite son's new effects were, so James, who stood outside the Orpheum smoking a series of cigarettes and counting heads, prayed there would be a second wave later.

When the line had been served, James glanced up and down the block until he began to look like he was awaiting a crowd – always a fatal posture for an artist's manager. Stubbing out his final cigarette, he returned to the theatre.

The girl inside the ticket booth, whose peripheral vision was excellent, noted his disappearance and returned to reading her *Movie Herald Weekly*, in which Rod La Rocque had a few choice words for Valentino.

The sun blotted out all at once, so she looked up. A huge man, bald, stood before her, looking at the easels, the posters, the woman herself, as if visiting an impoverished country.

'One ticket in the orchestra, please, for the *magic show*,' he said, his tone implying it was anything *but* a magic show.

'Eight dollars, please.'

'Eight . . . dollars. My word, this must be some kind of *magic show*, then. Young lady, spare my eight dollars, and please look on the comp list. I should be taken care of.'

'Okey-dokey. Whose guest are you?'

'Mr Carlo Roody.'

She flipped through some sheets of onionskin, yawning. 'He

doesn't have a guest list. Anyone else?'

He stared at her so long she wondered if he might never leave, and she'd have to start reading her magazine again with him still staring at her. 'The cheapest ticket, then.'

'Third gallery. It's fifty cents tonight.'

'Oh, a bargain.' He flicked five dimes at her.

She removed the bundle of 3C tickets and passed one to the man. 'Doors open at seven-thirty and the show is promptly at eight. And – you know, no animals are allowed?'

'Pardon?'

For a moment, she thought she'd seen him cradling a tiny dog, but now, clearly, he held nothing. She said, 'Um,' and then, in a drone, her line: 'Please don't reveal any details of the third act, when Carter beats the Devil.'

The bald man clicked his heels together. 'I am your servant,' he said.

Chapter 3

Carlo's girl had a sleek and well-maintained 1923 Cadillac speedster, or rather, her husband did. Its body was a deep blue that spoke of endless coats of polish, which the servants applied without complaining, for the owner traveled frequently, the odometer was easy to disconnect, and Sunset Beach was an easy destination.

Carter complimented the car's smooth suspension and handling twice on their way to Arbor Villa. Each time, Carlo said, 'Yeah, it's a good breezer.'

Throughout the trip, Carlo silently wondered what Carter suspected. A magician depended on deception, Carlo reasoned, and so being a snitch was just playing the game. It worked rather the same way he had borrowed the speedster. It was an easygoing philosophy, one that would serve him relatively well in the several hours he had left to live.

They arrived at the top of Fourth Avenue and pulled up on the shoulder of the road. Carter put his leather satchel over his shoulder and patted it, he explained, 'for luck.' The rest of their journey would be on foot. Borax's house, as they walked toward it, was never exactly silent; in addition to the birds and the howling of his many dogs, the mansion seemed to have audible noises of decay.

'This is the man's home? It's not that big,' Carlo whispered. He and Carter were a hundred yards away, on an old service road.

'It's two o'clock. Borax is at church and has taken his household staff with him. We have the place to ourselves for at least the next forty-five minutes but still, we'll approach without letting the cottages come into view. Someone or other might have stayed behind. Come here for a moment.' Carter leaned against a palm tree and dug through his jacket pocket. 'How do these look to you?'

Carlo took the eight pages of onionskin from Carter. They were filled with diagrams and equations heavy with Greek equations. 'Hey! It says "television." You already have the plans.'

'Thank you, excellent.' Carter tucked them into his satchel.

Carlo had but one expression of admiration – it was to turn out his lower lip and frown as if thinking carefully. He put it to use now, as Carter began to walk up the road again. Substituting fake plans. Clever, clever.

Carter took them off the beaten path, over tangled roots of teak trees that came from Kalimantan. No matter how deep the stack of dry brush he stepped through, the magician made almost no sound, and once, after avoiding a noisy patch of leaves, he turned and smiled when Carlo avoided it, too.

Their bushwhacking took them to an obscure corner of the west wing of Arbor Villa, where the date nut palms threw the house into perpetual shade. Neighborhood children had long ago broken most of the windows here. Carter glanced at likely places to enter and selected the remains of a bay window across which a moldering Navajo blanket was stretched. It was held in place with a few tacks, which popped out of the wood with a single, hard tug.

When they were inside, and their eyes had adjusted to the dimness – Borax was in no position to leave the electric lights on when he left the house – they listened for domestic noises. There were none, save the distant peacocks, whose calls made the atmosphere feel more desolate. They stood in a little-used parlor, floors covered with threadbare Turkish rugs, walls lined with books and paintings of sailing ships at sea. It smelled like mildew.

Carlo shook his head. 'A rich man should have better locks.'

'Shhh.'

'Where's the safe?'

Carter put his finger to his lips, then indicated that Carlo should follow exactly in his footsteps. They left the room – the door stood half open – and went into a musty hallway flanked by alcoves where suits of armor stood, their poleaxes looking ready to fall on passersby. This walk made Carlo nervous, as their path traversed so many similar-looking rooms and hallways he began to wonder if perhaps Carter was in fact looking for a safe at all. Perhaps he had a darker motive, a plan to confound poor Carlo here, perhaps even do away with him. Each time Carter's hand disappeared into his jacket, Carlo's throat tightened, relaxing only when he saw it was a pocket watch being consulted.

Finally, they stood in an ill-lit parlor – was it a different room than the one they'd broken into? – and Carter approached a bookcase. He extended his hand, then looked over his shoulder, concerned, 'Be a sport, Carlo, and tell me there's no one at the window.'

Carlo's head jerked to the window, which was covered by an entirely different design of blanket, and saw nothing. He looked back at his boss. 'Naw, there's a blanket—' In the moment he'd looked away, Carter had sprung the bookcase away from the wall, revealing a small, grey room with portland cement walls.

'Oh . . . I missed that,' Carlo moaned. 'You didn't show me how that happened.'

'That's a pity, Carlo. Come with me.'

Inside, the tall grey walls were saved from feeling oppressive only by high windows and friendly mementos that Borax had decorated with: photographs of friends, plaques of recognition from the City of Oakland, amateurish-looking oil paintings of birds and flowers and children.

'We have about twenty-five minutes,' Carter said. Inside these thick walls, he spoke in close to a normal voice. 'I'm going to concern myself with opening the safe. Your job is to keep your ears open for anyone returning early.'

They pulled the bookshelf on its track to within an inch of closing. Carlo stood braced against it, watching and listening, but also watching Carter, as he'd never seen anyone crack a safe before. He'd heard stories. When would Carter sandpaper down his fingertips?

Carter ran his palms across the embossed metal door, murmuring to himself, 'Puerorum spectatorum operatque studio,' adding, 'Incantations,' though he had actually been reciting an old Thacher fight song.

Borax's wall safe, a Schlage 1917 top-of-the-line model, was flush to the wall, sunk into the cement. Carter dragged two stools over in front of it, dropping his work bag down on the first, and himself down on the second. He unzipped the bag and gracefully pulled out not a stethoscope, as Carlo had anticipated, but a wine bottle.

'How do you open a safe with a wine bottle?'

Carter withdrew a corkscrew. He uncorked the bottle, and let it stand on the stool. Next, he took out a small bundle of newspaper, which he tore open to reveal a wineglass. He gently placed the glass next to the bottle and folded his arms. 'Red wine needs eight minutes to breathe,' he said, glancing at his fingernails. 'Borax showed me this hiding place several times. He was very proud of it.' He reached out with his right hand and twisted the wall safe's dial freely. Rather than watching this motion – he looked like a child spinning a top – his flat blue eyes locked on Carlo. 'He never let me close enough to see what combination he was entering, and I suppose the idea was that without that particular piece of information, he'd be *safe*.' On that word, Carter brought down the lever, and popped the door, which made a hydraulic gasp as it opened. Carlo looked at him with his lower lip flexed outward.

Carter poured himself a glass of wine and frowned at his watch. 'I'd hoped that would take six more minutes, but—' He half-saluted with the glass, ready to drink, then his eyes flicked toward the open safe. It took him a moment to form the words, and when they came out, they were terrible: 'You miserable *bastard*.'

'Boss?' Carlo couldn't have heard that correctly.

Carter stared inside the safe. He put the wine down.

'What?' Carlo left his post. He looked over Carter's shoulder. 'Huh,' he said. 'It's another safe.'

Inside the Schlage was a second safe, smaller in all dimensions, and secured to the larger model with a dry lather of mortar.

'Borax,' Carter whispered, 'where did you get an Olson Failsafe?'

'What's wrong?'

Carter held up his palm. They remained frozen, Carter holding his breath, quite literally, while Carlo's eyes darted from his boss, whose face was reddening, to the interior of the safe.

It wasn't much to look at – simply a metal door, a discolored bronze finish with a pattern of bulky oak leaves. To the left was the handle, to the right the familiar spinning knob, and above them, running the width of the door, an archaic-looking crest that read 'Failsafe' on a banner flanked by candelabras.

'Okay.' Carter drained his wine glass in a gulp. 'We're in trouble.'

'Can't you hear the tumblers on this one?'

'That would be the least of our problems.'

'You didn't bring a stethoscope, eh, Carter?'

'Stethoscopes are the magic wands of the cracking business.' He took a small leather pad from his pocket and flipped through pages of figures printed in his neat engineer's grid. As he ran his finger down the numbers, he began to explain their predicament: safe-cracking was a sham perpetuated by safecrackers. If they didn't physically blow a safe open somehow, it was more a matter of mathematical possibility, and patience.

'Safes are forgiving. If you enter a number within a couple of digits of the right one, you'll do fine, eventually.' He shook his head. 'And, generally speaking, it never even comes to that. Most people buy a very expensive safe, and then never change the factory preset.' He waved his pad. 'These are the presets I know of. Olson is of course a Norwegian design. Here we are. From the serial number, you can determine which progressions the Olson factory used, then you look on this table here . . .' He swallowed. 'So, for this model, the preset is five, fifteen, twenty.' He made no move. Instead, he continued to stare at the dial. 'The Schlage certainly was still at the preset,' he murmured, 'so the odds would be . . .'

He looked over at Carlo, who put on the same patient half-smile he wore during rehearsals. He'd been interested for a moment, but when it came down to details, his mind flew up, around the room, and out the window.

So Carter explained it more directly: 'This safe was designed to discourage safecrackers. You only have three chances to enter the right combination.'

'What happens if you just keep guessing?'

Carter didn't respond. The fact was, if some idiot entered the wrong combination on a Failsafe three times, the door would open on its own accord, and a vial of sulfuric acid would drop directly onto a plate treated with chlorate of potash and sugar. The resulting explosion would at the very least destroy the safe's contents. They were safes of last resort, designed at first for Russian nobility who lived in fear of ancestral documents falling into the hands of rioting peasants, and now exported mainly to diplomats from nations in which suicide was preferable to capture by the enemy. They were illegal in America; even bootleggers disliked them, for they often had to open their safes while intoxicated.

'Let's not think about that. Let us think,' Carter leaned

forward and turned the dial to five, 'positively. And hope that Borax was lazy.' He spun the dial left, to fifteen, then right to twenty. Somewhere out on the great, untended lawns, a peacock cried out twice, then Carter pushed the handle downward.

Nothing happened.

'Damn.' He poured a little more wine and took a sip. 'Borax doesn't know his birthday, so that's out.'

'Why not some lucky numbers he liked?'

'It could be, but Borax is a sentimental man. He'd choose a date that meant something to him.' A snap of his fingers. 'Teel's Marsh. March 16, 1875, the day God spoke to him.'

'What are you talking about?'

'That isn't helping me, Carlo.' He spun the dial freely, feeling the reeded edge between thumb and forefinger, stopping at three, then sixteen, then the long trip, more than 180 degrees, to seventy-five. His hand fell on the lever. He brought it down firmly.

There was an unsatisfying *clink* in response. He stood up and stretched and sighed, balling his fists up, and crossing his arms tightly across his chest. He paced, eyes on the mementos hanging from Borax's walls like he was in a museum. 'I'm open to possibilities for a third number,' he murmured.

'His birthday?' Carlo suggested quickly.

Carter stared at him.

'Wife's birthday?'

'Married twice. Loved them both.'

'Sixteen minutes,' Carlo said.

'That's no longer an issue. We'll be out of here one way or another.'

Carlo slumped against the wall and started fishing in his mouth for a corn kernel lodged between his molars. He felt Carter's focus begin to shift from the safe to him, as if he were doing something wrong. So he stood straight. 'Can I do anything?'

'Yes. Here's an idea. There are two pathways back to the house, front and rear. The rear path is cleared of debris, and that's how Borax usually comes and goes, but sometimes if the girls carry him, they go out the front.' He gave concise directions for how Carlo should go to the hall, turn right, then go up one flight of stairs – there was a narrow hallway from which one could see both paths,

429

all the way to the main road. 'Go quickly, and come back *more* quickly.'

Carlo pushed the bookcase forward on its casters, and graceful as a dancer, bounded from the room. Stairways tended to creak in their centers, so he padded up the edges of the frayed carpeting. The third-floor hall had windows facing the rear access road, which Carlo could see plainly, and Fourth Avenue on the north side. Far behind the loose tapestry of branches and dying leaves, cars and trucks whizzed on the boulevard.

Then he saw people on a pathway. Carlo, who had a quick eye, counted nineteen: a man in a wheelchair, a clergyman, and the rest all women wearing bonnets. The women stood in a semicircle, and the clergyman was jabbing his finger in the air. They were about a quarter-mile distant.

He sprinted back to join Carter, who had the book of presets open in his lap. 'Company,' Carlo said. He described what he'd seen.

'Lecturing by the front road? By the railcar, maybe? That's the one on vanity, and I believe it lasts less than five minutes. Help me with a date,' Carter said. 'Or duck.'

'Duck?' This caught Carlo's interest. 'Why?'

Carter hesitated. 'Try not to worry about this too much, but if we get the combination wrong, the safe will explode.'

Carlo stood upright, now impressed with the possibilities life had to offer. 'Explode?'

'Oh, yes. Any ideas?'

'Not his birthday,' he said slowly. He recalled the image of the old man in the wheelchair, listening to the sermon. 'Okay. Okay. A psalm, or a verse. Like 3:16, or . . .'

Carter nodded. 'A Bible verse. I wonder if there's a place where God says to Be Good.'

'Yeah, everywhere,' Carlo chuckled. Carter however faced him stonily, and so Carlo looked at his shoes.

A few awkward moments later, Carlo began to step backward, putting his toe against his other heel, arms extended like he was tightroping it. He looked at the walls. Here was an old photo of the Arbor Villa tennis courts. And there was a cute poster of a small white dog routing a huge bull mastiff, and Carlo squinted, reading the legend aloud, 'It's not the size of the *dog* in the *fight* that counts!' Yeah.' He looked at Carter, who was frowning, arms folded, at the safe.

'Damn it,' Carter whispered.

There was something written on the wall, in red ink. Carlo squinted at it. 'She never died.'

Carter turned his head slowly toward his assistant. 'Pardon?'

'Here,' Carlo flicked his forefinger toward the wall. 'What does that mean?' Someone had printed, crudely, with a fine bristle brush, that haunted phrase directly onto Borax's wall. *She never died.* Letters neither large nor small, just below eye level.

'Oh. That's a long story,' Carter began, and Carlo's face automatically receded into a mask of paying attention. 'A few years ago—' Then a smile broke across his face. 'Carlo, you're brilliant!'

'Thank you.'

'I could kiss you!'

'Eh,' he winced.

'That's just the sort of man Borax is. Black Christmas, which was 1917,' he said, hunched over the safe. 'Just the date he would commemorate. Twelve, twenty-five,' he said, drawing each syllable out as he spun the dial. Then he stole a glance at the now very involved Carlo, who hunched right behind him. 'Seventeen,' he said finally, and his hand reached out for the lever.

All was silent.

With his free hand, Carter gestured that Carlo should back away, to stand back from the safe, 'The corner,' he finally added, 'go all the way to the corner.'

Fascinated, Carlo walked backward.

'Here we go, success or failure, we'll know soon enough,' Carter said, and he pushed the lever down; it made a wonderful sighing sound, a sound of gears disengaging.

After all that intense effort, the room seemed lighter as the door swung open. Carlo noticed something was strange – Carter wasn't even touching the safe, but it was swinging open, easily, under its own power in fact.

'Down!' Carter jumped backward, tripped and fell, wrists out, to the stone floor, and Carlo threw himself to the side just as he heard a sound like a marble rolling down a tin chute. Something shattered, then a quiet puff of black smoke the size of a cabbage rolled lazily out of the safe, drifting toward the ceiling. It took less than a second.

Shakily, Carlo stood to see Carter, who was approaching the charred safe mouth slowly, his feet dragging along the floor. 'Oh,' Carter murmured. Inside the safe were charcoal-colored scraps of paper, some fringed with a word or two that had escaped, but otherwise all was ashes. Carter poked through the documents. He found ashes. He looked at his hands, which were smeared with soot.

'That was – that was something!' Carlo exclaimed, reminded of vaudeville sketches, where a tramp gives a prosperous man a loaded cigar. 'That was incredible . . . that was, hey – everything was destroyed! The plans are gone! Are you okay?'

'No.' Carter's eyes were all blue, the irises just the tiniest of pinpricks. He put his hand to his chin. 'What have I done,' he said. 'What have I done?' When his hand fell away, there was a smudge on his chin.

'Boss?' He'd never seen Carter with a smudge on his chin before.

'We have to get out of here.' But he made no move. 'Damn,' he said. 'I'm a damned fool.' His eyes began to well.

'We should get out of here. People will be coming.'

'It's just—' Carter peered into the safe again, eyes watering like a boy who's lost his prized baseball down the sewer grating. 'I can't believe I did that.'

Carlo pushed things into the satchel, muttering, 'Here's the wine, here's the fake notes, come on, Carter,' and put the whole package into Carter's arms. Carter accepted it, and said, 'Thank you,' and then, sounding numb, 'What have I done?'

He allowed Carlo to guide him out of the room, and as there were noises downstairs, he picked up the pace and by the time they'd found the room with the Navajo blanket in the window, Carter, cursing to himself, was all but racing to get away.

♣ ♦ ♥ ♠

Twenty-four hours earlier, Miss Olive White of the public library had a chore to perform. Since Carter the Great was opening, reporters had checked out many of the books that involved magic or magicians. She returned them to the shelves, flipping through them to look for pencil marks and stains left by shot glasses, clear signs they'd copied straight from the books rather than generate their own language to describe the show. As magic was magic to the average reader, no one much cared if the paper told them Carter would be performing a repertoire actually executed by Frederick Powell in 1890.

'Oh, you lazy men,' she murmured as she thumbed over a copy of a book by Robert-Houdin, its spine newly broken in many places.

Then the book fell open to an illustration of Robert-Houdin's business card. It was reproduced on the frontispiece of his *Memoirs*, with the legend 'macedoine calligraphique'. Spider-webbed, illegible, its form was somehow very familiar. But Miss White couldn't remember why. She would not have known it was a business card until she read the instructions the editors had provided. 'Bring this book right up to your nose, tilt the page away from you and look down it with one eye, like a telescope, from the bottom. What do you see? Turn it 45 degrees. What do you see? Keep turning. And what do you see?'

She followed the instructions with curiosity, and when she did so, she had such a start she actually dropped the book to the floor, cracking its poor spine yet again. She put her hand over her mouth.

'Wild surmise, Olive, wild surmise,' she murmured. She retrieved the book.

She closed the door to her office, opened up a letter she kept in a locked drawer, and placed a telephone call. Within a minute, she was talking to an operator at a switchboard in a Denver hotel.

That day was a busy one for the Treasury Department. After months of effort, agents had finally captured the *Billie Dove,* a lightweight powerboat with an engine modified so that even when laden down with barrels of hootch, it could outrun anything the government put in the water.

There was jubilation at the Mint, and at posts across the nation, as every agent, even those on the take, liked the feeling of a good capture. Late in the afternoon, however, a wire from the Denver office to Washington put a damper on things. It was an urgent message and was in no way related to magic: an agent had disappeared.

There was no indication of foul play, but the central office was deeply divided on whether this particular agent was one to go deliberately away without leave. So, noting that there was no cause for alarm yet, the bulletin was cautiously distributed throughout the nation: Agent Jack Griffin was missing.

Chapter 4

At four o'clock – four hours until curtain – James's dinner party was to begin. Generally, James's relationship with parties was similar to Carter's with magic shows: he lived for them. This afternoon, however, he felt quite differently. Before Carter's arrival, he'd been consulting his watch every five minutes. Soon after his brother came to the door and told him the story of the failed safecracking, James put his watch away, sat on the couch, and placed a cold washcloth over his eyes.

'We don't have time to worry about this,' Carter said.

James made no reply, which made Carter sorry. A bit of back-and-forth with his brother often made things seem better.

'You know, it *will* be all right.'

James sighed into his washcloth, and made a strange beckoning gesture with his fingers, as if inviting the fates to cast more down upon him.

Carter found himself annoyed. He'd reached deep into his imagination to present an all-new set of illusions, illusions quite beyond television, and was frankly dying for some appreciation. He said, 'Not everything has to rely on the television box.'

When James finally spoke, he did so slowly. 'There are two hundred unsold seats for tonight. And that's with all the comps we passed out. I swear that every nun and crippled child in the seven counties has a ticket to the show, and there are still two hundred . . .' He stood, rubbing his temples. 'And don't even ask me about the rest of the run.'

'Word of mouth—'

'If you put an elephant on a poster, the audience comes looking for an elephant. If you put a television on it, *even if they don't know what a television is*, they come looking for a television. It doesn't matter how great a magician you are, Charlie, but you are neither an elephant nor a television!'

Carter said quietly, 'I have *other* new illusions.'

'But nothing important!' With this, James froze, as if even he were startled at what he'd said.

Carter folded his arms. 'You know . . .' he said. And then nothing else.

'I'm sorry,' James sighed. He continued as he left the room, 'I'm just concerned for you.'

A few seconds later, Carter heard the shower start. He was left alone in the grand living area, feeling strangely like he was falling backward. He focused on various things: the vase of fresh lilies, the small Roman marble bust, then he realized his eyes were alighting on things he could accidentally knock over. But no – he was going some place beyond petty retributions now. He was beginning to gird himself for public performance, which meant shutting down small and social emotions.

The table was set for eight, using the cheap but festive Bauer plates. A large stew pot gently hiccupped in the kitchen. There were bouquets from opening-night well-wishers, all of them gathered around the maquette for the 'Everywhere' poster. Candles were lit, even though there was still the afternoon light, and red wine from Carter's own stock was breathing on the sideboard. Even though James had yelled, he had also prepared a feast and made the room feel like home.

Carter hadn't a clue whom James had invited tonight, and he knew better than to ask or even to attempt to wheedle the information out of Tom. Years ago he'd learned the excited, mock-pity look Tom could produce, with the accompanying, 'I'm sorry, that's a secret.'

He hoped Phoebe was invited. He hadn't seen enough of her in the past weeks. She lived in Oakland, and the recent burst of stage-craft required him to spend days and some nights at the Orpheum. He imagined introducing her to James. Then he imagined telling her how much James was annoying him, and even that minor intimacy made him feel a bit dizzy. It made shutting himself down for the performance that much harder. He imagined looking into her face, just to say 'hello,' and he felt slightly afraid; if he started talking to her he might never stop.

* * *

The first to arrive, at four o'clock on the nose, was Max Friz. He smelled of peppermint, and his clothes were clean and stiff, no doubt recently boiled over a firepot on the dock. Max had, rather improbably, brought a bunch of calla lilies. When he saw James already had calla lilies, his face fell, and he accepted a glass of wine, but had little further to say. Several minutes later, Philo came with Ledocq and Mrs Ledocq, with whom he'd been lodging. Carter greeted him warmly, noting that Philo smiled, but his eyes were looking somewhere beyond the room, as they had been for weeks.

After greetings had been exchanged, and James had accepted a basket of fruit from the Ledocqs, Carter and Ledocq stood aside from the others, by the fireplace.

Ledocq had a sore throat and was sucking on a lozenge. Nonetheless, he wanted to talk. 'Carlo's been telling the stage crew quite a story.' He mimicked Carlo's accent. 'Huge explosion, an' it almost *killed* us both.'

'If I'd killed him, husbands all over the globe would give me a tickertape parade. How go all the preparations?'

'If we were opening in three weeks, we'd be just about ready by then. Shellac, it's still drying. There's paint I've got boys fanning so it's tacky at least. It's a mess.' Ledocq coughed at length, until Carter asked if he were all right. '*Ma sacré toux*,' he whispered. 'Sand-soda-lime, the whole thing is murder on my throat—'

Carter held up a hand. Philo was approaching, shoulders slumped, hands in pockets. Carter touched him on the shoulder. 'Good afternoon, Philo.'

'Hello.'

'How is Pem?'

'She's fully recovered,' he said blankly, as he'd been saying for weeks. 'I'd like to go back to her, but she keeps telling me to stay.'

'She's a good woman,' Carter said.

'She is.' Philo looked up. 'James told me . . . the plans were destroyed.' Lately, his sentences bowed in the middle, as if their weight were unbearable. Whenever they talked, Carter wanted both to look away, and to tell him everything would be all right.

'It's a setback, to be sure. But not all is lost. I've been thinking – we have all the equipment except the flat-end tube. We're close, aren't we?'

Philo's eyes were on the andirons. 'Close, and far.'

'You know how to make it,' Carter murmured.

Ledocq said, 'I think the boy is tired.'

'You know, I do the impossible every night when I'm working.' Carter tried by force of will to make Philo meet his eye. But Philo was rooted on the andiron, which he touched gently with the tip of his shoe. 'It's not too late to help,' Carter said. 'I'd love it if my show inspired you to do something impossible.'

Now Philo looked up. It was a face hauntingly familiar to Carter: a polite smile, a mask that didn't quite cover the mouth of a black chasm. 'I used to know how to do that.'

'You can still—'

But Philo had already looked back down, where his foot was kicking against the fireplace bricks. 'I understand, Mr Carter. You and Mr Ledocq have been very kind. I can't produce what you'd like me to. I'm sorry.' Carter followed Philo's gaze – his foot dragged back and forth in a senseless pattern that Carter recognized. Like whittling sticks after Sarah had died. Philo was in a place that admitted no light.

Ledocq opened his mouth to speak, but Carter, with a single shake of his head, stopped him.

Carter said, 'It's okay, Philo.' And he and Ledocq left Philo alone.

When they were out of earshot, Carter said, 'I wish I could tell him that in the long run everything will be all right.'

'Why don't you tell *me* that, instead,' Ledocq whispered.

A few minutes later, James made a little speech welcoming everyone. With company to attend to, he stood taller than before, pouring wine or lemonade with vigor. 'This is the evening of inventors,' he said. 'I'm sure you'll have plenty to talk about.'

'*I* have something for them to talk about.' Tom stood in the living room. He waved a pamphlet in the air.

'Not that,' James sighed.

Tom shot him a look that told his partner 'I cannot be contained' and took advantage of a pause in conversation to read aloud. 'Now that you own a Victrola the whole world of music is open to you. *Everything* is yours from the magnificent pageantry of the grand opera to the wild swing of the jazz band – these come to you in your own home.' He paused. The entire room (save James, fuming) was adrift. 'We bought a Victrola last week,' Tom announced. 'I took it out of the box, it's in a thousand pieces, and I have instructions—'

At this, Ledocq began to chuckle.

Tom continued, 'I can't make heads or tails of how you put this junk together, so I was telling James as we have the greatest mechanical minds in the world here, wouldn't it be fun if everyone—'

'Give me that,' Ledocq whispered. 'Max, you help me. Philo, you don't have to if you don't want.'

Without inflection, Philo said, 'I can help,' leaving his post at the fireplace.

Mrs Ledocq blew between pursed lips. 'I don't know, you invite a man with a sore throat to dinner, and you make him do chores?'

While Philo read the instructions aloud ('Unfasten the taper tube by removing the brace from the end of the sound box crook'), Ledocq and Max sorted through the parts to determine what on earth a taper tube might be. Carter wondered if he might be of use in the kitchen.

But in the kitchen, Carter was told in no uncertain terms to go away. He reached to uncover a serving tray, and James slapped the back of his hand with a wooden spoon. 'Those are baked potatoes with cheese on them, and they aren't for you, they're for Baby.' When Carter protested that he wanted to help with dinner, James added that over the years he'd broken his weight in dishes, so he was invited to make himself useful by answering the doorbell whenever it rang. So Carter left, spirits oddly raised; at least James had returned to abusing him.

He stood at the edge of the living quarters, watching the knot of inventors contend with Mrs Ledocq, who had yanked the instructions away and, with amiable authority, was telling them what to do.

Carter heard Philo say, 'Hey, gents, she's right – that *is* the taper tube.'

'It is fun,' she nodded. 'I never get to do this at home. He always closes the door.' She said, 'Now, "After proper pivot setting has been secured, tighten the set screw." Lefty loosey, righty tighty, you know.'

Carter smiled and sipped his wine. He checked his watch and saw there were still hours until he needed to be at the stage door. He felt torn between participating in the social discourse to come and an almost grotesque impatience to close the doors, turn out the lights behind his eyes, and get the show started. The doorbell rang, giving him something to do. He threw the door open, readying a polite quip.

On the other side was Phoebe.

'Hello?'

'Hello!' He almost shouted it with joy.

'Oh, *hello*,' she cried in recognition, putting out a hand, which he took and more or less used to yank her across the threshold. She was a delightful study in contrasting simplicity and dash: though her face had been but lightly powdered, and she'd gone sans rouge, she also wore Angelus lipstick – 'shockingly scarlet' – and her hair had been very much *done*, straightened and held in place with chopsticks. She wore a beaded black silk dress that left an elegant amount of her throat bare.

'I'm so glad to see you,' he exclaimed.

'I'm glad someone is.' Her fingers flew across his palm, across his calluses.

She turned her head left and right, showing off from every angle, until Carter said: 'You look spectacular.'

'I did all this by myself, and not one girl at the Home noticed, and I wish I could forgive them for that, but—'

'How'd you get here?'

'Magic trick.'

Drying his hands on a towel, James came out of the kitchen. 'This must be Phoebe.'

'Are you James?'

James took her in, head to toe, and whistled. 'Dear God, but you're a dish.'

'Thank you,' she laughed.

'Charlie, you never told me she had such kissable lips. They're outstanding!'

'He leaves out important things,' Phoebe said.

'That smile! The taxi I sent arrived on time, I hope.'

'Shh. I told your brother it was all magic.'

440

'You are *so kissable*.' James leaned forward and kissed Phoebe on the lips. It seemed to strike her dumb, so he added, 'You'll have to excuse me, I've just come back from Paris.'

'That's a very good line,' Phoebe stammered. Carter laughed, delighted to see Phoebe knocked out by his brother.

'Everybody!' James clapped his hands and addressed the group by the Victrola. 'This is Miss Phoebe Kyle, and she is beautiful!'

Phoebe gave a shy little wave in their general direction.

'I'll fetch you a drink,' James said.

When he left, Phoebe said, 'Well, that was interesting.'

'You know, you two remind me of each other.'

'I have things to tell you. Can we go someplace?'

He nodded, and then said 'Yes' aloud, adding 'but perhaps we should wait until after dinner.'

'Oh dear, you're being reasonable.'

'It kills me, too.'

'You could show me the view.'

The idea seemed promising. 'Yes, I'd like that.'

With her arm linked to his, he walked her across the living quarters and opened the doors to the balcony that wrapped around three sides of the apartment. They were five stories up, so the view was rather magnificent from any position: the silent Sunday downtown skyscrapers behind them, the wilds of Telegraph Hill to the east, and then, extending to the bay, a vista of ramshackle roofs and whitewashed walls and clotheslines and wooden staircases painted green, the homes of North Beach Italian families. Because it was Sunday, the whole neighborhood smelled of oregano sauteing in olive oil, and young men were on every back porch, collarless, playing cards before dinner. Carter could see them laughing and he could see, behind them, in the gaps between the apartment houses, tendrils of fog reaching across the bay.

Carter glanced back inside the apartment. From their smiles and gestures, he could tell banter was flying between his brother and the Ledocqs. Philo stayed by the half-finished Victrola, and Carter could see him shaking his head, saying something to Tom.

'It feels like fall,' Phoebe said.

'I've noticed that quality to the light lately.'

'I used to notice it, too. And I can feel it still.'

'I've missed you.'

Her smile *was* terrific. 'Really?'

'Oh, yes. I've been working, but I always think about you. I've been inspired lately.' He told her a bit about the show. The opening card tricks, how he had a way to pick a card for the entire audience, and as he acted it out, it made her laugh in not quite the right places. She looked nervous to him, and her being nervous made him talk. 'I'll bring more people onstage than usual. I'll have a child throw knives at me, for instance.' Because she didn't say anything, he added, 'It should be fun.'

'Are any of the tricks dangerous?'

'No, not really,' he said.

'Are you sure?'

'I'm confident,' he said.

'Then I guess having knives flung at you by small-fry sounds fine.'

He touched her cheek. He hoped she would lean into it, as he remembered she had a subtle way of feeling his touch, but instead, she just seemed to look straight at him through her black glasses. This made him keep talking. 'I'd forgotten how you go about striking people dumb with wonder, but lately I've been paying attention to that sort of thing. I have old notebooks,' he said, looking off to the flat meadows atop Telegraph Hill. 'For years, my illusions weren't very good. They were so terrible I didn't even perform them in front of an audience. They were more like philosophical arguments with God. "How awful can things get," you know?'

'I have those sorts of talks every day. They've been coming out well, lately. I'm well-disposed toward the world when I don't want to destroy it.'

'That's exactly the balance,' he said excitedly. 'I had this trick, I wouldn't dignify it as an "illusion," it was with silk scarves – I would tear up colored silks very creatively, and then at the end, show how they'd been torn even more terribly than you thought. It may be magic, but it wasn't satisfying for an audience.'

She shook her head. She mouthed a 'No.'

Carter continued, 'I'd forgotten that a miracle is the type of magic an audience wants. A tragedy with a happy ending.'

Phoebe felt along the railing, hand over hand, until she had inched away from him. 'Was all that after your wife died?'

'Of course. Yes.' He paused. 'I haven't told you about her, have I?'

She shook her head.

'But you know about her anyway, don't you?'

She nodded.

'So, should that strike me as wonderful?'

'It's not wonderful.'

She looked like she was bracing herself for a punch. When he'd traveled to the Far East, he'd heard the Chinese knew the pressure points you could touch to ease pain, and Carter wished he'd paid more attention. He himself felt a lightness. He was looking at Telegraph Hill, directly behind Phoebe, where on an early morning in the spring of 1911, he had fallen in love with Sarah. Here he was less than a mile and over a decade away. What a strange world to live in. He thought of the boys and girls who looked for sweethearts at Mountain View Cemetery, and chorus girls who met their beaux behind scrim, and office romances that flourished in the buildings on Market Street, and he felt like there were little lights in alcoves here and there across the city, in cozy dens, in doorways during rainstorms, or even a chilly balcony on the Ferry building. Everywhere, little pairs of glowing lights. When you walked a city, wherever you looked, someone had probably fallen in love there.

'However you know about me,' Carter said, 'it *is* wonderful.'

'I'm not psychic, Charlie. I'm not a medium or a ghost—' The hair on her arms stood in a sea of gooseflesh. She hugged herself. 'I'm not this way, normally,' she declared. 'I'm very carefree, and I like your motorcycle and someday I'd like to dance with you.' The network of clips and pins that kept her bun in place was already failing, and her hair was beginning to take its natural course. Carter loved her. It was a feeling he hadn't expected to return to him, but here it was, a transformation, the dead heart now beating.

He began to say it. 'I—'

'I was one of Borax Smith's girls.' She managed each word with care, like she was testing it for resilience.

At first, it was as if she'd said she was from Kenosha, and Carter was ready to reply, 'Oh, yes, I've played there, I know it well.' But he realized what she had left unsaid.

'I didn't think it was fair,' she began, and then, 'I thought you should know.'

A thumping sound behind him, fingertips on glass. Carter turned around and saw his brother waving them in for dinner. When he looked back, he saw Phoebe's mouth was taut, and her hands braced on the railing like she was awaiting an earthquake. In a rush, for she'd been preparing this speech for a while, she said, 'I was there when you were sad. You told Borax all of your troubles. I was right there in the room sometimes, or the other girls told me what they'd heard. You made quite an impression on all of us.' Carter tried to remember her, but it was of course impossible – the bonnets, the veils, the silence. 'So that's how I know about you. I liked you back then, and I like you now. I've been such a pest at the Home, I'm just being eaten alive with guilt every moment you think I've got some kind of gift.'

'You're beautiful,' he whispered. He put his hands around her waist so that they met behind her. She stiffened.

'You can't mean that.'

He continued to hold her, until she finally let go of the railing and draped her hands on his shoulders. He felt her body releasing tension – he envisioned a picnic blanket catching the breeze, settling down toward the cool autumn grass.

'Are you telling me the truth?' she sighed. 'I can't see you, so . . . can you tell me again, maybe I'll hear it then.'

'You're a beautiful woman.'

She gripped his back with her hands. James knocked on the window again. Carter glared until he went away.

Her voice muffled by their hug, Phoebe asked, 'Is your brother mad at you?'

'He thinks I'm going to go bankrupt tonight.'

'Are you?'

'I think so.'

She murmured, 'That's good. I've had bad luck with men whose prospects are excellent.'

'I'm sorry but I have to ask you this – Phoebe, has Borax sent you to spy on me?'

'Really? You're serious? No. I haven't talked to him since I met you.'

444

'I robbed his safe this afternoon.'

'You've led a very interesting life.'

'I think you have, too.'

She put her lips against his throat, and he with no conscious thought began to stroke the back of her neck, which caused her whole body to press against his. Her lips touched his ear and her glasses scraped his cheek. 'I worry I'm not good enough for you.'

'Phoebe—' He closed his eyes.

'I can't see what you love doing the most in the world.'

'I know. But that forces me to behave differently. I can't be clever or simple.'

'I worry you might hurt me.'

He hesitated. 'You know that I – was – I was responsible for my wife dying.'

'That was an accident.' She said this with conviction, the same way she'd told him she knew he wasn't a ghost. He realized he'd needed to hear her say it. He'd needed that for longer than he knew. He brought his mouth to hers and they kissed until he realized the thundering sound in his ears was actually coming from inside the house, where there was a table full of company, on their feet, whistling and letting loose with randy applause.

At dinner, the conversation was amusing and the food uniformly excellent. The mood was sufficiently light that even Max Friz smiled once or twice. There were toasts to Carter and the show, telegrams to read from Houdini and Thurston and Goldin and Raymond. Ledocq had to leave the table early – he had to get to the theatre, he felt, or the earth would open up and a giant hand would yank the whole show into a chasm. But before he left, Carter read aloud a brief telegram. 'TO MONSIEUR LEDOCQ BREAK A LEG OR I'LL BREAK IT FOR YOU SINCERELY BENNY LEONARD.' Ledocq, touched to the point of tears, took the telegram and put it in his breast pocket and left without a word.

There was also a chatty message in French from a Leonetto Cappiello, whose name Carter didn't recognize. This caused James to lecture the guests on his brother's inadequacies in social situations, as Monsieur Cappiello had designed the 'Everywhere' poster, and Carter was about to make a tired response – for he no longer

445

wanted to be teased – when James finished with something close to an apology. 'My brother has been so busy designing illusions that will confound us all that I'm proud to be the one who keeps track of his things on earth for him.' The conversation segued into banter about Carter's obviously smitten self, and Phoebe's charms. Mrs Ledocq in particular said she'd never seen Charlie Carter looking so happy. Philo asked to be excused during the main course. He went and sat alone in the living room.

For a while, it was six people at the table, telling stories and asking questions of each other – for instance, Max wanted to know if Phoebe had a dog, which mystified her until, with the intervention of Tom (who'd heard about such a thing), she learned that the veterans blinded in the gas attacks were now able to walk on the most crowded sidewalks with the aid of trained guide dogs.

Over salad, discussion went back and forth about whether this was prudent or dignified, and as Phoebe learned more and more from Max – the blind in Germany could take their dogs on riverboats and buses and trains – she announced that she would get a dog, and furthermore she hoped it was a completely imprudent and undignified dog with a name like Bowser or Jingles, for only that type would suit her.

The table's laughter was met with the choral sounds of Handel's *Messiah*, which came from the living room. Then Philo walked to the table and sat down in his chair as if he'd done nothing. Tom shouted 'Hallelujah,' and, beside himself, ruffled Philo's hair.

For an hour, Carter sat amid friends and family. With the music playing, and the wine to drink, and a woman with whom he occasionally held hands under the table, this was his last time tonight to relax. It was well known among magicians that a man awaking to love was vulnerable to deadly mistakes.

♣ ◆ ♥ ♠

The last thing Griffin did before he left Denver was to send a certified parcel to his attorney in Bethesda, with instructions to open it if he went missing for more than a week. It contained all of his notes on the Carter investigation, including his suspicions that his superiors might be protecting the magician. He had scrawled at the bottom of the last sheet of paper: 'The wine bottle enclosed is visible in the uncropped *Examiner* photographs found herein. Its label is a "cabalistic" type visual puzzle that when viewed from an extreme angle shows the name of the vintner (Charles Carter), his profession (Magician), his places of residence (San Francisco, Oakland), and other phrases irrelevant to this investigation. Research confirms he received title to vineyards in Napa County at land forfeiture in December 1897. Witness Alhino saw a man (possibly Carter) delivering said bottle to Harding room that night.'

Even Griffin had to admit it was just a wine bottle. No trace of poison. But it put Carter in the room, maybe, and Carter hadn't mentioned being there. It wasn't enough to convict him, but Griffin was sure he could confront him and, if he had to, beat something out of him.

He was required to report for duty at 6 A.M. He telephoned the Northern Line train station and requested a one-way ticket on the 9:15 A.M. express, asking them to hold it for Jack Griffin. When agents swarmed the station, they hovered around the ticket office to no avail – Jack Griffin never arrived and his ticket went unclaimed. There being much gossip among the train crews, however, a Pullman porter heard the fuss and mentioned that a Mr Jack Griffin actually boarded the 7:25 and paid for a ticket to New Orleans.

Local authorities at every stop were alerted, and agents mobilized, but they needn't have bothered. Jack Griffin had learned a thing or two recently about misdirection: he disembarked from the 7:25 after one stop and walked a mile to an airstrip on which he saw a single Jenny. He entered the barracks and awoke the pilot, who'd been napping on his cot, and asked the groggy man how fast he could get to San Francisco. Half-awake, the pilot began his speech about how safe flying was and how many combat missions he'd flown in France – all Jenny pilots had exactly the same story, and it was built to suss out how much they could gouge their passenger – stopping only when Griffin started counting out ten-dollar bills.

'Dusk,' he said.

Chapter 5

Carter's driver dropped him at the Orpheum stage door at 6:30, and from that moment – for there was a page boy waiting for him on the sidewalk, and the page boy held a list of complaints – he dealt with crises. The red gels used on the stage lights were casting shadows unlike those they'd thrown during rehearsals. A water pipe over the stage had chosen that moment to leak. The lion was anxious. Cleo was unsure of her part in the Egyptian illusion: Could she try something called the Stanislavski method?

This last request was odd enough that Carter, supervising the loading of paper flowers into a cone, asked her to explain.

'You see,' she said, her voice much more exotic-sounding than it had seemed hours ago, 'I am not pretending to be an Egyptian princess – I actually *am* an Egyptian princess.'

'I follow. That would be fine.'

'It increases believability,' she added.

'Yes.' He dismissed her, watching the sequins on her headdress sparkle as she walked under the lights.

The stage manager approached. 'Mr Carter. The lion.'

And so Carter attended Baby, who indeed seemed more agitated than usual. He calmed down after a few reassuring words and one of James's baked potatoes with cheese.

The leak over the stage was taped up, the gels were swapped, and, though there was no end to the problems, Carter began to fade from the here-and-now into a quiet place where nothing could reach him.

He collared Albert and Esperanza and told them the company needed to block out a television-less version of the Devil's entrance just before act three; hence the interval following act two would be longer than usual. Would they mind performing the juggling bit from 'A Night in Old China' on the apron to cover for him? They were delighted: Did Carter have flash paper? He told them to hound Ledocq until they found some.

Then Ledocq moaned aloud to Carter about that development – the flash paper he'd made was volatile and tended to heat up by itself. Did they really want to risk Albert going up in flames? Carter paid enough attention to direct the conversation, but he was also listening to the other side of the curtain, where the orchestra, whom he was paying seventy dollars an hour, tuned up and read through the sheet music he'd provided.

Outside the theatre, on the sidewalk, boys paced back and forth, swinging school bells and wearing sandwich boards on which half-sheets of Carter's 'Everywhere' poster were pasted. The opening night audience, spilling a moderate way off the sidewalk, was waiting for the doors to swing open. Of the several hundred people who'd arrived early, there were men who wore diamond studs in their blouses, escorting women wearing pearl necklaces secured to their bodies the way Parisians did, with secret binding chains that discouraged theft. The thieves who worked in bump-and-run teams, impressed, stole the men's wallets instead.

There were street entertainers with their hats in front of them, among them: Nessie the blind accordion player, who attended each opening night, all over the city; and a young hobo, a *boho* hobo, a professor of *hobology*, he announced, who declaimed Shakespeare for anyone who would stop to listen.

Carter's complimentary tickets had gone far and wide, from Captain Willow, who hobbled along the sidewalk with his wife, to Philo, who came with Max Friz and Mrs Ledocq, to Jossie Dover, who looked smashing in a tuxedo, to the Chong family, whose daughters would play a small part in the show. Mayor Davie of Oakland and Mayor Rolph of San Francisco nearly collided, and after feigned politeness, tried to determine which of them had been given a better seat in the house.

Around the corner, in the alleyway, which had been kept scrupulously clean for the arrival of equipment and animals, the boys from the Shell station smoked cigarettes and drank gin with the girls they'd met in the graveyard, freshlings from Mills College who wore cloche hats and turned-down hose. 'Sure I know Carter,' Jimmy was saying to the girls. 'He's a good egg, he tells me how he does all his tricks.'

Exactly no one believed him. 'G'waaan,' the girls cried together.

A line of taxicabs two rows deep dropped passengers off under the marquee lights. From some of them came irritated men from the War Department and from others, shooting them the evil eye, came junior executives from RCA and Westinghouse. Word had come down that even though the plans for television were destroyed, smuts low on the totem pole had to report back with their own eyes that Carter was empty-handed. To one side of the entrance was a line of crippled children and their nurses, and to the other the fifty-cent ticket holders who talked about the great shows they had seen two or three seasons before, and which movie stars compared favorably to Mr Carter, and whether he'd actually killed the President, or whether it had been the widow Harding or his cabinet or the Reds, and, in a debate as old as the Phantom War Gun, was Charles Carter more a glamorous figure or tragic? Had he ever been as good a magician since his wife had died?

At 7:30, Carter took a final walk around the stage and the back-stage and then locked the door to his dressing room. This was a routine dating back many years – his final preparations would take him until two minutes before showtime.

He stripped to his undershirt and shorts. His work clothes hung from a hook just over his makeup mirror. He sat down and stood again, for his chair was unexpectedly yielding. He exclaimed aloud in simple happiness, as there was a large silk pillow on his seat. He reflected for a moment about the pleasures that headlining could bring, and then sat again, his makeup kit in front of him. Eye shadow, eyebrow pencil. He applied red dots to the corners of his eyes so they wouldn't disappear under the lights. Then on went the flexible greasepaint, mild as possible, capped with his secret weapon: Max Factor Society Makeup, a perfectly glareless powder. As it was made for civilians rather than the stage, other magicians hadn't caught on to it yet. The idea was for the audience to not even know he was wearing makeup.

He checked every pocket in his jacket, ready to resew or tear the seams of anything he needed to. But it was perfect, as, in a burst of industry three days ago, he'd lovingly stocked his clothes. With the familiar black wool suit around him, and his black tie done just *so*, the final step was to adjust his turban, just *so*. He felt around the folds of damask, ensuring nothing hidden was about to drop onto the stage.

When he was quite finished, he shot his sleeves, and looked at himself in the mirror again. He saw an unremarkable man from whom he would not expect miracles.

But it was only 7:45. Somehow, he'd prepared too quickly. He had nothing to do for fifteen minutes. Immediately, an anxiety so potent it had its own color – it seemed pinkish – rose in his chest and shoulders.

To combat that, he let out a contented-sounding sigh and put his feet up on his dressing room table in an approximation of looking relaxed. He attempted nostalgia: Ah, when had he last seen this dressing room? Four or five years ago, he'd had a nice week here, and he'd headlined here twice when he was still on Keith-Orpheum time. And 1911, now that was a remarkable show. He remembered his parents hovering over him here just before he'd debuted Blackmail, and how he'd exasperatedly wished they would just stay away on opening night.

They weren't here tonight. He couldn't in fact remember the last time they'd seen his show. They'd meant to come when he was in Rio nine months ago. He shrugged: he had James and Ledocq and a burgeoning romance, and yet, he'd once hoped to impress his parents, long ago. When you got older, did you actually need your parents less or did you just learn how to replace them?

The stage would be empty. He could go there. He folded up shop in the dressing room, turned off the lights, and closed the door. He walked down the narrow corridor, stagehands and property men shuffling past him and whispering to each other. He kept his head down until he passed Ledocq, whereupon he muttered that he was going to work now.

'You have your wallet?'

Carter patted his trouser pocket. 'Yes.'

'Good. Always take your wallet onstage.'

With that ritual finished, Ledocq patted him on the back.

The stage floor was built at a cunning angle, two degrees oblique from the audience point of view, so that it looked shallower, as if there would be no room for hiding, say, assistants or a second set of boxes. It was a collage of tape, traps, and marks to hit, and

Carter could feel as he strode across it which places gave way slightly and which were reinforced.

He stood dead center, by a small X fashioned from electrical tape beside which Albert had written, 'Here standeth our boss.' He smiled. There was a fire curtain behind him, green velvet, and, before him, a pair of musty draperies that would part in just minutes and show him off to the audience.

Carter was perfectly alone, and the isolation appealed to him. The orchestra was playing its preshow selections, a medley of waltzes and popular tunes. They came through the curtains muffled and mixed with the sounds of the audience, happy sounds, Carter thought. He fought back the urge to crack his knuckles.

'Hey.' Phoebe's voice. It took him a moment to locate her – she was standing in the wings, stage right. She was holding on to a handrail. Carter could hear the orchestra finish its final waltz. There was some applause, probably from the higher galleries, where the audience was unafraid to be excited. 'I'd kiss you for luck,' she said, 'but your makeup smells awful. Dear God, is that Society by Max Factor?'

'Shhh.'

'Have you tried Helena Rubinstein? She's very clever.'

He half-listened, unsure whether he had a deck of cards. He patted his jacket pocket, and found them.

'Is there any trick you do tonight that's dangerous?'

'Didn't you ask me that? They're all dangerous.'

'No, I mean, *severely*.'

He looked over his shoulder. When had the overture begun? It was in full swing now, and he had but a moment left before curtain. 'I'll have knives hurled at me at eight fifteen, and at eight twenty-five—'

'Please don't say that. I can't hear that kind of thing.'

'Well . . . bullet catching. That's the dangerous one.'

'Why is it?'

The music was swelling to a crescendo. Thirty seconds left. 'It's killed a few men onstage. Basically, there's a loaded gun, but you switch it with one that fires blanks. Chung Ling Soo used – never mind, we have a foolproof method to—'

'Please don't do it.'

'It's safe, Phoebe.' He touched her arm. 'Really. I don't take risks.'

She wrapped both her hands around his. 'I'm not letting you go until you at least consider it.'

He looked from her to the curtain, then back. The whole bullet-catching gag took two minutes and was deep into the third act. In fact, it was yesterday's business, a simple repeat of an effect he'd held over from last season. 'I can leave it out.'

Her shoulders dropped. 'I owe you something.'

'And what would that be?'

'The music's stopped,' she said, and smiled at him.

Chapter 6

The lights slowly dimmed and a single bonbon spotlight was brought up so it shone on the red velvet curtain. The focus drew narrower, tightening as there was a final explosion of kettledrums, and then, for the first time since the decade began, the grand draperies at the Orpheum Theatre parted for an evening-length show.

The spotlight fell on empty space. Carter the Great came to his mark from stage right, making small, sultanic salutes to the audience as the orchestra played the most familiar bars from 'Pomp and Circumstance.'

Between the time he found his mark and the time he spoke, he surveyed the audience in full. He had been through many opening nights, more than he could remember. On few of them had he felt like this. He mentally brought out the old checklist, . . . *am I too hot, no; am I too cold, no* . . . attempting to name the feeling, and then realized that the oddity was simply that he was *feeling*. He could feel Phoebe in the wings – he hadn't had someone waiting backstage for him in years. And there, the very back of the house, he saw empty seats. The sight struck him with weird urgency, as if his duty to entertain were quickly tripled.

The applause died down. He put his hands in his pockets. He curled and relaxed his toes inside his well-polished shoes.

'Ladies and Gentlemen, thank you for coming tonight.' The curtain closed behind him, so he was left on the apron to perform in-one. 'This is a very large theatre, and it deserves only the most massive and splendid illusions that cost many thousands of dollars to construct. I invite you all to witness this stupendous effect, an awe-inspiring spectacle ne'er before seen by human eyes. It will stun you. Behold,' he held on to the pause, 'a deck of cards.'

He showed in his right hand a deck of green Bicycle cards. There was almost complete silence of the uncertain sort, as it seemed an unassuming way to begin.

'May I have a volunteer from the audience?'

Carter picked a man from the fourth row, aisle seat, who trotted onto the stage as if he owned it.

'Good evening,' Carter said. 'What is your name, sir?'

'Patrick Smyth, with a "y."'

'Mr Smyth with a "y," please pick a card.' He fanned out his deck. 'Any card, of course, not just the card I want you to pick. Now don't show it to me. Thank you. Please put it back in the deck. Excellent.' One second later, Carter held up a nine of spades. 'Is this your card?'

'Yes, it is,' he said.

'Thank you, thank you,' Carter said, bowing completely out of proportion to the effect on the audience. The applause was akin to the sound of a newspaper rustling in the breeze. He came to a full upright posture, looking into the house with one eyebrow flexed. 'You know,' he said, as if in confidence, to Mr Smyth, 'the audience doesn't strike me as thrilled.'

Smyth shook his head.

'And it is my job to thrill them.'

'Indeed.'

'It did seem awfully easy, didn't it?'

'It wasn't a remarkable trick,' Smyth allowed. Carter had picked well, a man who had helpful critiques.

Carter shuffled the deck, looking lost in thought. 'Perhaps they suspect you're a confederate. Magicians, or so I'm told, use confederates. Have we ever met?'

'No, sir.'

'Are you on my payroll?'

'No, sir.'

'Walking down the street, have you ever seen me? I look something like this.' Carter turned in profile, as if that might help.

'I have not.'

'I'm not sure I believe you. I might be paying you to say that.'

'I'm perfectly trustworthy.'

'Which is the problem. If I had a confederate, he'd be perfectly trustworthy. How do I know then that you are *not* my confederate? I can't possibly amaze a sophisticated San Francisco audience until they know who my confederates might be.' Carter put

455

his hand to his chin. 'We must do something to flush all possible confederates out of the audience.' He snapped his fingers. 'Mr Smyth, you may return to your seat. A round of applause for the man who claims not to be on my payroll.'

Mr Smyth looked like he had a great deal more to discuss, even as he reluctantly took his seat back.

'Will everyone in the audience – and this goes for everyone – please look under their seats? One of you has five thousand dollars in gold bullion hidden there.' This last statement was an ad-lib. He imagined, somewhere backstage, James flipping through his showbook frantically. In the audience, Carter heard murmurs, and several isolated cries of astonishment as fingertips all over the theatre found that there was indeed something secreted under their seats. Carter continued, 'I'm sorry, did I say five thousand dollars in gold bullion? I meant everyone has decks of playing cards.' He heard groans and laughter, and returned to the regular script. 'Please unwrap your souvenir decks of cards. You'll notice they're rather thin. Hold them up. Thank you.'

It made a lovely sight, almost two thousand hands waving decks in the air. He directed everyone to open the boxes up and remove the twenty-one cards inside. 'They're normal playing cards except there's a rather plain-looking charlatan on the back. He's wearing a turban. He's drawn by Monsieur Leonetto Cappiello of Paris, France,' he added, another ad-lib he hoped James heard.

When everyone had removed their cards, he told the audience to pick a card from their decks. 'Now, please don't show it to me. You, sir, in Row S, five seats in, you're showing me your card! All right, I'm closing my eyes.' Carter put on a blindfold and continued. 'Now, I want you all to put your card back, right in the center of your decks. Exactly ten cards from the top, please. I'm going to make you do some math this evening, but it shouldn't be too frightening. I want you to cut your decks into piles.' He held up two fingers. 'Two piles. That's the math.'

All around the audience, men and women looked into their hands, following Carter's instructions, and making piles on their palms or on their knees. 'Actually,' Carter said, 'there is more math. Take the first three cards off the bottom . . . now take five from the top . . .' He continued in this vein. The audience shuffled and discarded pips as directed. The house was alive with the sounds of people counting as instructed. But far in the back of the theatre, in a seat in the third gallery, a man performed the maneuvers as if following the orders of a jail guard. And with each new instruction ('Cast aside the bottom card . . . now shuffle again . . .'), the man was heard to hiss, 'Oh, *please*,' until his neighbors told him to hush.

'Now, square your decks. This is the moment of truth. Take the top card off your decks, and look at it. Is that your card?'

The theatre sounded like the woodlands, as little trills and cries came through the air. For Carter had indeed led every person in the audience – save one, who had deliberately disobeyed – right to the card they'd chosen. He took off his blindfold. Almost two thousand cards were swinging in the air, a deep lawn of white and red and black flowers, people turning to each other to ask, 'How did that happen?'

'Have I chosen everyone's card then?' Carter smiled. 'Then it is as I'd hoped. You are *all* my confederates.' He bowed.

In the gallery, the bald man elbowed the woman to his right. 'What a blowhard,' he whispered.

'Shhh!'

'Don't you think the man's a blowhard?'

'Excuse me, sir.' It was an usher. He had a flashlight, and he pointed it directly in the man's face. 'Can you come with me, please?'

'I paid for this seat. Fifty cents.'

'Sir, please come with me.' The usher pulled his jacket back, showing off a blackjack. The bald man's eyes went from it to the usher's face.

'My, my. Two saps,' he said, and before inviting more dialogue, he stood. The usher was exactly his size, well over six feet. 'All right. I'm coming with you.'

He walked to the aisle, and as he passed, audience members grabbed at their ankles where he'd stepped on them. The usher pulled at his bicep.

The man regarded the usher's fingers. 'You should remove your hand.'

The usher said nothing more as he guided the man out of the gallery.

They made it like that as far as the staircase, which was dark, soundproofed, and curtained off. It was a staircase that led not only to the lobby, but to the roof.

'Would anyone here like to learn how to do magic tricks?' Carter asked brightly. As he spoke, his eyes were on the crippled children. Before the show, the nurses had informed him which children were sturdy and mobile enough for what he had in mind. Many of their hands went up, and they cried out in excitement. He listened carefully for those voices that would carry deep into the theatre.

To his delight, he heard one of them had deep gravel in his voice – he sounded like a gangster. He gestured that the boy should come join him onstage.

'What's your name?'

'Jake,' the boy growled. He was indeed a little gangster, perhaps seven years old, hands jammed down into trouser pockets undoubtedly stuffed with frogs and string and a pocket knife, eyeing Carter like he was figuring the odds on a dog fight.

'Jake, you sound like you're from New York City.'

'Naw. Lowah East Side.'

The audience roared, as it always did at children's misconceptions. Jake looked out at them as if he'd remember each and every one of their faces and take his revenge later.

'What are you doing in California, Jake?'

'I got az-mer.'

More laughter, which Carter hadn't wanted. He'd created this illusion to make a child happy to be onstage. It was vital to turn the tide in Jake's favor.

'Jake, let's teach you some magic to keep that asthma from bothering you, shall we?'

Phoebe Kyle was in the wings, listening, standing by the handrail, using it for balance. Onstage, Carter was teaching the boy how to hold a deck of cards 'just like a magician does.' But no matter how he gripped the deck, Jake couldn't make a card jump out the way Carter could. Just as it seemed Jake was about to become upset, Carter reassured him that magic was a long-term process, that practice and perseverance were the keys.

'I have every confidence in you. You must practice and practice and practice till sore. Only then are you ready to practice once more,' Carter half-said, half-chanted.

Phoebe heard someone treading lightly behind her. There had been light treads all evening long, so she paid this little attention until there was a hand at her elbow.

'Are you Miss Phoebe Kyle?' A young man's whisper. 'Western Union,' he whispered. 'Telegram.'

'Telegram?' The word seemed no more real when she said it. In fact, it seemed unlikely. 'For me?'

'Mr Ledocq, he pointed you out.'

She felt him putting a piece of paper in her hand. 'What does it say?'

He shrugged. 'We don't read 'em, ma'am.'

'I'm sorry, but I'm blind. Can you read it to me?' She passed it back to him.

'Oh.' A rustling. 'Huh. There's some mistake here. It's blank.' He passed it back to her. 'Sorry about that.' He turned on his heel with a squeak and trotted off.

Onstage, Carter was saying, 'Jake, you're ready for the next step, I think.'

Phoebe, who had many fears generally, was terrified by the idea of someone sending her a blank telegram. She held it like it was an envelope filled with scorpions, and then hesitantly she touched her fingertips to it. What she found made her more frightened: it wasn't blank at all. It was Braille.

'Now, Jake, cards are very difficult to practice with. So I'm going to move on to magic you can perform excellently and immediately. What do you say, sport?'

Jake nodded. Carter paid him close attention: he was patient, and serious, and hadn't yet cracked a smile. When he'd planned illusions for this show, Carter's earliest designs were scenarios for two small boys in a snowstorm, learning magic tricks, but raw autobiography never satisfies when half-disguised as entertainment – the important part was that, as a boy, he'd wanted to perform incredible illusions quickly. He engineered an effect that could turn a child into a sorcerer instantly.

An assistant wearing a fez – Albert – carried a table onstage and placed it near Carter. On the table was a bundle draped in velvet.

'This is the easiest type of magic to do right the first time.' Carter unwrapped the bundle and held the contents aloft in both his hands. 'Throwing knives at a living target.'

The curtain went up, showing off a set designed to look like Carter's study. Piles of books, the suit of armor from his last show, ancient lithographs and animal heads mounted on the walls. To the far left was a scholarly-looking desk on which there was a wise-looking stuffed owl. Behind the desk, along the wall, framed portraits of some of Carter's fellow magicians.

Carter took off his jacket and draped it over a coatrack just as Willie wheeled a backdrop painted with imps and devils on stage. 'So, here are your knives. I'll stand right here and you throw them at me.' Carter positioned himself against the backdrop, legs spread and arms akimbo.

Jake stood in the middle of the stage, uncertain what was expected of him. The table piled with knives was right behind him. He took in a shallow breath, a terrible little wheeze.

A second later, Carter exclaimed, 'What am I doing! I'm sorry, Jake, I didn't prepare you for this, did I?' He left the backdrop and went down on one knee, right next to Jake. 'This could have been very dangerous if I hadn't done this.' He took out a blindfold and showed it, both sides. The audience rumbled, half with laughter, half with horror, so Carter took the opportunity to murmur, 'Young man, you won't hurt me. No matter what you do, it's magic. I promise.'

'Okay.' Jake looked toward Carter trustingly, just like that. Carter wanted to hug him. He secured the blindfold around Jake's eyes so that its point hung down below his chin.

Carter returned to his pose, and, seeming to realize Jake couldn't find the knives when blindfolded, clapped twice. The assistant with the fez came to the boy's side.

'Just let your arm follow Albert's,' Carter called out. 'Just let it go limp, and he'll guide you.'

Albert's hand wrapped around Jake's, which was wrapped around the butt of the knife, then Jake's arm went back once, twice, and with the old heave-ho of a baseball pitcher, he threw with all of his might, right at Carter. There was a muffled impact, and a spotlight swept the stage for a few moments, finally discovering that Jake's first knife had gone considerably wide, in fact hitting a glossy, framed photo of Thurston square in the forehead.

There was considerable laughter from the front of the house. Carter called, 'Albert, those *are* the magic knives, aren't they?'

When it was confirmed that the knives were indeed magic, Jake was given a second chance. With Albert's arm guiding his, Jake's next throw hit the backdrop against which Carter stood, right between his elbow and his body. Carter was the first to applaud. 'Very good. Keep going!' he cried.

Jake's next four throws hit outside the knee, inside the knee, by the upstage elbow, and the last one popped a balloon Carter held in his teeth. Each of the impacts was accompanied by shrieks from the house – they generally diminished, save for a man in the seven-dollar seats who laughed himself into such red-faced hysteria that Carter actually addressed him from the stage. 'Sir, I don't know you, but I invite you to attend every one of my shows from now on.'

By the time the illusion was over, Jake was certainly not ready to leave the stage. Because Carter knew children delighted in the mess of it, he and Jake baked a cake in a man's hat. A great fog of flour spread into the audience while Jake's friends laughed the deep guffaws of children.

The finale of the first act, in which an upright piano was rolled onto the stage, was one Carter had birthed through sheer stubbornness, as Ledocq thought it was crazy. 'You put a piano onstage, you vanish it! You *must* vanish it! You must not' – his hands flew in the air as if describing exploding popcorn – 'it's a disaster.'

Carter had said, 'Anyone can make a piano vanish.'

When the piano was in place, Carter asked Jake if he knew how to play.

'Nah,' Jake rasped. With a few tricks under his belt, he seemed as virile as a cowboy.

'Are you sure? Have you had lessons?'

Jake shook his head.

'Have you ever played on a magic piano? No? Jake, have a seat on the bench there. Good lad. Can you reach the pedals?' His feet were in fact a good foot away from the floor. Carter spread his hands out on the keyboard. 'Just move your hands on the keys. Give it a try.'

Jake tentatively touched down his fingers on a few keys. It didn't sound particularly magic.

'Thank you, Jake. Now, be a good boy and play something for me, say, a nice, slow piece. It's all right, go ahead.' Jake fished for a key or two and looked up in astonishment as the piano began to make the most beautiful sounds. A nocturne.

'Hey!' His face twisted in delight.

'Very good. Familiar, too, isn't that Chopin?'

'Yeah?' Jake looked up at him.

'Keep moving your hands.' Carter asked Jake for a waltz and a rag, both of which he played impeccably. Just as the audience was sensing the kind of fraud it might be, Carter tugged loose the piano's paneling to show off the absence of a printed roll – this wasn't a player piano. He called for requests. Audience members called out for Irving Berlin tunes, then the 'Battle Hymn of the Republic,' 'Lost in the Moonlight.' But then someone called out for Liszt, and when Carter said this aloud, the piano began to play the *Benediction* that Sarah had played for him long ago, and Carter was pulled into his past. He saw two beautiful women running upstairs, hand-in-hand, and felt a dog putting her chin on his hand. He had woken up to discover the love of his life. He snapped back to the present, and he felt the demonstration had gone on long enough.

'Jake,' he said, 'you've become an excellent magician in twenty minutes, which is only twenty years less than it took me to reach adequacy.' As he spoke, he accepted a rolled-up purple velvet cloak from Willie. 'We're going to send you back into the world with all the arcane knowledge of the mystic arts at your disposal, but there's one more illusion you have to master before you can take my place here onstage.'

'Can I throw the knives again?'

'You never repeat anything onstage,' he said, and Jake nodded. They were having a conversation in front of two thousand people. How easy it was for a child if he was made comfortable. 'No, the skill I'm talking about is defeating the ordinary. For instance, here—' He gave the cloak a violent shake that scattered flower petals across the stage, and then he held it stiffly to his side, like a matador, and removed it – revealing a beautiful, smiling woman. She was dressed in a blue-sequined silk dress that ended just below the knee – not above, as Carter did not run that kind of show. She waved to the audience.

'See, Jake, that was unexpected. I struck a blow against the ordinary. This is my assistant, Madame Esperanza.' Carter took her by the hand and paraded her across the apron. He called over his shoulder, 'Now, young man, go to the piano bench and open it up and bring me what you find.'

All eyes were on Jake as he opened the bench and tugged at something. It took him two hands, but eventually he withdrew a long, heavy crosscut saw, a saw that stood almost as tall as he did. When he turned downstage to show it off, its lower end dragged on the boards. It was a two-man sort of saw.

Carter took it from Jake and stood it on its end. They made a pretty line-up just in front of the footlights: Jake, Carter, the saw, Esperanza.

'Jake, what would an ordinary magician do with that saw?'

'He'd saw the lady in half.'

'In halves, yes. Exactly! Now, you must *never* be ordinary. That's the rule.' And here was where Carter put into effect his odd little idea. Silently he thanked his mother for her insistence that he never saw through a girl – he'd been forced to think up something far more interesting. He explained that many magicians vanished pianos, and that this, too, was ordinary. But how ordinary was sawing a piano in halves?

'First, let's give the saw to Willie, shall we?' On cue, Willie walked in from the wings, and took the saw in hand.

'Second, we'll make sure Esperanza is out of harm's way. Wave good-bye, Esperanza.'

Esperanza, still smiling, waved to the audience as Carter threw the cloak over her and drew it away. The whole motion took less than a heartbeat, but she had disappeared. The applause was approving but also expectant: something was coming next.

Willie took the saw and walked to the far end of the piano. Carter said, 'Now, Jake, I need your help. Please hold this wand. Stand right here, back up a few feet, excellent. Now watch carefully.

When I give the signal, you must wave the wand, all right?'

Jake nodded. He was intent now. Carter felt like he'd made a lifelong apprentice. Willie brought the saw across the piano top, and waited.

Then, with the audience completely enrapt – was he actually going to saw it in halves? – Carter took one end of the saw, and Willie the other, and together they began to work it vigorously back and forth across the cherrywood surface atop the piano, and feathers of sawdust caught the lights, then fell to the floor.

It was indeed a bizarre sight to behold, magician and assistant pushing and pulling the great silver saw, and the audience at first laughed, for the performers looked quite awkward. But then the sound of the saw changed from a gritty and light kind of friction, to something far more distinct as the teeth points burned across metal parts. It was the sound of chaos at work: strings cut asunder, pinging like shot cords, then huge internal, muffled crashes, the collapsing of hammers and a spray of ivory chips as Carter brought the saw through the keyboard itself. By the time the saw was nearly through the piano's bottom foot, the laughter had changed to applause and full-throated cheers, and when the piano was separated in two halves, its rent guts gleaming under the lights, the Orpheum went wild.

Carter surveyed the audience, fighting back the urge to wipe his brow, for sawing a piano in halves had caused him to work up a certain perspiration. Considered from the audience point of view, all that work was destructive and yet strangely exhilarating. He heard whistles and happy noises, and he took a moment to beam. He had a simple fact at hand that Ledocq, a European, hadn't accounted for: if young Charles Carter had hated his piano lessons there was a fine chance that most of his audience had, too.

Then, over the piano, he threw a large grey silken sheet, a sheet he'd chosen for how it fell into place slowly, catching every air current, and he called, 'Jake, quickly, your wand!'

Jake waved it, and Carter pulled away the sheet, showing off the newly restored piano, on top of which Esperanza now sat, dipping her arms into a basket of brilliant red rose petals, and flinging them, a crimson snowstorm, into the fully excited house.

The applause was deafening, people even standing up to applaud, and the orchestra struck up a chorus of 'Roses, Glorious Roses.' The curtain dropped on the first act.

At that moment, three thousand feet directly overhead, a JN-4 airplane was making broad circles, its pilot rubbing his chin. His sole passenger was banging on the fuselage. Griffin had flown many times with his daughter, so he was no stranger to the discomforts of flight – the harsh winds, the way the goggles cut into his face, the sickening drops and turns, and, worst of all, the way all Jenny pilots were morons. In frustration, Griffin pounded again against the side of the plane.

'Hey!' The pilot, Captain Berger, bellowed over the guttural engine noise, 'Don't do that. I'm trying to think.'

Dusk had come and gone as they'd followed the Delta. Berger had kept yelling over his shoulder that even though they were late, Griffin should look at the way the setting sun played against the river, how it was like molten silver, or perhaps a tarnished mirror from better times.

'What? Just get me to San Francisco.'

Berger had been quiet for a while. When the sun had fully set in the west, Berger had spoken again. 'Did you know I write poetry?'

'Oh, God.'

'You know what it's about?' he had yelled.

Griffin hadn't answered.

'It's about airplanes.'

And from that moment on Captain Berger had recited his poetry.

He only stopped when they were over downtown San Francisco, and he was looking for the airstrip he was sure was just by the marina, though they seemed to have forgotten to light it tonight, and boy would he give Captain Stuart a piece of his mind about that. Then he, without skipping a beat, returned to his 'Ode on a Milk Route.'

The first act lasted exactly forty-six minutes. Miss White knew this, for she waited outside the theatre exactly that long. Even though Mr Griffin hadn't asked for a seat, she had two tickets for the rear orchestra in her purse, as she suspected he might want to watch the show incognito, and the Orpheum was such a lovely theatre in which to see a show.

She also had a small surprise for him.

She wasn't one to wait in vain – she detested the potboilers in which heroines did exactly that – and was ready to take her seat, alone, after only five minutes of pacing by the box office. But management stressed that there was no seating during the act, and she would have to wait until the first intermission. So she did her waiting outside.

She listened to the hobo, who was doing Gilbert and Sullivan's Major-General song, until he got to the tricky parts about 'the crimes of Heliogabalus.' When she noticed him skipping lyrics, he looked away and only mouthed the rest.

So then it was silent. It was a lonely feeling to stand on the sidewalk and hear muffled gasps of amazement from inside, or brief musical interludes, and when she heard 'Roses, Glorious Roses,' she suspected she had missed something special. Where was Mr Griffin?

Finally, she left his ticket, and the special something, at the box office. The girl inside barely looked up from her magazine to listen to Miss White's instructions, which were simple but in their precision reminiscent of the girl's least favorite teacher.

As Miss White entered the theatre, she was directed toward the orchestra. The Orpheum lobby was one she had looked forward to seeing again in all its splendor, but it made little impression on her tonight. She passed the great golden statues, and the murals of ersatz mythological scenes, and even the giant aquarium, a postwar addition that had been freshly stocked with coral and rare tropical fish. The whole time she was frowning.

She couldn't stop worrying, and so she found an usher. 'Excuse me?'

'Madame?' A tall, dignified man, he bowed from the waist.

'I've left a ticket with the box office for my friend Jack Griffin,' she said, 'but the girl didn't seem to pay attention. I'm worried she won't give it to him.'

'You needn't worry,' he said, reaching for her ticket as if to cut this interaction short.

'You see,' she leaned in and whispered, 'there's a backstage pass with the ticket. I want to make sure he gets it.'

At this, the usher fixed her with a stare that made her uncomfortable. 'A pass?' He blinked.

'An Annie Oakley. It came to me legitimately,' she said in a rush, as the brass buttons on his red uniform made her nervous. 'After the show, the library collects ephemera from the stage manager—'

'It's perfectly all right.' The usher reached out his palm, which was creviced and callused, and it took Miss White a moment to relinquish her ticket to him. 'I'll make sure your friend is taken care of,' he said.

Chapter 7

Carter took the path to his dressing room at a trot, checking his watch – the interval was eight minutes – and handing his turban to his dresser, who in turn handed him a towel and a glass of water. Ledocq stood in the hallway, arms folded.

'Am I fired?' Carter asked after a long swallow of water.

'I'll keep you on another week, maybe,' Ledocq whispered.

'Was I right?'

'Were you right? How could I know it would look so good from back there? I owe you a dollar.'

'Tell the pianist that next time if someone calls for Liszt, he should stick with the "Mephisto Waltz."' Carter opened the door to his dressing room. He saw Phoebe inside. He called over his shoulder to Ledocq, 'In the next interval, we need to do blocking for the entrance of the Devil.' Then, shutting the door, he said, 'How are you?'

She looked awful. She sat in the farthest chair, a shabby thing that had probably once been a prop, and she was clutching his silk pillow to her chest. 'You're in danger.'

'I'm cutting the bullet trick.' He went to the mirror, to check his makeup, which he'd sweated through. 'Were you listening to the first act? Was it acceptable?'

'I just received a telegram. From Borax.' Phoebe waved the yellow telegram in front of her. 'He says someone has been sent to kill you.'

'Might I see that?' He took it from her, opened it, and for a moment felt like he was onstage, or in a dream. 'I don't get the gag. There's nothing here.'

'It's in Braille.'

He muttered, 'How remarkable.' His mind spun for a moment – marked decks of cards, telepathy demonstrations – and then back to Phoebe, whose face was colorless.

468

'Why did he send something to you and not me?'

'Because he's devious.'

'Help me read it.'

She walked the pads of her fingertips across the embossed surface. 'Tell Carter Secret Service sent man to theatre to kill him.' When she was done, she looked toward him.

Carter said, 'He must be serious. That's eleven words, and you know how the rates go up after ten.'

'Please don't joke.'

Carter looked at the clock. 'I'm going to change my shirt. I hope that's all right.' He pulled off his jacket, and black tie, and then removed his collar stud and unwrapped the bands that made his sleeves appear to be fastened. When he was in his undershirt, he stretched out his bare arms and rolled his shoulders back to keep them loose. He spoke again. 'You only read me part of the telegram,' he said.

She drew in a breath, inhaling so deeply she arched her back, and then let it out slowly. Weakly, she murmured, 'It looked blank. I hoped you wouldn't notice. The gist of it,' she said, suddenly angry, 'is that Borax is a conniving fucker.' Her hand went over her mouth.

He froze with one arm in a sleeve. It wasn't the first time he'd heard the word from a woman – in fact, it reminded him of Sarah. He returned to dressing. When his shirt was buttoned, and his studs in place, he opened the door and whistled. A young page jumped into sight.

'Are you good with names?' Carter asked.

'Yes, sir!'

'Write these down. Hollis, Stutz, Samuelson, O'Brien, Starling. If any one of them tries to come into the theatre tonight, even if he has a badge and makes impressive noises about being with the law, don't let him in. In fact, if anyone has a badge and tries to come in, make sure I know about it.' When the boy was halfway down the hall, Carter whistled again. 'Add another name to the list – Griffin.'

He returned to the makeup table and sipped at the water. He could see Phoebe's reflection, surrounded by lightbulbs, one of which was burned out.

'From what I've heard, the four who dropped me in the bay are all peeling potatoes for Coolidge, or however they punish their own. And if Griffin has turned assassin, I think I can live with that particular challenge.' Another sip of water. 'So. Has Borax asked you to betray me somehow?'

'I don't know what you did to him. He's never asked me for a favor before.'

'So, would a "favor" mean betraying me?'

'He asked me to find out if you destroyed television on purpose.'

'Pardon?' He was so startled by the question, he didn't respond to a knock at the door.

'He seems to think it's – do you want to answer that?'

It was Ledocq, who silently pointed at his watch. Carter nodded, and closed the door, and leaned on it. 'Please go on.'

She read the telegram to herself. After a moment, she said, 'Just that he wants to know if you destroyed it on purpose.'

'What else did he say?'

Silence. Phoebe folded her hands in her lap.

'Oh dear God.' He drummed on the door with his palms.

'What if – what if I had done something awful once, and what if Borax knew about it? He would try to command my loyalty, wouldn't he? And remind me of it. Just a little.'

'I don't like secrets,' he declared.

This made Phoebe laugh. 'You love secrets. Would you come here so I can touch you?'

Like he was tearing himself from a pedestal, Carter left the door. He crouched before her. Her fingers worked from his hair – 'Oh,' she said, 'sweat' – to his face, like spider legs. When she had felt enough, her hands dropped to her lap. 'You don't trust me.'

He was aware of his breathing. Shallow, through his nose. 'What would you do in my position?'

She considered this. 'I would very *carefully* make love to a certain woman.' As this did not produce laughter, she added gravely, 'He wants to control me.'

'What does he have on you? More than just . . .'

She touched her finger to his lips. He crouched there, aware that it would be the easiest motion in the world to caress her, to put his hand on hers. He stood, finished dressing, and left the room, closing the door behind him without another word to her.

In the wings, he took an armful of hats from an assistant and stood half-wrapped in the act curtain while flats and scrim shot back and forth behind him. It was a complex act to stage, with multiple levels of scenery and drops mounted to pulleys that had to be raised or lowered at a moment's notice.

All he could think of was Phoebe. Everytime she peeled away one mystery, there were two more underneath. What hadn't she read to him? And destroying television on purpose? He considered this, listening to the incidental music. Why would Borax ask that odd question? Carter had asked the orchestra to choose pieces with a feeling of diminuendo. He didn't recognize what they were playing, something with strings and finger cymbals, almost Turkish in nature.

A hand fell on his shoulder. James.

'I've been avoiding you,' Carter said.

James nodded. He held a sheaf of papers. Carter recognized some of them as invoices he'd signed in the past several days. He squared his shoulders, ready with a fusillade of explanations. But James was quietly tapping the papers against his lips. He met Carter's eye tenderly, and said, in a voice so low the orchestra almost obscured it, 'Oh, my brother.'

That sent a chill down Carter's spine far more effectively than any lecture could. He put the hats down. 'Yes?'

'I'm very, very proud of you,' James said. 'It's truly a pleasure to have you as an older brother and I love you.'

They squeezed to one side to allow Cleo to find her mark onstage. 'But?'

He shook his head. 'No "buts," Charlie. The show has been wonderful tonight.' He stumbled over his next question: 'Did you manage . . . did you hold on to that expense journal?'

'Well, you know it was stolen, but I did replace it, and it's . . . it's somewhere.' He wanted to apologize. 'You know, the interval is almost over.'

James checked his wristwatch. 'We have time. Let me walk you through something here.' He unfolded a ledger sheet, and he moved his finger slowly from the left columns to the right. 'Given what you spent on start-up costs—'

'I didn't spend that much.'

'You left your checkbook at my house. And I found these receipts at Ledocq's. Let's not spoil this. Look, here's what you spent. And here's what you'll have to spend, each week, just to continue this run. And if you tour, here's salaries, and this is the minimum weekly cost of maintenance, and transportation and renting venues in the contiguous states.'

'I realize – I have to do well tonight. And I have to bring business in. I know that.'

'No. It's not that anymore.' James looked at him sadly, like he was explaining the rules of a game Carter had never understood. 'You just finished yourself off.'

Carter shook his head. The words literally made no sense in his ears.

'Even if you increased business dramatically – if you had the kind of houses Goldin does – you still couldn't recoup what you spent.'

'I'll tour for four years straight if I have to. James, I'm here, I'm back, I'm being creative – it can work. I'll make this work.'

'As I said, I'm proud of you. But we have to decide what you're going to do after tonight.'

'Tour! We'll play out the run, and tour.'

'Yes,' James replied, carefully. 'I just want you to have as good a time as you can tonight. It may be possible that you'll want to close up shop after we look at these numbers together.'

Carter looked at his brother. James, a Delphic oracle of sorts, intuitively and mysteriously understood money. Carter knew what understatement was and knew that his brother, who loved him, had seen a miserable and brief future for Carter's show of mystery. But James was also giving him a gift, letting him be *himself* for one more night.

Carter picked up the stack of hats from the table. He closed his eyes. 'So this could be a Viking funeral for me?'

'You know, most people never get a chance, even once, to do what they want for a living. You've always been lucky enough to follow your passion, and on behalf of most of the working world, I'd say there are far worse ways to go than in a blaze of glory.' James held on to both of Carter's shoulders. 'You have nothing to prove anymore. Enjoy it.'

* * *

When the curtain raised on the second act, the audience was treated to the same set as before – Carter's study. Nothing had changed – the knife still stuck straight from Thurston's face – but several more coatracks had appeared. Carter entered from stage left, causing a few quick, condensed laughs, as he was hard to see, obscured by much unusual hatwear.

'Ladies and Gentlemen,' he said, putting the hats on top of an unobtrusive table. 'Magic is a difficult business.' The words felt misshapen in his mouth. He delivered his patter like he was back in Macao and speaking it phonetically. He took aim with the brim of a bowler hat and tossed it onto the hook of the coatrack beside him. It was a toss of about six feet. He had scripted this act as if it were just fantasy, and yet his patter struck him like body blows. It was creeping in on him: he'd spent too much money. 'Each year the business gets harder.' He felt a lady's hat, with a short crown and long feather, hefting it for balance, then tossed it onto another hook. 'It's not as if I have many nonmagical skills.' A Stetson, black, whizzed from his fingertips, landing atop the bowler perfectly. Before it had even settled, Carter had tossed a beret to join them. The audience laughed, and he spoke as if begging to differ with them. 'I know, throwing hats, quite a skill. So you'd think!' And without even looking, he threw a Greek fisherman's cap directly behind him, where it alighted perfectly on another coatrack. In quick succession, each time without caring to look where he aimed, Carter threw a golfing cap, a flapper's cloche hat, a sombrero, and something quite silly, a coxcomb, onto the racks behind him, the coxcomb actually changing direction twice in midair before finding its place.

He held his next bit of patter for a moment, as the applause was unexpectedly generous. Then:

'See, that would be a magical skill and not one I could find gainful employment with. For I've often wondered whether I should retire.' He had rehearsed this sentence for weeks, it was as impersonal now as anything he had said onstage, and yet he was suddenly struck by how peculiar it felt to say. It was like he'd been psychic. Or like he'd known all along he was heading for disaster. 'If I couldn't be a magician,' he removed his turban, which made him feel more naked than he knew it would, 'I would be, of course,' he put on a government-issue canvas sunhat, 'a postman.'

This caused a roar – it was, he admitted to himself, a silly bit. He invited several young men onstage, asking them to remember, as they came forward, the seat numbers of people they wished to write letters to. He promised 'instantaneous delivery' anywhere within the theatre. The service, Carter promised, would be free the first time. As the men stood and wrote with fine Watermen pens Carter had provided at $2.49 each, he gave them final instructions: they should address the letters as they wished – say, to the blonde-haired girl with the pixie hat in row G; to the occupant of seat R16; even to a friend simply by name, no seat number. Each message was put into an envelope, sealed, and Carter vanished them all.

'You, sir,' he said to the first volunteer, 'look into my eyes. Ah, you are sending a letter to a Mr . . . a Mr William Harcourt, orchestra, row R. Seat 6 . . . no, seat 9!'

The man clapped his hands together and he shook his head as his friend in row R, seat 9 retrieved a letter he found under his chair.

'Sir, Mr Harcourt, if you are Mr Harcourt, will you please stand and read us all what your friend has written?'

Harcourt was a chubby sort, with a loose tie and jowls, and he read slowly, 'Dear Bill: I'm on stage! Best, Jim.'

Murmurs of acknowledgment, and then Carter repeated the routine with the next young man, who had apparently sent a drinking invitation to Mayor Davie, whose seat was in row F (one row ahead of an unimpressed-looking Mayor Rolph). Davie took up more time than necessary, bowing from the waist to all points on the globe before taking his seat, and while he acknowledged the Mayor with applause, Carter was thinking, *This is my Viking funeral.*

He pulled the third volunteer forward to better show him off under the lights. He stared deeply into the man's eyes. 'Your letter goes to the first gallery, row AA, seat 10.' He pointed his wand to the back of the house. 'The young lady there should find the note by her armrest.' The spotlights swept back just as a startled 'Oh!' came from that vicinity.

'What does your letter say, young lady?'

She stood, looking confused, a frown on her face as she read silently, and then she exploded, 'Yes! Yes! Oh, Billy, yes, of course I'll marry you!'

The applause was wild, and heaped upon it were 'awwww!' and 'how about that!' and 'congratulations,' and the young man onstage accepted handshakes from his fellow volunteers. Carter thought of Phoebe and imagined curling into her, holding her for comfort, but then he thought of Borax's telegram, and then mystery and suspicion; everywhere he turned something prevented him from finding comfort. And magic? Carter wondered if he'd been thinking magic would step in and save him or if all along he'd wanted a grand immolation.

He stood alone, and then a page brought him a glass of water. This was unscripted but he was indeed thirsty, so he drank it down. The page whispered, 'Stage door, library press pass, someone calling himself Griffin.'

Inwardly, Carter relaxed. It was only Griffin. Emergency canceled. Though he was onstage, Carter had no problem conducting a hushed conversation, as the audience would assume it would lead to business. 'Rumpled, right? Rather a bulldoggish sort?'

'No, bald. But we turned him away.'

Carter finished the glass of water. Griffin was traveling in disguise, then. He held the glass out as if asking for more. The page shrugged, as he didn't have a pitcher on him, and had felt clever for thinking of a way to go onstage. Carter said, with enough resonance that the audience could hear, 'Ahh, no matter. I'll do it myself.' He waved a hand over the glass and it was full again.

He addressed the house: 'Another occupation,' he said, holding the glass aloft, 'eternal optimist.' He tossed the glass at the page, who reached out to catch it, but it had turned to a trail of glitter. There was light, appreciative laughter, and Carter thought, *Lovely bit, keep it in*, and then realized he had nothing to keep it for. So he thought, *Enjoy it now. Enjoy it all now.*

When he was alone again on the apron, he flipped the postal worker's hat onto the rack and donned a pith helmet. 'Perhaps,' he said, 'I am better suited for the life of an Egyptologist.'

The orchestra, cued, began its fifteen-minute melange of Middle Eastern themes and Orientalia, and at the same time, stagehands were heaving on the ropes, sandbags rose into the air, and flats dropped down into position. The heaving of scenery was performed by a group of stagehands who were rugged. On the off season, they trained with weights, and their society behind the curtain was closed to the timid or the infirm. The six who worked tonight truly loved being on Carter's team.

Each piece of the set was on a winch and pulley, bag-dropped, counterbalanced by nests of fifty-pound bags of sand. The setup was called a 'Fairbanks,' for the reason that when a stagehand so wanted, he could stand upon a knot on the rope, untie as few or as many bags of sand as he wanted, and ride nearly to the rafters like Zorro as the scenery lowered.

There was no particular reason to ride that way, but because Carter allowed it, the team of men did so all night long, trading places at the top, jumping onto the ropes and riding back down later. With the mighty Egyptian set descending in its many pieces, the audience was deprived of a behind-the-scenes tableau of beauty: Carter's team swiftly riding ropes up to the catwalks and down to the stage again, simply because they could.

The sidewalk in front of the Orpheum was close to deserted. The crowds were gone, and the easels with the window cards had been brought into the lobby. The hobo was still there, picking with fingerless gloves through the change he'd received. A tall, bald man walked briskly away from the backstage entrance to the alley's mouth, and then stood there, hands on his hips, looking over his shoulder to deliver a devastating riposte to the stage-door buffoon who had turned him away.

He heard the sounds of running feet. 'Well!' he exclaimed, as Jack Griffin, necktie askew, raced past him.

Griffin slowed, put his hand out to the metal lip of the box office cage, and caught his breath. He was still trying to get his legs under him. Captain Berger had finally recognized a rectangle they'd passed a dozen times as the marina landing strip. From the marina, a taxi ride with a mad cab driver, and then the sprint down Market Street.

Griffin knew he couldn't show his badge to anyone, or give his name up, not with Carter's connections. And he wasn't about to try and force his way in. The easiest way inside would be simply buying a ticket.

He looked up, into the cage, which was empty. The girl had closed early.

'Oh, great! That's great!' He looked around. 'Hey, pal!'

'Yes?' The tall, bald man answered with some curiosity.

'You wouldn't have a ticket, would you?'

The man's face seemed to expand, eyebrows raising and mouth opening, all with pleasure. 'Ah, yes, thank you for reminding me. I *do* have a ticket.' And with that, the man walked to the entrance, and with a wave to Griffin, handed his ducat to an usher, after which he stood in the lobby and waved again.

Griffin watched as if someone had slipped him a dead fish. 'San Fran-*goddamn*-ciscans,' he said.

Meanwhile, inside, the bald man had a dry chuckle. He moved toward the doors to the orchestra section, but was turned away by the very usher who'd torn his ticket. 'You'll have to wait for the interval, sir.'

'I know that,' he sighed.

Seconds later, however, the usher said 'Hey!' as an infuriated Griffin was trying to muscle his way inside. In a phalanx, ushers from all points of the compass rushed toward the entryway to repel him. It took but a few seconds for Griffin to back off, straightening his jacket. He muttered, 'All right, all right, don't get excited on me,' and backed away, into the night.

When the usher in charge of the orchestra doors returned, he looked around, puzzled, as the lobby was empty. The bald man was gone.

A single oboe played sinuously with scant percussion, a triangle bell, perfect snake charmer music, while Carter prowled about the stage, holding aloft a torch that had been dipped in smokeless pitch.

'I've been reading much this past year about my namesake Howard Carter. He is, by the way, no relation, though I wish he were, for I'd like him to hire me. Excavator of Bani Hassan. And el Amarna, capital city of the glorious sovereignty of Akhenaten. Plunderer of Deir el Babri, the burial place of Queen Hatshepsut.' The stage around him was dark, though there were hints of statues and gold leaf inscriptions on towering obelisks. The oboe was joined by violins, which made an eerie screeching. 'He hunted up and down the Valley of the Kings like a man possessed, in search of the thrice-cursed tomb of the child king, Tutankhamun, Pharaoh of the Eighteenth Dynasty. He worked all day long and so as to discourage robbers, he slept at night in the caverns, with the bats. A year ago, he broke open the tomb, but we never heard what *actually* happened when he went into the three-thousand-year-old stygian darkness. Until tonight.'

Carter's torch went out. It was velvet black in the house, and silent. Not even a cough.

Finally, Carter spoke. 'Howard Carter's men asked him, "Can you see anything?" And he replied, "Yes, wonderful things."'

A dazzling burst of white light as all the spots in the house came up to show off stone walls on which hieroglyphs etched in gold extended to the high arch over the stage. Tremendous golden statues of Isis and Ramses flanked a great sarcophagus inlaid with precious stones, its head that of a great cat, caught in mid-snarl. Bats hovered and darted, leathery wings flapping.

Carter said mystic incantations, and this caused the life-sized portraits of mummies to come to life, shrieking and groaning until he said a second set of incantations that caused them to turn to dust.

Carter had the sarcophagus rolled toward him and rotated 180 degrees. He asked aloud what sacred mysteries this three thousand-year-old mummy would be protected by, and then he and his men threw open the lid. They jumped backward, and the audience gasped, for the inhabitant was in fact a roaring African lion.

'Let's close that back up,' Carter said and then, gingerly, they lowered the lid, and opened it again a heartbeat later. The lion was gone, and in his place was a towering and lovely woman who wore a jeweled headdress. She stepped out of the coffin with an imperious manner, ramrod straight and haughty, and when she paced around the stage, she walked Egyptian style (something Carter hadn't scripted, but he noted his approval of this Stanislavski method).

She stated that she was the one whom the Greeks called Thea Phiopater, reincarnation of Princess Akhanothep, of the Eighteenth Dynasty, and that her sleep having been disturbed, she was ready to curse Carter for all eternity unless he was able to set her spirit free.

Carter courageously accepted the challenge and had his men wrap her in bandages. When she was fully mummified (the winding movements around her limbs and torso were set to the whirling type of music preferred by dervishes), Carter stood her in the dead center of the stage. With his hands, he tilted her backward, and levitated her into the ether.

He ran a brass hoop over and around and past her floating form, gazing at her without blinking, as if she were held aloft by his concentration alone. He snapped his fingers and, like she was riding air currents, Princess Akhanothep drifted hither and yon, pacific, while the orchestra played the melancholy *Le Cygne* by Saint-Saëns.

Carter extended his fingertips and she floated over the heads of the first rows of the audience just long enough to confound them. He beckoned to the airborne girl, making slow and gentle motions, and she floated back to him.

'You are free!' he exclaimed, and pulled away the bandages. They fell to the stage, revealing something impossible: empty space. She had vanished!

There was raucous applause throughout the house, cut short when two spots swept to the back of the house, where the Princess now stood, arms extended over her head, dressed in long and extravagant Parisian silks, the hems of which she held in her hands – she appeared to have wings. 'Here I am, and I'm *free*!' She threw her head back and laughed gaily, and began a modernistic dance that took her down the center aisle, and back onto the stage, with the applause continuing the whole way.

With all eyes upon her – not only was her dancing impressive, but frankly, she was a choice piece of calico – the bald man standing by the back row frowned. Of course Carter would pull an 'It's Me' – type chestnut that produced a box jumper at the back of the theatre. He walked among the standing bodies – for Cleo was now bowing to a standing ovation – until he determined exactly where she'd appeared. He found it: a simple trap cut into the carpeted runner in the empty standing-room-only section. With the entire theatre otherwise occupied, he found it an easy matter to gimmick the trap open and drop down inside. He was in a tunnel. He had to crouch, but the pathway was illuminated by phosphorescent tape that clearly marked the route to the backstage area.

The main drape had come down; Carter pushed through it and, smiling, addressed his audience as they found their seats.

'Truth be told, Ladies and Gentlemen, dodging curses all the live-long day strikes me as a bit of a chore. I am a lazy man.' He removed the pith helmet and smoothed back his hair. 'I prefer the quiet life,' he said, producing a leather helmet and goggles, 'that of a stunt rider.' He wound a scarf around his neck and saluted the audience with a riding crop.

When the curtain opened next, the Egyptian tomb had been completely struck, and in its place was a very clean, almost ascetic set: a single large panel upon which a cold grey cityscape had been painted, Bauhaus style. The only props were a long wooden rampway and a metal platform fifteen feet in the air, the latter suspended over a shallow tank of water.

Carter crossed the stage, circling the tank, which came up to his knees.

'Ladies and Gentlemen, we are lucky to have with us tonight a magic cauldron, straight from the European continent. It is a good ten feet in diameter, but just eighteen inches deep. Nonetheless that is eighteen inches of *magic* water. But how exactly, you ask, is it magic? Please indulge me – welcome Miss Amanda Chong.'

Carter gestured upward, to the platform, where Amanda stood, in a robe. She wore a swim cap, and she gave a huge and fluttery wave to the audience, and she said, 'Hi! Hello!'

'Miss Chong,' Carter said, 'have we ever met before?'

'You live next door, Carter,' she cried, which received a big laugh.

'Are you on my payroll?'

She nodded with enthusiasm.

'Ah, you honest little girl. What am I paying you to do?'

She mimed making a dive into the tank.

'I'm paying you to dive off a fifteen-foot platform into eighteen inches of water?'

'Five dollars,' she grinned.

'Well, then, what are you waiting for? Oh, the incantation, of course.' The orchestra struck up a jaunty movement from *Water Music,* while Carter waved his arms over the tank, and said '*Ergo jubilatio, vivat floreatque media, media!*' then, to Amanda, 'Dive!'

She dropped her robe to the platform, showing off her fashionable black and red wool swimsuit. Bending her knees once, twice, three times, she bounded off the platform and with a perfect needle-nosed arc of her arms, swan dove into the tank.

The reaction was more a generalized gasp than enthusiasm, as it looked like Amanda had to have hit the bottom with some great force. Yet there was no sign of her, not even a bubble. While the audience was still craning their necks to see what had happened to her – she hadn't broken the surface – Carter rolled up his sleeves, and then threw both arms violently upward, in the direction of the platform, from which there was a puff of smoke. Almost immediately, people began to clap, slowly, because they could plainly see up there, waving charmingly, young Amanda Chong all over again, in her swimsuit, which was bone dry.

'Hi, Carter!' she called. Then the applause came, lengthy and relieved.

'Thank you. I'll see you back in Oakland,' he said as she climbed to the catwalk and left the stage.

'So,' Carter said, 'magic water,' with a shrug. 'Causes instantaneous transportation. Which doesn't matter as I'm not a magician anymore. I'm a stunt rider.' He was enjoying himself. He felt relaxed and *loose*, as if he could do no wrong.

Quietly, the motorcycle was wheeled in from the wings.

'Ladies and Gentlemen, behold a triumph of European engineering,' he cried. 'The BMW R32, an extravagant machine, reliable, steady, and true at speeds of eighty miles per hour. It is the preferred mount for those of us who are no longer magicians but stunt riders.'

As he spoke, he walked around the motorcycle, flicking on the petcock.

'I should tell you a bold fact: this is the only BMW in all of America. They are just now making their debut in Paris, and eventually some clever rich men here will find one. But for now, I have the *only* BMW in all of America.' He used the riding crop to trace an imaginary pathway. 'I am going to ride this motorcycle in a spiral, increasing my speed steadily, until I have achieved full velocity, eighty miles per hour, at which point, I will go up the rampway you see before you, and fly through the air, landing on that six-foot-square platform that hangs from the rafters. And I shall come to a full stop immediately. At least,' he added, 'that would be prudent.'

In the audience, in a row seven back from the stage, Max Friz squirmed between Philo and Mrs Ledocq. Friz shook his head. 'Eighty miles per hour? He cannot go that fast in this small space.' Mrs Ledocq put her finger to her lips, and Max turned to the audience members behind him. 'He cannot go eighty miles per hour in this small space,' he explained, but his protest was cut short as Carter, mounting, lowered his goggles and kicked the engine over and gunned it to a thunderous roar. Easing off on the throttle, Carter nodded at the conductor, who gestured to the trumpet section. They launched into the opening of the *William Tell Overture* and Carter began his slow and steady spiral outward.

The spotlights swirled around the stage in circles as if he were hard to find. With full attention on him, only the extremely canny noticed, and puzzled at, drapery arising around the platform hanging over the stage. If Carter were going to ride onto the platform, wouldn't he crash into the curtains?

Carter spiralled from tight circles to wider arcs, suddenly swinging out to the very lip of the stage, and then back to the wings, and then with a mighty roar, he was on the rampway, motoring upward, accompanied by flashes from small red and green and blue fireworks, and the motorcycle was climbing through the air, describing a perfect parabola toward the platform, the audience holding its breath, some already moving their palms together to applaud, the orchestra blasting the *Overture*'s brassy crescendo, and then rider and machine came down, fatally short, missing the platform entirely and splashing into the water tank. The impact sent tidal waves cascading over the sides, washing across the stage. Those in the first three rows were treated to sprays of water as if they were standing on the prow of a boat.

For long seconds, the surface of the tank churned, and just as the depth of this accident became apparent – Max Friz was frozen solid, hands clutching his head – there was a puff of smoke, and high over the stage the drapery around the platform fell away to reveal Charles Carter and motorcycle, unharmed.

He waved, and he called out, 'Magic water,' and bowed from the waist; the orchestra played out the finale of the Rossini piece while the audience, standing for the second time that night, gave up their applause and their cheers.

When some time had passed, and he was able to be heard over the clapping, Carter declared, 'You let me know I'm a magician after all. Thank you.'

Outside the theatre, Griffin paced. He couldn't even pace in silence, for the hobo on the sidewalk had decided Griffin seemed like a good mark, and had started mangling Mark Antony's soliloquy. He managed only a few lines before losing steam, and he started complaining instead. 'I played here. This was before the movies, back when a man's voice was his ticket. I had excellent diction. The women, I tell you, they were all over me, Tessie Wall's girls, *and* Jessie Hayman's. Murdoch, hated him. He was a mean man. That honey pot. He was, he was, Iago.' He paused here, eyes battling back and forth as if trying to retrieve a suitable monologue from *Othello*. Finally, he looked at Griffin. 'Spare a nickel?'

'I'll give you a quarter if you be quiet for a minute.'

The hobo nodded. Griffin dug in his pocket and handed over a quarter. The hobo opened his mouth to say thank you, then thought better of breaking his vow of silence. Instead, he sat down on the curb and absently cupped his elbows in his palms.

Griffin looked down the alleyway. A fire escape. He turned his head back – it went all the way to the roof. The roof had to have a fire exit, then. Access. He made a pyramid of garbage cans – harder to balance than he'd expected – and stood on the top one, which was just high enough to pull himself onto the fire escape.

The whole way up, he found some small relief in how assiduously he'd been doing push-ups and sit-ups lately. When he reached the roof, he was hardly fatigued. There were taller buildings that hulked over the roof. The huge Orpheum Theatre sign, with its thousands of white lightbulbs, hummed. He saw the hump of the fire exit door and a pile of rags in front of it.

He jogged across the tar paper, shoes sticking, and then he slowed when he realized the pile of rags had arms and legs.

Griffin reached inside his jacket to unsnap the strap of leather that ran across the butt of his Colt. The theatre sign blinked on one letter at a time, then all the letters shimmered before the whole cycle started again, so the rooftop structures – air vents, mostly, and the fire exit – were thrown first into light, then darkness.

Griffin could see the man's body, clothed only in an undershirt, shorts, socks, and garters. The head lay at an unnatural angle, neck broken, eyes open. No, not open. The sign lit up, O-R-P-H-E-U-M, and Griffin saw pennies against the dead man's eyes.

Something was wrong with those pennies. He picked one up. It was a copper token the size of a quarter. On one side was a lion, rampant. 'Will You Have Her As Your Bride?' was the inscription. On the other side was a profile portrait of a proud-looking man holding a small canine, surrounded by the legend, 'The More I Know of People, the More I Love My Dog.'

Griffin's heart sickened. What kind of a freak had done this? He tried the fire exit door. It was, as per his usual luck, locked from the inside.

He walked around the roof carefully, recalling he hadn't seen windows as he'd come up the fire escape.

His eyes lit on a structure that he took at first for an airshaft. Then he thought it was something else, and then he explained it to himself as an airshaft again, for there was no reason for a theatre to have anything other than a ventilation device up here.

But this was too large for an airshaft. 'What the hell,' he murmured as he approached it. He shook his head. By the time he was six feet away, he had confirmed exactly what it was.

Not again, he thought.

The backstage area, from the very rear wall to the closed fire curtain, and from wing to wing, was boiling over with people carrying things, no better sign that this was indeed opening night. Carter stood in his shirtsleeves (he'd torn his jacket at the shoulder and a seamstress busily repaired it), directing his cast and crew with a precision that was in no way cold. Despite what James had said, he could hardly accept that this was his last night, especially when he was enjoying himself so much.

'All right, we need military discipline, my friends. Esperanza, Albert, the audience will be patient for about nine minutes, so wait until then, then go to the apron with your props and put on your routine.'

'Sure,' Esperanza said. Albert, who was a cutup, curtseyed toward his boss and started to run off hand-in-hand with Esperanza until Carter called to him:

'No, not yet, we need you for a moment. We're reblocking the Devil's entrance.'

'Hey, that's me!' Albert raced back, and walked through his cues patiently, with Carter's hands on his shoulders, directing him where to stand. They were surrounded by electricians, the script girl, and the stage manager, who was ready to write down new items for the prop schedule. Ledocq hovered, but did not participate. He drank a glass of water.

Carter said, 'If we're introducing the Devil by conventional means, we should at least use a splashy kind of lighting. We'll base it on last season's rigging. Do we still have the schematics? Excellent. Tell me, how are the electrics?' Carter asked his grips and, to a man, they said there was no danger of fuses blowing, as the Orpheum had been refitted with novel and highly sophisticated knob-and-tube wiring.

Carter blinked. 'All right, I'll take your word for it,' he said, looking over their shoulders at Ledocq, who nodded in confirmation. 'Splendid. What's next?'

The stage manager reminded him they had to drain the water tank that night, which made Ledocq clear his throat, and explain, blushing, it was a lot of water, and the plumbers had asked them to only attach it to the sewer drainpipe when the theatre audience had departed and the toilets were no longer flushing.

'Yes,' Carter said, 'very uplifting. There's something else to change. What is it? Ah, the bullet catching, of course. We're cutting that.'

When he said this, he saw Ledocq frowning at him, but he also heard a single pair of hands clapping and a familiar voice crying 'Hoo ray.' Phoebe was sitting in a chair, half-hidden by curtains. 'You kept your promise,' she said.

The prop man went to the table upon which were laid the loads of flowers, the silks, the bird cages, and such, and he segregated the pistols onto a shelf for the items to be cut.

'Anything else?'

'The ending,' Ledocq said.

'Ah, yes,' Carter replied. 'Is my jacket ready yet?' The seamstress shook her head.

'Might I go now, boss?' Albert stretched his arms. 'I feel like using up that *flash paper*.' He smiled at Ledocq.

'Albert, that is volatile flash paper,' Ledocq sighed. 'I have told you this more than once. Are you juggling the torches?' Albert nodded enthusiastically. Ledocq said, 'I hope I'm in your will.'

'Albert, you're a madman, go now, enjoy, please.' Carter waved him away. He rubbed his palms together. 'So . . . who do we need for this? Carlo and Scott and Willie . . . and . . . that's all, right, Carlo and Scott and Willie?'

The script girl nodded. The three men approached for a huddle. Simultaneously, Tom and James approached, leading Phoebe between them. James had a final pat on the back in mind, and Tom wanted to complain to Carter that though he'd opened the tomb of Tutankhamun, there'd been nary a peep from King Tut himself. But all that was put on hold, because James saw that Scott was holding an odd metal sort of basket.

'I'm sorry,' James said, pointing, 'but what is that?'

Scott waved it in the air, an effort that took both hands. 'It's called a brank.'

James squinted as if listening for faint music.

'Carter,' Tom started, 'you didn't give us our King Tut.'

'James?' Carter asked.

'Didn't Dad have drawings of a brank or something on his wall?'

'Yes. Why, do you remember anything else about it?'

James said to Phoebe, 'He's always bringing up things I don't remember.' Then, to his brother, 'No, I don't remember. What are you doing with it tonight?'

'I'm imprisoned in it just before Willie here cuts my head off.' Carter patted Willie on his ruddy cheek.

'Well, that's nice,' James said. 'Listen, the show has been marvelous so far—'

'Cutting off your head?' Phoebe looked toward Carter. 'Cutting off your head,' she said again, this time drawing out the words like they described an exotic and awful delicacy.

'It's a trifle,' explained Carter.

Carlo made a grand head-chopping motion on Carter's throat,

adding *whoomph* as a sound effect.

'Actually,' James said, flipping through the few remaining pages of the script, 'I'm just not sure about that as a finale.'

'Why? Carlo, Scott, Willie, you can go, we're all up to speed, I think.'

With the crew gone, James continued, 'I'm worried about the very end of the show. People enjoy resolution.'

'My head comes off, and then I come back onstage.'

'Excuse me,' Phoebe said. 'Can you please tell me why cutting off your head isn't dangerous?'

'It's far safer than the bullet-catching.' He considered telling her he wouldn't be killed tonight, they'd turned away a Secret Service agent at the stage door, and it had only been Agent Griffin all along, but she looked so peeved he didn't want to risk it. 'James, I don't understand what you're saying.'

'Thematically,' he said, and then acknowledged Carter's look of surprise. 'Yes, yes, for once I'm able to see a theme here. I'm quite involved in your show tonight, it's been superior. And I just think that the way you have it blocked, it lacks some kind of magical *punch* at the end. People will be riled up when they see you die, and . . . you haven't really thought out the coming-back part, have you? It's blah.'

Carter took Phoebe's hand, saying, 'Let's leave my brother to his bad feelings. I'll explain the illusion to you.'

'Thank you.'

But James stopped them. 'No. The illusion reminds me of the worse side of the things you dream up. Like Blackmail. It performs the function of an illusion, but it's not satisfying.'

'Oh, an argument with God,' Phoebe interjected. 'I've had those,' then 'Ah! Yes!' – she gripped Carter's arm.

'What?' He was feeling impatient.

'Say. *Did* you destroy television on purpose?'

James clapped his hands to his mouth. 'You dear woman! Maybe he did!'

Carter's mouth fell open. 'You're kidding me.'

'Aha, yes.' James picked up the thread. 'If movies hurt the magic business, maybe you worry that television would do the same, or worse.'

'As if I would behave that way. ' Carter hissed, 'That's absurd.'

'Yes it is,' Phoebe answered. She said to James, 'I don't think it's conscious on his part,' and James nodded quickly, replying to her, 'Yes, I told him to make it a Viking funeral tonight, only I didn't know how truly I spoke, you know,' which caused Phoebe to say, 'He has self-destructive notions and he can be very sad, have you noticed how sad he can be?'

As Phoebe and James continued to discuss him, Carter said, 'Why is it everyone I know sounds exactly like my mother? My every motive is utterly transparent and I do *not* stand a chance. Might I just kill myself now?'

James came up to Carter and poked him in the chest. 'Don't let this be a peculiar punishment-suicide trick. Peculiar isn't good.'

'It's not a trick, it's an illusion.' Carter took Phoebe's hand. 'Phoebe, I'm going to show you the illusion, and I'm going to walk you though everything that happens, and I'm going to show you the safety mechanism, just so you know how safe I'm going to be.'

Phoebe hesitated. 'All right,' she said.

Carter and Phoebe walked away from James and, on the catwalk, a figure stepped along on the balls of his feet, following from above, as Phoebe wasn't the only person interested in seeing how the safety mechanisms worked.

Chapter 8

Meanwhile, on stage, Albert and Esperanza were finishing their routine. As he was too excited to pace himself, Albert had used most of the flash paper in the first thirty seconds. The finale, therefore, though fiery, was flash paper–free: an inspired bit in which they threw back and forth six knives and a burning torch. Each time Esperanza received the torch, she used it to light a candle downstage, and each time Albert caught it, he attempted without success to light a cigar he gripped in his mouth. He kept bringing the flames up to his face, which elicited quick shrieks from the fainthearted, and when it ignited, there were cheers.

The couple shared a quick tango by the light of all the candles, and then bowed. When they straightened, Albert said, 'Ladies and Gentlemen, we bring you the end of Carter the Great's show, his finale.'

Esperanza said, 'To preserve the mystery for future audiences, management asks that you please not reveal any details of the act that follows.'

The lights fell and at the same time, the curtains were drawn fully open. The stage was bare. Carter ambled out from stage right, hands in pockets, lingering. He had a smile on his face, and the smile truly came from his soul, for he had the profound sense, *inexplicably* given how much financial trouble he was in, that he was in exactly the right place, doing, God knew why, exactly the right thing.

'Ladies and Gentlemen,' he said softly, 'it has been wonderful. But now it's time to say good night.' He teared up, just slightly. There was silence out there, as the audience knew this couldn't be it, not yet, Carter wouldn't cheat them that way, and he realized what sort of pact he had with them: he would treat them fairly in ways that life itself would not. 'We have had our fun, and I have proven myself the greatest magician of any age. I am prepared to send you all back home unless a greater wizard than I should appear.'

There was a brilliant flash, far more brilliant than last season, it made Carter wince in fact, and then a great roiling sulphurous cloud; the Devil himself joined him onstage.

So it began: the ending of the Carter the Great Paragon Show of Mystery, the all-new, all-different spectacular, the show with fifteen carloads of scenic effects and tons of ponderous impedimenta. In the wings and under the stage, prop men waited with newspapers and ducks and eggs, and Cleo tucked her long hair under a blonde flapper wig so she could be put into the Gone! chair, and Esperanza, too, put on a wig to be her double. And men rode the Fairbanks up and down silently and Scott and Willie suited up to be bearded Hindu yoga men, and the cannons were rolled into position, loads of flowers at the ready. From the flies to the crawl spaces, every square inch out of the audience line of sight was packed: here was the cage for the doves, there were the screen and projector and slides for Carter's hand shadows, here was a cage lined with straw, goats and pigs and sheep within, ready to be released when the hand shadows came to life. And, listening carefully to every sound was Phoebe Kyle.

The music was fiery, and brash, with cymbals clashing and the lead violinist showing off Paganini-like hemi-demi-semiquavers. Carter was handed his rod and reel so he could materialize fish from just over his audience's heads, and at the same time down from the flies came the instruments the Devil used for *Night on Bald Mountain*.

'Go!' said the script girl, and Scott and Willie went onstage, where they were drilled through to great applause and astonishment, and then it was time for them to be loaded into the cannons, and they raced to backstage to change for their next bits. The partitioned dressing room was so small only one of them at a time could go in; since Scott had to get back onstage first, he changed first. He came out in black, and said to Willie, 'Well, do I look like the Devil's thug?'

Willie nodded. He pulled the curtains carefully shut. He faced a rack of hanging costumes, most of them black, all in a row, all packed so closely together that getting one out was a struggle. He reached out for his executioner's cloak and mask, and it seemed to resist him. He checked for snags, then pulled it out easily, utterly unprepared for the blackjack that came hurling out with it.

Onstage, things were building toward the new climax. First was Gone!, wherein Carter put Cleo into a chair, which began to rise, and when he fired a pistol, she disappeared. The Devil put a finger up in the air, indicating he had but one trick left, and he nodded smugly, confident it was so good Carter could in no way approach his presentation. Carter chuckled, as Albert was so expressive in pantomime that he seemed to make the fixed mask of the Devil smile, glare, glower, simply by his posture.

'So,' Carter said, part of the script now, 'one last trick, and I have to beat it?'

A nod.

'Or else . . .'

A more significant nod, which caused nervous laughter.

'Very well.'

The Devil removed a silk handkerchief from his pocket. He turned it front and back to show it was an ordinary white handkerchief. Carefully, he extended his index finger and draped the handkerchief over it, and looked at Carter.

Carter shrugged. 'So far, I believe I can beat you flat.'

The Devil's finger described circles in the air, greater and greater circles, the handkerchief spinning at the tip, and as it spun, amazingly, it began to grow. It took several seconds for the audience to realize what was happening, but when they did, there was a great, mass intake of breath. He spun and spun the handkerchief until it was the size of a napkin, then a towel, then a bedsheet, and finally Carter had to stand back, as the silk expanded to the size of a small tent, which fell down over the Devil himself and continued spinning. The edges dragged on the stage, but slowly, slowly now, the material began to rise, and rise, and rise – revealing a street carousel. The silk had become a ribbed tent over the carousel, which had four seats, two of them in the shape of zebras, and two in the shape of bears, and in each seat there rode a beautiful woman in a sequined dress. The women held glasses of champagne and laughed, ran their hands through their bobbed hair, and pouted their lips in a display of vampish chorine sex appeal.

The carousel ground to a halt. The girls got off and joined the Devil, standing two on each side of him, all of them linking arms. The carousel was wheeled away, and the stage from the front of the apron to its deepest recesses was pitch black and empty, save for the troupe of players.

The Devil gestured magnanimously with his palm. He'd done his trick. Now it was Carter's turn.

'So all I have to do is something more extravagant than producing a carousel with two zebras, two bears, and four beautiful girls serving champagne?'

The Devil rocked on his heels, rubbing his hands together.

Carter snapped his fingers. It wasn't a dramatic sort of snap, and it wasn't even accompanied by fanfare or flashes of light. Nonetheless, one quarter of a second later, there was an elephant onstage.

The effect was so startling, there were cries from several members of the orchestra and even the players were stunned. It certainly hadn't looked that good in rehearsal. One moment, the stage was empty, the next, an elephant!

In the back of the house, Ledocq stood, arms tightly around his waist, and holding his breath. When the crowd burst into cheers, he exhaled.

People whistled, they stomped their feet, they laughed out loud. Many an elephant had vanished onstage – but *appearing* like that? Carter asked the audience, 'How many people preferred the carousel business?' and the applause continued unabated, and he asked, 'How many liked my friend Tug the elephant?' and the crowd whistled mightily, doubling and redoubling their applause.

The showgirls left the Devil, and all draped themselves on the elephant.

Carter said to the Devil, 'Thank you. The elephant wins. Good night,' and he escorted the women and Tug offstage.

Left alone, the Devil began to fume, and the orchestra struck up a passage from *Don Juan in Hell* to accompany him.

Carter ran ahead into the wings. As Tug passed Phoebe, she reached out and stroked his flank.

She said, 'You can keep your chorus girls, I'm holding hands with Tug tonight.'

Drinking down a glass of water, he said, 'You know, it's a disaster tonight, I'm simply going into debt to my eyeballs for the rest of my life, but . . . this is fun. I'm having a terrific time. I've found a rhythm to work in, it's terrific. I have to go back on in a moment, then we're wrapped. Have I mentioned I'm having fun? Lord, I'm talking a lot. Say something to me.'

She smiled. 'I like you.'

'I love you,' he said. It just came out, like a dove slipping out of his sleeve. He couldn't take it back, and so he breathed slowly, willing the silence to mean something sweet. When seconds had passed, he added, 'Did you hear—'

'Yes.' She rubbed her hands like he'd shut a window on her fingers.

'There's all kinds of things you can say back. . . "Go soak your head." I can help you think of others.'

'I don't want to tell you that, but . . . we'll talk later.'

'Of course.'

There was but one effect left, a final illusion about which all of San Francisco would be talking in the coming days. There would be much explanation by those who had seen it to those who hadn't. And then those people, years later, would claim to have been there, too. No wonder so few witnesses could agree on what exactly had transpired, a situation that drove the police to use gross expletives in their private reports.

In response to the materialization of the elephant, the Devil threw a tantrum. He commenced juggling three small human skulls that burst into flames and while the orchestra played the 'Mephisto Waltz,' the lights came down, and with the skulls describing a higher and higher arc, the Devil made rude gestures that caused sparks and jets of flame to leap from his fingertips.

Amazingly, as the Devil juggled, the flaming skulls went high enough to arc behind the proscenium arch, and, before anyone much noticed how this had happened, he was juggling two, then one, and then his hands were empty. James, with a snifter of brandy, stood on the catwalk by the prop man whose job was to catch the skulls in a long fishnet and drop them into a tub of wet sand.

With the audience occupied by this display of pyrotechnics, Cleo and Esperanza ran back and forth with sparkling flares, and, behind the act curtain, the stage crew rolled a tremendous rig to the center of the stage. It stood a story tall. It consisted of a wooden staircase leading to a scaffold caped with black velvet.

Carter took his position in the wings. He took deep, cleansing breaths. The makeup stinging his eyes, he looked up to the catwalk, and saluted James. He even hissed 'James,' hoping for a simple wave back, but James wasn't looking in his direction. He was, instead, enjoying the Devil's final outburst, in which he opened a deck of Carter's souvenir cards and burned them to a crisp, and then, in a ham-ish performance that made the audience roar with laughter, mimed sawing a piano in half and threw his hands in the air as if to ask what the big idea was!

Carter walked out and joined him at center stage. The Devil grabbed him by the shoulders and shook him until, by sheer sorcery, a pair of shiny handcuffs bound his wrists behind his back. Then the Devil pumped his fist in the air. He pointed into the shadows that had grown deep behind him: here was the mighty rig that took up so much of the stage, the staircase that led up to a cloaked object. On the Devil's command, the cloak fell away to show off the guillotine.

Beside the guillotine was a man dressed in a black robe. He wore a black hood into which eyeholes had been cut, and he stood with his hands on his hips and legs spread wide.

Ledocq, who paced where the standing-room-only patrons would have stood, frowned at this reveal. Next time, they should bring the white spots up first, and then add red when the audience's eyes adjusted. The executioner should have a white rope as a sash. Moreover, Willie was only illuminated from the chest down. He seemed to have missed his mark – either that, or he'd grown six inches.

There were three men on the stage: Carter and the Devil by the apron, and, standing up by the guillotine, the executioner.

'Well, an original guillotine built by Tobias Schmidt,' Carter said ruefully. 'If I have to go, I should go first class.' He held for the nervous laughter. He looked at the Devil. 'Might I go up there and have a look around before—'

The Devil folded his arms and shook his head.

'Someone should examine that to make sure it's safe,' Carter declared. He took a step toward the footlights. 'Will the smartest man in the audience please come onstage?'

It was an ancient line, and no one tonight recognized it. But he'd thought it appropriate to bring back. The spotlights swept the audience until they all joined at once near the center of row G. Sitting there, squinting, and then pointing at himself as if to ask 'You don't mean me?' was Philo Farnsworth.

'Yes, Ladies and Gentlemen, we have a special guest. Mr Philo Farnsworth. A newlywed from Beaver City, Utah.' Mrs Ledocq urged Philo out of his seat – he made more than a passing show of resistance – and prodded him to go up the aisle. 'Mr Farnsworth,' Carter continued, 'is an engineer and an inventor, and it's a privilege to have him in my audience.'

When Philo was onstage, Carter directed him to walk up the staircase to the scaffold on which the guillotine stood. 'As you can see, Ladies and Gentlemen, there is nine feet of space between the scaffold and the stage. This means no place to hide, no hidden compartments, no way out, in short.

'Mr Farnsworth,' he called, 'what say you?' Philo stood by the executioner who, with a flourish, invited him to examine his device. Philo adjusted his eyeglasses, and knocked on the crossbeam and the posts, and respectfully tapped his finger against the blade itself.

'It seems real,' he said.

'I paid $750 for it,' Carter said, 'it had better be real. Please come back down here. I don't want to get blood on you.'

More nervous laughter from the crowd. Philo took the stairs briskly, returning to the stage.

'Philo,' Carter said, 'I want you to be my eyes down here.'

'Okay, Mr Carter.'

'If anything should happen to go wrong, you're the next generation, you get to carry on my wizardry.'

Color blotching his cheeks, Philo seemed unsure of where to look – Carter, the guillotine, or the audience, which was growing restless and anxious. The Devil beckoned with his fingertips, and two loutish brutes entered, dragging behind them the brank.

Carter regarded the Devil coldly. 'As for you, sir, my magic is greater than yours by far. You may try to cut off my head, but that will only annoy me. I'll come back to haunt you!' His eyebrows flexed. He could see Phoebe standing in the wings. It was hard to gauge her expression. He wished he could wink at her to reassure her. How strange to fall in love with a woman who would never see him. She hadn't said 'I love you' and part of him felt loneliness, his lifelong companion, and the other part fully understood why she was so wary of love, and then the Devil's henchmen went to work. One threw a rough sack over Carter's head – there were no holes, not even for his eyes, not even for him to breathe – and atop that, they fitted the brank.

The audience murmured; there was a great shifting around and uncomfortable whispering. Carter, blinded and bound, was led to the edge of the stage by the two thugs, one on each elbow, and his struggles against them seemed real and forceful enough. They walked him in a circuit around the stage, and then, plainly visible from every seat in the house, they marched him up the stairs. The orchestra, which had been playing ascending staccato notes for long minutes, broke into Mozart's *Requiem*. Ledocq, from the back of the theatre, continued to stare at the executioner. What was wrong with this picture?

Struggling, step by step, the thugs guided their captive to the scaffold. They leaned him over the trestle and opened wide the fitted form of the lunette into which the brank just fit. Then down went the lunette, touching the back of his neck, and it was clasped shut with an impressive sliding bolt.

The thugs trotted away. Now the only upright forms atop the scaffolding were the executioner and the guillotine itself, its victim strapped in with no way to escape. The orchestra held on to the same eight measures, repeating them with increasing volume. The executioner looked down at the cuffed hands that flexed, the narrow back, the trapped head, and he listened to the music. It was the largest audience he had played in years, and easily his most enjoyable role. He was a natural.

'After being severed from the spinal cord,' he whispered, 'the brain will still function for several seconds. Or so I understand.'

A jolt, brank smacking against the guillotine frame. 'Who is that?'

The bald man said quietly, 'Mysterioso.'

A drumroll, the rest of the orchestra stopped dead, and here was a moment of terrible magic history. Philo, onstage, wondered how on earth Carter would get out of this. James gazed down from the catwalk, next to Tom, who was reading a newspaper. James was suddenly struck with a vision of the brank and a pillory. Something vague and unpleasant began to bother him, like he was the one himself being trapped. In the wings, Phoebe was counting the seconds until the show would be over, for she suddenly felt like a dolt and hoped to trade with Carter those soft words that she had not yet said. Max Friz had grabbed Mrs Ledocq's hand and was squeezing it. Olive White, who had been waiting for Mr Griffin until this moment, had completely forgotten about all else except what was transpiring before her eyes. And throughout the audience, the dignitaries, the friends of Carter, the neighbors, and critics fixated on the guillotine. Even the men from RCA and the War Department ceased for just a few moments to be involved in the game of business and were leaning forward in their seats. James squinted to see past the lights, to look into the audience, and he no longer felt trapped – he took an emotional reading of the theatre, the hot and the cold anticipation, and he felt an ancient, almost forgotten pride, being shoulder-to-shoulder in a grand enterprise, even if for the last time. The whole house was engaged in the moment – save Ledocq.

Ledocq was watching critically until he saw the executioner *speaking*. He wasn't supposed to do that. The timing was so crucial he'd threatened to fire Willie if he were even five seconds behind schedule. And then, with the drumroll, he saw something so horrible he felt bile rising in his throat – Willie pulling the safety pin out of the guillotine.

He cried 'No!' aloud, clapping his hands – the audience around him, several people called 'No!' as well, all caught in the thrill of it – and Ledocq managed to take several steps toward the stage before the executioner's gloved hand reached out and made a leisurely pull on the release cord.

There was a cold metallic sound like ice skates skidding, and then a heavy tumble into the wicker basket.

The audience gasped, for it seemed very realistic. Ledocq was in the aisle, but now there was a crowd, standing, for him to push through. As he moved forward, he also strained to see onstage. Willie – but he knew it wasn't Willie – had fished into the basket, and now grabbed the brank by its crown and held it aloft, some dark form lolling inside like a sleeping bird.

'Behold!' the executioner cried, which was part of the script, a fact that Ledocq clung to. It was not Willie's voice, he knew this with all his heart. He pushed people aside. The audience fell silent enough to hear that the kettledrums were building again. The executioner spoke slowly. Surrounding the stage, black bunting was beginning to fall away, revealing polished glass surfaces. 'Carter!' the executioner cried. Then, 'the Great!' A weird blue glow began all over the house, its source uncertain. 'Is!' and then 'Dead!'

Draperies and coverings around the arch fluttered to the ground like discarded feathers, revealing two dozen oddly shaped globes that wrapped around the stage as if they were massive lightbulbs on a marquee. They crackled with opalescent blue fire. The executioner, trophy extended toward the audience, was plunged into darkness, which seemed to startle him.

Philo, who had felt small, stood alone on the apron of the stage. His head turned from globe to globe, and he felt his skin moving on its own accord, for he suddenly understood what was happening.

Each globe, flattened at the end, went brilliant and blue, rich with horizontal veins, and each gradually came into focus so it contained the spirit image of Charles Carter, two dozen of him all around the stage, and then Carter's mouth opened, and said, 'Carter the Great . . . is . . . Everywhere!' They could hear him, the enunciation was perfect, clear as a gramophone recording, a voice from the other side.

There were screams as the spirit turned from left to right, all of his images in unison, and then, looking straight on at the audience, made a broad and unmistakable wink. A flash, and then all the images at once extinguished.

The stage went dark. Philo watched the receding blue dots glow in each of the flat-ended tubes, and for the first time in his life, his mind was utterly blank. He then regarded the audience, which was on its feet, but smothered, draped in dead silence, the children in front holding on to their nannies with fear, and, gradually, he could hear strong voices, those of men, but just fragments, whispers, 'impossible' and 'never seen anything like' and 'what was that?' Then the women began to speak, and the children were asking questions. The curtains behind Philo drifted closed; he hardly paid attention.

Then, finally, it felt like hours had passed, the applause began. It was like nothing Philo had ever heard, not just full, not just exuberant, but seeming to feed on itself, growing in intensity, as if the theatre wouldn't actually contain the flood of emotion, as if it would burst outward and down the street, to fill the city and sweep like tidal waves through its outlying reaches with joy and marvel. 'More! More!' And it continued to grow, just grow unchecked. Applause always ended, its nature was ephemeral. But Philo began to feel like this reaction would never end. Never. Years from now, he would still be here, center stage.

The actor playing the Devil was at his side suddenly. When had he left the stage? When had he returned? Philo looked at his mask for long seconds. 'Hello,' he choked.

The Devil put his finger to his lips and swept a hand across the panorama that was his audience, the standing ovation, and he looked at Philo as if to say 'enjoy this.'

Philo nodded. The Devil put an arm around his shoulder.

A moment later, the Devil put one hand below the chin of his mask, tugging it free and revealing the face of Charles Carter.

A fresh wave of cheers burst forth, *Bravo!* and *Carter!* and simple, wordless cries of exhalation.

Tears ran down Philo's face. He could hardly make his voice work. He was reduced to pointing at the flat-ended viewing screens. 'How?' he managed to say, and then 'Impossible.'

'Yes, you told us that, but then we went ahead and made them anyway.'

Philo continued to stare at Carter as if he hadn't heard him. The cheers and thunder of feet pounding the gallery floorboards could have drowned out anything.

Carter looked Philo in the eye and said, 'It was magic.'

Chapter 9

The 'it was magic' explanation, while poetic, was hardly enough for James, who had many questions. James was just one of the many who crowded Carter the moment the show curtain closed – Albert, Esperanza, Cleo, Scott, Max Friz, Mrs Ledocq were all shaking his hand or rubbing his head and Phoebe was swept toward this knot of people – someone dumped water over Carter, good-naturedly, and even the men who rode Fairbanks for a living wanted to touch Carter, to confirm he was alive.

Carter grinned at them all and made the thumbs-up sign to Ledocq, who circled the group with a frown, disappearing behind the curtain where the guillotine illusion was housed. Normally, Carter would have followed, as he was one to gravitate toward any possible error in an otherwise spotless performance. Yet here he was at the center of such assorted carrying-on that he simply let himself go and enjoy the moment.

James successfully fought his way to his brother's ear. 'And what was that nonsense about Borax's safe?'

'Hello, James! Did you see the finale?'

'Yes, and—'

'Satisfying, wasn't it? Not at all suicidal, was it?'

'Yes, you certainly showed me,' James replied. 'Now, why the charade at Borax's?'

'Not a charade. I opened the safe when Carlo wasn't there and swapped in the fakes. That's what burned up. I wanted them to think it was all destroyed. I hope Philo liked it, do you think he liked it? Where is Carlo? I'd like to apologize for the deception and then fire him.'

At the edge of the crowd, Tom tapped Philo on the shoulder. 'There's a vigorous-looking group of men out there who want to meet you. Young men in suits.'

Philo's eyes widened.

When it counted, he was still possessed of the protective instincts of a football hero: Tom said, laconically, 'I'll go with you.'

James announced that all concerned should reconvene immediately at Coppa's, upstairs, for a proper wingding. And with this, some attempts were made to start striking the set, but Carter would have none of it. 'Everyone,' he cried, 'go and drink before James wises up.'

The stage door was propped open for the groups of people who began to spill out, most of them in makeup, even those who hadn't appeared onstage, for it was quite the mark of sophistication to be seen late at night at Coppa's, upstairs, still in your stage wear. So down from the catwalks came the remaining stagehands and out from the shadows the grips and assistants, all of them chattering and ready to play. Albert wouldn't let Carter alone, asking him several times if he'd ever *actually* intended to replace his entrance with that set of glass globes, and Carter confessed that no, that had been a bit of misdirection; they'd been planning to use it with the guillotine all along. 'So your job is safe. Take Madame Esperanza out and dance with her at Coppa's. You can tango there and cause a scandal if necessary. But!' Carter blocked his way, and gave him the evil eye until Albert surrendered his remaining flash paper, three pieces of it.

As if he'd been waiting all night to say it, Albert declared, 'Now I can't get three sheets to the wind,' which provoked groans and promises that Carter would one day fire him.

Next to leave was Max Friz, who had made a complete circle around his R32, head craned, blowing kisses up to the platform where it rested. When he was gone, Carter approached Phoebe, who'd been standing in place for quite some time.

'Hello,' he said.

'I hear you were magnificent.'

'Well . . . yes.'

'It's hard to understand it exactly, but congratulations.'

'Thank you.' He hadn't recovered from the unanswered 'I love you.'

'Charlie, I feel like God's own heel. I'd like to explain.'

'I need to find Ledocq, so let's park you . . . where? Oh, here.' He sat her in the Gone! chair.

She touched the wires behind the chair back. 'Are you about to make me disappear?'

'You're safe. Wait here.' Carter looked for Ledocq, with whom he would pack the television apparatus, but he was distractedly thinking about Phoebe and wondering if she were going to say 'I love you,' so he went in wide circles until Ledocq found him first.

'Come with me,' he said, pulling Carter through the curtains and up the stairs to the guillotine's scaffolding. Ledocq explained what he'd seen during the illusion: someone, having taken Willie's place, pulled out the safety pin.

'That's odd,' Carter said.

'But this, here, this is bizarre.'

All of the black velvet around the guillotine was gone, pulled up by its edges. The wicker basket was also gone. There was stage blood smeared on the guillotine's base. It looked like someone had fumbled the job of cleaning it.

'We'll ask Willie what happened,' Carter said.

'Willie, I'm not so interested in. Where's Carlo?'

'On top of the nearest chorus girl. He never stays after the show. He's always afraid someone will ask him to help lift something.' Carter smiled; Ledocq did not. 'You don't mean— You don't think someone cut off Carlo's head?'

'Someone, thinking it was you.'

'You're such a *grandmother*. Bubbie! We turned that flatfoot Griffin away at the stage door – that's the assassin Borax was prattling about.'

'But look at this – who would take all this away unless there was blood on it?'

'That's very, very Gothic of you.' As he spoke, he was otherwise engaged: he wanted to hear Phoebe say 'I love you.' Until then, his universe was hopelessly out of skew. 'Let's go to Coppa's. *L'Chaim*.'

'We should find Carlo and Willie.'

'Willie is probably back at his flat by now. He's not much of a debutante. Let's pack up television.'

Outside, the exodus from the stage door merged with the crowd that lingered by the marquee, alive with laughter and people telling each other about Carter's marvelous illusions. How had he done that final one, with the crystal balls? Uncanny. Some of the children were studying the decks of cards they'd received, wondering how exactly one became a magician. The nurses and their charges left in buses, and there were passengers sharing taxis and trolley cars.

Walking slowly, head turning from left to right in hopes of meeting a certain pair of brown eyes, Olive White was trying to make the best of things. She hoped that she could still share whatever adventure Agent Griffin had found.

Soon, the hobo was one of her remaining few companions. She recognized him. He'd been an actor once. Chase . . . something. 'I played here. I had excellent diction. Murdoch, hated him.'

She paced back and forth, turning on her heel, using her rolled-up program to bat against her shoulder. She admitted to herself that he wasn't going to come. Yet he wasn't an insensitive man. He would telephone her and explain what had happened.

'Before the movies came,' the hobo was saying. 'Before then, a man's voice was what he could profit by. Murdoch, hated him.' Olive handed him a quarter. She wouldn't wait. That would be lovesick. She crossed the street at the corner. Chase's sad patter continued. 'Used to have some guy dress up as Santa Claus, and come down the chimney, like that mattered when the movies were here.'

Just as Carter and Ledocq were packing the last of the television equipment into a safe box, they heard a tremendous *thump* overhead.

'What was that?' Ledocq asked.

'Carlo, dismounting. Now amscray, we'll meet you there.'

'I need to—'

Carter snapped Ledocq's suspenders as if trying to wake him up and handed him his overcoat. 'Good-bye! This is *au revoir*, not *adieu*.'

Ledocq complained that Carter wasn't being sensible. 'If I'm gone, you two will be alone in this . . .' As those words left his mouth, his white eyebrows went north, and he said, 'Ahhh!'

'I never could fool you,' Carter said. 'Now leave.'

The moment he left, Tom and James came backstage from the house, Philo between them. Tom held a stack of business cards on behalf of Philo, who looked in the most positive sense like a man who'd come through a hurricane.

'Charlie, did you speak with Albee yet?' asked James.

Carter wondered if he'd heard that question correctly; it seemed to have come from the wrong decade. 'No.'

'There were a couple of his junior agents in the audience. They're coming to Coppa's.'

'Albee? Vaudeville?' He hadn't a clue how to feel about that, so he said it again and watched James.

'They always need a headliner to compete with the movies. And the television box might be something audiences want to see.'

'And they have money?'

'Apparently so. They're a bit desperate.' James began to explain – less up front, but guaranteed work for nine months, no problems renting theatres, and such. This wasn't a rescue, and Carter shouldn't regard it as such, for it wouldn't solve his problems, but it did postpone them for a while. Though the news was tepid, Carter felt creeping excitement. He would still entertain.

'Tragedies with happy endings,' he interrupted. 'Never under-estimate them.'

'I can't pretend to understand it.'

'Business is better than you thought?' When James nodded, Carter pushed it with, 'Better than Thurston?' And James shook his head. There was further back-clapping and teasing, as Carter maneuvered the remaining company to the stage door. He smiled at all, and agreed that there would be many toasts tonight, and he would be there soon, save seats for him and Phoebe, and he pushed them through the door, good-bye.

After he closed the stage door, he locked it to keep anyone from remembering a scarf.

The stage – his stage – was a smashing panorama, from Baby pacing in his cage to the flats and scrim flanking him, and the curtains all around, and among all the ingenious devices and props was Phoebe, in the Gone! chair.

'I wish I were a photographer,' he said. 'You make a lovely portrait.'

'Do I?'

'Yes.' He wanted to describe all that he saw, but he wasn't born to that sort of explanation and got tangled, and he finally bent over and delivered her a kiss.

She pulled him down to his knees. 'Listen,' she said, and when she said nothing more, he began to listen to the noises in the theatre. Creaks, the lion, the elephant chained up in her private room, but mostly, what he heard sounded like a heartbeat. 'I promised myself,' she said, 'that I couldn't say "I love you" to another man, not unless I knew,' she swallowed, 'simply knew.' She didn't say what she needed to know. 'I love you, Charlie.'

They kissed then, him in his dinner jacket, on his knees before her, and she leaning forward in her chair. Their hands moved over wool and silk and skin. His hand was on her calf, and they kissed more with his hand on her knee, and then inside and above her knee, and then time moved much faster, and Carter and Phoebe made small noises deep in their mouths as they breathed.

She kissed his palm. 'Such nice hands.'

He listened again. 'It's quiet. It hasn't been quiet for a while.'

'It's not totally quiet,' she whispered. 'I can hear electricity. Right now.'

'Really?'

She nodded. 'When it's very still, I can hear electricity. The wiring hums.'

'You're *so* interesting. What other skills do you have?'

'Only one, but I do it exceptionally well.'

'Come here and tell me about that.'

A moment later, Phoebe pulled back. 'What's that noise?'

'That's Baby. He's fussing.'

'Why?'

'He's been fussing all night.'

She tilted her head. 'Can I meet him again?'

He brushed off his knees, stretching, as he escorted her to the cage. 'He's sweet, but he's getting old.'

They were at the bars of the cage. Baby paced back and forth and let out a discontented sort of growl.

'Is that him not liking me?'

'No, that's him being a prima donna. Here, a secret weapon.' He handed her a baked potato with cheese on it, and instructed her to place it between the bars.

She held it for a moment like he'd handed her a rubber chicken. 'A baked potato? With cheese on it?'

'I know. I tell myself baked potato must taste like raw zebra. Either that or he's gone soft.'

Gently, she placed Baby's treat on the floor of the cage. 'Baby,' she said, cautiously. 'It's the woman who fed you roast beef.' The lion ignored her. He continued to make circuits, toenails clicking. Carter was confused and a bit disappointed; Baby was usually gracious company with women.

Phoebe held on to the bars. She asked Carter, 'Do you miss Sarah?'

'Yes. But something's changed. When I was in the packing crate in the bay—'

She laughed. 'I *so* look forward to more stories that begin like that.'

'You know, Baby is spooked. He's like that sometimes after a show. Let's go to Coppa's and come back when he's ready for visitors.'

Phoebe agreed. She took Carter's arm.

They stepped away from the cage. The stage door was only fifteen feet away.

'So, when you were in the packing crate, what happened?'

'I started to understand how you can feel sad sometimes and also keep living.'

'While you were underwater.'

'It's hard to explain.'

They were just three strides from the door. She was to his left, arm around his waist, and his hand rested against her lower back. 'You must try,' she said. 'I'm very interested.' His head was cocked, as he considered his next words.

A blur, something dropped from above, clattering and metallic. Phoebe jumped. It rolled, colliding with the stage door.

'What was that?' she asked.

It was the brank, and it was occupied. In the second it took Carter to understand what was inside, he thought how unrealistic it looked, how to be truly frightening, it should have looked the way Harding's had onstage, with brighter eyes and a messier wound to the throat.

'Something fell,' he said as if it had been a flowerpot. Walls and buttresses went up in his mind, he knew he would unlock the stage door and shove her through.

'Then why—' she said before what looked like a sack of wet laundry fell to the stage, right between them and the stage door, boots bouncing once as the legs found crazy, broken angles. Carter pulled her back by the shoulders, causing her to cry out.

There was motion on the catwalk, someone moving gracefully down the ladder by the back wall, one hand on the rungs, the other holding a pistol. There was now a head, a body, and a man with a gun between them and the stage door.

'Stand behind me,' Carter murmured in a way that would not carry far. It was his most calming voice, and using it made him feel some slight control. 'This is a man from the Secret Service who's after me. Just follow my steps,' making sure his body shielded hers.

'Charlie?'

'Follow my lead.' She was silent. Good. Carter had underestimated his opponent – Griffin had become more violent, but still, Carter felt ease, ease as solid as a cornerstone. But then the earth around it began to shake: a woman he loved was in danger, again, and beyond that thought was chaos. He counted his pulse, breathing in though his nose, out through his mouth. He had no weapons. Could he hide her somewhere? He felt her tensing.

The man dropped to the floor. Though he was still in shadow, he didn't look at all like Griffin. He pulled a second pistol from the waist of his trousers. Carter recognized them now: the guns from the bullet-catching bit. They were terribly inaccurate, hard to aim, and only one was loaded with a real bullet. All in all, lucky. But then luck like this was relative.

'Hello, Carter.' The man stepped over the corpse and walked, guns extended, toward Carter and Phoebe.

It was in no way Griffin. Carter didn't recognize him. Where was the excited command to reach for the sky? The man seemed in no hurry. He wore work pants and a stiff cotton shirt, and a motoring jacket far too small for him that Carter recognized: it was from his own wardrobe. The man was completely bald and had dyed his Vandyke jet black. His skin was weathered like a sundial.

The man looked around the stage, almost smiling. 'You must have wondered often whether you'd completely destroyed me.'

Carter put his face up against all the Secret Service agents he knew, and came up blank. He was about to say he had not the faintest clue what he was talking about, which would have been fatal – the man would have shot him for not remembering. But at that moment, Baby made his weak little moan, and the man turned to him and said, 'Hello, *Baby*.'

Carter blinked. The face in front of him came into sudden focus, and he felt chills, and immediate, ancient anger. A dozen years ago. Here, this very stage. Mysterioso. Obnoxious, cretinous, the man who represented to Carter all that was dark and unworthy in magic. But Mysterioso had changed, somehow – something in him seemed harder and wilder; he'd aged like the windward side of a mountain. Still, Carter could handle Mysterioso.

'Aren't you going to introduce me to the lady?'

'I don't know her name. She's blind, she got lost in the theatre, and I'm trying to help her leave.'

'She could have left *much* faster if you hadn't insisted on kissing her and philosophizing afterward.' As Carter had no reply – he was remembering that *Houdini*, not he, had handled Mysterioso – Mysterioso continued, 'I believe he called you Phoebe. Phoebe, will you please come out from behind your man?'

She took a broad, sidelong step. She looked quite steady, her mouth a deep frown, arms folded over her stomach. She wasn't about to say or do anything out of fear.

'Thank you,' Mysterioso said. 'You *are* lovely.'

Something awful bloomed in his chest. 'So?' he demanded. 'Who are you working for?'

Mysterioso simply looked around the stage. He pushed his lips out, evaluating what he saw. 'That levitation you have, is that a Kellar?'

'No, it's my own design.'

'Oh, *please*, it's a Kellar, anyone can see you stole it.'

'I *didn't*.' Eyes burning, Carter suddenly felt twenty-three years old again. He had to struggle to stay cool.

'It's a Kellar,' Mysterioso concluded to his own satisfaction. 'Now,' he brought both pistols up, 'which of these is loaded?'

'Neither.'

He shook his head. 'No. If you'd used them in the act, neither would be loaded. But you didn't, so one has a live round.'

Phoebe said 'Damn' under her breath.

'What was that?' Mysterioso raised his eyebrows.

'They're both empty,' Carter said.

'Then you won't mind if I shoot one at each of you. Actually, Miss Phoebe, because your friend says it's safe, I'm going to shoot both of them at you.'

'No!'

Carter's moment of panic seemed to delight Mysterioso, who brought the barrel of one gun to his lips, as if kissing it for being such a good boy. 'Ah, you *do* love her. Which gun, Carter? Phoebe, is Carter a good liar?' Old memories percolated icily in the back of Carter's mind. Mysterioso was playing Blackmail with him, and with live ammunition in the gun.

Carter said, 'The pistol with the trigger guard in the shape of a diamond, do you see it?' As long as Carter talked, he could think rapidly, but all that came to him was that he didn't want Phoebe to be shot, which was exactly what Mysterioso was set on doing. The pistols shot .22 rounds. 'Do you see how one has a heart, the other a diamond?' If Mysterioso shot him instead of Phoebe, he could survive and charge the props table, where there were a half-dozen throwing knives. 'The diamond is the live round.'

'Oh God,' Phoebe said.

'Thank you, Carter,' Mysterioso said. 'But I like my original plan.' Both guns turned to Phoebe. Carter stepped in front of her. Mysterioso pulled the triggers back. Carter gritted his teeth.

'Drop your weapons now!' It was a loud voice, one used to shouting. Carter squinted into the shadows. He saw a figure staggering toward the light. Unbelievable!

Agent Griffin, begrimed and greyish black from head to toe. His clothes were torn and, as he walked onto the stage, he left footprints etched in ash.

Mysterioso looked at Griffin, whose Colt .45 was steady and cocked, a round in the chamber. Mysterioso, who had some experience with insane anger, saw it in Griffin's eyes. 'Well,' he whispered. 'My my.' He sounded impressed. He took the pistols by their butts and carefully put them on the floor. Griffin kicked them away.

'Are we saved?' Phoebe asked.

'Yes.' Carter waved. 'Agent Griffin. Hello!'

'Charles Carter,' Griffin declared, 'you are under arrest for the murder of President Warren Gamaliel Harding. Place your hands behind your neck.'

Carter didn't move. He was so surprised, he couldn't move. 'Excuse me?'

Mysterioso barked, 'What are you talking about?' He looked at Carter with a mixture of jealousy and respect. 'Carter, did you really kill—'

'Look, you grimp,' Griffin snapped, 'I don't know who you are but if you say another word, I'm going to blow a hole in your chest so big I'll be able to read the phone book through you.' Griffin glared at him, a thousand-degree stare. Then, in a singsong voice, he added, 'Yeah, I *do* have a ticket, thanks for reminding me.' Asshole.'

Mysterioso intook breath, ready with a reply, and Griffin pointed the gun at his solar plexus.

'Just say it. One word. Just one.'

Mysterioso closed his eyes and let out a disappointed sigh.

Carter put his hands behind his head. 'Agent Griffin, may I speak?'

'What?'

'Phoebe here is blind. Do you mind if she sits?'

Griffin shrugged. Carter walked Phoebe to the Gone! chair and helped her sit down. He put her hands on the frame of the chair. When she folded them in her lap, he returned them to the frame and held them there, pressing his fingers into her palms before letting go.

Carter returned to his pose, hands behind his head. 'Why are you arresting me?'

Griffin spat soot onto the floor. 'The wine bottle.' As soon as he said it, it seemed hopelessly inadequate. A wine bottle. Still, even if it took all night, he'd make Carter confess.

Carter's response was unexpected. 'The wine bottle. That's amazing. I'm amazed.'

'What's he talking about?' Phoebe shouted. Mysterioso opened his mouth, then thought again, and closed it.

'Quiet,' Griffin said, though not above feeling proud.

Phoebe said, 'Charlie, this is where you tell him you didn't do it.'

But Carter said nothing. To Griffin, Carter looked pleased, like he was basking in getting caught. But Griffin still hadn't heard a confession. He had no more evidence than the bottle. So he bluffed. 'The only thing I don't know is who you were working for – the Duchess or one of the politicos.'

'Ahh,' Carter replied. 'I see. What can I say about that?'

Phoebe shouted, 'What about "I'm not guilty"?'

'It's not that simple,' Carter murmured. 'I'm thinking.' He shook something into his hand. A tin. Mysterioso frowned at it.

'What's that?' Griffin waved his gun.

'I'm having a peppermint. I'm trying to think.' Carter shook the tin. 'They're called PEZ. Would you like one?'

'PEZ!' Griffin exclaimed. 'Why you—' He growled, as it dawned on him, 'The Germans. Of course.'

'Pardon? No, I'm—'

As this colloquy had taken no small attention away from him, Mysterioso shouted, 'Carter, come now, you didn't really—'

'Hey, Barrymore, I said not another word out of you!' Griffin fished in his jacket. 'You're under arrest, too. Put these on.' He threw a pair of handcuffs at Mysterioso, who caught them with one cool hand.

'What are you doing?' Carter asked.

'Cuffing him. Put 'em on, pal.'

'You can't be serious!'

'You're next, so shut your yap.'

'He'll get right out!'

'Hey, these are *government regulation* cuffs,' Griffin explained. 'You guys can't dick your way out of them.'

Carter could only stare: he was face to face with ignorance. If he survived, Griffin could someday make an outstanding audience member.

And then, looking at Griffin the whole time, concentration written on his face as if asking for reassurance that he was doing it correctly, Mysterioso secured one wrist, then the other. He extended his hands. He looked toward the floorboards, radiating a luster of schoolboy shame.

Griffin got out a second pair of cuffs, which he would use to secure Mysterioso to an overhead pipe. He holstered his gun.

'Don't get near him, Griffin.'

Griffin said, 'It's—' and Mysterioso grabbed Griffin's wrists and gave them a quick shake. Griffin looked surprised, as that simple motion made the handcuffs jump off Mysterioso's wrists and onto his own. While Griffin stared at them, Mysterioso's hand dipped into Griffin's jacket and pulled out his gun.

Mysterioso said 'Pardon,' and shot Griffin in the side.

Carter flinched. The report was awful and with it came a *thump* across the room. Baby had fallen over. Griffin looked at Mysterioso with an accusatory expression. *Poor Griffin,* Carter thought. He saw in Griffin's eyes, before they closed, disappointment with the world. Then the agent collapsed. Mysterioso paid Griffin no mind – instead he looked with interest into the lion's cage.

Phoebe. Carter took a single step backward and hit the button for the Gone! chair so that Phoebe, with a gasp, was fired upward as if from a slingshot. She vanished.

Mysterioso didn't notice at first. He was too engaged by the sight of Baby stretched out. He looked away to brush soot off his clothes, and then returned to his curious stare.

This was a moment Carter could have used to engineer Mysterioso's defeat. Instead he was fixated on Griffin, who writhed on the floor. As he bled, Carter began to float. He'd never seen a man shot before. Suddenly his own rules of conduct, the outcomes he believed in, seemed frail and naive. Mysterioso had gone places Carter could never go. He wasn't sure how to fight that.

Then it didn't matter. The gun was pointing at him. 'I had one bullet and now I have five,' Mysterioso said, but his mind was elsewhere. 'You trained Baby to fall over when there's a gunshot?'

'Yes, or a loud enough clap.'

'How does he stand up?'

'I clap twice.'

'What if anyone else claps?'

Carter said, 'Why don't you try?'

'No. I'd have to put my gun down, so you do it. Clap.'

'There's a man dying here.'

'I should hope so. Now clap.'

Carter gave a pair of dispirited claps. Baby lurched onto his haunches. Mysterioso watched him.

'That's very interesting. Oh, and I see your girl is missing. What was she riding, a de Kolta?'

'Yes.'

He squinted. 'I don't see a trap. But I do see a lift, so maybe it's a Gone! effect. Finding a blind woman on a catwalk. Yes, that should tax me no end.' He jerked his chin toward the stage. 'I still don't understand your Kellar device.'

Carter was about to rise to that bait, and then thought, *He's just a bully.* Granted, a bully with a gun, but the thought gave him slight comfort. 'I'm not telling you how everything works.' As he spoke, he saw Griffin's mouth tying into a grimace. In the shadows, it was hard for Carter to see how extensive Griffin's wound was, though the layer of soot on his torn shirt was now sticky with gore. He was on his side, knees bent, his body forming a harbor for a pool of blood.

Mysterioso approached Carter. When he was still a few steps away, he paused. 'You'll try something,' he murmured. With his free hand, he unbuttoned his shirt to the waist, showing off a hand-made sort of sling. Sitting in the sling was a dog.

'Oh my God,' Carter murmured. Mysterioso took the dog out of the sling and put him on the floor. The dog stretched his front legs and yawned. 'Handsome,' Carter said.

'Handsome III,' Mysterioso corrected. 'Who's my little man? Who's my little man? Sit, Handsome. *Good boy!*'

With Handsome sitting at what his master judged was a safe distance from the treacherous Charles Carter, Mysterioso fished in Griffin's pockets and found a second pair of cuffs. Extracting them, he felt under Griffin's jaw. He frowned. 'No, no,' he chided, and gave Griffin a brutal kick in the back. Griffin groaned, which seemed to relieve Mysterioso.

'Handsome! Go get din-din!' And the little dog bolted from his spot, settling daintily at the edge of the pool of blood, from which he began to drink noisily.

Carter's stomach turned upside down.

Mysterioso threw the cuffs at him. 'Put one cuff on your left wrist. Leave the other one free.'

At gunpoint, Mysterioso led Carter to the wooden backdrop he had used for the knife-throwing act. Carter could smell him now, cheap cologne over dark earthen smells, like a man who'd slept in barns and ditches. 'Twelve years,' Mysterioso said. 'Twelve years of you using my act and living the high life.'

'Like hell.'

'Oh, I'm sure you had many troubles,' he yawned. His black eyes focused on Carter. Twelve years ago, Carter had seen in them contempt and ego. But now, unexpectedly, he was looking into a void. There was nothing in those eyes. 'Do you know what I did? I left the country. And where did I go? Go on, guess.'

'I don't know.' Carter swallowed. He was feeling oddly lost, like the emptiness was spreading from Mysterioso's eyes, and was obliterating all that he knew for certain.

'Really. The most obvious place.' Mysterioso grabbed the free end of the handcuffs and fastened it to a squat metal U-bar that jutted from the flat around waist level. 'Guess.'

'India,' Carter said blankly.

'Exactly. I did exactly what all of us pretend to do. I went to India to learn magic at the feet of holy men. I went there for years, Carter, and while you were riding high, having the easy life, five thousand a week—'

'I never—'

'Be quiet.' Mysterioso pointed the Colt at his throat. Carter knew he would pull the trigger whenever he felt like it. Carter had a hand free, but his mind was foggy with images of ancient maps he'd seen of a flat world, with arrows to the edges and 'here be dragons' promised for those who left the known behind. Mysterioso had gone *beyond*. There was no predicate to that, simply that no matter the map, geographic or psychic, Mysterioso had gone beyond any known point. 'I traveled by donkey to the obscure cesspools, the vermin-infested caves and slums, and you know what the holy men taught? Do you? *Inner peace*. Enlightenment. Can you imagine? I just wanted one bloody, miserable thing no one else knew, anything, teach me to carve a boy to

514

pieces and restore him, show me the real Indian rope trick, but no! *Yoga! Come on!'*

The gun went level with Carter's solar plexus; with his other hand, Mysterioso grabbed Carter's right hand and held it far over his head, against the backdrop. That sickly cologne made Carter choke. 'Go on! Stand up straight, up on your tippy-toes,' he spat. 'Stretch!'

It was an odd request. There was really no way for one magician to detain another. No one was sure what someone else could escape from. So Carter went willingly, not nearly as afraid as he should have been. He'd had years of experience doing one thing while observing another, so he pressed his back against the flat, and stretched up on his toes, his hand directly overhead, and he saw Griffin lift his head slightly, then drop it. Griffin had another pair of handcuffs. Perhaps Griffin had a second gun. Carter looked for signs of movement where the Gone! chair had parked and saw none. All this observation while at the same time figuring when he could best slip the cuffs. Mysterioso dug the gun into Carter's gut. 'Do you know what this gun is good for?'

'No,' Carter whispered.

'Misdirection,' Mysterioso said, which caused Carter to look down. It was no longer the gun pressed against him – it was the handle of one of his throwing knives. The moment this substitution registered, Mysterioso brought it up and out into an arc and then drove it, blade first, through Carter's hand. Mysterioso stepped back to admire the sight.

Carter never even heard the sound it must have made. A mild vibration traveled up his wrist, a sensation that trembled and widened as it found his mouth, which went taut in surprise. His hand was pinned over his head like he was the brightest student in the class. He stared without a thought in his head. The world became very wobbly, a poorly threaded projector, his vision skipping with each heartbeat.

There was some kind of motion around him but he had no clue what it was, as he was being poured out of his body. A memory, a fragment: a winter evening at the library, Thacher School, bare tree branches shaking outside in the rain, which poured down the windows, wind whistling past the building, him huddled over *Gray's*

Anatomy until the electric lights flickered once, twice, and then out, casting into darkness the etching of the transverse section of the carpus. He'd seen, snugly fit together like a cross-section of a cell, the skin, the tendons, vessels and nerves, the ligaments, flexors, muscles and bones cozied together, and then, when the lights went out, all that mortal power fizzled, just as he had once imagined shaking Horace Goldin's portrait until the accoutrements of magic – the doves, the scarves, the coins and imps – spilled out and left an empty man.

He awaited pain, but felt none. Instead, fear began to spread. When pain came, it would be horrible. The application of will against the physical body, his hand was hopeless, and his will washed away, too, and in its place, a tidal wave now of thunderous, pounding, vicious pain.

Carter still hadn't made a sound, and Mysterioso put his hands on his hips. 'Oh, come on, that's *got* to hurt.'

And *yes,* as conscious thought returned to him, the pain was there and with it the visceral message from body to brain and back again, sickly fear of further harm, but also a challenge, one Carter automatically clung to, *do not* give this man satisfaction.

He breathed in through his nose and out his mouth. Labored. Clenched teeth that he fought to unclench.

'My employers,' Mysterioso said, crossing his arms and leaning against a support pillar, 'are going to allow me to keep all of your devices. Well, whatever I don't destroy.' He looked at his nails.

Carter rasped, with words that sounded measured, 'Are you going after Houdini, too?'

Mysterioso considered this. He looked all around, alighting on Griffin (who wasn't moving). 'I'm sorry, are you making conversation until someone rescues you, or are you just making conversation? Houdini did what he had to do and I respect that. You, you were just Houdini's punk, a cheap kard and koin opportunist who lucked into a momentary crown. So by the skill and determination that you don't possess, I'm taking it all back. Audacious, no?'

He winced. That word. Three syllables. *Audacieux,* as it came to him for no particular reason in French. It brought him somewhere primal. *Jamais tromper pas la repout pour l'audace.* As Mysterioso turned away, Carter shouted, his eyes sealed shut with concentration, 'Never mistake obnoxiousness for audacity!'

Mysterioso kept walking. Over his shoulder, he muttered, 'Yes, yes, familiar advice.' He had reached the brick wall, and begun following something. 'Who was that, Professor Hoffman?'

Ottawa Keyes. Carter's eyes snapped open.

He watched Mysterioso, who counted off steps from the fuse box and down the wall – then looked at how he was pinned, the easy hand first: left hand, handcuff around a U-bar. No special tools needed, which was good because Carter's special tools were up his other sleeve. Striking the cuff against a hard surface could release him. Mysterioso had cuffed him with the U-bar a good distance from the floor. With enough slack, he could use the U-bar itself.

He remembered how every night he'd worried about Annabelle's hands, how she could have broken bones so easily by fighting. His morning ritual of olive oil and milk. A piece of him had been killed. There was no way to feel how *entirely* that was going to ruin him. He moved his thumb. He *could* move his thumb.

Mysterioso held a fire ax. Carter took a deep breath. When Mysterioso came near enough to swing it, he would kick as hard as he could, but even that wouldn't be enough.

Mysterioso walked past him with the fire ax. Then back to the fuse box, which he popped open. He brought down a lever. The left side of the stage was plunged into darkness. He brought it back up; then he did the same with the right, then the overheads, then levers that seemed to do nothing, perhaps connected to the outside power, and then he brought the house lights up and down. 'Ah,' he said, 'that's it.'

Mysterioso walked along the wall about thirty feet, and then brought his ax over his head and down once, causing the blade to spark against the metal fasteners. He threw the ax aside and pried back on the now-severed power line. He pulled it from its braces, which popped away like buttons, walking back to the fuse box, where he brought the power lever back on again. He now held, like a garden hose, forty feet of live cable, two 120-volt lines at 180 degrees out of phase, wrapped around a neutral, making 240 volts.

Carter bit down. He was not to be axed, but electrocuted. But then Mysterioso yelled, 'Hey, Carter, how do you make the lion roar?'

Griffin had never been shot before. In his youth, he'd dreamed about it. Now, with the shock wearing off, all he could think for long minutes was how stupid he felt. Shot for no reason. Jack Griffin, idiot. There was now something definitive for his gravestone. It didn't even hurt that much – he just felt weak. Moving might have been possible, but certainly wasn't worth it.

He heard the two magicians talking. He watched as a little dog with diseased-looking skin lapped up his blood.

Griffin's entire world filled up with the dog. He formed a complex relationship with him. He was thinking maybe he had actually lived his whole life for *this* moment, not the glory he'd hoped to die for, and the dog had lived its whole life without any foresight whatever. And here they were, the man who was always wrong, splayed before an animal. *Now I'm food for a vampire dog*, which seemed a fitting destiny. As Handsome grew bolder, actually standing in the blood, Griffin looked at the gauzy patches of white hair over his pink and grey skin. He saw a grey spot on the dog's flank that looked like Florida. The world was a wonder. God's infinite plan included the duplication of the state of Florida on a dog's rump.

Then Handsome was overcome by greed and stepped directly to the source of his meal, Griffin's side wound. Griffin felt sharp teeth on him, and his reflexes kicked in. A convulsive jerk. It was enough. Handsome recoiled, made a full circle, and watched Griffin from afar. If a dog's eyes could make judgments, these were sizing him up, determining whether he was too dangerous to eat.

The little dog's nose went in the air, and his lip curled. Without further preamble he trotted off.

Griffin chuckled, deep in his throat. He wasn't meat yet.

'Griffin! Griffin? Can you hear me?'

He saw Carter, who was pinned just a few feet to his left, stealing glances at him, while Mysterioso was far away in the shadows, playing with the fuse box again.

Carter whispered, 'Can you stand? Do you have another gun? Can you help me pull this knife out of the board?'

The answer to all those questions was no. But Griffin did feel a little stronger.

'Griffin,' he hissed, 'crawl to the lion cage. Pull the pin. It's by the floor.'

Mysterioso, satisfied that the lines would do, faced the cage. But Baby had gotten as far away as possible and sat with his back to him. Shocking the lion without seeing his face would never do. 'Come, Baby. Come here.'

'Griffin, let the lion loose,' Carter whispered, head turned away from Mysterioso, speaking so quietly Griffin could barely hear him.

A wounded man letting a lion loose. At the word of a presidential assassin. Griffin glared at him with all the contempt he could muster.

Carter looked to the cage, and to Griffin, beseechingly. 'I'll confess to killing the President. Let the lion loose.'

Mysterioso reached into the cage with one hand and poked at the baked potato, of which a few bites had been taken. 'Food, Baby. Come for food.' He heard a quick yip, its source somewhere nearby. Then a steady little whine that was somewhat muffled.

'Little man, where are you?' he asked with concern. This was not Handsome's sweet play bark. It sounded strange.

He looked all around, at the crates and the dozens of places Handsome could be lost, then at the cage again. He saw a trail of tiny footprints outlined in Griffin's blood. They led directly to a box near the cage, then into the cage, to the baked potato. The potato, now unattended, had a single dog-sized bite taken out of it.

'Little man?' Mysterioso asked anxiously.

Baby turned around slowly. Lions cannot grin, but Baby looked like he was grinning, for his mouth was open just wide enough to show off how well his great incisors made a cage for Handsome, who was alive and panting in his mouth.

'No!' Mysterioso dropped the power line. 'No! No!' He waved his arms in front of him as if surrendering. Baby sat down, all four legs down, looking like a sphinx, teeth – and dog – bared.

They froze like that, Mysterioso afraid to move, as if any motion would alarm Baby. Finally, inspired, he brought his palms together. *Clap*.

Baby started chewing.

Mysterioso let out a wounded scream. His knees collapsing under him, he bent forward until his face was against the stage. His lungs filled with air and he screamed – agonized, horrified – again.

Carter, who had been fruitlessly banging his cuffed wrist against the backdrop, paused. He saw Baby chewing and heard Mysterioso, and knew what had happened. He loved his pets and could have felt sorry for Mysterioso, the way he had once years ago after Blackmail, but he didn't. *Good,* he thought, and turned his attention to the hand overhead, which had entirely drained of blood. It no longer felt like his hand but like a wooden paddle someone had attached to his wrist.

Over the stage, Phoebe was trying to get her bearings. The chair had come to a full stop after just a second of violent upward motion, as if fired out of a cannon. She had sat, hands gripping the wooden arms, listening to the voices below.

She had heard Mysterioso asking about Baby, and then Carter clapping. She listened closer for clues to her own location. Even when she was a girl, and still had her sight, she had realized she could *hear* objects. She had risen from bed with her eyes closed and knew, somehow, where the walls were, where the bureau was.

When she went blind, she learned that nearly every blind person had that proximity sense as a child and hoped it would help them, but it didn't. Still, there were the magical few who could find their way around Lake Merritt. They made her terribly jealous. For her, finding her way around unfamiliar surroundings was hit or miss, and so here, over the stage, she put her toes out first, gingerly.

The chair could be alone, hanging by a wire, in empty space. There was in fact empty space under her feet. A fluttery feeling radiated to her palms. She pointed with her toes, walking them through the air. They hit something solid.

She took her shoes off and put them in her lap. She removed her stockings and balled them into her shoes. Using her bare feet, she felt along the edges – it was a wooden platform and it seemed to extend as far as her feet could reach. If Carter could remain calm, so could she. They would work together. She had to believe that. She lifted herself out of her chair and put both feet on the wood. She got on her knees and felt with her hands. Glad she hadn't taken a broad step, for it wasn't a platform, just a plank eighteen inches wide.

She left her shoes behind and tucked the hem of her dress into her waistband so she could crawl forward. She crawled very slowly, listening to the sounds below her. When she heard Carter yell, 'Never mistake obnoxiousness for audacity,' she grinned. He was a fighter.

The plank ended, and then Phoebe, confirming it led to a wider platform with a railing, stood. She smelled gasoline and exhaust, and when her hands touched rubber, and metal, she knew exactly where she was. She could hear, below, almost directly below, Mysterioso call out, 'Little man, where are you?'

She ran her hands all over it, trying to turn everything she felt into a weapon. Headlamp, handlebars, the seats, the engine, the tires. What was in the panniers? They were empty. Why didn't motorcycles come with machine guns and flamethrowers?

She heard Mysterioso scream. It sounded like keening. He was close by. How close?

If she started the motorcycle, and made it go over the platform, she could drop it on him.

It was a crazy idea. There was no way to accurately drop a motorcycle off the platform and onto a specific person who was standing nearby. Yet she had no further ideas. Locating the throttle was easy. Next she had to find the petcock and the kickstarter.

Mysterioso hovered by the cage. He was silent. Carter watched him carefully while thinking about his hand, which he continued to imagine being made of wood. An image of releasing himself came to mind; he banished it. He didn't like the way that particular release worked.

Inside the cage, Baby was still chewing sporadically. Mysterioso picked up the power line. Carter shook his head, as if that would help. He called out, 'Don't do it,' which at least made the other magician look his way, eyes brimming.

Making a warrior's cry, Mysterioso brought the 240-volt line against the bars of the cage. Baby switched from chewing to licking his paw and bringing it over his face to clean himself. Mysterioso yelled again, banging his cable against the cage. But it wasn't grounded, and the current passed through harmlessly.

Mysterioso dropped the cable. He saw motion on the other side of the cage. He walked there, and saw, now collapsed on the floor, Agent Griffin. He was on his side, hands still cuffed, arms over his head, like a swimmer caught in mid-dive.

Mysterioso drew his gun and aimed it, then paused. Griffin was holding something in his hand. An eye hook.

He turned fast, but not fast enough, for Baby had already launched against the cage's door, which swung open and knocked Mysterioso down.

Carter yelled encouragement as Baby jumped from the cage. Above the stage, Phoebe had found the petcock, and the throttle, and she stood astride the motorcycle, her bare foot finding the kickstarter. She pushed down tentatively. A purr, the sound of something spinning. But nothing else.

Miraculously, Mysterioso managed to hold on to his gun, and as he pushed himself upright, he looked for the lion but did not see him until Baby was on him. Baby roared, and a spiked paw the size of a frying pan knocked Mysterioso in the face. The gun skittered across the floor. Baby snarled and placed his jaws around Mysterioso's chest, ready to dig in.

Phoebe kicked the motorcycle over. The engine came to life. It coughed. Then, carburetors flooding, it backfired.

Baby fell over.

Carter watched with sheer disbelief. One moment, savagery; the next, the lion groaned and collapsed and his enemy was saved. He unthinkingly tried to bring his hands together to clap – of course he couldn't. Trembling with adrenaline, Mysterioso crab-walked backward, eyes on the lion, whose eyes were closed, stomach rising and falling peacefully.

Mysterioso sat upright. He looked himself over, finding cuts and tears, but all his limbs accounted for. He laughed. Bits of Handsome's hair clung to his Vandyke.

He glanced at Carter slyly, and then looked toward the sound of the motorcycle engine. Carter strained against the knife again. He saw his enemy shading his eyes as he looked upward, taking slow paces.

Over the engine noise, Phoebe could hear very little. Someone nearby, speaking to her.

'You can come out now, Phoebe,' Mysterioso called. 'I won't hurt you.' She seethed: he spoke as if she were a child. This gave her an idea. It began with pretending they were both idiots.

'Stand where I can see you,' she said.

'See me?'

Carter yelled, 'Hey!' for though he couldn't hear the conversation – the engine drowned them out – the thought of Phoebe speaking to Mysterioso terrified him.

'See me?' Mysterioso shook his head. 'Is there a place on God's green earth where you can see me?'

'That's not nice,' she said. She was thinking, *Please underestimate me.*

'I apologize.' She could hear from the sound of his voice that he was walking in circles below the platform, looking for ways up, or at least looking for her silhouette. And even from this height, she could smell his cheap cologne.

She said, 'Just stand in front of the platform.'

'How did you start the motorcycle?'

'Please, I'm very frightened. I need to know I can trust you.'

Mysterioso took a step. He hesitated. Standing directly in front of a running motorcycle? He thought not. He stopped to the left-hand side of the platform and folded his arms. 'I'm standing right here,' he said.

'Where?'

'Right here.' He tilted his head back.

Phoebe, gasoline line in hand, took careful aim at the voice and drained the full fourteen-liter tank directly onto Mysterioso. He caught the first dump in his face, the rest on his head and shoulders.

Phoebe killed the engine. Sputtering, Mysterioso half-slid, half-staggered away from her. She listened to this, unsure how satisfied to feel.

With the engine off, she heard Carter yelling her name.

'I've dowsed him in fuel,' she yelled. 'Can you get him?'

'Yes!' Carter said, 'Good work!' but he wasn't eager to tell her he was pinned to a board like a beetle. He saw a form moving haltingly up the ladder on the far wall. 'Phoebe, get away from the platform. Go up the rope ladder.'

After he said that, he was silent. He was no good to anyone staying here. And he realized the only thing that kept him trapped was that he was holding on to magic. How would a magician get away? He would have a gimmick. Or an accomplice. Baby would stay in a heap until he clapped. Griffin was unconscious or worse. A magician would use cunning, natural forces, optics, physics, he would use his physical body, which he'd trained to perform what seemed impossible. But Carter was freed of being a magician.

Now, he had to do something horrible. He began to turn his mind off, bringing the cold, anatomical terms into focus. Mysterioso had planted the knife vertically, between his middle and index fingers, in the valley of the second palmar interosseous, probably turning the second and third shafts of the metacarpi into shrapnel. His hand – a cozy array of levers and pulleys whose delicate motion had helped Carter find some peace. He said a silent good-bye to them.

He lifted both heels up. Tucked his knees against his chest. He managed to bend his arm and hung there for a moment, the pressure causing a new fountain of blood as his weight dragged him down a quarter inch, a half inch, opening the gouge around the knife. Not enough. Full weight, tugging, still, unrelenting, a terrible limitless pain jolting down his arm. He dropped to the ground.

Arm now down, feeling began to return – he hadn't even been aware how blessedly numb he'd been. He couldn't look. He touched his left fingertips to his right hand and confirmed he had ripped a hole from his palm upward and through the line of bones and cartilage between his fingers, which seemed to hang inappropriately from his hand. With the crème-colored silks in his pocket, he improvised a bandage that immediately became a map of another world, red oceans spilling over white continents. Mechanically, his left hand went up his right sleeve and pulled out a wire. He inserted it and the cuffs fell to the ground.

He looked at the knife in the board and thought about ripping it out. Too difficult. He saw Mysterioso overhead leaping from the ladder and onto the top of a piece of the Egyptian scenery, walking across it.

The props table. No matches. No self-lighting candles. The other five throwing knives were gone. Albert had used them all during the show. Albert who was such a fire bug.

Carter touched his pockets. Flash paper. The three sheets he'd taken from Albert. He had those. They only worked intermittently, with the right friction, and had less flame than a match head, perfect when you needed to dazzle the eye. But Albert had juggled torches without igniting these three papers – they were almost useless. The bullet-catching pistols, where were they?

Looking overhead – Mysterioso was spiderlike, crawling up a ladder stealthily; Carter couldn't see Phoebe, but he hoped she had found cover somewhere impenetrable. Carter returned to the middle of the stage, where Mysterioso had laid the pistols down. He looked on the black-matted floor, under a triad of spotlights that gave perfect illumination for yards, but they were gone. He remembered Griffin had kicked them away. He heard quick footsteps overhead, two kinds, one light, the other in heavy boots. One-handed, bleeding, armed with three sheets of flash paper, he set off toward the rafters, where his last battle awaited.

Rather, he tried. He ended up making a wide circle. Things were getting fuzzy. Climbing a ladder one handed? There was an elevator, but it was parked at the top of the highest catwalk.

He looked upward. There were levels of catwalks and flies crossing like tree branches. There were banks of lights. He saw, suspended over the stage, the statues from the Egyptian illusion. He stared at them. Brilliant, golden, heavy.

The rope ladder Phoebe had found went several vertical yards up to an iron walkway that felt cold against her feet. She padded along, hands on the waist-high railing, attuned to the slightest vibrations in the metal. She could hear small aquatic sounds, hollow and echoing, which meant she was over the water tank. What was near that? What was useful?

A sudden clang of boots on metal. The close seasick smell of gasoline. She clutched at the railing. She was forty feet in the air.

'I'm unarmed,' she said in a small voice.

'Good,' he replied and drew back his fist. But there was a turbine-like sound of the Ramses statue dropping on its cable, and Mysterioso turned his head in anticipation of seeing it crash to the stage.

There followed a panoply of things in motion, taken together as inevitable as the figures on a giant village clockworks striking the hour: Mysterioso's head turning downward, toward the stage, and Charles Carter, riding the Fairbanks rope, propelling upward. Mysterioso, ready to wrestle with him, took a step toward Phoebe, who tripped, yelling as she fell onto the catwalk. Mysterioso gripped the railing so that if Carter pried him away, they would fall forty feet together. The natural motion of the rope forced Carter up and out, in a parabola, and he jumped, feet planted just outside the railing, on the edge of the catwalk, and grabbed Mysterioso in a bear hug, one arm under the armpit, the other squeezing him around the neck. With arms linked, jerking with his own dead weight, Carter pulled him over the railing.

The plaster statue smashed onto the stage, coming apart into chicken wire and powder. Phoebe was alone. She held tightly to the still-shaking catwalk. She had no idea what had happened. She didn't hear the impact of bodies.

'Charlie?'

Below the catwalk, spread out in all dimensions, with wires and filaments as translucent and complex as a spider web, was the asrah levitation device that Carter, not Kellar, had designed. Despite its delicacy – under the stage lights, it was of course invisible – it was as strong as high-tensile fishing wire. It was a net stretched between springs tense enough to launch boulders over distant battlements. Carter and Mysterioso had landed in its embrace, bouncing slightly, and safely, twenty-five feet over the stage. But each was tangled in threads they couldn't see. Two bloody, contorted men seeming to float in the ether as if waiting for a giant arachnid.

Mysterioso fought to get his hand in his pocket; the wires around his wrists cut into him, but he was able to pull out his knife. Carter was bound in a nearly fetal position, facing him, neck and feet just out of reach of the knife that Mysterioso swung. He swung it again, closer.

'Holy—' Mysterioso suffered an unexpected shake and bounce. He'd accidentally severed some of the lines that kept him from falling headfirst onto the stage. He froze.

Carter felt himself bob. It was almost soothing. He'd been greatly excited a moment before, but the ascent and tumble had brought a fresh spray of blood from his hand; it was actually trickling now, draining out, dripping down his sleeve, and it was hurting less by the minute. That wasn't good. But it was very very hard to fight. Around the edges of his eyes, the sights were breaking into dots and dashes. He saw between these particles something eternal, warm and quiet.

'Phoebe,' Carter said calmly. He had a plan. He had better say it now. 'Go to the end of the catwalk. There's an elevator there. Take it down to the stage, and go get help.'

He was watching the slow passes Mysterioso made at him with his knife. In spite of the care he took, the blade severed another filament, and Carter felt tension in the net increase. It felt ready to pull apart, but still Carter was feeling warm, and safe, and very numb. In the fading footlights of his vision, he could see how everything he'd ever known was just props and scrim, how reality wasn't action and friction and motion, but a winding down. Entropy, Ledocq's evidence of the creator. Carter could see it, and it was all right. He looked at the man wrapped up with him and tried to broadcast those feelings forth. Mysterioso's eyes narrowed and then, violently, he lunged at Carter, regardless of the consequence to himself. Carter was thrown right and left and down as cords were cut, and there were curtains drawing shut in his mind. He wanted to go home, to sleep. It would feel much better to give up, give in. Then he remembered faintly that this was exactly the Devil's advice. What if all this sweet winding down was the way the Devil buried *wonder*? Wonder was life. The knife came at him again. He had one piece of business left. He reached into his pocket after Mysterioso's knife arm thrust forward. The blade came close, right to the point of Carter's chin, and that's when Carter rubbed flash paper vigorously against Mysterioso's stabbing arm.

There was a fizzle of white magnesium sparks, which went out immediately. But now in their place was a low blue flame. The gasoline that had soaked Mysterioso's clothing caught fire, igniting like a gas jet, and he screamed. The smells of scorching cotton and burning rubber brought Carter to full attention – since he had bear-hugged Mysterioso on the catwalk, there was gasoline on him, too. He struggled in the net, trying to put distance between them. Mysterioso jerked around like a puppet, and then in horror Carter realized the mistake he'd made, for the remaining asrah wires were burning like candlewicks, tiny flames traveling along the supports. He was tossed to the left, then flung upward. He flailed in the air, flying, limbs madly grabbing at nothing. He hit a wall face first, then dropped to the stage.

Instead of swinging out, Mysterioso dropped straight down and into the water tank. Aviation fuel will burn on water, but not underneath; the initial splash revived him, and he gulped down a breath, lay under the surface, and shed his burning clothes. He would stay under as long as he could, and as a magician, Mysterioso could hold his breath for a very long time indeed.

When Mysterioso surfaced, there were small patches of flaming cloth on the water, but the rest had extinguished. He took stock: he was dirty, and cut, and clawed, and had minor burns – otherwise he was at peak capacity. Though the edges of the tank were only eighteen inches deep, it sloped inward so he stood in about four feet of water. He felt the bottom with his toe until he located one of the throwing knives that had fallen in with him. He heard echoing sounds – footsteps, clapping, like hesitant applause. He caught his breath. He peered out – there were curls of smoke in places and, under the lights, they were impenetrable.

'Hello?'

Mysterioso heard Phoebe's voice. She was close by. He said nothing. Carter, unconscious and in a heap, couldn't answer her.

'Carter?' Her voice, sounding slightly panicked. 'Are you in the tank?'

Mysterioso splashed around, then, splashed long and hard. Where was she?

'I'm over here. Take my hand,' she said calmly. He watched for her through the smoke – there she was, drumming on the side of the tank. She smiled. 'Let's get out of here.'

He walked over to her, his right hand extended, left hand loosely wrapped around the butt of his throwing knife.

Mysterioso reached out toward Phoebe, and he took into his hand not her hand but the 240-volt power line she had located by its buzzing on the floor.

A power line against the bars of a cage may not be grounded, but a power line in water is grounded very well indeed. Mysterioso's eyebrows stood on end, his teeth jammed shut on his tongue, and every muscle in his body clenched beyond their limits, curling and contorting. In his last five seconds of consciousness, he felt his eardrums burst and the vitreous in his eyeballs begin to melt away. Then, though strictly speaking, dead, he continued to stand with his hand wrapped around the line until gravity made him keel over, and the water around him boiled.

Carter awoke with jumbled impressions of where he was. In a crate? Lights in his eyes. Onstage. Someone was saying he was fine. His head felt like it had been crushed, and he was afraid to move it, remembering a long-forgotten fear of Tug accidentally stepping on him.

'Charlie, it's okay, you're fine.'

'Phoebe?'

'Yes. We're safe. We're okay.'

He considered this. 'Are you safe?'

'Mmm-hmm.'

It was a large stage. There were many obstacles all over it. 'How did you find me?'

'I clapped, and Baby more or less towed me here.' Carter was on his back, his head in her lap. Baby was stretched out behind them like they were relaxing at a picnic. 'Then I heard someone moving in the water tank—'

He remembered his hand. 'I'm bleeding to death.'

'I don't think so. We'll get you to a doctor.'

'Oh.' His vision was blurred, so he blinked, and it cleared. 'You clapped and Baby got up?'

'Yes.'

'He must like you.' He could hear a percolating sound, like bubbles, and there was a sweet odor in the air. 'What's that smell?'

'Mysterioso, boiling,' she said.

He tried to get a sense of her face, but given his blurry vision, it was difficult.

'Are you all right?'

'I'm very good. You hurt your hand.'

'Is he dead?'

'I killed him,' she said, swallowing. If he hadn't been listening for it, he wouldn't have heard the catch in her voice.

'And you're all right?'

She shrugged.

He remembered more. 'Where's Griffin?'

'I opened the stage door. There was a man out there, someone named Chase. He called for an ambulance.'

Carter sat up. He held his head, which throbbed.

Leaning on Phoebe, he limped the dozen steps to Griffin's side, and knelt.

Griffin, pale, looked at him. He moved his hands, still cuffed. He was weak. He tried to bring his hands up. Carter noted that Griffin was holding the bullet-catching pistol. He couldn't quite lift it.

'You're under arrest,' Griffin whispered.

That Griffin was holding the pistol with a blank round in it made Carter feel a yearning in the back of his throat. He put his hands up in the air. 'I'll go quietly now,' he said.

Chapter 10

The next morning's headlines could – perhaps – easily be imagined. When a magician once implicated in murdering the President is found with a dead rival (electrocuted), a dead assistant (decapitated), another assistant bound and gagged (Willie, unconscious in the wardrobe), a dead usher (broken neck, and in semi-undress), and a wounded Secret Service agent, the accumulation of details is almost hypnotic. If you added sex – and there was *indeed* sex, in the form of a blind woman in a torn evening dress pushed up into her waistband – an almost holy silence would overcome the managements of the *Call-Bulletin,* the *Chronicle,* and the *Examiner.*

So the headlines of November 5, 1923, were in their way revealing. The *Chronicle*'s front page described Secretary Mellon's scandalous new plan for taxation. There was also a scientific report on the supernormal effects of sodium dihydrogen phosphate, an energy drink given to German shock troops during battle. One man apparently held back a tank while on 'Peppo,' as they called it. The *Call-Telegram* focused on the annual meeting of the British Association for the Advancement of Science, at which Sir Ernest Rutherford deflated all hopes of ever bombarding atoms so as to drive away electrons and thus create vast supplies of energy. The *Examiner,* in a daring exposé, revealed that a Fifth Avenue storefront in New York was actually a 'birth control' clinic and chided citizens for its existence.

Carter was mentioned nowhere. The *San Francisco Law Journal* in its biweekly *Police Blotter,* listed a homicide/justifiable homicide at the address of the Orpheum Theatre, but there were no further details. Of course, there were whispers . . .

Saint Mary's was the hospital closest to the theatre, but their physicians were undistinguished. Carter requested that the ambulance take Griffin and himself to a small facility at the crest of Lone

Mountain, the least developed of San Francisco's hills, the one with the best views. The hospital there, in the shape of a Spanish cross, had but thirty-two rooms on two floors. Many faced the ocean, and all had excellent sunlight and breezes. The floor in the transepts was done in hexagonal tilework, and at the center, a two-story open and airy plaza, there was mosaic of a Mucha princess, Saint Agatha, patron of nursing. There was a grand piano, too, for during the War, this hospital had answered speculation about which amenities most aided convalescence: it encouraged music, sunlight, a view of the ocean, mobility, and an ancient form of exercise called 't'ai chi'.

Carter was X-rayed. No fractures were found in his skull, though he was warned to stay awake for twenty-four hours in case of concussion. Then he was given morphine, and his wound was topically treated with cocaine and cleansed with flavine compounds by a doctor who, while stitching up his hand and fitting him with a Thomas splint, kept repeating, 'Well, it looks like God got a piece of you.' Carter began exactly two minutes after his last injection to think of the doctor as fascinatingly handsome, skilled, and spiritually enlightened.

Griffin was taken to surgery. The bullet had caught him below his navel, lodging in his intestine. Before the War, he would have died, as no one had operated on the gut. It was as mysterious an example of God's work as the brain. Luckily, Dr Boone, who operated on Griffin, had trained on the battlefields of Flanders.

Boone debrided the wound and irrigated it with Dakin's solution of sodium hypochlorite and boric acid. Then he was free to operate on the bowel, remove the bullet, and primary-suture the damaged lengths of intestine with kangaroo thread. The final layering of plaster of Paris immobilized the wounded area, and as he applied it, Boone drew deep sighs of relief, for he was never sure a patient would survive such an operation.

At five o'clock in the morning, Griffin was pronounced stable. He was sent to a room with a saline-glucose drip. Boone showered and joined his fellow surgeons – doctors Wilbur and Cooper – in the chapel, where they saw in the dawn with prayers.

At the same time, Carter sat on the piano bench under the skylight. He was dressed in clean clothes he'd had sent from his house, but he'd forgotten to ask for shoes, so he wore the same smoky, scuffed dress boots from the night before. He ghost-fingered chords and watched the chapel doors. Soon, they opened and out came doctors Boone, Wilbur, and Cooper.

'Gentlemen,' he called, saluting them with the arm that was now splinted and bandaged to his elbow. 'A word?'

Carter introduced himself and asked for the best possible care for Jack Griffin. The doctors dismissively agreed to this: all patients received excellent care here. They might have added that they as physicians were used to very important patients.

'He's a Secret Service agent,' Carter said, 'wounded in the line of duty.'

At this there were illuminated cries, 'of course' and 'yes,' for they were all very patriotic.

'His superiors have been informed, and they know he's going to make a full recovery,' Carter said, stressing 'full recovery' so much that it seemed insulting.

Dr Boone, who had a long face and a beard like Lincoln, intoned, 'How was the agent wounded?'

'He was in the process of arresting me.' Carter grinned. His audience shifted on their feet, betraying a confusion that he enjoyed. 'He was arresting me for the murder of President Harding.'

Doctors Boone, Wilbur, and Cooper exchanged silent glances. Wilbur, who suffered gastric distress under even mild circumstances, hiccupped.

'Oh, yes!' Carter said as if remembering. 'You're the doctors who signed the late President's death certificate.'

'Sir,' Cooper said, saying it as slowly as a one-syllable word could be said, for he had a Kentucky accent, 'I must say I'm confused about our priorities. Shouldn't we have you arrested?'

'Oh, yes, absolutely, I'd be very excited to present all I know about the case.' Carter beamed. 'But perhaps the most sober course is to let Griffin present his evidence to his superiors and let justice take its course.'

He gave them time to work this out silently; eventually they all realized Carter was assuring them, rather arcanely but persuasively, that they would be safe. Carter had a great deal to say, more than usual, and after he began to repeat himself on the topic of how he was sure Griffin had distributed his evidence in a great many places in case he didn't make a full recovery, the doctors said Carter was free to be discharged whenever he wanted, but instead Carter followed Boone down the hallway (he was strangely attracted to the man's Lincoln beard) and, close to tears, told him, 'Do look out for Griffin,' concluding, meaningfully, 'he's the best audience I've ever had.'

A few minutes later, he knocked softly on the door of one of the thirty-two rooms. Resting on a featherbed, though not exactly asleep, was Phoebe. She still wore her evening dress. She'd washed her face of the charcoal and grime from the previous evening. Her eyeglasses were folded on the night table.

'Are we done?' she asked, her voice groggy, raising herself up on an elbow.

'You have to keep me awake for twenty-four hours.'

She sat up. 'I can do that.'

The beach was his idea. She asked if he were obsessed with beaches, reminding him he'd attempted to take her to Neptune Beach in the dead of summer. 'I like the beach,' he said in full explanation.

Ocean Beach in November, an hour after dawn, was an empty playground. Two people alone, walking barefoot in the surf. Up by the retaining wall was a still life: a pair of socks, a pair of silk hose, and two pairs of evening shoes, scuffed and battered. The day was warm, though not so warm that Phoebe didn't accept Carter's jacket as they walked in their bare feet to the waterline.

'The last time I borrowed your jacket—' she began.

'If you try to go this time,' he said slowly, 'I'm going to sit on top of you and squash you like a sandwich.'

She poked her tongue into her cheek. 'Charles, did you really kill the President?'

'That's a complicated question.'

'No, it's not.'

'How terribly do you want to know?'

'I'm prepared to behave very badly.'

The tide was out, so there was a wide swath of dry sand, then damp and yielding sand, then the hard-packed sand on which seashells and driftwood were littered. Carter felt all the gradations from hard to soft underfoot, as he imagined Phoebe feeling them.

Seagulls carried mollusks from the shore and to the concrete pathways, dropping them so they shattered, and they could have their breakfast.

'I'm amazed by everything,' he said.

'Said the man on cocaine and morphine. All you need is some marijuana and you could join a jazz band.'

His hand was throbbing, as was his head. He had a glass vial with pills in it, but he didn't want to take them.

Phoebe approached the tide, and backed away. 'Say, how does my dress look, anyway?'

'I owe you a new one. You should go in the water if you want.'

'Can you afford to buy me a new dress?'

'I think so. Even with the hand,' he waved his splint.

'Did the doctors tell you how it will heal?'

He nodded. 'They can do amazing things these days. They said something about attaching tendons to other muscles and reeducating the hand . . . but . . .' His voice trailed off, because what the doctors could do struck him as somehow irrelevant. 'Also, there's a magician, I've been trying to remember his name all night, who worked the Continent a hundred years ago with two fingers missing. I'm hoping he wrote a pamphlet. But . . .' Again, he left the word hanging.

Phoebe stood with her body pointing toward the ocean, knees bent, her skirt hiked an inch or so up, her face toward him, listening, and then the surf rushed up over her ankles, which made her cry out. She dropped the end of her dress so that its very edge was buoyed on the water. 'I should just accept it,' she said, returning to walking, carefully, south, water sluicing around her feet. Carter rolled his trousers to his knees.

'You said "but" a minute ago,' she said.

He couldn't retrieve what he meant. 'You remember how I said I liked how you couldn't see what I did for a living? It's like that.' He'd never seen an X ray of himself before. He'd been surprised to find his inner workings were exactly the same as the next man's. It made him peculiarly optimistic. 'I love magic, it's wonderful, but when it came down to it last night, you were more important.' He was thinking how life was all motion and transformation. From boy to magician and no way to turn back. And from a husband into a widower, and again, there was no turning back. His soul was once choked with grief that had now vanished by a method he hardly understood. He stood with one hand operative, the other ruined. It made him feel like he might be both a magician *and* a man.

She took his left hand. They walked for a few feet, and then Carter stopped to kiss her.

'That's nice,' Phoebe sighed, for his hand had cupped her breast. A moment later, she stood outside of his embrace. 'I need to think,' she said.

'That's a bad idea,' and again she found his hand on her breast.

'Please tell me there aren't forty Marines and a school bus full of children hiding downwind. Charlie, if we went to bed, you'd fall asleep afterward and I couldn't have that on my conscience, I'd feel like a praying mantis.'

'I'm willing to risk it.'

'How hard did you get hit in the head, anyway?'

'Not hard enough.'

She took his arm and forcefully started them to walking again. She told him to imagine the waves against his feet as God's own cold shower. She asked him to describe the ocean: Were there any ships at sea? Tramp steamers or yachts or liners? Where did he think the ships were going?

The sun hit the pebbles and shells so they glowed. Even the chains of kelp draped across the sand looked fertile and sweet like grapevines.

She was being quiet. A stiffness to her walk, and then she whispered, 'Excuse me' and walked directly inland. He followed her.

When she was in dry sand, she sat, knees up, her head braced against them, expression hidden. Her thicket of black hair rustled in the breeze.

He sat beside her, sat on her right in case he needed to reach out and comfort her. How long did they sit that way? Carter, for whom time was increasingly elastic, put his arm around her. She folded up her glasses and dropped them into a battered leather case.

'I killed a man,' she said, sounding sickly.

He nodded. 'I thought you seemed too cool about it.'

'What? Mysterioso. No, not him.'

'So you've killed someone before?' he chuckled. Somehow the drugs had made him misinterpret her, which amused him.

'I can't believe I'm actually telling someone this.'

He hadn't misunderstood. His mind jumped from word to word: manslaughter, self-defense, traffic accident, buck fever.

'I was so sure I could just tell you I was thirty-one years old. I didn't know what kind of path I was taking when I said that. I used to imagine I would dictate my memoirs when I was eighty to some bright-eyed girl who was sent to the Home to look after cranky old Phoebe, and I imagined telling her about the man I murdered, and her being terribly scared of me.' She shook her head. 'You shouldn't feel guilty about Sarah. That was an accident. I killed a man on purpose.'

'Every time a layer gets peeled away,' he murmured.

'You don't have to hear this. We can keep on walking.'

Carter felt inadequate – as with the long-ago brank, he wanted to know, and *not* to know. 'Who was he?'

'This was back when I could see. His name was—' She said nothing further. Carter was prepared to know the name. He felt, to his marrow, that he and Phoebe were made for such coincidence. She sighed, 'John Osborn.' Then, 'Dr John Osborn.'

Carter squinted. No, he'd never heard that name.

'My Johnnie,' she continued. She said more: she had loved him, and he was a sweet and pure soul, and he said he was going to marry her even though his family had forced him to become engaged to another. 'It's an old story,' she said, drawing designs in the sand, 'which didn't help me much when I ended up at Borax's. "Oh, you, too," one woman after another with exactly the same story. And I kept trying to explain that it was different, it had happened to me. Me!'

She asked if he remembered how Borax had a wonderful stream that ran by the cottages, and if you followed it long enough it became a wild pool where ducks sometimes waded in pairs. At the edge of the pool pine needles and oak leaves and the occasional branch settled in a tiny harbor. Every day, there was a greater accumulation. It began to feel like her own private project, like she was supervising the construction of a new world. But as she watched one afternoon everything emptied, all the leaves, everything, back into the stream, and disappeared over the rocks. And it caused her to burst into tears because she realized she was no more important than anything else.

'Of course,' she whispered, 'there was this very sad mahatma who kept coming by. I used to wish I could see him do something. I thought it would cheer both of us up.'

Carter heard barking in the distance – coming up from the south at a brisk trot, along the shoreline, were some dogs. There was no sign of an owner, but this wasn't a surprise, for there were many strays here, living on fish and food thrown to them from the Cliff House, to the north. 'Were you still there when I performed?'

'You performed at Borax's?'

The dogs were crossing in front of them. One was tall and shaggy, and the other white and low to the ground. They sniffed at the seaweed together, and then tugged on either end of a stick before the taller one seemed to hear an attractive noise to the north. He barked, and the other one followed him, and they vanished over a sand dune. Carter cleared his throat. 'Shortly after Black Christmas. What, a week after? Something about that woman's story . . . I think you keep being reborn and you never know when. I was inspired to return to magic by the story of that poor woman dying and so I performed for the women then.'

She pursed her lips. Her bottle-green eyes, eyes like emeralds, eyes like oceans, they were watering. 'Oh, sweetheart. Oh Charlie,' she whispered. 'I never died.'

He was about to correct her. It was like she'd sung a popular song, only gotten the lyrics wrong, and he was just about to say, 'No, it's *she* never died,' when all of a sudden he could hardly think at all.

'I inspired you?' she whispered.

He swallowed. 'You're the woman who . . .'

'I am.'

'But they said you died.'

'Everyone thinks that.'

'I don't understand.' He played the details in his head: a man coming back for his woman, then locking her in a cabin, burning it to the ground, killing her. He began to feel anger at Borax. He'd made Carter buy into a sad story.

'Everything Borax said was true,' Phoebe said, 'except one thing. Johnnie didn't escape to Mexico.' She swallowed. 'I might have to stop, but I'll try. After Johnnie had stabbed me. In the stomach. The knife was so slippery with my blood, he dropped it. I stabbed him right through the throat. And I ran out of the cabin, which was on fire. I was losing blood. The flames went past me, and I had to get through them, so I crawled, and the smoke was making me cough. I felt if I coughed hard enough, I'd come apart. Then I saw I was almost out of it, just a little ways to go, and I was thinking, my love had wanted to murder me, and this was the worst thing that could ever happen. That's when I ran through the burning poison oak.'

Her blind eyes were directed toward the dunes, beyond which the dogs were barking. Every once in a while, one or the other raced within view, then away again. Carter watched her turn in profile. She looked remote and classical, like an image stamped on a coin.

She didn't tell him the rest, though he could imagine it. Borax hiding her from the prosecution reserved for unwed, immoral girls who stabbed respectable men. A life at the Home, where the choices were piety or bitterness. Gin. He felt very small, a child playing with pretty seashells while all around him roiled the great undiscovered and depthless ocean.

'You're the trade.' He straightened.

'What?'

'Borax told me he would trade me something for television. He meant you.'

'Ah, how nice to be chattel.' She shook her head. 'He did help keep me away from jail. He reminded me of that in his telegram. I think he was trying to trade me and keep my loyalty at the same time. How nice to be Borax.'

'That's the part you wouldn't tell me about, then?'

She nodded. 'The funny thing is how life can find you again despite yourself. I was going to marry a doctor, and then I thought I was going to wear a veil at Borax's, and then I was drunk and blind, and then I was accepting how alone I was. Then who do I meet? A magician. And I love you. I didn't know I could do that again.'

'Hold on.' Carter focused very hard on the sand in front of him. Then on her. 'If you – wait.'

'I'm waiting.'

'If I understand your story, your name can't possibly be Phoebe Kyle.'

'It isn't.'

He looked at a pelican splashing into the ocean. He looked up, tilting his head back, looking straight into the air. He wanted to know. He didn't want to know. 'Is your name—'

'No.'

She was smiling. In fact, she began to chuckle. He pressed on, 'It's not—'

'No. But wouldn't that be amazing if it *were* Sarah?' She was tickled by the idea, and continued to laugh. 'I come to you prophecy-free.'

'The prophecy-free life,' he said. 'I like that.' He picked up sand and made a fist of it. Drained it out, like an hourglass. Swept up another fistful of sand, let it drain again.

They sat in the sand in their tattered and stained evening clothes, discussing their scars. And Phoebe told him something he'd never heard: in China, the women who'd had their feet bound could recognize their kind from across the marketplace from how they walked. Their loping motion, the lotus gait, bespoke a life of suffering, or beauty, depending on how one accounted for it. 'You have that,' she said. 'I knew it the first moment we met.'

It broke his heart. He wanted to protect her and dazzle her with kisses and restore her sight and give her back all the things she had lost. Which he couldn't. 'We have it together,' he said.

'That's why we can talk.'

They had the rest of the day to stay awake. South, there was a café that Carter knew where they sold Italian coffee. Beyond that his plans were vague.

There were never moments in your life when you actually saw something end, for whether you knew it or not something else was always flowering. Never a disappearance, always a transformation.

In his youth, Carter had believed everything was possible. Then in grief, he believed everything was impossible. And now, the very moment he stood, pulling Phoebe up with him, he felt that when you had lived enough of your life, there was no difference between the two.

Curtain

In offering a farewell to the public, you should not wait till there are none left to receive it.

— ROBERT-HOUDIN

The *San Francisco Chronicle* of August 27, 1924, ran a story on page one with the headline 'Local Man Invents Radio with Pictures; Calls It Television.' Only one word of this headline was disputable, and it was inaccuracy for the sake of civic pride – Philo had been working in a laboratory on Green Street long enough that he was claimed as 'local.'

The remainder of the article summarized his great achievement, with quotations from financiers and notable scientists from the University of California. Briefly mentioned was a live demonstration held that day at the Palace of the Legion of Honor. Philo had worked out the faulty schema that had tended to make his invention untrustworthy, so now it was just a matter of increasing the fidelity of transmission.

The show at the Legion of Honor was for the general public. The idea here was less science than spectacle, and to that end, his connections in San Francisco had leased the services of many interesting performers, each of whom stood before the camera for but a few minutes. Fifty people at a time could fit in the auditorium with the television set, and well over a thousand came that day, so there was a line down the side of the building, and into the park, where hawkers sold hot dogs and taffy apples.

Every fifteen minutes or so, a group was ushered out into the sun, and another group went in, doffing their boaters, adjusting their eyes to the darkness, and then squinting at the small blue flickering images with deep horizontal veins. And when their time was over, a new audience came in.

The show lasted from noon until dusk, with ventriloquists, chorus girls in spangles, comedians in black shoe polish, political speeches

542

by the mayors of San Francisco and Oakland, fencing demonstrations by masters of the épée, a pair of boxers who sparred rather unconvincingly, and of course one magician.

Like all the performers, Carter was startled at the room he had to perform in – it was the size of a phone booth – and the necessary makeup – to be seen by the camera, his face had to be painted a brilliant purple. The heat under the lights was unbelievable, but Carter was luckier than the ventriloquist, who had left his dummy on the stool unattended for five minutes. It melted.

Carter did a one-handed close-up routine involving coins and cards. He could not see himself or how he looked to the audience, but he smiled (his teeth were painted red) and hoped for the best. When his time was up, he bowed quietly and left the broadcasting studio, peeking in at the audience, which sat transfixed by the three-inch screen now occupied by puppets fashioned from hosiery.

He stripped off his makeup. He needed to go outside, and quickly. He saw James and Philo standing with a small group of men in the shade of a willow tree, so he went to join them. They were all smoking cigarettes and having a friendly chat, and when he approached, James introduced him all around: several were managers for various aspects of Radio Corporation of America. The rest worked in military laboratories. Carter gave them polite nods. He accepted a cigarette from one of them, who said his performance just now had been spectacular. Soon after, the man admitted he hadn't seen it himself, but still, the audience must have loved it.

Since Philo had retained patent attorneys, his relationship with the corporations had improved. They wanted to fund his research into broadcasting sound and color images. Furthermore, the army seemed to have worked out their differences with their industrial competitors, and they now were quite friendly with each other. They'd rather struck up an alliance in fact. As part of their deal with Philo, they paid Carter not to perform the television illusion. This, coupled with his vaudeville appearances (he had debuted four new illusions in as many months), lent him a vague stability that James explained to him as 'adequate.' So Carter listened to the impeccably dressed young men share their views with Philo. He found himself massaging his right hand, which ached.

He excused himself. There was a vista nearby, a view of the park, and his shoes crunched over gravel as he made for it.

A moment later, he heard James whistle behind him.

'You aren't happy,' James said.

'I didn't say that.'

'You have your way.'

They had reached a vista: a gentle slope of pasture, and then hills dotted with small houses. Carter stood here for a moment, and then asked James what would happen next with Philo.

'Well, he's filed for a number of patents. He's talking to the right people, people who can develop them.'

'They'll eat him alive.'

'You've done everything you can. He owns all the rights to the devices for seventeen years. Perhaps he'll become extremely wealthy.' James looked at his brother then the ground. 'Maybe.'

'Have you been watching the television performances?'

'Somewhat. But it hurts my eyes.' James rubbed at his tear ducts to prove this, and, because he sensed the next question, he added, 'I saw some of your act.'

'Some?'

'I did mention my eyes hurt, didn't I?'

'I think the audience hated my routine.'

'They didn't. But they didn't love it, either, I can't claim that. They were . . . apathetic, I suppose.'

Just then, a new group left the auditorium. Several boys in knee pants ran back to the end of the line, and their parents called out to warn them that this was the last time.

'James?'

'Yes?'

'Nineteen forty-one,' Carter said. 'That's when the patents move into the public domain, correct?' When James nodded, Carter said, 'RCA will keep it from mass production until then.'

'I'm sorry to say you're beginning to understand business.'

'Nineteen forty-one,' Carter declared. 'That's how long I have.'

'Well, you see, Philo—' he paused. 'How long *you* have?'

Carter blinked. His hands were deep into his pockets. He began to walk, James coming with him along the pathway, Carter looking at the Durants and Packards and Model Ts parked on the shoulder of the road, but hardly seeing them. James put his arm around his brother's shoulder. They walked together.

But seventeen years, properly considered, was a very long time for adventure. To begin: September 1924, Lakeside Park, Oakland, was the site of a wedding.

Carter had envisioned a small, dignified ceremony. Phoebe listened to him carefully, eliciting every detail – perhaps a string quartet, a guest list of ten, quiet moderation – and she told him in no uncertain terms that this would never do.

Lakeside Park, the site of their meeting, was transformed in a way Oakland had dreamed of: it was beautiful. The boathouse walls were covered with trellises of jasmine and stargazers, a pathway between the oak trees had been strewn with rose petals, and there was in the air both the music of laughter and actual music in the form of Sid LeProtti's So Different Jazz Band, which Phoebe had engaged.

A few days before the wedding, Carter was sitting in his workshop in a kind of quiet panic. He had invited only friends who were in no way associated with the magic fraternity, for he knew how *that* group behaved around ceremony. Then, with a single knock at the door, his preparations went straight to hell, for standing there in the morning sunshine was Howard Thurston. Thurston was grinning – he grinned much of the time, for he had recently had his face lifted – and held in his hand an invitation to the wedding. Phoebe had sent it, with a request that he bring as many magicians as possible.

This meant Carter was treated to a wedding rehearsal that was far more complicated than most. Thurston fought like a tiger to be Carter's best man, not because they were close, but because he was wicked. He loved being married so much, he said, he'd done it three times himself. Of course, a more likely explanation was his behavior on the road – he kept a trunk on each tour that he gradually filled with ladies' underpants on which he had written the owners' names and corresponding letter grades.

'Howard, I'm so sorry,' Carter said to him, truly sounding sorry, 'James is going to be my best man.'

So Thurston planned Carter's bachelor party instead. It was held in San Francisco and was exceptional only in that the groom, who had changed not one whit since the days of Jessie Hayman's parlor house, did not attend.

Carter had photographs of his first wedding in an album his parents kept for him. He'd never looked at them. First, he'd been touring, and then they were too painful to look at. He and Sarah had married in a Lawrenceville, Kansas, church, with their families in attendance, and there was a picnic afterward. He looked through the photographs now, and saw on his face and his bride's anticipation of a bright future.

Once he'd been afraid that seeing these photos might ignite a kind of sadness that could never be extinguished. Instead, two days before he married Phoebe, he looked through the album and wished he could shout back to the young couple he saw, 'It will be brief, but you'll have a remarkable time together.' He had changed; his heart was overflowing with benedictions. Since meeting Phoebe, he was anticipating the future again, and yet he wasn't a fool.

Then, on a lovely fall morning, he felt like he'd simply gone into a coma, and recovered at the altar in front of 155 people, dressed in his morning coat and listening to an unexpectedly poignant version of Pachelbel's *Canon* performed on trumpet, trombone, banjo, clarinet, alto sax, and washboard.

Phoebe wore white roses threaded through her hair and clutched a spray of exotic flowers. She wore white, a simple silk dress with beaded fringe, but no buttons or lace. She did not wear a veil – she'd had enough of them – so her face showed fantastically white, like marble, during her walk down the aisle.

No one gave her away. She had been quite insistent on this point. She was led to the altar by her new companion, a German shepherd named Lili Marlene.

When she stood next to him, Carter whistled, fully unconscious of having done so, which caused quite a ripple of laughter. James later described him as a man who raced through the vows for he could not wait for the kiss.

The reception was an odd collision among past, present, and future: introducing Thurston to Lee Duncan, who had trained Lili Marlene, or his father to Philo and Pem, who had come up from Hollywood, where they had established another laboratory. There were blind men and women with their faces pointing toward the sun, enjoying the jazz music, which included intermittent dancing and vocal stylings by Lottie Brown.

At some point, Phoebe disappeared. Carter couldn't find her anywhere. Ledocq was the last one who'd seen her – she'd asked him to look after Lili Marlene, and he was amusing himself by teaching her commands in Yiddish. Mrs Ledocq wasn't so sure this was a good idea, but even she was impressed that it took but two pieces of cheese for the dog to learn *schmooze*, offering her paw to shake.

Carter saw Phoebe's purse on a table, and his father sitting near it, like a lookout. So he approached him.

'Have you seen my wife?' Carter asked.

His father looked up with a smile that anticipated the delivery of agonizing news. 'She's currently taking a walk with *my* wife.'

Carter sighed, drawing up a chair. 'God only knows—'

'Where Lillian is concerned, I'm not so sure he does,' Mr Carter interrupted. They laughed together. But after a moment, they had nothing more to say, and each man found himself reaching for a second smile while the music played in the distance. Carter withdrew his pocket watch and pulled the repeater lever. It was 5:37.

Mr Carter squinted. 'When did you get that watch?'

'This? I've shown you this.'

'No, you never have.'

Carter thought about it. And he realized that, no, it was a story they'd never shared. 'Nineteen eleven. Albee gave it to me.'

'Is that an Edward Koehn?'

In surprise, he asked, 'How did you know?'

Mr Carter reached for the watch. 'That's simple. It sounded like angels. Hand it over.'

'Do you own one?'

'I have three of them,' Mr Carter declared, looking satisfied as he inspected the dramatic masks. 'But none as fine as this,' he hastened to add. He opened it and tilted it back and forth to better read the name the dial detailed. 'This isn't a jeweler's name, it's – oh!' He looked at his son, pursing his lips. 'Now I'm *certain* you haven't told me this story.' Before Carter could say anything, his father continued, 'Perhaps I should ask on a day when you aren't getting married.'

Carter accepted the watch back. He said, 'I've missed having you and Mom at my shows, you know. I'm glad you're here.'

'Yes, well, we're proud of you,' he replied, tightly. A moment later, he added, with somewhat more intent, 'I've heard you were just paid a nice lump sum – have you considered how you might invest it?'

Carter shook his head. 'I need some advice.'

'We'll discuss it then.'

A few moments later, Carter spied Phoebe, arm in arm with his mother, returning from the boathouse. They were approaching the table, but first they stopped by Ledocq, who was teaching Lili Marlene to *plotz*, at which command she was supposed to roll on her back.

'What are you doing to my dog?' Phoebe asked suspiciously.

'You have a very smart dog here,' Ledocq said, sounding a little guilty. 'It's good for her to learn another language.' He handed the dog on her stiff leather strap over to Phoebe, who, in a mock huff, walked with Mrs Carter to join their husbands.

Carter eyed his mother, as she could still without effort make him feel roughly seven years old. She smiled. 'Phoebe is wonderful.' She listed Phoebe's graces and predicted wonderful things for their future. Carter awaited the moment she would become theatrical or turn to psychological analysis, but his mother surprised him and did nothing but beam.

Astonishingly, there was a late arrival of sorts by none other than Houdini. It was actually a messenger bearing a gift that Houdini said in a note had to be opened straightaway. So bride and groom took a few moments from the reception line to cut along the packing tape to reveal – a photograph of Houdini! It was inscribed 'To the lucky bride and groom, may this token watch over you for many years to come!'

'Well, that was extraordinary,' Carter sighed, tossing the photograph onto the gift table.

James picked it up. 'He paid for it to be framed – that *is* extraordinary. And holy smokes!' His eyes popped open. 'Tom, come here!'

Tom came, and when he saw the photo, he yelled 'No!' for in Houdini's photograph, he was wearing a red-as-rouge necktie.

This fact, long into the afternoon, was a recurrent topic of discussion. All a group of two or three guests had to do was fall silent, and James or Tom would accost them to ask if they'd seen Houdini's red necktie. Few understood the ramifications, but those who did – the members of Sid LeProtti's So Different Jazz Band, for instance – agreed that a man who chained himself into milk cans, and who liked to be locked nude in jail cells, was certainly one to watch.

Luckily for Carter, bored with that subject, Phoebe was quick to distribute the bouquet. She had a certain method in mind, and to effect it, she requested help from a pair of women, wives of members of the Society of American Magicians Golden Gate Assembly. They helped direct her arms as she turned her back to the crowd. She counted 'One! Two! Three!' and threw her bouquet with all of her might and in midair, it became a hail of bouquets, and like the best of all blessings, each of the women caught at least one.

When they cut the cake, a young man threw a cloth over it, whipped it away, and the cake was whole again. Gales of laughter, followed by a second attempt to cut it, another treatment with the cloth, and, yes, it was restored again. Finally, solemnly, Phoebe cut into the cake, removed a piece, and stood back as a flutter of wings passed her – a single white dove.

Carter witnessed this with mouth open, for he hadn't expected it. He said, 'I am in the hands of a master,' which caused one of her hundred-thousand-dollar smiles.

There was much to drink, champagne from France, a bottle of which Mayor Davie seized as 'evidence,' placing it in the bushes for safekeeping. As the afternoon became evening, strings of colored lights were turned on in the trees, and the music drifted across the lake, to East Oakland, and Brooklyn beyond it, and it was like sending up smoke signals: friends of Sid LeProtti, men who'd brought their saxophone cases or their own drumsticks, seemed to come out of nowhere, saying 'Sid, I knew it was you, I could hear you all the way from Fourth Avenue,' and sitting in themselves on the slow, dreamy waltzes, or the classical numbers like 'Pique-

Dame,' or the complex modern syncopations of Sid's own 'Canadian Capers.' Lottie Brown led the crowd through the dances San Francisco had invented: the Texas Tommy and the Turkey Trot, the Bunny Hug and the Two-Fist Stomp.

Not everyone danced. After he was thoroughly knackered, Carter turned his bride – she was uninterested in ceasing to dance for even a single moment on her wedding day – over to James. Carter noticed one man who hung to the side and, even though he had seconds of roast beef and cake, seemed to be not so much *participating* as fulfilling a loathsome duty.

Carter approached a table where he sat alone, toying with the remains of a slice of raspberry cake. 'Mr Griffin,' Carter said.

Griffin regarded him.

'How are you feeling today? You haven't said much.'

'You don't want to know what I've got to say.'

'But I do.'

Griffin squinted. 'All right. Why aren't you in jail?'

'Ahh.' He scratched his nose. 'You have noticed it's my wedding day? Did you congratulate the bride at least?'

'I'm not a chump,' he growled. 'Plus, I—'

'Your lady friend made sure you did?'

A shrug, and then Griffin dug his fork into the cake frosting, leaving a trail of divots.

'Tell me, Mr Griffin, weren't you promoted recently? I don't know how the Service works, but understand you were kicked upstairs.'

'Bureau chief,' he said. 'Small office, Los Angeles, it isn't much.'

'But, suddenly, you're appreciated.'

The band was playing 'Gin Bottle Blues,' a fairly upbeat version, which had the dance floor quite occupied. Carter listened to the music while Griffin stared at him.

'Making me bureau chief doesn't change what I know.' He looked at his hands on the table, playing with his fork.

'May I?' Carter produced a silver dollar and placed it in his palm. He squeezed it shut, tapped it twice, and opened up his palm, showing off . . . a silver dollar.

Griffin met his eye and confirmed that, yes, a trick had been performed in its entirety. Before he could say anything, Carter said, 'Now watch again. Watch closely.'

This time, Griffin saw it. The silver dollar in his palm was minted in San Francisco. But when he squeezed it, the mint mark had changed to Denver.

'There,' the magician concluded.

'You're a goddamned lunatic,' Griffin muttered.

Carter laughed. 'Now, now. I just wanted to point out that some tricks are very subtle. Too subtle. It's not satisfying for me as a performer if I do something and no one even notices the effect. So I have to say, I'm beholden to you. When I brought the wine to the President's room, I was sure the world would see the bottle in the newspaper and talk would ensue. Foul play that could never be proven no matter how hard they looked. But they cropped the photograph, and there was no call for any sort of inquest. I was very disappointed. You're the only person who even knew a trick had been performed.'

Bang, Griffin slapped the table so that the silverware jumped. 'I might just shoot you myself, see what kind of trick you think that is.'

'Oh, but Mr Griffin, I didn't kill the President.'

'If not you, then you helped somehow.'

'What I mean is, nobody killed him.'

'What, suicide? Right,' Griffin said. He stared at the dance floor. Olive White was performing a noteworthy foxtrot with, of all people, Max Friz.

'You see that man with the droopy mustache?'

'A Kraut,' Griffin replied, in a tone that managed to pity Max Friz and condemn Carter for knowing him.

'He's not what you'd call a dancing fool, but there he is. His motorcycle has done well.'

'So?'

'So he's dancing with your lady friend. You should be dancing with her.' At the mention of Olive, Griffin thawed about five degrees, but no more. Carter put both silver dollars on the table. He turned an empty chair backward and put his legs up. 'So let me tell you what happened,' he whispered. 'President Harding was quite worried the night I met him. He kept asking what I'd do if I knew—'

'Of a terrible scandal, yeah, I know.'

Carter smiled, sincerely proud. 'You *do* know. There were so many scandals brewing around him, and he wanted to tell me all of them and, well, he wanted to tell *everyone* about them. He was quite afraid he would be murdered by his men. He felt that if they didn't get him, his wife would.' Carter hesitated. 'I hope you knew that he had affairs.'

'Go on.'

'As a rule I tend not to get involved with world leaders. They have problems. But he would only give me the television blueprints if I helped him out of his jam. He kept saying, "Mr Carter, surely you can make a President disappear."' Carter rubbed at his ruined hand and whispered, 'When I see Thurston next, I bet *he* could do it.' A very wily man, that Harding, when he wanted to be.'

'I don't believe this Shinola.'

'That's perfectly fine. I thought about it during my act, how to make a man who was so universally loved, and also in such danger from so many places, vanish off the face of the earth. And I hit on a wonderful solution – pit the sides against each other. He'd been asking so many people "what would you do" about his problems that he was annoying his cabinet. I realized that if he were dead, they wouldn't ask any questions.'

'They had *me* asking questions,' Griffin said.

Carter's blue eyes softened with empathy. 'That's exactly right, Mr Griffin. You were absolutely the most qualified agent they wanted going anywhere near the evidence.'

'Oh.' Whatever else Griffin was going to say caught in his throat.

'After the show, I went to the hotel. My plan involved Harding confessing all to his wife. Of course, she knew all, the Duchess isn't a fool. He had a diary I asked him to make an entry for – did you see his diary? Never mind. After midnight, she called that Starling and – do you like Colonel Starling?'

'None of your business.'

'He's a dangerous man. I don't understand him, but he's dangerous. But that's neither here nor there. She just told Starling rather coldly that Warren had stopped breathing, and she supposed he should send up a doctor when he could. Just like that. "When he could." It was magnificent. He could tell, right over the phone wires, she'd poisoned him. You know what he did? He sent for a doctor twenty minutes later! And when the doctors came, she wouldn't let them near the body. She announced that her Warren was dead, and that she was grieving, then she closed the door.'

'Carter, you expect me to believe that none of those physicians even examined the body? They signed oaths that—'

'When they asked – meekly – about collecting the body, she told them she'd already arranged for cremation. Then slammed the door right on them! They didn't ask questions. What could they assume but she'd poisoned him. And that was a family matter – a *first* family matter. Best to keep a distance and ask no questions. I watched from the closet.'

'So you're saying everyone – my boss included – wanted the President dead.'

'So he wouldn't discuss the scandals, yes.'

'Why all the manpower chasing you down to Baja, then?'

'I fled, that's why.'

'And if you didn't kill the President, why did you flee?'

A brilliant smile, a payday smile. 'Misdirection.'

Griffin said nothing else. He had nothing else to say about this insane story. The band finished their tune and received generous applause from those on the lawn. 'So is this a confession or what?'

'The next morning, I took Mr Harding to my flat and he waited there until the arrangements I made panned out. I knew a place he could go. You know, he truly loved his wife. Truly. It was incredible to see how much she loved him. She agreed to go to Washington and Marion and burn everything that could incriminate him. People will always think she poisoned him, but she risked all that just so she could join him again later.'

Griffin wasn't sure he'd heard right. 'Later?'

'Soon enough, the Duchess will die. She'll choose a hot news day when everyone's forgotten her. Then, she'll join him quietly, to live their lives out. It was the least I could do for a man who gave me such an interesting illusion. Well, two illusions if you count his death.' Carter produced an envelope. He patted it against his lips. 'Do you know what a deadman's switch is? Of course you do. From the moment I agreed to make the President disappear until I was assured I wouldn't be hurt by anyone, I had a deadman's switch kind of arrangement. I have a man who pretends to be my florist who does small favors for me, and he held on to this. If anything had happened to me, it would have gone right to Hearst. And elsewhere, in case Hearst wasn't interested. Would you like to see it?'

Griffin shook his head. No, he didn't want to see it. Carter stood. He tapped the envelope against the table.

'Well, I'm going to give this to you. Starling once told me that you'd tried very hard to protect the President – Mr McKinley – and that you'd failed. I can imagine how that hurt.'

'You can't—'

'If we'd met under different circumstances, I'd have stories to tell. But it's my wedding day. I'll leave you this envelope. And perhaps you'd like to use it to protect the President. It's up to you.'

Carter dropped it on the table, by the centerpiece, white roses with a candle at the center. Griffin watched him walk back onto the lawn, where he met up again with his wife.

The envelope was sealed shut. With the music playing and couples dancing under the lights, Griffin tore open the end and pulled out a strip of negatives and one eight-by-ten print. There, on the deck of a house he recognized, with Lake Merritt in the background, stood Warren Gamaliel Harding. He wore dungarees and a workman's jacket. He held a newspaper, the *Examiner*, from Friday, August third, with the tremendous headline announcing his death. His expression was that of a man who had just been rescued and was not sure he deserved it.

Griffin looked up – Carter was dancing with Phoebe, the band was playing, people were in line for more drinks. He had no idea what to do.

He saw Olive. Not for the first time, she made a beckoning gesture, for she was sure he was a fine dancer, and she had made him promise to be good today. He looked at the photograph. He stood. He nodded at Olive. She yelled at him, through the crowd, 'That's the spirit!'

Before he left the table, he put the photograph and negatives back in the envelope, which he held in his hand just high enough over the candleflame so that it caught almost immediately. The emulsion on the film made excited green and violet sparks, and when it was fully consumed, Jack Griffin draped his jacket over his chair, for the night was young.

At stroke of eight, Howard Thurston whispered into Carter and Phoebe's ears that it was time for them to leave. Carter protested the method. 'I was hoping for a life of quiet dignity.'

Phoebe said, 'This is what you're getting instead, so love it.'

With a fanfare of trumpets and trombones, the newlyweds were led onto a platform at the edge of the lawn, where Thurston and junior members of the Golden Gate Assembly shackled them together. 'Matrimony!' Thurston yelled, 'the one trap from which there *is* no escape.'

The couple was turned into a regular hardware store of chains and restraints. They were helped into a black and red lacquer cabinet decorated with dragons and Chinese sages, and finally, a huge iron ball was rolled into the cabinet, and its length of chain wrapped around them both.

'Maestro,' Thurston signaled, and a snare drum began to roll. Thurston shut and bolted the cabinet. There was a puff of smoke, and as he threw the door open, there was a loud clang as manacles hit the floor: Carter and Phoebe were gone!

Thurston rolled back his sleeves and extended his magic wand toward the road by the lawn, and there was the sound of an engine starting and a clatter of tin cans as a brand-new Willits-Overland convertible pulled into view. It was frosted with wedding wishes, and wisecracks, and was chauffeured away, its backseat overflowing with three passengers: Lili Marlene, nose into the breeze and, looking behind them and waving until they could no longer be seen, Charles and Phoebe Carter, waving good-bye, good-bye everyone, on the road to performing the greatest trick of them all, that of living happily ever after.

♣ ♦ ♥ ♠

And here this story of Charles Carter comes to an end, but for one detail:

On November 20, 1924, with the newspapers obsessing over Calvin Coolidge winning the general election, Florence Harding, the Duchess, died.

There was little notice. She was by all accounts an unknowable woman, and with so few clues to go on, the obituary artists reserved both judgment and comment. Her death marked yet another end to the troublesome Harding reign, so: the sooner she was gone, the better. There was no funeral train, there were no hymns sung by strangers. Services were brief and private.

Like her late husband, she was cremated and, like her late husband, there was no autopsy; the death certificate promised she had died of myocarditis and chronic nephritis. A funerary urn was placed in a crypt in Marion, Ohio, next to the urn that was etched 'Harding, Warren Gamaliel,' and that was still guarded, as a courtesy, by the Tenth Infantry detachment.

Soon after, workmen chipped her final resting date into a marble slab, and this was the quiet end of the Hardings' sad public dynasty.

History records that in 1925 the Mergui Archipelago, east of the Andaman Sea, was the twilight habitat of the pirate Tulang. He was no longer the man who had faced down Charles Carter. Ravished by syphilis, his skin withered as if aging a decade for every human year that had passed, Tulang had good days and bad. His crew was tired.

In late January 1925, a poorly armed narrow-seas ocean freighter was about to drop anchor in the leeward bay of a small island off the Thai peninsula when it was seized by Tulang. He pointed the tip of his sword to the Captain's chin, and for that moment, it was as if the old days were back, but then a fog settled onto the pirate, and he had to be led through the manifest twice before remembering what he had come aboard for.

'Your wares!' cried Tulang. 'We will help ourselves to what you bring to the market.' Because the ship had come all the way from the United States, the men were excited – who knew what treasures might be aboard? The pirates brought the crew to the deck, along with an elderly woman who was being sent away from America to live with distant relations.

Tulang's second in command, Samuel, a newly Christian Thai with genuine fondness for his leader, took control here, grabbing the Captain of the ship by the neck and rough-handling him belowdecks, past the sweltering heat of the engines, boilers, and fuel bunkers to the cool, stale air of the cargo hold. Reluctantly, the Captain took him to the packing crates containing the majority of their shipment: fifty gross of rake heads.

Samuel pried open the first crate with a crowbar. He didn't know what a rake was. The Captain demonstrated – when the factory in Thailand fashioned the right kind of dowel, it would fit here, and when you needed to make a pile of leaves, it worked like so.

'That's all you have? Oh, Jesus Christ!' Samuel cried. 'These rakes aren't even complete? Just the heads?'

'Just the heads.'

'Jesus Christ! What else do you have? Guns?'

The Captain shrugged. 'We were supposed to get fifty gross of hoe heads, too. They were too late.'

'What's in there?' Samuel waved at another part of the hold, which was padlocked.

The Captain jangled some keys

When the metal door opened, Samuel winced from the odor of dung. Inside the hold was an elephant. 'You're bringing an *elephant* to Thailand?' The Captain solemnly nodded. Samuel said, 'Who brings an *elephant* to Thailand? They have enough elephants.'

The Captain explained that this was a retired animal owned by a magician who would no longer use her in his act. They were anchored at this island, in fact, to drop the elephant here. The elephant and the old woman.

Moving into the hold, but still keeping his distance from the elephant, for he was unsure how well it was trained, Samuel noted it had no tusks, which meant no ivory, and if it were retired, it was too old to work, so what use was it?

He touched his hand to his pistol. Shooting it would teach the captains of freighters to carry better things in their holds than rake heads and elephants.

The elephant raised one foot, which was shackled to a length of chain, and stamped it on the floor of the hold. If he shot and killed it, how would the freighter crew ever get it out of the hold? The effort would be immense. It would make the crew very angry. This ship might next time travel armed.

Still, the idea of shooting it was attractive, for Samuel couldn't remember the last time he'd shot his pistol, and Tulang would be excited to know what he'd done.

'There's also wine,' the Captain said, grudgingly.

'What?'

'A case of it. But it's from America. It isn't from France.'

Samuel considered this. 'What kind of wine?'

The Captain took Samuel across the hold, to a packing crate that had on it, like all wine from America, the stenciled notation 'For Sacramental Use Only.'

'Jesus Christ! This is – is this for communion?'

'I don't know. It's also from the magician.'

'It says *sacramental*. That's holy wine.'

Samuel felt a light growing inside of him. Cracking open the crate, as gingerly as a crowbar would allow, brushing aside the straw bedding, it was like a manger scene to him. The glint of glass. He pulled forth a bottle, with its strange cabalistic markings, and felt a hand on his shoulder that he could only call divine. There was plunder in this world, and then there was the world beyond this one. What were the odds of finding a case of communion wine? The air in the hold suddenly smelled sweet. This wasn't luck, it was a blessing to share. He wanted to spare the elephant's life, and the lives of everyone he could.

'Help me with this,' he said to the Captain, squatting down to better get a grip on the crate.

On deck, Tulang was asleep in the sun. His crew and the freighter's stood in small groups, telling stories of misfortune, while the elderly woman, who had found shade, cored and ate an apple.

When Samuel brought up the wine, there was rejoicing all around, for the pirates had seen little alcohol recently. Samuel tried to describe why this wine was different than the rest, that they shouldn't gulp it, but as his mates seized bottle after bottle from the packing straw, breaking them open and singing old songs as they drank, even he had to admit that God's plan was infinitely odd – the most mysterious element of them all, joy, could enter this life profanely.

Soon, the pirates felt friendly enough to share their wine with the freighter's crew, and by the time the sun had swollen at the western horizon, the two crews had begun to visit each other's ships. There were rowdy bunches of newly made friends wrestling playfully on both ships' decks and card players were in both sets of crew quarters, and someone on the pirate's ship broke out guitars and accordions and drums that were passed around so all the old songs could be played. The ships were anchored side by side, and the tide was waning so that the bay below them grew a paler blue with each passing moment. Tiny Koh Pheung Thawng was the site of the largest party it had ever witnessed.

As for the witnesses themselves – the only spectators at first were goats and dogs and pigs who came out of the tangle of palm trees and tall grasses to scratch themselves and watch the commotion with puzzled eyes. Then the island's few human residents, a married couple and another man, all elderly, all white people who'd been baked brown by the sun, came to the beach.

Finally, when the heat had given way to a cooling breeze, and torches were lighted on the beach, the pirates and the freighter crew decided in the spirit of cooperation that now was the perfect time to send the elephant on its way.

Getting an elephant from a freighter at anchor to a beach was a surprisingly simple task. The ship's pilot, who had been a mahout in youth, brought the elephant from the hold and walked her to the bow of the ship, where he climbed onto her shoulders and waited for exactly the right wave to pass. He prodded her outward, into the waves, and then man and elephant fell together into the ocean with a tremendous splash that doused the groups on the ship and caused those on the beach to cheer.

She swam the remaining hundred yards while, at the same time, a dinghy was lowered from the ship and crewmen began to row the old woman to shore. In the end, it was a good-natured race: which would get to the beach first? It was a busy beach now, as the dogs and pigs were in a frenzy of early evening play. There was a campfire, and the husband played guitar as the wife clapped her hands to the simple tune that rolled across the bay, 'Three Blind Mice.' And there was the other man, the one with a high stomach, a nut-brown and happy man with a thicket of grey hair, waving and smiling. Walking into the surf, the breakers foaming past his hips, he waved at the pirates and the freighter crew, at the elephant and the woman in the dingy, he waved at everything in his view.

* * *

At the same time, on the ship, Tulang slept. Exhausted into dementia, he'd been carried to his bed, and his men had lovingly placed a bottle of wine next to him.

He awoke to the familiar throbbing of the engines. At this moment, his mind was back, completely, with an acuity that alcohol had once brought him in his youth. He was unsure what year it was. His eyes fixed on the wine bottle, and from this angle, he could clearly see the phrase: Charles Carter, Magician.

Carter the Great, he mused, now drifting out of clarity and into the past. 'Bring up the package,' he said aloud. Then, grinning, 'Life in Jakarta would be hard on her.' With a chuckle, Tulang slowly fell back into his dream, one he had almost nightly, about a day so many years ago, the day of the greatest magic show he had ever seen.

$p$rogram $n$otes

All of the magic appearing herein was performed (or attempted) during the craft's golden age, the 1890s to the 1920s. A nod and a word, however: key details have sometimes been poeticized. If, for instance, you use Carter's methods to escape from a packing crate, you should expect a less felicitous outcome.

Likewise, I've subjected history to vanishes, immolations, and other acts of misdirection. You'd be surprised, however, at how often history was far more interesting than anything I could have made up. Should you wish to read a more sober view of such adventures as Philo Farnsworth's, I direct you to the biography section of your local bookstore.

Though you're never supposed to show how you did a trick, it would be folly not to pull back the curtain and lead a hearty round of applause for *Carter the Great* by Mike Caveney, an astonishing in-depth biography of the real Charles J. Carter. Mike is an excellent historian, collector, and gentleman. Every book by his company, Magic Words, is wonderful reading.

The past five years have been a blur of microfiche, used-book stores, arcane libraries, and eBay bidding wars in the service of better understanding the world of Charles Carter. A few of the magicians whose writing I consulted include Nevil Maskelyne, David Devant, Robert-Houdin, Howard Thurston, F. B. Nightingale, Augustus Rapp, T. Nelson Downs, James Randi, Harry Kellar, Ottawa Keyes, Ricky Jay, and Walter Gibson. A complete list of resources combed over, and in some cases scrupulously ignored, would fill its own book. However, some works so influenced me that I'd like them to get their day in the sun (if the sun can be said to be shining for anyone other than the author at the end of a 560-page manuscript):

Milbourne Christopher, *The Illustrated History of Magic*; Alice Morse Earle, *Curious Punishments of Bygone Days*; Curt Gentry, *The Madams of San Francisco*; Rachel P. Maines, *The Technology of Orgasm*; Harpo Marx, *Harpo Speaks*; David Price, *Magic: A Pictorial History of Conjurers in the Theater*; Francis Russell, *The Shadow of Blooming Grove: Warren G. Harding in His Times*; Kenneth Silvermann, *Houdini!!!*; Edmund Starling, *Starling of the White House*; Herbert Yardley, *American Black Chamber*.

Since I started this book in February 1996, I have written and rewritten attempts at thanking specific people for their support, and yet I'm no closer to expressing the gratitude I feel. We begin with abject groveling toward Bill Sturm, lord of the Oakland History Room, for leading me to periodicals, files, maps, photos, city directories, and a photograph of lonely old Joe Sullivan.

Thank you to Irv Seaver Motorcycles, owners and explicators of a 1923 BMW R32, serial number 41.

Carolyn Birnbaum helped me out immeasurably. Thank you.

Michael Edwards and Norm and Lupe Nielsen were my ambassadors to the world of magic history. Ken Trombly answered many questions. Charles Greene III is the Pierce-Arrow of magic collectors.

Larry Finkler walked me through a certain display of electrical mayhem.

Inspiration came from the unbeatable troika of genius storytellers: Stan Lee, Jack Kirby, and Steve Ditko.

Aimee Bender, the prestidigitator of processing, and Teal '4' Minton are two of the best friends a guy could have. I look forward to more dinners and laughter around great oak tables. Let us all smoke fine cigars.

Friendship, readership, and relentless support came from Melanie Clayton, Mike Sears, Cy Voris, and Rob Stolzer; shots in the arm from the East Bay Express, the Squaw Valley Community of Writers, Ann Heiney, and the UC Irvine Composition programs. Richard Kyle provided enthusiasm then inspiration then (unexpectedly) cold, hard cash that allowed me to continue writing. Kathryn Chetkovich gave me a quiet place to stay for several crucial weeks of writing, rewriting, and squeegeeing the shower tiles. I am grateful to Jonathan Franzen, the spirit of St Louis, who tucked a copy of *Carter* into his cockpit and milk ran it to Colonel Susan Golomb, Ninja Assassin, who, under cover of the night, led me to Leigh Haber, who, with a pass of her magic wand, vanished scrofulous rabbits and cross-eyed box jumpers from my act. A quick and altogether incomplete thank-you to Cassie, Phil, Conan, Jane, Casey, and everyone else at Hyperion whose enthusiasm shaped this book.

The UC Irvine Creative Writing program was the greatest learning experience of my life. Thank you to everyone who ever came to a reading, said something nice to me, or *thought* of saying something nice to me. Specific thank-yous to Phil Hay and Danzy Senna (Los Torritos Diablos); Judith Grossman, Wilton Barnhardt, Margot Livesey, Michelle Latiolais, and Geoffrey Wolff, white-bearded wizard who wasn't satisfied unless I wrote beyond my abilities. Arielle Read, sultana of the MFA program, deserves a chocolate chip cookie from everyone who applies to the program.

When I was three years old, my father used to sit me on the bathroom sink and, while he clipped my toenails, tell me stories about genies in bottles and guys who walked into bars and pulled piano players out of their pockets. Around the same era, my mother let me sit in her lap and type gibberish on her old Olivetti. Then she would circle the words I'd accidentally spelled. I think everyone can see what that led to. The writing life has never gotten better. I love you both.

Also, thank you to the members of my audience who cannot read: Ernie, Batgirl, the ghost of Other Kitty, Lilly Marlene (who indeed spells it differently than her ancestor), Basel the beagle, Henry the tyrant of Flintshire Road, and Damned Spot. We are all siblings under the skin!

Finally: Sebold. Mind reader, levitator, secret weapon, gadfly, butterfly. Artist's model, box jumper, diva, high-wire aerialist. Quick-change artiste, sensation of the ages, and inquirer into the spirit world. Critic, effects-builder, manager, diva, oracle, mistress of escapes, queen of the mysteries, fellow conjurer, class act, and have I said 'diva' already? Friend, sister, secret weapon, paramour. Wife! I love you – let's take over this evil planet and make it a playground.

☆☆   ☆☆   ☆☆

Ladies and gentlemen, for your entertainment,

we present

from Glen David Gold's new novel

★★ SUNNYSIDE ★★

the opening reel,

starring
Charlie Chaplin,

a family of lighthouse keepers,
a dangerous young girl
from Texas,
a snooty train engineer,
the entire country of America

and 800 more
Charlie Chaplins.

☆☆   ☆☆   ☆☆

Newsreel for
November 12, 1916

A Day's Pleasure

☆   ☆   ☆

It was quite a large war. It was stupendously big and very distant. The public really was not inclined to pay much attention to it . . . We had grown used to the shouting. This perfectly understandable and honest public attitude was reflected more accurately and frankly in the motion picture than in any other institution.

— Terry Ramsaye
film historian and publicist (1925)

☆   ☆   ☆

1

At its northernmost limit, the California coastline suffered a winter of brutal winds pitched against iron-clad fog, and roiling seas whose whiplash could scar a man's cheek as quickly as a cat-o'-nine-tails. Since the Gold Rush, mariners had run aground, and those who survived the splintering impact were often pulped when the tides tore them across the terrible strata of the volcanic landscape. For protection, the State had erected a score of lighthouses staffed with teams of three or four families who rotated duties that lasted into the day and into the night. The changing of the guard, as it were, was especially treacherous in some locations, such as Crescent City, accessible only by a tombolo that was flooded in high tide, or Point Bonita, whose wooden walkway, even after the mildest storm, tended to faint dead away from the loose soil of its mountaintop and tumble into the sea.

Until the advent of navigational radio, communication with the mainland was spotty. God help the man who broke his leg on the Farallon Islands between the weekly supply-ship visits. But the peril of the European War had meant Crosley crystal-receiver radio sets and quenched spark systems with an eight-hundred-mile range for all who lived and worked on the coastlines, and so, on Sunday, November 12, 1916, just below the Oregon border, at the St. George Reef Lighthouse, eight miles off the California coast, there began an explosion of radio, telephone, and telegraph operations unprecedented in American history.

At high tide, roughly five o'clock in the morning, it was over an hour before dawn. The sweeping eighty-thousand-candlepower light from the third-order lens cast the frothing sea from shore to horizon into the high contrast of white against black for some moments, then back into full pitch-darkness. Two strong men in caps and slickers rowed the station boat toward the crown of stone upon which the lighthouse stood. Their passenger, her corpulent form bundled beneath a treated canvas sail, her arms crossed around her morning pitcher of coffee, was the Second Assistant Keeper, Emily Wheeler. As the light rotated, there was a stroboscopic effect which illuminated her progress cutting across the sea foam that lay like frosting above the crags and crevasses of the ancient reef.

Emily Wheeler, in the third generation of a family of California lighthouse keepers, was a difficult woman, but, as with all difficult women who could demand such isolated work, her desire was immediately granted. Of course, send her to a rock miles off the coastline, go with the governor's blessings.

But, unlike other such women, she had thought to make her own uniform. She wore it under the sail and her layers of slickers and inflatable vests. It was navy wool, with simple gold braid at the throat, and there was a smart, matching cap under which she tucked the foundry-steel braid of her hair. After considerable thought about stripes – she didn't want to seem conceited, yet she also wanted to acknowledge her duties – she had given herself the rank of sergeant.

Her lighthouse was the world's most expensive, nine years in the making, a cylindrical housing hewn from living granite, a 115-foot caisson tower as sturdy as a medieval fortress, its imposing skin interrupted only by the balistrariac slits of loophole windows. And at the very top, capped with iron painted a brilliant red, was its lantern room, in which rotated the Fresnel lens, as faceted as a sultana's engagement diamond, and which, like the eye of Argus, was chambered myriad ways, as close to omniscience as technology could dare. There was no better light in America.

To be the sergeant sharing charge of such a great beast was an honor and a responsibility to which Emily Wheeler was equal, and to be a woman superior to men was a life she made no secret of enjoying. In fact, to gain their confidence, she was known to pander to their prejudices, in effect putting her own gender up for sale. ('Gentlemen,' she said on her first day, 'I do not give the orders. The sea gives the orders, and we are at the mercy of *her* unpredictable ways.')

She was clearheaded in a crisis, and had organized the rescue of many a wayward sailor. However, it was her habit in the boring hours to engineer small crises herself. A twitching filament on the reserve lantern was occasion for much shouting; cleaning the fog signal's air compressor meant at least three separate fits of panic. It was thus the curse of her men to wish on every shift for an actual disaster.

Since no one could live comfortably at the station for more than a week, the four keeper families passed much of their lives in cottage-style duplexes on the coast, on the dunes just above the shoreline. Husbands and wives and children were eternally, twice a day, with the waxing and waning tides, handing off hot meals and kissing each other goodbye.

Eight miles from shore, the station boat now settled into place on the leeward side of the lighthouse, which made a wedge-shaped windscreen, a small pool of calm. The men in the boat flashed their tiny lantern, and in response there was a groan from the crane housing overhead, and a winch dropped down a cargo net, into which Sergeant Wheeler stepped. Another exchange of lights, and then the crane withdrew, bringing her aloft. It was during the long moments when she swung in the wind, and the spray of the sea managed to slap at her face and neck, that she most enjoyed her job at the very edge of the map. 'I am the westernmost woman in the country' – an idea she extinguished when the cargo net placed her on granite. Trouble.

Leland, her assistant, helped her unbuckle the harness and step out of the cargo net. 'We have a problem, Mom.'

Leland was always on duty at the same time she was, less a personal choice than a request of the other families. He was twenty-four years old, talk at the lighthouse had deemed him 'unfairly handsome,' and he had wrecked two surreys on the dunes near the cottages while impressing girls. Further, he had a propensity for mail-ordering sheet music from San Francisco, *jazz rags,* which he insisted on playing on the clarinet most afternoons, and he was known to visit the picture show three consecutive days to memorize the details of photoplays rather than stay at home and help his grandmother, who had the vapors. It was hoped Sergeant Wheeler would provide discipline.

'What's wrong?'

'Craft adrift. About a mile west-northwest.'

'Anyone on it?'

Leland hesitated. He was generally quick with a quip, which

melted Emily's heart too much and prevented any actual discipline from occurring. So now she looked at him not just as a sergeant, but as a worried mother. Finally, he said, 'You should come see.'

They passed through the portico into the engine room and took the elevator to the cramped observation chamber just below the lantern room. It shared common glass with the lightbox one story above. There were two men already present, a father and a son of the Field family, pushing each other away from their only telescope worth a damn, the Alvan Clark with a two-inch lens. While Emily removed her slicker, and polished the wet from her glasses, two more assistants came into the room, having heard excitement was brewing.

'Where's the craft?' Emily asked.

'It's ten o'clock, a mile out,' answered the elder Field.

'And it's manned?'

Field looked to his son, who looked to Leland, who nodded.

'Is it the invasion?' For this had been a topic of discussion, at first hypothetically and of late a grim certainty.

'No, it's just one man. Alone.'

Frowning, Emily pulled the phone from the wall and called to the lantern room, asking them to fix the lens so that it shone at ten o'clock, and to send up the code flags, prepare for a series of two-flag signals, and notify all surrounding vessels via radio telephony that a rescue was in progress.

The engine ground down with the easing of a clock spring, and the white light went steady upon the churning seas. The fog, which most days was a woolen overcoat, this morning was but a beaded mist easily torn through, and even without the telescope, Emily could see a small boat bobbing in the swells.

'Lord! It's just a skiff, an open skiff,' she whispered. She made fluttering gestures to push back the group around the Alvan Clark, and they exchanged glances of anticipation. This was either a real crisis or one about to be shouted into existence. Emily applied her eye to the eyepiece, blinked, and ran her fingers along the reeded focus knob, making a blur, and then, in a perfectly circular iris, she saw, with a clarity that made her gasp, Charlie Chaplin.

She jolted a step backward, looking to the window without the aid of magnification, as if the telescope might have somehow fabricated this vision. She could see the boat, now rocking on the crests of ever-increasing waves as it came closer, and there was indeed a solitary figure aboard. He was dressed in baggy black trousers, a tight morning coat. He had a mustache. A cane. A derby.

'Is that . . .' She swallowed.

'We were thinking it looks like Charlie Chaplin,' Leland said, with the shame of a boy caught believing in fairies.

Emily gulped coffee, searching for it to kick like gin, and then she looked again through the telescope. The lighthouse provided a brilliant spotlight that swept away all color in the flood of illumination, casting its view into glowing white or penumbral mystery; there was no missing the open skiff, its single sail patched and sagging, its occupant shuffling from stem to stern, toes out, gingerly leaping over each oarlock's thwart. He was rubbing his chin, and waggling his mustache as if itched by a puzzling thought, and in the several seconds Emily watched speechlessly, a gust of wind swung the ruined sail so that it hit him in his rear end, causing him to jump in place. He realized what had hit him, he tipped his hat as if he and the sail were engaged in polite social discourse, and he returned to his bowlegged pacing.

'We have to rescue him,' Leland finally said.

'Yes,' Emily whispered.

'Could it be someone *dressed* as Charlie Chaplin?' asked the elder Field, who always saw the blank physics of a situation, but even his voice had doubts. Each assistant took turns looking at the little fellow in the skiff, and each had to agree, one could certainly dress like Chaplin, and even act like Chaplin – there were contests and so on – but in the view of their telescope's eye, there were no hesitations, no awkward attempts to remain graceful. This man was not pretending or attempting to convince them of his identity. Further, they were battling against logic with their desire to believe it was true. In the end, what was right before their eyes won.

'Well,' Leland said, helplessly showing off what he knew from the magazines, 'that is definitely Charles Spencer Chaplin.' Then he whispered, 'Son of a gun. There's a hole in the hull.'

He knew this because Chaplin was now using a tin cup to bail out water. As the boat drifted closer to the rocks, waves dumped over the bowl, so the bailing was useless and frantic. Chaplin

573

removed his hat to use it as a ladle, and now both his arms became pistons flinging water away as the sea drew his boat closer and closer to its doom.

Emily's hand went to her mouth. 'There's a hole in his derby, too!'

'Perhaps he's making a movie here,' suggested Field.

'I'm going,' Leland said. Before his mother had a chance to object, he had shot to the exit, and his boots made the authoritative peal of cathedral bells as he sprinted down the circular metal staircase.

'Leland, come back,' she cried, as mothers have always called to their children who in turn were called to the brutal seas, but in truth she hardly wanted to stop him. To stop him smacked of that phantom discipline she could not muster. Moreover, he was going to aid a helpless sailor, an act that throbbed with responsibility.

For his own part, Leland could not have been dissuaded, because the chance to rescue Charlie Chaplin would never come again. On the porch where the launch boats hung, he slipped into his flotation vest and jumped into the rowboat behind Johnson, who always wore a cameo of the Blessed Virgin on the outside of his protective clothing. With Johnson in first position, Leland took second position in the oarlocks, and signaled to the crane house to drop them to the sea.

For long minutes, two pairs of youthful arms rowed in splendid unison, threading the boat between spires and jags until it faced the open sea. Leland spotted the skiff ahead; it was drifting toward *la pared de la muerte*. Many points along the coast were known as the Wall of Death; this one had reasons for the name so convincing that the antediluvian Tolowa fishermen had described it thusly, and centuries later the Russian otter-hunters had agreed – *stayna greebel*, of course – for, no matter the tide, a wicked current drew anything in its grip magnetically shoreward, with unexpected speed. When you were still in the swells a quarter mile away from the obvious rocks, in the sickening drop of a trough, the half-submerged wall would be thrown erect before you, and there was a vortex into which all boats would be sucked down, then spat up against it, dashing what remained into bits.

Sergeant Emily Wheeler watched with pride and fear as her boy's rescue boat rose and fell with the ocean, oars moving it foot by foot toward Chaplin's skiff. She was anticipating the outcome – the shoreline, sunrise, seagulls chasing the spindrift, Chaplin on a driftwood log with a blanket draped over his shoulders, sipping coffee laced with brandy, and shaking from the fear and pleasure of having been rescued.

At the same time, arms fatigued and cold, Leland was staring through his partner, Johnson, considering the shape that the gratitude of Mr. Charlie Chaplin might take. He imagined lecturing Chaplin; he had read *Motion Picture Weekly*, and he knew the difference between pretending to be on a dinghy in the movies, and testing your luck on such spirited seas as those near St. George Reef. 'But you know, Mr. Chaplin,' he would say, 'this does make quite a scenario, don't you think?' And how else could Charlie respond but to stand from his log, place one arm up on Wheeler's solid shoulder, pump his hand, and say, 'I hadn't considered it, Leland Wheeler, but you're right,' and 'Leland Wheeler is a splendid kind of name. Come to the studio – we need strong arms and strong jawlines,' and Leland constructed and reconstructed these statements with different kinds of English accents, from Ascot-races lordly to cockney chauffeur, since he wasn't quite sure what Chaplin sounded like, eventually settling on the accent he'd heard a slapstick comedian use at the Redding Music Hall, British with a Jewish or Gypsy tint, he didn't really know the specifics; but such speculation swirled in its own vortices, and he concluded first that this rescue might be his own salvation, then: might there be a filmed re-enactment, but this time with *bathing beauties*?

It is the nature of wishes and their potential fulfillment to travel faster than anything shackled to earth, especially a rowboat straining against a current that all but groaned in its desire to blow into *la pared de la muerte*. So Leland Wheeler's mind could travel from sea to shore to the road leading seven hundred miles south to the bare ankles of the engaging backlot sirens who fluttered and yawned at the Mutual Studios of Los Angeles, in the approximate time it took Chaplin's boat to be sucked into the whirlpool and begin an awful, irresistible spin.

Leland was calling out to Johnson, who called back; Leland could hear just the harder consonants of a prayer. Chaplin noticed them – he visibly perked up, stood, and leaned forward until the boat tipped, and he was forced, hands on hat, to lean back. He smiled, recognizing not the danger but the rescue, and he again tipped his hat, face breaking into the smile of one about to be saved. But his boat was already turning, turning slowly, turning almost gently, in obedience to Coriolis, and the men in the rowboat were shouting themselves hoarse, and Chaplin, in order to keep them in sight, began to march in place, counterclockwise. He was in effect stationary, even as the boat was beginning to spin under his feet. Leland shouted, 'No!'

Chaplin cocked his ear as if trying to listen, holding to his temple his useless tin cup as if it were an ear trumpet, and, with the boat's rotation increasing, he stepped up his own counterrotations until he was all but a blur.

The swells drew back. The boat stopped, Chaplin continuing to spin until he toppled over. With acrobatic momentum, the tumble carried him upright, and he stood, arms in fists at his sides, looking as if he had just triumphed over the sea. He did not see what loomed behind. With the weight of a mudslide, a wave crashed down upon the boat, and Charlie Chaplin was blown below the surface.

Pressure mounting against it like the thumb and forefinger of Uranus, the hull of the skiff rocketed out of the depths, sailed six feet over the waves, and crashed into shards like a wine bottle against the Wall of Death.

The sun was beginning to rise; there wasn't yet its actual glow or warmth, but instead the gray promise of daylight. The lighthouse beam was thus fading in comparison with natural light, and the many colors of the sea were being restored: the olive bulbs of kelp atop the rich obsidian rocks, the emerald nightmare that was the sea, the lapis of the dawn skies. Leland and his companion rowed in place. They had lost their spirit. How terrible it was that God had created in humans the urge for compassion, a sensation that nature itself withheld.

The simplest pairs of code flags rode up the station's monkey pole, the blue-and-white 'A' and yellow 'Q,' then the powder flag and St. George's Cross: boat lost, man overboard. An emotionless message, all was lost, all was lost. The St. George Reef telegraph operator, weeping, began to tap out a note to the naval station to the south, and to all the ships at sea, a spotty and impressionistic account whose clarity was far outweighed by its emotional devastation. And yet, at the same time, he was receiving something that was not a response, that made no sense, a message of dots and dashes from the east.

From *la pared de la muerte* there was a quick bubbling, and Leland pointed, just as his mother, eyes red and wet with tears, swung the telescope to see what he witnessed: surfacing, dome up, the battered black derby, with a single strand of seaweed, like a rose upon a coffin.

Then rained down the next wave, and the hat was lost forever.

2

Three thousand four hundred miles eastward, it was nine o'clock in the morning. The autumn sun stretched thinly over Manhattan, and yet, as per local legend, it had still arranged itself so that 350 Fifth Avenue, the Waldorf=Astoria, did not fall into shadow.

At the Waldorf, breakfast was served. In its block-long kitchens, steam rose from copper kettles, Florida oranges rolled down pipe shafts to be cleaved for the juicer, the alchemical preparations for champagne truffles brought gourmet Pierre Revel from his usual tufted seat in the Hamilton Lounge into the kitchen for consultations on proper mincing of the negretto, a platoon of mushroom-hatted chefs from Brussels frowned as they tasted hollandaise sauce puddled on greenbrier-wood ladles, and a legion of metal whisks fluffed up sauces for the orders of eggs Benedict that Park Avenue doctors now prescribed as a morning antidote for the social side of the night before.

Then there was the sound of three chimes.

Cups froze, suspended in the air. A single chime meant a message for a guest in a room the size of a suite or smaller. Two chimes meant the message was for a guest in the Maidenhead Suite or even one of the penthouses. Conversations now began to dissolve like honey in warm water, for no one could quite remember having heard *three* chimes before.

A pageboy in white chinoise-silk gloves again struck the soft rubber mallet against his three-note glockenspiel. He called out, 'Mr. Chaplin. Paging Charlie Chaplin.' Which, in an instant, caused a ripple. Heads craned, and then, upon realizing what their owners had done, cheeks reddened.

And then the pageboy was gone, down the speckled Bidjar runner and into the lobby, where he again struck his three tones, and called out the name of Mr. Chaplin.

In the Colorado Rockies, at the Grand Imperial Hotel, which had indeed looked imperial in its mining days, the manager uncorked the intercom tube that, in theory, addressed all public areas – in practice, it worked about as well as stretching two tin cans along a length of string – and called, in a voice whose transposition along the ether made it shimmer like a mirage, 'Will Charlie Chaplin please come to the lobby?'

And in the Alexandria Hotel of Los Angeles, California, a boy in a red pillbox hat cupped his hand to his jaw and cried, 'Paging Charlie Chaplin. Charlie Chaplin, please report to the concierge desk.' In a boarding house on the slopes of Butte, Montana, a land-lady gingerly knocked on the door of the large bunk room, and cleared her throat so that the men in every dank cot could hear. 'Is there a Charlie Chaplin here this morning?'

From the languid playpens of the Florida Gables to the great clap-board Outer Bank inns, from the flophouses of the Bowery to the pilgrims' resorts near the Great Salt Lake, there were pages for Mr. Charlie Chaplin. According to the *Boston Globe,* Chaplin was sought that morning in over eight hundred hotels.

3

Also that morning, on iron tracks through which sifted the East Texas dust, a sturdy 4-6-2 steam locomotive chugged eastward at forty miles per hour, towing its coal tender, four passenger cars, and caboose on the main route of the Beaumont, Sour Lake and Western Railway line. This was nicknamed among those who knew it best the Belch, Slow Leak and Wheeze. Constructed during a flurry of interest in connecting the Midwest to the Gulf (the morning the line opened, its Missouri station was proclaimed 'The Port of Kansas City'), it had been bought and sold and gone into receivership so often that the workers now demanded to be paid in cash. Still, service was mostly friendly, a 'what the hey' cama-raderie which accepted as a noble truth that, should you have business aboard the Belch, Slow Leak and Wheeze, you deserved commiseration.

On the train today were a handful of passengers, an engineer, his assistant, a conductor, two soused brakemen, an indolent fireman, and a seething porter who continually flipped a coin to determine if his sweetheart had been faithless.

In the very rear, facing the receding horizon, alone, feet dangling through the iron rails of the caboose, eyes disconsolate and ill-focused, moped one Hugo Black. He was twenty-three years old. He wore the brown-and-elephant-gray overalls of the Beaumont, Sour Lake and Western Railway junior engineering staff as if they were prisoner's stripes.

Below a pencil-thin mustache, his mouth was moving; one schooled in the art of lip-reading would find that Hugo was silently pronouncing villainous curses upon the world. In café French. His mastery of the idiom was astonishing, especially in that he had never been to France. He was mourning how moments ago the ill-glued spine of his Flaubert had caught in the wind. As the train rattled past Batson, pages of *Madame Bovary* scattered behind, fluttering into brambles as if brilliant French literature were simply a by-product of steam locomotion.

Hugo no longer had business on this train. He was the son of a professor at the University of Michigan. Hugo Black *père* was a scholar of mechanics, specializing in the design of railway trains. 'I am an engineer of engineers,' he had said, often, with the eternal hope that he might be found witty, and his son, after cringing through many summers of local railway work, had upon his graduation from college spread his wings as far from home as adventure allowed, seeking at first distant colleagues of his father's on the Chicago, Milwaukee & St. Paul, then the Lehigh Valley, and even two weeks on the Sinnemahoning tending to the needs of a splendid Mikado locomotive. But he consistently found his services were no longer required.

Between jobs, he returned to Michigan for cotillion season, tall and striking in a dinner jacket, with or without vents, executing flashy scarlet waltzes or Viennese rumbas. His family lived not quite in Grosse Pointe, or even quite on Jefferson Avenue, but two blocks away from the Immortals, in a house not quite as fine as the rest.

This left his mother eternally vigilant as to class, grace, and aesthetic choices.

Hugo was unsure exactly when he lost his fellow employees on the Belch, Slow Leak and Wheeze, though no one had appreciated the wreath of prairie roses he had braided himself and hung over the staff lockers. Even after he had explained they were created in accordance with William Morris's principles of workplace ablative motifs, his fellow workers could not be said to embrace him. He understood and he tried to be patient, for he wanted to be helpful. But when he volunteered to while away the hours by reading aloud from John Ruskin, they asked that he no longer assist with the boiler, the wheel maintenance, the loading and unloading of baggage, but sit in the back and please be quiet. It was the 'please' that killed. His rejection so complete it inspired *politeness*.

There, on the lonely caboose, with the last of the pages gone, and the book binding empty as a corn husk, Hugo considered whether he could at least announce he'd been reading Flaubert in the original French. He had no one to say it to, and so, instead, he let his heels smack against the car's empty coupling until he felt the vibrations ping up his shins, and he slumped while the train found the final slow curve along the Neches River, into the disaster awaiting them at Beaumont.

If the train cut through any particular atmosphere, it was the same suspended tension throughout the forty-eight states, an indrawn breath not yet expelled. The last week's presidential election had been fraught. There were recounts and challenges, and long days later, Woodrow Wilson was declared the winner, and the relief was palpable. America was still at peace.

But when there was a long-enough lull – all it took was another day or so, news from Europe drifting onto the front pages again – it wasn't really silent anymore. Wayward winds blew to shore the terrible sounds of mortar fire, cries of wounded men, the lacquer tang of poison gas. America was on edge, everywhere, as if every man were glancing toward his rifle and then toward the neighboring barn, hearing cries of pain at sunset, and knowing that before morning came he was charged with the responsibility of shooting the family horse. One day – but when? – America would have to put old Europe out of its misery.

In the meantime, today, Sunday, the surprise guest, the picnic – this came as not just a respite but a blessing for the citizens of Beaumont, Texas. At the Beaumont train station, the burbling crowd drowned out the purple mourning doves cooing on the statues to Progress and Industry. Church bells were swinging as ineffectively as if the clappers had been stolen, for no one was at church.

There was a crow's nest fifty feet west of the station, and in it was a twelve-year-old girl who had courage and a spyglass. She wore exceptionally clean overalls and boots that had never known mud, and she had wind-burned skin, a brown-eyed stare pegged to eternity, and black hair that went easily into pigtails, and this was the single obedient part of her.

Her name was Rebecca Golod, and her fertile kin, all of them industrious, energetic, and argumentative, had come to Texas from the steppes of Russia ten years before, with stops in Toronto (not very friendly), Detroit (the same), Chicago (too many other Jews – it was like Russia all over again), and Biloxi (who wanted to live in Biloxi?). The Golods owned an entire block of Beaumont stores now, with cousins and nieces and nephews who flowed through the Russia-to-Texas pipeline as efficiently as any light sweet crude. Had there been a family crest, it would have shown two rampant hawks with beaks pinching each other's necks.

Roughly half of the family was crooked. The shady half was perpetually blackmailing the noble half to pay off gambling debts, drinking bills, schemes to open opium dens. Rebecca's spyglass was the only keepsake her grandfather had successfully smuggled out of Russia, having lost even the family samovar to guards at the Austrian border. She had determined that, among the screaming and shouting, she could distinguish herself, and still induce the kind of rage that seemed to mean that your parents truly loved you, by becoming the quietest, most humble, and most *honest* of all Golods. The type of girl who had organized her dolls by height (then, as she assigned them personalities, in order of their self-discipline), she decided she could be entrusted with delicate things, and so the spyglass was freed from Grandfather's closet and now comfortably dangled on a chain around her neck.

As one relative, then another spotted her in the crow's nest, each wailed as if hit in the foot with a mallet, looked for someone else in the family to blame, then called for her to come down and hand the spyglass back to Grandfather, but Rebecca put her finger to her lips, looked piqued, as if they were embarrassing her, and returned to looking for the 8:16 train.

On the platform, the Marine Band rehearsed 'When the Saints Go Marching In' and its tricky segue to the 'Spindletop Fight Song' near a table covered with checked cotton cloth, and on it chicken salad, baked beans, and, finally, their surfaces domed and ready to burst like volcanoes, perhaps a quarter acre of freshly baked pies. The finest people in town, those who had built their homes in The Oaks, lingered by their chauffeur-driven automobiles, for they had their own plans to spirit the guest toward private luncheons with blue-etched china plates shipped from Dresden and on them the amazing fact of tiny, round sandwiches that had *no crusts*.

Beaumont was home to the Spindletop gusher, whose eruption in 1901 had spilled a million barrels of oil even before it was capped. This was exciting to everyone, from the local boys who had found that dancing in the geyser was a fantastic method of causing their mothers to faint, to the petroleum companies – Humble, Gulf, Texas – who had generated wealth beyond reason.

'Thus,' Mayor Knight whispered, rehearsing, finger in the air as if slicing through prevailing winds, bringing insight and prosperity, 'were Texas a giant, you could lay her upon the bosom of Europe. And, with her head in repose upon the mountains of Norway, with London resting in one palm and Warsaw in the other, she could easily bathe her ponderous feet in the blue waters of the Mediterranean Sea. So, on behalf of the people of Beaumont, proud home of the Spindletop gusher' – he considered the delightful morning he'd had at the Pine Tree Café – '*and* home to the tastiest flapjacks in Jefferson County, we invite you, Charlie Chaplin, to take light refreshment and a morning drink with us.'

'TRAIN'S COMING!' The yell came up from a fleet of boys running down the track. Rebecca frowned. With the naked eye, she could clearly see the steam from the smokebox chimney that floated over a locomotive shimmering in the distance, and yet she hadn't been able to see it through the spyglass. And then she saw that the lens was host to a wicked, spidery crack. She was tempted to shout down that the family heirloom was a piece of junk. Instead, she capped the lens, wondering with increasing anger how long her grandfather had kept its obsolescence from them; how betrayed she felt, what a *farbrekher* he was; then, lowering the spyglass into its protective leather satchel, she was chilled. Wasn't there a moment, climbing up, when she'd felt it strike the lodgepole-pine stand? Hard?

Since she was always so careful, she decided that this hadn't actually happened.

The band assembled into neat rows flanking the strongest boy in the twelfth grade, who wore a bass drum strapped to his belly, and who beat on it with a joyous rhythm from the heart of East Texas. There were last-minute panicked repinnings of bunting that had diabolically chosen this moment to sag, and all the town spilled onto the platform in a mass, from the patients at the Ralston Confederate Retirement Home in their wicker-strap wheelchairs to the girls who had turned out in their best dresses, dresses so fine that when the newspaper accounts described the catastrophe to come, they still spent inches serenading local color ('Miss Kate Ogden, pink albatross and white velvet; Miss Fannie Stewart, pink velvet; Miss Hattie Chapman, pale-lavender teatime dress'), and all the girls, no matter how much they hated the others' high-handed ways, stood linking arms so that – hang your light refreshment and a morning drink – *they* would be the most inviting sight for Chaplin's eye.

The 8:16 eased into the station with a belch and slow leak of steam, and then, as promised, a wheeze of ancient brakes. The conductor stood at the exit door, watch heavy in his hand, as if his weighing the correct time might explain this massive crowd.

Rebecca threaded her way between adults until she was in sight of the caboose, where there stood a young man with a razor's-edge mustache and a baroque nose. He put his hands on his hips and fixed the crowd with an angry, disappointed look. Rebecca almost gasped. She thought he had the condemning weight of storybook nobility, a landowner ashamed of his serfs. She wondered if Charlie Chaplin traveled with, among his many friends, royalty.

The band launched into 'Over There,' which annoyed Mayor Knight: there had been discussion of why exactly Chaplin hadn't enlisted, and he wanted to extend the feeling of welcome rather than guilt. 'Play something else! Anything!' he yelled.

'There he is!' The cry came from the throat of a sensible man, Dr. Franklin, and the crowd pressed forward, and a figure appeared at the head of a passenger car. That it was Eugenia Burkhardt in her daisy pokebonnet, returning from her trip to Houston, in no way diminished Beaumont's enthusiasm. Eugenia, who had never thought much of Beaumont, ignored the hands pulling at her, and the questions of where Chaplin was, until she finally rapped her umbrella against Bethyl Taylor, who was trying to hug her.

By the caboose, Rebecca tentatively waved at her elegant stranger, who was of course Hugo Black, in the hope he might wave back. She had a hunch, which had crept up on her as hunches did for children in folktales who listened to the advice given by magic mirrors or voices whispering from wells: the multitudes around her were missing an actual prince in their midst.

'That's him!' This time the cry came from many places. Nonetheless, the person leaving the train was only mournful Joe Nailer, in his only good suit, who waved glumly, as if crowds greeted him every day of his life.

Whenever there was motion inside the train, ripples went through the crowds on the platform, and Rebecca was jostled, which required her to give narrow looks to many of her neighbors. A conductor in a sharp black cap yelled at her prince, who snapped to attention as no prince ever would.

From here, it was a small leap for her to suspect that Charlie Chaplin wasn't really on the train.

When the porter opened the baggage compartment, a half dozen people fell over, trying to see inside, as if Chaplin – of course! – were traveling under the train like a railway rat, perhaps to surprise them in costume.

'Folks! Folks, stand back from the train!' This was obeyed easily enough – they had to give him some room, that was understandable. Still, it took some time, and the conductor continued, 'The train cannot leave the station until there is room, so please stand back.'

The crowd did not stand back: they were here to see Chaplin, who was here to see them.

'Where's Charlie?' a girlish voice cried. It was Rebecca Golod.

The question took seed. 'Where's Charlie?' It was an easy name to join in on, two syllables, and it seemed so friendly at first, 'Charlie, Char-lie, Char-lie.'

The conductor consulted with the engineer, and two redcaps stepped up to see what was the matter. Rebecca noticed her young man join them. Within moments, the uniformed men had finally found a use for their imperious-looking college-educated charge, Hugo Black: it was his job to disperse the crowd.

This Hugo took to with vigor, fluttering the backs of his hands at the crowd as if shooing an insistent hobo's dog away from a freshly glazed ham. The chant of 'Char-lie, Char-lie, Char-lie' went darker.

The engineer blew the steam whistle, readying the train to go. Farmhands lifted their friends onto their shoulders, and they beat against the train, drumming their palms on the sheet metal in an apoplectic dissonance that caused Hugo to wince. Bravely, he began to lecture from the iron steps of the passenger car, adapting freely from a *Ladies' Home Journal* essay he'd read by Mrs. Alfred Astor about how easily sidewalk etiquette was achieved on Park Avenue, and he explained into the din how those simple lessons of common courtesy dictated that the crowd should disperse. Remembering the impact of the word, he added, 'Please!'

He saw just one person looking his way: a little girl. He cocked his head and raised his eyebrows, and he smiled. Humbly, he thought. Her own eyebrows went south, eyes narrowing as if squeezing the last of daylight from them.

Hugo then saw what was around her neck. It was so incongruous his voice spoke on its own accord. 'Good grief! Is that a Zeiss Optical spyglass?'

His heartbeat, which had been hammering in nervousness, mellowed. To see this in Texas made the rest of the world oblique; he felt suspended in a bubble outside of which all was blurred and vague. A Zeiss Optical spyglass was the pride of European technology, a salute to Old World charm and warmth, a slender fluted slide with a reeded edge calibrated for sensitive fingers. His father had one, calling it 'too sweet for the workaday,' and they had used it on weekends together, looking for birds. He remembered his father's hand on his shoulder. 'Pardon,' he asked, for the girl had said something.

'It's my grandfather's,' she whispered again. He could just barely hear her voice, though she had tiptoed closer, two strides away from his stairs.

'I'm sure it is, but—' He broke off, for his own voice was submerged by the tuba player of the band, who had let out an emotive blat of frustration. Hugo swallowed. 'I have one, too. At home. I'll be careful.'

Hugo had been forgotten by everyone, save Rebecca. Somewhere behind her, someone dropped a bottle, which caused her to look over her shoulder to see one of the hoodlum children, an enormous sixth-grader who was rumored to be twenty-two years old, picking up a hank of broken railway tie and testing for tensile strength by whacking it against one of his callused palms.

As Rebecca approached, Hugo glanced toward the exits, since it was apparent people were walking away. He thought his lecture had worked. But there were actually two distressing developments. First, people were linking arms on the track ahead (putting down blankets so they could sit without dirtying themselves), and, second, the departing Beaumont citizens were only walking as far as the brickyard, where the proprietor, jangling his ring of keys, waved them in.

Hugo, innocent of this view, whispered to Rebecca, 'May I hold your Zeiss Optical spyglass?'

There was no reason to let this man touch such a valuable object, but Rebecca realized with a merciless crackle up her spine that such thinking did not become a Golod. Wordlessly, she removed the spyglass from its case, and then took the chain from around her neck, like slipping off a bridle.

Rebecca felt as light and generous as if supported by angels, and Hugo reached for it, cupping his hand as Rebecca confidently, with a determination beyond her years, dropped the spyglass, lens first, onto the concrete platform.

It rolled in a semicircle.

Rebecca found her voice. It was a low, almost subsonic moan that ascended in volume and timbre until it sounded as epic and awful as the misery of a garroted winter wolf.

'You – broke – my – spyglass!'

She was aware, without turning, of the shadow behind her, the way any animal could sense the presence of kin. It was the shadow of someone huge. Hugo was so transfixed by the squalling girl that he went dimwitted. He caught a blur: a left hand that had, on the bitter spring mornings on the steppes of Drohitchen, during troubled whelpings, pulled calves from their mothers' wombs with a single tug, found Hugo's shirt collar. It yanked him forward and off the train.

This was excellent news, briefly, in that the first brick hurtling through the air missed Hugo. It thudded against the train cab stairs just as Hugo's entire field of vision filled with a permafrost of impenetrable white beard surrounding a pit of angry teeth that had known only Russian frontier dentists. This was Abraham Golod, Rebecca's grandfather, owner of the spyglass, and as his left fist continued to reel in Hugo by the collar, his right fist, black as an ironmonger's mallet, punched him in the face. Hugo's head snapped back, his legs buckled under his weight as if they were blades of grass, he heard warbling birds and gamboling children, and he wanted to tell them hello, but he was already unconscious.

Rebecca stood wide-eyed, nostrils flaring and mouth open as if every sense were eager to take in all available wisdom from this moment. Had she actually blamed her tarnished prince for the spyglass? How awful of her! Had that resulted in her slithering out of trouble? How not-quite-awful. Her grandfather grabbed her by the arm. When she resisted, he threw her over his shoulder and strode through the crowd toward their Ford flatbed truck, his shattered spyglass now in one fist.

'Today you ride in the back!'

'But, Grandpa—'

'With the vegetables. In the back!'

Their discussion went unnoticed, the air already gone dusty red, a convocation of bricks soaring in parabolas, colliding with the train, bouncing off sheet metal, cracking windows.

'Char-lie! Char-lie! Char-lie!'

While ranchers clambered in through the window frames, wildcat workers fanned into a passenger car, coughing the name like bloodhounds treeing a fugitive. Luggage compartments were thrown open, and each successive valise, portmanteau, and Dutch satchel that was discovered not to be Charlie Chaplin was heaved out the

.dow, until the skies over the platform were heavy with the rain necktics, trousers, crêpe de chine smocks. Travelers and train workers were marched down the aisles and to the platform, where the crowds demanded, 'Where is he?' and did not listen to the answers.

The portmanteaux and satchels were thrown back first, and, in a savage response to the man who had so terribly dismissed their hospitality, came the light refreshments and pitchers of beer. And then a single pie. It half disintegrated on the way, crust and filling slapping against the train like an upsplash of mud.

Hugo, who could not account for several recent minutes, was crawling, bloody as an anchorite, from the train and toward daylight at the edge of the mob. He arose near the picnic tables. His face felt as if he'd slept on a clothes iron.

He watched the crowd swarm over the train: passenger-car seats were ripped open, their straw stuffing used as kindling, and then, with a careful sprinkle of the God-given, plentiful, and rich local gasoline, the train was set afire.

The rest of the assault – pipes beating on the train, bricks, harassment of passengers – came to a halt, for the spectacle of the burning train was impressive. Hugo had never actually seen a mob before, but this certainly confirmed all he had heard about them. There was a stiff crackle, and he flinched before a sound like rivets popping, the fire finding a cache of ammunition in someone's suitcase.

But passenger cars made poor targets for arson; once the seats and wallpaper were consumed, there was just a no-longer-exciting trickle of smoke going skyward. By then, word had passed through the crowd that perhaps they had made a mistake and it would be best to go home.

When a horde lost its purpose, it was like the sun disappearing in a fog bank. The entire town brushed past Hugo, finding fascinating objects in the middle of the lowlands to stare at. He looked to the picnic tables, where there still sat the quarter acre of pies. His eye was swelling shut, his nose was clotting with blood, there was a bruise that throbbed from his jaw to his cheekbone, and he was running his tongue from tooth to tooth, testing them all for number and fixity.

And yet the pies smelled delicious. The nearest was sweating, its

vents swollen with a deep-blueberry ooze. Hugo wondered [.
person decided to throw a pie. And why was that supposed t
funny?

With a flick of his eyes, he grabbed a pie in each hand. He limpe
with determination to a pillar draped with bunting, where he carefully
sat with a groan, cross-legged. The pies were slightly warm, and
the smell of strawberries and rhubarb was overwhelming. He exca-
vated a palmful of custard filling. The taste was glorious, tempered
only by the trouble he had working his jaw. Then he took another
pawful of the sticky fruit and crust, and closed his eyes. Heaven.

The train had been destroyed, but he laughed, for he had hated
everyone on the train. He glanced toward the station-agent cottage,
alive with telegraph activity. As soon as they were done reporting
the damages to the company, he would need to wire his father. He
put a sticky fist under his chin. He realized, with a shudder, that
he needed another goddamned job.

Meanwhile, in the station-agent cottage, the telegraph operator was
taking notes with confusion while men all around gave combative
monologues punctuated with foul gestures. Beyond the current emergency was something far larger. The engineer, cheek smeared with
soot, was telephoning other train operators down the line. On railways across the country that did not link to East Texas, Chaplin
had also been expected!

Further, the railways were not the only places people had gathered
and been disappointed. There were riots on the docks of the Gulf
of Mexico, and in Rye, New York, at an airstrip, a mob had tipped
over an airplane he was supposed to be on, snapping off the propeller
and rolling it down a muddy hillside.

The next week's *Beaumont Sentinel* ran a full account with photos
of the unfortunate event. After a chronology of the riot, Beaumont's
first, was a statement from Mayor French admitting they had been
confused. 'What we are trying to ascertain is why we all thought
Chaplin was coming. I would swear the Widow Candless said so,
but she says she heard it from me.'

So Beaumont, in the course of a few hours, had gone from prosperity and the prospect of fame, to being the home of a burnt-out
shell of a passenger train. The cars sat on the siding with occasional

, of smoke and ash rising into the air, and when the winds
led toward town, people would stiffen in embarrassment, then
continue on their way.

They were not alone. The next day, the *Kansas City Star* asked
in its headline, 'HAD YOU THE CHAPLIN-ITIS?' There was an account
of his being paged in over eight hundred hotels, the failed rescue at
sea off the California coast, his anticipated arrival at train stations,
and below was an artist's conception of that day's commotion in
Kansas City, when Chaplin had been seen wreaking havoc at the
baseball field, knocking down an outfielder as he dove for a fly ball.
He stumbled through a church picnic in Knoxville, and in New
York City, at 31st and Sixth Avenue, he tied up traffic during a
manic boxing match with a hotheaded bruiser of a cop. He was
seen clutching the mane of a horse galloping across a field in West
Virginia, and falling into a vat of offal in a Chicago stockyard. And
then he was gone.

☆　☆　☆

Such is the nature of the inexplicable that, as long as it does not
involve money, it can be ignored. Within several weeks, the Chaplin-
itis was forgotten, except for one small report.

A circular was issued by the American Society for Psychical
Research, a group founded in 1885 in Boston by curious men,
including, as they never failed to mention, William James, dean of
skeptical inquiry and father of American psychology. After his death,
it had become much more satisfying for the remaining founders to
believe than to *evaluate,* and currently the Society was tilting toward
defense of the ethereal world. The circular on Chaplin was written
by a Professor Bamfylde Moore Carew ('the Bohemian rhapsodist,'
as he was known).

Charlie Chaplin, Professor Carew wrote,

has become an American obsession, and among young and
active minds, Chaplin is a subject of constantly recurrent
thought. We find beyond peradventure that on Nov. 12 there
existed a Chaplin impulse, which extended the length and
breadth of the continent.

After several expository paragraphs (including a rhetorical blackjack taken to the knees of his enemies in physics, psychology, and *Scientific American*), Carew concluded:

> There is a new, immediate medium which we do not yet under-
> stand the psychology behind, the filmed photoplay. For the first
> time, our 'hero' has fame not predicated on his presence before
> us, but upon a technology that renders him both real and im-
> aginary. Not since the days of the prophets have we all so
> swiftly agreed that a single entity, one suffering many of life's
> mishaps, can answer so many of our needs. We needed Charlie
> Chaplin to be our alter ego – or perhaps simply our ego itself
> – and so he came to us. Psychologists, those alarmists, call it
> mass hysteria. I call it a shared dream, a fairy tale, the birth
> of a myth. Today is a new beginning.

There Professor Carew's argument finished, never to be examined
or expanded. He did not indicate what exactly was beginning. No
one seems to have inquired. Instead, the moment was over, and the
world and all its inhabitants could move on.

Unless, of course, you happened to be one particular person.

A Q&A with Glen David Gold about
Carter Beats the Devil

What inspired you to write about Carter the Great?

About ten years ago, my father bought me a magic poster from the 1920s as a birthday present and it featured a magician called Carter the Great in a scene called 'Carter Beats the Devil'. I was living in San Francisco at the time and I did a little bit of research into who this guy that I looked at on my wall every day was. It turned out he was in San Francisco in the 1920s, and I was very interested in what a magician's life would have been like in the 1920s. That's when I started researching Carter the Great.

Where did you draw the line between fact and fiction?

Being asked that question really makes me feel like I've done my job – now I'll tell you why I'm going to evade it! It reminds me of sitting in the audience watching a magic trick thinking: 'where did fact and fiction begin there? At which point did my imagination take over?' It made me realise why magicians don't reveal the secrets of how they do their tricks.

I realised early on that even I didn't want to know how these tricks are done. I was much more interested in effect. There are a few times – for example, a point towards the end of the first half of the book when a trick involving a woman being shot through a wall is performed – where I get very technical. If you read it, it seems to make perfect sense about how the trick works, and you would feel like an educated audience member if you had that information and saw the trick performed. But it is also just poeticized enough so that if you actually tried to perform the trick you wouldn't be able to do it, as you would be missing some vital information. This seems to fit in th one of the major themes of the book – that of misdirection and lusion.

Did you feel any loyalty to Carter's memory?

In a sense, yes I did. He was one of the biggest magicians of his time, he could bring a town out to his shows. Yet today nobody has heard of him, so I like the idea of bringing his name back into public knowledge.

There are two strands to the novel: on one hand, there is the life of Carter the Great; on the other, a look back at America during the 1920 and 30s. Which aspect came first to you?

I've always been fascinated by history, and in particular the 1920s. I've always had an affinity for the time, probably because I used to watch Marx Brothers movies with my father in the middle of the night when I was a little boy! Living in San Francisco, and looking at the history of the place . . . the 1920s were a very interesting time there too. Once I'd got the history, Carter came shortly after.

In the novel, you analyse the great rivalry between magicians. Does that exist today?

I'm looking forward to finding that out. I don't know that many magicians yet, but those that I have spoken to have been wonderful about the book. They are excited about the novel and are opening their doors to me. I'm really hoping to eavesdrop and see what gossip I can pick up from them!

In amongst the rivalry between the magicians, did you find that there was also a camaraderie?

I think that if you respect what a person does, then you end up liking them to some degree. One of the stories I love concerns Houdini, who everybody wanted to know but was extremely difficult to get along with. He had a dog, a pretty horrible mongrel, which had some puppies. He gave them away to these people, who were really happy that they had a puppy given to them by the great Houdini, when in fact he just wanted to get rid of them.

As an outsider, how did you manage to get access to the Magic Circle?

That was one of the hardest things, because magicians really do guard their secrets carefully and they were not too interested in talking to me. Of the five years I spent researching the novel, I would say two and a half years were spent trying to answer that very same question.

Was there any point in it all when you thought you had taken on too big a task?

Every second. But the novel was this self-generating world. Every time I sat down to work on a scene I had new ideas, and they kept playing themselves out. It's kinda like seeing a bend in a road, and you think that you will carry on until the road stops – my road happened to last 760 manuscript pages.

The press release for Carter requested that 'members of the press do not reveal details of your third act.' Now that you share this desire, one which governs the careers of magicians, do you have a different perspective on how the illusions are created?

Oh, absolutely. At first, I wanted to know how they did everything, but now that I know how some things are done I realise that the secrecy actually protects the audience. There is a part in the novel where a character needs to know how you make an elephant vanish, and Carter says: 'I think sometimes that not knowing protects the audience more than it does the magician.' There is something about that view; the audience think that they want to know, but what is much more important is surrendering to the magician and wondering. You really want to wonder . . . you see a trick and then spend the rest of the day asking yourself how it was done. That keeps you alive.

Does the fact that you know some of the secrets spoil your enjoyment, or enhance your respect for those that can do it?

It gives me much more of an appreciation for the skill and showmanship involved. There is an American magician named Ricky Jay. I saw a performance by him where he spoke a lot about historical magic, and he introduced many tricks by telling the audience that it was first performed by a particular magician in the past. With some of the tricks, I had actually read books by the magicians who had devised them. Therefore I knew some of the secrets, yet as I watched Ricky Jay I still couldn't see how he did it. That makes me twice as amazed. One of his tricks involved giving 15 decks of cards to 15 different people in the audience. He then asked them to select a card, and then he found each card in a different way, one after the other. Now, that's just mind-blowing, but I think I know how he did some of them . . . but I don't know for sure. To see magic taken to that level amazed me all over again.

Knowing some of the secrets of magic, could you perform any of the tricks?

No way. The way the tricks are learnt is that the magician will sit down for four hours a day, every day, for three years just performing a motion, or a combination of movements, in front of a mirror until he is able to do it in such a way that you can't tell it has been done. There is a tremendous amount of skill involved, so that things that seem impossible are actually quite real.

Why do we never see biographies of magicians – they must have stories to tell?

Magicians want to tell their stories, but they don't want the public to know how they did their biggest tricks. They want to brag about it at the same time, so what they do is they print up these minute numbers – probably only 250 to 500 copies – of their autobiographies and price them astronomically. If you really want to know the secrets of these tricks you have to pay a lot of money to find out.

A lot of my student loan went on the research into the novel, especially buying some of these books. Usually I was rewarded by finding some little anecdote, or detail. A bit later I found out that there were slightly cheaper ways of doing some of the things I did, but it was too late to change things!

This Q&A first appeared on samedaybooks.co.uk in 2001.

Glen David Gold

Glen David Gold was born in Hollywood and raised in San Francisco, where he began his life-long love of the strange and dazzling aspects of history. His first novel, *Carter Beats the Devil*, was shortlisted for the *Guardian* First Book Award, and has been translated into 14 languages. His short stories and essays have appeared in *McSweeney's*, *Playboy*, and the *New York Times Magazine*. His second novel, *Sunnyside*, was published in 2009. He lives in San Francisco with his wife, Alice Sebold.